Nicola Thorne was born in Cape Town, South Africa. Her father was English and her mother a New Zealander, and she was brought up and educated in England. She graduated in Sociology at the London School of Economics, but always wanted to pursue a literary career and worked as a reader and editor while writing her first novels. In 1975 she left publishing to write full time. *Affairs of Love* is her eighth and most recent novel to be published under the pseudonym Nicola Thorne. She lives in St John's Wood, London.

D0892501

By the same author

The Girls
In Love
Bridie Climbing
A Woman Like Us
The Perfect Wife and Mother
Where the Rivers Meet
Affairs of Love

NICOLA THORNE

The Daughters of the House

PANTHER
Granada Publishing

Panther Books
Granada Publishing Ltd
8 Grafton Street, London W1X 3LA

Published by Panther Books 1982
Reprinted 1985

First published in Great Britain by
Granada Publishing 1981

Copyright © Nicola Thorne 1981

ISBN 0-583-13317-7

Printed and bound in Great Britain by
Collins, Glasgow

Set in Times

All rights reserved. No part of this publication may
be reproduced, stored in a retrieval system, or
transmitted, in any form, or by any means, electronic,
mechanical, photocopying, recording or otherwise,
without the prior permission of the publishers.

This book is sold subject to the conditions that it
shall not, by way of trade or otherwise, be lent,
re-sold, hired out or otherwise circulated
without the publisher's prior consent in any
form of binding or cover other than that in
which it is published and without a similar
condition including this condition being imposed
on the subsequent purchaser.

For Irene Pain
in gratitude for many years of friendship and support

CHAPTER ONE

The Queen was not due until noon, but everyone had to be in their seats by ten. Even the Duke of Wellington was there punctually. A great roar greeted his arrival from the amiable crowd, many of whom had spent all night in the park, dossing down under the trees in the rain. There were few enough free delights for the mass of the people, and excitement had been mounting since the glass palace had started to rise only nine months before.

The Vestrey family arrived just before the Duke and stood respectfully aside in the shade of the great cast iron Coalbrookdale Gates as he prepared to make his entrance. He was a surprisingly small man, resplendent in his Field-Marshal's uniform, slightly stooped by age but his large beaked nose thrust high into the air, his sharp eyes missing nothing. His hair though white was thick like a young man's and his stick seemed a mere adornment rather than a support.

'Morning, Vestrey,' the Duke observed. 'Mrs Vestrey. Your labour is complete now, George.'

'Not mine, your Grace,' George Vestrey bowed deprecatingly, towering over the great warrior. 'Mine was a very small part.'

'I daresay; but I heard your contribution was valuable. I have been here almost every day, you know. I have observed every stage in its construction through binoculars from my study window. Remarkable. A house of glass, amazing. Never been one before on this scale.'

The Duke touched his nose and tapped his stick on the floor. The Beefeaters at the gates prepared to stand aside for him and the crowd, waiting in the transept and along the galleries, grew restless because of his delayed arrival.

'Respects to your father, Vestrey,' the Duke said as his servant righted the sash of his Garter ribbon. 'I hear he is failing. Well, it comes to us all. My birthday you know. Never thought I would live to see it.'

'Many happy returns to your Grace, many long years to enjoy the affection of the Nation.'

The old man fixed George Vestrey with his penetrating gaze. 'I don't think I've long Vestrey; but it's been a good life. Family well? I see they are all here.'

The Duke looked approvingly at the women grouped respectfully around him. Even at his age he still had an eye for beauty and the Vestrey girls were noted for their looks. 'Take after their mother, I see. Lovely.'

'I have not *all* my family with me, sir. Three remain at home.'

'Indeed? I didn't realize there were so many. My own family are a source of constant joy to me; it gets better as you get older.'

The Duke clasped George Vestrey's arm, smiled once more at the women, and then marched slowly into the north transept while the excited crowd rose to their feet and cheered.

Some said there were upwards of half a million people in the park on the day of the opening of the Great Exhibition, garnered from all corners of London, indeed from the whole kingdom. The industrious poor considered they had earned a day out, and came with their picnic baskets, their flagons of ale, their numerous children, relations and dogs to have a good time. The less industrious poor, of whom there were a good many, the thieves, would-be assassins and pickpockets, the whores, petty criminals and ne'er-do-wells – they were all there, too, for it was a working day for them, a busy profitable day with a little entertainment to be had on the side.

The carriages had been rolling in since early morning, admitted by the top-hatted police constables who patrolled the fence that Mr Paxton had thoughtfully constructed around his lovely house of glass. Many of the privileged few who were actually to attend the opening ceremony – and a fine fuss there had been about that, for the Prince Consort had wanted a private ceremony – walked across the park to avoid the traffic jams that silted up the gates into the park and stretched as far as the Strand.

Oh what a day it was to be, even though rain had fallen first thing! Mr Paxton's Crystal Palace, towering over the trees, gleamed like newly minted coin, its white paint picked out in the deepest blue, its acres of sheet glass reflecting the sky, the trees, the houses opposite in Princes Gate, many of whose residents had objected so vigorously to its presence – some were actually supposed to have moved out. Hundreds of flags, representing the many nations taking part, fluttered from poles placed at intervals along the rising levels of the roof. On the Serpentine a fleet of small boats surrounded a fully manned frigate which was primed to give a miniature salute, and in a far corner of the park Charles Spencer was preparing to rise above the Palace in his giant balloon.

In every tree lurked numerous urchins who also crammed the roof and gardens of Apsley House by permission of its owner the Duke of Wellington, the hero of Waterloo and now, in the twilight of his life, one of the most honoured men in the Kingdom, who was celebrating his eighty-second birthday.

Eighty-two, the Duke was eighty-two! Quickly word got round, and some stood on their seats to catch a glimpse of him as he prepared to join the illustrious crowd grouped round the stately dais in the north transept, covered by a carpet which had been worked in Berlin wool by a hundred and fifty ladies. Upon it stood the gold chair of state draped in crimson and gold, and above it the octagonal *baldacchino* covered in blue satin hung from the ceiling. In the background towered one of the two giant elms that had been left in the building – together with some smaller ones – and which the temperate conditions inside the great glasshouse had brought into full leaf well before time. The Duke had disposed of the problem created by the birds nestling in its branches. 'Try sparrow hawks, ma'am,' he told the Queen.

Agnes Vestrey looked nervous and plucked at her husband's coat sleeve.

'Pray George, do not let us go in yet! I will feel they are cheering us.'

'My dear we shall be quite ignored, I assure you. An[d] see, the Cabinet are forming behind us and we don't wan[t] to join *their* train either!'

'I told you we should have come earlier George. I ar[e] quite embarrassed.'

'Mama, people have eyes only for the Duke,' her daughte[r] Caroline said comfortingly. 'And see . . . there is Lor[d] Stanley and oh Mama, the Prime Minister . . .'

Mrs Vestrey looked back anxiously at the Cabinet i[n] their green Windsor uniforms which had been designed b[y] the Prince Consort. She bowed to Lord Granville as he[r] husband acknowledged a smile from Lord John Russel[l] the Prime Minister, before ushering his brood through th[e] great iron gates into the body of the palace.

Nothing that she had seen or heard had prepared Agne[s] Vestrey for the sight she now beheld as her husband, tak[-]ing her arm, escorted her slowly along the transept toward[s] the dais. She greeted people she knew, bowing and smiling but her eyes were glancing upwards to the huge arche[d] roof of the transept, to the galleries crammed with peopl[e] some of whom were observing the scene in the nave throug[h] binoculars. Between the partitions gorgeous carpets hun[g] from the highest girders and the crystal of huge chandelier[s] reflecting the light that flooded in from all sides of th[e] building, glittered and twinkled in kaleidoscopic profusion o[f] greens, purples and golds, reds, ambers and topaz. Ahea[d] of them Mr Osler's remarkable three-tiered crystal foun[-]tain, a centrepiece of the Exhibition, seemed to capture th[e] quintessential spirit of the concept of Mr Paxton's vas[t] creation.

Standing twenty-eight feet high it looked enormous, bu[t] so skilled and delicate was the working that the water, leap[-]ing out of its topmost flute and cascading down the ornat[e] levels to the large basin in which it stood, seemed lik[e] molten glass, the very stuff of which the fountain was made The theme of light and air was reflected in the fountain and in the wonder on the faces of those who gazed at it a[s] Agnes did before her husband whispered to her.

'My dear, we are holding people up.'

Agnes glanced round apologetically, smiling at Mr[s]

Gladstone just behind her and murmured, 'I am so transfixed by everything I see.'

'You have almost two hours to observe it better.' George Vestrey glanced at his watch. 'Ah, here are your places, in the front as I was promised. You will see my dears that only ladies have the privilege of seats. The men have to stand.'

'But where will you stand Papa?' Caroline Vestrey looked about her with concern.

'I have to stand with the members of my commission my dear, by the side of the dais. See, Mr Cole is already there chatting to Mr Dilkes. James and Oliver will be over there where you can see them. I think we shall all have a splendid view.'

Agnes Vestrey sat down on the hard seat and motioned for her daughters to sit on either side of her, Caroline the eldest to the left of Jane, the youngest of those present. She folded her hands in her lap and smiled up at her husband.

'You hurry off and join your colleagues, George. We shall see you afterwards.'

George bowed and, escorting his sons to their place under one of the galleries, quickly made his way to the dais where Mr Cole, one of the instigators of the Exhibition, hurried over to take his hand.

'George, I am so glad you arrived early! Are your family happy with their seats?'

'Very happy, Henry. Am I to thank you for this as for so much else?'

'It is kind of you, but ...'

George Vestrey held up his arms and gesticulated to the glories that surrounded them.

'When I think that so much of this is due to you, and you yet have time to see to the seats of my humble family ...'

Henry Cole laughed and took his friend's arm. 'I assure you, George, I did not *personally* see to it. Those who allocated seats were told to ensure that the families of members of the various commissions had good views.'

'I still think it too bad that none of those who are exhibiting or who built it are present.'

'Oh, they are represented, my dear George, by men such as Mr Fox, Mr Henderson and Mr Chance who employed

11

them, after all. And the diplomatic corps represent foreign exhibitors, and there are sufficient of us here to represent the English. Don't worry, the common people don't think about these things. They don't expect it. They will be in the park making merry, drinking beer and enjoying themselves.'

The crowd round the dais got thicker as the Cabinet and members of the diplomatic corps took their places.

Every seat in the place was now filled and the galleries were packed. In the west nave, where the British exhibits were placed, the flags of each participating town added even more to the riot of colour provided by the dresses of the ladies, hanging carpets and the trophies of Spitalfields silks, the uniforms of the military, members of the Household and other functionaries. George, who had watched every step made towards the completion of the Exhibition, would never have believed that anything so breathtakingly spectacular could have been achieved in such a short time. He was well pleased. He gave a sigh of satisfaction as he finished having a word with Mr Scott Russell, the secretary of his commission, and looked over towards his family sitting to the right but almost in front of him.

Agnes, Emily and Caroline had their heads bent in conversation, Jane was staring in front of her and James was pointing out items of interest to Oliver who was keenly interested in everything about the Exhibition and had the day off from Eton to attend it.

Yes, he had much to be satisfied with, much to be pleased about, George Vestrey thought to himself. He was a worthy member of the community and he had a happy and secure family life. He was a Member of Parliament, an active, useful man. However, in some ways he was a dissatisfied one. What he strove after George Vestrey never really knew and, looking across at his third daughter Jane, he wondered if in her he had created the conscience he basically lacked.

Jane had no time for the Exhibition. She had said so loudly and often, and she was only here out of respect for her parents' wishes. She thought it was a waste of time and money, a further exploitation of the working poor who had slaved in not, unhealthy factories to create many of the

12

wares on display. When her father tried to reason with her that prosperity for the country made every section better off she would have none of it.

Jane saw her father's glance, and waved. His face softened. Radical at heart she may be; but she was a beautiful girl – slim and graceful, with dark colouring and thick, black, curly hair. There were, in his family, the dark Vestreys and the fair Vestreys, the former taking after their father, the latter their mother. But the one most like him, in looks as well as in spirit, was Jane. Her skin was the deep amber colour of a ripe olive, rich and iridescent, her eyes a darker brown flecked with tiny specks of green. She had a long slim neck, a tilted chin, an imperious arch to her eyebrows and a trim straight lipline that gave her such singular beauty when it relaxed in a smile. It was a mouth of character and determination, hinting at inflexibility, a certain vigorous determination to have her own way.

His second daughter, Emily, was the fairest of his brood – the opposite of Jane, in looks and temperament. But then their mother and father were very different too and Jane and Emily were always bent on opposition, their tastes as dissimilar as their looks. Emily's most striking feature was her golden hair; it massed about her head as though all the pins and womanly artefacts at hand could not contain it. Little wisps of it blew off her forehead, curled about her ears, or flew from the neat ringlets massed at the nape of her neck. Her eyes were a shade of blue that was difficult to define because it seemed to vary according to the light. When it was bright they appeared cerulean, like a field of fresh cornflowers. But at night they resembled sapphires, gleaming with the opalescent quality of that mysterious jewel. It was this feature that gave Emily her fascination, especially her power over men, and because of this was a determinant of the kind of person she was. The colour of her skin provided the perfect setting for her eyes. Like her mother's, it was fair, with a transparent quality that made it glow and vibrate. It had the bloom of apricot skin, and thus avoided that chalk-like pallor which was so much the rage among her contemporaries.

Caroline's appearance harmonized with that of each of

13

her two younger sisters. Her colouring was not as well de
fined as either of theirs. Her skin, though not as fair a
Emily's, was much lighter than Jane's. It had the warm
brown tinge common to people who live on the Mediter
ranean. It seemed to proclaim her as the out-of-doors gir
she was, living by the sea, enjoying riding and long walk
along the Kentish coast. Her hair had the same lustrou
quality as her sisters'; but it had the highly polished shee
of a horse chestnut that has fallen from the tree at the ver
end of autumn and only when it has reached a deep, ful
reddish-brown maturity. Caroline had a feature shared b
no other Vestrey: high cheekbones that seemed to draw
up her eyes and give them a slightly provocative slant. A
times this had the disconcerting effect of making her seem
of oriental origin, rather than a sprig of the English aristo
cracy, and the calm, unhurried way in which she moved
enhanced this impression. Her mouth, however, owed noth
ing to the east. It was wide and full and made her expres
sion seem permanently pleasant and at ease, so that even
when she was sad or angry it helped her to mask her
feelings.

Thus the three eldest daughters of Chetwell Place, the
Vestrey family home, were lovingly contemplated by their
father as they waited, with differing degrees of interest and
excitement, for the ceremonial to begin. Caroline looked
alert but composed, content to let time take its course
Emily was gazing about her, fluttering her lashes, hoping to
see and be seen by as many handsome men as possible
Jane tapped her feet impatiently on the floor of the nave
giving deep sighs and little murmurs of irritation to the
vexation of her mother who kept on digging her sharply
but surreptitiously, in the ribs.

Yet by now nearly everyone inside the hall – some twenty
to thirty thousand people were estimated to be there – was
getting restless. There was a lot of coughing and using of
handkerchiefs. One or two people fainted in the heat. I
got even hotter when the sun came out and blazed down
upon the crimson carpet along the nave and the banners
which hung so proudly over the British exhibits.

Suddenly outside a cheer could be heard which grew in

14

volume until it became a roar. The atmosphere in the glass
house underwent an imperceptible change, and everyone
stopped coughing and blowing and shifting about and became more attentive. The Duke of Wellington stopped chatting loudly to the Archbishop of Canterbury and raised his
peaked nose in the air as though sniffing for quarry. Mr
Cole, who simply could not stop organizing things as he
had, most satisfactorily, from the very beginning, fell unnaturally still; and Mr Paxton took his place rather pro-
minently on the outside of the group round the dais as
though ready to receive all the tributes he, rightly, thought
to be due to him.

'The Queen, the Queen . . .' The whispers started and
gathered force, circulating around and around so that the
great glass palace reverberated like the whispering gallery
in St Paul's Cathedral. A salute of guns boomed from outside and a few nervous heads were raised towards the sheer
glass roof, some remembering the Astronomer Royal's pre-
diction, among others, that a place made of glass could not
possibly withstand the forces of wind, rain or those caused
artificially by man.

But now it was too late. Mr Paxton claimed to have foreseen everything, measured everything, tested everything.
Not a pane of glass had been broken during the violent
storms in January. Three hundred men had jumped up and
down on portions of the gallery for several minutes in the
presence of the Queen, the Prince and their children; a
corps of sappers had double marched on them and trolleys
of cannon balls had been trundled to and fro. Despite all
those Jeremiahs who had called the Crystal Palace a sieve,
an oven, a lightning conductor, a house of cards, it was here
and they were in it, and Mr Paxton's words had to be taken
on trust.

On this day of its opening his confidence was justified.
The man who had started his working life as a gardener's
boy had pulled off a miracle. Here it was in all its glory,
shimmering inside and out, not merely a crystal palace, but
a fairy palace to delight and enchant those who had tickets
for the opening, who thronged about outside or who gazed
at it from the top of Highgate Hill in the north of London

or Sydenham Hill in the south. It shone like a huge glittering jewel in the May sun that eventually blazed forth, just in tim to greet the arrival of Queen Victoria.

A peal of trumpets rang out as the Royal Standard wa broken from the top of the building, surmounting all th other flags that flew there, and the spectators inside spon taneously broke into a triumphant rendering of the Nationa Anthem. Then, briefly, there was a silence of electrifying intensity, when it seemed as though everyone had stopped breathing. To a wave of applause and roars from the crowd the Queen appeared through the great Coalbrookdale Gate holding the little Prince of Wales, dressed in full Highland dress, by the hand.

She was preceded by the architect of the Exhibition, the Prince Consort, looking grave and composed despite his triumph, the Princess Royal at his side nervously clutching his hand. The Princess's dress was of lace over white satin and she wore a small wreath of pink wild roses in her hair But all eyes were for the diminutive form of the Queer walking majestically in the wake of her beloved husband turning to right and left with nods and smiles, so joyful a sharing his success that everyone, even those who didn't like him, rejoiced with her. She wore a gown of pink and silver, with the broad Garter ribbon across her bosom, and on her head was a diamond ray diadem with a little crowr at the back from which two feathers protruded.

Once on the dais, surrounded by equerries and ladies-in waiting, the Royal Family, who included the Queen's mother the Duchess of Kent, graceful and elegant in a white dress and some visiting relations, stood in a prayerful attitude while the National Anthem was sung again. This time it was led by a choir of a thousand voices, and the thunderous swell of an organ. When this was finished the Prince stepped down from the dais and, facing his wife, who remained standing throughout listening to him with an expression of ineffable sweetness and indulgence, delivered an address prepared for the occasion by the Royal Commissioners. To this long and verbose report, during which there was much shuffling and clearing of throats, the Queen delivered a short and gracious reply which was followed by a prayer intoned by the Archbishop of Canterbury. Then the organ, and massed choirs burst forth once more in a joyful rendering of the Hallelujah Chorus from the Messiah.

George Vestrey took his place in the procession among the various commissioners, the diplomatic corps and members of the Household, some of whom walked awkwardly backwards. Ahead of him the Duke of Wellington had his arm firmly through that of the Marquess of Anglesey and was talking at the top of his voice to his old comrade in arms. They had fought together at Waterloo when the Marquess, then Lord Uxbridge, had had a leg blown off. But since then they had undergone a period of estrangement. Everyone was pleased to see they were friends again. On either side of the nave the crowds clapped and cheered and waved their handkerchiefs. The sound of the organ vied with that of a military band placed at one end which did its best to render the march from *Athalie*.

Above, in the galleries, many of those pressed so closely together leaned perilously over to have a better view of the procession as it wove slowly past the great Coalbrookdale Dome with its statue of the Eagle Slayer shooting his arrow in the air; past Ross's great telescope and the giant lighthouse reflector; past the huge colourful trophy of Spitalfields silks splendidly and effectively draped against a column of mirrors, past Apsley Pallet's huge chandelier which hung at a length of twenty-four feet, the Seeley fountain and the huge, and some thought very ugly and ostentatious, statue of Lord Eldon and his brother Lord Stowell carved by Watson from a single block of marble.

At the end of the west nave was a giant model of the Liverpool docks ornamented with sixteen hundred fully rigged ships and, as the procession wheeled round this to make its way back through the nave, George caught the eye of young Flora Macdonald, who walked just behind the Queen to whom she was in waiting, and smiled. But young Flora was too busy and intent on her duties to relax for a minute and George was rewarded instead by a beautiful smile from Lady Douro, Wellington's daughter-in-law, who was also in attendance on the Queen and was far more experienced in coping with those things than young Flora.

17

In fact she might have thought the smile was meant for her. Like her father-in-law, George Vestrey was also known to have an eye for the ladies.

Once more the procession passed the crystal fountain and entered the eastern nave which housed the foreign exhibits, many of them still unpacked, so that the scene was one of considerable disorder. Indeed the Russian exhibits, frozen up for the winter, were not to arrive until June and its whole court was entirely bare. No matter. The foreigners who had contrived somehow to remain cheered Her Majesty, many French voices loudly calling out *'Vive la Reine!'* to which the Queen, who had hardly ever stopped smiling, such was her pride in the work of her beloved Albert, gave a gracious and delighted wave.

Yet the suite of rooms furnished by Leistler of Vienna was nearly finished, and The Amazon, the colossal bronze zinc sculpture by Professor Kiss, was in place. The Queen even paused for a moment and gazed at it with obvious admiration, as it towered above her and the assembled concourse. There was a plastic tableau of a rural fête at Rosenau, Prince Albert's birthplace, towards which the Queen looked with veneration – she would spend a lot of time there on her many subsequent visits to the Exhibition – but she averted her eyes from the nude figure of a female slave by Hiram Power which graced the American section of the Exhibition.

As the dignitaries walked along the east nave, some of them beginning to wilt a little now in the heat, two foreign organs made their contribution to the gaiety, playing vigorously and harmoniously but not together. Thus the din, except to the Duke of Wellington who was hard of hearing, was almost unbearable.

The procession took about forty minutes to cover the east and west naves, and when it returned and re-formed round the Royal family on the dais it could be seen that many of the participants, as well as the spectators, were wiping tears of happiness from their eyes. The Queen seemed almost unable to speak, though she still did not take advantage of the State chair placed on the dais. She remained standing while the Prince Consort hurriedly asked

18

Lord Breadalbane to declare the Exhibition open, which he did in a loud voice crying, 'Her Majesty commands me to declare this Exhibition open.' There was a further flourish of trumpets and, to a great roar from the assembly, the Royal family departed back through the Coalbrookdale Gates to be greeted by further cheers from the masses outside.

But even before the Queen had passed through the gates, the crowd surged over the barriers and charged helter-skelter towards the wonderful array of exhibits housed in the various galleries and courts throughout the Palace.

Oliver had already disappeared in the direction of the machinery section as George tried to regroup his family in the bustle. His wife, Jane and Caroline were together but Emily had also disappeared while James was talking to two friends. The sun streaming through the glass roof, and the presence of so many hundreds of bodies pressed close together, had contrived to make the atmosphere in the Palace oppressive and George mopped his brow.

'I think we should not stay any longer today. We will return tomorrow for a closer look at the exhibits, my love, if you wish.'

Agnes nodded. 'Let us get out of here as quickly as we can, or I think I shall faint from exhaustion. Where *is* Emily? Where *is* Oliver? Oh those children . . . Caroline, my dear . . .'

'Certainly, Mama.' Caroline, the capable one, so dependable, set off at a brisk trot into the west nave where she thought she could see the bright dress of her sister.

It was no surprise to find that Emily had a male companion. Of the three elder Vestrey sisters Emily was the natural flirt, the one whom men picked out in a crowded room, the one whose ball card was most quickly filled. Subconsciously Emily gave off that aura that women do whose prime reason for existence appears to be to please men. They are not always beautiful, but they have a peculiar allure that makes them recognizable, desirable to men. Emily Vestrey, however, was enchanting. She was quite irresistible because of the way she moved, the instinctive gestures she made, the tilt of her golden head and the inviting look in those eyes whose colour varied according to the light.

Caroline's heart sank as she saw that look and the reason for it: Rawdon Foxton, the eldest son of Lord and Lady Foxton. The Foxtons and the Vestreys were near neighbours, the Foxton estate being just over the border in Sussex a few miles from Rye. Foxtons and Vestreys had intermingled all their lives; attended one another's parties, gone on joint excursions, were presented at the same time, shared the same school, in the case of the boys, and the same regiment in the case of Rawdon and James.

The first to leave the schoolroom, Caroline was also the first Vestrey girl to be aware of Rawdon as something other than a friend and familiar. He was the same age as her brother, a year older than she, and as soon as the down on his chin gave place to luxuriant whiskers, and the upper lip showed the mark of a razor, Caroline was aware of a new interest whenever she saw him, a hitherto unfamiliar restraint when they were together.

But if Caroline kept her feelings to herself, Emily did not. If anything she was conscious of Rawdon as a man before she had left the schoolroom and at fifteen made a special effort with her toilet whenever he was expected. Under the camouflage of Emily's forwardness Caroline was able to conceal her own interest so that, subtly and unbeknown to the family, scarcely to the girls themselves, a rivalry between Caroline and Emily commenced for the heart of the heir to Lord Foxton.

And once again here he was captivated by Emily, his mouth parted in a smile that hovered on the brink of laughter, his eyes riveted on her as Emily recounted some anecdote with those expressive gestures of her elegant hands. Caroline, though she deplored its cause, recognized the jealousy in her heart and her voice rose sharply as she spoke.

'Emily, Mama is fatigued and wishes to go.'

'Oh,' Emily reddened, 'but Rawdon has just offered to escort me round the Exhibition.'

'I offered to escort you *all* round the Exhibition,' Rawdon protested laughingly. 'But none of you were to be found.'

'Papa says we must go, thank you Rawdon. Mama is hot and threatens to faint if we do not leave soon.'

'Oh but may I not . . .'

'No, you may *not*, Emily. Please. You know Grandpapa is unwell, and lunch will be waiting.'

'You are staying in Park Street?' Rawdon asked.

'Yes, until Saturday. We are to spend all tomorrow at the Exhibition and the evening at Lady Newmark's ball, but Papa wants to be home after that for he has some local function to attend on Sunday.'

'Then may I see you here tomorrow? *All* of you?'

Caroline inclined her head, looking at Emily. 'Let us meet by Mr Osler's fountain at ten; but first we must check with Papa. Oh Oliver! He is completely lost. Now where would he be?'

'I saw Master Oliver Vestrey disappear in the direction of the engineering section, if I am not mistaken. Does your young brother incline that way?'

'Oh, he is very interested in science. Could you take us there?'

Rawdon led the way confidently along the west nave and into one of the galleries which led off it and resembled a huge shed full of machinery. Giant presses, wheels and pieces of equipment loomed up, none of them as yet in working order so that, apart from the hum of people and the clatter of boxes being opened, everything was still. Oliver Vestrey, tall for his sixteen years, was standing by himself, hands clasped behind his back staring at a colossal piece of machinery several feet taller than him. He was so lost in concentration that he failed to hear his sister's voice until she seized him by the shoulder and shook him.

'Oliver!'

'Oh Caroline . . . is it not *magnificent*?' Oliver ignored her obvious irritation and his arm swept reverentially towards the machine. 'This is the great hydraulic press, its object is to manipulate the chains which raise the tubes of the Britannia Bridge over the Menai Straits. See Caroline . . .'

'It *is* marvellous, Oliver, quite wonderful. But we are to leave at once. We have all day at the Exhibition tomorrow.'

'But I want to come back today!'

'Then you must ask Papa if James may take you. Hurry now. Mama is almost fainting with fatigue.'

Oliver reluctantly lowered his eyes from the hydraulic press and looked wistfully about at the many machines which surrounded this monster like so many small fish around a shark. Some of them were beginning to turn and whirl as their operatives finished oiling some vital part, or fixing a bolt or tightening a final screw.

When they returned to the transept Agnes Vestrey had sat down again and was fanning her hot face with the programme for the opening. George Vestrey was also puce, but more from vexation than heat and Jane was tapping her feet, her air just as bored as when they first arrived. Their father started up as he saw his family return, but the reprimand died on his lips when he saw the Honourable Rawdon Foxton.

'Ah Rawdon . . . I see you have recovered my erring family for me.'

'Partly, sir.' The young man smiled and bowed towards Mrs Vestrey. 'I trust you enjoyed the opening, Mrs Vestrey?'

'I enjoyed it excessively, Rawdon, but now I am fatigued and hungry . . .'

'So I hear ma'am, so I hear. May I escort you to your carriage?'

'We *walked*, my boy,' George said. ''Tis but ten minutes to Park Street and we came up by train. There was a queue of carriages in our street at seven this morning, so we were well advised to travel the way we did. No, I think we have had enough of the Exhibition for today. Now tomorrow . . .'

'Oh Papa *please*.' Oliver's eager young face was difficult to ignore.

'I will gladly take him round the Exhibition this afternoon sir, together with any other of your family who would care to join me. James?'

'No, I have had enough of exhibitions for today. I shall go to my club.'

James was restless. The pretty girls were too docile because of the presence of their mamas, and there were too many ugly ones as well as old ladies and doddering men

22

about. James was easily recognizable as the Vestrey heir, the firstborn. He was as tall as his father but had inherited his mother's looks, her fair skin and ash blonde hair, those deep blue eyes, that straight nose and slightly pugnacious mouth. Agnes's mouth was not pugnacious; it was more inclined to petulance – the deep downward turn of the permanently aggrieved; but one could see, in her son, where the contours came from.

James had a military bearing, a straight back and a rather fixed expression. He looked, as he was, self-centred and self-assured. James had never seemed to be afflicted by doubts or troubles of any kind. From early years he had exhibited a clear-cut certainty about the world and his place in it that had led him inevitably into the army where he now enjoyed a Captain's command.

It was strange to find a man like this a close friend of someone like Rawdon Foxton. It seemed an attraction of opposites.

'You're an idle fellow, James,' Rawdon said good humouredly. 'This is the age of progress.'

'Progress be damned,' James said stifling a yawn. 'Caroline will go with you.' But his sister shook her head.

'No, I have had sufficient for today. I'm getting one of Mama's headaches.'

'And Jane thinks too many of the exhibits were produced by exploiting the workers and does not wish to return again,' her father said wryly.

'Well, they were,' Jane retorted angrily. 'The conditions in the factories are such that we should feel ashamed to be here.'

'But surely if our prosperity increases, the wages and conditions of the workers will improve?'

Much as he admired her beauty Rawdon was irritated by Jane. Perhaps he knew that, unlike her two sisters, she was unimpressed by him. Although Caroline was not as blatant as Emily in her admiration, Rawdon could see the effect he had on her. In a way he was even more flattered that a girl of Caroline's qualities could find him interesting. Emily was known as a flirt, but Caroline was serious and

23

reserved. Her beauty was quieter than Emily's, less flamboyant, her charms not so obvious. One felt that she would not give her affections so easily, so he prized them more.

Yet Jane he considered, in common with many, the loveliest of the eldest Vestrey girls – the loveliest and the most annoying. She was quick and clever, but her tongue could sting and her looks wither. A man felt uncomfortable in her presence. She was desirable but intolerable, at least for someone like him who admired spirit in a woman as long as it was within the bounds of convention. His normally amiable expression showed incipient hostility as she considered her reply, measuring her words and looking at him with her large, limpid but unsusceptible eyes.

'With free trade we have absolutely *no* protection,' Jane continued unabashed. 'The importation of foreign goods only encourages commercial competition, *not* better wages.'

'Come come, this is no time for economics,' her father said quickly. 'Rawdon, will you join us for luncheon? And then Oliver and whoever wants can return to the Exhibition with you. I shall take forty winks and then go to my club, and my wife I am sure will spend the rest of the day resting.'

Outside the crowd still swarmed round the Crystal Palace like busy worker ants. Already long queues were forming at the three main entrances despite the high cost of admission on the first day. In the clear sunshine the Crystal Palace looked enchanting in its fresh paint, the flags of all the participating countries waving in the breeze. There was a mêlée of carriages arriving and departing, men on horseback, and a posse of policemen trying to maintain law and order.

The Crystal Palace was three times the length of St Paul's Cathedral, contained two hundred and ninety-three thousand, six hundred and fifty-five panes of glass put in place by an ingenious glazing waggon designed by Mr Paxton which ran on wheels, and four thousand, five hundred tons of iron, both cast and wrought. Some six hundred thousand cubic feet of timber had been used and twenty-four miles of guttering.

Such were the statistics expounded by the Honourable George Vestrey as he strolled along with his family who gasped with admiration at every new piece of information, scarcely able to wrench their eyes away as they walked the length of the vast edifice towards Park Lane and home. And the entire building could be taken down and erected elsewhere. It was a miracle of modern scientific construction.

It was certainly something to be proud of, a tribute to the endeavours of man. Whatever Jane said or thought, people could only be better off, especially those belonging to a nation which had given birth to such a stunning manifestation of skill and initiative, such a monument to the marvels of progress in this year of grace 1851.

CHAPTER TWO

Mr Ruskin agreed with Jane Vestrey that the Exhibition was an absurd waste of time but, more importantly, much of it was sure to be in execrable taste. He was not so worried about the waste of public money as about the exploitation of the working classes. Since leaving Oxford he had been kept in considerable comfort by his father, who also maintained an establishment in Park Street for him and his wife and made them an ample allowance. However John Ruskin possessed an incipient social conscience which was to surprise some of those who considered that he only lived for art.

The fortune of Mr Ruskin senior was built on commerce; he was in the wine trade. Normally this fact would have been enough to bar their entry into the kind of society in which people such as the Vestreys mixed. But times were changing. Young Mr Ruskin, the author of *Modern Painters*, was considered very clever and his wife, in addition, very beautiful. Moreover she had been presented to the Queen and they had both attended drawing rooms at Buckingham Palace. Many men admired Mrs Ruskin, and these included some from the very pinnacle of society such as the Marquess of Lansdowne. It was through him that they had been invited to Lady Newmark's ball.

But the Ruskins were known to the Vestreys anyway, being neighbours in Mayfair. Vivacious Mrs Ruskin had the entrée almost anywhere, and was a friend of Lady Eastlake who was very close to the Honourable Ruth Vestrey who looked after her brother Lord Vestrey.

Mr Ruskin didn't care for dancing and Jane was quite happy to sit out with him while his wife danced every dance with a different man. Mr Ruskin conversed with Jane Vestrey and appeared to take no notice of what was going on on the ballroom floor. He seemed profoundly bored with the whole thing; yet occasionally he had to do what

26

Effie wanted to do and this included escorting her to evening parties.

Lady Newmark's ball to mark the opening of the Great Exhibition was one of the events of the season; everyone was there. It was held in their large house in Grosvenor Street and a marquee had been erected on the lawn outside to accommodate the overflow of guests for supper. John Ruskin had felt like a fish out of water until he had spotted Jane Vestrey sitting beside her great aunt and mother, her hands folded in her lap, her expression one of considerable *ennui*.

'And where are your beautiful sisters tonight?' Mr Ruskin looked at Jane appraisingly. 'And pray do not think you are *not* included in this category, Miss Jane. The names of the lovely Vestrey sisters are, I know, on the lips of every eligible young man – and some who are not eligible either.'

Jane accepted the compliment calmly, returning his gaze, not with a blush as most young women would, but with a look of candour. 'Mr Ruskin, do not deceive *me* with your flattery when you are known to be married to one of the most admired women in society.'

'Ah . . .'

John Ruskin leaned back on the slender Chippendale chair and stared thoughtfully at a well-polished toe, turning it to catch the reflections of the glittering candelabra. In watching the dancers he had not failed to observe his wife animatedly dancing with an attractive man. But he was quite used to this. Effie was an outrageous flirt. It happened all the time in Italy where they had recently passed several months. Men were always in love with Effie and she responded to them; but he trusted her because of the agreement they had to go their own ways while appearing to be a devoted couple.

'There I am fortunate indeed, Miss Jane. Effie is *very* lovely and, as you say, justly admired.'

Was there sadness in his tone? Or resignation? Jane couldn't decide, but his pale blue eyes avoided hers and he went on turning his pointed shoe this way and that, as though mesmerized by it.

'Ah *there* is Caroline! See, Mr Ruskin?' Jane gestured with her hand, being careful not to point. 'Dancing with Rawdon Foxton.'

Mr Ruskin raised his head and stared in the direction she had indicated.

'They make an attractive pair,' he observed. 'Is there an understanding?'

'Oh no! Rawdon is an old family friend. Lord and Lady Foxton are old friends of Mama and Papa. We have known all the Foxtons all our lives.'

'But see how they look at each other,' Mr Ruskin murmured, glancing at the girl beside him. He saw the very fixed expression, the pursed lips. Jane would be a very difficult person to convince of anything she did not want to know.

'Do you disapprove of romance, Miss Jane? Is it too frivolous for you?'

'Of *course* I do not disapprove of romance, Mr Ruskin! But I assure you there is nothing like that between Caroline and Rawdon. He is my brother's closest friend.'

'But your brother isn't dancing with him.' Mr Ruskin persevered gently. 'See how they look at each other as though they were quite unaware of anyone else in the room.'

Others besides Mr Ruskin had observed the manner in which Rawdon and Caroline moved, seeming almost to flow together in perfect harmony on the tide of Mr Strauss's waltz. The heads of wise dowagers used to observing such things in the course of countless similar balls over the years nodded in agreement: they were a very well-matched pair, exceptional even in that dazzling company by virtue of their height, the graceful way they moved together and the comparability of their striking looks.

Caroline, the eldest, was also the tallest of the Vestrey girls. Some thought she was too tall for a woman; but she moved so lightly and with such grace, and her figure was so perfectly proportioned that her height was an enhancement to her looks, rather than a disadvantage as in the case of the Foxton daughters, where their extra inches contrived only to make them look gaunt and skinny. Caroline's thick chestnut ringlets bobbed on bare white shoulders perfectly framed by a ball gown of blue wild silk threaded with silver. Her brown eyes sparkled with excitement and the exertion of the dance had produced a becoming flush on her clear white skin.

Rawdon Foxton gripped her very firmly, one white gloved hand in the small of her back, the other clasping her fingers. His carriage and figure were military in bearing and his black dress coat and narrow black trousers set off to advantage his white satin waistcoat embroidered with thick gold thread and the many flounces of his high lace cravat.

'Mr Foxton is in the army?'

'He is in the same regiment as my brother, the Third Battalion of the Grenadier Guards.'

'Ah, the Guards. It is interesting what the Guards do to a man. One can always tell.'

Jane looked at him with a slight air of bewilderment as though not knowing whether to believe him or not. Yet Mr Ruskin seemed perfectly serious.

'You could actually *tell* he is in the Guards?'

'Oh, undoubtedly. It is the stance, the thrust of the chin, above all the self confidence at being in a regiment so close to the monarch, so privileged. Surely you must notice it with your brother?'

Yes, Mr Ruskin's eyes were twinkling. She saw not only genuine amusement but also a derision. She had only met Mr Ruskin a few times, but he always made the same impression, that somehow he was unfathomable, too detached and aloof to be real. He had a high intellectual forehead, and rather vague blue eyes surmounted by thick brows. His lower lip was full, his nose aquiline, his looks quite regular, and yet despite all this something about him was not quite right . . . But she enjoyed his conversation and the relief in talking to him instead of pivoting round and round the ballroom with one inane young man after another.

'Yet you are not at all interested in that kind of thing are you, Mr Ruskin?'

Mr Ruskin raised the bushy eyebrows. 'What kind of thing exactly, Miss Vestrey?'

'Oh, to do with the military, you know . . .'

'I have *very* little in common with military gentlemen.

But my wife, I believe, finds them quite entertaining. She was very taken by General Radetsky and Marshal Marmont during our stay in Venice. And they, I believe, with her.'

Mr Ruskin gave a wry smile and looked at Jane who realized then what was peculiar about Mr Ruskin. He did not look at her as most men did – as a man looks, appreciating the charms of an attractive woman. Mr Ruskin was cold; there was no doubt about that. Perhaps that was why Effie played about such a lot.

'But Rawdon Foxton is very erudite as well,' Jane said defensively. 'He distinguished himself as a scholar at Eton, and read Classics for two years at Oxford before deciding on an Army career. Despite their very different personalities he has always been very close to my brother James. James is a madcap and Rawdon the opposite. They balance each other out and share a love of sports and the active life. Rawdon is very attached to my sisters too . . .'

'But not to you, Miss Jane? And yet you defend him so well?' Mr Ruskin looked at her again with that same cold, impersonal smile.

'No, Rawdon is not attached to me, nor I to him. We argue a lot. Emily and Caroline play up to him a little. I am not a person whose object in life it is to please men. I do not mean to say that Caroline is either. Caroline is friendly and polite to everyone; but Emily . . . Emily is a completely different person when men are around.'

'So Caroline is your favourite!'

'Oh yes! Caroline is so dependable and conscientious; Emily will always put herself before others. Caroline has always taken her family duties very seriously. She has helped to bring us up, under Mama of course.'

Jane sighed and looked to where her mother was sitting with Aunt Ruth and a bevy of older ladies, the dowagers who always liked to keep an eye on the behaviour of their juniors. Mama had nearly not come because she had felt one of her headaches to be imminent. Mama nearly always ailed when they were in London and her father, bursting with vitality and rude health, nearly always became impatient with her. There had been a scene; then Papa had simmered down and Mama had decided to recover almost at the same time, which usually happened too.

Yet Mama was not really delicate. She was as strong as an ox. But if she didn't want to do anything, or see anyone, or go anywhere she always took refuge in vague ill health, and this was trying to a naturally robust and vigorous family. For as many years as Jane could remember, it was Caroline the family really relied on. Caroline who took over when Mama had one of her heads or a peculiar feeling in her chest that made her go and lie down. Caroline who made peace when their parents had one of their many arguments and father swept out of the room slamming doors behind him. Yet with all this she could still say it was a happy united home.

Jane turned from looking at Mrs Vestrey, dimpling and pretty in a dress of yellow tarlatan with many flounces and laces, and observed a young man approaching Mr Ruskin, yet his eyes were looking past Mr Ruskin to her. She felt herself flush and was angry with herself for doing so, but there was a peculiar intensity about the young man's gaze, a bold directness that was unnerving.

'Mr Ruskin, sir.' The young man bowed and Mr Ruskin, deep in thought, once more started up.

'Why Jeremy, you startled me. I was lost in admiration of all the beauty surrounding me, all the colours of the dresses and the candles. Now let me see, do you know Miss Jane Vestrey?' Ruskin turned to the girl beside him and the young man bowed and took her hand.

'Jeremy is a very talented young artist, Miss Vestrey. Jeremy Pagan. Also a friend of the Eastlakes, I think. Lately returned from Italy.'

Jane, her features once more composed, smiled at the young man and saw how he looked at her as he raised his head. She was not unused to the admiring glances of young men, but this somehow disturbed her and despite the heat of the room she felt a cold frisson up her spine.

'How do you do, Miss Vestrey?'

'How do you do, Mr Pagan?'

'Might I have the pleasure of a dance? If Mr Ruskin has no objection?'

'I have no objection, my dear boy. But I believe Miss Vestrey does not care to dance. She finds it decadent.'

'Dec . . .' Jeremy Pagan appeared unable to believe his ears.

'Miss Vestrey is a radical. A convert to the work of Mr Mill and Mr Bentham, a disciple of Miss Martineau and, like that excellent lady, she declares that it is not her object in life to please men . . .'

Jane, who rarely blushed, did so again and put her hands to her cheeks. 'Mr Ruskin! Desist! You make a mockery of me. I *do* like dancing and it has nothing to do with being radical. It was just that I knew you did not care to dance and I preferred to talk to you. So you see I *do* like to please men.'

She gave him a smile that showed herself every bit as capable of flirtatiousness as her sister Emily, and Mr Ruskin felt himself pale. Her potential frightened him; a woman as intelligent as she was charming and beautiful. Someone whose force of character was as formidable as Lady Eastlake whom he detested or Lady Trevelyan, his dear friend Pauline, whom he loved, yet so much younger than either. And Effie was so empty-headed, so vain, so out of tune with his own temperament. Would that he could pay court to Jane Vestrey . . . He sighed and swung back on his chair.

'Now you are flattering *me*, Miss Jane. Indeed I have seldom been more entertained, or indeed instructed. You hold in an advanced form many of the views that I myself have been slow in formulating. Your condemnation of the exploitation of the labouring classes is only too justified. Now did you ever consider *that*, Jeremy?'

Jeremy Pagan reluctantly removed his gaze from Jane and looked impatiently at his mentor.

'About the conditions in the factories; the low pay, the long hours and inadequate health facilities. Did you ever think of all that when you admired a piece of furniture or some intricate object made of glass or metal, or maybe the clothes you wear – how much the people were paid who actually made them? Whether free trade, by encouraging competition, drives down the wages paid to the workers?'

'No, I confess I never did.'

32

'There, that is the artist in you! But I did. So it can be done. A social conscience is quite consistent with aesthetic appreciation. Now I see my wife is returning and doubtless she would like me to take her to supper. If Miss Vestrey will allow you a dance perhaps you will join us later in the marquee on the lawn?'

'I should be delighted, Mr Ruskin. Mrs Ruskin . . .'

Effie swept up, her face crimson, her shoulders heaving with exertion.

'John, I am absolutely parched . . . why, Jeremy, when did you get to London?'

'Only a few days ago, Mrs Ruskin. I am lodging with Millais in Gower Street. You must know him.'

'I have heard of him, of course, and admire his work,' John Ruskin said, apparently on his wife's behalf, 'although we have not yet had the chance to meet. I am preparing a letter to *The Times* in defence of his work and that of his friend and fellow artist Holman Hunt whose work exhibited at the Royal Academy has been so savagely attacked by the critics. I felt that more notice would be taken of my defence of them if I had no personal acquaintance with them. But I look forward to meeting these – er – founders of the pre-Raphaelite Brotherhood soon. Rossetti too, of course. Tell them that.'

'I will, Mr Ruskin.'

Effie's feet had not stopped tapping to the music and she took her husband's arm impatiently. Jane thought she was indeed an excitable, nervous young woman appearing to have little in common with her taciturn scholarly husband.

'John, pray take me to supper. I am famished and thirsty. Jeremy, are you joining us, and Miss Vestrey?'

Effie looked coolly at Jane Vestrey whose dark beauty she considered a serious rival to her own acknowledged looks.

'Thank you, Mrs Ruskin, but I have promised Mr Pagan a dance. Afterwards perhaps . . .'

'John, there is Pauline Trevelyan. Pauline . . .'

Mrs Ruskin darted away without saying goodbye and John, shrugging his shoulders in a gesture of submission, followed her.

'How do you know the Ruskins?' Jeremy asked, leading Jane to the floor.

'Mrs Ruskin is a friend of my aunt who is very literary. They also live in Park Street near my grandfather's house and are almost neighbours, separated I think by two gardens. Do you like her?'

'Mrs Ruskin? I like her well enough but find her superficial. She is always bent on creating an effect, and she likes male admiration excessively. I would be driven mad if I were her husband. I seldom saw two such dissimilar people married. I knew them in Venice from whence I only returned last week. Mrs Ruskin was all over the town while Mr Ruskin was working on his book. There was quite a lot of talk about *her*; but she takes care not to create scandal. No, they are ill suited. But how is it I have missed you, Miss Vestrey?'

Jane was aware of his arm around her waist, the strong grip of his hand on her shoulder.

'We do not live in town, though I am to be presented this year and we will come up for the season, staying with my grandfather.'

'A radical – being presented?'

'Oh please, do not resume that mockery, Mr Pagan. I am interested in the condition of the people, in the many injustices in our society; but if I were not presented it would deeply offend my parents. Both my mother and my sisters were before me, and my younger sisters will be after me. My aunt is a friend of the Queen's mother, a former lady-in-waiting. There are certain ways in which I must conform, and I do.'

'I think you are altogether admirable, Miss Vestrey. A beauty with a social conscience. Indeed an unusual combination, at least in my experience.'

Emily Vestrey danced furiously all evening, in an effort to try and forget that Rawdon Foxton had asked Caroline to dance and not her. She had spent the entire day in Rawdon's company at the Exhibition listening attentively to his commentary on the exhibits, laughing in the right places, admiring the range of his knowledge, the depth of his under-

34

standing of the most intricate processes of machinery – and Caroline had not even been there! She had had him entirely to herself, well, Oliver too of course, and Papa and Aunt Ruth for part of the time. But Caroline, no. She had stayed at home to look after Grandpapa and so give Aunt the chance to get out.

Rawdon couldn't have been more obliging, attentive, patient, when she didn't quite understand, thoughtful when she wanted something to eat or drink; anyone would have thought he was a man half in love. And yet the very first thing that had happened when they entered the ballroom as a family was that Rawdon, in conversation with Lord New-mark, had excused himself as soon as he saw them and darted over to claim Caroline for the first dance.

Not only the first, either. Emily glanced over her shoulder. They had not stopped dancing all evening. She trod heavily on her partner's foot and did not apologize even when he winced. In a few more minutes she would tread on the other.

Caroline knew that she should marry. In many ways she was ready for marriage and she wanted to marry; to have her own establishment, her own family. In every way Rawdon Foxton was right. He was the right age, he was accomplished, even erudite. He was wealthy and the heir to a barony – not that the last two mattered very much to her, though Mama said how nice it was, when one had become accustomed to something, to know that one would not lose it. His father's estates were not far from their own in Kent; so she would even be near her family.

Rawdon always appeared to Caroline to be on the verge of speaking to her; and then something held him back. He would gaze at her very intently – as he was now for instance – and then he would shift his gaze or start talking rapidly about something quite impersonal. He had never touched her except in the dance, or tried to draw nearer to her in any way. But she sensed, she knew, that Rawdon felt the way she did about him. It was something she could not put into words.

She felt this union with him now as, perfectly suited, they waltzed so well together and she knew how many eyes were upon them. She knew they made a fine couple and that

35

Mama was hopeful, and her best friend Sybil Foxton desired nothing more in the whole world.

The music stopped and they stood gazing at each other. There was a high colour on Rawdon's cheeks and he breathed very quickly; his hands still clasping hers tightly. His clear grey eyes gazed into hers, tenderly, questioningly and that slight smile of unspoken interrogation hovered on his lips. His thick black hair curled over his ears into long side-whiskers and Caroline thought how everything about Rawdon was clear and well defined, there was nothing blurred or indecisive. His dress was always faultlessly correct whether it was military or civilian, as now; and in a regiment which recruited men for their height he was one of the tallest, his body lithe and muscular.

His hand pressed hers more tightly and the colour rose in his cheeks while his eyes shone brightly. She knew he would speak now, and she caught her breath, suddenly averting her eyes because, now that the moment had come, it was unexpected.

'Caroline, I . . .' Rawdon coughed and hesitated and as Caroline swiftly raised her eyes to encourage him she heard that voice, saw that figure that always seemed to come between Rawdon and herself.

'Caroline, *are* you coming to supper? And Rawdon, you have not danced one dance with me all evening. Did I tire you too much during the day?'

Emily pouted prettily, her eyes flashing at Rawdon, one hand still resting in that of her partner.

'Let me have *one* dance with Rawdon. Caroline, you dance with Charlie Parker here and then we can all go and join Mama and Papa at supper.'

The moment had passed. Caroline saw Rawdon give a small resigned shrug, trying to catch her eyes as Charlie Parker, a practised lady-killer, whirled her easily onto the floor.

'Your sister is in love with that fellow, you know,' Charles Parker said after a few turns of the dance floor. He was a good dancer and Caroline, at ease in his arm, hardly heard what he said.

'I beg your pardon?'

'Emily. She can't stop looking at Rawdon . . .'

'But she is dancing with him.'

'Even when she isn't. When she was dancing with *me* she was looking at him all the time. Didn't you notice?'

Yes, Caroline had noticed. She was always aware of Rawdon and Emily when they were together. Yet, reserved and conscious of her position as the eldest daughter of the house, Caroline considered it undignified to be a rival with her younger sister for the affections of the same man. She did not wear her heart on her sleeve; it was not her way. If anything, she even tried to make it easy for them to be together as she had today when Grandpapa was perfectly all right with his nurse and the servants, and Caroline had been quite eager herself to see the Exhibition again, especially with Rawdon.

So why did she do it? To test Rawdon? To challenge him to prove that he loved her and not Emily? Or was it because she wasn't sure herself, and the fact it was her duty to marry first seemed to vie with another ambition – to be different, to make something of her life? But this she concealed from her family and almost succeeded in keeping hidden from herself, because it seemed such an impossible thing to realize.

'They do look well together,' she murmured gazing in the direction pointed by Charles.

'Will they make a match do you think? He is always at your house, I hear.'

'He is James's best friend!' Caroline replied indignantly, her face flushing.

'Ah, is *that* the only reason?'

Caroline knew she felt angry because anyone should think that Rawdon came to see Emily and not her. Was she so much less pleasing than Emily then? And Emily looked particularly well tonight, her hair and skin enhanced by a dress she had designed herself of turquoise moiré silk. She danced so gaily, so vigorously that her ringlets flew about her head and the high colour of her face and her sparkling eyes made her the very embodiment of happiness, a girl in love.

And Emily *did* fascinate Rawdon; he gazed at her sister

37

just as ardently as Caroline had seen him looking at her. Caroline felt a twinge of jealousy mingled with something deeper. Anger, perhaps, and sadness too that somehow the evening had been spoilt; that magical moment when Rawdon had grasped her hand and gazed into her eyes was gone.

The dance seemed interminable for Caroline, but when it was over she made her way eagerly with Charles to the door leading to the garden closely followed by a chattering, ebullient Emily and a smiling Rawdon.

And it was thus that Agnes Vestrey saw them entering the marquee and the moment remained etched on her mind. She had expected *Caroline* to burst in with Rawdon. Having seen them dancing together she knew how satisfactory it was, and had gone off to the supper room with the hope that what she and Sybil wanted so much would come to pass.

Lady Foxton wanted the eldest Vestrey girl for a daughter-in-law. She wanted Caroline, who was beautiful but also dependable and conscientious, as Emily was not. Emily of course was young and, in time, no doubt would lose some of those exuberant spirits that made her appear a little forgetful of her duties, and deficient in the respect she should show to her elders and betters. Emily, very decidedly, put self first.

Agnes Vestrey would have been quite happy whichever daughter Rawdon chose, for he was the sort of man any mother would welcome as a son-in-law. He was not only very attractive, wealthy and well born; he was nice, in a way that many of James's brother officers were not. He was fun and of a happy disposition; but he did not womanize, as far as was known, and he had a social conscience and an appetite for hard work.

Much as they loved one another, devoted as they all were as a family, the Vestrey women shared a common quality as far as the revelation of intimate feelings was concerned: they did not discuss them. Mother did not talk to daughters, or sister to sister. They did not know how to. Love was a new and powerful emotion to the girls, full of mystery and suspected dangers. To their mother it was also fearful, and dangerous indeed because of its intimate aspects which the girls knew nothing about and Agnes, to her sorrow, only too much.

Yet women had to marry and bear children; they had to move away from their families and become wives and mothers. If so, who better than someone like Rawdon Foxton to whom to entrust a beloved daughter? Agnes smiled indulgently as they all came in. Whichever daughter Rawdon chose she would be happy.

George Vestrey got up as his children came into the tent and a servant brought up more chairs, while Rawdon and Charles led the girls to the buffet and James got them glasses of champagne. It was a jolly family party that sat down to eat and Aunt Ruth, who led quite an active life despite the tie of grandfather, declared she had seldom had a better time all year.

'Where is Jane?' her father enquired, looking towards the door.

'Papa is not happy unless he has all his brood about him.'

'Not at all, Emily dear, but someone espied her engaged in earnest conversation with Mr Ruskin and I was wondering if she was about to join the Brotherhood!'

'Do not mock it, my dear George,' his aunt said reprovingly. 'Mr Ruskin is *not* one of the members of the Brotherhood though Pauline Trevelyan tells me he thoroughly approves of them. John Millais is a most enchanting young man, and very talented.'

'But Jane can't paint!'

'You don't have to be able to paint to appreciate art. Here she is and . . .'

Ruth Vestrey moved to make way for Jane who came in with a tall, very artistic-looking young man close behind her. His hair was a good deal longer than the fashion for young men and his side-whiskers of equal length and abundance. He had a lofty forehead, deepset dark eyes, underscored by dark shadows on his very pale skin, a long thin nose and a thin bloodless mouth. His dress, though correct, was as arresting as his appearance, his suit being of dark blue over an embroidered waistcoat. A very large white necktie was loosely tied round a high collar.

Jane, Agnes was relieved to see, was happy and smiling which made a change in this most unpredictable and moody of her children. Jane had not wanted to come to London, or to see the Exhibition or to go to Lady Newmark's ball, nor did she want to be presented at court or have her London season. She had made it perfectly clear that she would do all these things only because her parents expected her to do them.

Life with Jane was an unending round of battles lost or gained. She was one of the reasons her mother retired so often to her room with a headache and left Caroline to cope. There was just no logic or reasoning with Jane. Despite her social conscience, her concern for suffering mankind, she appeared to have very little care for the effect of her views on her family, the suffering her thoughtless behaviour caused her mother.

'Father, may I present Mr Jeremy Pagan, a friend of Mr Ruskin's.'

George stood up and shook hands with the young man, introducing him to his wife and aunt who smiled and said:

'I *have* heard of Mr Pagan. He is a very talented young painter, a friend of Mr Millais and Mr Hunt. Lately returned from Venice, I understand?'

Jeremy Pagan drew up a chair and placed it next to Ruth Vestrey.

'I am most honoured, Miss Vestrey that you appear to know so much about me. I have not yet had an exhibition.'

'But you intend to, I understand. You have been working hard in Italy?'

'Indeed. I have brought back many canvases with me. But the glory of my exhibition, the pride of place shall be given to a portrait of Miss Jane Vestrey, if she will allow.'

Jane laughed and a hand nervously clasped the lace fichu at her bosom.

'Mr Pagan! This is the first I have heard of it, father, I assure you.'

George Vestrey seemed nonplussed and looked to his wife for support. She gave him no help. Trust Jane to grab all this attention for herself, when she had hoped, watching them dance, that Rawdon might declare himself for

Caroline. Or did he prefer Emily after all? Looking at the three of them now it was hard to tell. Rawdon and Emily were talking with the greatest animation and Caroline, wholly relaxed and composed, was listening to one of the funny stories for which Sir Charles Parker, a well known wit, was famous. Her face was happy as though anticipating the laughter which would come when Charles reached the end, and the reputation of some unfortunate politician or socialite crashed to the ground.

Rawdon undoubtedly found Emily fascinating. That he enjoyed her company was clear whenever he came to the house and she made it her business to monopolize him and claim his attention. Whereas Caroline always held back; indeed she appeared slightly indifferent, treating him rather like the old family friend than a prospective beau.

It was difficult to know with Caroline. Of all the girls she was the most adept at concealing emotion, at hiding her feelings. Maybe Caroline did not really care after all? Besides, Agnes thought, she would miss Caroline. Maybe Emily should be the first one to go, unusual as it would be before the eldest sister had married. That would leave Caroline at home to cope with Jane and naughty little Patrick.

'I hope you don't have any objection, sir,' Mr Pagan said eagerly. 'Miss Vestrey has been telling me of your home by the sea in Kent, and I wondered if I could do my portrait of her against that background and, if so, if I may start soon?'

George Vestrey nervously tugged an earlobe and again silently besought advice from his wife, who suddenly said, very sensibly, 'Why does Mr Pagan not call at Park Street and talk it over with Aunt Ruth? It all seems very sudden to me and Aunt Ruth will advise you, George, as to what she thinks fit.'

George beamed at his wife with gratitude and relief.

'What a capital plan, my dear. Would you do that, Mr Pagan, and my aunt will consult with me in due course.'

'But I thought if it could be settled now sir . . .'

'My dear young man, my daughter's beauty will, I hope, not fade before you have had the chance to put brush to canvas, should that come about, and it will give us all time to consider the matter, and the suitability. I am not sure yet as to what course I shall take. Now would you like to escort Jane to the buffet and, James, kindly procure another bottle of champagne.'

James, who had good-humouredly been listening to the proceedings, laughed and got up.

'Certainly father and then, with your permission, I shall return to the ballroom and catch myself another filly.'

'James!' his mother protested, 'you know I dislike such language. Women are *not* horses, whatever you may think.'

'Sorry, Mama.' James sidled away still smiling. Like Jane he was merely performing his social duties here tonight to please his parents. What he really preferred was an evening playing cards with his fellow officers or visiting one of the entertainment complexes, such as Vauxhall, the Flora Gardens in Camberwell or the Cremorne in Chelsea, in order to acquire a woman for a night's pleasure. James thoroughly enjoyed his uncomplicated, masculine life lived in the company of his peers and loose women. He had very little interest at present in the young ladies provided by the society into which it was expected he would eventually marry as, of course, he would.

James returned with the champagne and more glasses on a tray and then, excusing himself, went upstairs to try and find one of the less dull society beauties to dance with.

Despite the late night the Vestrey family were up early next morning to catch the train to Folkestone. A hurried breakfast was eaten and good-byes were said to Grandpapa and Aunt Ruth while the carriage waited outside to take them to Charing Cross Station. Good-byes were brief for they would soon be back. Jane was to be presented at one of the Queen's afternoon drawing rooms in June and Papa had promised a few weeks of jollity in London to mark the occasion.

Only Oliver stayed behind. He was to spend one more night in his grandfather's house and be driven over to Eton the following day by coach. He came to see them off at the station and, feeling very grown up, waved them off as the train steamed out of the platform. Then he was driven back in solitary splendour to Vestrey House.

Except for some desultory conversation the journey home was undertaken in almost total silence. Everyone was tired, mostly thoughtful and Mama wasn't feeling well. Papa had had a little too much port the previous night and was liverish in consequence, and the three girls were wrapped in their own very different thoughts.

But as soon as they were approaching Folkestone and saw the sight of gulls wheeling over the bay, hearts rose again; and the sight of Ben Hall and the Vestrey coach waiting for them restored them to good heart. For, whatever might temporarily divide them as a family, they were all united by a love of Chetwell Place, the family home since the thirteenth century.

And it was a home, not a palace and not a castle. It was not even very large because the original house had almost been destroyed when the newly-knighted Sir Peter Vestrey had rebuilt his mansion in a style he considered fitting to one who had been made Squire of the Body to Henry VIII. His son had cemented the family position and fortune under Elizabeth and had been part-pirate and part-courtier, sailing with Sir Francis Drake and bringing back plunder to his Kentish home, before going up to London to strut about the court.

Since then the Vestreys had always been associated with the reigning monarch, although Sir John Vestrey had foolishly sailed into exile with James II. Fortunately for the family, Sir John had soon died in Holland and had been succeeded by his son, Richard, who had very different ideas of loyalty, and firmly supported the later Stuarts and the Hanoverian succession from then on.

Sir Richard had been created first Baron Vestrey by George I, who was establishing his cronies around him to cement his hold on the throne. Sir Richard had even gone over to Hanover to help bring back the new king, while his brothers and cousins helped to keep down the Jacobite rumblings stirring at home.

Throughout the eighteenth century Vestreys had held minor positions at court without contributing anything very remarkable to the progress of society in the country as a whole. There were no prominent Vestrey politicians or soldiers, though the Honourable Gerard Vestrey had been killed at Waterloo. This was one of the reasons the family knew the Duke of Wellington so well, because he had personally told the then Lord Vestrey of the death of his son, brother to the present Lord Vestrey, the fifth baron. Gerard had served with the Duke during the whole of the campaign in the Peninsula, and everyone had thought him destined for high honour in the army, until a bullet from a French gun got him defending the chateau of Hougemount with his fellow Coldstreamers on the field of Waterloo.

The Vestreys were not among the richest families in the land, but they were very well off. The third and fourth Barons Vestrey had not only increased the lands and farms round Chetwell Place but had also supported the growing industrialization in the midlands and the north by careful investment. The present baron had been among the first to invest in railway shares and sell them at a handsome profit before one of the frequent collapses of that particular market.

Chetwell Place occupied a commanding position on the cliffs between Folkestone and the ancient cinque port of Hythe. On one side lay the sea and on the other the rolling valleys of the Kentish countryside, the acres of woodland and farmland owned by the Vestreys, and the river Chet which gave the house its name. The first Chetwell Place had stood in the valley, or 'well' of the Chet, away from the sea winds. But Sir Peter who started to rebuild it moved it higher up, so that seen from one side it looked like a fortress, a battlement against the sea, and from the other a gracious country house.

Its lack of uniformity was part of its charm. Made mostly of red brick from the sixteenth century, it had many half-timbered gables and turrets of uneven height, with decorated chimneys which rose at random from the parapets making it look in parts like a medieval castle. The windows were all square-headed, placed at irregular intervals about the fabric of the house and the large oval porch, made of golden Bath stone from Somerset yet fitting harmoniously

44

in with the rest, stood at the base of one of the towers to the left of the house.

The house was built at an angle facing south-west so that, seen either from the coast road or the valley on the other side, it presented a harmonious mingling of the gracious and the warlike, part country home and part fortress. This latter aspect had been intended to frighten Napoleon when he contemplated the invasion of England, and the military canal at Hythe which had been constructed to repel him, lay not far away.

Chetwell Place was one of the reasons why the Vestrey family spent so little time in London. Indeed, Agnes scarcely went there at all except for some parliamentary and court functions and part of the season, and when her girls had been small she never even went there then. When Parliament was sitting George stayed in Park Street, but only for half of the week. It was the thought of being separated from his beloved home that had weighed uppermost in his mind when he declined the offers, made from time to time, to take a more important part in running the affairs of the country.

They could see it from the coast road, glowing in the sun of early afternoon. The sea was like a silver mirror, scarcely a wave rippling its calm surface from the point at far Dungeness to the white cliffs of Folkestone harbour. On a clear day like today the French coast could be seen, a thin white ribbon in the far distance and as they entered the drive between the tall wrought-iron gates, an eighteenth-century addition, the familiar feeling of homecoming and welcome engulfed them all and made them smile at one another, the tiredness and vexations of life forgotten.

But all was not well at home. There was something about the way the housekeeper Mrs Oakshott hovered in the porch clasping and unclasping her hands and ran out to greet them as Ben halted the coach in the drive. Agnes felt a spasm of apprehension, and was the first to scramble across the legs of her daughters and alight.

'What is it, Mary? Is all not well?'

'Oh ma'am. It is Miss Deborah. She developed a fever yesterday and has spent a restless night. The doctor was

45

here this morning and he will come again. It is the scarlet fever. He says none of the children must go near her.'

Caroline, the next out of the carriage, caught her mother's arm as she stumbled and for a moment leaned against her. She thought she had fainted.

'Mama, are you all right?' Caroline said in alarm. 'There is no need to worry. The disease will take its course. Jessica Tangent only recovered from it last month.'

'Yes, but how many *more* have died from it? My younger brother for one. And he was Debbie's age. Oh my God, I had a feeling all was not well. An apprehension I cannot explain . . .'

'There, Mama there. I will come with you to Debbie.'

'But Doctor Woodlove said . . .'

'I care not what he said. Mama, you are so pale.'

Caroline looked with renewed concern at her mother who was half sagging in her arms and, at a signal from her, her father came running over to be told the news. He put his arm round his wife's shoulder just as she crumpled completely and fainted.

It was the journey, the heat, the fatigue. Mama had gone to bed too late, she had been too tired. Agnes was put to bed immediately when she was taken into the house and Dr Woodlove found he had two patients when he came later that afternoon. After examining Mama he spent a long time with Papa who looked very grave at dinner that night, and Caroline could hardly wait to be alone with him afterwards. She sensed that his unease was due to Mama's condition and not Debbie's, who apparently only had what was hoped would be a mild attack of fever.

Papa took Caroline with him into his study and shut the door. He poured himself a large glass of port and went and stood in front of the fire.

'It is as she feared, my dear Caroline,' he said looking at her solemnly. 'For although a child is naturally a joy sent by God, it was not wished by either of us that your mother should conceive again.'

Caroline gazed at her father with consternation, and quickly sat down.

'Mama is with *child*, father?'

46

'Yes. She thought as much; she feared as much, which was why she has not been feeling well.'

'But Mama . . .'

'Your mother is but forty-one, Caroline. It is not too old to bear children, alas. Oh God, why do these things have to come to us as a punishment for pleasure?' Her father leaned his head against the mantel and Caroline observed, for the first time in her life so far as she could recall, that he was crying.

She quickly went over to him and put a hand timidly on his arm. 'A punishment, father? What can you mean? Is a child not to be welcomed?'

'Not now,' her father said, wiping his eyes. 'Not now. Your mother's last two confinements have been difficult ones; both times she lost the babies, Caroline, as you know. In all she has lost four children at birth or shortly after and she has miscarried three times at various points in her life. There is scarcely a year since we were married, nearly a quarter of a century ago, that your mother has not been pregnant or suffering from the effects of pregnancy.'

'But it is *three* years since Mama's last baby died, Papa. Little Nigel who lived for a week.'

'Three years. Aye. We had hoped that by now . . . I have hitherto abstained, my dear Caroline. I do not want to go into these matters of so delicate a nature for a young girl; but you are mature. I believe you may be contemplating marriage. You must know these things . . .'

'Of course, Papa,' Caroline said gently. 'You can talk to me. You know you can.'

'But it is not easy for a man to abstain. A full-blooded man with normal appetites such as I have. Your mother begged me not to, but I did. And now this. Yes, it *is* a punishment, Caroline. It is not a blessing. God is punishing me for the baseness of my nature, the crudeness of my desires.'

'Papa, Papa . . . Let us welcome the new baby and make Mama happy. Perhaps it will be the last, after all.'

'Oh, it will,' her father said grimly. 'God has taught me a lesson. There will be no more succumbing to temptation. Now go and see your mother my dear, and then tell your

47

sisters; but say nothing of what else I have said. That is something I wish you to keep to yourself, the outpouring of your father's tortured soul. Just say that Mama is with child and we are very happy about it.'

But Mama was not happy, so much was obvious when she was able to get up and walk about the house, which was not for nearly two weeks. And then she walked about like an old woman bent and feeble, sharp tempered and easily prone to tears. Moreover she avoided Papa's company and was short and snappish with him when in it. Caroline alone knew why. Mama had asked Papa not to, and his own base nature had brought this calamity about. He had said so. It was his fault, his weakness. And now look at the effect on Mama and him; the whole household was in gloom, and Debbie was very slow to get better and had several more crises before she did.

Caroline now had to face up to what for many years she had refused to consider, all those years when she had been growing up and Mama had had one baby or pregnancy after the other: that the relationship between men and women was a mystifying one that frequently led to unhappiness. It was not based on equality, but on the needs a man had and women apparently did not. It had made Mama like an old woman, a nervous irritable creature whose looks were fast disappearing, and everyone knew that in her youth Mama had been very beautiful. Yet she was younger than father and he was still a fine upright figure of a man, youthful and good looking. This desire that men had, which they sometimes could not, it seemed, control, destroyed women but not themselves. Was it fair?

During the months that she looked after Mama before her confinement Caroline had many moments in which she reflected on the sad fact that it was not. That the world in so far as it concerned men and women was very uneven, and that the women invariably – perhaps inevitably – came off worst.

To some extent also, it subtly altered the way she felt about Rawdon Foxton.

CHAPTER THREE

The aftermath of the homecoming following the opening of the Great Exhibition had a profound effect on the Vestrey family; it was like a tide that, encroaching slowly, only leaves its residue to be seen when it has ebbed again.

Caroline would often fix mid-1851 as a turning point in her life, before which it appeared, in retrospect, simple and uncluttered like a perpetual summer. After that there were many storms, and periods of unceasing rain and cold clinging mists.

The most immediate change was that, because of Mama's feebleness, her mantle fell firmly and inexorably on Caroline. Mama's 'heads' and vague feelings of being unwell had now crystallized into something solid and substantial. Mama was frequently tired and physically sick. She spent a large part of the day in bed or confined to her room. She withdrew into herself and sought comfort from reading religious works, and gazing for hour after hour at the sea as though she derived from it a solace that nothing human could give her.

She withdrew most of all from Papa who, some days when he was at home, didn't see her at all, and now he was at home less and less and stayed at Park Street more and more. Lord John Russell was trying to persuade him to join his Whig party and offered him a place in the Cabinet; even the Queen and Prince Albert intervened because of the impression George Vestrey had made on all with whom he had worked over the Exhibition. He was now no longer considered a lightweight, but a man with an important contribution to make.

But George did not want to change his party. Although he was from the solid landowning aristocracy, from which the great Whig peers came, he was at heart a reformer. He was a friend and admirer of Benjamin Disraeli, the author of *Sybil*, whose radical 'Young England' party he supported. Disraeli was the outstanding adornment of the Tory party and one who, although he had not yet had office, surely would one day. It was an age when the distinction between the parties was very fine and overlapped a good deal; some Whigs were for protection and some Tories for free trade and vice versa. Men could often be lured from one party to another.

But the bulk of both parties was composed of the solid middle class with at one extreme the aristocracy, who still mainly led them, and at the other the mass of the working population most of whom had no vote at all. Because of the guilt he felt about Agnes George threw himself more and more into the political world. He had promised Agnes there would be no more children after Nigel died, that the years left to them would be free of babies and the misery of childbirth, the grief of infant death.

But, as he had confessed to Caroline, he was a normal man, and the torments of the flesh had been such that at length he had gone to his wife and broken his promise. The result had been an increasing alienation because of his demands, even though he still loved her and he knew that she adored him. That was why Agnes had been so tetchy of late, so prone to vague feelings of ill-health and headaches. Beneath the apparently calm surface of their marriage, their intimate life was a perpetual state of war.

Agnes Vestrey had been the daughter of a near neighbour and friend of his father, Sir William Tangent, who farmed hundreds of acres on the Kent and Sussex border. The Vestreys and the Tangents had played together throughout their childhood and Agnes, the eldest and the most beautiful, had been George's choice ever since he was first aware of the stirrings of attraction between men and women.

They could scarcely wait for her seventeenth birthday to be married, and his father made over to him Chetwell Place in order to spend most of his time in the sunnier climate of Italy for, all his life, Henry fifth Baron Vestrey had been in poor health. Now he had more or less come home to die, or to try and prolong his life with the medical treatment only available in London; but few thought that this would be effective or last for long.

In many ways George Vestrey felt a young man, at the peak of his powers. His reproductive life spanned twenty-three years – he had fathered a child at twenty and now he had fathered another, yet unborn. He was fit, he was vigorous, he knew he looked younger than his years. Pretty women smiled at him and one or two of the bolder kind made no secret of his attraction for them. Yet, whereas he was young and felt it, Agnes had entered middle age – her hair was tinged with grey and her face was lined. Her figure was a little stodgy and laced tightly in with stiff corsets, and she wore a lot of powder and rouge on her face.

So, although he felt almost the man he had been twenty-three years ago, she was nowhere like the same woman. Between that time and this for her there was an enormous gulf, whereas for him there was none at all, or very little. And so the difference showed in their relationship – she envied him his freedom, and she resented the demands that he made on her physically, particularly because of the consequences which had been so painful, so dire and so heartbreaking of late. Now that her eldest children were old enough for matrimony she wanted no more young babies in the house and, after the death of Nigel, George had promised her that their relationship would be as brother and sister, close but not carnal.

But such a promise was hard to keep. He did not love her like a brother, but like a husband. The fact that he could not treat her like a true wife made him nervous and he frequently lost his temper. In the same way the unnatural relationship affected her too and she became shrewish and sharp, a prey to illness real and imagined. The results of their abstinence had not been harmonious to the family, and George knew that in many trifling ways they all felt it.

But breaking the abstinence had in reality made matters even worse. A temporary gratification on his part had led to what she most feared. After three months of a normal relationship with his wife she was pregnant again and now the result was worse than ever. She treated him with a frozen reserve, as though he were a stranger, and he felt guilty and ashamed of his desires whenever he saw the reproach, the suffering in her eyes.

Thus it came about that, during the summer, the family

gradually divided. As Agnes could not present Jane her great aunt would bring her out; and Emily begged to be allowed to chaperone Jane although many thought that it was Emily who needed chaperoning. With their father they would go up to London usually on a Monday and come back on the Friday unless there were balls or parties in which case they would not come home at all. But most people went to their estates for the last half of the week and London was quiet even in the season, or at the end of it as it was now.

At the end of the season Emily, exhausted by balls, parties, soirées and the endless variety of social life offered to the rich, went to Saltmarsh Castle to stay with Harriet Foxton, Rawdon's younger sister, who was her particular friend.

The Foxton sisters were not well endowed. Nature had not favoured them as it had their three brothers, or their mother, still considered a beauty in her forties. The Foxton height which was an advantage in a man was not so in a woman, and the girls were tall and lanky with small breasts and narrow boyish hips.

Harriet Foxton and her elder sister Jennifer had tried to compensate for nature's cruelty by cultivating things of the mind. They played and sang well, wrote verse and composed novels of great length and complexity. One day they hoped they would surprise the world with their versatility like Mrs Gaskell or the Brontë sisters who were so lionized by society.

Emily hoped that during her week at Saltmarsh Rawdon would visit his family. She thought it would show whether he cared for her or not; whether he would fulfil the unspoken promise his behaviour had seemed to suggest all the times they had danced together during the season. With Caroline out of the way, safe at home, she had had a wonderful time, because Jane the debutante was no rival for Rawdon's affections. They didn't get on.

'Rawdon considers Jane too like a man,' Harriet explained one afternoon as the girls sat over their embroidery in the drawing room. Lady Foxton had gone to Rye to buy materials and Lord Foxton was taking his customary afternoon nap.

'A man!' Emily exclaimed indignantly. 'My sister is not in the least like a man. I have heard that she was considered the Debutante of the Year, exceeding even the popularity of Lady Frances Colchester.'

'*She* has no brains at all,' Jennifer said, cutting one of her silks with a pair of tiny scissors and spreading out her work on her lap to admire it. 'There, I think the castle comes up very well.'

Emily and Harriet jumped up and bent over Jennifer, admiring the picture of Saltmarsh Castle she had designed herself and which she was working in tapestry as a large antimacassar.

'You are clever, Jenny!' Emily exclaimed with enthusiasm. 'Now *you* have plenty of brains. I couldn't see Frances Colchester designing anything like that.'

'Ah, but I would exchange a few of my brains for Lady Frances's success on the ballroom floor.'

'Really?' Emily stepped back and looked at Jenny who, avoiding her eyes, adjusted her steel spectacles and examined her tapestry with exaggerated care. 'I thought you did not care about that kind of thing, Jen?'

Jenny was twenty-four. It was difficult to be a plain young unmarried woman of that age and not care, however hard one tried.

'Of course I care that I do not attract men. I see no contradiction between brains and beauty except that I have too much of one and not enough of the other. Of course I care that I sit out at dances more often than others and that my brother dragoons all his friends into dancing with me. I care that I have to sit at home, to the despair of Mama who wishes I were married and making her a grandmother. Harriet still has time, but I am getting old.'

'Oh Jen,' Harriet threw her arms round her sister and hugged her. 'You know that is not true. Why, Parthe and Flo Nightingale are about *thirty* and they are not married.'

'But that is through choice,' Jenny said, 'at least as far as Florence is concerned. She does not wish to marry, but to devote her life to some great cause. She has turned down a number of men. I have never had the opportunity of turning down anybody.'

'Well, Aunt Ruth says that Florence Nightingale is slightly mad,' Emily said, going to the window and looking out at the smoothly kept lawn. 'She says all the family are touched and their mother most of all. Aunt Ruth has known Mrs Nightingale since she was a girl. She didn't get married until she was very old either – over thirty! So there.'

'It isn't that I wish to marry *particularly*,' Jennifer said, smoothing back a wisp of stray hair that had fallen across her brow. 'It is that I feel I should. What else can I do with my life? What is there to do?'

'Maybe you should send one of your books to Miss Brontë,' Harriet said, 'and ask her opinion of it.'

'Or Mr Thackeray,' Emily sat down on the low bench that stood under the window. 'Papa knows him quite well. Or why not just a publisher, like Mr Smith who publishes Miss Brontë?'

'Yes, just send it off,' Harriet jumped up and down. 'Oh that is such a capital plan, Emily!'

Jenny gazed at them with wonder, a finger on her lip.

'But I never thought of that.'

'Why ever not?' Emily enquired. 'Books are meant to be read.'

'What will Mama say?'

'Do not ask her until you have a publisher.'

'Oh, if I were a published author, it would give me . . . such purpose!' Jenny said. 'It would mean so much to me.'

Emily gazed at her friend, as though she saw beneath those plain, homely looks to the passionate, unhappy woman beneath. It was difficult to know what it would be like to be Jennifer, with her large Foxton nose and the wide Foxton mouth that made the men attractive but the girls uncomely. None of the Foxton men were conventionally handsome in that there was nothing regular or clean-cut in their looks. But the unevenness of line, the seeming lack of harmony produced an effect that women appeared to find almost irresistibly attractive. Even old Lord Foxton was handsome in a craggy kind of way. Not that he was very old; but he was older than Papa whom she considered very youthful.

'Miss Brontë is not married either,' Emily went on helpfully, trying hard to think of all the happy or successful unmarried women she knew.

'But she is particularly plain, I hear,' Harriet said. 'She is very small. Tiny.'

Emily laughed.

'It is only because you are so tall, Harry, that you consider that a disadvantage.'

'Some consider it a disadvantage in us.' Jenny squinted myopically at her silks, holding them up to the light. 'Now *if* I could get just the right colour for the watch towers . . . But I must say I prefer to be tall than small. Being tall has advantages. Yes, I will send my manuscript to Mr Smith. Rawdon can take it back for me when he goes to London.'

'Rawdon is coming?' Emily enquired slowly, hoping with a shrug of indifference to conceal her interest.

'Did Mama not tell you? He and James are coming for two days, arriving this afternoon.'

Jennifer blushed a little as she mentioned James and turned her head from the light.

'Oh, *James* is coming too?' Harriet said, looking meaningfully at Emily. 'We shall have quite a little flutter in the dovecotes.'

'I can't think what you mean.' Jennifer selected her silk and began to thread the needle, bringing it closer to her eyes.

'Well, Emily is in love with Rawdon and I know that you fancy James.'

'*I* fancy James . . ?'

'*I* in love with Rawdon . . ?'

The two girls burst out indignantly with one accord, Jennifer dropping her needle and Emily rising swiftly from the bench where she had been idling.

'Oh come. I know you girls. Emily danced with Rawdon all the season.'

'Rawdon and I are old friends,' Emily protested. 'He is like a brother to our family, as you are like sisters.'

'And is James like a brother to you, Jenny?'

Harriet leaned over, unsuccessfully trying to catch Jennifer's eye.

'It is true I *am* fond of James; but he is not the least

interested in me. He is kind to me and asks me to dance; but that is all.'

Emily sighed.

'I am afraid that James is untrustworthy, Jenny. He is a ladies' man. You must not lose your heart to James.'

'I can think of no two more dissimilar people,' Harriet said brutally. 'James is beautiful and dashing and Jenny is plain and withdrawn . . .'

Emily gave a horrified gasp as Jennifer rose and dashed her tapestry into Harriet's face, belabouring her with it as though it had been a whip. As Harriet crouched trying to protect her spectacles Emily ran forward and seized Jennifer about the waist drawing her back.

'Oh Jenny, Jenny . . . you must not. Stop!'

Jennifer struggled and, on account of her strength, at first succeeded in resisting Emily, but Harriet managed to retreat out of aim and Jenny let the mangled, utterly ruined piece of needlework hang loosely by her side. Then she burst into tears and Emily instinctively turned her head to her bosom patting her shoulder.

'There. There. It was a very cruel thing of Harriet to say, and untrue.'

'It *is* true,' Harriet said from the safety of the other side of the room. 'Jenny pretends not to care for men but she yearns for James; just because he is so bad and has such a wicked reputation. Papa says he goes to brothels. There!'

Emily felt herself affronted by the attack on her brother. She gently led the still sobbing Jennifer to a chair and made her sit down. Then she turned and, crossing her hands in front, drew herself up and looked at Harriet.

'James's private life is no concern of ours, Harriet. At least if he goes to brothels, which I abhor, he is not defiling virtuous young women. I do not understand a man's needs which are different from our own. But James has a good heart. He is very kind, and if he is also impulsive and sensual then all I can say is that it is a part of his nature and he is very discreet about it. If Rawdon said anything then . . .'

'Rawdon, Rawdon,' a voice said as the door opened. 'Do I hear my name taken in vain?'

'Rawdon!' Harriet flew over to him and he opened his arms to embrace her.

Emily was glad of the diversion because it enabled her to recover from the shock his sudden appearance gave her. It was the effect his presence always had upon her that made her know without any doubt that she was in love. She didn't feel like this about other men; but seeing Rawdon across a room or suddenly enter one briefly took her breath away.

Rawdon always looked grave when he came into a room, though with an agreeable expression on his face as though he had to impart serious but not unpleasant news. He invariably had his hands clasped behind his back, and his firm square jaw thrust into the air as though he did nothing without purpose. Yes, Rawdon was very purposeful, very masculine, Emily thought not for the first time, as he gently put Harriet aside and went over to where Jenny, still tear-stained, was sitting on the couch. His deep-set eyes were so obscured by the shadow cast by his high forehead and springy eyebrows that, without being near him, one could hardly make out their colour.

Emily knew the colour from the many times they had waltzed together or he had leaned close to talk to her. They were a clear and most unusual colour of grey with maybe just a suspicion of green when they flashed, as they often did. His nose was long and broad, flattening towards his cheeks rather like a pugilist. His mouth was wide and his upper lip full and sensuous, overlapping the lower one which was rather narrow and aesthetic as though expressive of the ambivalent nature of a strong yet gentle man.

Rawdon was leaning down staring at Jenny, his legs apart, his hands behind his back. He was dressed for riding with a full frock coat, a high lace cravat and long black shining boots. Jennifer would not meet his eyes and her head sank on her chest in an attitude of abasement.

'Jenny? Tears?' Rawdon said, but Jenny did not reply.

Rawdon straightened up and came over to Emily bowing slightly, his hands still behind his back.

'Emily, it is charming to find you here. Now what were you saying about me as I came in?'

Emily was aware of that strong masculine aroma that aroused in her feelings to which she dared not give a name. She stared boldly into his face and gave him the smile that she knew was special for him, because no one affected her as he did.

'*If* you want to know, Rawdon, we were not talking about you but about James. Where is he?' She made a great charade of looking over his shoulder as though expecting at any moment to see her brother enter.

'James is at Chetwell. We escorted Jane there, and James decided to stay because your mother complained she never saw him and it made her ill. He sent a letter with his apologies to Mama who I understand is in Rye. And Papa, is he well?'

Rawdon looked over at Jenny who still sat with her head bowed.

'Papa is tired,' Harriet said. 'He had a little twinge of pain around the heart last night and Mama said he should rest more.'

'Ah!' A look of anxiety passed briefly over Rawdon's face as he turned again to Emily. 'But if you were talking about James how did I . . .'

'You were at *Cherwell?*' Emily interrupted angrily, as though he had been visiting forbidden places.

'Is there anything wrong with that?'

Rawdon smiled, and Emily wondered if she saw a mischievous light in his eyes.

'I was under the impression that you and James were coming straight here.'

'Ah, you had forgotten about Jane. No, I spent the night there and left the coach and came over today on horseback. Your Mama would have me escort you back in a day or two and then James and I return to London. Our regiment is going on manoeuvres very shortly.'

'Oh.' The thought of Rawdon alone with Caroline was somehow mitigated by the knowledge that he was here to take her home and that, until then, she would have him for at least two days.

'Now what were you saying . . .'

'Oh Rawdon, it is too delicate to explain!' Emily said

impatiently. 'We were talking about James and your name came up. That is all.'

'We were saying that it is known James goes to brothels,' Harriet said with a nervous glance in the direction of her sister, as though fearful that she would once more jump up and berate her. 'Papa said so, and we thought you told him.'

Emily reddened and turned her face away from the light.

'Oh Harriet! I wish you would not. It is not delicate to talk like that.'

'Indeed it is not,' Rawdon said severely, 'and if you think such information came from me I assure you you are mistaken. I would never speak like that about a friend and comrade to anyone, let alone my father. I am quite shocked. Is this why Jenny is in tears? I do not wonder.'

'No, that has nothing to do with James,' Harriet said, beginning to flounder. 'Well yes, in a way it has.' She stopped and looked again at Jenny.

Emily decided matters had gone far enough. She moved swiftly over to Jenny and took her hand. Then she looked straight into Rawdon's eyes.

'We were having a little female chat, Rawdon dear. Why do you not go up and see your Papa?'

Rawdon frowned, then smiled. With consummate female tact Emily had provided just the answer.

Saltmarsh Castle was a grim baronial structure going back to Anglo-Saxon times when the sea had come as far as Rye. Foxtons had lived in it since King John granted it to a war-like ancestor of theirs who had supported him against the barons. Over the centuries the sea had retreated and the castle now stood on a promontory in a fertile wooded valley, through which meandered a stream that had its source high in the Sussex Downs.

The Foxton home was still surrounded by a moat and battlements, which had been allowed to crumble since it was no longer necessary to protect the local citizenry from marauders both within and without the kingdom. In olden times they had driven their animals up the hill and stayed secure within the walls, sleeping under makeshift dwellings made of skin and wood set up in the outer bailey. An inner and outer bailey still existed and so did the huge watch-towers constructed by the warlike Sir Ranulf Foxton who had supported Bad King John. Between them stood the original part of the Keep, the huge main doorway surmounted by the Foxton arms and protected by a portcullis which, though never raised or lowered now, was still kept in working order.

Were it not for the lure of the Foxton family, or rather its heir, Emily would never have stayed at Saltmarsh if she could help it. With its small rooms and the thick, forbidding walls it seemed to be more like a prison than a home. It lacked the elegance and spaciousness of Chetwell with its tall windows and broad sweeping vistas of the sea and the countryside of Kent.

But there was plenty to do at Saltmarsh. There was riding and walking and visits to the farm and, for Emily, there was the very important task of contriving to spend as much time with Rawdon as she could without seeming to try very hard.

Emily had many of the qualities of a much older and more sophisticated woman. They seemed quite natural to her; it was as though she were born with them. She knew how to interest men by pretending to ignore them; and then, when she had them in thrall, she knew how to keep them by the exercise of her charm and an almost instinctive knowledge of feminine wiles. She could make Rawdon Foxton feel at his ease with her because they had known each other all their lives. Thus she could subtly intrude in his life in a way she would never have dared had he been a comparative stranger. The difficulty was making him aware of her as a desirable woman rather than a friend of the family, an intimate of his sisters.

Emily had a very good seat on a horse and she loved riding. She rode better than her sisters and much better than the Foxton girls who were awkward on horseback and not able to go very fast because of their poor eyesight. The way to get Rawdon's exclusive attention was to go riding. Emily decided on her strategy that night as she lay in her narrow bed in the small tower room, and the next morning she was up early dressed in her riding habit which she brought with her because she rode in Hyde Park as well as the country.

Lady Foxton, who had spent the night worrying about her husband, was up early too and surprised to see Emily as she sat in the morning room pouring tea.

'Emily, child. It is just past seven. Could you not sleep?'

'I slept very well, Aunt. But I love to ride before breakfast. May I?'

'Of course. The grooms will be glad of your help, exercising the horses. What a pity you did not mention this last night. Rawdon might have gone with you.'

Sybil Foxton looked slyly at Emily. In her severe black riding habit with her hair drawn hard back into a prim chignon at the nape of her neck, she looked almost more lovely than she did in a ball gown with her ringlets tossing and her blue eyes sparkling. Her habit was made of black grosgrain with a full skirt and tight high buttoned jacket that accentuated her well developed bosom. Her black beaver hat had a spotted muslin veil tied loosely round the brim, trailing stylishly behind her. She could have been dressed for an important meet rather than a morning canter on her own.

But then Emily was always correctly attired, at whatever hour, whatever the occasion, because she thought you could never be sure when you would need to show yourself at your best.

Emily patted her neat bun and adjusted her veil in the mirror.

'I'm sure Rawdon needs to sleep Aunt Sybil, if only to get ready for all those manoeuvres.'

Sybil smiled to herself. Emily would never give anything away, though it was obvious to her that she cared for her eldest son. Anyone watching her at the dinner table last night needed no further proof, although it was done very subtly and obvious only to someone as experienced in the ways of the world as Sybil Foxton.

'I will get one of the footmen to escort you to the stables my dear, and be sure a groom accompanies you.'

But when she got to the stables which were in the valley below the steep walls of the castle, Emily found a state of great activity at the centre of which, to her secret delight, was Rawdon Foxton. He was dressed informally in open-necked shirt and riding breeches, leading his horses around the field while assorted grooms and servants scurried about with pails and brushes and various accoutrements.

Emily gazed at him with pleasure before he observed her, her mouth partly open, a deep sigh of happiness on her lips. It was so much nicer for being unplanned and therefore unexpected. She walked up to the stables and began to chat to the head groom before Rawdon returned, leading a mare from the far side of the meadow. She was selecting a mount when Rawdon hailed her and when she looked at him she endeavoured to appear both surprised and detached.

'Rawdon! I did not recognize you in that garb. I thought you were one of the grooms.' She gave a pert smile as the head groom, taking care to control his features, helped her onto her sidesaddle.

'Shall I accompany you, Miss?'

'If you would, Jordan. Lady Foxton particularly asked me not to ride alone.'

'Well I shall ride with you, dammit,' Rawdon said, gesturing to the groom. 'Saddle Midnight for me please, Jordan.' Then, making an elaborate bow to Emily he said: 'I hope it does not inconvenience you, Miss Vestrey. I shall be sure to travel some paces behind.'

Emily laughed delightedly and, taking the reins of her horse, nudged its flank and sped off down the meadow by the side of the stream. She felt a thrill of anticipation, a wild sense of abandon as the horse's hooves thudded beneath her and the blurred outline of the leafy trees passed on either side. She could hear the sound of hooves behind her and flicked her whip against the roan's neck calling to it to go faster. Ahead there was a turn in the valley which led to the sea and a small bridge crossed the stream. Emily slowed down to walking pace and glanced behind to where Rawdon was still thundering across the meadow after her. Emily moistened her lips with satisfaction and took her horse onto the bridge just as Rawdon was forced to slow down too.

From where she stood the Castle towered over the valley,

the twin perpendicular watchtowers looming like sentinels. Ahead the valley narrowed so much that the trees on either side almost converged to form a vault like the sculpted tracery of a gothic cathedral. The sun filtering through the trees illuminated the left bank, while the other was in deep shadow. The stream broadened at this point and only a narrow bridle path ran along one side.

'We can only canter from here on,' Rawdon said, leading his horse up to her. 'But when we get to the shore we can gallop as fast as we like!'

The wind had brought colour to their faces, though Emily's veil had swirled about her head so that it partly concealed her face. Her glowing pink cheeks and the glint of her eyes through the mysterious veil made Rawdon suddenly aware of her deeply desirable femininity. It was a quality he had hitherto not perceived in the girl he had grown up with, the friend of his sisters with whom he enjoyed dancing because she did it so well. The picture she presented as she stood with her horse against the background of the variegated greens of the trees, the abundance of wild flowers, the contrasting patches of light and shade, was infinitely alluring. She seemed to him someone of whom he had only just become aware, a new exciting, completely different person.

Observing his look Emily drew herself up, tilting her head and allowing that flirtatious smile, whose efficacy she knew, to play upon her lips. But as he came nearer she was assailed by a fit of shyness and she turned to stroke her horse's nose thus avoiding the penetrating look in his eyes. She was aware of Rawdon's hand reaching out to stroke the horse, of his proximity and that strong masculine aroma that was like nothing she knew from Papa or her brothers or anyone else. She suddenly realized they had never been alone together. There had always been people thronging about them, on the dance floor, in the various homes where they met and talked and laughed; but never quite alone as here.

'Come, let me lead your horse over the bridge,' Rawdon said, gently patting the animal's flank and taking its bridle in his hand. Emily followed thoughtfully after him, and when they were on the path Rawdon turned and deftly helped her mount, taking care not to indicate his enhanced awareness of her by an unfamiliar gesture that might seem like a caress. Then when she was seated sidesaddle he vaulted on his horse as though to emphasize the difference between them: that she was a fragile delicate woman and he was a vigorous muscular man.

But Emily liked being fragile; she enjoyed her feminine role. She had no wish to write books or serve humanity or be anything other than the wife of someone like Rawdon Foxton, the chatelaine of his castle and the mother of his children. It would be pleasant to marry someone slightly more elevated; an earl or a duke perhaps; but Rawdon would suit very well, a baron as Papa would be one day and with a similar estate and income. Besides, he was so attractive.

They rode in silence through the valley until it grew broader and in the distance they could see the wide expanse of Camber sands and to the right, perched on its hilltop, the ancient town of Rye. Emily stopped her horse to glance behind and Rawdon drew abreast of her. Together they looked back through the valley to where the crenellated tops of the twin watchtowers could be seen rising above the trees.

'It is a very beautiful morning,' Rawdon said. 'What a good thing we came. Did you know I was out?'

'No,' Emily said truthfully. 'And your mother thought you were still in bed. I always like to ride in the morning. At Chetwell I do every day, unless I've had a very late night. I never saw the castle look so splendid,' she said as an afterthought.

'I don't think you like it very much, do you, Emily?'

'Oh yes!' Emily said quickly. 'Whatever gave you that idea?'

It was very important that Rawdon should think she liked his home.

'Jennifer said you found it frightening.'

'That is Jenny's imagination,' Emily said lightly, letting her horse break into a slow trot. 'You know that she has written a novel she wishes to send to a publisher?'

'I know that she has written novels but not that she wanted to see them published.' Rawdon sighed and the expression of contentment left his face. 'Poor Jenny. I wish she could find a husband.'

Yes, Emily wished she could find a husband too. Rawdon's unmarried sisters would only stay at home and be a burden when Rawdon married.

'Jenny could be quite pretty if she did her hair differently, wore more becoming clothes and only used her glasses when she really needed to.'

'But she is too tall and thin.'

'If she chose more flattering clothes and went to a better dressmaker, it would conceal the disadvantage of her figure.'

Rawdon looked at the trim waist and firm mature bustline of the woman next to him. The proportions of her figure were quite admirable. With her hair neatly set in a chignon, her pert hard little riding hat and the feminine veil, her profile was distinctly alluring.

'Perhaps Jenny and Harriet would let you advise them,' Rawdon said impulsively. 'Do you think . . . ?'

'Oh no,' Emily said guardedly. 'Besides, I would not presume. I think it is up to your mother, who has perfect dress sense and beauty into the bargain.'

'I think mother is disappointed in the girls,' Rawdon said quietly. 'And her disappointment shows. She is too apologetic for them.'

Emily avoided a direct answer. Relations between mothers and daughters were delicate enough, as she well knew, without her interference.

'Maybe Jenny will be a famous writer like Miss Brontë!'

'But I do not *want* her to be like Miss Brontë!' Rawdon flicked his crop against his horse's neck causing it to break into a brisk trot. 'I want her to be like any other woman. Like you . . .'

He looked at Emily and she met his gaze. She felt very sure of her attraction for him, of the hold she had suddenly and quite unexpectedly acquired. She knew she was beautiful and clever and witty and she must use her time at Saltmarsh to press home the advantage she had gained, possibly to the extent of getting Rawdon to declare himself. Oh, if he asked Papa when he took her home . . .

Her hope showed on her face and it occurred to Rawdon that he had overplayed his hand. After all, it was a beautiful morning and Emily had a perfect seat on a horse. She was vibrant with her youthful good looks, and the habit she wore was particularly becoming. He was proving too susceptible and before he knew where he was he would be saying something foolish.

'I mean a *normal* girl like you and Caroline. Ordinary normal girls with the usual accomplishments that young women have.'

'But not Jane, I notice,' Emily said artfully, seeing the confusion on his face.

'Well, Jane is not exactly normal. Jane and Jenny have a lot in common except that Jane is a beauty and Jenny is not. I could not live with Jane at all. She tries to be too smart.'

'You do like women to be in a mould, do you not, Rawdon?'

He looked at her with surprise. 'A mould? How do you mean, a mould?'

'Well, to conform. Do you expect all men to be alike too?'

'Oh come, Emily. You are chaffing me. Everyone is different, man or woman. No, I do not wish for moulds; but I like women to want womanly things, to be like women and if possible to look pleasing. My sister wants to be a novelist and she does not attract men. That is not what I want at all. For *her* sake. And Jane will have a lot of difficulties in her life with her views and opinions which she does not conceal. Why, she was even presuming to argue with Lord Palmerston at Mrs Gladstone's the other night! Your father was quite put out.'

Emily laughed with delight and turned her horse towards the sea. 'I think men like a woman with spirit. Do not Caroline and I have spirit too?'

'Of course you have! But I cannot see either you or Caroline arguing with the Foreign Secretary.'

'But Lord Palmerston likes pretty women. He would

enjoy an encounter with Jane, just to see the colour in her cheeks and the sparkle in her eyes. He is an old roué.'

Emily looked at him flirtatiously and Rawdon knew he was becoming more enmeshed by the minute. It had been unwise of him to come after Emily. He should at least have brought a groom. They had never been alone together and there was good reason for the customs of society. He would be paying court to Emily Vestrey before he knew what he was doing. He did not wish to marry yet. He had never even thought of it, despite the hints of his mother. He was too unsure of what he was doing in life, whether to stay in the army or leave, or transfer to a regiment that offered more action. His only weakness, and he knew he was not unique, concerned the needs of the flesh. These he kept in check by vigorous exercise and discipline and the occasional visit to a good house patronized only by the nobility. He would have liked a mistress as some of his brother officers had; a married woman who had performed her childbearing duties, and whose husband looked elsewhere. But Rawdon eschewed the involvement that this kind of relationship entailed – the present-giving, the subterfuge, the inevitability of emotional entanglement.

His mother often reminded him that the prettiest girls were soon snapped up; there were many marrying in their teens. Someone like Emily Vestrey, or her sister Caroline, would not be around forever.

Emily had put her horse into a gallop and was heading out across the white sands towards the sea. She was a temptress, no doubt about that. She knew how beautiful she looked, how well she sat on a horse. She was trying to get him to fall in love with her.

Rawdon suddenly felt an impulsive surge of the heart. Well, why not? Maybe it would, after all, be the solution to many of his problems. He would leave the army and join the diplomatic service as his father wanted, and Emily would accompany him to posts overseas, Moscow or Berlin or Vienna, and be a perfect, beautiful hostess, an adornment, an asset to him. Emily would do that sort of thing so well, and if he waited . . . A lot of young men were already after Emily Vestrey and it was only his vanity that made him think she cared that little bit extra for him now.

Yes, he would pursue her; he would court her and when he was sure his feelings were reciprocated he would propose, maybe before Christmas. His parents would be delighted.

Emily was now a dot on the horizon and Rawdon suddenly became alarmed. She was going too fast; she would fall and break her skull. Already he thought of her as his future bride. He began to call after her and spurred his horse to a gallop.

Emily realized that, by trying to impress, she was going too fast and pulled on the reins. For a moment she had a feeling of panic and a vision of the horse tearing into the sea or maybe it would never stop and ride on to Hythe. That would never do. She pulled hard at the bit, and to her relief the horse slowed down, until she was able to look behind and see with satisfaction Rawdon pounding after her. She meant him to chase her; to chase her hard. She wouldn't give him too much of a run; but he must realize she could choose almost anybody and she wanted to be married, to have her own establishment and her own place in society. She felt that Rawdon was still not sure what he wanted, and he must be helped to make up his mind.

She turned round and began to canter gently away from the sea towards him until she could hear the hard breathing of his horse and see the exertion and anxiety on his face, which was rather set and grim as though he had feared she had bolted. She prepared a welcoming smile for him when, out of the trees through which they had come, someone else was riding hard towards them. Yes, there was no mistake, and as he drew nearer she saw it was one of the grooms from the castle. Obviously Lady Foxton, scandalized at Emily disappearing alone with her son, had quickly sent an escort. It didn't matter: she felt she had done a very good morning's work.

As Rawdon came up to her and slowed down she pointed with her crop. 'Look! Your Mama has sent an escort.'

'Oh, but Mama would not do such a thing. It must be something else.'

Rawdon smiled confidently at Emily to show her that they now had a new relationship though she might not yet be aware of it. He would take his time; but he would be very sure. He wanted her.

The groom was panting and Rawdon's happiness evaporated in a frisson of alarm.

'Is something wrong, Jordan?' he called, and trotted up to the rider. Emily became apprehensive too and went slowly after him.

'Mr Rawdon, sir,' the groom gasped. 'You are to come straight away to the castle. Your father has been taken ill and the doctor sent for. Your mother found him collapsed in his bed. He is very bad Mr Rawdon, sir. Very ill.'

CHAPTER FOUR

Jeremy Pagan having, by sheer persistence, succeeded in obtaining permission to paint Jane, had set her leaning against a great elm that crested the brow of the hill of Chetwell Park. In the background was the splendid sweep of the sea, and he placed Jane slightly in profile so that she appeared to be gazing at some distant spot between the sea and the cliffs at Folkestone. To accentuate Jane's special type of beauty he had her dressed very demurely in mauve poplin print, the neat *basquin* bodice buttoned to the waist with a V neckline, and a turned-down collar edged with a narrow frill of Brussels lace. Beneath the low *décolletage* was a *chemisette* made of tulle, also frilled and puffed and fastened at the wrists below the bell-shaped sleeves of her bodice. The long skirt gathered at the waist fell to the ground and, just below knee length, there was an ornamental border of deep purple stitching encircling the dress. Over her shoulders she wore a plain white Indian shawl which at the back resembled a cowl heavily fringed with thick silk tassels. Her hair was loose and hung over her shoulders and her hands were clasped in front of her, one foot also slightly before the other.

On a day such as this she was a vision of beauty and he painted furiously to recapture the moment, the conditions that were so right, sunny but dark under the elm so that he had part of her face in the shade. He wanted to get the background right here, and the figure he could finish in London working in the studio that Millais had let him use in Gower Street.

Millais had just met the Ruskins and was very taken by them, particularly Effie, and they by him. They wanted him to come abroad to Switzerland with them and he spent most of his time at their house in Park Street. What had started as gratitude for Ruskin's defence of the pre-Raphaelite brotherhood in *The Times* had turned into friendship. But, in Jeremy's opinion, Ruskin was a cold fish, and Millais a hot blooded and passionate man. He didn't see the friendship succeeding, though it would be useful for Millais to be well thought of by such an eminent art critic at Ruskin.

Jane was wonderful to paint, such a good subject. They spoke little and, unlike most women of his acquaintance, she seemed perfectly happy absorbed in her own thoughts. When she did say something it was interesting and to the point, or some intelligent comment on a remark of his. They got on very well. Jeremy's thoughts had even turned to love though he had no intention of getting married for years, and a girl such as Jane Vestrey would never be allowed alone in the company of a young unattached man. Her sister had accompanied her to the preliminary sketches in London, and what a chatterbox she had been!

The sister was coming over now, walking across the lawn with a large bonnet to protect her from the sun. She also had on a white spotted poplin dress and in front of her ran a couple of dogs while by her side were the youngest Vestreys. Seen from the corner of his eye Jeremy thought it was a charming picture – English upper class country life at its best. Behind the advancing sister – he saw now that it was Caroline not Emily, for which thank God – was the red stone pile of Chetwell Place, a monument to English wealth and the continuing dominance of the aristocracy.

Gracious living appealed to Jeremy Pagan. Like Mr Ruskin his father too was a merchant, but not such a successful one. There was enough however to send young Jeremy to Rugby where he was found to have a talent for art, and a little more was scraped together to pay for instruction in London and later in Italy where Jeremy spent his early twenties.

Now he had returned home to make his fortune as a fashionable painter, and the ease with which he had captured Miss Jane Vestrey made him optimistic about his future, for Millais had told him what he already knew, that his talent was outstanding. False modesty was not among Jeremy Pagan's attributes.

Young Patrick Vestrey broke away from his sister and

nearly knocked over Jeremy's palette as he cannoned into him, the barking dogs nagging excitedly at his heels. Jane turned round in alarm as Jeremy recovered his stance but not his composure.

'Get away from here!' he snapped and Master Patrick, unused to being addressed in such terms, stood his ground and stuck out his tongue.

'Patrick!' Caroline cried reprovingly, seizing her young brother by the arm and dragging him away from the easel. 'I *do* apologize, Mr Pagan. Patrick has no sense of art.'

Jeremy had laid down his brush but could not conceal his irritation. The day had been so perfect, the mood and moment just right. Now Jane had lost the particular stance he had worked so hard to arrange, and was smiling at her impudent young brother. The dogs were sniffing round the legs of the easel and one had already relieved itself there to the vast amusement of Clare, who was trying unsuccessfully to stifle her giggles into her cupped hands. Jeremy ran his fingers through his hair and gazed despairingly at the sky.

'I can see we have disturbed you, Mr Pagan,' Caroline said apologetically, 'but my Great Aunt Ruth has arrived unexpectedly from London and we are to have luncheon early. Papa begged me to interrupt you and say that you may have all the time you wish later for the portrait.'

Jeremy's irritation changed swiftly to good humour. He had, after all, to placate his wealthy and influential patrons. Any show of churlishness would be remembered. He wiped his brow on a paint-stained handkerchief and gave them all the benefit of his dazzling and charming smile.

'Forgive me Miss Vestrey, but when I am absorbed in my work, young boys, *and* dogs . . .'

, 'I know, *and* interruptions. Emily and Papa will doubtless return with Aunt Ruth tomorrow or the day after and if that is not sufficient time for you, and Jane consents, you may stay down here.'

'Jane consents, I should think she would!' Jane stretched her arms and took a deep breath. 'Do you think it is not preferable to that nonsense in London of partying and so forth? Thank God when the season is over.'

72

Jeremy laughed, wiping his brushes carefully before placing them in his box.

'I am afraid Miss Jane is a socialist. She would reform the world and have everyone at work. No idle women or bored men. My father, you know, knew Miss Martineau in Norwich before her father died and she came to live in London.'

'Really? You never told me that.' Jane brushed back her hair from where the wind had blown it across her forehead.

'Yes. Mr Martineau was a cloth manufacturer before the collapse of his business and my father knew him very well. No-one expected Miss Martineau to achieve such fame. He said she was a very singular young woman, but ill-formed and as deaf as a post.'

'Oh I should *so* like to meet her!' Jane clasped her hands together. 'I have read so many of her articles in *Household Words* which Mr Dickens edits, and also in *The Leader* and *Once A Week*. Her famous tales of political economy made an impression on me in the schoolroom.'

'And how does a very young lady from the aristocracy have such seditious works in the *schoolroom*?' Jeremy said mockingly, tucking his canvas carefully under his arm as Caroline prepared to lead the way back to the house.

'Oh, Miss Martineau is not seditious,' Caroline said, taking Patrick's hand and giving him a little shake to stop him from repeatedly sticking out his tongue at Jeremy. 'Father has always approved of Miss Martineau and also of Mr Bentham and Mr Mill who were also read in the schoolroom as were Mrs Gaskell and Mr Carlyle.'

'Only the Misses Brontë were forbidden in the schoolroom,' Jane said wryly, 'because they dwelt on *passion* and not on politics.'

'And have *you* read the Misses Brontë?'

'Of course, including *Wuthering Heights* which is really quite shocking.'

'You find it shocking, Miss Jane? I am surprised.'

'No *I* do not find it shocking; but *it* is shocking. No-one thinks it could be written by an unmarried woman who had not experienced the things she writes about. And Miss

73

Emily Brontë died unmarried, therefore...' Jane shrugged her shoulders and smiled.

'Therefore she is considered shocking.'

'Exactly. She was shocking. But *Jane Eyre* is my favourite. It is about a girl who is merely a governess and falls in love with the father of her charge. It is *very* passionate. We have all read it; but Mama does not know, and you must not tell her.'

'I would not dream of it.' Jeremy stepped back as Jane went into the porch, a smile upon his lips. So far he and Jane had discussed all sorts of things, but never passion. He must bring up the works of the Misses Brontë again.

This was one of Mama's good days. Indeed the latter half of the week had been altogether better and she was even quite nice to Papa and was now being very agreeable to Great Aunt Ruth. The family had already sat down when the others appeared in the dining room, as hours for meals were very much a fixed part of life at Chetwell Place, Papa having a passion for punctuality. He ostentatiously looked at his large repeater watch as Caroline, Jane and Mr Pagan slipped into place. The younger children still ate separately from the rest of the family except on Sundays when Papa liked to observe their progress as regards table manners.

'Excuse us Papa; but I think luncheon was a *little* early.'

'I said it would be early Caroline, and I asked you...'

'You must pardon me, Papa. I changed and went into the garden as soon as I could. Deborah was not well last night and I had a very busy morning.'

'Debbie is ill again?' Her father's face puckered with anxiety as he rang the bell and a stream of well-trained servants entered through the door that led into the kitchen quarters, carrying an assortment of dishes.

'She has a cough as a result of her fever, Papa. It kept her awake half the night.'

'Then Doctor Woodlove must be called again, a specialist consulted maybe. All my children have always enjoyed excellent health.' Papa poured himself some claret as Mama raised her eyes to heaven, observed only by Caroline and Aunt Ruth. It was Papa's insistence on good health that made Mama's life both such a trial to herself and a trial to him. Papa had never known a day's illness in his life and did not expect others to. Maybe his childhood memories of his semi-invalid father had made him determined that his life and household should be ordered differently.

'Now Aunt Ruth, you have not told us the object of your visit, except to say that it is not about father who, if anything, is a little better than he was. I am happy to hear it. I sometimes wonder if the country would not suit father better than London.'

'You mean *here*, George?' Aunt Ruth said incredulously, while Agnes shuffled in her chair.

'Well, where else?' George said. 'We have no other country house that I know of.'

'Oh, it is impossible . . .' Agnes began, but Aunt Ruth gave her a reassuring smile and said: 'You know your father loves London, George. When he can he likes to go to his club or have a drive in the park. Besides, he is near his doctors.'

'We have good doctors here,' George said, placing his glass firmly on the table as though to indicate that that was the end of the matter.

Ruth sighed. Though she loved her nephew dearly she did not find him an easy man. Her brother always having been delicate meant that his eldest son had somehow grown up as an autocrat, having taken over the reins from a very early age. George was a liberal in politics, a reformist at heart as he was always fond of telling people; but in the bosom of his family he was absolute master, fond and loving husband, father and brother that he was. However, to move his father was clearly ridiculous. So George must have suggested it merely to provoke Agnes.

Ruth had always maintained her independence, her own status as the eldest daughter of the house until the others married. Even then she kept the respect that they had always felt for her. No one ever thought to pity her, let alone despise her for remaining unmarried.

It had not been from choice. A good-looking woman still at sixty, Ruth had been a beauty toasted throughout London as one of the adornments of the season when she was presented. But she was in no hurry to cast her cap, and flirted with all the young bachelors who anxiously pressed their suits during those heady days of the Regency when the whole tenor of Court life was laughter, fun and not a little debauchery.

But when at last she fell in love it was seriously, and as far as she was concerned for good. Her suitor was a fellow officer of her brother Gerard Vestrey, Sir Archibald McLeish of an old Scottish Jacobite family, yet loyal now to the monarchy and serving with the Coldstream Guards. They were engaged and just to be married when Napoleon escaped from Elba and landed at Golfe Juan. The wedding was postponed for a month while Archie dashed off to join his regiment in Belgium.

Like Gerard, Archie McLeish fell at Waterloo and Ruth never looked seriously at another man or sought to replace him in her memory and her affections. She had been twenty-five at the time of Waterloo; already her mother was dead and she became her father's right hand, his help and his nurse. She travelled abroad with him, becoming a fond aunt and support to all her nieces and nephews who brought their troubles to her. Then when her father died and Henry Vestrey was also widowed, his young wife dying from tuberculosis at the age of twenty-nine, she began to look after him, and had done so ever since, helping to bring up his children and see them well placed in life.

George had always been difficult, gifted, a bit lazy, very idealistic. George was the most handsome of all the Vestrey boys and at one time great things were expected of him, an early place in the Cabinet. But George frittered away his time doing this and that and travelling a lot. His enthusiasms for collecting paintings and horses were about equal and it was not until his forties, his family already partly grown up, that he settled down and became useful on the Committee formed by Prince Albert to put into effect his ideas for a Great Exhibition. Now everyone was talking about George as though he was some up and coming young politician instead of a middle-aged man, almost a grandfather. Almost.

Ruth Vestrey spent a lot of time worrying about her great nieces, the three elder Vestrey girls. Too much time, she

76

knew. She worried about Jane because with her spectacular good looks she had such a wild and unconventional streak. Her views were too pronounced and she did not care who she upset when she voiced them. She spent as much time arguing with statesmen as she did dancing with subalterns, and seemed to prefer the company of the former too. It seemed such a waste because surely a very brilliant marriage could otherwise have been predicted for her. Maybe she would grow out of them.

She worried about Emily who had been so unhappy and withdrawn since Lord Foxton suffered his heart attack while she was staying at Saltmarsh the previous month. Her grief had been quite excessive, seeing that Lord Foxton was not even a relation – or had she hoped he might be her father-in-law? If so, and it would be nice, it would not happen yet. Rawdon had leave from the army to look after the estate and his mother during his father's very slow convalescence, and had far too much on his mind to think of marriage.

Then there was Caroline. Aunt Ruth dreaded to see happen to her eldest niece what had happened to her.

For a few years Ruth had broken away, and some of her happiest days had been spent in waiting to the Queen's mother, the Duchess of Kent, whom she knew well, and from whom she had just received a letter.

She would tell them about it now and not wait to say it in private to Agnes and George as she had intended. She knew that, strictly speaking, she was incorrect; but she hoped that the weight, the importance of what she had to say would be seized upon by the other members of the family to counteract the inevitable possessiveness of Agnes. It would give Caroline the break she needed before the demands of her home grew more stifling. Agnes would grow more and more clinging especially as she had developed this antipathy for George. And if her baby lived she would never allow Caroline away from her side.

'You're talking nonsense, George and, as you must know it, I shan't argue. I am here to bring you news of a very singular honour.'

Ruth produced a letter from the small reticule she still

77

insisted on carrying, even though they were out of fashion. For her generation they were regarded as essential.

As though aware of the importance of the occasion everyone put down their knives and forks and waited expectantly on her words, with the exception of Jeremy Pagan in whom a morning out of doors had engendered a ferocious appetite. Ruth unfolded the letter and glanced at Caroline, her face enigmatic.

'I have received a letter from the Queen.' Ruth studied the letter for effect as she knew the contents by heart. 'And Her Majesty, mindful of the personal service our family has performed for the Royal Family in time past, and particularly my own years of waiting on her dear mother, asks that Caroline should be allowed to join her maids-of-honour following Lady Maud Watling's retirement to be married. There.' Ruth sat back, her smile of satisfaction showing her confidence that her family would share her pleasure.

But their reactions were very different, and rather unexpected. To start with no-one appeared at all pleased, as one would have anticipated at receiving a summons from royalty. Papa took a draught of wine and looked anxiously at his wife who had leaned back in her seat closing her eyes and clutching her stomach as though experiencing a spasm of pain. Well, Ruth thought grimly, one could have expected *that*! George's hesitancy too of course. But Caroline's face expressed various and confused emotions, while Emily looked sulky and Jane indifferent, secure in the knowledge that if anyone were to go into waiting it would never be she.

'Well?' Ruth said after the silence had gone on for long enough and even Jeremy Pagan had stopped eating.

'I know not what to say,' George Vestrey said, sitting back and mopping his brow with his napkin. 'I wish you would have mentioned this to me beforehand, Aunt Ruth.'

'I did it deliberately at the table,' Ruth said, carefully pausing to take a sip of her wine. 'I wanted to see how you would all react. Well, I have.' She patted her lips grimly. 'And I am shocked. This family has a tradition of service to the Royal Family going back for over a hundred years, if not longer. It is a singular honour Her Majesty proposes. Think you that there are not hundreds of suitable young women she could choose from, who would have jumped up and down at such a command and not sat glumly staring in front of them as Caroline does now? The Queen made a point of telling me how pleased Prince Albert was with your father's work for the Exhibition, and what pleasure it would give her to cement the affection she has for this family – yes, Her Majesty used the word "affection" – by getting to know Caroline better.'

'It is not that I am not honoured, Aunt Ruth.' Caroline spoke at last looking at her aunt straight in the eyes. 'But I think you know that I am unable to leave home, because of Mama. This is the reason I did not come to London for the rest of the season. You know that, Aunt.'

'I know it my dear. I know very well what you are thinking and I can only commend you for it. But you would never be asked again. It is not only an honour, but a chance to meet some of the most interesting people in the country, I may say the world. You never know to whom you will be sitting next at dinner : a German Prince, a French minister, an Indian Maharajah. I found the experience fascinating and it increased my interest in world affairs which I have never lost.'

'I cannot leave Mama. I have given my word.'

Yes, she had promised one evening soon after Mama knew about the baby, that she would see her through this bad time, that she would never let her down. Mama had been crying, saying that she did not know what she would do and Caroline had taken her hand and promised to stay with her, no matter what happened. And in the few short weeks since she made that promise she had received an invitation to join the service of the Queen.

But a promise was a promise. As the eldest daughter it was her duty, her privilege, to keep her word no matter what the cost. It was how she had been brought up; it was expected of her.

'Could not *Emily* take your place at home?' Aunt Ruth said pointedly. 'She is but a year younger than you.'

'Emily?' Mama said, unable to keep the tone of shocked horror out of her voice. 'Emily may only be a year younger than Caroline, but she hasn't the *slightest* idea how to run a home, look after the children or take care of me. You know that, Aunt Ruth.'

Emily had the grace to blush and sat fiddling with her spoon as the servants quietly cleared the plates from the main course and started to serve dessert. Emily knew she had been very difficult and had infuriated everyone because they didn't know why. She had never got over the shock of the sudden end to her idyll on the beach when she was sure that Rawdon had stopped seeing her as an old family friend and was thinking of something else. The day had seemed so charged with the promise of happiness; of the prospect of a continuation of this new intimacy; of long walks and quiet chats between them; of a growing together that was not possible anywhere else but in his own home where his mother, she was quite sure, favoured their match and would leave them alone.

Lord Foxton had nearly died and she had scarcely seen Rawdon again before James came to take her home, summoned urgently by Lady Foxton. And since then she had not heard from him directly although she had written several little notes expressing her worry and anxiety for his father. Only Jenny had written to say that 'the family' were grateful for her concern and that Papa was slowly recovering. Slowly. Too slowly for Emily.

'And suppose Caroline married and was not here? What would you do then, Agnes? Emily must be made aware of these things, the duties of a daughter of the house. I know Emily likes parties and dances and enjoying herself, but one day even *she* may be married and mistress of a home . . . and if she goes on flirting with young men the way she does I think it may be sooner than she expects!'

Emily avoided her aunt's eye. If only she were right!

'I could look after Mama.' Jane's voice was quiet, unexpected. Everyone looked at her. Her healthy outdoor colour had gone and she looked pale. But if Jane felt confident in her ability to perform the duties of the eldest daughter it was not shared by the other members of her family, particularly her mother who felt herself developing palpitations at the very idea of Jane attempting to take Caroline's place. She put a hand to her bosom and started breathing very quickly.

80

'Out of the question,' she said faintly, and Caroline looking at her with concern said quickly, reassuringly, 'Neither Jane nor Emily could really look after Mama. Well, if it came to it they could, but it is not necessary. Mama wants me and I gave her my word. That is sufficient. However, Aunt, I have another plan which would save the family's honour in the eyes of the Queen. *Emily* would be very suitable at Court. What is more she would love it in a way that I, I confess, would not.'

'Oh!' Emily cried, clasping her hands together. Her depression had suddenly fallen away as, almost instantaneously, the prospect of a new world opened up before her. She did not hesitate. She knew it was right for her, for her character. She was not one to spend months moping around for a man who did not even send her one little note to thank her for her thoughts. Because her thoughts were for him; not his father. Surely he must know that? 'Oh I would *love* it, Caroline. Aunt, is it possible?'

Aunt Ruth looked taken aback and began to wish that she had talked this over in private with George and Agnes after all. But the idea even without reflection was not a bad one. The office of maid-of-honour was unexacting and the long hours of idleness at the Court might suit Emily admirably. Besides, she got on well with children, and the royal nursery was rapidly filling; she danced beautifully and was always bright and amusing. Yes, Emily was really a better choice than Caroline, now that she thought about it.

Both George and Agnes had smiles on their faces and the tense atmosphere round the table relaxed.

'Would it be possible, Aunt Ruth?' George murmured. 'It would solve the problem admirably.'

'You would like me to suggest Emily in place of Caroline?'

'It would be *wonderful* if you could, dear Aunt Ruth,' Agnes said eagerly, her palpitations already beginning to subside. 'It would be ideal, would it not, Emily? You would love it at Court?'

'Oh I would *love* it, Mama! It is full of the most handsome young men and, of course, I am devoted to Her Majesty, the Prince and their children.'

'It would not do to refuse outright,' George said. 'It

would look very bad for us all. Maybe if you went to see the Queen personally and explained the situation? Is that possible, Aunt Ruth?' George was as relieved as everyone else at the prospect of Emily returning to normal. Of course Emily was bored; that was the explanation. After the hectic season she had not enough to do.

'I will see,' Ruth Vestrey said. 'I will have to think what is the best way to approach Her Majesty; but she will be sympathetic I know and sensible of Caroline's duty to her mother in the circumstances. She may of course prefer to ask another fortunate young girl; but I think it will be all right. I think she will have Emily.'

CHAPTER FIVE

Fond as she was of Caroline, the Queen in many ways preferred Emily Vestrey and was pleased to grant Aunt Ruth's request. Although Caroline was the eldest and had to be asked first, Emily was the prettiest and the gayest of the three elder Vestrey girls. She was a wonderful dancer, she painted well, she had a lovely singing voice and was an accomplished pianist. Caroline was rather grave, in the Queen's opinion, and somehow she couldn't see her entering as enthusiastically into the somewhat frivolous spirit of the evenings at Windsor, Osborne and Buckingham Palace as Emily.

It was well known that Prince Albert had once hoped to make the Court the centre of intellectual activity to which men of distinction would come as in days past. Successful in influencing the Queen in so many other things, he had failed in this. So Court evenings after dinner were spent in playing games, dancing or singing the duets which the Queen loved so much. Albert joined in all this with a good heart, but he preferred earnest discussions behind closed doors with the men of the suite whenever he got the opportunity, or playing four-handed chess in the far corner of the room away from the babble.

At the time of Emily's appointment Queen Victoria was thirty-two years old and had been on the throne of England for fourteen years. Since 1839 she had been happily married to her cousin Prince Albert of Saxe-Coburg Gotha and they already had seven children, the youngest Arthur, a baby of a year old.

The English Court was a model of sobriety, rectitude and, some thought, dullness. The days of the four Georges, the scandals of Court life, the debauchery and open licentiousness were buried in the past. Queen Adelaide, the wife of Victoria's Uncle William, who reigned for the seven years between the death of George IV and her own accession, had begun this trend towards respectability even though her husband had sired ten children by his mistress Mrs Jordan before he married her. But, more than anyone, the Queen's mother the Duchess of Kent had cemented it. She had kept her daughter strictly separated from Court life until that momentous day in 1837 when Lord Conyngham and Archbishop Howley had called at dawn at Kensington Palace to tell her that she was Queen.

Prince Albert's background gave him much in common with the Queen. His father was a rake and his mother, who was much younger, was also given to extra-marital amours. Pretty, bubbling Princess Louise was sent away and never allowed to see her children again, rather like the wife of George I. However she was at least allowed to remarry, whereas Sophia was shut up in a prison for thirty-seven years and died there. Victoria had also been brought up without a parent; her father had died soon after she was born.

They both seemed to long for a settled family life and thus embodied the spirit of the age – hard work, respectability and innocent amusements. It suited the Queen's family as it suited her subjects: prosperity and industry centred round a stable home life, after the upheavals of the industrial revolution and the effects of the Napoleonic wars.

Emily Vestrey was the ideal Victorian girl – accomplished but not too clever, not too docile but not in the least ambitious. Or rather she was ambitious but only in the sense that she wanted what every normal, well brought up girl wanted – a carefree girlhood followed by a good marriage to a reliable, respectable man like her father who would care for her and protect her, and whom she could admire and respect as the Queen admired and respected Albert.

Emily loved life at Court. Her only grief was that the periods in waiting were only for a month at a time and not longer. From the moment the carriage bowled through the gates of Windsor Castle and her new life began she thrived on it and rapidly became a favourite with the Queen, the Prince and all the senior members of the Court such as the Duchess of Norfolk, Lady Douro and Lady Canning.

At Court Emily came into her own. Caroline was not there to control her nor Jane to annoy her, nor the boys to tease her nor the little ones to plague her. She was a person in her own right, a member of the Royal Household, and she wore the Maid-of-Honour badge, a miniature of the Queen surrounded by diamonds, on her left shoulder. The duties of the maids-of-honour were slight: to put the Queen's bouquet by her at table; to ride, drive or walk with the Queen whenever she wished, and the Queen had a passion for fresh air; to accompany her at the piano or sing with or for her; and to be agreeable at all times.

The trivia of Court life enchanted Emily. She loved the gossip, the ceremony, the endless hours standing about looking pleasant, the antics of the Royal children, always strictly controlled by their governess Lady Caroline Barrington; the games and dances played every night after dinner. Her French and German were good and improved as she was often placed next to a distinguished visiting foreigner at dinner. She loved the Queen, admired the Prince and got on well with all the members of the Household so that she soon became a pet. The Court became to her an enclosed privileged world where she was cherished, protected and loved.

Emily did not forget about Rawdon Foxton; but nor did she see him in perspective. She was angry with him. There *had* been something between them that day in the valley and on the beach and it was important. It was no use pretending it had not happened; it was no freak of her imagination. So why had his father's illness, serious as it was, made such a difference? He had simply severed communications as though nothing had happened. In a similar circumstance Emily could never envisage herself behaving as he had. He was running away.

No matter. Emily was convinced that this was not the end of her and Rawdon Foxton, and she was quite happy to bide her time. Moreover she would not give him the satisfaction of languishing at home. She was an active, busy, important person : a member of the court.

She wrote enthusiastic letters home detailing her life; little stories about the Queen and Prince, something they or the Royal children said, what she wore, who was at dinner, what games they played afterwards.

Agnes Vestrey, lying on her couch by a window which overlooked the sea, could not hear enough about Court life and read her daughter's letters eagerly as soon as they arrived.

'See, and she went riding with the Queen for an hour and a half in the park! Then she was commanded to Her Majesty's room to accompany her at a duet composed by the Prince!'

Emily's letters did her mother good. The colour came into her cheeks and her eyes momentarily regained the sparkle that Caroline remembered from her childhood. Mama was so pretty, so vivacious when they'd been small, always laughing, always busy and bustling about. It was only when Caroline had reached girlhood that Mama started to be solemn and to scold and nag; her nostalgic memory of childhood was one of pure joy, though of course it couldn't all have been like that. But since she had been in her teens Mama had had three babies who had died, and two miscarriages. The deterioration in Mama's looks had begun then, imperceptible at first, as changes are when they concern people with whom you live.

It was only when she compared Mama to Papa that the changes became marked. Papa was as she remembered him as a child, tall, alert, handsome; but Mama was very different. Mama had shrunk, and grown almost old.

'Oh, the Queen and the Prince have been playing whist together *again*. And the Prince *once* more scolded the Queen and she vows she is afraid of playing with him!'

Mama prattled on, brought alive by the antics at Court. Listening to the endless accounts of drives, walks, dances, rides, who said what to whom, Caroline felt not the slightest bit of envy or regret that she had lost her place to Emily. It all sounded so trivial, so tedious, so purposeless. Caroline put down her embroidery and went to puff up a cushion that had fallen behind Mama's back. Then she stood for a while by her mother's side and looked out at the sea, while Mama continued to read the account of life at Osborne in a breathless, excited voice. The sea which stretched before her would be calm there too, yet not only that but a complete world separated her from her sister Emily.

But what did she have instead? Was what she had so much better? This isolation, this confinement to the house and looking after Mama? Papa had taken the younger children to Scotland in September. James had gone on leave to Italy with two friends, and Jane was now being painted by, it seemed, the entire pre-Raphaelite brotherhood either here or in London, and had entered a new and exciting world of artists, writers and intellectuals.

But Caroline ... nothing had happened to Caroline at all. She felt she was living in a world that was neither limbo, hell nor heaven. Mama had stopped speaking and was looking at her.

'Car, you look so sad? Are you miserable because you gave your place to Emily?'

'Car' was mother's term of endearment for her; nobody else in the family used it but Mama, and then only on special occasions when she was feeling tender or Caroline needed comfort. Mama put out a hand and Caroline clasped it, squeezing it to reassure Mama.

'No Mama, of course not! Life at court would *never* have suited me at all! Dutiful as I would have been to the Queen, and honoured to have served her, I could never have borne the tedium of the life. And I neither dance, sing nor play as well as Emily. I think she is perfectly suited.'

'She *is*.' Mama dropped Caroline's hand and looked thoughtfully out of the window. 'It is ideal for Emily and, nervous though I am about it, Jane has found an ideal niche for her tastes and inclinations. Have you noticed how much less moody she is of late? Maybe it is out of consideration for me, but she does not seem to vex me half as much. You don't think she is in love with Jeremy Pagan do you, Car? He would never do for a husband.'

'I don't think *he* is in love, I think he is too absorbed in himself. I think Jane does like him a little; he is so unlike the men we are used to.'

'Oh Car, pray don't say that.'

'Mama, it will not lead to a marriage, maybe merely a

disappointment for Jane. I think he has no intention of settling. Like our James, he wants a good time.'

'That is men, of course,' Agnes said, setting her mouth grimly. 'Few of them have any sense of responsibility. Rawdon Foxton I must say is an exception. He is very suitable; I like Rawdon very much. Do you think, dearest Car, that there was anything between him and Emily when she stayed at Saltmarsh?'

Caroline looked sharply at her mother.

'Whyever should you say that, Mama?'

'Because Emily was so *low* after that; in such poor spirits.'

'I thought it was because the sudden illness of Uncle Edgar gave her a shock. It must have been very unpleasant to be there when it happened. She is so close to Harriet. Also I think she was bored here. Emily likes a good time.'

'Did she say *nothing* to you about Rawdon?'

'Nothing, Mama, I assure you; but then Emily wouldn't, you know that. She would keep it to herself.'

Yes, she would. Agnes looked speculatively at her eldest daughter, soon to be twenty-one.

'Car, did you ever entertain any feeling for Rawdon? I mean . . .'

'Oh Mama!' Caroline bent down to tuck her mother's blanket around her and also to give herself something to do to hide her confusion. 'Of course I *like* Rawdon; but I haven't seen him for months. He is hardly courting me. So if I did like him it would be rather frustrating.'

'But you do like him a little?'

'Of course I like him, Mama. As a friend of . . .'

'Not *only* as a friend, Car. He would be a very suitable husband. If Edgar does die, and I pray he will not but the attack was such a severe one, there is no doubt that Rawdon would leave the Army. He would be very near. He would be looking for a wife.'

Caroline straightened up. It was suddenly rather an interesting idea. She would be near Mama, and . . .

'It is sheer speculation, Mama.'

'But it would be nice.'

Yes, it would be nice, but she would not say so to her

mother or she would never hear the end of it. And it would very soon be heard at Saltmarsh too.

'But oh Car, not yet. Not until I am well again. You would not leave me.'

'Of course I would not, Mama.' Caroline pressed the soft white hand comfortingly. 'And it is all very remote and not likely to happen, as far as I can see. Rawdon has never indicated to me at all that he cared for me particularly. I know he likes me; but then he likes Emily. He seems to like girls quite well. And I think he is so *very* attractive, that he could marry anyone he chose.'

'But you are attractive too, darling. Do not underestimate your looks. I know Sybil would be very pleased if he married you.'

'*Me?* She has said so, Mama?'

'Or Emily,' Agnes said casually. 'I know she would like him to marry into our family. We have always been so close. And we *do* know he won't choose Jane!'

'They never got on.' Caroline smiled, happy to change the subject. 'Even in the nursery. But you know it is strange, because he loves Jenny so and she is intellectual and argumentative, and yet Jane irritates him.'

'That is different, my dear. He has a tender brotherly love for his sister. He is protective towards her. She is no threat. But Jane threatens him.'

'How do you mean, Mama?'

Agnes's perspicacity was unusual in one who seemed to observe so little and think so much of herself; but on occasions she surprised her daughters.

'Well, Jane is a beauty. Rawdon likes her as a beautiful girl; but her intellect threatens his masculine self-confidence. Jane behaves like another man, and yet she isn't. He can't understand it.'

'Oh Mama, I think you have Rawdon too much on your mind. If you ask me Rawdon hardly ever thinks of our family. He would probably be amazed if he could hear this conversation. Now don't worry Mama, and don't *plan*. I will be here for a long time I assure you, and Emily is safe with the Queen who does not like her maids-of-honour to marry too soon. We shall probably all three end up old maids.'

'Oh God forbid!' Agnes said with horror. 'Really Car dear, you will start my palpitations again.'

Agnes looked with mock sternness at her daughter. Then she drew her shawl round her and settled back against the cushions Caroline had arranged for her.

Caroline was such a comfort and so good in the house. With four other daughters – and all of them beauties, even young Clare – would it matter if Caroline stayed at home for ever to look after her father and mother in their old age? Would it really matter, after all, if Caroline did *not* marry? Look at Aunt Ruth; no one despised her or pitied her and what a help she had been to her father and now her brother. All the family loved her and admired her. Maybe Caroline would be like Aunt Ruth, a dependable person who would give up her own personal happiness for the comfort of those around her.

And, after all, what was personal happiness? Agnes shifted on the couch and felt her swollen belly. She dreaded the birth more than she had dreaded anything in her life. When it came to it, this was what personal happiness resulted in and Caroline was well out of it. Maybe she should not mention Rawdon to Caroline again. Caroline was well provided for and would always have status, particularly when her father succeeded to the title. Caroline had no real need to marry. She would be lucky to be spared the sufferings her mother had had, if she remained an old maid like her Great Aunt Ruth.

His father's illness was a severe crisis for Rawdon. This was not only because he loved his father and did not want him to die; but it had happened just when he felt he was making some decision about his life. One moment he had decided to leave the army, embark on a diplomatic career and marry Emily Vestrey; the next he was suddenly called upon to resume the responsibilities of the head of the family with a very real likelihood that this would be for good.

But Lord Foxton did not die; nor did he really recover. His attack was so severe that he was an invalid for weeks, with Lady Foxton constantly by his side and Rawdon needed to manage the large estate and the various Foxton business interests. The Foxtons had no London home so Rawdon stayed in his old lodgings when he was in town which was not often.

Life suddenly became so different that Rawdon hardly had time to think. It was only when he could take stock that he realized he didn't really want to think. He had put Emily Vestrey and the diplomatic career out of his mind. He was content to be governed by circumstances.

Jennifer grew even closer to her brother. He had no-one else to depend on, in whom to confide. He told her about Emily and she was the only one he told. Jennifer thought it was not the time to think of marriage and he should not encourage Emily. The next thing was that they heard she had joined the court. So maybe she hadn't taken him very seriously after all.

It was Harriet who proposed a visit to Aunt Agnes to see how she was. It was late in October and the baby was about due. Sybil had not seen her friend since her husband's illness and the proposal for a visit was welcomed, especially by Caroline who liked the Foxton girls and missed company, with her sisters in London. It had never occurred to her that Rawdon would come too.

'This is the first time I have been away since Papa's illness,' Rawdon announced towards the end of lunch, 'except for some business visits to London and to arrange indefinite leave with my commanding officer.'

'Do you miss the army?' Mama had not come down to lunch and Caroline sat at the head of the table as hostess. Rawdon faced her at the other end with the Foxton ladies in between. The smaller Vestrey children lunched alone. Caroline had been surprised to see Rawdon, but not flustered. She realized that her duties had made her put him out of her mind, everything out of her mind except care for the house and concern for Mama now that her time approached.

She was in Mama's place; in *loco parentis*. The mistress of the house. With Rawdon she was impersonal and detached, remembering who she was and who he was. They both had new and overwhelming responsibilities.

'I have not had time to think about it, Caroline,' Rawdon

replied, conscious of the poised and very assured woman at the other end of the table. He had hardly seen her since the opening of the Great Exhibition and since then he had almost fallen in love with her sister. Had he really? He wasn't quite sure. He sometimes thought it must have been an aberration brought on by the glory of the morning. He wouldn't know until he saw her again. 'I regard it as a kind of extended leave. I do not wish to lose my seniority so, as soon as father is well, I will go back. As for missing it . . .' He shrugged.

'Rawdon is very conscious of his duty, Caroline,' his mother said, 'and you will know what that means. While he is needed at home, it is where his place is. May we go up and see your Mama now?'

'Will you not take coffee, Aunt?' Caroline looked at the butler who came forward to receive his orders.

'May we take it with your Mama?'

'Of course. I will have it sent up.'

'I think I should *not* visit your Mama,' Rawdon said tactfully. 'Please give her my respects. If I may I will take a turn in the garden until Mama and my sisters come down.'

Caroline inclined her head. 'Please do as you wish, Rawdon. I will have coffee sent into you in the drawing room, and you may smoke or do as you like.'

Caroline led the way upstairs while Jennifer and Harriet followed dutifully in their mother's wake.

After an hour of listening to a repetition of all Mama's woes during the last few months, Caroline grew restless. Outside the sky was blue and she thought of Rawdon pacing about on the lawn. Aunt Sybil was sitting close to Mama's bed listening attentively to every detail and every now and then either shaking or nodding her head, whatever was required. The 'ohs' and 'ahs' were getting wearisome.

'Would you like to take a stroll outside?' she whispered to Jennifer.

Jennifer shook her head. 'I think Aunt Agnes likes an audience. Besides, I *am* intrigued. I never knew such an old woman to have a baby.'

Caroline frowned and lowered her voice. 'Pray do not let

her hear you say that. She is not really old you know. Harriet?'

But Harriet shook her head, saying nothing, her eyes riveted on Agnes. Life was far too remote for the Foxton girls for them to want to forgo all these dramatic details of Agnes's confinement.

'I shall just go and arrange tea,' Caroline said, getting up. 'If you will excuse me Mama.'

Agnes waved a hand and told them about the little show of blood that made the doctor think she was going to lose the baby, and how George was quickly summoned from London.

'Oh,' they all gasped and drew their chairs a little nearer the bed. Caroline, who had been there when it happened and had heard about it countless times since, quickly left the room. She made a show of going into the kitchen and arranging for tea to be sent up; but all the time she knew she wanted to go to Rawdon. She could imagine him walking on the lawn, maybe taking a stroll down to the farm. From the kitchen she went to the drawing-room and out of the French doors onto the lawn.

It was a perfect autumn day and, in the slight breeze, the brown leaves fluttered from the trees, adding to the thick carpet on the ground. She could see Rawdon right on the brow of the hill, his back to her staring out to sea. Would it seem very forward to go up to him? What excuse could she give? Suddenly he turned and started to stroll back; then he saw her standing on the terrace and, raising his hand, beckoned to her. She began to walk slowly up to him, hoping by her measured tread to still the rapid beating of her heart. It really was quite absurd to feel like this. She was too alone at Chetwell; too cut off. She remembered what Mama had said about Aunt Sybil wanting Rawdon to marry a Vestrey girl. She tried to put away such absurd ideas.

Rawdon was puffing at a cigar. The smoke rose about his head and he wafted it away as she came up to him with an elegant inconsequential gesture. The good-humoured smile on his face seemed to have a special welcome as she climbed the last few steps up the hill and then stood looking at him.

'Did you want me, Rawdon?'

'I?' Rawdon looked surprised. 'No. I saw you standing there and, well, I thought you would come and join me. Is your Mama well?'

'Very well, considering. Jennifer thinks she is very old to have a baby!'

Rawdon laughed and looked appreciatively at Caroline. There was something so natural about her. They fell into step, easily, together.

'Jenny is very protected; but how old is your Mama?'

'She is forty-one.'

'Then she is rather old, is she not?'

Caroline shrugged. The conversation was verging on the indelicate. Since when had she had this particular awareness of Rawdon? She screwed up her eyes in an effort to remember. He mistook her expression.

'I am sorry. It is none of my business. I merely thought that beyond a certain age women could not conceive. I am very ignorant of these matters.'

'I am too.'

Caroline smiled at him again and as she turned he looked keenly at her profile. She was very different from Emily. She was taller, rather more substantially built but without Emily's prominent bustline. Their colouring was completely different – Emily pale and fair; Caroline with a glowing, rather brown skin and that glorious chestnut hair. Emily's jawline was pert and mischievous, Caroline's softer but firm. When she had turned to him her brown eyes, the corners slightly elongated, had the velvety softness of the heart of an orchid. Caroline looked vaguely oriental with her long slanting eyes and her brown skin. It was very unusual and rather intriguing. What he liked about her was this absence of false modesty. She did not blush or avert her eyes when they discussed childbirth or her mother's age. She looked at him directly. She was a capable, sensible person; she would make a good mother herself.

For a moment Rawdon thought rather uncomfortably of Emily. No, he hadn't behaved very well; he must be more circumspect with her sister.

'And Emily is happy at Court?'

'Oh, very happy. And Jane is being painted for the Royal Academy!'

'And you, Caroline?'

Rawdon stopped and looked at her. He threw his cigar into the bushes. It had long ago gone out and was quite cold. Caroline stopped too and looked up at him. He was standing on a slight hill and looked even taller than he was. Somehow he seemed to dominate her and she was aware of his power, his unfamiliar maleness.

'I am happy caring for Mama. Why? Should I not be?'

'No indeed. I am relieved to hear it. Only, I know how it is to be tied to the house. Even after two months I grow fretful.'

'So you *do* want to be back in the army?'

They continued walking again towards the sea, going downhill this time. In the distance Hythe Bay curved over towards Dungeness. Beyond that, well out of sight, lay Camber Sands and Rye Harbour.

'No, I don't *exactly* want to be back in the army. To tell you the truth I was thinking of buying myself out, just before Papa became ill. I thought I might try and be a diplomat. There is not much doing, you know, for a man to use his head in the army. It is all drill and manoeuvres and guard duties. Oh, do not misunderstand me! I know James loves the life . . .'

'But James is a very different person from you,' Caroline said quietly. 'Of course I do not misunderstand. You must find it very frustrating.'

'Only at times,' Rawdon said carefully. 'Only at times. If we had more action it would be different; but I don't think there will be a war for years.'

'Oh I don't know. Papa is worried about Turkey.'

'Turkey? There will be no war in Turkey; or one not worth fighting. What on earth would we have to do in Turkey?'

'You will have to ask Papa. He is very knowledgeable about it.'

'You are not like your sister. She would be lecturing me immediately about the rights and wrongs of the affair.'

'You mean Jane?'

Rawdon looked slightly discomforted. 'Well, I did not mean Emily. You know that.'

'Of course I know. I was teasing. Jane, as far as I know,

is not the least interested in the Eastern Question. Her time is taken up with the Pre-Raphaelites.'

But Caroline had found out what she wanted to know. She had seen the slight flush on Rawdon's cheeks, the way he had dropped his eyes as he had mentioned Emily's name. Maybe Rawdon had something to do with Emily's strange mood, and her eager departure for Court. Had she thrown her cap at Rawdon, to have it tossed back into the ring? Or had *he* made the advances and she had rebuffed him? How could one know?

'I think we should go back to the house for tea!' she said. 'See, your sister is waving from Mama's window.'

After they had all gone Caroline felt a sense of emptiness. It was as though she had received an answer she did not wish to have. Rawdon was not interested in her, involved with her, but with her sister Emily.

CHAPTER SIX

Jane Vestrey was not in love with Jeremy Pagan, but she was intrigued by him and his circle. Wherever she went she was carefully chaperoned by Aunt Ruth or Emily when she was not in waiting, or Caroline if she was painted at home. But the whole world of art and artists introduced her to an entirely new aspect of life, a freedom and a lack of formality that was new to her in the society she was used to. Then there were so many unconventional relationships that went on beneath the surface of lives that still paid lip-service to conformity.

It was rumoured that all was not well with the Ruskin marriage; that he neglected her and that she was much taken by John Millais. Writers and artists mixed very freely in this new world and women were listened to as people of importance who had something to say. Jane met briefly the philosopher John Stuart Mill with his wife Harriet whom he had just married, but with whom he had been openly in love for many years while her husband Mr Taylor was alive. Apparently there had been no secret at all about that. Mrs Mill was very clever too, and of considerable help to her husband in writing his philosophical books. Moreover, they were both very much in favour of women having equal rights with men. When Mr Mill had married Harriet he had made a written contract to the effect that he had no rights over her whatsoever, and that she was free to dispose of her time and herself as she wished.

Some thought it very odd in the circles in which Jane now moved; but some thought it perfectly natural and long overdue. Some had very advanced ideas that women should have not only the right to their own property after marriage, but the same rights as men to their children after divorce and even the right to vote. At one gathering Jane caught a glimpse of the beautiful but notorious Mrs Norton who campaigned for women's rights through her novels and pamphlets, but because her name had been linked with Lord Melbourne and Mr Herbert she was not received in polite society. Even the liberal-minded Aunt Ruth hurried Jane away in case she should somehow be corrupted by being in the same room as a woman with such a reputation.

It was a new world for Jane, a new life. It was so different from Emily's stifling, closed world that the two girls found even less in common than they had before. Caroline was more than ever a buffer between them, while Mama kept to her room whenever they both happened to be at home at the same time which, fortunately, was not often.

Although he was proud of her, Jeremy Pagan began to be jealous of the success that Jane enjoyed with his fellow artists, all of whom seemed to consider her fair game for their brushes or pencils. Jane so obviously relished her triumph it was difficult to do anything about it. To show his resentment would mean revealing his own possessiveness, his lack of detachment. Yet all these sittings that Jane undertook for Rossetti, Holman Hunt or Millais, even though they were mostly sketches, meant that it kept her from his major work, the full length portrait of her that he wanted to submit to the Royal Academy the following March.

It was November. Emily, having completed her first waiting at Court, was now Jane's escort. Emily could talk of nothing but the Court and her success and Jane listened with a faint smile of derision on her face as she sat for Jeremy to complete the rich details of her dress. The background had been finished in the summer.

Jeremy found Emily's chatter almost unbearable and he kept on throwing down his brush in a gesture of frustration that was not lost on Jane. But she maintained her smile; her detached, enigmatic smile. And she *was* enigmatic, aloof, cold. Nevertheless he sensed he was falling in love with her, despite his resolution never to become involved with anyone who wished matrimony. He knew his jealousy sprang from the feeling he had about her, the resentment that other men should paint, should desire what belonged to him.

And there was no question that he could ever have her, even if he offered marriage. Her father would never permit it. He had no fortune, no status. The fact that he was a clever painter would have little weight with the future Lord Vestrey. Jeremy knew that well enough; he could go so far, but no further. He was welcome so long as he kept his place.

There was an unaccustomed silence in the studio which Millais had lent him in Gower Street. It was a dull day and the light was bad; the rain that shone on the grey roofs of the nearby mews seemed the brightest thing about. Emily was fidgeting and looking to the door and Jane, without turning her head, said:

'Emily, you want something? You have finished talking!'

'I just wondered,' Emily said timidly, 'if it would be all right if I popped out for a few moments, just into Bedford Square. An acquaintance of mine, Philippa Cardew, lives there and has begged me to look in whenever I am in London. I met her at Court through her father Sir Algernon Cardew, one of the Queen's . . .'

'Oh yes. Pray go,' Jeremy said, wiping his brush on a rag with more energy than he had displayed all morning. 'I can then concentrate on this stuff without forever having to hear what the Queen said to Prince Albert or he to her.'

Emily flushed and snatched up her bag. ' I would go with pleasure were it not that Aunt Ruth said . . .'

'Aunt Ruth said you must never leave me along with a man,' Jane mimicked Aunt Ruth's tone with amusement.

'Oh no I didn't mean *that*. I know it is all right.'

'Maybe the Queen wouldn't like it,' Jeremy said knitting his brows in an effort at concentration. 'But then need she ever know, or do you feel you have to tell her *everything*?'

'I do not like your tone, Mr Pagan,' Emily said, getting up. 'If you do not take care this conversation will be reported to my father who will see that Jane is never allowed to come here again. He is very particular about the manners of the young men I or my sisters see, I assure you.'

'Oh Emily!' Jane said, looking apologetically at Jeremy. 'That is no way to talk. It . . . it is almost rude.'

'But *he* is rude. He is mocking the Queen, who after all is my mistress. I cannot tolerate that. Also you know quite well that my task is to chaperone you. Aunt Ruth *did* say

99

you must never be alone with a man, and Papa too; I am neglecting my duty if I leave you now.'

'Then stay,' Jane said tossing her head and resuming her pose. 'I care not. 'Twas you suggested going to see your friend.'

'I am so bored,' Emily said, evidently in a position where she did not know what to do. 'You are both quite uninterested in what I have to say yet make no conversation of your own. If I had half an hour with Philippa, how quickly the time would fly . . .'

Jeremy sighed deeply and looked at Jane.

'Your sister will come to no harm with me, I assure you, Miss Vestrey. We shall be as professional when you are gone as we are while you are here. Mr Millais's servant will escort you to Bedford Square to be sure *you* come to no harm on that possibly hazardous journey, which forethought will, I hope, earn me the gratitude of your father. The parlour maid will be in earshot here and we will leave the door open. Now if you are satisfied kindly ring the bell and inform William you wish to be escorted to Bedford Square.'

William, when summoned, listened to his instructions with his head dutifully bent. The elder Mr Millais and his wife were both out and it was a very dull and boring day in the house with only the silver to clean. He was glad to escort Miss Vestrey across the road to the square and would stay there for as long as she wished. He held the door open for her and Emily swished out, pausing only to say that she would be back in an hour.

After she had gone Jeremy continued his work as though she were still there. He had never been alone with Jane, or hardly ever, since they had met the previous May. There had been the odd walk in the garden, or the painting sessions under the elm tree; but one always had the feeling that the many windows of the house concealed hundreds of pairs of eyes keeping watch over the couple in the park.

Yet, the atmosphere had changed. Jane was aware of it too. There was introduced by Emily's departure an atmosphere of expectation in the room, of an indefinable undercurrent of intrigue. Slowly he began to feel that if he did

100

not make use of this time such an opportunity would not recur, but he did not know what to say. What did he want to say?

'The customs of our age are really absurd.' Jane broke the silence for him, voicing what he felt. 'It must strike you so, more than me.'

'Oh? How so?' Jeremy carefully daubed paint on the canvas aware that the pace of his heartbeat had quickened.

'You must know what I mean. This constriction that prevents the sexes getting to know each other better, or even talking in a normal way.'

'It is particularly so with your class, if I may say so,' Jeremy murmured, pretending that the matter did not concern him very much. 'Not all females are chaperoned so carefully. I don't quite know what we men are expected to do to an unprotected woman . . .'

Jane's peal of laughter broke the tension. Jeremy caught the look in her eyes and smiled.

'Still, we wanted her to go away, didn't we?' Jane said softly and Jeremy restlessly threw down his brush and went over to her, meeting the grave look in her eyes.

'I find so little in common with your sister,' Jeremy said, his voice tight. 'I . . . I don't quite know what to say now. You intrigue me, you interest me and yet . . . It is just that Jane, I am not desirous of marriage. I am in no position to marry.'

'Marriage?' Jane said, the astonishment in her voice so genuine that he was taken by surprise. 'I have *no* wish to marry either. I am but eighteen, and although I know it is not an unreasonable age to marry – my mother was seventeen – it is the last thing I want. I am talking about friendship, Jeremy, not marriage.'

'But, then, we are friends!' Jeremy's confusion at the surprising turn of events left him on the defensive.

'I am protesting at the way a man and woman cannot properly be friends, close friends, without people thinking they must marry. If you were a girl we could spend hours together chatting. The very fact that we cannot, that we must resort to lies and subterfuge and the presence of my sister or aunt, introduces an element in the relationships between men and women that inevitably renders them artificial. If we were to spend a lot of time together, talking as we should like, exchanging views about life, books, pictures, people would think we wanted to marry. Yet if *I* were a married woman like Effie Ruskin, we could be friends in that way. Is it not absurd?'

'It *is* absurd,' Jeremy said, but he reached for her hand nevertheless. He felt her start and tremble, the atmosphere between them growing oppressive.

'You are *not* helping me to prove my point,' Jane said unsteadily. 'You are doing just what I did not want you to do.'

'It is very difficult to do otherwise,' Jeremy murmured, his face close to hers. 'I find you so attractive, Jane. I do not desire mere friendship with you. Yet I know what you say is true, and I am in no position to marry and your father would not allow it even if I were. But just to be friends with you is very difficult for me.'

Jane Vestrey, eighteen years of age, thought this was a most interesting situation. It uncannily resembled the novels of the Misses Brontë, where the strong undercurrents of passion were scarcely concealed beneath the polite words of social intercourse. In a book it made one catch one's breath and a curious commotion commenced in one's breast. But now this was real and she sat back in her chair, her body taut and expectant, and gazed at Jeremy Pagan who was really saying that he wanted to make love to her. That, she supposed, was what he was saying. It was far more satisfying than a novel.

Jane's knowledge of love was based on books, on her inner thoughts and feelings. It was an exciting state between men and women that had nothing to do with marriage, like that of her parents, or the many babies that marriages produced. Beyond that Jane was as ignorant as her sisters, her cousins, friends or any other well brought-up young ladies of her age and position. She never discussed it with her mother or sisters; but it preoccupied her mind. It interested her to learn about Mr Mill and Mrs Taylor, Mr and Mrs Ruskin and why her Aunt hurried past Mrs Norton at Lady Trevelyan's reception.

She knew it was grand and melodramatic and her own passionate nature cried out for it.

'I would like you to kiss me,' she said to Jeremy suddenly leaning forward, her eyes bright and fearless. 'I would like to know what it is like.'

Jeremy was taken aback by her prosaic approach to such a delicate matter as a first kiss, usually the result of much subtle thought and innocent insinuation until the lady under attack yielded, with at least a show of reluctance. He might have expected this of Jane, but such an opportunity, though unlikely to recur, caught him unawares. He stepped forward and hesitantly cupping her face between his long hands, gently kissed her lips. She did not close her eyes but remained staring at him, as though determined to miss nothing, and the curiosity and merriment in her eyes acted as a brake on any notions he might have had about unleashing his ardour. Besides he was uncertain himself, never having been invited to kiss a woman in circumstances quite like this.

'Is that all?' Jane said, as he stepped back as carefully as he had approached her, as though determined not to miss his step and make the occasion one for comedy.

'It is enough,' he said guardedly, 'to begin with.'

'I was wrong,' Jane said disappointedly. 'I should have sat back. Let myself go, like this . . .' She draped herself melodramatically against the seat and Jeremy burst out laughing.

'You should be an actress. Then you would soon find out all about passion.' He took up his brushes again and dabbed thoughtfully at his canvas, trying by his conversation to still the rapid beating of his heart. Even the brief, chaste touch of her lips had been enough to electrify him.

'Why?'

'Actresses are notoriously "loose".'

'Oh I know; but do they know *all* about passion?'

'Apparently. That is why one must be very careful of them. Young men too are warned about actresses.'

'I should like to know about passion,' Jane said slowly, resuming her pose when she saw how business-like he had become. 'Do you know about it?'

Jeremy decided that enough was enough, for the moment. He screwed up his eyes in a frown.

'My grandfather might not be a lord, my dear Miss Jane, but there are some things that men and women do not discuss together – at this stage. Passion is one of them.'

Jane heeded the warning in his voice. Despite the fact that he was an artist, she suspected that Jeremy Pagan was at heart a conventional young man and that she would put a strain on their friendship if she said any more.

Mama started labour unexpectedly in the middle of the week. Apart from the servants Caroline was alone in the house; her father and sisters were in London and the younger children were spending the day after lessons with the Tangents at the rectory half a mile away.

Having had so many babies Mama knew quite well what to do, except for one factor: this time she was terrified. She expected to die and the baby to die too. She always had this fear at the back of her mind and, as she grew bigger, she dwelt on it more and more until she became morbid and could think of nothing else. She wrote many letters of farewell, a long one to George and her sister-in-law, Dorothy Tangent, and some of varying length to her children and relatives. A particularly long one went to Caroline bequeathing her mantle to her, although there was little she could tell her about running a house or looking after children. Whenever Caroline came into the room she put them away and tried to be cheerful and calm. But inside she was terrified; there was a great aching void in her heart, not resignation, but fear of death.

If only she could talk about it she thought it would help, but she couldn't. She knew Caroline was afraid too, and was too close to be able to help her. If she went Caroline would be on her own; she would be the mother. She knew that was why Caroline was frightened too.

Caroline sensed her mother's fear; but she did not know how to help her. She couldn't introduce it first as a topic of conversation and she knew that Mama never would. Mama, so used to hiding her real feelings, would deny it and pretend to be calm. She wanted to tell Mama that it would be all right; but there had been four dead babies and several miscarriages. The best thing to do seemed to be to say nothing and hope.

Agnes gave a cry of pain when she started labour. It came as a fierce spasm across her belly and went round to her back. It was dusk and Caroline had been drawing the curtains. 'No,' Agnes called out trying to restrain Caroline, because she didn't want the last vestiges of daylight to be extinguished. She thought she would never see it again and the drawn curtains represented the end of her life.

Caroline helped Mama into bed and rang the bell for the maid. This set the whole household in motion. Mary the housekeeper came running up and Ben Hall was sent for the doctor. On the way back he was to stop at the rectory and bring Mrs Tangent. The children would stay there until Mama was delivered safely.

Now Agnes told her about her fear, told them both, Mary and Caroline, as they sat on each side of the bed, holding her hands with the many rings, the gold and platinum bands on the soft white flesh which plucked pathetically, spasmodically at the sheets. Her fear came rushing out and she told them where the letters were and her will and what she wanted done with her personal things and her jewels. Caroline, dry eyed, listened with foreboding to her mother's outpourings. She longed to give her courage, but she felt none herself. The pupils of Mama's bright blue eyes were large with fear and her nose and her mouth were pinched as though she could smell and taste death. Mama's belly heaved up and down and Mary stroked it and said 'there, there' while her eyes anxiously looked towards the door as though wondering where the doctor could be.

But Agnes's fear finally gave Caroline courage. She felt at first a faint sense of resolution and confidence gnawing at the anxiety until it surged through her, driving away the fear and replacing it altogether. She stopped staring anxiously at her mother, kneading her trembling hands which seemed both to feed and reinforce their mutual dread. She pushed her chair away from the bed and stood up, smoothing her skirts with hands that were suddenly steady and firm. She gazed down at Mama with a calm face, the trace of a smile on her lips, her eyes serene. The hand she put on Mama's brow was cool and capable.

'Mama, you will be all right,' she said. 'There is no need to be frightened. Try and relax, and breathe deeply and think of happiness and sunshine. The happiness of a new brother or sister for us, a son or daughter for Papa, and think of us all gathering round the new baby. Next summer it will be nine months old, crawling maybe and Clare who loves babies will nurse it and . . .'

Mama's eyes, fastened on Caroline's face, cleared and the fear left them. She stared at her daughter who was giving her such unexpected confidence, such hope. Why had Caroline not spoken to her like this before? Her very attitude, the way she stood seemed like an assurance, a guarantee that neither she nor her baby would die. Caroline was like a rock, steadfast and sure. Mama grasped her hand and the doctor who came into the room at that moment saw with surprise that Agnes Vestrey was taking all this in her stride. Despite the suffering she had endured during the pregnancy she was now calm and hopeful, a changed woman. Her pulse was strong and steady and her skin, except for some beads of perspiration on her forehead, cool and dry. Dorothy Tangent, standing behind him, was surprised too, and glad. She knew how afraid Agnes had really been, but it had been so difficult to talk. She took Caroline's arm to lead her outside; but a spasm crossed Agnes's face when she saw the motion and Caroline smiled at her aunt and shook her head.

'I will stay with Mama, Aunt, in the room, and if she needs me I am here.' And Agnes relaxed and smiled again even though the contractions were quicker and more painful. Dorothy, shocked, was about to protest until the doctor, seeing that the birth was imminent, shook his head. Dorothy quickly left the room in a turmoil of emotion at such unnatural behaviour on the part of her hitherto protected niece.

Caroline held Agnes's hand all through the birth and never avoided the sight or felt disgust or shame. She admired the skill of the doctor, the calm, expert way in which he spoke to Mama and told her what to do, the serene, un-

106

flurried confidence of Mama who had been through this many times before. Caroline, holding tight to her mother's hand, reflected that women of the lower orders were quite used to the experiences of birth and death that upper class women were protected from. She knew about suffering and sickness, but nothing about these elemental activities that were hidden behind a heavy veil of secrecy. It seemed unnatural, now that she thought about it; but up until now she never had, all the time while Mama was having her babies and she was carefully protected away out of sight somewhere in the house or at Aunt Dorothy's.

Caroline thought it was a beautiful experience and she never turned her eyes away at all except to look at her mother and comfort her with her steady reassuring smile. As the baby was born, her expression was so ecstatic that Mama's turned from agony to joy and they both cried out as, their hands still tightly clasped, the doctor held up the baby and gave its bottom a loud smack.

For Agnes Vestrey the birth of her daughter Rebecca was not only joyful, it was memorable, just because Caroline had been there, to give her such strength. But, from then on, she would need her eldest daughter more than ever.

George Smith, that amiable and concerned young publisher, did not feel able to undertake the work of Miss Foxton. He returned the manuscript of her three-volume novel with a brief note of regret. He gave no reason. Rawdon found her sitting by the opened parcel staring at the letter which, silently, she gave him to read.

Rawdon quickly perusing the contents shrugged his shoulders and patted her on the back.

'There are other publishers, Jenny. Or we can ask George Vestrey to talk to Thackeray.'

'Why should Mr Thackeray help me when Mr Smith won't?'

'He might have a different opinion. I tell you what, we can go over tomorrow. Uncle George and James are at Chetwell. I know because James wrote to me that they were going to see the baby.'

'But it is too soon after the birth for us to go.'

'Nonsense, that was a month ago. They will be pleased to see us. I shall send Jordan over with a note to see if we are welcome.'

'You know *you* are always welcome, Rawdon.'

Jennifer leaned heavily on the personal pronoun and carried her manuscript over to the piano, carefully placing the letter on top of it.

'Why I more particularly than you?' Rawdon glanced after her, but he knew the answer.

'I think you have ensnared both of the Vestrey girls.'

'Well, I didn't ensnare Emily for long. She immediately went and joined the Court.'

'Caroline is different. Emily has a hard streak in her. Do not be deceived by Caroline's practicality. Caroline likes you.'

Jennifer and Harriet went quite frequently over to Chetwell to borrow books from the large library and also to see the Tangent family who lived nearby, the Reverend John Tangent being the brother of Lady Vestrey. Jennifer knew that Caroline always looked for Rawdon when they appeared and observed the flash of disappointment in her eyes when she saw they were alone.

'I like Caroline,' Rawdon said, turning as the door opened and his mother came into the room looking about her for some embroidery she had mislaid.

'I couldn't help overhearing,' Sybil Foxton said, rescuing her work from the recesses of a deep armchair. 'I *am* glad you like Caroline, Rawdon. She would be very suitable.'

'Oh *Mama*, we were not talking about weddings,' Rawdon said with an air of disgust. 'I like Caroline and I like the Vestreys as a family. I like Uncle George and Aunt Agnes, and James and . . .'

'But Caroline would still be very suitable,' Sybil Foxton said, smiling at her eldest son with equanimity. 'And now that the baby is born she is free. Agnes will soon be up and about though I hear she is slow in recovering her strength. Pray God it will be the last child she has. She is too old.'

'We thought of going over tomorrow, Mama, to pay our respects. James is there and I should like to see him. Will you accompany us, Mama?'

Lady Foxton did not reply, her eyes on the manuscript on top of the piano.

'What is this?'

'Oh,' Jennifer flew over to the piano and stood in front of the untidy parcel. 'It is nothing, Mama.'

'Why don't you tell Mother?' Rawdon said quietly. 'It is nothing of which to be ashamed. Jenny has submitted one of her novels to a publisher, Mama. He has rejected it.'

'Oh *why* did you say . . .' Jennifer stamped her foot on the floor and rushed out of the room. Sybil gazed after her and then grimaced at Rawdon.

'I wish she would confide in me. I am her mother and I love her too.'

'I know, Mama.' Rawdon went up to his mother and gazed into her eyes. 'She wants to please you. She wants to be beautiful and clever, and she cannot stand to be neither.'

'But she *is* clever. Just because her book has been rejected once, why should she be so upset? There are other publishers are there not? I would like to help her, Rawdon, to get it published if that is what she wants.'

'Mama, that is capital of you!' Rawdon allowed himself a rare display of emotion and hugged her. 'Jenny thinks you do not approve of her writing. That you would like her to be happy and settled in matrimony.'

'Well of course I would like that best of all.' Sybil Foxton sighed and read the letter on top of the manuscript, sighing again when she put it down. 'I do not give up hope because Jenny can look nice when she tries. Only she never seems to try, thinking that men should like her as she is. If only she had the looks of the Vestrey girls! Sometimes I am positively jealous of that family. Each girl so very different to look at, yet a beauty. But then George and Agnes were considered a very handsome couple. Of course so were your father and I . . .' She trailed off and gazed at Rawdon. 'Life is not very fair is it? My daughters' looks are a great source of grief to me; but you, dear Rawdon, a great source of pleasure. You are the ideal son. What I would have done without you these last weeks I do not know.'

She went up to him and put a hand on his cheek. He clasped it between his and kissed it.

'You are very lovely, Mama, and I love you. I wish you could always be happy, and when Papa is well . . .'

Sybil Foxton shook her head and, pressing his hand, released it. She sat on the sofa, her body straight, her hands clasped on her lap. 'I don't think your Papa will ever completely recover, Rawdon. He is only fifty-six, but the doctors say his heart is badly damaged. You must face it; he is going to be an invalid and more will fall on your shoulders.'

Rawdon sat next to her, taking her hand in his. 'You are saying you want me to leave the army, Mama?'

Sybil nodded and Rawdon saw that the beautiful eyes, from which the colour of his own came, were filled with tears. 'I *would* like you to marry too, Rawdon.'

'Oh Mama! There you go again.'

Rawdon tried to laugh it off; but in his heart he felt once again the turmoil that he thought he had been so near to resolving that summer.

'I am serious about Caroline Vestrey,' his mother went on. 'She is in every way very suitable and she is free, for the moment. Once she starts partying in London . . . she will be snapped up. I would like you to marry Caroline. We would all like it – your father and I, Agnes and George.'

'You have all discussed it?' Rawdon said incredulously to hide his embarrassment.

'Not as such, and not together. But I know how they feel, and how we feel. Your father would like to see you settled should anything happen to him. Caroline would be ideal. The girls like her, and so do your brothers. And I like her and I should need her help. She would be so kind to us all. I don't think you could improve on Caroline. You would be fortunate to get her.'

Rawdon got up and paced to the window, standing for some time looking at the smooth sward of lawn which stretched from the house to the crumbling walls of the inner bailey. On one side were the ruins of the old knight's chapel. This was his heritage, his birthright. All this would be his one day, a day that, sadly, might not be too long delayed. Yes, Caroline was very suitable. Then he thought of Emily on the horse chasing out to sea, the way she looked over her shoulder at him, those eyes tantilizingly concealed by her little veil, their message very clear.

'Do you not like Emily, mother?'

'Emily?' Lady Foxton said in some surprise. 'You prefer Emily to Caroline?'

'I don't know.'

'Well, what an extraordinary thing to say, my darling. You mean you like *both* sisters?'

'In a way, yes.' Rawdon put his hands in his pockets and began pacing the room. 'I find Emily very attractive. Oh, Caroline is beautiful too and I like Caroline's nature better, at least I think I do. I agree with all you have to say about Caroline; but I don't know. I feel therefore I am not ready to marry, Mother.'

'Of course you are ready to marry, Rawdon. You are twenty-three. It is a good age to marry. Oh, I grant a man can be a lot older and it is no bad thing; but you have re-sponsibilities that others do not have – James Vestrey for instance, if you are thinking of him. I pity the girl *he* marries, that is all.'

'Jenny would like to marry James,' Rawdon said quietly. 'I think she wants to go over tomorrow to see him rather than ask his Papa about Thackeray.'

'Oh, I know how Jenny feels about James. It is obvious when they are together. Of course it is hopelessly unsuitable even if Jenny were his type, which she is not. We know quite well what sort of women James Vestrey prefers!'

'But when it comes to settling down he will not choose that kind of woman, Mama. He will look for someone well born, but beautiful because he will not need a fortune. I'm afraid he will not look at our Jen or at Harriet, who is a more suitable age.'

The Foxtons the following day found the Vestrey family not as well or as cheerful as they had hoped they would be, following the recent addition of a new member.

'It is that Mama has not recovered as we hoped,' Caroline explained, as they took off their cloaks in the drawing room, where a large fire welcomed them in from the cold. 'She is very weak. When the time came to get up she seemed all right; but then after a few days she complained of weakness in the knees and one day she fainted in the drawing room when Aunt Dorothy Tangent was here with Polly.'

'May we see her?' Sybil Foxton said with concern.

'I think *you* may, Aunt Sybil, but no one else, if you don't mind. Mama must be kept very quiet although the doctor says he can find no physical cause for her malaise.'

'Your mother must have no more children,' Sybil said severely, looking at George Vestrey who had kept in the background while Caroline explained the situation to the Foxtons.

'Of course there will be no more children, Sybil,' he said, his face colouring faintly. 'That is quite well understood.'

'We are here, sir, to ask you a favour,' Rawdon said quickly. 'That is, besides coming to pay our respects to you and Aunt Agnes and the family. Jenny has written a novel. We wondered if you could talk to Mr Thackeray about it. We understand he is an acquaintance of yours.'

George frowned. 'Well, we belong to the same club . . .'

'I am sure Papa will help, won't you Papa?' Caroline said eagerly. 'You would talk to Mr Thackeray about Jenny?'

'But Mr Thackeray is not a publisher.' George was clearly reluctant.

'No, but his recommendation would be of enormous help in getting it placed,' Caroline said. 'You can see that, Papa.'

'Please Uncle George, do not incommode yourself,' Jenny began frostily when James, who had been leaning against the wall, burst into laughter.

'*Jenny* an author! Well well.'

'What is funny about it?' Harriet said, her cheeks bright with colour. 'Is it so very unusual for a woman to want to write?'

James grimaced and dug his hands in his pockets as though he did not want to say as much, but thought the answer was probably yes.

Jenny was staring at James in dismay when there was a commotion outside the door and Jane entered with the new baby in her arms. Its nurse, who seemed to think that Jane was not quite a responsible enough person to have charge of her young sister, fussed behind her. All the women got up with one accord and rushed over to the new arrival and Jane, flushed with concern and pride, took Rebecca over to the window and parted the shawls so that everyone could see the baby's face.

Rebecca Vestrey was asleep. She had the tranquil contented look of the youngest of a large family. Even at four weeks old she seemed aware of the privilege of her position; the fact that as the most recent arrival and, hopefully, the last, she would always be fussed over and adored. Her chubby little lips were pouted in an expression of satisfaction and the long lashes on her pink cheeks already curled upwards as a portent of future beauty. Her head was covered by very soft fair curls.

'What colour are her eyes?' Sybil whispered, her face puckered adoringly.

'Blue. She is going to be a fair-haired blue-eyed Vestrey like Emily. But I think she favours *me* most of all.'

Jane dimpled and, laughing, looked over at her father who kept his distance from his new daughter, as though still suffering from the remorse of being responsible for her. Rawdon stood at the back of the crowd, an expression of benign amusement on his face. Suddenly he saw Caroline standing across from him and his smile broadened. He had caught an expression on her face as she looked at the baby that he had never seen before – sublime love, maternal tenderness and care. He felt it would be very nice to have Caroline feel like that about oneself; to see that expression more often. He sidled around the back of the crowd towards her.

'I think my mother is as proud of the baby as though she bore her.'

'We all love her; especially Papa. See how proud he looks.'

'I thought he looked a bit ashamed.'

Caroline stared at Rawdon indignantly before seeing the teasing looking in his eyes.

'You must not joke about my father, Rawdon. He really is quite pleased despite all the fuss.'

Rawdon fell silent looking at Caroline. Surrounded by his family and hers in the drawing-room at Chetwell he felt at home. These were all familiars, people he had known all his life. Supposing he let her go and she did marry someone else? How would he feel then? Even in this crowd with her father, her brother and her sisters she seemed to be someone apart – a symbol of womanhood, courageous, capable, loving. If his father continued to be an invalid and he had to leave the army, who better than someone like Caroline by his side – in control, strong, embracing everyone with the warmth of her love, her soft motherly personality?

Miss Rebecca Vestrey suddenly woke to the fact that she was once more the object of a crowd of admirers. The Tangent family came over *en masse* almost every day to worship, and now here were another lot. Her little cheeks puckered and she seemed uncertain whether to laugh or cry. She gazed up at Jane and decided to cry. She let out an enormous howl and Jane looked about her with concern. A crying baby was so much more difficult to cope with than a sleeping one.

Caroline moved swiftly through the throng and held out her arms. Gladly, thankfully, Jane gave the baby to her and as if knowing how secure she was, in what good hands, Rebecca Vestrey settled down again to sleep.

CHAPTER SEVEN

In January Lord Foxton suffered another mild heart attack. Before that he had been progressing so well that Rawdon had made plans for rejoining his regiment. At Christmas he was even able to come downstairs and gently partake of the family celebrations which were purposely kept at a low key. He did not go over to Chetwell, but saw the younger Vestreys when they came to lunch on Boxing Day. George had stayed behind with Agnes who did not feel up to making the journey. Emily was in waiting at Windsor that Christmas and Rawdon realized he had not seen her since the summer.

But he had seen a lot of Caroline. He sometimes rode over to see her, making some sort of excuse about collecting books for his sisters. In December she was twenty-one and had an evening party attended only by her family, the Tangents and the Foxtons. Emily had already gone into waiting.

For Caroline Rawdon's visits, his increased signs of interest, became an important part of her life, because her mother simply did not get better. She was querulous and demanding and given to fits of tears and deep depressions which went on for days. Sometimes she refused to see anyone other than Caroline. Her husband found himself cut off with the rest. He realized that the only way to get over his misery about Agnes was to throw himself more deeply into his work.

Jane was still being courted by the cream of the artistic world. She had visited Sir Calverley and Lady Trevelyan at their home at Wallington in Northumberland – a sign of great favour. She met all the writers and artists of talent whom the fashionable and influential found amusing – the Rossettis, William Scott and, of course, the Ruskins. Lady Trevelyan, a good deal younger than her husband, thought Jane a great find – she admired her artistry, her intelligence; but above all her beauty. In that world it was important to be surrounded by beauty as well as talent.

Away from all this, hardly aware of its existence, Caroline felt increasingly cut off from the world. As her mother's dependence on her tightened, she began to look on her beloved home as a prison. Rawdon's visits offered her relief because she liked to see and talk to him; and also hope, because, just possibly, one day he might take her away. Of course that would not offer real freedom either, in the sense that she would have his invalid father and his two sisters to consider. She had a feeling that the latter, as long as they remained unmarried, would cling to their home, resisting all attempts to introduce them to society, creating little barriers and making difficulties at every turn. But she would have Rawdon with her; they would be two instead of one. She would not feel as alone as she did now.

After his father's second heart attack Rawdon sensed that his life was narrowing. He too was confined. To go over to Chetwell was not only good exercise, but the perfect escape. It was just long enough for a good canter, and he was always sure of a welcome. He looked forward to the expression on Caroline's face as she hurried to greet him, or rose from her chair and came over towards him, her arms extended in greeting – almost as though she wished to embrace him.

Yet still he did not propose. It was, he reasoned, because she would obviously have to refuse him. Yet it was also impossible to be sure of his own feelings because there was always the picture of Emily at the back of his mind.

'But Agnes cannot stay in bed all her life!' his mother protested. 'Caroline *must* return to London and go into society again.'

'Perhaps she does not want to,' Jennifer said, looking at her brother who was gazing moodily into the fire in the drawing room at Saltmarsh. It had been a bitter February and he felt hemmed in by sickness and cold, a feeling that sometimes brought him close to despair. It would all be so much better, his mother said, if he would declare himself.

It would cheer them all up to have a wedding to look forward to.

'It is not so simple. I do not know how Caroline feels, Mama.'

'Is *that* what is holding you back? Or is it how *you* feel?'

There was that glade dappled in the August sunshine and the big roan hunter bearing a slim fair-haired girl who raced out to the sea. He galloped after her, and he was going to fall in love with her and change his life. He closed his eyes and could see vividly that bright summer day, such a contrast to the gloom and biting cold of this winter. Summer and Emily, winter and Caroline . . . yes, the two sisters represented two different moods for him. Responsibility and folly. He loved them both. How could he tell his mother he loved two women equally? That the one he wanted to live with, but the other he found exciting. He was ashamed of the animal side of him to which Emily appealed. He knew it was carnal and that he would like her as a mistress rather than a wife. Everyone knew that this baser side of man was only important in marriage as far as the begetting of children was concerned. Nice women like his mother, his sisters and Caroline would not expect to be treated like whores. The very thought disgusted him. But with Emily . . .

'Someone should find out how Caroline feels,' Jennifer said. 'I will ask her if you like.'

'Oh no. Pray do not!' Rawdon exclaimed. 'I beg you not to mention it to her. She will think you are an emissary. Besides, I doubt she would give you a truthful answer. The Vestrey women do not wear their hearts on their sleeves.'

Except Emily, he thought. Emily. Once, just briefly, she had shown him her heart.

Rebecca was not christened until the spring of that year because it had been such a bad winter and Agnes Vestrey's health had deteriorated even further.

Caroline realized sometime after Christmas that her mother was probably going to stay like this for as long as she could, maybe the rest of her life. Mama looked blooming lying there in bed, pretty and even young again; but as soon as she put her feet to the floor she turned very pale and swayed, and whoever was with her had to rush and tuck her back into bed. Mama thus ruled the household from her bed, though she left the organization to Caroline. She received the children during the day at certain stated intervals and if they stayed too long she got one of her bad heads.

Papa was strictly a visitor too and Caroline noticed how Mama only liked to have him there when others were in the room with him. Papa now had his own room on another floor, and gradually all his things were removed from the bedroom he had formerly shared with his wife, and from the dressing room next door, to the new large room on the second floor.

Then Caroline knew that her mother and father would never share a bedroom again and the reason why. Rebecca was a gift, a dream, a child of God – but she had to be the last. Mama was much too delicate to consider any other possibility. Everyone was told that Papa was moving to enable Mama to sleep better; but Caroline knew the real reason. Papa had to remove himself from temptation, from that weakness of which he had accused himself before.

By the spring the situation was accepted and the routine settled. Occasionally Mama got up for an hour or two, but never when Papa was there. His very presence in the house seemed to make her worse. Papa didn't realize this because he was away such a lot. He thought that Mama was always like this, a bedstricken invalid. Papa still reproached himself for bringing this condition on Mama, even though Rebecca was such a joy to them all. Looking at him on that day, just after Easter when the baby was christened at Chetwell Church by her uncle, the Reverend John Tangent, Caroline thought that now it was Mama who looked younger, while Papa had aged. His side whiskers were going grey and the lines at the corners of his eyes and mouth had deepened as though incised with a knife.

A large family party had assembled for the christening and Caroline had spent days organizing the food, preparing the rooms for the guests and looking after Mama who found it absolutely impossible to put a foot out of bed. But

118

now it was a beautiful April day, the breeze blew gently in from the sea and everyone was in the church except Grandpapa, who was failing fast, and Mama who was quite unable to leave the house but had promised to try and get down for the party afterwards.

The girls all had new dresses and bonnets and James looked very smart in a fly fronted overcoat with a velvet collar and narrow trousers in a loud check underneath. He wore a shining top hat and carried a cane. He looked quite a swell. Aunt Ruth was there, also in a new bonnet and a skirt with one of the large hoops which were becoming increasingly fashionable. A few politicians were there, Rawdon and the entire Foxton family and many notabilities from the neighbourhood. The Queen had sent a comforter made of silver and emblazoned with the Royal arms. Surely no baby teeth would ever be allowed to cut themselves on *that*?

The reception afterwards was held in the drawing-room on the ground floor and, due to the mildness of the day, the doors were thrown open onto the terrace and people wandered in and out with glasses of champagne and cucumber sandwiches in their hands. Mama was there already when they arrived, to everyone's delight, comfortably seated in a chair, dressed in a becoming spring-like dress of spotted muslin with a matching cap in the fanchon style with floating ribbons dangling behind. She looked years younger than anyone had seen her for a long time. Mama laughed and chatted and drank quite a lot of champagne, which was remarked on by some of those who thought it could not possibly be good for someone in such a delicate state of health.

Great Aunt Ruth had not seen Agnes Vestrey since the previous summer when her condition then had made her think she would not survive the impending birth. Now she saw that things were very different as she sat in her upright chair chatting to Lady Foxton, who was watching the ineffectual attempts of poor Jennifer to capture the attention of James. In this she was rivalled by his cousin Polly Tangent who was not only three years younger than Jennifer but much prettier.

The Tangent family had a hard struggle not to let the clever, talented and good-looking Vestreys eclipse them. Not that the Vestreys intended to assert themselves, having a very deep and genuine affection for their mother's brother and his family. They had been brought up together; shared games and books and played together; attended the same lessons with the same governess or tutor, paid for by the Vestreys, and the eldest boys were at Eton paid for by Sir Marcus Tangent, John and Agnes's eldest brother. He farmed the many acres left to him by his father on the Sussex border but always seemed oppressed by domestic cares and debt. He had even more children than George Vestrey, but a very strong and dominating wife who had them all perfectly under control as well as her husband. She had no time at all for Agnes Vestrey taking to her bed in this ridiculous manner and said as much to Miss Ruth Vestrey and Lady Foxton, who were hobnobbing away in a corner of the room with a bottle of champagne and a huge plate of sandwiches between them.

'There is nothing wrong with Agnes that I can see,' Felicity Tangent boomed so that half the room could hear, but luckily not Agnes, though Felicity would not have minded in the least.

'It is her legs,' Lady Foxton whispered delicately. 'She has a weakness in them.'

'Stuff.' Felicity Tangent sat down beside them, grabbing a sandwich which she munched furiously. All her brood had been told to eat as much as they could at the Vestreys because there was only mutton stew for dinner. Aunt Ruth had little time for Lady Tangent so said nothing, but her eyes had hardly ever left her niece by marriage, and would roam from her to her husband who wandered amiably about making sure everyone was comfortable and well provided for.

Despite the beauty of the day, his pride in his family and his evident joy in the new baby, Ruth knew that her nephew was unhappy. It was not so much what he said to her. Fond as he was of his aunt, years of inbuilt reserve, of tradition meant that men of the upper classes were for the most part very reserved when it came to expressing emotions and feelings even in private. It was the way he behaved when he was in London, throwing himself into his work and working late into the night. In February there had been a government crisis brought on initially by the behaviour of Lord Palmerston and his undisguised enthusiasm for the *coup d'état* of Louis Napoleon in France. Lord Derby was now Prime Minister with Mr Disraeli, George's friend, at the Exchequer. George had been given a post in the Treasury which he took very seriously. It seemed that, at last, he was aiming for a high place in the government now that the Conservatives were in power.

'Agnes enjoys the attention she has acquired and does not mean to give it up,' Lady Tangent continued. 'She makes herself important, an object of concern. And moreover she keeps her eldest daughter tied to her apron strings. Caroline is already twenty-one. She will never get a husband if she stays at home and does not go out into society. Her mother was younger than Caroline is now when *she* was born, and James was already a year old!'

'I do not think Caroline will have difficulty finding a husband when she is ready.' Sybil Foxton peered over the rim of her champagne glass at her friend. 'She has a beauty that will not fade.'

'Besides, Caroline is particularly nice natured,' her great aunt said approvingly. 'Emily and Jane are both deficient in that respect, being too self-centred. Look at Emily now: she has made a little court for herself as though she were at Windsor.'

Rawdon had hardly taken his eyes off Emily in church. He had been particularly well placed to observe her because he was one of Rebecca's godfathers – Agnes Vestrey so wanted to draw him into the family in some way or another – and he stood behind the font, from which position he was able to watch Emily in the front row. He thought she looked like the perfect emanation of spring in a *redingote* style dress of white batiste, overprinted with tiny spring flowers. Her wide-brimmed bonnet, tied under the chin with a huge bow, made an oval-shaped frame for her face which was entirely disarming in its simple beauty. Her large eyes, the colour of fresh violets, protested her

121

innocence and her pink, full, bow-shaped mouth was severely pursed in an attitude of pious concentration as she followed the service. Had she, he wondered, knowingly cultivated that expression of solemnity, subtly blended with a quality of enticement as though such purity expected to be robbed of its innocence? Did she know, as she lifted her eyes to sing the hymns or utter the responses, what the effect would be? Was it calculated or was it unconscious? He did not know. More than any woman Emily combined in her personality, for Rawdon, sweet innocence with mystery. It was a highly erotic combination, but whether she was conscious of it or not one was never quite sure.

Every nuance of expression, every gesture Emily made in church or anywhere else that day was made with Rawdon in mind. She knew he was still susceptible as he stood behind the font in his pale beautifully cut grey morning suit and elaborately tied pearl coloured necktie. He carried his top hat in his hand and everything about him from his thick black hair to his shiny black shoes looked well groomed and cared for. He appeared older than he had in August yet this maturity made him look more distinguished, a man of the world. Emily had dressed for him, and how she behaved was governed by the hope that he was looking at her whether it was in church or now in the drawing-room. But she had never once looked directly at him. It was part of her act of appearing not to care.

Emily was a wonderful raconteuse, a facility that had developed during her time at Court when she was expected to entertain and hold her own with the most difficult of Her Majesty's guests. And court life now provided a wonderful subject for her art – there was such a fund of amusing and entertaining stories, so many visits and adventures to recount.

After the ceremony Emily had driven off in a carriage with her sisters and cousins, and the men walked up the hill to Chetwell, Rawdon talking to James and James's cousin Dalton Tangent. Emily was already surrounded by her circle of admirers when Rawdon came into the drawing-room. He saw her immediately, but he would take his time. There was, he knew already, an implicit undercurrent of excitement between them, even though they had not exchanged a word.

When would Rawdon come? Emily glanced between the bodies that stood in front of her and saw him talking to Jane and Polly Tangent. But without his head turning, his eyes kept on swivelling in her direction, and then he started gradually to make his way over towards her, bowing and exchanging small talk with people he knew. Emily judged it was time to wave. The charade had served its purpose. She waved. Rawdon pretended, without much conviction, to see her for the very first time and, excusing himself to an acquaintance, walked over to her. The throng seemed to stand to one side instinctively, like the parting of the Red Sea for the Israelites to enter the Promised Land.

Rawdon bent and, taking her hand, kissed it, aware of her answering pressure. They gazed at each other warily, testing the ground.

'I was sorry to hear about your father, Rawdon,' Emily said matter-of-factly. 'The second attack was quite dreadful. You were just about to return to the army, James says.'

'Indeed I was, Emily. Thank you for your concern.'

'And how is he now?'

'I think he is better than the doctors expected. He walks quite well and his mind of course is ever alert.'

'It must have been a terrible time for you, Rawdon.'

'It has not been easy. Such a cold winter too, and so little to do except support my mother and sisters. Tim has had his first two terms at Oxford and Ben is still at Eton.'

'Where he and Oliver are particularly friendly, I hear.'

'They seem to get on well. Now you must tell me all about the Court. I am quite a backwoods man, I assure you.'

Emily dispersed her admirers with a glance and a wave and she and Rawdon moved towards the terrace.

Sybil Foxton had watched them with some disquiet. She had seen all the manoeuvring that went on between them, had been aware of Rawdon's glances across the room and Emily's pretended indifference.

'Emily is a little enchantress,' she whispered to Ruth Vestrey. 'She is after Rawdon.'

'Really?' Aunt Ruth peered over towards the French windows and saw them just disappearing onto the terrace. 'Oh no, I assure you Sybil dear, Emily has no designs on Rawdon. She is devoted to the Queen and her career at Court. She does not think of settling down. Emily has always been flirtatious, you know that, Sybil. She does like men about her. The men at Court I know are a little disappointing; rather staid and many of them elderly. Emily does seem to need male admirers. But there is nothing serious.'

'I am not so sure,' Sybil murmured. 'I would be so heartbroken for Caroline's sake.'

Aunt Ruth enjoyed a gossip. Although she was at the centre of things in London she missed a lot of what went on in the country.

'Have Caroline and Rawdon been – er – meeting?'

'Oh yes. He comes over here quite often on the pretext of using the library or enquiring after Agnes's health. I think he really comes to see Caroline. I hoped he would have spoken to her by now. I don't know why he hesitates. Perhaps it *is* Emily after all.'

'He would be very fortunate whichever of my nieces he gets, if either,' Aunt Ruth said firmly. 'The Queen thinks most highly of Emily. She is exemplary in her duties.'

Caroline moved quietly about the room, seeing that all was well, that there was enough to eat and drink and that everyone was comfortable. Her baby sister had been taken up to sleep and she had seen that she was all right and Mama not too tired. But Mama appeared particularly well and Papa stood behind her like a proud bridegroom. Both her parents seemed, for that day at least, to have recovered their youth.

Jane conscientiously performed the duties of a daughter of the house, introducing people who did not know each other, who felt left out.

'The aunts are all having a good natter,' she whispered to Caroline as they met in the middle of the floor.

'Talking about us no doubt, when are we going to get married and how little time there is left.'

Jane giggled. 'Aunt Dorothy has already lectured me

about Jeremy Pagan. She said artists are quite beyond the pale and not at all respectable.'

'She should know you well enough by now to realize that would make them irresistible.'

'Oh, I shall definitely marry an artist,' Jane said, 'and live in a garret.'

'Did you not ask Jeremy today?'

'No. Why should I? This is family except for some close family friends and I would not call *him* that.'

'I think you are tiring of Mr Pagan,' Caroline hissed.

Jane fluttered her long black lashes in mock astonishment. 'I tired of him weeks ago, dearest Caroline. You are very out of touch.'

'Yes, I am.' Caroline's face was solemn. 'I am the little country sister, out of touch and out of mind.'

'Oh, Caroline.' Jane looked crestfallen. 'You *must* come back to London! Mama is sapping your strength.'

'Someone must stay and look after her,' Caroline said. 'Who else is there but me? Besides . . .' She looked towards the French windows. She had just seen the backs of Emily and Rawdon disappearing through them and had felt nothing but extreme agitation ever since.

Jane followed her look. 'I know there have been compensations,' she said.

'Whatever do you mean?'

'Jennifer says Rawdon comes over here quite frequently.'

'Oh, that is to borrow books. Jenny should know; they are for her, but the roads have often been too bad for travel.'

'Perhaps she *sends* him on purpose.'

'You mean as a matchmaker?' Caroline smiled ruefully. 'Oh no. I don't think Rawdon is interested in me – at least not when Emily is around. Now look Jane, the Mayor of Hythe is preparing to take his leave. Would you see him to his carriage?'

Not when Emily is around . . . Caroline had been dreading the arrival of her sister. She knew how she would look and behave and that she would flirt with all the men; that Rawdon would be drawn to her like a magnet and would find his way over to her, as he had done. She had to stifle the wild urge to go after them, and had made herself very busy, pretending indifference. It was ridiculous to be jealous of one's sister. Ridiculous and petty. If Rawdon wanted Emily and she him, why, that was that.

'Rawdon and Emily are on the terrace,' Jennifer Foxton whispered slyly in her ear.

'Really?' Caroline looked at her good humouredly and leaned over to stop one of the footmen.

'Hawkins, would you clear the glasses from that small table and put some fresh sandwiches and cakes on it?'

'Very good, miss.' Hawkins, splendidly dressed for the occasion in the rarely used Vestrey livery, slid obediently away.

She must be busy, detached, capable. 'Now, Jennifer?'

'I said Rawdon and Emily...'

'But Jenny dear why should they *not* be together? They have not seen each other for months. Emily has a lot to tell Rawdon about the Court, and he about your father...'

'They *slipped* away together...'

'Oh Jenny, don't be melodramatic. They did not slip. They walked and everyone saw them, myself included. Pray do not tittle-tattle. Oh, Papa, how is Mama bearing up?'

Caroline turned with relief to her father, who had been avoiding Jennifer and thought that, with Caroline there, the bad news he had to impart might be mitigated.

'Mama is fine my dear. She likes a party as we all know.' George cleared his throat and smiled at them both. 'Well Jenny, you look very well. It is a good party is it not?'

'Very good, Uncle George, as befits a happy occasion.' Was there implied scorn in Jenny's eyes? Difficult to know, it was so hard to fathom her.

George coughed again and looked at Caroline for help. But as she did not know what help he wanted she could not give it, and stared bewilderedly at him.

'My dear Jenny, I have some rather, well I suppose you would say bad news...'

'Mr Thackeray does not like my book,' Jenny said in a monotone, staring at the floor.

'It isn't exactly that my dear. He does not feel qualified

to *judge,* that is it. Yes that was the expression he used. "I am not qualified to *judge* such a work, Vestrey. Miss Foxton would do well to send it to a lady novelist or someone who publishes such works." He thanked you very much for letting him see it; but I am sorry to say I have brought it back with me together with his kindest personal regards.'

'He did not like it, Uncle George.'

'No, no, my dear. He was not qualified . . .'

'It *was* perhaps a mistake,' Caroline said gently. 'Mr Thackeray is such a busy man; perhaps he did not have time . . .'

'Oh Caroline, pray do not treat me like a baby!' Jenny burst out and, clearly on the verge of tears, brushed past Caroline and her father and went rapidly to the door.

'What has happened to Jenny?' Harriet rushed over to Caroline as George looked at the door in dismay.

'Mr Thackeray does not like her book.'

'He said he could not *judge,*' George protested.

'Oh that is an excuse, Papa. You know it. You should not have told her now. 'Twas not the right time. Or you should have let me break it to her.' Caroline looked distractedly at the door wondering what to do.

'Rawdon shall talk to her,' Harriet said firmly. 'He knows how best to handle Jenny's moods.'

Harriet made for the terrace and Caroline followed slowly.

Rawdon had his hands clasped eagerly about his knees and was sitting on the balustrade of the terrace looking at Emily. She sat higher up in a chair and was talking with such verve and animation that she might have been entertaining a large audience. Rawdon thought that she would never stop talking because she did not want to renew their intimacy; so he just gazed up at her and listened. He found her remoteness quite tantalizing.

'Then the Prince took the Princess Royal by the hand and do you know . . . why Harry, what a look on your face! Has something happened?'

'Jenny has run off in tears, Rawdon. You had best go after her.'

Rawdon got up immediately and looked over Harriet's shoulder at Caroline coming after her.

'What is it, Caroline?'

'I'm afraid Papa broke the news that Mr Thackeray felt he could not praise Jenny's novel. He did it rather abruptly and at the wrong time and she was upset.'

'Oh dear.' Rawdon grimaced and looked at Emily. 'I must go and see to her. You must finish the story afterwards. I am dying to know how the Queen reacted to *that*.'

He swiftly left the terrace while Emily, suddenly deflated, sat sulkily fiddling with the bows of her bonnet, gazing towards the sea.

CHAPTER EIGHT

Rawdon and James, who was still on leave, met frequently in the days after the christening to go fishing or shooting or for long rides. Rawdon took his duties seriously and spent long hours over estate affairs. Because he loved animals he had a great interest in the livestock; but he also saw how important other aspects of managing an estate were – the maintenance of buildings, particularly the old castle, the farming of the land, the care of the orchards and hop fields which made up the many hundreds of acres owned by his father.

Then there were various business interests, for his provident father had not been content to sit on inherited wealth, but made it work by investing in the many new aspects of the industrial revolution. He had shares in coalfields and in tin mines and, because of the proximity of the important ports of Dover and Folkestone, he had put a lot of money into harbour development, and the building of ships that plied across the Channel increasing England's wealth.

But despite all his preoccupations Rawdon managed to see a lot of his friend and often they were accompanied by his sisters, or the Vestrey girls, Emily and Jane. Caroline stayed at home because of the burden of her domestic duties and also because she was afraid, and ashamed, of betraying her jealousy of her sister.

'It is ridiculous the way Mama stays in her bed,' Jane said one day as they were arranging flowers in the large cool pantry at the side of the house. 'You see how well she was at the christening.'

'Still, Mama *is* ill,' Caroline said carefully. 'Whether it is in her mind or her body I don't know. But this is my place. I have to be here. Besides, what else can I do?' She took a large bunch of daffodils and began sorting through the stems.

'You are becoming like Jenny who says that all the time.'

'Well what *is* there to do?'

Jane picked up a daffodil and held it to her face, striking a comical attitude. 'You could be an artist's model.'

'Jane!' Caroline burst out laughing. 'Can you think of nothing serious to say?'

'Or a poet. But pray do not try being a lady novelist until Jenny has had her work accepted, as I think she would kill you. Or . . .' She gazed at Caroline. 'You could be the wife of Rawdon Foxton.'

Caroline looked at her, pausing in the middle of her work. 'Could I?'

'Oh yes. He *appears* to be all over Emily, but I think that is to conceal his love for you.'

'He does it very well then,' Caroline said tartly. 'For I scarcely see him, now that Emily is here.'

'And James. He really wants to be with James; he misses his comrades. Emily just tags along.'

But Emily didn't just tag along. She was trying to impress Rawdon with her versatility. She rode well, she fished, she sketched, she kept the conversational ball rolling; she had a tremendous knowledge of contemporary events. She could almost tell you what various ministers and heads of state were thinking. She wanted to show Rawdon what a fine wife she would make, not just someone who did the flowers and bore children.

And Rawdon was impressed. He liked to ride behind her so that he could observe her figure on a horse, or sit opposite her at table or when they picnicked so that he could see the expressions on her mobile face, drink in the beauty of those violet eyes. But he could never quite recapture the mood of that August day. For one thing they always had company – young ladies and gentlemen were, by custom, never left alone. Sometimes they were joined by Harriet or Polly Tangent, but Jennifer never stirred outside, sunk in a mood of depression. Since Mr Thackeray had been so unkind about her book she preferred to sit in her room looking at the wall. Rawdon was very worried about Jenny.

'A picnic,' Emily suggested when she heard how Jenny locked the door and refused even to admit Rawdon. 'Jenny loves a picnic. The weather is so glorious. Tell her James will be there and Polly and Ben and Oliver. Oh yes! A great family picnic! It is just what Jen needs to get over her melancholy.'

Rawdon looked at her with gratitude. He was lying on the grass while she sat on a small stool sketching. James had gone to put the horses away and Polly to collect Jane and Caroline so that they could have tea out of doors.

'You are good, Emily. You really are thoughtful.'

'Well, I care about Jenny,' Emily said, looking at her sketch pad then at him, making deft strokes. 'She is in a very depressed state. I think how lucky I am with my life. I never have a moment of gloom and then I think of Mama and Jen and know how lucky I am.'

Rawdon wanted to put out a hand and touch her. He wanted to take her in his arms and kiss her. Her presence was so tantalizing.

'Do you know we are alone?' he murmured looking around.

Emily felt her heart beat faster. 'It is like the beach,' she said, 'that day on the beach.'

'It was important for you too?'

'Of course.'

'Then why did you never...'

'Why did *you* never?' Emily said reproachfully. 'You never replied to my letters.'

'I had so much on my mind. And you too, have the Court. I thought you were avoiding me.'

Emily looked at the drawing she had made of him, holding it away from her and putting her head on one side. 'There. That is you.'

'Me?' Rawdon leapt up and leaned over her shoulder. This was the closest he had ever been to her apart from dancing, certainly the most intimate moment. She smelt so fresh and there was a delicate hint of perfume. Her white shoulders seemed an invitation to further intimacy, and he could see the swell of her breasts through the white muslin fichu that she wore in the open V necked bodice, a style she favoured because she knew it showed off her figure so well. Her hair parted in the middle formed little bunches of ringlets caught up by a blue bow behind each ear, and he could see the fine hairs below her hairline and a thin film of sweat on her skin.

Rawdon closed his eyes. His desire for Emily was almost overwhelming. It was wrong. He did not think of her properly, with the respect that was her due. His carnal thoughts disgusted him. He moved away from her and glanced down at the drawing which, as though unaware of the turmoil she was creating, she held up for him to see.

'It is a fair likeness,' he admitted.

'See, I have caught your high brow and that wicked gleam in your eyes . . .'

She glanced flirtatiously up at him and Rawdon swallowed. Every feature of her was so sharp, so desirable. Her bodice accentuated her tiny waist and . . .

'Why Rawdon, you look quite pale.'

Emily thought he was trembling and he seemed to be trying to suppress some deep emotion. 'Has the picture offended you?'

'Of course not. It is an admirable likeness. It is only that I think you flatter me. I am surely not such a handsome fellow!'

'You are *very* vain,' Emily said primly, pretending to smack him with the paper, and the very familiarity of the gesture took them back to the schoolroom again and the mood was broken.

The picnic was held the day before James's leave finished, and Oliver and Benjamin were due back at school. Tim was staying with Oxford friends and the very young Vestreys were not allowed to come. A spot had been selected on the cliffs between Chetwell and Folkestone, not too high above the sea but sufficiently far up to give a lovely view. The selected spot was sheltered by the trees of tropical pine which grew in such profusion along that part of the south coast.

The Foxtons arrived in the middle of the morning. Rawdon escorted the coach with his sisters, and then there was a great deal of commotion while it was decided who should ride and who walk and who wanted to be taken over by coach.

In the end Rawdon, James, Benjamin and Oliver went on

horseback; Emily and Jane walked, while Caroline went with Debbie, Harriet and Jennifer by coach because Deborah's cough had worsened again and Caroline was anxious she should not exert herself. Into the coach too were packed the hampers for the picnic.

The men were already there when the coach arrived, the horses tethered to the trees, and in the distance the party of women could be seen toiling up the hill. Caroline felt lighthearted and happy despite the anxiety that always beset her about Debbie when her cough was bad. She was sure too she had grown thinner and there were bright spots of pink on her cheeks.

Jenny said nothing on the way over, but Harriet prattled non-stop because Papa was so much better and Rawdon was talking of rejoining his regiment.

The men collected round the coach as it arrived, Rawdon assisting Jenny, Harriet and Debbie to alight and then coming back for Caroline. He held up his hand and looked at her just as she glanced down to be sure she had her foot on the little flight of steps. The sun burnished her hair making it gleam like copper and her wide slanting eyes and soft brown skin reminded him of a picture he had once seen of an oriental madonna gazing with that knowing, yet unfathomable, expression that hinted at all the mysteries of womanhood. Caroline bit her lower lip in concentration as she descended carefully, firmly clasping his hand until she was on the ground.

'Thank you, Rawdon.'

She smiled at him, but he was reluctant to let go of her hand. It was firm and strong, long and supple. The nails were short and well kept, the little half moons clearly visible and very white against her brown skin.

'Thank you, Rawdon,' Caroline said again more loudly, looking at him with a puzzled expression. 'Rawdon, are you lost in thought?'

'Oh forgive me.' Rawdon released her hand and stepped back. 'You remind me of a picture, Caroline, did I ever tell you?'

'No?' Caroline looked at him curiously.

'It is Byzantine I think. The Madonna and Child.'

'And I am like a Byzantine Madonna?' Caroline's tone seemed to reprove him. 'I don't know whether to be flattered or insulted.'

'Flattered, I assure you.'

'Come on Rawdon,' Benjamin said boisterously. 'Stop all that billing and cooing and help carry these things.'

'I'll thank you to remember your manners, young man,' Rawdon said smiling. 'That is what we brought you young lads for, to carry things while we bill and coo.'

He looked good humouredly at his younger brother and Caroline laughed delightedly. Her heart seemed so light, though she knew it was absurd. She had been aware of Rawdon's expression, almost as though she could read his thoughts, and felt the firm pressure of his hand.

'We are going to swim,' Oliver Vestrey announced, and started to undo his shirt.

'Oliver, please!' Caroline chided. 'You remove your clothes *out* of sight if you don't mind.'

'But it was just the top part, Caroline.'

'Please, Oliver!' she said sharply and looked with dismay at Rawdon.

'They are terrible, those pups. Thank God I am not their housemaster.' He made a gesture with his hands to shoo them away. Caroline felt that somehow they were sharing a parental role; that it brought them closer together. She looked fondly after his and her young brothers.

Oliver Vestrey was just seventeen yet he was as tall as his brother James and almost as muscular as Rawdon, a man six years his senior. Oliver had thick honey coloured hair like Emily and deep blue eyes, fair skin that reddened easily and high ascetic cheekbones. He looked what he was, a combination of an athlete and a scholar. He was a fine boxer, an oarsman, a fencer, a rider, yet he had a love for the classics that astonished his teachers. Caroline adored Oliver because, due to his versatility, his nature was very contradictory. He had been a difficult boy and now his moods alternated between high elation, when he wanted to ride and swim and hunt all day, and deep contemplation when he wanted to read and sit gazing out of the window.

Oliver loved family life and was more disturbed by his

mother's withdrawal than anyone but Caroline knew. He enjoyed seeing the family happy and together surrounded by relatives and animals with Mama and Papa at their right place at the centre. Today was the sort of day Oliver loved and he charged around shadow boxing with Ben and James, teasing Debbie because she wanted to sit and look and not run around.

The two girls came to the top of the cliff, hot and panting, and Emily threw herself on the ground.

'I didn't realize it was as long. Water, water.'

Oliver crept up on her from behind with a bowl of cold water in his hand and was just about to throw it over her when Caroline screamed a warning, and Emily sat up in alarm, just avoiding the water which cascaded over her head and soaked the rug on which she had been lying.

'Oliver! You will be sent home . . .' Caroline wagged a finger menacingly at him while Emily struggled to her feet and ran after him trying to hit him with a stick she had picked up from the ground.

'Monster! How *dare* you!'

It was a happy time. The young men finally managed to change without shocking anyone's sensibilities and went down the narrow cliff path to swim; the picnic was elaborately set out; the girls made daisy chains and collected wild flowers and Rawdon lay on his back and looked at the sky. James, Jane and Harriet went off for a walk and Caroline leaned up against a tree and thought she had not been so content for a long time.

As she closed her eyes the sun beat upon her face and she was aware of the intensity of the smells and sounds of summer. Everything was enhanced by the beauty of the day. Through half open eyes she saw Folkestone Bay shimmering below and way on the far horizon the thin ribbon of coastline that was France. One or two fishing boats trailed lazily through the water, and the French packet pulled slowly out of the harbour *en route* for Boulogne.

Beside her Debbie coughed and brought her back to reality. She sat up and looked at her little sister who seemed half asleep too, and unaware of her coughing. Caroline laid her gently on the rug and smoothed the hair from her brow.

'Is she asleep?' Rawdon whispered.

'She is very tired. She did not have a good night. I don't think I should have allowed her to come.'

'She would have been very disappointed,' Emily said. 'She likes to be with the boys even though they take no notice of her. What cruel beasts they are.'

'Would someone call the boys,' Caroline got to her feet and tied an apron round her dress. 'In fact call everyone. It is time we ate.'

Emily had been sitting near Rawdon looking at him lying in the grass. After lunch she would try and get him to take a walk with her; perhaps the feel of pebbles beneath his feet would awaken memories of the summer. When it came to it Emily had been least in favour of the picnic of anyone even though she had suggested it, because she would have to share Rawdon.

Rawdon went to the top of the cliff and called down to where the boys were frisking in the water watched by Harriet and James.

'Lunch,' Rawdon put his hands to his mouth to form a hailer. 'Lunch everyone.'

Jenny had said nothing since she arrived but sat on the ground leaning against a tree. Her face was pale and her mouth clenched, and as she stared out to sea her eyes never wavered. Caroline had suggested she went for a walk but she didn't stir.

'Do you think Jenny's all right?' she whispered to Jane, who had returned first, as they sat together cutting bread and large thick slices of ham to lay on them.

'She is depressed, Rawdon says.' Then aloud to Jenny: 'Jen, are you all right? Could you butter some bread?'

Jennifer looked apathetically over at them but then turned her head towards the sea very deliberately as though she knew she was being rude.

'Oh come on, Jen,' Rawdon said. 'You are really like death's head at the feast.'

Jennifer gave a gasp and, putting her head in her hands, burst into tears. Caroline put down her knife and, gathering up her skirts, rushed over to her and knelt beside her.

'Oh Jenny!'

'I shouldn't have come,' Jennifer sobbed. 'I am making you all miserable.'

'*We* are not miserable at all,' Emily said firmly. 'It is you who are miserable, Jen. If you want to be by yourself you may and we will bring you a plate of food.'

'No, no,' Jane said, frowning at Emily. 'Jenny must come and sit with us. Try and be happy, Jenny. Life is good.'

'For you maybe,' Jennifer said. 'What is good in it for me?'

Rawdon looked uncomfortable and seemed about to say something when the dripping figures of Benjamin and Oliver appeared and Caroline sent them into the bushes to dry and change. Shortly afterwards James and Harriet came puffing up the cliff and Jennifer was forgotten. In fact the circle round the rug extended so much that it embraced her and she didn't have to move from her place by the tree. But she ate nothing and in the end Caroline gave up coaxing her and got on with her own meal.

Jennifer cast a shadow over the event. It was such a beautiful day and everyone wanted so much to be happy that her sullen face could not somehow be ignored. Emily resented it because of the effect it had on Rawdon, and when everyone was quiet and dozing after the good food she said, 'You really should not have come, Jenny, if you are determined to be so miserable. You should stay at home and mope by yourself.'

Jennifer appeared not to hear and Rawdon frowned at Emily.

'You shouldn't say that, Emily,' he whispered. 'I did all I could to persuade her to come.'

'Just because people don't like your book,' Emily said sharply, and Caroline leaned over and tapped her arm.

'Emily, please don't provoke . . .'

'I am *not* being provocative,' Emily said, 'but truthful. Look, everyone else is silent.'

'Everyone is sleepy,' Jane said calmly. 'Lie down and go to sleep, Emily.'

'I want to go for a walk,' Emily said getting up. 'Anyone coming with me?' She looked at Rawdon, but he avoided her eyes.

'I'll come with you,' James was always restless, 'or I shall sleep away the afternoon.'

'We are going to play cricket on Sandgate beach.' Oliver went to the coach to get the bats and stumps which he had carefully stowed away. 'Come on, Rawdon. You can field, and James, we need you as a bat. You girls can watch and cheer.'

'The cheek,' Emily said. But, like everyone else, she found Oliver's good humour infectious. 'Oh all right, I'll come and cheer. It is too hot for walking anyway. Jane? Harriet? Jenny?'

'I'll stay here with Jenny and Deborah,' Caroline said, 'and we can watch you from a distance. You will have to move along the beach because the tide is coming in. Emily and Jane, will you help clear up for a few minutes?'

'*I* have been asked to watch the cricket,' Emily said. 'Come on, Rawdon. I need a strong hand to help me down that path. It is terribly steep.'

Caroline suddenly felt very irritated by Emily, by her rudeness to Jennifer, by the way she had sat so close to Rawdon during the meal, the glances she gave him. Now she was going to watch the cricket just because he was playing.

'Emily, I want you to help me *first*, please,' Caroline said trying to keep her mounting irritation under control. 'Then you can go and watch the cricket. I'm sure you are really quite capable of getting down the path yourself.'

'Oh, very well. But Rawdon wait for me, please,' Emily commanded, swooping down and gathering up some plates. 'We should have brought a servant. When we go on picnics with the Queen . . .'

'Well we are not with the Queen now,' Caroline said trying to remain calm.

'That is *quite* obvious.' Emily's face was beginning to turn red. 'The Court does thing so much better.'

Caroline stood up and put her hands on her hips. 'Then I wish you would stay with the Court, Emily, and leave us in peace. Maybe you could ask for a permanent position with the Queen and you could be at Court where they do things *so* much better *all* the time. I for one am sick of

138

hearing about the Court and how well things are done there.'

Emily was kneeling on the ground stacking a pile of plates. She raised her head and stared incredulously at her sister.

'Whoops!' Oliver said. 'A first-class family brawl. I'm off. Come on, Ben.' He threw the cricket bat to the younger Foxton and the two of them scampered down the cliff path and were soon out of sight.

'I'm going too,' James said. 'Come on Debbie, I'll give you a lift.' James scooped Debbie into his arms, pretending she was very heavy, which made her laugh, and staggered with her to the cliff path.

'Really, Caroline,' Emily spoke very quietly, 'I am distressed at what you say. I thought you approved of the Court. Are you by any chance jealous of me?'

'No I am *not* jealous,' Caroline said stamping her foot. 'Just sick of the airs and graces you give yourself. Ever since you have been at Court you have become more and more self-centred. We are not your servants, Emily.'

'I said we should have *brought* servants.' Emily tried to sound reasonable.

'Come on, Harriet,' Rawdon said. 'I think this is between sisters. Emily, shout if you can't manage the cliff. Jenny, are you sure you won't come?'

Jenny didn't even shake her head.

'I'm coming too,' Jane said. 'This isn't between sisters – just *those* sisters.' She scrambled down after Rawdon and Harriet and vanished out of sight.

'Now *what* have you done!' Emily said, her voice sounding shrewish. 'Made a fool of me with Rawdon.'

'I made a fool of you?'

'He was quite disgusted with you, and embarrassed. If you carry on in this fashion Rawdon will not wish to come to Chetwell. He is too much of a gentleman to stand you behaving like a fishwife.'

'At least I don't behave like a strumpet. The way you ogle him all the time is nauseating.'

'How can I help it if Rawdon admires me? I don't have to ogle him. He can't take his eyes off me.'

Caroline felt so enraged she could hardly speak. She

could never recall feeling so out of control, as though she wanted to throw something at Emily or hurl her over the cliff. She moved menacingly towards Emily, who hurriedly stepped backwards. Jennifer had meanwhile stopped staring at the sea and was watching the row with interest, her eyes going from one contestant to the other.

'Rawdon doesn't really care for either of you,' she said. 'You are wasting your time fighting over him. Rawdon confides in me and I know.' Both girls stopped glaring at each other and stared at her. 'Rawdon is going back to the army and hopes to be sent abroad. He has no plans at all for marriage. You *are* making fools of yourselves if you think he will have either of you.'

Caroline had forgotten all about Jennifer sitting slumped by the tree. She felt mortified and humiliated about what had happened. 'I don't think we are talking about Rawdon caring for either of us, Jenny. For I am sure this is how we feel about him. As a family friend.'

'It is not how *Emily* feels about him then,' Jennifer said spitefully. 'Emily is in love with Rawdon and she told me so.'

'I did not tell you *any* such thing.' Emily went very red and stamped her foot on the ground. 'You are a spiteful frustrated little cat, Jenny Foxton, eaten up with jealousy because you are so plain and no one wants your silly books.'

'Oh Emily.' Caroline grabbed her sister's hand and pulled her back.

'Emily, you must not talk like that. It is not true.'

'It *is* true. She wants Rawdon to herself, anyone can see that. She doesn't want anyone else at Saltmarsh so that she can rule the roost with her fads and moods. If anyone loves Rawdon it is Jenny. She is in love with her brother and *that* is obscene. All the time he is anxious about her health, her moods. She won't leave him alone, or give him any peace.'

As she was speaking Jennifer got up as though propelled by some slow-moving mechanism. She walked over to Emily and Caroline tightly grasped her arm, frightened of the look on Jennifer's pale, taut face. Emily appeared frightened too and moved closer to Caroline for protection. When Jennifer was a few inches from Emily she stood staring at her, her eyes travelling over her as though taking in every feature, every graceful contour that she so pitifully lacked. Jennifer towered over Emily and her height made her look ungainly and frightening. Then, still with the same mesmeric movement, she leaned over and spat straight into Emily's eyes, and was about to spit again when Caroline cried out and put herself between Emily and Jennifer.

'Oh no, Jenny. No!' she cried in horror. 'Emily did not mean what she said. Oh please don't . . .'

Jennifer stared hard at Caroline but said nothing. Then she turned and started walking swiftly along the cliff towards Folkestone.

'Oh!' was all Emily could exclaim, paralysed with shock.

Caroline quickly fetched a cloth and tenderly wiped the spittle from her eyes which she had instinctively closed. 'There is nothing much there, Emily. It has all gone. Oh, what a horrible thing to happen.'

'She is deranged,' Emily said, 'she is quite mad.'

Caroline looked anxiously around for Jennifer and saw her beginning to run along the cliff towards the leas. Her head was thrown back and her arms extended in front of her, flailing about as though she didn't know where she was going.

'Emily, I am worried about Jenny. Look at her.'

Emily opened her eyes and looked in the direction Caroline was pointing. Jenny had turned now and was running towards the sea.

'She is going to jump!' Caroline screamed. 'Oh my God, what have we done?'

She ran to the cliff path and, cupping her hands to her mouth, began to scream towards the tiny figures playing below on the beach. The tide had come right up to the foot of the cliff and the players had moved along the shore. Caroline started to race down the path towards the Sandgate beach shouting and waving her arms but her voice was carried away by the wind. Emily, horrified but powerless, was the only one to follow with her eyes the figure of Jennifer as it disappeared over the edge of the cliff.

By the time Caroline reached the beach everyone was running towards her.

'Jenny has jumped over the cliff,' she said, falling upon James who reached her first. 'She simply ran right towards it.'

'Oh my God.' Rawdon raced towards the sea, taking off his jacket, followed by James and Oliver. Benjamin, transfixed, remained with Harriet, who had started weeping, and Jane, who was trying to comfort her.

'She cannot have jumped into the sea,' James called. 'It does not reach the edge of the cliff.'

They rounded the point and though the tide was full a long stretch of sand ran as far as the eye could see towards Folkestone harbour. Caroline, who had joined them, closed her eyes. The cliff sloped at an angle so that Jennifer must have fallen onto hard rock or pebbles.

But there was no sign of a body lying on the shore. Their eyes scanned the cliffs, but they saw nothing, no movement.

'Are you *sure*?' Rawdon said, looking at Caroline. 'May she not just have been going for a walk?'

'Well, she ran towards the edge. Oh, thank God, maybe she . . .'

They looked up and above them Emily was waving and calling though they could not hear what she said. She was pointing in the direction of the cliff but they could still see nothing. It sloped away from them. Rawdon started up the cliff path, the young boys clambering vigorously ahead of him. Emily ran down to greet them, meeting them half way.

'Jenny has fallen against some scrub or bushes,' Emily panted. 'She is lying very near the top of the cliff. She has not fallen far.'

'Is she all right?' Rawdon gasped.

'I think so,' Emily said, looking helplessly at her sisters. Oliver and Benjamin shot along the cliff like sure-footed mountain goats and found Jennifer, as Emily had said, very near the top. She had simply rolled into some bushes, the cliff continuing its gradual slope away from her towards the beach. As they got there Jennifer was lying quite still, the boys standing awkwardly on either side of her.

Caroline knelt down and put a hand on her breast. 'She is breathing. I think she has fainted.' She stood up and looked back up the cliff. The slope was so slight that they could walk it easily. 'I don't think she has done herself much harm.'

'She did it on *purpose*?' Rawdon said, looking incredulously at Caroline.

'I think she was distressed; by our row; by her depression. However she must have known she could not do herself much harm. It was a gesture.'

But what a gesture. As Caroline turned she looked at Emily, who had started to cry again. Jennifer had certainly brought things to a head.

CHAPTER NINE

They took Jennifer back to Chetwell where Dr Woodlove was called to see her. She had sprained her ankle and wrist but was all right. She claimed to have no recollection of her fall although Caroline thought she wasn't unconscious when they found her; just shocked.

They tried to keep Jennifer for the night at Chetwell to spare her father; but she refused to stay. Even Agnes was concerned enough to get up and go and see her, but the sight of someone taking more attention than herself drove her back to bed, where she had palpitations for half an hour. Jennifer said scarcely anything to anyone.

Rawdon took her back in the carriage, leaving Benjamin to bring the horse on which he had ridden over. It was a very quiet and distressing end to what had been planned as a perfect day. No one but Caroline and Emily could understand it, or why it had happened.

Jennifer seemed glad of an excuse to stay in bed and be fussed over by Mama, Rawdon, her brother and sister and the doctors. A doctor specializing in nervous diseases was to be sent from Tunbridge Wells to see her; but Jenny was already very much better. Her dramatic action had quite cheered her up – that and the thought that now she was at the centre of things, the household revolving around her and not Papa or Rawdon.

Rawdon sat by her bed a good deal. He felt responsible for what had happened. He read to her and encouraged her to talk, to speak about her writing and her ambitions. He thought it was Mr Thackeray who had sent her over the cliff.

'No,' Jennifer shook her head firmly and seized Rawdon's hand. It was the third day after the accident and she felt so warm and comfortable in bed. ' 'Twas not Mr Thackeray, Rawdon. It was Emily.'

'Emily?' Rawdon sat up sharply. 'You mean the row between Caroline and Emily?'

'No. Emily said I was jealous because I was so plain and no one wanted my "silly old" books. I felt mad. I can't explain it, Rawdon, but it made me mad to look at her, so lovely and fancied by everyone, saying that to *me*. I felt I wanted to kill her, but she was protected by Caroline and all of you, so it would have to be me. Both of us could not go on living.'

Tears started from Jenny's eyes and Rawdon reached for one of his big handkerchiefs and delicately dabbed at them.

'I think I can understand you Jenny; but I cannot understand Emily.'

'She loves *you*. They both do. They were fighting for you.'

'Oh Jenny, I cannot believe that. You must have misheard.'

'No, I heard correctly. Emily accused Caroline of spoiling the day, and Caroline said she was a strumpet ogling you all the time.'

Rawdon closed his eyes. He could almost see the scene, the girls as he had left them going for each other. He should never have gone.

'When I tried to stop them,' Jennifer said carefully, skilfully editing the truth, 'they attacked me.'

'It is the end of us and the Vestreys,' Rawdon murmured disconsolately. 'Oh, my poor Jenny.' He took her hand and pressed it.

'Neither of them would have been good for you, Rawdon,' Jennifer said with answering pressure. 'Neither of them is any good. You should stay here with Mama, Harriet and me. We will look after you.'

George Vestrey had come down as soon as he heard of the accident and had driven over with James to enquire after Jenny; but Jenny wouldn't see them. The attitude of the Foxton family greatly disturbed George, the iciness of Sybil, the bare civility of Rawdon. On the way back James decided to tell his father the truth about what had happened.

'*Emily* to say that? But I can't believe it.' George looked out of the window at the lovely familiar countryside fragrant in its spring glory.

145

'She was provoked, Papa. Besides, the girl was deranged. She said nothing all day.'

James was very angry. He and Rawdon had had words outside the house, each defending the behaviour of their sisters. James hated domestic crises, things going wrong. He liked an ordered, settled world when he could get on with his own pursuits. By now he should have been back with his regiment; but he had had to extend his leave.

'I'm afraid it is our family who has upset Jenny,' George said grimly. 'Who, pray, suggested I should speak to Thackeray? He thought the book was dreadful. He said he only read a bit of it and that was awful. They had no right to ask me. It demeaned me in Thackeray's eyes, that I should peddle such rubbish.'

'I think their intentions were good, Papa. Emily also suggested the picnic for her sake. They only meant to help, to be friendly.'

'Well, they have caused a rift between our families, and we have known each other since before all you children were born. I have never known Sybil Foxton so distant. She was scarcely polite. Now I know why. Plain indeed. Jennifer *is* exceedingly plain, but there is no need to tell her so to her face.'

'What are you going to do about Mama, Papa, talking of invalids?' James's eyes fastened on his father.

'Why, your mother will get better in time.'

'Do you think so, Papa?'

'Of course. She was too old for a child.'

'It is *May*, Papa. Rebecca is six months old. It is the effect on Caroline that worries me. She is nervous and on edge. She should not be asked to take the full responsibility for Mama. The girls should help more. When Emily is not in waiting she should be here and Caroline should get up to town. I think the whole household needs a shakeup, Papa. You are too preoccupied to see it.'

George looked indignantly at his eldest son. They had always got on; but in a distant way, never really taking the trouble to understand each other. James, even as a small boy, was always very self sufficient, undemonstrative. He seemed very happy with life and with himself; but it was difficult to know what really went on in his mind.

146

'Are you criticizing me, James?' George said, drawing his brows together.

'No, Papa. I respect you and admire your work. I know you are busy. But I think things are happening here that you do not know about, and I think that Caroline will suffer.'

'I cannot let that happen,' George said anxiously, looking out of the window. Then he put a hand lightly on James's knee, being careful not to show too much affection. 'Thank you, James for being good enough to draw this matter to my attention.'

Agnes, not knowing the reason for the family meeting, sat up in bed looking very bright and alert. It was something to do with the Foxtons – that silly girl falling over a cliff to make an exhibition of herself. Caroline had said she was depressed. Well she, Agnes, could tell them all about depression and she, Agnes Vestrey, didn't go hurling herself over cliffs or out of windows. Besides, she was far too comfortable. She selected a chocolate from the large box George had bought her and snuggled under the bedclothes as the family trooped in.

Her white frilled nightgown was tied at the neck by a large silk bow and there was a profusion of lace at her throat and wrists. Her cap, also of lace trimmed with ribbon which floated behind, concealed most of her blonde hair which lay in ringlets over her left shoulder.

'You all look very solemn,' Agnes said nervously. 'Do not tell me poor Jenny is worse?'

'No, she is progressing my dear.' George reached out and patted her hands, which were soft and very white like uncooked pastry. On her fingers were the plain gold and platinum rings that Agnes always wore, including her wedding band which was very shiny and smooth after all these years.

'I can't understand how it happened.' Agnes shook her head. 'The poor girl's nerves must be shattered. She is *so* plain and I think that makes her jealous . . .'

'Oh Mama, *please* do not!' Emily shook her head violently and put it in her hands, while Agnes looked at her with astonishment. 'It was *I* who caused the whole thing. I said she was plain. Oh Mama, I have ruined my life.'

147

Emily threw herself across her mother's bed and Agnes gazed at George in alarm, putting a hand on her chest to feel the beating of her heart. Caroline leaned over Emily and drew her back into a chair, keeping an arm round her shoulders.

'You *said* she was plain? To her face? Oh la.' Agnes reached for her smelling salts and vigorously shook the bottle under her nose, pausing to take deep breaths. 'Oh la. What misfortune. Why ever did you say such a thing?'

'I was provoked. Oh Mama, I can't talk about it. Rawdon Foxton will never speak to us again.'

'None of the Foxtons will most like,' George said gloomily. 'Maybe Rawdon will talk to James eventually, if he goes back to the army.'

Agnes replaced the bottle on the table by the bed and waved her heavily laced handkerchief airily about her.

'Well, we have plenty of other friends, although I did think Rawdon was very interested in Caroline.'

'No Mama, he was interested in me, *me*.' Emily leaned towards her mother, her finger pointing earnestly at herself, her face streaked with tears. 'He was about to propose.'

There was a profound silence in the room. Caroline felt herself flushing and squeezed Emily's shoulders very tightly.

'But I assure you,' Agnes continued blandly, 'Rawdon came over here regularly to see Caroline. He pretended it was to ask after me; but I knew better. I used to observe them walking on the terrace below.'

Emily threw back her chair and stared at her sister. 'So you *were* playing with Rawdon's affections while I was away! Taking advantage of my absence. Oh fie, Caroline! But Rawdon prefers me, he always has done. And now you and Jenny have driven him away forever.'

Emily rushed out of the room leaving Caroline standing gazing down at her empty chair.

'Is that true my dear?' George gave a slight apologetic cough and spoke very gently.

Caroline raised her eyes and looked at her father. 'I can't answer truthfully, Papa. I *did* think Rawdon liked me. I also think he likes Emily. He is very civil to us both, preferring neither one nor the other.'

148

'Lucky dog!' George said tapping his snuff box, while Agnes regarded him severely.

'Not "lucky dog" at all George. Philanderer is the word, playing with both my daughters.'

'Oh Rawdon was doing nothing of the sort, Mama,' James said testily, looking at his vest watch. He had hoped to have a game of billiards with his father before bed. 'He is no philanderer.'

'Has he confided anything to you?' Agnes said hopefully.

'No.' James drew himself up like the Guardsman he was. 'And I would not expect him to. Men do not discuss that kind of thing, Mama. I do think however that Rawdon likes my sisters, and maybe he is unable to choose between them.'

'I like that,' Jane said bitterly. 'That they are to be *chosen*. Do they not have a say in the choosing?'

'Of *course* they do,' George said, 'but *they* may both like Rawdon Foxton too. But that really is enough of that. Caroline is too embarrassed.' He looked at Caroline but she avoided his eyes. 'Now the next thing, my dear Agnes,' George said patting her hand again in that brotherly way, 'is to get you well. Caroline must be out and about more. It does her no good cooped up here. James says so and I agree. There are plenty of young men in London for Caroline to take her mind off Rawdon Foxton. Now that the good weather is here you should be thinking of getting up and about.'

'Oh I do want to, George. How I *hate* it being confined to my bed all the time. I like to be up and about, as you know.'

Agnes flung her hands in the air as though to indicate just *how* much she wished to be free to run about all over the place, to be busy and bustling about the house.

'Doctor Woodlove is going to get a specialist from London to see you, my dear. It may just be a matter of getting your legs accustomed to walking; something quite simple that the doctor will be able to tell you.'

Agnes looked not quite so happy again. The little furrow on the brow had become a permanent crease and she sank slowly into the bed drawing up the sheet as though for protection.

'He will not *do* anything Mama, you may be sure,'

Caroline said noticing her gesture. 'Just an examination and an opinion.'

'My spine was affected by the birth,' Agnes said petulantly. 'Nothing can be done about it at all. Everyone knows that.'

George leaned forward, smiling fondly.

'But you *want* to be better my love, do you not?'

'Of *course* I want to be better!' Agnes said crossly. 'Who in their senses *would* want to be confined to their bed or a chair all day? Who could possibly want *that*?'

'Then you will see the doctor, my dear,' her husband replied smoothly. 'He is a first rate man they say.'

Jane had been pacing up and down at the far end of the room, hardly listening to what was going on. Her chin was sunk on her chest and she whirled the ends of her shawl absentmindedly as she walked. When there was a pause in the conversation she stopped and came into the light of the oil lamp which burned by the side of her mother's bed, her face very white and strained.

'I want to tell you that I have come to a decision, Mama. I have not told Papa or anyone because I wanted you to hear it too. But I wish now to take Caroline's place. I have been selfish for too long, and I see how it has affected her. She is too stifled here, too alone. Maybe she has dreamed of Rawdon Foxton for this reason. Why not? He is very eligible, though I myself would not care for a man of such rigid and conventional views. But, as Papa says, if Caroline gets to London more often she can have a wider choice. She has been confined to the house for a year now, Mama. I wish to replace her.'

Once more there was a heavy silence as everyone stared at Jane. Agnes began her nervous plucking of the sheet with the fingers of one hand, agitatedly running the other through the golden bubbles of hair on her forehead.

'Replace Caroline?' she said weakly. 'How can you replace Caroline? She is my eldest daughter; she knows how to do everything, what to do when I have an attack. She is irreplaceable.'

'She does *not* want to leave you, Mama . . .'

Agnes looked relieved and smoothed the sheet instead

150

of plucking at it; a little smile of contentment eased the anxious crease on her brow.

'Oh that is very good. I knew she ...'

'But James and I want her to, Mama!' Jane interrupted her. 'We have discussed it. Emily has her place with the Queen; but I am free. Besides, I am tiring of the artistic world. I can see my duty for the time being, until you are really well, lies here. I know you *are* unwell, Mama, and need looking after. I am willing to take Caroline's place. I am quite able, Mama, to do so and ready. I have nothing in the world to do except devote my life to you.'

The tone of Jane's voice, though firm, was pleasant enough but to Agnes's ears it was harsh and threatening. She put a hand to her breast and felt her heart leaping within, up and down in a fierce palpitation. George had got up to face Jane, his eyes gleaming, his hand stretched towards her.

'I think it is a capital suggestion,' he said, taking her hand and beaming at his eldest son. 'Good of you and Jane to be so concerned, James.'

'But no-one consulted *me*, Papa,' Caroline said in a small strained voice, 'and my name has been bandied about enough tonight. It is assumed I am in love with Rawdon Foxton and have a desperate need to go to London now that he is to go out of my life.' Caroline grasped the back of the chair vacated by Emily, her knuckles glowing whitely. 'Well, I am not at all sure that I am, or was, in love with Rawdon Foxton, Papa. If he did not know his own mind I certainly did not know mine. I have given Mama my word that I will stay here until she is better. I am anxious about Debbie who is far from well. I feel I have a duty here, Papa, as the eldest daughter, and I am glad to fulfil it.'

George appeared to brush aside her remarks by an expansive wave of the hand.

'My dear, your emotions are quite rightly your own affair and we have no right to intrude, except that I as your father am concerned for your happiness as are your Mama, your brothers and your sisters. I think, or thought, Rawdon a fine fellow and would not cavil to have him for a son-in-law. However, your seclusion here is a point well made by James and Jane. Your sister is nineteen. She is perfectly able to take your place looking after the affairs of the household. She has nothing to do, as she says, and her young men can come down and paint her here. Emily will be left free for her duties at Court and . . .'

Mama gave a gasp and slumped right down on the pillow, her head hanging sideways over the edge of the bed. Caroline, anticipating the movement, was by her side, lifting her head and gently sliding her back into the centre of the bed. She put a hand on Agnes's chest and could feel the heart pumping up and down in a frenzy of excitement.

'There, Mama. Jane, fetch a cold compress please.'

Jane ran to the tallboy where she poured some cold water from the jug into the basin and, soaking a cloth in it, brought it over to Caroline. Caroline pressed the damp cloth on Mama's forehead, and then on her wrists, while she motioned to the others to leave the room.

'May I stay?' George whispered.

'You must *all* go,' she said. 'Mama has fainted.'

As they tiptoed from the room Agnes's eyelids fluttered and when her eyes opened they looked anxiously towards the door, then up to Caroline. She put a hand to her heart and breathed deeply, the colour gradually coming back to her face.

'There Mama. There.' Caroline stroked back the curls which were damp now, the rouge·smudged on Mama's cheeks, the fetching little lace fanchon cap slightly askew.

'I will be dead in six months,' Agnes murmured weakly. 'I have not long to live. I know it.'

'Not with me here, Mama. Not with me.'

Her mother reached up and grasped her shoulders, quite strongly considering she was so ill, and pressed her daughter to her.

'No not with *you* Caroline. But you are going to leave me. It is not right that I should stand in the way of your happiness.'

'I cannot leave you Mama. I have promised I will not until you are really well, maybe in another few months. We will see what the doctor from London says.'

'It is not that I don't love Jane,' Agnes said after a while, pressing Caroline's hand. 'It is just that . . . she is so *hard*. She would let me suffer, I know. Whereas you, you anticipate every movement. Jane is quite a different sort of person.'

'I know, Mama.' Caroline patted her hand, went on smoothing her brow. She thought how lovely Mama was and yet how frail. It would be cruel to leave her mother to the mercies of Jane. The two had never understood each other at all. It simply would not do.

She settled her mother for the night, helping her to take the rouge and powder off her face, sponging her lightly – noting now that the heart was perfectly steady and regular, even strong – getting her into a serviceable nightgown made of cambric and more suitable for actually sleeping. Then she put one or two curl papers into Mama's hair, gave her her medicines and a drink of cordial, lowered the pillows so they were not too high for sleeping and then settled Mama gently back upon them, the bedclothes pulled up to her chin. Mama looked so pretty and fragile lying there, sweetly scented, her blonde hair spread on the white pillows, her face bereft of makeup, quite white and translucent, like an angel.

Agnes's eyelashes fluttered sleepily and she gazed up at Caroline smiling that little smile of contentment, sighing deeply. She put up a hand and Caroline clasped it and held it until Mama's eyes shut and she fell into a deep regular sleep. Then she blew out the lamp and tiptoed quietly out of the room.

CHAPTER TEN

In King's Road, Chelsea, the Cremorne Gardens offered a variety of pleasures to Londoners of all sorts and descriptions. The better class of women never went there, or only some of the more daring ones in disguise. But gentlemen from the very top drawer often went there for a few hours of relaxation; to drink, have their fortunes told, watch the water pageants, medieval tournaments or other amusements, or maybe to pick up a woman either for an hour or two or the whole night.

Many of London's young working class women went to the Cremorne, to forget the endless hours they spent at a work bench, or bent over some intricate piece of embroidery or stitching without adequate ventilation or in poor light. They mostly came from the poorer parts of the city; but some of them were quite respectable hardworking girls and the Cremorne, like other pleasure gardens, offered one of the few means open to them of carefree enjoyment. If they were lucky they quickly picked up a man and their drinks and amusements were paid for in exchange for a few kisses or a quick grope under one of the trees in the park. If they fancied a man they might go off with him, and men of all kinds were there for the taking, rich, poor, good and bad.

James Vestrey was already half drunk when he got to the Cremorne with a crowd of fellow officers. After a good dinner they had been to Charles Morton's novelty, a newly opened music hall, The Canterbury, which offered first rate entertainment, songs, jokes, ballads and a comic turn or two.

Rawdon Foxton alone of his brother officers was not drunk; but he was tired and he wanted to go home. He had just rejoined his regiment and this occasion was an attempt on the part of James to make up. Rawdon had thought it churlish to refuse. Besides, he liked James; he liked the whole Vestrey family despite everything. As Jenny had improved, due to the constant attention she received, he

154

was able to see how trying she could be. She was petty and demanding and self indulgent. She wanted him and her mother and no-one else.

Rawdon had known that he had to get away from home or he would begin to go mad, like Jenny. He felt, privately, that Jenny had been deranged when she jumped down the cliff: a temporary derangement, but a derangement all the same. But she was his sister and his blood, and no Vestrey, however fascinating, could be allowed to taunt her and get away with it. Just because she was plain and unsuccessful she had to be protected; but she could be very trying all the same. She was going to turn into another Agnes Vestrey.

He and James were brother officers. They wanted no part of the petty quarrels between women. They had agreed about that and drunk a glass of champagne. Even if he never spoke to the Vestrey girls again he and James were friends for life. But he did want to speak to the Vestrey girls again. If they cared for him, as Jenny said, he cared for them; but a little break would do none of them any harm. It would give them time to sort things out.

Rawdon had tried hard to get drunk with the boys; but he was not in the mood and besides the Cremorne had a sobering effect on him. He hated the place. There was such a crush inside that it was almost impossible to move, and people were pushing and shoving, crying and shouting, pinching and kissing, as half the crowd seemed to want to move forwards while the other wanted to go back. The air was pungent with the smell of drink, cheap scent, horse manure and unwashed bodies. The noise was infernal with the medley of a merry-go-round, several organ grinders and crashing bands apparently rivalling each other to see who could play the loudest. From one of the stands came the clash of jousting knights and the roar of the onlookers as one was toppled from his horse. The multifarious coloured lights were both dim and garish, and a large red spotlight revolved round and round, inflaming faces one moment, casting them in furtive gloom the next.

Yet the crowd was very good natured; there was much scuffling but no fighting. Occasionally a woman screamed but mostly their laughs were high pitched, flirtatious and appreciative. Sweat poured from everyone's faces, hats were askew on damp heads, and the cheap make-up of the women streaked down their faces, while portly pot-bellied men mopped their crimson brows and the strands of hair vainly matted across their bald pates.

James had already secured a fresh bottle of champagne and a fairly secluded table and his companions slumped around it, breathing heavily, their faces wet with perspiration, their waistcoats undone across their gleaming evening shirts. James had also procured a girl, as well as the champagne, and was chatting her up filling her glass as fast as he could. Her 'friend' was sidling up to the table, waiting to be commandeered by another of James's comrades.

James, with a full glass of champagne, then turned to two more girls who sat alone at the next table and, hunched together, they hung on every word he said, their eyes greedily fixed on the bottle before him, on the inebriated faces of his companions.

'Here, more champagne!' James roared and held his glass aloft in the air. 'A toast. To Pleasure. To Forgetfulness. Rawdon, you old misery, go and fetch another bottle of champagne and some glasses for our lady friends. And then get one yourself, a girl I mean. Here, ladies, come and sit with us.' James bowed towards them with exaggerated politeness and the girls, giggling, eagerly joined him, one draping an arm around his neck.

Rawdon was glad to escape to the bar and took his time purchasing two bottles of champagne and some glasses, ignoring the waiter who fussed round him offering to carry them.

It was so hot and sticky that he longed for some pure air and he decided to leave the bottles on the table and make his way home, walking by the side of the river to his rooms off Whitehall which he kept as a refuge from the barracks by the Palace. He struggled through the friendly, jostling crowd, deftly avoiding a drunk who tried to wrest the bottles from under his arm, and placed them on the table. Now each of his brother officers had been joined by a woman. James was entwined with his, his mouth pressed against hers, an eager hand exploring inside her *décolletage*.

156

James briefly parted from his doxy to wave in the direction of a woman sitting on her own, pointing at Rawdon.

'This one is for you. She . . .'

Rawdon put down the bottles and glasses, smiled at the girl, shook his head and slipped her a coin.

'I am going home, James. I have a headache and fancy a walk to clear it. Fred, can you and James and the others get home? Can you . . .'

Rawdon's voice was drowned in a commotion that came from a booth in the far corner. Suddenly a man slumped to the ground, his arms still round the woman he had been kissing, who fell spreadeagled on top of him, her hat awry, a string of broken artificial pearls cascading all over the inert body of her partner. She put a hand up to her face and screamed.

Rawdon stared at the man on the floor and then, with two bounds, he went over to him and, kneeling, lifted his head looking at him anxiously. Then he put a hand inside his coat and felt his heart. By the time he had helped the man onto the seat the woman had stopped screaming, and the crowd who had briefly stopped talking, laughing and kissing to see what was amiss resumed their activities. Such occurrences were not uncommon as the night wore on.

'Is 'e all right?' the man's companion said. 'Oh my gawd. I noo 'e 'ad too much but, cor, 'e didn' 'alf give me a turn. I thort 'e was dead. 'Art failure or somethink.'

'He is merely drunk,' Rawdon said briefly. 'Have you been with him long?'

"Alf an hour. 'E got through a bottle and a half of champagne, and 'e was tight already. I 'ad the other.' The girl gave an unladylike burp.

Rawdon took a sovereign and gave it to the girl. Looking at it she bit it and put it inside her bosom, her face sullen.

"E wanted me for the night. It would have cost more.'

'You're lucky you got that,' Rawdon said curtly. '*I* owe you nothing. Now be off with you.'

The man had started to lean over again and Rawdon saw that he was, indeed, dead drunk. He was a big man and Rawdon knew he couldn't manage him alone. He looked at James in desperation and then at the others. It had to be

James. He would not want the others to know. He propped the man carefully against the back of the bench and went over to James, shaking him by the shoulder. James had made progress with his young woman whose skirts were now over her knees, her legs straddled wide. Rawdon could see one stocking halfway down her leg, and a dirty petticoat half torn. He felt almost sick with disgust and shook James again.

'James, sober up!'

'Waa . . . what?' James said, turning to him groggily. 'Be a sport, Rawdon, leave us alone.'

'James, this is urgent. Sober up.'

'Waa . . . what is urgent?' James looked around, trying to focus his eyes.

'Your father!' Rawdon hissed. 'Your father is over there. Dead drunk. Out like a light. I can't shift him without your help.'

The very word 'father' had an electrifying effect on James who seemed to sober up within a second of hearing it. He sprang up from his seat and his girl nearly crashed over on her face. The odour of her sticky, unwashed body was almost overpowering and, remembering the torn petticoat and black stocking, the glimpse of a frayed black suspender, Rawdon felt so nauseous that he thought he would vomit. However he made sure the girl was all right, helped her to right herself, gave her a coin and hustled James across the floor to the far booth.

George Vestrey sat against the bench, his head back, his mouth open, snoring heartily. From his mouth a thin stream of liquid trickled across his chin and down onto his spotless white evening shirt. Rawdon saw that his watch chain hung loosely and guessed that his watch had been removed. Of the girl who was with him there was no sign. James stared, aghast, at his father, his own face puce and running with perspiration.

'Father.' He turned to Rawdon. 'How in the name of God did he get here?'

'The same way as we did, I suppose. He was with a coarse strumpet who has made off with his timepiece by the look of things.' Rawdon shrugged. 'Now James, you take one arm and I the other and we'll get him to a cab. Are you all right?'

'I'm all right. I never felt more sober in my life. God in heaven Rawdon, *father* of all people. I never ever knew him the worse for drink, never mind in a place like this. Supposing he were recognized?'

'That is what I thought,' Rawdon said bending down and putting his shoulder under George Vestrey's right arm.

'Now heave. Steady.'

The three men, the one in the middle supported by the other two, staggered towards the entrance hoping no one would notice them. It seemed their luck was in and everyone was too intent on enjoying themselves to care.

George Vestrey sat for a long time by the side of his father's bed. The old man was completely bedridden now and spent his time either asleep or in that state that is neither sleeping nor waking. He could hear very little of what went on, but his eyes were still good and when he was awake he looked round with the lively curiosity of a young baby. George hated to see his father sink into this state of near senility and wished that he would go.

Yet he did not want him to go. He not only loved him, because he had been closer to him than any of his children, but the title would now fall on him, sixth Baron Vestrey. It would make very little difference to his circumstances except that he would own the house in Park Street, and he would have to give up his seat in the House of Commons for the House of Lords. He would also have the responsibility for Great Aunt Ruth, but that would be a light burden.

The old man gave a sigh and George leaned over and gazed into his face. His cheeks were cavernous and there were little bubbles at his mouth as his breathing became stertorous. His valet kept him shaved, and his sparse hair neatly combed. He was washed every day, his nightshirt changed and he was frequently moved to prevent bed sores. Everything that could be done to ease his father's passage from this world was being done. It was just a question of time.

There was a light step behind him and he felt a hand on his shoulder.

'Come and have luncheon, George. Peter will sit with your father.'

159

Peter was his devoted valet and servant who had been with him for thirty years. Peter loved his master as much as his family did and he hovered now just inside the door, his kind face sad and concerned.

'He is no worse, Peter,' George said passing him. 'We shall not be long.'

Peter bowed and George followed Ruth slowly down into the dining room and took his seat at the table, by custom not the head because that was left for his father even though he would never take it again.

'The girls are coming up by the afternoon train,' Aunt Ruth said, unfolding her napkin. 'Matthew is meeting them.'

'Kind of you to arrange it, Aunt Ruth,' George said looking at the beefsteak pie. He was not at all hungry.

'Lucky they were not here last night, George.'

George picked at the food on his plate with his knife and fork. The sight of it gave him nausea. He had felt terrible all morning, ever since he woke up with a pain in his head and an awful taste in his mouth. He could remember very little about the previous night except going to Cremorne Gardens alone after dining at his club.

'Yes, it was fortunate. Good of Rawdon and James to bring me home. They seem to have made it up. I'm glad. I always liked young Foxton.'

'You were in a terrible state, George. They had to carry you up the stairs.'

George put down his knife and fork and took a long draught of water. He bowed his head.

'I know Aunt Ruth, and I'm sorry. It will not happen again.'

'But it has happened *before,* George. It has happened twice since Christmas, only you were not quite as insensible as you were last night. Then you saw yourself home, even though I heard you stumbling up the stairs. But what about all the nights you do not come home at all, George? I know about those as well, you know.'

George flung his napkin on the table and got up. Luncheon was usually taken *à deux* when they were alone and after they had brought in the food the servants left them to serve themselves.

'Aunt Ruth I am of age, you know, to do as I please. What I do . . .'

'Is none of my affair, I suppose you're going to say.' Aunt Ruth pursed her lips staring gimlet-eyed at her nephew. 'But it *is*, George. It *is*, when you are found drunk and insensible in a place of ill repute with a woman who was doubtless a prostitute. Oh I know all about it. James was very upset. To find his father in such a condition has disturbed him very much.'

'But he was there too.'

'James is a young man, George. He has every right to sow his wild oats, as they say. It is natural. Or rather nothing that you or I can say or do will stop him. But imagine finding his *father* there, a member of the House of Commons, with a place in the government. Think of the consequences if one of your opponents had seen you; if it had come to the ears of the Queen, what would have been Emily's position? Did you think of that? I can't imagine you taking such a risk. And consorting with these common women, George. Consider the danger to your health. Oh, it is not to be borne.' Aunt Ruth put her hands to her face and shuddered.

'I am a man, Aunt Ruth. I must have an outlet. Agnes denies me, as you know.'

Aunt Ruth had finished eating and put her knife and fork neatly on her plate. She had a small appetite but what she ate she enjoyed. She drew the fruit dish towards her and began to peel a pear.

'I know all about Agnes, George, and you cannot blame her. She is too old to go on having babies. She has become a nervous and physical wreck. No George, I have been thinking about this problem, and I know it is one, believe me. I was born in the years before the Regency you know, and our mothers and fathers had a very different attitude to this kind of thing, a more practical one.' Aunt Ruth finished peeling the pear and cut it into neat quarters before she attacked it with her knife and fork. 'You must have a mistress, George, a clean respectable woman who will not only satisfy your physical cravings but will give you affection too. Agnes provides neither of these, as far

161

as I can see. She seems to treat you now as one of the children.'

George stopped his pacing and sat down again staring hard at his aunt.

'A *mistress*?'

'A proper, established mistress,' Aunt Ruth said firmly. 'Many people do it, though they do not talk about it. When you inherit from Henry, and alas it will not be long, you will have enough money to set one up in a nice little house in St John's Wood or Chelsea. I believe that is where rich men keep their mistresses. You will buy her a little house and she will maintain a small establishment, a maid, a cook, that sort of thing. No need for a coach. It will be quite sufficient and will not cost a fortune. Then maybe after a few years when she realizes you are not a threat Agnes will get out of bed and resume normal life again, and release Caroline to marry whom she pleases if she is not too old.'

Aunt Ruth rang the bell and got up from the table.

'Let us take coffee in the morning room, George.'

She swept out and George, his hands in his pockets, his head throbbing more painfully than before, followed her. In the morning room, which looked onto the pretty garden at the back of the house, Aunt Ruth poured coffee from the tray that had been left on one of the many small tables that proliferated in the room. Aunt Ruth, confined so much to the house, had recently developed a passion for re-decoration and modernization. Most of the furniture that belonged to the Regency was being discarded in favour of the new fashionable style of heavy, solid furniture intricately carved and ornamented in the naturalistic style with a profusion of fauna and flora, or scenes from the Bible or the classics. It had reached its zenith in the Great Exhibition. Everyone was buying it and Aunt Ruth felt that Vestrey House had to keep abreast of the times.

Furnishings were massive, in proportion to the Victorian love of measuring success by worldly goods. The more prosperous the country grew the grander and more magnificent the furniture, with an emphasis on heavy oak, padouk and mahogany and drapes made of thick silk, velvet or damask. The wallpaper was increasingly elaborate and covered with paintings by fashionable artists and gradually, with time on her hands, Aunt Ruth had gone from room to room. The old style classical furniture by Hepplewhite, Chippendale and Adam was sent to the sale room and modern pieces brought from leading manufacturers such as Gillows, William Watts, Smees, Collinson and Locke, or the well known firm of Crace in Wigmore Street where Aunt Ruth liked to go and browse.

George did not know whether he altogether approved of the many baskets, pots of plants, china ornaments, knick-knacks and bric à brac, boxes made of papier-mâché, baskets, hassocks and ceramics that one tripped over wherever one went, or the fringed damask drapes covering the piano and on the mantelshelves which Ruth had recently introduced. Sometimes his nostrils were assailed by a huge Pampas grass sticking out of an elaborate vase fashioned by Herbert Minton in majolica, or ivy hanging wantonly from a decorated jug moulded from glazed Staffordshire ware brushed against his head. The curtains in the drawing-room were also of heavy crimson worked with thick gold thread and looped by gold ropes with enormous tassels. Sometimes he thought the new fashion stifling, and he went over and flung open the French windows that led into the garden.

Aunt Ruth attributed the action to his bad head. She put his cup on a table by the side of one of the new deep easy chairs which had a long heavy fringe round the bottom to conceal the legs, which some people considered rather indecorous, such was the climate of the age. For herself she selected one of the new upright mahogany Elizabethan chairs, with the seat and back panel of tent-stitched embroidery done in a flower motif.

'I see I have embarrassed you, George. But I am your aunt, you know. I know about these things even though you might imagine me protected from the world, as I have never married.'

'You are serious that I should take a mistress?' George came back into the room and took up his cup without sitting down.

'It seems to be an eminently practical idea. A woman

for whom you have some affection – take care not to have too much – who will see to your needs and desires, help you to relax after a heavy day in the House. Your marriage is over, George, from the point of view of that kind of thing so you may as well forget it . . .'

'But I love Agnes. She is my wife.'

Aunt Ruth put down her cup and delicately wiped her mouth on a napkin. She gazed at her long ringless fingers and wondered if she was doing the right thing.

'I know you love Agnes, George. It is admirable and very correct. But Agnes will not be a wife to you again, in that special way. She will not have you in her bed, I can tell you that. She is quite determined upon it. As you say, you are a normal man with the usual appetites that men have and expect to see gratified, not that I understand them but that is neither here nor there. I *know* about them and that they exist. Now I do not like the thought of you consorting with women of the type your son and his friend found you with last night. You must feel disgust and reproach yourself constantly, as doubtless you do. I have in mind some nice respectable woman who, for various reasons, is not married; who is not well off but who nevertheless craves affection and comfort.'

'You have someone in *mind*?' George's lips were half twisted in cynical amusement. 'You have been planning this whole thing?'

Aunt Ruth shifted in her chair a trifle uncomfortably. It was indeed a very delicate matter they were discussing.

'It is the idea I have in mind George, not so much as someone specific; but yes, since you ask, I do know of a lady who would be just the person. She is very respectable, of gentle birth but not gentry. Her father was a prosperous merchant whose business crashed in the twenties when so many people had trouble. She became a governess; then she married, but her husband was sickly and died of consumption after she had nursed him devotedly. She is now looking for a position as a governess again and that is how I came to meet her. She is a friend of Mrs Miller and her daughter Lady Carter, is looking for a governess. However Mrs Ashburne, Hilary Ashburne the lady in question, is not everyone's choice of a governess.'

'Why, is she so very ugly?' George lolled against the mantelpiece, his good humour gradually being restored, his hands in his pockets.

'On the contrary, she is *very* pretty. And as she has been married and is – er experienced so to say, she is not everybody's choice. She is certainly not Lady Carter's who has turned her down. I happen to know that Mrs Ashburne is in very dire straits indeed and has no roof over her head save what is provided by kind friends.'

'And what age is this – er Mrs Ashburne?'

'She is about thirty, George. A good age; not a child and yet not too old. She is intelligent and well educated; she is very amiable, has a nice disposition and as I say is extremely pretty. But she has no fortune and no access to unmarried men who would support her. She is too old for that. Her position is desperate.'

'And how do you propose to contrive this liaison?'

'By introducing her to you, dear George. I am going to invite her to stay. Then, if you like each other, it is up to you to make the arrangements.'

'I think you are very immoral, Aunt Ruth.' George's head had cleared and he felt suddenly better. Whether it was Aunt Ruth's idea or not he could not say; but he felt springier, livelier and altogether more youthful than he had half an hour ago. 'I think the name for it is procuress.'

Aunt Ruth's hands fluttered up to the large cameo brooch at her throat and a very faint blush appeared on her cheeks.

'That *is* cruel, George,' she said quietly. 'I feel that I am doing a service not only to you and your family but to dear Mrs Ashburne who has very little opportunity in this life at all. There is nothing crude or distasteful in what I propose. There is no compulsion. It is not like visiting a house of assignation or consorting with prostitutes in the pleasure gardens. Mrs Ashburne will be here as my guest and if you and she do not take to each other . . .' Aunt Ruth got up and gave a majestic shrug. 'Now I must have my rest and you go back to Henry. Peter has some errands to do this afternoon.'

Debbie stirred in her sleep and Caroline gently wiped the

sweat from her face. For so many days she had felt near to tears, yet she could not cry. She really marked the day of the picnic as the occasion when Debbie started to deteriorate. The shock and the confusion, the sight of Jenny's apparently lifeless body being brought up the cliff, had seemed to disturb her more than anybody.

Caroline felt she hated Jennifer Foxton for the harm she had brought to her family: for the fact that she and Emily no longer spoke to each other; that Rawdon no longer visited nor Aunt Sybil come to see Mama. Moreover they were no longer referred to as 'aunt' or 'uncle' any more – those courtesy titles born of affection, because they were not really related. They were called Lord and Lady Foxton, when anyone mentioned them at all.

Jane, upset by her mother's reaction to her self sacrifice, had flounced back to London and was now at Wallington with the Trevelyans and a host of artistic young men and comely, intelligent women.

And now here she was, alone again, with the sick and the dying. For Debbie was dying. Caroline knew it. She would never voice it to herself or others, but she knew it was true. The doctor came in frequently and shook his head whenever he did; and Debbie grew thinner and the bright spots on her cheeks larger, and her eyes more opaque and feverish.

Debbie was now fourteen. She had always been delicate, possessed of an almost frenetic love of life since she was a baby, as though she knew she would not make old bones. Debbie was an ash-blonde Vestrey, her hair midway between Emily's bright golden curls and the wiry blond hair that all the boys shared. Her cheekbones were high like Oliver's and her face had the sculptural beauty of Emily, but with more calm than invaded the expression of that restless girl. Debbie's large blue eyes were paler than Emily's, and she had a *retroussé* nose and a pronounced dimple in her chin.

Yet somehow Debbie had not yet made much impact on the house, maybe because she was overshadowed by her various elder sisters and the sheer naughtiness of Clare who enjoyed the privilege of being the youngest. Rebecca had yet to make an impression. Debbie, though fun loving, was always good; never naughty, never mischievous. She was apt to be overlooked. She did not try to call attention to herself. In character she was most like Caroline, and they loved each other accordingly because they shared so many qualities. She had a sense of inner joy that somehow Caroline felt should have warned them that she would not live long.

Debbie stirred and opened her eyes. The dry cough started again and Caroline raised her on her pillow, giving her a glass of water. It was very hot even though all the windows were open and the night air blew in from the sea. Debbie lay back and looked at Caroline.

'You look tired, Caroline.'

'Well I'm not,' Caroline said cheerfully. 'I had a long rest this afternoon while Polly was here.'

Her cousin, Polly Tangent, shared the nursing of Deborah with her, and came over every day to relieve her. Mama dared not come too near her in case she got something.

'When I get well I shall look after *you*.'

'But I do not need looking after, precious.' Caroline leaned over and drew the sheet down to her waist. 'There, is that cooler?'

'You are very sad, Caroline, aren't you?' Debbie reached for her hand and squeezed it. Caroline thought: 'Oh God this is it. She knows she is dying.'

'No darling.'

'You look sad, always. Is it because of Mama or because Rawdon Foxton never comes to call?'

'Well, Mama is getting better, like you, and Rawdon has rejoined his regiment. He is with James because his Papa is so much better.'

'And Jenny, the one who fell down the cliff?'

'She is better too.'

'But you never see them.'

'No.'

'Is it because you had a row or because of Rawdon?'

'A little of everything. There.' Caroline stroked her cheek. 'Try and go to sleep again.'

167

'I would like you and Rawdon Foxton to get married and live here. Then you would never go away.'

'I will never go away anyway,' Caroline said as she blew out the candle and resumed her vigil by Debbie's bed. In the dark the tears that she had held back started to pour down her face; but she clung to the hot little hand, listening to the heavy laboured breathing, until dawn stole into the room.

Not only George, but his daughters Jane and Emily took to Hilary Ashburne who arrived to stay shortly after Aunt Ruth's conversation with her nephew. The girls thought she had come as Aunt Ruth's companion to help ease the hours of sitting with Grandpapa, and indeed Mrs Ashburne entered into her unspecified household duties with a diligence and capability that impressed everyone. She was not obtrusive, she was not servile, she did not talk too much or too little. She had a gay infectious laugh which was not heard too often or in the wrong place or at the wrong time, and her conversation could be most erudite without being overweight or boring. She was well read, the classics as well as contemporary writers, and she was *au fait* not only with the political situation in England but in the rest of the European continent too.

When she was first introduced to the Vestrey family Hilary Ashburne was exactly thirty years of age, a little taller than average with fair hair that had a natural curl so that it was difficult to control in the sleek style with centre parting, draped smoothly round the ears then in fashion. Her complexion was healthy, her skin glowed with the care of someone concerned about her appearance and she had very dark blue eyes that often twinkled with merriment. Her figure was good, not too thin but not ample, with a pleasingly firm bosom that made her look at once slightly matronly and capable but about which there was also, for those who cared to observe these things, a hint of voluptuousness. It was possible to imagine that, somehow, with her hair unbraided and her form uncorseted the delights thereby revealed would be enough to turn the head of the least susceptible of men.

168

George was determined not to be impressed by Mrs Ashburne and for the first few days after her arrival stayed at Chetwell Place as though to confirm to himself his devotion to his wife.

When he did return to town for business he was most perfunctory towards her, polite but hardly ever smiling. He was out a good deal for luncheon and dinner and did his best to keep out of Mrs Ashburne's way.

In June Emily left for Osborne for her tour of waiting and Jane, dividing her time between London and home, found herself frequently in Mrs Ashburne's company. They visited galleries together, attended tea parties and discussed the latest novels of Mr Dickens and Mr Thackeray and their social theories.

Jane was increasingly dissatisfied with her life. Since her mother had rejected her she felt useless and guilty about the role that Caroline played at home. The social life bored and irritated her and even the artistic and literary parties she managed to find dull.

Hilary Ashburne seemed to understand Jane and the two became confidantes, Hilary talking a little about her life in the past, her time as a governess, her happy but all too brief marriage and the lack of any prospects she seemed to have for the future. Not that she complained. She stated this as a fact and accepted her lot.

'But for the goodness of your aunt, I would not even have a home and I cannot stay here forever.'

They were walking in the park towards the Serpentine. The great Crystal Palace, scene of the Exhibition the previous year, towered above the trees, still shining splendidly in the sunshine though bereft of flags. The previous month it had been decided in Parliament that Mr Paxton's glass house would have to come down, even though Papa had been among those who thought it should remain in the park as a place of amusement. But the Prince was against it and Mr Paxton was known to be devising other schemes to keep his beloved creation intact.

The thick green fronds that covered the trees partly obscured the Crystal Palace, but provided here and there tantalizing glimpses of it across the water of the Serpentine.

The birds nesting high up in the branches swirled about, diving to the ground for twigs or pieces of dead grass. The fat pigeons strutted about cooing, some amorously inclined looking for a mate, their chests puffed out, the curious ritual dance of courtship performed in front of dozens of startled-looking hens.

It was a warm midsummer day and the parasols were up, as families perambulated in the park and dozens of riders, men and women, boys and girls, took up the main thorough-fare. Carriages jostled with the riders on horseback, most people intent, through the colours and variety of dress, on being seen and admired. After lunch every day of the week Hyde Park was like a busy market place but here the wares on offer were human or animal and not strictly for sale. Most days at this time Jane and Hilary, sometimes accompanied by Great Aunt Ruth, stepped out from Park Street to walk in the park. At night there was usually a party or a ball, for the season was in full swing and Jane, accompanied by Papa and Aunt Ruth, obediently attended while Hilary Ashburne sat with Grandpapa, sometimes until the early hours.

Thinking of this Jane replied warmly, 'But Mrs Ashburne, you are doing such a *service* to Great Aunt Ruth. She seems to have a new lease of life since you came. She can do so much more that she could not do before and, although I detest the stupid balls and parties of the season she thrives on them, and Papa likes us to be seen there.'

'You *detest* them, Miss Jane?' Mrs Ashburne looked curiously at the girl beside her.

'I find them tedious and irksome; the young men boring to distraction, the women trivial and vain. I feel so lost and out of place at times; so resentful of being a woman. Do you not think, Mrs Ashburne, that women have not a fair place in the scheme of things?'

Hilary Ashburne stopped to wave deferentially to an acquaintance, also a friend of Mrs Miller's. She had gone for an interview as a governess to her small children but had not got the post. Hilary thought that women's lot *was* very unfair in the scheme of things, but she was surprised to hear the young daughter of a wealthy aristocrat say as much.

'I would have thought you had everything in the world, Miss Jane. A loving family, beautiful homes, money, anything you want. You have beauty and have been painted so that everyone goes to see your picture in the Academy. You are well educated and your father treats you as an equal, discussing important things with you. How can *you* consider the lot of women unfair?'

'It is not only women such as I,' Jane said carefully. 'It is women such as *you*, who have no family or fortune and there are many more of you than there are of me. But you are a gentlewoman. I am also concerned about the women in the poorer sections of society who toil all day in factories and small back rooms, who have too many children and drunken brutish husbands, who live in damp, rat-infested slums, freezing in winter and hot in summer. I indeed am fortunate compared to people like this.

'But women are unable to get beyond a certain level, Mrs Ashburne. We are simply destined to marry and be an adornment at some man's table, the mother of his children, the mistress of his house. We have no other destiny even if we wished. We cannot be Members of Parliament, or business men, writers, yes some, but that is difficult too. We have no vote, no right to our own money on marriage, and then if the marriage is not successful no means of redress, though Papa says there is a movement afoot to remedy this. Papa says that in a generation or two the position of women will be very different; but it is slow in coming. I cannot see it coming at all.'

'What is it you want to do, Miss Jane?' Hilary Ashburne said gently. 'Do you want to write or be a Member of Parliament, to indulge in commerce or the professions? Do you not think these things are well enough done by men?'

'Oh yes, you do not understand. I think we should have the right to do them too.'

'To be *doctors*!' Mrs Ashburne seemed most entertained by the comical notion.

'Why not? And why not be a Member of Parliament? After all, we have a Queen on the throne.'

'Yes, but she does not rule.'

'According to my sister she has a great deal of influence

171

on her statesmen, owing to the years she has been on the throne. It is not only the Prince who knows what is going on in affairs of state; the Queen spends hours at her desk and intervenes most strongly. It is said that her personal dislike of Lord Palmerston caused his resignation as Foreign Secretary before Christmas. If Queen Victoria can do it, why cannot we?'

'I think women *have* a place,' Mrs Ashburne said cautiously, 'but I am impressed by what you say. I have never thought of it, I confess. Simply that it is women's lot to do these things, that they have their place and. so have men. It is an ordered scheme of things, having its origin in the laws of God! "By the sweat of thy brow shalt thou earn thy bread".'

'Miss Jane Vestrey!' The voice came from behind, interrupting the concentration of the two women who turned in the direction from which the sound had come. Jeremy Pagan stood just behind them, and beside him was a rather plump woman of middle years who leaned heavily on a stick and appeared none too robust, as the other arm was firmly linked in Jeremy's. Due to the disposition of nature she was decidedly plain although it was difficult to say exactly why. Her eyes were a greyish green that was not displeasing and she had an abundance of brown hair though streaked with grey. Her face was unhealthily chalky-white and a very square jaw made her look decidedly unfeminine, though forceful and determined.

She wore a most unbecoming black bonnet and a long black cloak that concealed her dress but fell just short of the ankles of her elastic-sided black boots. She was staring intensely at Jane who found her alarming, and tried to avoid her by looking at the woman's companion.

'Jeremy, we have not seen you for such an age!'

'I have been in the Lake District my dear, oh what glories in that country! I saw Dorothy Wordsworth and it was there that I met again my family's old friend Miss Harriet Martineau who allowed me to accompany her to London on a brief visit. I fetched her today to have a walk in the Park as I promised, seeing it is so fine.'

Jeremy turned in the direction of his companion who, to

172

Jane's consternation, whipped a large ear trumpet from beneath her cloak and stuck it into her ear.

'What?' she boomed.

'I was telling this young lady about you, Miss Martineau. May I present Miss Jane Vestrey and . . .'

'Mrs Hilary Ashburne,' Jane said her face crimsoning in the presence of the great Harriet Martineau, fierce champion of the American slaves, expert in political economy, fearless supporter of women's rights, critic of the Royal Family. There was very little that Harriet Martineau did not know or on which she was not an expert, and she was one of the most famous intellectual women in the country.

'Vestrey?' Miss Martineau said. 'I know the name.'

'Her father is the Honourable George Vestrey, Miss Martineau. He was on the committee for the Exhibition and now has a place in Mr Disraeli's Treasury.'

'I have heard of him.' Miss Martineau nodded. 'I read the parliamentary reports. Was this not the young woman whose portrait you painted for the Royal Academy, Jeremy? It is a good likeness. She is beautiful.' Miss Martineau nodded abruptly and seemed prepared to resume her walk as she stuck her ear trumpet back under her cloak and took up her stick.

'Oh, Miss Martineau,' Jane said quickly. 'I have so wished to meet you. I am an admirer of yours.'

Miss Martineau had missed all this, but the expression on Jane's face interested her and she produced her ear trumpet again so that Jane had to repeat what she had said. Miss Martineau looked gratified and her face grew a little pinker.

'I am flattered, my dear, that a young girl who is an aristocrat as well as a beauty should admire an old woman like me. I have spent so much of my life – I have attained my half century you know – talking to people whose minds are as deaf as my poor ears. You must be *very* singular, my dear.'

'She is,' Jeremy said with enthusiasm. 'She is a socialist, a radical.'

'Indeed?' Miss Martineau beamed. 'By socialist you would have to tell me what you mean, as there are so many varieties of socialism, not all of which I approve; but a radical is a good sign. My dear, you must come and have tea with me. I am staying with my cousin Richard Martineau in Westbourne Terrace, but only for a short while. I am here to see Mr Hunt about writing leaders for the *Daily News*. Can you come to tea *today*?'

'Oh? I would have to tell my aunt. I . . .'

'But *I* could tell your aunt, Miss Jane,' Hilary Ashburne said eagerly, noticing that the great woman had little interest in her. 'If Mr Pagan and Miss Martineau will accompany you I can run back and tell your aunt where you are.'

'And I will bring her home,' Jeremy said eagerly. 'Oh that would be *capital*.'

'Then that is settled,' Miss Martineau said. 'I am getting tired and cold. Fetch a cab for us, Jeremy and you run along dear, and say what you have to say to this young girl's aunt. Nice to have met you.'

Miss Martineau dismissed Hilary with a sweet smile and then she tucked her arm through Jane's and led her to a bench. 'Now you must tell me all about yourself, I can see you are a most intelligent young lady.'

CHAPTER ELEVEN

Jane always looked back to her tea with Miss Martineau as a crucial moment in her life. She had never met anyone so positive as Miss Martineau, with so many ideas and views on such a variety of subjects. Miss Martineau even expatiated on the virtues of mesmerism which had cured her of a serious illness. There was nothing she did not seem to know about and her views were informed, vital and interesting.

'Of *course* women are trodden on,' Miss Martineau opined over a cigarette after her tea. Jane had never seen a woman smoking a cigarette before; it was unheard of. 'It is their *own* fault. They want to be men's playthings, so they are played with, their views discounted. Look at me. I am merely the daughter of a manufacturer of bombazine cloth whose business failed in the twenties. My father was dead by 1826 at which age I was twenty-four, deaf, having suffered from bad health most of my life. I was no beauty so my face was not a gateway to fortune; this was an advantage. But I had my brain which my father, in his foresight, had sought to cultivate. I was one of seven and my brothers and sisters with the exception of one, James, were all healthy and strong. You would have thought that I would have been eclipsed; but not I. I sought to exploit my only attribute – my intellect. I found I could write and I enjoyed writing. I came to London and as you know my tales of political economy brought me fame.

'I was able to support not only myself but my mother. Now I live in a house in Ambleside that I built myself and, although my health has never been good, it has never deterred me from enjoying life to the full. I have never married but I have not regretted it – I was engaged once to a minister, but he went mad, poor fellow. Then I believed in God and thought it was a sign; now I no longer do, but I still think that by his death my feet were set on the right path.'

'You do not believe in religion at all, Miss Martineau?'

Jane by this time found herself seated at the great woman's feet, her arm leaning against her chair, a plate of cakes untouched at her side. Miss Martineau dominated the room because her cousin was out, and Jeremy sat on a small pouffe between Miss Martineau and Jane where he could surreptitiously study the latter's glorious profile.

'The publication last year of Miss Martineau's *Letters and Laws on Man's Nature and Development* which she wrote with Mr Atkinson caused a considerable stir,' Jeremy said. 'I believe also a rupture with your family and many friends, you said, Miss Martineau?'

'Oh goodness yes!' Miss Martineau said with enthusiasm. 'My family, though, I regret. I found the attack by my brother James in the *Prospective Review* hard to take, but James and I had been growing apart for some years. He is a Unitarian Minister and my intellectual views and opinions have become increasingly repugnant to him. Many people whose views I normally respect have felt themselves called upon to criticize my work though pretending to admire some of its qualities. No, I see true religion in the brotherhood of society, the fellowship we have for one another. Christianity is simply the means used by the clergy to maintain their position in society. And Mr Chambers' *Natural History of Creation* which he published in I think 1844, the year I was cured by mesmerism of my debilitating illness, confirmed that revealed religion is based only on false premises.'

Miss Martineau's face glowed with excitement and Jane also observed that when she became agitated she seemed to hear, whether she was using her ear trumpet or not.

However there was not much of an occasion to talk while Miss Martineau held the floor and the trumpet was little used. She seemed to revel in the sound of her own voice. It was rumoured that when the story teller Mr Hans Christian Andersen had visited London in 1847 he had to lie down for the rest of the afternoon after meeting Miss Martineau at a garden party. She not only rejoiced in the flow of words; she excelled in it. She had a voice of great beauty as well as force and, because everything she had to say was so new, so interesting, so unusual, Jane did not mind at all and hung upon every word.

But at length even Miss Martineau came to a stop. The shadows lengthened in the garden outside and a servant came in to light the lamp in the room. Jane looked up and realized the time.

'Oh, I must go. Aunt Ruth will be expecting me for dinner.'

'You live in London with your aunt, dear?' Miss Martineau enquired kindly.

'No. My grandfather has a house in Park Street which is presided over by my aunt. He is very ill. Papa uses the house a lot, especially during Parliament and I am up for the season.' Jane hung her head, 'I am sorry to say.'

'Why are you sorry, dear?' Miss Martineau seemed not to have heard quite well and jammed her trumpet to her ear, her face showing her perplexity. 'Do not young girls like dancing and that sort of thing? I thought they did.'

'Jane is no *ordinary* young girl, Miss Martineau,' Jeremy said with amusement. 'I told you she was a radical.'

'Then you must *do* something girl, if you are a radical,' Miss Martineau said briskly. 'It is no use loafing and idling about, disliking what you are doing. I agree it is sheer waste of time, at least to my way of thinking. But what do you want to do?'

Jane sank back on the floor again and folded her arms about her knees, her eyes gazing into the embers of the fire which had not been built up because it was such a warm day.

'I want a completely different life, Miss Martineau. I would like to be of some use; to visit the sick and help the poor, but in a real practical way, not as lady bountiful. To be among them, not seeing them from afar. I would really like to improve the lot of people; but I cannot stir Papa into believing I am serious and the very thought makes Mama ill, and she is already an invalid.'

'Your mother is an invalid?' Miss Martineau said with interest. 'Pray what is her affliction?'

'She has paralysis of the legs following the birth of my youngest sister. She cannot walk or get out of bed.'

177

'She must try mesmerism,' Miss Martineau said firmly. 'I will send her one of the best practitioners, Mr Spencer Hall who miraculously brought about my cure, or Henry Atkinson with whom I wrote my letters. He is a most gifted young man.'

'Mama does not want to get better,' Jane said abruptly, only realizing afterwards what she had said.

'I *beg* your pardon?' Miss Martineau screwed her trumpet more firmly into her ear and frowned. 'Did I hear you say she does not *wish* to recover? When there is so much to be gained from an active life that one cannot have as an invalid? How well I know this, bedridden as I was for years at Tynemouth.'

'I may be wrong,' Jane said, 'and it is true that Mama cannot move her legs, but I think she likes the attention we all give her since she has become an invalid. Above all she has the total devotion of my sister who is tied to the house.'

'Your sister stays to look after your mother?' Miss Martineau asked in surprise. 'Are there not others who can do this if your sister feels tied?'

'I offered to do it myself, but Mama has a special attachment to Caroline,' Jane said. 'Caroline was even present at the birth of our youngest sister, which greatly shocked a lot of people, because Mama could not bear to be alone; she was frightened. Caroline gives her strength and when Mama is very ill she is the only one who can make her better. Mama is in bed nearly all the time now.'

'Mmmm.' Miss Martineau pursed her lips grimly. 'This is almost a definite case of hysteria, where mesmerism can work wonders. But what does your father say?'

'Very little. Mama is afraid to have another baby. She sleeps by herself and Papa is hardly ever allowed to see her.'

Miss Martineau, who loved a good gossip, leaned forward. 'Then she must be taught birth control,' she said gazing to the ceiling as one calling upon the prophets to witness, even though she did not believe in them. 'Oh do not look so shocked child; it exists, you know, but no-one will admit it. It is considered a forbidden subject and *I* have been frequently attacked for expressing my views. It is the only solution to the problem of overpopulation among the

178

working classes, but people of all kinds can benefit from it too. I think if I had an hour's conversation with your mother and then Mr Atkinson came to see her she would be a changed person.'

'I will try and arrange it,' Jane said getting up. 'If only for the chance to see you again and listen to your views.' She held out her hand and the older woman grasped it, pressing it and smiling. 'You have changed my life, Miss Martineau. From now on I will *find* ways to act. I must make myself useful.'

'I hope you do dear, but you are a pretty girl. I warrant you have any number of admirers. Hold out though against the slavery inflicted on women by matrimony for as long as you can. I can see that, like mine was, your father is an enlightened man who has not neglected your mind. There is a great need for women to resist the evils of society, the ignominious position they hold. Write to me, my dear, come and see me in Ambleside. You are welcome at any time and when I come to London again, and if you can arrange it, I will try and see your mother. But at the moment I am undertaking a vast task, the translation of one of the works of Monsieur Comte the French philosopher, so that I do not expect to journey south again for some time. But come and see me, my dear, and *write*. Now Jeremy fetch a cab to take Miss Vestrey home and see you do not linger. Oh, I saw the look in your eyes,' Miss Martineau wagged a finger in his direction, 'but you are not good enough for her, I know that; she is a very special person.'

Miss Martineau looked directly into Jane's eyes and her gaze was solemn, unsmiling. Years later Jane often remembered that look and wondered if, somehow, Miss Martineau was able to divine what life held in store for her.

As she tripped back across the park Hilary Ashburne thought that it was all very well for people to talk, but when it came to the crunch their actions belied their words. As soon as Jane Vestrey met up with the important Miss Martineau her views on equality underwent a transformation, so that Hilary, who was very clearly subservient, was made to feel more so by being despatched back to make excuses for the younger girl. Hilary Ashburne would have enjoyed telling her friends, the few she had, that she had engaged in conversation with one of the most famous women of the age. She was sure she was just as capable of holding her own with her as Jane Vestrey. But no; because of her domestic inferior status she was sent back to the house. It was true she had volunteered; but it had been not only eagerly accepted, but taken for granted. The theory and the practice, as usual, turned to her disadvantage.

Hilary Ashburne was quite used to this; she expected nothing else. She had no money and nowhere to live, so even the best intentioned people exploited her whether they meant to or not and she was quite sure that Jane, whom she liked, did not mean to. It was simply that if one had everything, one could simply not assume the skin of someone who had nothing, or very little. It was true that Hilary was a gentlewoman; but gentility did not get you very far. Now the kindness of the Honourable Ruth Vestrey, though well meant and sincere, was gradually turning her into a superior unpaid domestic servant. She had become a sort of gratuitous companion who ate with the family and was accepted as one of them, but who was not asked to balls or the best parties or to converse with a distinguished female member of the intelligentsia.

Hilary hurried up the stairs and through the door of Vestrey House which stood open. Somewhat to her surprise the butler appeared in the hall as soon as she entered, his face looking worn and concerned.

'Oh Mrs Ashburne, I thought you were Miss Vestrey. We have sent for her. His lordship has taken a sudden turn for the worse.'

'Is anyone with him?'

'Only Mr Vestrey. The doctor has been and gone saving there is no more he can do. We are not sure where Miss Vestrey is. She took the coach and went out without saying. Have you any idea, madam?'

'I have none at all, I'm afraid. I had better see if there is anything I can do.'

Hilary hurried upstairs pausing only to take off her

bonnet and cloak. Outside Lord Vestrey's door she paused and, taking a deep breath, smoothed her dress and tidied her hair. The door was slightly ajar and she pushed it open. The old man's breathing was light and laboured and George Vestrey sat hunched in his chair by the side of the bed. Hilary tiptoed up to him and stood behind him.

'Aunt Ruth?'

'It is I, Mr Vestrey, Mrs Ashburne. Is there anything I can do?'

George Vestrey got up and turned to face her, indicating the seat he had just vacated.

'Do sit down, Mrs Ashburne. It is good of you to come.'

'I came back, sir, from the park. Your daughter, Miss Jane, has met Mr Pagan and Miss Martineau in the park and been invited for tea. She begged me to tell her aunt where she was.'

'Miss Martineau. *The* Miss Martineau?'

'Yes, sir. It appears she is a friend of Mr Pagan.'

'Some of us call her Miss Martinet,' George said, the strain on his face momentarily giving place to a smile, 'but still there is no denying her capability. Oh well, I suppose no harm can come of it.' George drew up a chair and sat next to Mrs Ashburne. 'Father is going. The doctor says we can do nothing and he is comfortable.'

Hilary looked at the face so familiar to her through the many hours of watching she had done herself. She felt she knew him intimately despite the short time she had been there, despite the fact that he had seldom spoken a word that made sense, so long had she gazed at his countenance while the others had been out or asleep. It seemed she saw the whole of the Vestrey family history in his physiognomy; the pride, the intelligence, the arrogance of nobility which all of his family bore to a greater or lesser extent but Jane, she thought, most of all. Jane's very certainty that she was right about everything, that her views were the most important, seemed to bear the stamp of arrogance, even though she would be horrified if she were told this. Even her sister, Emily, for all her airs and graces had a natural charm and grace which seemed to pre-empt arrogance. Mrs Ashburne had never met Caroline or the others.

'He is very peaceful, Mr Vestrey.'

George looked at her sideways, noting the tilt of her head, the pile of attractive blonde hair slightly wispish as though she had been running in the open air. From this position too he saw her bosom to advantage, noting the firm heavy swell just by the armpits. He closed his eyes guiltily at the vision of Mrs Ashburne in the nude that had come unbidden to his mind. 'Oh father, forgive me,' he said inwardly. His father had never looked at another woman even though his mother had died relatively young. He was a pillar of rectitude and morality, as George ought to be.

Yet he, his father's eldest son, had fallen grievously. He was tormented too often and for too long by the stirrings of the flesh until he had been forced to go after women of the streets, like a parched man seeking water. Afterwards the guilt and self disgust were unbearable too, so that for days, sometimes weeks, he reproached himself whenever he thought of it. He worked furiously hard to banish the memory from his mind of those common women and the terrible lodging houses on and off the Haymarket they had taken him to. But then the memory dimmed and the need became overpowering again and he sought them out once more.

Mrs Ashburne smelt very clean; there was a good wholesome odour of Pears soap about her, not the cheap stink of the street women. Mrs Ashburne emanated health, virtue, respectability, intelligence and, he had to admit it, a certain sensuality that he had been aware of since she had first come to the house. He found her very attractive indeed, pleasing and desirable. But the idea that Aunt Ruth had . . .

His father's breathing changed and the rattle began in his throat that George had so dreaded. His eyes filled with tears and he took the thin hand, so white and delicate it looked like rice paper. He was aware of the sympathy on Mrs Ashburne's handsome face, her unspoken comradeliness. With such a woman like that by your side . . . Could it be *possible*? He was so alone, so lonely. But would she want it, could she conceivably tolerate it? What about Agnes? Was it *right*?

182

A spasm passed through his father and George knelt by the side of the bed gently taking the old man's head in his arms, cradling it, frantically wanting, despite the odds, to keep him in this world. Mrs Ashburne knelt too and bowed her head. The tears flooded down George's face and he wept for all the love he had had for his father, all the memories of a happy and contented youth and manhood due to him. For the many years his father was abroad they had corresponded, long warm letters, never very intimate, but full of affection. They understood each other so well.

'Never had a man more perfect a father,' he murmured and pressed his head very close. The rattle had stopped and the room seemed very still. George looked at his father's eyes and saw that, very dim now, they seemed fixed on a spot high on the wall in front of him.

'He has gone, sir,' Mrs Ashburne said, her voice composed. 'Your father is dead.'

George held his head and swayed back and forth on his knees, trying desperately to blink away the tears. Then he drew down the thin translucent lids over the eyes that already no longer looked familiar, which he would never see again.

Mrs Ashburne got to her feet and turned to go.

'Stay,' George said abruptly. 'It is consoling to have you with me. Please do not go. Do you mind?'

Mrs Ashburne looked at him and smiled, a deep, sympathetic smile that although warm was just right for the occasion, had just that trace of tender sympathy and regret. She would always know what to do; she would never let one down.

'Of course I will stay, Lord Vestrey,' she said, 'for as long as you want me. I am flattered that you should need me.'

George's heart suddenly filled with gratitude towards this kind, good self-effacing woman and, feeling strengthened, he stood up and kissed his father tenderly on both cheeks. He was not going to be alone, after all.

No matter how cold it was, and it was a bitter autumn, Jane Vestrey rose very early every morning and was driven by Matthew over to Soho. So that she should not be seen arriving by carriage he stopped at the top of Poland Street and escorted her the rest of the way. At four he came to pick her up again in the same discreet way, sometimes accompanied by Emily or Aunt Ruth who came out of curiosity. Compared to the sedate *ambiance* of Mayfair the busy, narrow teeming streets of Soho were like another world.

The Poland Street Mission was run by a friend of Miss Martineau's, Isabella Goodey. In her youth Miss Martineau had been a strong Unitarian and the Poland Street Mission, though strictly non-denominational as so many of those whom it tried to help had no religion at all, had been started and was supported by the Unitarian Church.

Isabella Goodey was a friend of a Unitarian minister, the Reverend William Gaskell, husband of the novelist Mrs Gaskell who in turn was a friend of Miss Martineau. It took Miss Martineau no time at all, after arriving home the previous summer, to get the wheels in motion that led to Jane Vestrey's interest in the Poland Street Mission.

It had been decided not to tell her mother what Jane did while she was up in town. Mama thought she was still sitting to painters, carefully chaperoned, or attending literary parties, teas and salons; but Jane had almost given up that kind of thing and worked at the mission with the devotion of a zealot. Papa knew and Aunt Ruth, Caroline and Emily, but no-one dared tell Mama especially as she was now able to get up for a few hours a day and everyone thought the strength to her legs was returning. Mama was so improved these days as long as nothing disturbed the even tenor of a life made and controlled by the capability of Caroline. The baby was thriving, the younger children were happy, though Deborah's health continued to cause concern. Papa seemed to have accepted the situation with Mama with good grace, and she began allowing him in her room for a chat because he never even so much as whispered the idea that he should move back into her bedroom. He had obviously learned his lesson, in Agnes's opinion, and his work kept him fully occupied.

In December Lord Aberdeen had succeeded Lord Derby as the Prime Minister of a coalition government with Mr

Gladstone as Chancellor and Lord John Russell as Foreign Secretary. Although his friend Mr Disraeli had gone from office, Lord Aberdeen had a high opinion of the new Lord Vestrey who spoke for foreign affairs in the House of Lords, as Lord John was a member of the Commons. Papa seemed so happy and calm, so fulfilled that the family were relieved the situation with Mama no longer upset him so much. Obviously one could get used to anything.

Papa sometimes came to the Poland Street Mission and Jane took him into the houses of the very poor to see just what conditions were like. No room of the tiny cramped houses had less than six or seven souls in it; there were outside privies often shared by three or four houses, and all of them used the pump in Broad Street which was the only source of water.

At the back of Poland Street was the workhouse and so dismal were the conditions there that the sick, the homeless and the destitute preferred, if they could, to sleep in the alleys that ran through Soho like rabbit warrens, than take shelter there. Whole families encamped together and were practically supported by the food and clothes which came from the Poland Street Mission.

Jane worked tirelessly among the inhabitants of the mean, cold, rat-infested houses of Soho with their poverty-stricken inhabitants. At first her nausea and disgust with what she found were such that she preferred to stay in the Mission House dispensing food to those who came for it. But gradually as the weeks wore on and the winter grew worse, her compassion overcame her fastidiousness, and she was also ashamed that of all the helpers she was the one who stayed in the Mission House. Many well brought-up young women, some of the nobility such as she, did several hours a week at the Mission, being brought and collected in their carriages like Jane or accompanied by servants. Lady Pamela Fairclough, a married lady, even brought her butler and maid, not to look after the needy, but to follow her about making sure that she did not soil the hem of her dress in the litter-filled streets or dirty her hands. Isabella Goodey soon told Lady Pamela Fairclough, a deeply religious woman, that she felt her duties were probably best directed towards her family and not the poor. Lady Pamela was impressed by this good counsel and left, assured that it was the will of God.

Isabella Goodey was a tall gaunt girl who had had small-pox in her teens and, if she had ever had looks, she had lost them then. Her face was deeply pitted, her features were haggard, but her expression was one of such serenity and natural goodness, her eyes so full of gentleness and compassion that all who saw her were convinced that she was beautiful. Her father, though a gentleman, had not been content to waste away his days in idleness, hunting and spending long, useless hours in his club. England had grown rich on its commerce and, seeing the opportunities, he had invested in a glass-making business which finally came out of the doldrums just when Sir Robert Peel repealed the tax on glass, and was one of the main sub-contractors for Mr Paxton's Crystal Palace. He was remotely known to George Vestrey because of his predisposition to good works. A son, a twin to Isabella, worked with him in his business. He was a widower and a devoted family man.

Foundress and director of the Mission, Isabella was one of those who was neither driven to work nor accompanied by a maid. She would walk through the streets of Marylebone and St Giles from her home in Queen Anne Street, appalled by the overcrowding and poverty of so much of one of the richest cities in the world.

The railway boom had meant that the construction of the tracks and the great main line stations had cut quite ruthlessly through the already overcrowded parts of London. These were parts that coincidentally housed the poorest people and so the land was relatively cheap to buy. Houses had been bulldozed with utter disregard for any resettlement programme, and their inhabitants tipped into other parts of London like so many fishes spilling out of a net. Neither government nor city institutions, nor those who built the railways, gave a thought for what happened to those who were so summarily dispossessed – there was a pious, vague hope that they would move out of London and so ease the congestion. Unhappily they could not and did not; they crowded in upon already overcrowded houses so as to be near their places of work. The efforts to do something about the situation fell to voluntary bodies and philanthropic individuals of whom, it is true, there were a good many.

However the problem was so vast that no amount of philanthropy could take the place of a well-organized policy of urban resettlement, and the 'model dwellings' that sprang up under the aegis of such men as George Peabody and Henry Roberts were like tiny stones in a vast pond. Even the Prince Consort had designed a 'model dwelling' which had been proudly shown at the Great Exhibition; but the problems of the real poor remained unsolved. Those who could afford the rent for a model dwelling were the more prosperous sections of the population, skilled artisans and craftsmen who looked down upon those who merely laboured and possessed no trade. In fact the artisans felt that the unskilled should keep to their place, just as much as those a little up the scale felt the artisans should keep to theirs. It was a strictly hierarchical world where the aristocrat looked down upon gentry, the gentry looked down upon those engaged in trade, and so on until the very bottom was reached. It was only there among the very poor that any kind of camaraderie obtained, and that was hard to find.

Jane found it most among the children who played together in the streets. Watching them at hopscotch, makeshift skittles or kicking a bundle of rags fashioned in the shape of a ball, she sometimes wished they would never grow up but remain in this blessed state of ignorance forever. But it was not really ignorance; it did not extend to the facts of life or the conditions of everyday existence. They slept in the same room as their mothers and fathers, their brothers and sisters, sometimes their grandparents and aunts and uncles as well. They knew all there was to know about birth, disease, life and death, poverty and hunger. Procreation was such a natural process to them, through continually observing it in the close confines of their quarters, that as soon as they were old enough they started experimenting, imitating their elders in the street, rather like the pigeons, caring not who observed them.

In the six months that Jane had been involved in the Poland Street Mission she felt that she had never really been alive before, never so aware. All her own girlhood ignorance vanished as she saw the effects of hunger, disease and overpopulation everywhere she went.

She tried to interest her father in the welfare of the poor, but although sympathetic he said that enough people were engaged upon this already and his business was in foreign affairs where a troublesome situation was blowing up in Turkey. He said he would put Jane in touch with Lord Palmerston's son-in-law Lord Shaftesbury; but somehow either he or Lord Palmerston or Lord Shaftesbury were always too busy. All were, by their natures, very busy people. As her bitterness and disillusion increased Jane came to despise the inactivity of authority which did so little and some of whose laws even made matters worse.

Isabella Goodey remained sanguine and optimistic. She believed in the goodness of God and the worth of man, despite all the evidence that daily surrounded her to the contrary. Even those she helped were not always grateful – if you weren't looking they stole from you if they could, or poked their tongues out when you turned your back. Some men attacked you, so it was a rule that the numerous helpers travelled about in pairs when they left the house. The Mission House was bare because of theft and the tables and chairs were secured, where possible, to the floor.

Soho not only contained the destitute, those who came to the Mission, but people of every kind including many who earned an honest living in the numerous small factories with which Soho abounded. Every kind of trade and manufactory could be found there: tailoring, dressmaking, glovemaking and millinery; foundries where goods of iron, brass or silver were made to grace the homes of the wealthy; printers and bookbinders, stationers, pawnbrokers, watchmakers, candlemakers, coal merchants, mechanics, and manufacturers of cakes and fancy sweetmeats to spoil the palates of those who could afford them. In addition there were shops selling goods of every conceivable kind – fresh meat and fish, imported wines, fruit, vegetables, ironmongery, hardware, haberdashery and household goods.

Soho also fed the service industries situated in the centre of London. Since the opening of the railways, hotels, practically unknown before then, proliferated. Restaurants opened and the houses of the rich needed chimney-sweeps and men to empty their dustbins. Not all the men and women employed in hotels lived in and they had to be as near to their work as possible. So they swarmed into St Giles, Soho and Covent Garden, itself the greatest market in the world for fruit, flowers and vegetables, employing hundreds of porters to handle the wares which came from the country or the continent of Europe. All had to live nearby in order to be on time for work when the hours were long, sometimes from six in the morning until ten at night.

The poor who had opted out or who were too weak or ill ended up at the workhouse. There families were separated, mothers and children from husbands and fathers or, more pathetic, a couple who had lived together all their lives and were too old and sick to cope any longer. Together with all this flotsam and jetsam of society, Soho also gave refuge to the many exiles who had fled to England following the 1848 upheavals. Dressed in long dark clothes, sporting beards, wearing unfamiliarly shaped hats, they walked along the streets with jerky, self-effacing movements diving into doorways or up dark alleys with careful backward glances to be sure they were not being followed. For there were spies as well as those spied upon, informers, traitors and the usual interplay and intrigue of exile politics and manoeuvrings in a foreign country.

Jane realized, during those months, in a way that nothing else could make her realize, the gulf between the rich and not only the poor, but the various gradations of poor among whom she worked. Far better than the novels of Mr Disraeli, Dickens or Mrs Gaskell, far more than the speeches of Mr Bright or Lord Shaftesbury or the philanthropy of Miss Coutts or Mr Peabody, the actual reality of life as she saw it and knew it to be turned Jane Vestrey from a well-meaning young noblewoman with vague ideas about poverty and doing good to an embittered radical determined to try and change things.

But how could one go about this fundamental change; for the whole structure of society must be altered and destroyed? No-one was trying to do that, that she knew of; the Chartists had attempted it but finally failed. She felt that what was needed was a revolution such as had taken place in so many continental countries in 1848, but they had failed too. The workers must rise up, but how? How, when the rich controlled all the resources and means of production and the workers, badly paid and because of this badly fed and badly housed, eked out a mere existence to keep alive?

By the end of the year Isabella Goodey was becoming very worried about Jane Vestrey. Not only about her appearance – she had lost weight and her eyes burnt as though lit by a fever – but about her views which she freely expressed, sometimes quite shaking the Mission's director.

Instead of being content to visit the poor and sick taking them nourishing broth and warm clothes, she spent a good deal of time talking to the better-off workers, trying to get them to protest against their lot. In fact sometimes Isabella thought Jane spent more time talking and arguing than in physically doing good. One day she said as much when there had been an epidemic of influenza because of the wintry conditions and many of her helpers had fallen ill. This meant that, reluctantly, she had to break the rule about her walkers going about in pairs and Jane accordingly disappeared with an urn of soup and some bread just after eight in the morning and did not return until mid-afternoon. Isabella met her at the door, her hands on her hips, ready for one of her rare displays of anger.

'And just where have you been, Miss Vestrey?'

'I beg your pardon?' Jane said, her eyes raised with surprise at Isabella's tone.

'You left here at eight. It is now a quarter to three. I would have expected six journeys with soup and bread in that time, not one. I am worked off my feet. I only have two people to help me including the cook.'

Jane looked tired; her face was unnaturally white and

there were dark circles under her eyes. Even her hair seemed to have lost its lustre and hung damply over her forehead with droplets of the day's rain clinging to it. She tossed off her cloak and drew off her gloves after setting the urn down on the floor. She threw herself in one of the few chairs that remained and put her head in her hands.

'Oh Isabella, what *is* the use? Do you really think we achieve anything? I spent all day with Mrs Ticehurst whose baby died last night. It was still there in the room; they cannot afford to have it buried and must wait for it to be taken away by the authorities, and buried in a pauper's grave. Good Dr Snow did all he could, but it was useless. It is her fourth child to die and she already has six more. It is impossible to feed and look after them all. When I think of my Mama and the fuss when her babies died. The doctor came and my Uncle the rector, and Papa was there and there was such a grand funeral and a feast to follow and Mama was pampered and cosseted in bed as she is now. If Mama could see *this* she would not survive. Yet Mrs Ticehurst's husband is a clerk who because of ill health has not had work for a year. He is not an uneducated man.'

'But Jane, you can't spend all day talking to these people, no matter how bad the circumstances. If we did that we would never achieve anything!'

'I don't think we *do* achieve anything,' Jane said matter-of-factly. 'We are just covering the wounds, not healing the body. This is a palliative not a cure; in a way it is self defeating.

'Sir Charles Trevelyan, Lady Trevelyan's brother-in-law, told me not long ago that when he was at the Treasury he stopped grants to the distressed Irish Unions during the potato famine in order that they should help themselves and not become dependent on government aid. Yet he is not a bad man. My father likes him. It is just his idea that people should help themselves. But what if they can't?'

'There is some logic in what he says.' Isabella pulled her shawl round her shoulders because the fire was low and as they left at nightfall she had not wanted to waste valuable coal building it up. 'I can see the reasoning behind it. But *we* know that when people are defeated by the conditions of their lives they lack the will to do anything about it. They cannot better themselves and their apathy becomes total. If we leave these people they will starve, not go out and try and get work which is not there anyway for many of them. Their children will die first, they always do. I know Mr Ticehurst. I used to know him when he lived on the whole of the first floor of the house in Broad Street and had a good income as a clerk with a firm of lawyers in Golden Square. Then he became ill and he moved his family into one room and let the others to lodgers. He will soon go to the workhouse and his family with him.'

'Maggie Ticehurst is a spirited girl,' Jane said. 'She works as a kitchen maid at Bentley's Hotel and brings home all her money. She is just seventeen. But she was even *glad* that the baby died because there will be one less mouth to feed. Her father never gets out of bed now that his lungs are so bad.'

'Let us hope there will not be more children in that case,' Isabella said, pursing her mouth.

'If Miss Martineau could see all *this*,' Jane went on, 'she would realize what a gulf there is between the theory and the actuality.'

'Don't be bitter about Harriet Martineau, Jane,' Isabella said. 'She is a very good woman even though she no longer has her religious faith. Mr Gaskell says she has lost it by being too cerebral, that God wants us to be like children, trusting and confident in our hearts towards Him. The Bible says as much. But she does a lot of good by her writing especially now in her regular leaders in the *Daily News*. Miss Martineau has done *much* good in many small ways. Not only is her influence at large profound, but in the many kindnesses she does to those who are less well off than she, to the poor and those who work for her. Now Jane, let us get home and please, tomorrow, try and do your normal number of visits. Though I confess I am anxious when you are out by yourself. I hope Sarah will soon be back.'

Isabella put a hand on her arm and Jane saw how careworn she had become. If ever she knew a saint it was in the person of the woman who stood before her. She knew that Isabella gave most of her personal income for poor relief and towards the upkeep of the Mission, that once she got home she spent hours writing to people begging for money. Isabella was the soul of pure goodness but, in her own heart, Jane knew that she despaired of Isabella's well-meaning attempts to remedy the situation that called for an earthquake, if that were possible, in the social system.

'Let me take you home in the carriage,' Jane said. 'You look worn out.'

'I'll say "yes" for today as it is almost dark. Does your coachman always wait for you?'

'Oh yes, he will have been there for an hour.' Jane got on her cloak and poured water onto the embers in the grate watching the smoke hiss up the chimney. 'I despise myself you know; but if I didn't let Matthew bring me Papa would stop me coming altogether. As it is he doesn't know that Matthew waits for me at the top of the street. And yet you always walk alone.'

'Well, I am a big woman,' Isabella said with a laugh, 'and no beauty. Anyone would think twice before assaulting me. Also I have my parasol under my cloak just in case.'

Isabella took it from the corner beside the fireplace and thrust it out menacingly. Jane laughed and blew out the lamp. As Isabella locked the door of the Mission securely behind her she waited for her on the pavement. Then she tucked her hand in her arm as they walked up the street the short distance to where Matthew was waiting.

CHAPTER TWELVE

The bright, very bright red blood appeared on Debbie's pillow just as Caroline was preparing to receive the family for Christmas. Emily had told them how Prince Albert loved decorations and had introduced the idea of a special tree covered with candles from his boyhood memories in Rosenau. Caroline had one of the gardeners dig up a large fir from the Chetwell estate, and had it placed in the hall by the side of the open fireplace where a great log fire crackled all day from late November onwards. Every day she and the children added something to the tree, just as the Royal family did.

It was a grey morning as Caroline drew back Debbie's curtains and looked out at the mist which hid the sea from view. The trees dripped with moisture and the garden had a tired neglected look with skeletal rose trees, some still with their heads on, and dejected clumps of long dead flowers. But for the fact that it was nearly Christmas Caroline would have allowed herself to succumb altogether to depression. Already the winter seemed long and it had scarcely begun.

Life at Chetwell was routine. All routine. Mama insisted on a very strict regime and everything ran as though in obedience to many unseen clocks. Meals were at hours fixed to the minute, even when Caroline ate alone, in order to fit in with the children's school hours, also strictly adhered to, and the demands of a large household.

It wasn't that she felt lonely, because the smaller children were demanding, time consuming but also life giving. Mama was like a small child too. There were so many things that only Caroline could apparently do properly and she was forever at Mama's beck and call.

But all that winter Caroline worried about Debbie. She had so many fevers, so many days when she stayed in bed or by the fire in her room and did not come down at all.

She grew thinner and her skin seemed illuminated by an inner fire that was burning her out. Yet no-one wanted to believe she was dying; it was simply not to be thought of, not possible at all. Vestreys were strong and robust and did not have the illnesses of other people. Mama was not really a true Vestrey, which was why she ailed. All the other Vestreys were expected to be like Papa, strong and hearty until they slipped away from old age.

Caroline turned from the window and went over to summon the maid to light the fire. These days she liked to call Debbie herself, to see how she was and help her to start the day. It was still a dark morning and it wasn't until Caroline went over to the sleeping child's bed that she saw the bright lung blood on the pillow. But it wasn't spotted as it had been before; as her handkerchiefs sometimes were. It was soaked.

Caroline felt a catch in her throat and knelt by the side of the bed staring at Debbie's face. In a way she hoped she had died in her sleep; but the thin trickle of blood from her mouth hadn't congealed and her shallow rasping breathing showed she was alive.

Quickly Caroline went to the washstand and poured water into the basin, bringing it to the bedside. She began lightly to sponge Debbie's face and as she did the child woke and started to cough. The blood ran from her mouth in a torrent and her frightened eyes implored Caroline to help her. Caroline stifled her panic and murmured soothingly, holding her to her chest so that she did not choke on the blood. 'Oh God,' she prayed inwardly, 'do not let her suffer. Please God take her before the agony begins.'

Caroline clasped her little sister tightly to her breast stroking her hair, saying gentle comforting things until the spasm ceased and the terrible flow began to diminish.

'Oh Lord, Miss!' The maid, Joan, dropped the logs she was carrying and held her apron to her face as she saw Caroline hugging her sister while a great stain of blood spread over the front of her dress and down her skirt. 'Is she gone, Miss?'

'No, Joan,' Caroline said very calmly. 'Please send Ben for Dr Woodlove, and tell him to be very quick. Then ask

Mrs Oakshott to come and see me. My sister has had an unfortunate spasm but she will recover.'

Caroline looked at Debbie's face and saw great tears beginning to well up through her closed, screwed up eyes. She kissed her cheek and sat her on the side of the bed. Like her dress, Debbie's white nightgown was covered in blood. There were patches on the sheets and the floor. It was like some sort of carnage, as though murder had taken place.

And it was murder, Caroline thought bitterly, the death of a young girl. God *was* cruel; he was not just and merciful as her uncle said.

By noon John and Dorothy Tangent had come over, all the Vestrey family had been sent for and the doctor had come and gone. He thought it was a matter of hours, not days. He gave Debbie a sedative and she lay drowsily in a clean bed with fresh linen and all traces of the horrible blood removed. She was never to be left alone – Aunt Dorothy or Polly or Mrs Oakshott would help see to that.

The Vestreys arrived from London by the last train. Luckily they had all been foregathering at Park Street to come down for Christmas. Emily was not in waiting, and Jane had her last day at the Mission. She had wanted to work over Christmas because, she said, the ordinary people had no joy at Christmas time, but her father wouldn't permit it. Only James was missing, and he had been sent for and would come first thing the next day which was also Caroline's birthday.

Caroline woke up on the morning of her birthday and forgot what day it was. Everything had been forgotten in the drama of Debbie's terrible illness. All she thought of, on waking, was Debbie and she put on a robe and ran along the corridor, Aunt Dorothy and Polly having agreed to share the night's vigil.

Polly's head sagged on her chest as Caroline tiptoed into the room dreading what she might find. But Debbie slept peacefully, her head turned to one side, a hand on her chin as though she was thinking. Her long lashes curled up from her hot cheek on which Caroline lightly laid a hand. Polly started up and rubbed her eyes.

'Oh Caroline. I dropped off. I assure you it was only for a few seconds.'

'That's all right,' Caroline whispered, her hand lingering on the burning skin. 'She has a fever.'

'She was wakeful in the night but not fretful. She had two doses of the medicine Dr Woodlove prescribed. It has calmed her.'

Caroline went to the window and drew the curtains. It was just like yesterday, damp and with a clinging mist that swirled in from the sea as though it would penetrate every corner of the house. Caroline shivered and wrapped her robe closer around her. Then she went to poke some life into the fire.

The door opened and Jane stole in also in her robe. There were dark rings round her eyes and she looked as though she hadn't slept. She ran a hand through her tousled hair.

'How is she?'

'She slept pretty well. There has been no more haemorrhage.'

'Thank God.' Jane went over and kissed her little sister's cheek. 'She's very hot.'

'She has a fever. Polly, you go and get some sleep and Jane and I will take over. Or maybe you could knock on Emily's door and ask her to get dressed? Then she can watch while we do the same.'

Polly got up and limped across the room clasping her back. 'Oh, I feel so stiff. I didn't sleep, Caroline, really.'

'It doesn't matter if you did. You would have woken immediately anything happened. Dear Polly.' Caroline put a hand on her cousin's shoulder and kissed her. She could see that Polly was restraining her tears with difficulty. The night vigil was an awful burden and she should have done it herself. But with the arrival of her family, the subsequent solemn conference in the drawing-room, she had almost broken down herself – and she must not. They all depended on her, all of them – Papa as well as her brothers and sisters. She must be strong. For them it was more of a shock than for her, because she had lived daily with the certain knowledge of Debbie's impending death for weeks, months, ever since the picnic. Nothing had really gone well since the picnic. 'There Poll, go and get Emily.'

She pushed her gently to the door but Polly had scarcely gone before Emily appeared. She was fully dressed, her hair neatly in place, everything about her as it should be just in case, it seemed, she was wanted, by anyone, her family, her friends or the Queen of England. But Emily could not conceal her own pallor and her first act was to look fearfully at Debbie's bed.

'She had a good night,' Caroline whispered. 'There has been no more bleeding.'

Emily sat in a chair by the bed, flopped in it as though she was almost too worn out to stand a minute longer. She put her hands to her cheeks and stared up at her sisters.

'Oh Caroline, it is too awful. Why did you not *say*?'

'What could I say? She suddenly got worse; but she has not been well since the summer. You must have seen the way she has been going down?'

Caroline moved nearer to Emily so as to keep her voice low in case Debbie should wake. But *had* Emily seen? Her visits home had been so few and so brief. She had gone to Italy in the summer with the family of one of her best friends. Then she had gone straight into waiting. Emily had hardly been here at all, and when she had it was clear that she still harboured resentment against Caroline because of the row. They were almost like strangers rather than sisters. Now Emily seemed the most heartbroken because her own preoccupations had kept her from knowing what everyone else knew. She shook her head.

'You should have *said*.' She put her hand out and took Caroline's. 'Oh Caroline, we have been too far apart. You have been here and I have been so *thoughtless*. I hardly slept at all. If the Queen knew what a selfish monster I was she would send me away. I can hardly look at myself in the mirror.'

It was terrible when the proud became abject, worse than all the suffering one had endured oneself. Caroline was suddenly filled with love for Emily, her beautiful, wayward, selfish but always very human sister. She wanted to spare her suffering now.

'Emily, there was nothing you could do, darling. Nothing anyone could do. We could not all stay at home moping. I have a lot to do with the little ones, with the baby and Mama. I have not just sat about thinking of Debbie. And of course some days she seemed so much better. It has not been all gloomy, I assure you! For Debbie's sake we have kept cheerful.'

'Did Mama know how bad it was?' Emily clung to her sister's hand as though to a lifeline.

'I could never tell Mama the truth, you know that. Mama has to be kept cheerful otherwise she goes under so quickly; then everything is worse than before.'

'Mama doesn't know *now*?'

'Not really. Papa is going to tell her today. I couldn't face it.'

Jane stood looking down at Debbie listening to the murmur of voices behind her. She had seen a lot of suffering in the past few months; but this was worse than anything because it was so close; her own sister. How would she have coped if she had stayed at home? Not well. In her own way she was as selfish, as self-absorbed as Emily. However it was no time now for beating breasts. That would come later.

'She is waking up,' she said and they gathered round as Debbie's eyes flickered and tried to focus. She seemed unsure where she was and when she saw her sisters standing by her bed, she gave them a beautiful smile.

'Oh you are all here already! You came for Caroline's birthday! I knew you would.'

Debbie sat up slowly, with difficulty, her little face pink with fever but it could have been excitement. She groped under her pillow and drew out a small parcel carefully wrapped in green tissue paper. Shyly she held it out.

'Happy birthday, Caroline. I made this for you.'

'Oh darling!' Caroline took the present and quickly undid the tissue. Carefully placed in its folds was a handkerchief beautifully embroidered and bordered with lace. In one corner, also hand embroidered, were the initials CV. Tucked between the folds of the handkerchief was a small card, hand painted in a geometrical pattern of the kind worked on a sampler and inside, in Debbie's strangely mature handwriting, 'To my darling sister Caroline on her birthday.'

Caroline closed her eyes and pressed the handkerchief. 'Oh God, let Debbie live.' Then she bent down and sitting on her bed took her in her arms and held her.

'This is a lovely surprise, my darling. All the nicer because I didn't expect anything.'

'You didn't *know* I was doing it?' Debbie looked at her with childish anxiety mingled with excitement and pride.

'No, I promise. I knew nothing.'

'Polly was sworn to secrecy,' Debbie said. 'She swore . . .' Debbie stopped, seized by a fit of coughing. Caroline held her, feeling the hot little body and then the sticky wet substance that ran down the neck of her gown.

'Get a cloth quickly,' she said to Jane; but Emily ran to the washstand and brought a towel giving it to Caroline, who held it to Debbie's mouth as she coughed and choked in an awful never-ending spasm.

When the bleeding subsided at last Debbie appeared only half conscious. Caroline laid her gently on the bed and the sisters removed her stained nightgown and bathed her face. They worked quietly and quickly, without fuss or unseemly haste, sisters together, composed, knowing just what to do.

Then they changed the bed with clean sheets from the linen cupboard until the only blood that could be seen was on Caroline. Later when Emily was sitting by Debbie's bed holding her hot dry hand Caroline came back, bathed and dressed and looked for the handkerchief so lovingly worked and dropped in the crisis. It lay just under the bed, and on the corner initialled 'CV' was a spot of bright lung blood. Caroline crumpled the handkerchief and tucked it into her bosom. She would keep it all her life, like a precious relic. 'Please God, don't let her die on my birthday.'

Later Debbie rallied and began demanding a party for Caroline – the reason, she thought, they were all here. 'It is so lovely to have the family here all together,' she said. 'Oh do ask Mama to come to the party.'

Agnes was persuaded to come downstairs with difficulty. It was too cold, she was too ill. Caroline, called in to cajole when George failed, all but lost her temper with her. To her surprise she found it more effective than all her pleas. Mama was cowed into submission.

At four o'clock James, who had arrived at noon, carried his little sister lovingly downstairs and laid her on the couch in the drawing room near the fire. He covered her with a rug and sat at her head so that she leaned against him. When she saw James had arrived Debbie was rapturous. Seeing her so happy made him feel she could not possibly be going to die.

The little ones had no knowledge of the gravity of Debbie's illness. They were brought in precisely at four by their nurse and they scampered up to her and started to climb on the couch to be shooed off by James. Oliver stared gravely at Debbie, cocking his head on one side.

'You look interesting, madam. See that you do not become accustomed to this easy style of life.'

Debbie giggled and patted the place beside her next to James. 'Come sit here Oliver. Oh isn't it exciting to have a party for Caroline's birthday!'

When all the children were assembled George and Agnes made a formal entry, the latter leaning heavily on her husband's arm. Agnes had not been downstairs for weeks; but she had taken enormous care with her toilette assisted by her maid, by Emily and by Jane.

Agnes looked as though she was about to grace some elegant London tea party in the height of the season. She wore a silk shoulder wrap of the same dark blue taffeta as her dress which had a bustle and a long full skirt underneath. Her silk cap was ruched complete with a lace *bavolet*, the ribbon strings tying under her chin in a bow. Her hair, parted in the middle, had the usual little curls at the side of her face and under the cap. She wore powder and quite a lot of rouge and the hand that was not through George's arm clasped a stout cane.

Caroline felt a catch in her throat as Agnes and George walked in. It was difficult for them to hide their sadness, and Agnes wasn't trying very hard. She looked soulfully at Debbie on the couch and her tragic expression alarmed Caroline because of the effect it might have on Debbie.

But Debbie was in the grip of an elation common to her condition. She seemed almost bursting with joy. She had every member of her beloved family about her – her elder brothers whom she idolized, her elder sisters whom she loved and admired, and the little ones on whom she doted. Only Rebecca was missing and she was brought in by her nurse and placed in Mama's arms as soon as she was seated.

Then with great solemnity the doors were thrown open and cook came in with the large cake she had hurriedly baked, on which were twenty-two candles. Beyond her a procession of maids and footmen brought in trays full of cakes and jellies, sandwiches, tarts, fruit pies, sweetmeats and a variety of cordials as well as a large silver urn of tea.

It was such a bustling happy scene that Caroline almost forgot that inner core of sadness that was so much part of her existence. You went about your daily routine, the many things you had to do and for a long time, sometimes hours on end, you forgot about the emptiness inside you, that nagging sense of doom and unhappiness. Debbie. Mama didn't affect her in that way because, basically, however much she loved her she had to admit that Mama was a nuisance. She would go on like this forever, but she wouldn't die. Debbie never referred, or hardly at all, to her sickness; yet she was doomed to a short life. No, Debbie was at the heart of the fear that always lurked inside Caroline's heart.

But today was a happy day. Games were organized, musical chairs, blind man's buff and then charades to settle everyone down. Even Mama could be seen to relax and her face became quite animated. Of course Mama didn't play, and neither did Debbie; but all the rest did, including Papa, who seemed to enjoy himself most. When the noisy games were over Agnes gave the baby to Jane to nurse so that she could play Consequences because it didn't involve getting up, just a lot of fun with pencil and paper.

Patrick poured his cordial all over one of the cats, who had sneaked in, and was sent out for bad behaviour; and Clare laughed so much she had to be patted vigorously on the back in case she choked. Emily played the piano for the

202

musical games and Caroline, as usual, kept an eye on everything, trying to forget the heaviness in her heart.

Then the candles on the cake were lit and Papa nodded to James, who left the room returning, after a few moments, with the butler. Between them they carried two bottles of champagne in large silver coolers, with the best crystal glasses on an enormous crested silver tray. James drew the corks amid cheers and more laughter and as Emily played 'Happy Birthday', Caroline, face flushed with happiness, blew out the candles and everyone sang and cheered.

'Goodness,' Agnes said, putting her hands to her ears at last. 'They will hear all this revelry down in Sandgate.' She lifted her glass. 'A special happy birthday to you, my dearest Caroline. Without you I don't know what I should do.'

She lifted her glass and Caroline went over to her and kissed her.

'Thank you, Mama. Thank you all, for being here on my birthday. Thank you, James, for making the special effort and Debbie for coming downstairs when you didn't feel too well this morning. Thank you all, my family for your presents, your love, and ...'

Caroline choked. She remembered the inner hurt, the nagging sadness that would never leave her. They were not here because of her but because of Debbie. It was a death feast. Emily saw the tears come into Caroline's eyes and thumped the piano vigorously. All the family cheered again and took up the refrain deliberately because Caroline had been so overcome with emotion. 'Happy birthday to you. Happy birthday dear Caroline ...'

Debbie half lay in James's arms. It was difficult for her to sing. If she did she was afraid that the blood would start again and spoil the party; so she just lay there mouthing the words, smiling, feeling very happy and secure with her family around her.

Then Papa got up and took his glass holding it high in the air. Papa's eyes were moist and he looked almost overcome; Emily kept her fingers poised over the keyboard in case she would have to come crashing down on them again any moment. But Papa steadied himself.

'It gives me great happiness my children, my beloved

wife,' he bowed to Agnes, 'to have you all together around me on this happy occasion, Caroline's twenty-second birthday. Last year was happy but I think this is even better. My dear children, your mother and I thank God for the blessing you have been to us, that you *are* and I do not exclude – ' and here George dodged as a paper dart came whizzing in his direction – 'Patrick who really is the naughtiest Vestrey of you all!'

The children roared with laughter and Patrick went red.

'Who is the best, Papa?' Clare piped up. 'Oh tell us who is the best.'

George took a fortifying sip of champagne and smiled at her. 'If you want me to say *you* I won't; but you are all good in my eyes, lovely children, a pride to any father. If on this special day I say who is the best then, because it is her birthday and because she is my eldest daughter, I say Caroline. Caroline who has taken on so much to help Mama, to help me ...'.

'And me Papa! Don't forget me.'

George looked tenderly at the little face, vibrant and happy, but too highly coloured.

'I *don't* forget you, my dear Debbie.'

'I mean how Caroline helps me, Papa, when I am ill. When I am well I shall take Caroline's place so that she can go back to London and have a good time like Emily and Jane. I shall ...'

The emotion caused Debbie to start coughing again and, fearing a haemorrhage, Caroline went over to her. But James held her strongly in his arms, smoothing the hair back from her brow.

'Thank you, Papa,' Caroline said, sensing his agony. 'Thank you very much for what you have said. Thank you all; but Debbie must go upstairs and rest.'

'And I too,' Agnes said looking at George and tapping her stick on the floor. 'This has quite exhausted me.'

'You have done remarkably well, Mama,' Caroline said evenly. 'Could you not stay down to dine with Papa and the family on this special day?'

'Oh yes, Agnes!' George exclaimed. 'We have not dined together for months.'

Agnes leaned back in her chair and dabbed at her face. 'I am quite surprised at you even *suggesting* such a thing, Caroline. You know that I am very far from well. I . . .'

James carefully picked up Debbie and carried her over to her parents bending down so that they could see her face. George leaned over and kissed her, but Agnes turned her face away.

'I dare not kiss you, darling child, for fear of infection,' she said touching her cheek with her soft beringed fingers. 'It would be the death of your Mama if she caught a chill. Oh dearest you are so hot! Caroline do you know how hot she is?'

'She does have a fever, Mama. She has had all day.'

'Then should she have been brought down here? I mean the risk of infection . . .'

For the first time that afternoon the smile left Debbie's face. Her chin began to tremble and she gazed at her mother. 'Oh Mama, I did not mean . . .'

'That is absolute nonsense, Mama,' Caroline said firmly. 'There is not the slightest risk of infection. You need have no concern for your health which really is quite robust, Mama. James, pray take Debbie upstairs, and I will come and see to her in a few minutes.'

As though to make up for Agnes the family gathered round to kiss Debbie. The little ones came first standing on tiptoe even though James crouched down, then Oliver, Emily and Jane. Papa kissed her last again and his lips lingered on her cheek.

'God bless you my darling daughter and make you well . . . and happy.'

Debbie reached out and clasped his hand. 'Oh I am happy Papa – happy! This has been such a lovely day.'

James kissed her last, almost crushing her in his arms and then lightly singing 'Happy birthday to you tra la', he ran out of the room and Debbie could be heard giggling all the way upstairs.

Caroline turned to the children's nurse who had been quietly embroidering in a corner.

'Hunter, would you take Master Patrick and Miss Clare back to the nursery and send Paget for Miss Rebecca.'

She turned to her youngest brother and sister and brought them up to their parents from whom they received hugs and kisses, before she ushered them to the door.

'Good night, Mama.'

'Good night, Papa.'

'Good night. Good night.'

Caroline closed the door and walked slowly back into the room, her eyes fixed on her mother. She stood in front of her, breathing hard. 'I do not know how you could have done that to Debbie, Mama. Denied your dying daughter a kiss. Maybe the last you will ever give her.'

George started up but Caroline held out her hand. 'I wish to say this Papa, because I am so tired of Mama and her unspeakable selfishness. But I endure it so long as it affects only me and no one else. However when I see my sick little sister putting up her angelic face to be kissed and Mama *turning* away . . .' For a moment Caroline looked as though her still extended hand might hit her mother, but she let it fall to her side. 'Turning away. I don't know how you could do something so monstrous.'

'Caroline, you are too upset . . .' Emily put a restraining hand on her arm and tried to lead her away, but Caroline wrenched herself free.

'I feel I have to say this to Mama, Emily. I want Mama to know how I feel about it!'

Agnes had been looking at her daughter with an offended expression. It seemed at first as if she did not completely comprehend the words, but she began dabbing at her face with her handkerchief, tugging at the fichu at her neck.

'Oh George, I feel so unwell. Pray stop her.'

'A dying girl, Mama, your own flesh and blood . . .'

Caroline leaned threateningly over her mother, who began to gasp.

'Caroline, please stop. I feel so unwell. My heart is hammering. You know Debbie is not dying. She cannot die. She looked so well. Whereas I am ill and diseased. If I should pick up the least infection . . .'

'Mama I say . . .'

George, who had been standing next to his wife, suddenly

held up his hand. 'Caroline, I forbid you to continue. Your Mama is too distressed. Pray leave the room.'

Caroline stared rebelliously at her father.

'I say leave the room, Caroline. You are my daughter and I command it. Then, Emily, you and Jane may take your mother to her room and help her into bed.'

Caroline walked swiftly out of the room while Jane and Emily helped a trembling Agnes from her chair. Oliver gave her an arm to lean on and Jane supported her on the other. Emily tucked her shoulder wrap around her and took her stick. George pecked her on the cheek and then stood to one side as they went out of the room. He closed the door after them and went quickly to the whisky decanter which stood on a small table by the window. He found he was trembling and his hand shook as he poured the amber liquid into a crystal glass. Then he went over to the window and stared into the December darkness, pressing his forehead against the pane to cool it.

'Oh Hilary,' he murmured, 'I wish you were here. My darling, darling Hilary.'

Caroline did not come down for dinner, but sent a message saying she was sitting with Deborah. Her dinner was brought up for her and she ate it without appetite beside her sister, who now looked utterly exhausted.

'You overdid it, darling. I should never have let you go.'

'But it was so lovely, Caroline. It was such a wonderful party. And Mama looked so well, don't you think? I didn't mind her not kissing me at all. I would never want Mama to be ill again through any fault of mine.'

Caroline wondered at the ability of the young to forgive. Or did they not properly perceive? It was difficult to know. Perhaps it was that their critical faculties stopped when it came to parents or loved ones because they needed them. Perhaps she genuinely thought that her mother's attitude was reasonable because she loved her and needed her approval.

After dinner Emily and Jane came up. They were subdued. Dinner had been strained because James was furious with Caroline for speaking as she had to their mother, and he and George had had a row because her father defended his daughter on the grounds of strain. Both James and Papa had accordingly had a lot to drink which made them more quarrelsome than ever.

It seemed so incongruous, the family quarrelling and Debbie looking so happy. She lay against the white pillow, her white lawn nightgown tied with a fresh pink bow at her neck. Her hair was brushed back from her forehead and Caroline dabbed her with Eau de Cologne to refresh her hot cheeks. The three sisters then came to say goodnight, kneeling by the side of the bed to kiss her.

'Goodnight, darling.'

'Goodnight, Jane.'

'Sleep well, precious. God bless you.'

'Thank you, Emily. Good night.'

Finally came Caroline, who knelt longer than the others, holding both Debbie's hands in hers, leaning over to kiss her cheeks. For a long time Debbie looked at her, her expression tender and tranquil.

'Am I not lucky to have such a family, such sisters to look after me? I love you all so much.'

Caroline couldn't speak. She swallowed hard and pressed the thin hands between hers.

'God bless you, my darling little sister. Sleep well.'

Debbie fell immediately into a calm sleep. Caroline had not seen her looking so beautiful, so at peace, for a long time. In fact it was an expression she had never seen. Jane and Emily remarked on it, but it alarmed her.

'I will sit with her tonight.'

'Oh Caroline, you are so tired. Let me,' Emily said.

'No. I wish it.'

'Do not punish yourself for what you said to Mama. I thought you were quite right.' Jane looked comfortingly at her sister. 'So does Emily and so, I think, does Papa. The boys are on Mama's side.'

'I think Oliver was quite shocked,' Emily said. 'Of course he does not have to put up with Mama like you do.'

'I shouldn't have said it,' Caroline said simply, looking at each in turn. 'It was wrong and unwise. Mama is not really in her right mind, I have decided, and isn't entirely responsible for what she does. I will apologize to her tomorrow and to Papa and the boys. I was simply so vexed.' She turned and gazed at Debbie. 'You see, I love her so much. I hated Mama then for hurting her. But afterwards I realized that, in Debbie's eyes, Mama can do no wrong. She was not hurt or upset by her. It was natural to her that, being ill, Mama should want to take care. So my outburst was unnecessary and upset everyone, especially Papa. And him, of anyone, I do not wish to hurt.'

For a long time that night Caroline sat by the window looking out to the sea. It was full moon and the fog had gone. Maybe it would come back with the dawn; but it was calm and peaceful outside, the vastness of the sea stretching to the horizon, timeless and comforting. She fell asleep, looking at the sea and not by Debbie's bedside as she had intended. When she awoke there was a thick white cloud of mist in front of her and the birds were singing with the first light of dawn. The fire had gone out and she was very cold.

She got up quickly and went over to the bed. Debbie lay there just as she had when they said goodnight, her face turned slightly to one side on the pillow, her long lashes curling up on her very white cheeks. Caroline froze. Debbie's body was too still and the pink flush of fever Caroline was so accustomed to had left her face. Maybe she was better.

But as she leaned down to touch her she knew. Debbie was dead.

Caroline threw herself on her sister's body and burst into a torrent of weeping. She had wanted to comfort her, to hold her as she went. But as the room grew brighter she sat up on the bed and looked at the lifeless form. Maybe God *was* good. He had taken her without suffering and when she was happy. Caroline kissed her sister's cold hands and then went to break the news to the family.

Only the candles on the Christmas tree continued to burn over Christmas. The festive decorations were taken down and replaced with black crêpe. The candles remaining were a silent tribute to Debbie's memory. Caroline insisted on it.

Debbie was buried two days after Christmas and only the family were there, the Vestreys and the Tangents. It was a cold grey day, dry but without mist. A cheerless, lifeless English winter's day. Debbie was buried in the Vestrey vault by the last Vestrey baby who had only time to be christened after his birth.

In the grief and shock of Debbie's death everyone forgot about the night Caroline had been so rude to Mama. Even Mama seemed to forget because Caroline was the only one with the strength to support her in her grief. She needed her. Caroline apologized and Mama said it was all right. Had she known that Debbie was really dying she would have kissed her no matter what, she assured Caroline. There had been something very pathetic in the way Agnes gazed up at her daughter, as though trying to seek her forgiveness for an omission she could never repair.

In the awful days that followed Debbie's death everyone leaned on Caroline, George most of all. Caroline had no time for tears. In a way she had been weeping in her heart for months.

Early in January Caroline was sitting in one of the parlours doing the household accounts. Jane was riding with James and Emily, who had a slight cold, kept her company, doing her embroidery. There was a knock on the door and the butler entered.

'Mr Rawdon Foxton is in the hall, Miss Vestrey. He has called to offer his condolences to you and your family and hopes you will receive him. Miss Foxton is with him.'

Emily jumped up and threw her embroidery into the chair.

'Of course you will say no! What impudence to come without sending a note.'

Caroline remained where she was, staring at the bureau on which her papers were spread. Then she put a hand on her bodice and smoothed her dress, getting up as she did so.

'Of course we must see them, Emily. They must have made an effort. Besides, James and Rawdon get on very well.'

210

'Then he should have asked to see James. *I* shall not see them.'

'Very well. Bryce, please show Mr and Miss Foxton into the drawing-room and I will be with them directly.'

'Very good, Miss.'

Bryce withdrew, closing the door while Emily, her face puce with anger, flounced up and down.

'How you can see them I don't know! Have you no pride? Remember she spat; spat in my face. She spat in your sister's face and never sent an apology.'

'But you never apologized for what you said.'

'But spitting! Oh, it was so vile.' Emily touched her cheek as though recalling the episode. 'And as for him, when he pretended to love me . . .'

'Did he?' Caroline raised an eyebrow. 'Did he really say he loved you?'

Emily stopped walking about and retrieved her needle-work. 'Not in so many words; but it was obvious to anyone with eyes. He was about to declare himself, I know. His behaviour since has been quite abominable.'

'Then I will see him and listen courteously to him. I must go, Emily. You can stay here.'

Caroline went out of the room without waiting for a reply. She walked slowly along the corridor into the hall, past the tree and the fireplace, until she stood by the drawing-room door, aware of the quick pace of her heart.

Rawdon was standing with his back to the fire, Jennifer sitting in a chair. He wore a grey suit with a grey Tweedside overcoat and a black muffler. He carried a grey top hat in his hand. Jennifer was dressed in a brown cage-crinoline with a brown fichu at the neck and a brown pelisse with bell-shaped sleeves. Her brown bonnet lacked any adornment except for the brown ribbons under her chin. She got up as Caroline came in and looked timidly up at Rawdon, moving closer to him as though for protection.

Caroline went straight over to her and kissed her cheek. 'Welcome, Jenny.'

This seemed such an unexpected gesture that Jennifer stroked the spot that Caroline had kissed as though in

211

wonderment. Caroline gave her hand to Rawdon and he bent low and kissed it.

'You are most welcome, Rawdon!'

'You are very kind to receive us, Caroline. I should have sent a note; but we only just heard. I came straight away.'

'This morning,' Jennifer said her eyes filling with tears. 'Our shepherd Matthew had heard it by devious means through one of your servants. We came at once; we didn't hesitate.'

'It is *very* good of you to come,' Caroline said. 'James and Jane are riding. But Papa is upstairs.'

'Do not disturb your father,' Rawdon said quickly, recalling the last occasion on which he had seen Lord Vestrey. George had sent him a note to thank him; but it would still be an awkward meeting. 'We merely wanted to give you and your family our heartfelt condolences.'

'Heartfelt,' Jennifer echoed. 'It is too terrible when I recall Deborah's youth and beauty. How is your poor Mama bearing up, Caroline?'

'Oh Mama is quite inconsolable; but she did go to the funeral and happily she was able to come downstairs for tea the day that Debbie died. Debbie seemed to make a special effort because all the family were there and even to be fairly well, but that night she passed quietly away in her sleep.'

'Your birthday?' Rawdon murmured.

Caroline flushed, avoiding his eyes.

'How kind of you to remember.'

'I wanted to send a gift. Jenny thought it better not to.'

So Rawdon was still guided by his sister. Caroline looked him straight in the eye. The old attraction was still there. If anything she felt it more strongly because she had not seen him for so long. Since the picnic. That accursed picnic.

'I am so glad Lord Foxton's health has improved so much.'

'It is quite miraculous,' Rawdon said. 'He can do almost everything he did before. Dr Gully performed miracles with his water cure in Bath.'

'Maybe I should suggest it to Mama?' Caroline murmured.

'Your mother still ails?'

'I think she *is* a little better, but she has become accustomed to ill health.'

'So you are still here all the time?'

'Oh yes. And I am in charge of the nursery and the schoolroom and, of course, Debbie until . . .'

Suddenly she remembered; but that inner pain had become another sort of feeling; no longer apprehension but certainty. She would go upstairs and Debbie would not be there; wherever she looked she would not find her. Debbie was at peace and there was no more suffering as Uncle John had said in his fine funeral sermon:

. . . there shall be no more death, neither sorrow nor crying, neither shall there be any more pain: for the former things are passed away.

The ones who remain are the ones who still suffer, because of the void that Debbie has left. She has given such joy in her short life, such an example to her sisters, you, the daughters of the house who remain.

And God shall wipe away all tears from their eyes.

Caroline blew her nose, shielding her eyes from Rawdon because whenever she thought of Debbie the tears still came. God had not yet allowed her to remember her sister without grief.

'Well anyway I am very busy, and I hear you have returned to your regiment, Rawdon?'

'Yes, my father, thankfully, is much better.'

'And you will stay in the army?'

Rawdon looked at her and she saw the quizzical light in his eyes. Was he appraising her or was there admiration or some unspoken question? She could not tell.

'Circumstances being what they are I shall remain. For the time being.'

There was the sound of horses' hooves and Jennifer ran to the window.

'Oh, here are Jane and James!' Jennifer turned to Caroline. 'But where is Emily? Is she at Court?'

'Emily is upstairs,' Caroline said, hesitating only for a moment. 'I *think* she must be with Mama.'

'Will she come down?' Rawdon stuck his chin in the air and stared at Caroline. Caroline shrugged.

'I know not.'

'She has not forgotten?' Rawdon went on. 'Or forgiven? It was a long time ago.'

'I think a note ... of apology might have helped.'

Caroline spoke quickly because she was anxious not to give an offence. Jennifer reacted with immediate indignation as Caroline knew she might.

'But *I* was deeply offended too. *I* was abused.'

'Yes but – ' Caroline hesitated. 'There was something you did. Something ...'

'Jenny *did* something?' Rawdon said looking at his sister with surprise. 'I thought it was Jenny who was offended by Emily? With the passage of time and increasing good health Jenny is prepared to overlook what Emily said and ...'

'That is all very well, Rawdon.' Caroline pursed her mouth. 'But Jennifer, doubtless provoked as she was, made a gesture that is not the sort of thing one expects of a lady, however provoked. So ...'

'What sort of gesture?' Rawdon demanded, looking severely at his sister.

'I prefer not to say.' Caroline folded her hands neatly across her waist. 'If you do not know I do not consider it my duty to tell you.'

'What sort of gesture, Jenny? I must know.' Rawdon's bewilderment was making him angry. Jennifer lowered her head.

'I spat at her.'

The silence was profound. Outside James and Jane could be heard talking as they came nearer to the house.

'*Spat?*' Rawdon roared. 'My sister *spat* at someone?'

Jennifer nodded her head, her chin crumpling, a prelude to tears. Caroline felt sorry for her.

'She was very provoked. I say it is six of one and half a dozen of the other; but Emily will not come down. Her nature is not so forgiving. I will talk to her and then, maybe a letter ...'

'I am bitterly ashamed,' Rawdon went up to Caroline and took her hand. 'I had no idea, having only heard Jenny's version. Jenny shall write to Emily, and so shall I. Whatever Emily said nothing, nothing justifies something like *that*.'

Caroline raised her head and looked slowly at Rawdon, aware of the pressure of his hands.

'I *am* glad. We'd all like a reconciliation, I know. Even Emily.'

For a few moments they gazed at each other, neither knowing what else to say.

CHAPTER THIRTEEN

The Tangent family, or its individual members, scarcely ever got to London. This was partly due to their impecunious circumstances, and partly because the Rector and his wife loathed the city. So it was convenient to nurture in their children this dislike of the metropolis, because they couldn't afford to go there anyway.

Jane Vestrey heard the noise in the upstairs drawing-room as Cornwall the butler helped her off with her cloak. After Deborah's death her work became even more important because it left so little time for thinking. She pitied Caroline who stayed at home, more alone than ever now without Debbie who had become a companion to her. Mama was becoming more and more difficult. Not only was she bereaved, but she was also eaten by guilt and remorse because she hadn't even been aware her daughter was near death.

Papa only went to Chetwell as a duty. The memories it brought back of Debbie were too painful and, besides, Mama was no companion to him any more.

'We have company, Cornwall?'

'Your relatives from Chetwell, Miss Jane, also your sister Miss Emily is due here for the evening and I believe Mr James, and Mr Rawdon Foxton are also expected.'

Jane's hands flew to her face. 'Oh, I completely forgot they were coming! Pray do not say I am here until I have changed. Please send Gertrude to me at once.'

Jane hurried up the stairs while the butler went to the servants' quarters to find her maid. Jane felt tired and she had a headache; all sorts of pressures seemed to afflict her and she had no idea how to resolve them.

She had had another argument with Isabella about her habit of lingering with certain families. She was accused of preferring the good of the few to that of the many. Miss Goodey pointed out that one of the mentors she was fond of quoting, Mr John Stuart Mill, would not have approved at all. Yet Jane felt it was important to befriend certain individuals, like the Ticehursts for example, so that they felt someone really cared about them.

Besides, so many were apathetic; you could really do nothing for them at all. You could not get through to them. With the few she did become close to she felt that she really shared somehow the hardships of their appalling lives. Or did she? She looked at herself in the mirror as her maid Gertrude appeared at the door with a jug of hot water and helped her to wash and dress. She brushed her long hair until she had restored the gleam and gradually in this pampered, kindly, familiar world Jane's colour returned to her face and the sparkle to her eyes.

'You have been *very* tired of late, Miss,' Gertrude scolded her. 'It won't do for you, you know. Better give up that work, if you ask me, and have a few weeks in the country.'

'If you'd have seen the people I saw today, Gertie, you would think it wrong to live like this. Sometimes I am ashamed of myself, of my life.'

Gertrude brushed her mistress's ringlets round her fingers, giving them a final pat. 'Them people are used to it, Miss. They know no different. That is what you forget. Same as I am used to my life. We all have our proper places. I am a great believer in that.'

Jane looked at the girl who was about her own age. She'd been her maid for over a year yet she had never had a glimmer of curiosity about her.

'How long have you been in service, Gertie?'

'Since I was twelve, Miss.'

'Twelve! That is *very* young. And you never wanted anything else?'

'Never, Miss. I am glad to be where I am, grateful to have such a nice position in a best house.'

'Best house?' Jane laughed. 'What is a best house?'

'Oh it is the house of a lord, Miss, or someone very important. The best, you understand? And there are few better than Lord Vestrey.'

'Oh, there are *many* higher than Lord Vestrey!' Jane laughed. 'He is but a baron. There are viscounts, earls,

217

marquesses, dukes. There is a whole hierarchy of nobility.'

'This is a best house as far as I am concerned, Miss. I would wish nowhere else.'

Jane looked at Gertie and realized that although she was so familiar, so close, she scarcely knew her. She never spoke to her about her personal life, but would chat about her own or what had happened to her that day. It was as though she had never thought of servants as having personal lives of their own at all. They were simply there to serve her family. She was suddenly stricken with a sense of shame. It was only her work in Soho that had opened her eyes to the existence of another order, and they need not all be desperately poor like the Ticehursts.

'Do you ever wish to change, Gertie? To marry perhaps?'

Gertie blushed and looked at her feet. 'Well Miss, that's as maybe. But I am happy as I am. Will that be all, Miss?'

In Gertie's reply Jane recognized an implied criticism of herself, although the servant would never have intended it to be taken as such. It was simply that she was not accustomed to being asked personal questions by her mistress, nor about herself. Her mistress took it for granted that all was well with her, that she had no real views or opinions of much importance. Her function was to care for Miss Jane, her clothes and personal effects and listen to her chatter as she brushed her hair at night. Last year it had been all about the parties, the literary gatherings, the painting sessions. Now it was all about Soho and the terrible conditions of the poor. Miss Jane had not changed; only the subjects that concerned her had. She never seemed to wonder if Gertie had a private life at all, or what she did or thought. Gertie was quite used to it. She didn't expect anything else. In fact she preferred the gossip about parties to all this talk about the poor.

Rawdon Foxton and James had just been admitted and were standing in the hall as Jane came down the stairs.

She held out her arms: 'James, this is a lovely surprise and Rawdon too! He is not as frequent a visitor as he used to be.' She shook hands. 'It is a family party indeed. What is the occasion?'

'Oh, Uncle John wanted to see a doctor about his chest

and Aunt Dorothy thought she would buy a new bonnet. Something like that. Polly came up to see *you* and Dalton was invited to be here with us. Come, my little sister, and tell me your news. Jane has become a worker you know,' he said turning to Rawdon who bowed his head.

'I know. Caroline was telling me all about it. I was at home last week and went over to Chetwell to pay my respects as usual. She says they are worried about you, Jane, that you do too much, that there is fear of disease or contamination where you work.'

George Vestrey flung open the drawing-room doors and saw them walking up the stairs. 'I wondered where you were,' he called. 'Come in, come in.' He stood back and kissed his daughter, shook hands with James and Rawdon and brought them into the room.

'I am sorry to be so late, Papa. I had such a busy day at the Mission.' Jane went over and embraced her aunts, uncle and cousins.

'Jane takes her work very seriously,' Aunt Ruth said brightly to try and disguise the worry she felt, always would feel, about this almost frightening dedication of Jane's, so unlike the worldly, rather vain little girl she used to know.

'Too seriously,' George said. 'It is undermining your health in the opinion of Aunt Ruth. You look pale my dear, and are growing too thin.'

'Oh, but the *dedication*,' Polly said. 'I admire it so much. Jane do you think I might come with you and see the work you do, if Papa will allow?'

Polly looked at her father, Agnes's brother, whom many years of ill health and relative poverty had made into a mild docile man, anxious not to give offence. He felt very beholden to his brother-in-law for his security, the help he had given with the children's education, his many kindnesses and acts of thoughtfulness and, above all, the forbearance and generosity he had shown Agnes since the onset of her debilitating illness.

Considering the strain he knew he was under, the grief he had felt at his daughter's death, John Tangent thought George looked remarkably well. It was true he had preferment in the new government; he was a voice in foreign affairs even though Lord Clarendon had succeeded Lord John Russell as Foreign Secretary. He had no financial worries as John Tangent so often did and, even though Agnes and the plight of Caroline were a constant worry and Jane a problem, he really had a very good life. But even taking all these considerations into account he looked relaxed and blooming, a man very satisfied with life indeed.

'Of course I will allow it, my dear. I would like to come myself one day and see this good work.'

'Even though it is run by Dissenters?' Jane said slyly.

'*Because* it is run by Dissenters, my dear Jane,' John Tangent said charitably. 'We have a lot to learn from the good these people do. The Quakers, the Unitarians, Evangelicals of all kinds, sometimes put the mission of our own established Church to shame. Is it not so, George?'

'Whether or not it is true, John, the Dissenters always *try* and make us think their work is better than ours. I am sure that is due to religious rivalry.' George looked at his watch. 'I think we will not wait for Emily any more or the dinner will be spoilt. James will you ring for Cornwall and say we shall eat now?'

Everyone admired the decorations in the dining-room recently completed by Great Aunt Ruth with the connivance of an interior decorator recommended by Mr Ruskin, who was alleged to have remarked 'wherever you can rest, there decorate'. The plain green silk lined walls had been replaced by a heavy flocked wallpaper showing an assemblage of pendant dead game, hounds, stags at bay and all the symbols of the chase. Aunt Ruth had wondered about the effect of this on people's appetites, but Mr Taylor, the decorator, had thought it in admirable taste especially when almost covered by prints and paintings, Regency miniatures and portraits of the family. A thick Brussels carpet with a floral motif had replaced the plain Regency gold which had been there since the reign of George III. But Aunt Ruth's pride and joy was the vast mahogany sideboard carved by Messrs Cooke of Warwick illustrating scenes from classical Greek mythology appertaining to the prowess of Diana, the goddess of the Hunt. This had been specially commissioned to go with the wallpaper and even now Aunt Ruth had never dared tell her nephew the cost. It was one of the very few pieces in London of such complexity and Mr Ruskin kept on bringing all his artistic friends to see it. A huge semi-circular mirror set at the back reflected the rest of the room making it seem twice as large.

This piece completely eclipsed the large new circular table and the balloon-backed dining chairs, also of mahogany, with moulded backs, leaf carved straps and seats upholstered in velour. These had only been used twice before and Aunt Ruth looked gratified as her guests exclaimed over the beauty and skilled workmanship of the new furniture, particularly Aunt Dorothy who shared Mr Ruskin's taste and his admiration of Mr Taylor.

'Your refurnishing is a masterpiece of taste and imagination,' Aunt Dorothy said with enthusiasm. 'I so admire it.'

'I think it too cluttered myself,' George said accepting his soup from Cornwall. 'But then I am old fashioned. I am thankful that Agnes is totally uninterested in refurbishing Chetwell Place.'

'How *is* Mama?' Jane said, keeping her eyes on her plate. Jane had not been home for three weeks, pleading a heavy cold which Mama was naturally most anxious not to catch.

'She is *tolerably* well my dear, so long as she maintains her routine. There must be no excitement, no change, nothing untoward. She even gets up for a few hours each day and last weekend sat in the drawing-room for an hour in the afternoon.'

'Miss Martineau has written to me about a practitioner of mesmerism who she thinks would cure Mama. A Mrs Chetwynd. She highly recommends her.'

Her father put down his spoon and mopped the soup which had spilled on his chin, his expression one of horror.

'Mesmerism! I have never heard such nonsense. I would not let a mesmerist near your mother.'

'But why *not* Papa? Do you not wish her to be cured?'

'It is all folderol, is it not, John? I appeal to you.'

The Reverend John Tangent carefully wiped his lips, his

eyes remaining withdrawn and cautious; he was so anxious not to say the wrong thing.

'There *are* a lot of people who have much to say for mesmerism and its allied science of phrenology, the study of bumps of the head. I would not have any objection to it myself if a positive relief in the condition of a sufferer were to result. Agnes for instance, if she were to recover the use of her legs ...'

'Miss Martineau thinks that Mama is a good subject,' Jane said, 'because of what I have told her about the condition. She says mesmerism is particularly suitable for cases that might be caused by hysteria.'

Jane was aware of the silence that followed her outburst, which she knew was delivered with force and a conviction that her family would not approve of. Papa signalled for Cornwall to serve the next course and James looked very angry and drank half a glass of wine at a gulp. Just then there was a commotion in the hall and the dining room door opened and Emily flew in still with her cloak and bonnet, peeling off her gloves, her face red with cold.

'Oh Aunt, do forgive! Her Majesty was to have gone to the theatre, but cancelled the arrangement because she is indisposed. Or rather she is *not* indisposed but the Prince Consort is reluctant to allow her to go out into a crowded theatre on such a cold night when she is so near her confinement. However I told Her Majesty that we had a family dinner party and she *insisted* that I should go and the Prince himself ordered the coach to take me. It will return for me at half past ten.'

Emily threw her cloak with a smile to one of the footmen and sat down without ceremony patting her hair as she did.

'Am I forgiven, Aunt Ruth? Papa?'

'Of course you are my dear,' Aunt Ruth said, signalling to Cornwall. 'How very gracious of the Queen. I trust she is well?'

'Oh she is *very* well. And very excited. And the Prince, he is so sweet with her, so considerate. We go back to Windsor tomorrow. She was here on political business. She is very vexed at the moment about the actions of the refugees in this country, people like Kossuth and Mazzini to whom we have given shelter, and who abuse our hospitality by their threats and agitation.'

'My dear I do not think you should gossip about affairs of state if you will pardon my saying so, particularly as this affects the Royal Household. Such things are confidential.'

'But Papa they are of concern to *everyone*. There is nothing confidential. You told me yourself that you thought Lord Palmerston was wrong to receive Mr Kossuth. And then there is the business with Russia and Turkey. I know the Prince is most anxious in case the situation there should lead to war.'

'War!' said James eagerly. 'Capital. Time we had a good war, eh Rawdon?'

'I confess I would not object to seeing action,' Rawdon said slowly, 'providing it was not on a great scale. I do not think this country would benefit from a war, do you sir?'

George Vestrey, thankful to get Emily away from her potentially indiscreet disclosures about the views of the Royal Family, leaned back in his chair.

'This country was nearly brought to its knees by the Napoleonic wars. No, I do not want to see war again. But we have treaty obligations towards France and Turkey, and I know Lord Aberdeen is anxious about the expansionist policies of Russia. The Tsar Nicholas is an ambitious, arrogant man. Not an easy person to deal with. I would not see a war on any scale myself, maybe a skirmish or two in some remote place beyond the Dardanelles. Just to keep up appearances, but not a full scale war. Definitely not.'

'Then may we be sent there,' James said. 'I am tired of peacetime soldiering, although there is a rumour that we may be sent to India. Now that I should like!'

Rawdon Foxton listened to James as he pattered on about seeing action, and to his father's theories about the political situation. He was thinking once again about buying himself out of the army and entering the Diplomatic Corps. There was no telling how much freedom he would have before he inherited from his father. Although much improved, he knew that Lord Foxton could go at any moment, because the considerable damage done to his heart could never be repaired. There was all this talk about the possibility of war in the Balkans, but it never got much further and George Vestrey seemed to be saying it never would. The army satisfied neither his desire for travel nor action, consisting as it did of endless ceremonial duties at Buckingham Palace or Windsor Castle, or excursions into Wales or Scotland on exercises that were purposeless with no war to fight.

He gazed across the table at Emily who seemed indifferent to his presence. After a brief nod when she had come in she had not looked in his direction. Maybe he was still not forgiven. Yet there had been a letter – two, one from Jenny and one from him. There had been a reply, on Windsor Castle stationery, thanking them and saying that as far as she was concerned the matter was forgotten and she for her part apologized for any hurt she may unwittingly have caused.

May . . . it was an ironic word. Her hurtful words had sent Jenny over the cliff and caused a major row between the families. But he couldn't take his eyes off Emily; without returning his gaze she seemed aware of him and, by her movements, to indicate that she was. The graceful flourish of her hands in conversation, the sweep of her neckline, the way she turned her white shoulder and held her head, all seemed subtly geared to ensure that he paid more attention to her than his food or what was going on around the table.

Emily, he thought, had developed extraordinarily since she had been in waiting. It had seemed to make her mature as a woman. She was also more poised, more attractive. She was certainly astonishingly pretty with her golden hair decorously parted in the middle and plaited behind her ears, and her large beautiful eyes. Her dress this evening was a rich yellow velvet because it had been so cold and her skin the colour of warm pink marble.

Afterwards in the upstairs drawing-room Rawdon gravitated towards Emily after she had dutifully entertained the company, and thrilled Aunt Ruth, by playing a new piece that the Prince Consort had specially composed for Queen

Victoria. Emily was talking to Jane and Polly, trying not to yawn at the very notion of visiting the starving poor in their homes and bringing them food.

From the corner of her eye, Emily observed Rawdon Foxton approaching. She had not been unaware either of his glances across the dinner table.

As soon as she entered the dining-room and saw Rawdon Foxton at the table Emily had known that she still felt the same way about him. He was special for her. She only smiled briefly at him and then ignored him for the rest of the meal, but she knew that every movement of her face or body made him aware of her presence. Although she scarcely glanced at him she thought of nothing and no-one else. Even when he stood beside her now, half bowing a greeting, she wouldn't interrupt her conversation.

'But in this weather, Jane!' she exclaimed loudly. 'It is so *freezing*. Even the Prince has a heavy cold. I cannot support the idea of the risks you take. And to what purpose? Everyone knows the poor will not help themselves, with very few exceptions. Is it not so, Rawdon?'

'Is what not so, Emily?' Rawdon said, standing very close to her, on the edge of the circle.

'It is so bitterly cold to visit the poor.'

'No, Emily,' Jane corrected in her firm humourless voice, 'you were saying that the poor will not help themselves.'

Emily flushed beneath her sister's withering gaze and the obvious disapproval of her cousin Polly.

'Well that is *my* opinion and others have said it too. The poor are lazy as well as stupid and many of them evil. That is the undeserving poor. I know there *are* deserving poor, those who through illness and misfortune have fallen on bad times. I do not include them, of course.'

'I think you know very little about the poor,' Jane said hotly. 'And since you have moved in these exalted circles you care nothing either. What does the Queen care about the poor, pampered and spoilt as she is?'

'How *dare* you talk like that about Her Majesty,' Emily said heatedly. 'It is tantamount to *treason* as far as I am concerned. She is the kindest, tenderest soul alive, always aware of the hardships or illnesses of those who work on her estates.'

'Yes but they have work do they not? The people I know have none nor any chance of it. I spent a lot of time today with the family of a man who is a trained clerical worker. He used to be a clerk in a lawyer's office, can read and write. Yet he developed consumption and was thrown out of work. He was reduced to giving up his comfortable home and letting rooms. Now he and all his family live in one room. The mother is feeble and has just lost a baby. They are gentlefolk down on their luck.'

'But is the workhouse not for people like that?' Emily said magnanimously, looking again to Rawdon for assistance. 'People who cannot help their bad luck? I have nothing but pity for them and would gladly take them a bowl of soup and warm clothes.'

'Have you *ever* seen a workhouse, Emily? Families are separated, the women in one part, the men in another. If you love your husband, your male children, think what it is like to be separated from them.' Jane's rather pale face was now quite pink, and her eyes flashed dangerously.

Emily shrugged deprecatingly. 'Well, it can't be helped can it? If they must they must.'

Jane stamped her foot and turned away from her sister and Polly, after a moment, followed her. Emily, hanging her head in mock dismay, made a mimic of pawing the floor with one dainty foot.

'I have said the wrong thing haven't I, Rawdon?'

Rawdon was looking angrily after Jane, her display of imperious bad temper quite familiar to him. The fact that her mother couldn't bear to be nursed by her was enough condemnation as far as he was concerned. Despite her beauty, her natural verve, she was, he thought, a most unfeminine woman, almost unnatural. And now Caroline had to be sacrificed while Jane devoted her life to the anonymous poor she didn't even know and who were sure not even to be grateful.

'Your sister has a hot temper,' Rawdon said. 'One day it is sure to get her into trouble.'

'I don't understand Jane,' Emily said leading him to one

226

of Aunt Ruth's new large and comfortable sofas. 'You know she was never the one in our family to whom one went in need. She would laugh if you fell or be scornful if Mama or someone made you cry. Why is it that Jane should now show this tenderness and compassion for the deprived? I confess I do not understand it. Yet it has not made her gentler, it has made her harder. There is a very bitter quality about Jane that frightens me as I know it does Aunt Ruth, or Papa if he would notice it. Why should Jane be bitter? She has a number of admirers and can choose any life she likes in society. Why does she choose this, which will soon make her an outcast if it does not kill her?'

'I don't know,' Rawdon said smiling. 'You Vestrey girls are all a puzzle to me.'

'Surely not I,' Emily said dimpling. 'I am *very* straightforward, Rawdon.'

Rawdon looked at her thoughtfully.

'Yes. Yes, perhaps you are the most straightforward of all, Emily. You do not complicate your life with good causes and sacrifices.'

'You mean Caroline too,' Emily said looking at him through lowered lashes. The little minx, she *was* flirting with him.

'Yes, I do mean Caroline.'

'But Mama needs her. Mama really does. People may think she is pretending; but I know she is ill. I have seen her fall and the pain on her face when she didn't want people to know. That makes it even harder for her, that people do not really think she is sick.'

'Caroline has a hard life,' Rawdon said, realizing that they were conversing with the naturalness of old friends, as though there had never been any break between them. 'Since the death of Debbie, Caroline always seems to look sad. But she never complains. She always presents a front of calm and good humour.'

'Caroline would,' Emily said. 'She regards it as her duty never to give way. But that is how we Vestreys were brought up. Even as children we were careful to hide our emotions. It comes from the Vestrey side because Mama is very emotional; but Papa is very controlled. You can see how controlled he is just by looking at him.'

Rawdon looked at the tall, rather striking figure standing talking to Polly and John Tangent. He had always thought George Vestrey a warm sincere person but, it was true, tightly controlled, except on the night he had found him insensible through drink on the floor of the Cremorne Gardens with a woman of ill repute by his side. That night had never been mentioned between them except that the then Mr Vestrey had sent a note thanking him for his services, which had been unspecified. Such a thing like that would embarrass George Vestrey more than most people, to lose control in that way and be seen by his son and a friend.

'Your father looks very well.' Rawdon thought it was time to change the subject. He was uncomfortable talking about Caroline to her sister, especially as he was so unsure of her sister's feelings. 'High office suits him.'

Papa came over to them at that point as though divining that he was being talked about. He had his timepiece in his hand. It was just ten o'clock.

'I must go, my dear Emily. I wish to say goodbye, and kindly give my respectful homage to Her Majesty and the Prince.'

'I shall, Papa. The Queen always wishes to be kindly remembered to you and Mama. She always asks after Mama's health. But going already, Papa? Where to, pray, at this time of night?'

'I am going back to my office in Whitehall for some hours with my papers. The Eastern Question is very vexing to those of us who have to do with it.'

'I cannot really understand it at all, Papa. It is to do with religion the Prince says, the guardianship of the Holy Places.'

'It is much more complicated than that my dear, though it is a fact to be sure that the Turks are infidels and the Russians consider themselves the guardians of the members of the Greek Orthodox Church in the Ottoman Empire. Whereas France considers herself the protector of the *Latin* or Roman Catholics in the Ottoman Empire. That is to say, the custody of the Holy Places in Jerusalem is a matter of some dispute. But it also concerns the territorial ambitions of the Tsar Nicholas who would reassert his power over the Sultan by putting more principalities under Russian domination.'

'And where is Britain in all this, sir?' Rawdon enquired.

'Well, we do not want to see Russia extend her domination into Europe even though in January of this year the Tsar offered us Egypt and Crete in return for letting him have his way with Turkey. Lord John, of course, rejected them out of hand and Lord Clarendon has just confirmed it. Moreover, Lord John sent back the former British Ambassador to Constantinople, Lord Stratford de Redcliffe, who he believes knows how to deal with Russia. You remember Lord Stratford, my dear?'

'He was at Court quite recently, Papa. He is *exceedingly* pompous and made us all laugh – secretly of course. He is called the "great Elchi" and the Queen considered him rather comical. Oh dear, I must not gossip again. It will be the undoing of me.'

Lord Vestrey had consulted his timepiece again and kissing his daughter, shook Rawdon by the hand. In a way he was very thankful for the service Rawdon and James had performed for him nearly a year ago. Then it had seemed shocking that his son and a friend should find him in such a state. But it had proved beneficial. Strange were the ways of fate. He smiled warmly at Rawdon. 'I am so glad you are coming regularly to see us again, Rawdon. 'Twas an unfortunate affair between the women of our families. All over and forgotten now?'

'Of course, sir.' Rawdon smiled; but it was no longer 'Uncle George'.

Clapping him on the shoulder, George then went over to take farewell of the rest of the company before hurrying out of the room.

'George works *so* hard,' Aunt Dorothy said watching him go. 'I fear for his health.'

'Oh I think George is very robust,' Aunt Ruth said reassuringly with a slight smile. 'I would not worry on his behalf, dear. Now Polly, will you go tomorrow with Jane?'

'Yes Miss Vestrey, if I may. Dalton says he will come too to protect us. Do you think James would come, Miss Vestrey?'

'You must ask him, dear. I know not what his duties may be.'

She beckoned to her nephew who was stifling a yawn and also looking at his watch. He knew not whether to go to one of the brothels in Windmill Street or stay at home for the night. He was intrigued by his father rushing off, supposedly to his office in Whitehall. He very much doubted the truth of that story. It had given him ideas. But it was a dismal business going to a brothel by yourself even if you were known, and he was a regular client in a good many now. He wished Rawdon were more of a sport in matters like that. James heard Aunt Ruth calling and obediently went over to her.

'Aunt?' He clicked his heels and gave a mock salute.

'My dear, could you escort your cousins and sister to Soho tomorrow? Polly would like to have you there.'

Polly blushed and lowered her eyes. She felt sometimes her feelings for her cousin were too obvious; but he always regarded her with the affection of a playmate. He treated her with the fond chaffing indifference that he had towards his sisters.

All the Tangent children were fair because the colouring of both their parents was light and when John Tangent had had any hair it was curly and blond. But in his middle age the top was completely bald and the curls, now the colour of pepper and salt, formed a fringe round his cravat and, with his gold half moon spectacles gave him the appearance of a bishop. Alas, he was never likely to be that.

Polly was petite, much shorter and finer boned than the Vestrey girls and, although her health had always been robust, she looked delicate. She had large violet eyes, pale translucent skin and a pretty bow shaped mouth, always smiling. Polly was her mother's helpmeet, but she would never be forced to stay at home because Dorothy was so capable that one could never imagine her retiring to her bed for months on end.

Dorothy had been more aware than anyone of the shadow

of the Vestreys over the Tangents at the rectory half a mile away from Chetwell Place. She was herself the daughter of a north country clergyman to whom John Tangent had been curate shortly after his ordination. She had known nothing of the powerful Vestreys when they had become engaged even though his sister Agnes had already been married to George Vestrey for three years. They had stayed in the north, and John was not offered the living of Chetwell Church until it was clear that the northern climate had a bad effect on his consumptive constitution and a recommendation to the south and sea air made a move to Kent vital.

But the Vestreys were never intentionally overpowering, Dorothy knew that. Pretty, flighty Agnes never attempted to play the *grande dame* or lord it over her sister-in-law and she adored her brother. Dorothy Tangent was one of the few women George Vestrey felt comfortable and at home with. The children had been brought up together and shared books and games and, when they were young, childish secrets. Did they share them now? Dorothy shook her head sadly to herself.

Her eldest son, Dalton, had once been close to the Vestrey boys; but maturity had made them grow apart. Dalton was careful and scholarly, self effacing and religious. His father had wanted him to go into the church because his second son, Frederick, had gone into the army straight from school. But Dalton did not feel called to the church. He was attracted to the law and Dorothy encouraged this with all her heart imagining that a successful law career could lead to all kinds of things, the House of Commons maybe or eventually a seat on the Bench: Mr Justice Tangent. It had a very nice ring, Dorothy always thought. But above all Dorothy wanted a good marriage for Dalton more than for any of her children. If Dalton could marry money it would make a great difference to his prospects; give him the time he needed to establish a practice.

Besides, Dalton was good-looking. He was not as tall as James Vestrey, but he was slender and looked ascetic with a clever, lofty forehead and a long thin nose. He was a modish young man and liked to dress well; he entertained modestly, in accordance with his means, in his chambers in Doughty Street near to Gray's Inn where he had been a pupil to Sir Smithers Rawlings, QC, one of the keenest lawyers practising at the Chancery Bar. He was now Sir Smithers' devil and the great man thought highly of his clever and eager pupil. There was absolutely no money for an inexperienced young man to make at the Bar and Sir Arthur Tangent had reluctantly dug heavily into his pocket to help support Dalton in the hope that eventually his investment would pay dividends. No, there was no real worry about Dalton. But at twenty-two a rich wife would help a good deal to launch him on his career. Dorothy determined to have a word with George about it as soon as she could get him alone; very hard these days, he seemed so busy.

Then there could be another good match – an excellent one, in fact – if only James would cease to regard his cousin as a sister and come to appreciate her real feminine charms, as a lot of young men did. Of course he had a bad reputation as a womanizer; but that would pass with age. It did no real harm to a man. Polly was the same age as Emily and just as pretty, Dorothy thought prettier, with more character. The eldest son of the rector of a big church in Folkestone had offered for her when she was only seventeen, but Polly didn't want to marry a clergyman. She said even if she loved the young man in question, which she didn't, she would never want the life of a rector's wife with its endless drudgery and lack of money. She regarded her Vestrey cousins with love. She also envied them because they would never know, could never imagine what it was like to be the daughter of the rectory, and the eldest daughter at that, with all the responsibilities of cutting corners and altering clothes that had to be passed on from the eldest down.

Polly yearned for the life that Emily had. To be a member of the Royal Household, to circulate in this rich, dazzling and privileged world was something she could only dream about. Emily had promised to invite her to Windsor but so far had not kept her promise, and there was never any chance at all that Polly Tangent could conceivably be invited to be a maid-of-honour. Between the Vestreys and the Tangents there was all the difference that Jane found among the many social classes that inhabited the mean little houses in Soho, only on not quite such a gigantic or tragic a scale. The Tangents were gentry, but poor; the Vestreys were nobility and really very rich, especially since George had inherited.

All the good things that happened to them, in Polly's opinion, came from the Vestreys. The classes at Chetwell Place – the great house up the hill – when they had been children; the parties and games there, especially at Christmas time when they all went back for Christmas dinner after Papa had taken the morning service in church. The visits to London were only possible because they could stay at Vestrey House, and Papa's medical bills were discreetly paid by Uncle George while Aunt Agnes had given Mama a pound towards a new bonnet. Oh, the Vestreys never talked about it, or ever mentioned money. As far as they were concerned there was no difference between themselves and the Tangents at all. But to Polly, vital, eager and ambitious to better herself, just in the way that Mama was ambitious for Dalton and Fred, there was all the difference in the world.

James said he would be delighted to escort the party to Soho. It would be a lark. He had never been there, but had heard a lot about it. Or rather he *had* been there, he said meaningfully, but not visiting the poor. Poor, exactly, ha! ha! no indeed. This was said with a hearty laugh and a wink, a sly movement of the mouth. The whispered insinuations about James's private life made him even more glamorous in Polly's eyes and her heart leapt when he consented to come. She wondered idly if he were not looking at her this evening with a slightly different expression from the one she was used to. There was an appreciative little gleam that she had never noticed before, and she thought he had been particularly attentive to her at dinner. Or was she imagining it?

The party broke up just after the Queen's carriage came to collect Emily at ten-thirty and she was seen off at the door by her family who could not but be impressed by the coachman and postilion, the discreet Royal crest on the door of the brougham.

Rawdon and Emily had had no further opportunity to talk during the evening; but as she looked out of the carriage window she was aware of him standing in the hall, his hands behind his back, his grave face looking at her with an enigmatic expression. She saw him half raise his arm in farewell and she smiled and waved back, rather as the Queen was accustomed to acknowledging the homage of her subjects.

Emily was well pleased with the evening, and sank back on the comfortably upholstered seat of the Royal coach, her face flushed, her eyes closed. They had re-established contact; they had not referred to the events which had parted them and there was, she thought, in Rawdon's eyes, in his obvious appreciation of her, great promise for the future.

Shortly after she left, James put on his hat and, nonchalantly swinging his stick, went off into the night with a jaunty air. Rawdon was apparently not to accompany him. Muffling himself against the cold he said goodnight and went the other way, the firm brisk tap of his stick echoing through the damp deserted streets.

CHAPTER FOURTEEN

George Vestrey let his hand travel down the body of his mistress from the curve of her full breasts to the crease between her loins. He felt her tremble, even though he knew she was asleep. She was every bit as voluptuous and enticing as he had known she would be that day he, to his lingering shame, had had carnal thoughts about her at his father's death bed.

But, oh, his father would have approved of Hilary, he was sure of that. She was so tactful, so discreet, so exactly right in every way. Why, she kept his marriage together; she was so understanding and positive about Agnes, so helpful in her suggestions, modestly put, in telling George what to do and what to say. It was really owing to her that he and Agnes had remained friends – no not remained, *become,* that was the word.

In his heart, of recent years, his love for Agnes had warred with a feeling of hatred because of the great tussle he had to get her to allow him his rights as a husband, followed by all the reproaches afterwards when she conceived. Distressed though he was to admit it, he had hated Agnes for this for years and yet, as a good and dutiful husband, it was his behaviour that had seemed so wrong. It had caused him such qualms of conscience.

Agnes had never enjoyed the marital act. She endured it for his sake, he supposed. He didn't know for sure because of course, they had never discussed it. No Vestrey ever talked about intimate things of that nature and, presumably, no Tangent either, as Agnes had never mentioned it. But he knew she didn't enjoy it, because her body sometimes trembled in the dark as he had mounted her and he knew it wasn't through passion. What she had done was from duty and in fear, and afterwards she turned her back to him and often he thought she was weeping. Agnes always managed to make him ashamed of his behaviour; as though he had committed some unnatural and unclean act.

But it never seemed to lessen her love for him. Like all well brought-up girls, she knew that her function was to obey her husband in all his demands; he had rights over her body and soul. He had never run his hands over Agnes's naked body as he did now with Hilary. That would not have seemed right at all, and was certainly not expected. He had never even seen her nude. What they did in the confines of their marital bed was under the sheets in the dark, with her long nightdress bunched over her hips and then quickly and furtively lowered when he had finished.

To tell the truth, he had been slightly scandalized when Hilary had shown herself to him naked. She had done it very subtly and even modestly, if you could call that sort of thing modest. But she hadn't objected to his exploration, first in the dark, of all the parts of her body, even of his kissing her breasts. Then one day he had arrived at noon and she had allowed him to make love to her. Even with the curtains drawn he had seen it all, everything, and gazed at her with excitement as she permitted him to pull back the sheets as she lay on the bed, completely nude, one leg just slightly apart from the other.

He wondered at the time if a really decent, modest woman would behave like that and if he had been right about Hilary. George Vestrey had been conditioned not only by his upbringing and marriage, but by the prevailing view that although pleasure in sexual intercourse was natural and right for men, it was quite different for well brought-up women whose prime duties were as good wives and mothers and not instruments for carnal pleasure. They were not meant to enjoy themselves at all. This was confined to loose women and the lower orders who were, accordingly, not respected for it. The female was idealized, a sort of Victorian and, of course, Protestant Virgin Mary; undefiled, inviolate and yet a mother.

Agnes's marital behaviour, although painful to George, was understood by him. He expected that his mother had behaved like that and that in due course his daughters would. They would not be instructed in what was expected of them on marriage, and to most refined girls it came as something of a shock from which they seldom recovered.

George never questioned this state of things because no-one, let alone a Vestrey, ever discussed it; there was no literature on the subject, except in the pornography which flourished at the same time as morals became so strict, and some medical writings which were misleading if not downright inaccurate.

Of course George had seen naked women, or partly naked, indecently exposed for the purpose of sheer lust in the hot sordid little rooms in the Haymarket and Windmill Street that he had frequented since the birth of Rebecca. Before that he had never been unfaithful to Agnes, even during the months she had refused him, in the intervals when the three dead babies were born.

It would never have occurred to him then to have gone to a brothel, and when he did he regretted and was deeply ashamed of the carnal impulses of his passionate nature. Being a religious man he often prayed to be delivered from them, to be pure as he was sure other men were, to be worthy of Agnes and her love. But it was no use. God did not hear him and sent no soothing balm to alleviate his torments.

His torments were not really eased by consorting with prostitutes. Although his carnal appetite was assuaged his nausea and sense of self-disgust increased that he should have to consort with women who were so lewd, debased and often dirty. As the French historian Hipollyte Taine was later to say, when travelling through Britain in the sixties, the gulf which separated virtue from debauchery was sheer; there was no ladder from one to the other as there was in France. Though he did not know it, George Vestrey, when he set up his mistress in a little house in St John's Wood, was making such a ladder, and imitating thousands of Frenchmen to whom a respectable mistress and a domestic establishment apart from his lawful one was almost taken for granted.

It had really been a business arrangement at the start, a question of mutual convenience. George wanted a clean, respectable sexual partner and Hilary wanted security. There was mutual regard, but no expression, at first anyway, of anything more. There was something so tactful, discreet and admirable about Hilary and George was so generous, grateful and methodical that respect soon developed into affection especially as they suited each other so well, not only physically but temperamentally.

Agnes had always a tendency to hysteria throughout their married life; she was very emotional and easily flew off the handle. Hilary was the epitome of calm and good sense; she was acquiescent but never cringing or subservient. George was very business-like. He made his proposition, was accepted after a decent interval (not more than a day or two) and then he made over to her a lump sum of money and *carte blanche* to purchase one of the new little villas being built behind high walls in St John's Wood.

Since Nash's development in Regent Street and Regent's Park in the earlier years of the century, the area immediately north of the Park with its fields and woods and leafy lanes had increased in popularity. It was away from the heavily built-up, over-populated streets of the City, yet close enough to it to be accessible by carriage for those successful men of business who increasingly wished to live in one place and work in another.

St John's Wood, thus, by the middle of the century, was a well laid-out garden suburb with separate and semi-detached villas in their own areas of garden, presenting a contrast to the terraced houses of the town. Because of its beauty it attracted people of all kinds including a considerable number of artists and writers and gentlemen who, for reasons of discretion, liked to keep their mistresses well away from their homes, yet within reach.

As a widow Hilary had a sort of respectability already. She came no-one knew from where, but obviously in comfortable circumstances, in a hired brougham with a maid and a quantity of luggage, the house having been previously carpeted and furnished throughout by Waring and Gillow.

But St John's Wood was not a curious place. Many people, though she did not know it, were in the same circumstances as herself, ostensibly widows or maiden ladies living in seclusion, but really under the protection of a nobleman or a man of wealth. People did not chat across walls in St John's Wood; but went very quietly and circumspectly about their business. For many months Hilary Ashburne would not even have recognized her neighbours, and for years she did not know who lived across the road.

Carriages came and went at night or during the day, depositing their occupants for an hour or two and then returning to pick them up. No-one asked questions, there was very little to see.

Hilary loved her house from the moment she stepped out of the carriage, opened the wrought iron gate set in the wall and saw it standing in a patch of garden with a small magnolia tree leaning to one side. It was a perfectly symmetrical house with, at the top of a short flight of stairs, a main door surmounted by a Corinthian portico. There were two windows at either side of the door on the ground floor and three on the first, one over the door. There was no attic but an adequate basement with a kitchen and scullery and two rooms for the cook and the maid. It was a fair sized house, big enough for a small family. George had opened an account for her at Mr Coutts' bank and she engaged a lawyer, acting on her own, so that no-one would know about her protector or where her money came from. After the basic furnishings were finished she added to them over the months with an assortment of small *objets d'art*, bric à brac and paintings, stuffed animals, papier mâché boxes and a variety of plants and ferns spilling out of urns and vases, rather like Aunt Ruth was doing in Park Street, but on a smaller scale.

Aunt Ruth never let on that she had arranged the whole thing. She was, she averred, delighted to hear of Mrs Ashburne's good fortune in the shape of an unexpected legacy from a relative and promised to come and visit her in her new home where she hoped she would be very happy. If anyone deserved good fortune it was Mrs Ashburne, Aunt Ruth opined, and she saw her off with a wave and a smile and begged her to keep in touch.

George had nothing to do with choosing the house or the furnishings. At first he was not at all sure he was doing the right thing. Supposing he and Mrs Ashburne didn't suit? After all, they hardly knew each other and, of course, had never been to bed together. It was rather like a second marriage, in George's opinion, and he was fearful of a similar outcome. But Aunt Ruth was most reassuring on the subject. She felt she had chosen well.

Aunt Ruth was right. From the moment of George's first visit, with a large bunch of flowers and some sweetmeats from Bentincks in Wigmore Street tastefully arranged in a box with a large violet bow, things went well. The first day he came for tea there were two kinds, Indian and China, served in delicate porcelain cups, cucumber sandwiches and little cakes. There was no question of anything carnal then either, except that Mrs Ashburne's charm and dignity turned what could have been an awkward visit into a pleasant one, and impressed him more and more, as did her intelligence on the next visit which was to dinner. On that occasion he was allowed to put an arm round her waist and he actually kissed her, trembling with passion, afraid of ruining it all with precipitate haste. In order to cleanse himself, to be worthy of this excellent lady he had not been near a brothel for weeks.

On the third occasion, they went upstairs after dinner, or rather she did first and when he reached her bedroom she was already in bed, looking very pale and nervous in a white flannel nightgown with lace at the neck. He hadn't felt too sure of himself either and, after blowing out the lamp, quickly undressed in the dark and rather fell upon her as he was used to doing with Agnes, in order to get it over as quickly as he could. It was not a great success on that occasion and he left soon afterwards, mortified and afraid he had disgusted her as he did his wife.

But after that things improved – they could hardly have been worse, in Hilary's opinion. She was not a virgin, but she had not had a very satisfactory marriage with a man who was an invalid, a consumptive from his youth. Yet she was a very sensual woman, as George had divined. Accordingly, as the prime purpose of this charade was to afford Lord Vestrey carnal satisfaction – otherwise she would not be here at all, no house, no maid, nothing – she set about giving the matter some serious thought and doing her best to please him.

It was not very difficult. He was a handsome man, very attractive to her, personally fresh and fastidious, with clean underlinen every day as one would expect from a gentleman. He was clumsy at making love and he spent himself very quickly. Afterward he seemed to feel ashamed of himself and gradually she got him to talk about it as she lay there, feeling unfulfilled and frustrated. Then she began to touch his body tentatively with her hands and she would lean over and kiss him, taking the initiative which he found quite delightful, as well as the fact that he was allowed to touch her too, to stroke and caress her.

For a long time she came up before him and he would undress in the dark and leap into bed; but after that day when they made love in the daylight things were never the same again. They were delightful. They became more frank and open with each other, undressing in the same room and at the same time, or maybe he would undress her first and embrace her naked body as she stood so statuesquely on the floor. He would kneel down and kiss her rather as a votary worshipping some Grecian goddess. With her pleasingly rotund body, not fat but rounded in just the right places, the buttocks, the hips and the breasts, and with her long unbraided hair she did indeed resemble some ancient deity such as the Victorian sculptors were continually representing. She had a very tiny waist that was pleasing too and a pair of really superb legs such that George Vestrev had never seen in his life, let alone imagined.

Then at last they abandoned themselves to carnal pleasure. The flinging of himself on her stopped completely, because there was no need to get it over with. It could last quite a long time and the longer it lasted the better; and Hilary enjoyed it too. Her excitement and pleasure was the most astonishing, most gratifying part. She enjoyed making love as much as he did, and she was always finding new ways of pleasing him and then he would do something that particularly delighted her. The mutual discovery and pleasure was so excellent, so good, that the guilt vanished completely.

The fear and the shame went too and in a very few months George, sixth Baron Vestrey, did indeed become a new man as his friends and relations had noticed. He was happy and satisfied in love and in work and did not neglect his family either or lose his concern for his poor sick wife Agnes.

Agnes. George lay in the dark thinking about her. It would soon be dawn and he would walk to the end of the road where a tired Matthew would be waiting with his horse. He would have to find some way of doing this that did not incommode Matthew so much; maybe hire stables somewhere. He wanted to make love to Hilary again; her body beside him was so enticing, so he kissed her gently and murmured words of love in her ear. Hilary stirred and even instinctively, half asleep, put her arms about him. Gently, with the skill and practice he had learned like some diligent student of the art of love, he spread himself upon her and loved her, as she moved and sighed with pleasure and contentment.

A blackbird was singing as he got out of bed and started to dress. It didn't seem at all strange now to dress in front of Hilary and sometimes she got out of bed and passed him his things, looking very enticing, either naked or in a transparent robe of some flimsy stuff. But this morning it was very cold and she lay propped up against the pillows, just with her breasts exposed and her long hair unbraided and lying across her shoulders, because she knew he liked that, and watched him.

Yes, she was very fortunate in having such a handsome, accomplished man for a lover. His black curly hair had not a trace of grey in it and his clean-shaven skin had a healthy vigorous glow. He had a long, very straight nose, a firm but well-shaped mouth and the most beautiful dark eyes, deep set and brilliant, under his rather thick but well arched brows.

His body was firm and unflabby, his chest well covered with thick dark hair. George Vestrey was over six feet tall and dressed or undressed he was a fine figure of a man; needless to say it had not taken Hilary very long to fall in love with him. This made it easier, but also more difficult. It made it easier to please him, to prepare the food he liked, the wine he preferred, to make the little intimate suppers, dinners or lunches he so enjoyed. And then she spent hours preparing herself with the degree of fastidiousness and with regard to the fashions he liked. It was very pleasurable being a mistress, even though one had to be constantly available to the demands of a man with very powerful passions that needed to be frequently satisfied.

It made it harder in that she knew she would never have any more than she had now – a house, a maid, a cook and as much money as she wanted. Her lover hardly ever stayed the night, or if he did left at dawn and his family, whom she would never be able to meet again, took up a fair proportion of his life. She was not at all jealous of his wife even though she knew he still loved her. But it was, he assured her, now the love of a brother for a sister. He had no desire ever to know her carnally again, and nor, of course, had she.

Hilary Ashburne knew that she should consider herself very fortunate that, at the age of thirty without a penny to her name, no home and no support, she should have secured a lover who was not only a nobleman and very rich, but also kind, tender and considerate. Being a settled family man he would not wander or consort with prostitutes or take another mistress. She didn't think he would ever discard her, or not for many years. He was no philanderer. Her mission, her sole function in life was now, and for as long as she could see, to exist to satisfy George, Lord Vestrey, and whether she liked it or not that was what she was going to do. But loving him made it just that little bit more difficult not to wish for more. Thinking constantly about a man made you want to be with him always, to be received with him in society among his friends. And she knew that would never happen. Never, ever. It was foolish even to think of it.

George sat on the side of the bed putting on his boots. He was tired, but satisfied and happy. A brisk canter through the park and along Baker Street to Park Street, a bath, a shave and a good breakfast and he would feel invigorated, knowing that he was a successful man in the prime of life. He had an important position in the government, a fine family as a proof of his virility, and a lovely young mistress, who seemed to adore him, as a proof of his continuing vigour.

When he saw her lying against the pillow watching him, his heart turned over with an emotion that was not solely desire, but he knew was akin to love. He already adored her in the sense of worshipping her beautiful body, for the sheer carnal pleasure she gave him; but Aunt Ruth had been very particular in warning him not to let his emotions become engaged, not to be so foolish as to fall in love. Men did very silly things in that state and, in Aunt Ruth's opinion, George had no time for it. He must regard Hilary Ashburne as a sort of superior servant which, as a kept woman, was strictly what she was. Such people, although necessary, were really to be pitied and despised. George must never allow himself to fall in love.

George tried to remember Aunt Ruth's warning; but no, his heart was melting. He looked forward more and more to his visits, to seeing her, just to be with her. He hated leaving her, especially if he knew it was some time before he could come again, if he was going to Chetwell, or government business was too pressing and he had to go to Windsor or Osborne to see the Queen.

Hilary had her breasts just showing above the line of the lace edged sheet, plump like ripe gourds, firm and full underneath, by the armpits, as he had known they would be when he had glanced at her sideways such a long time ago. The tips were elongated like fresh raspberries ready for picking. The aureole was large and brownish-coloured and then the milky white line continued up to her firm throat.

Her long fair hair rested across her shoulders making her look at once wanton and chaste, as though she was trying vainly, but not very hard, like Botticelli's Venus, to hide her nakedness. He threw himself across her form and kissed each erect nipple, longing to take it in his mouth and start to make love to her again. From the light in her eyes, the way she shifted beneath the bedclothes, he knew that she wished it too.

'I can't, my love,' he said. 'No one will believe I have been working all night in the office.'

'Do they now?' Hilary sounded amused.

'No one dare ask. You cannot question Papa, whatever you may think.'

He adopted the firm tone of the strict Victorian father and got up off his knees after kissing her breasts once again, then her full generous mouth. He put on his jacket and straightened his waistcoat, glancing at his watch as he fastened his chain through the centre button.

'I meant to talk to you about Jane.'

'Jane?' Hilary looked up, her eyes still lazy with love. 'What has she done?'

'She is being very difficult. This Soho thing has gone to her head. She has become quite wild.'

'Then you must stop it, George. As you said, you are her father with full control over her.'

George gave a rueful smile. 'Not *my* daughter Jane. I don't think anyone could quite control her. I pity her husband, if she has one which I sometimes doubt. Jane has always had her own way. There is something about her, almost as though she were possessed. She is fanatical. It has always been the same with each new enthusiasm.'

'But you *must* put a stop to it, George. Send her to Chetwell. Insist.'

'But Agnes cannot stand her about. She has really taken against Jane. I think she still fears Caroline might leave her and Jane take her place. Whereas she used to have turns when she saw me, it is now Jane who brings them on, while I am accepted because I am no danger, thanks to you, my love.' He blew her a kiss. 'Anyway, Jane wants Agnes to see a mesmerist. Miss Martineau thinks she will cure her.'

'A mesmerist!' Hilary laughed. 'Whatever is that?'

'Oh you must have heard of it. It is named after a German, Herr Franz Mesmer, who had some new-fangled technique for curing the sick. I know very little about it myself; but Miss Martineau has a famous cure she swears was brought about by it, and Emily tells me even the Queen and Prince have expressed interest. And Prince Albert is no fool, as I well know through working with him.'

'Well, let this Mesmer person see Lady Vestrey.' Hilary always referred to Agnes by her title, never her Christian name.

245

'Mesmer is dead, my love, or so I believe, but he has many adherents in this country. Apparently a Mrs Chetwynd who lives in Tunbridge Wells and is known in the south for her remarkable cures is a friend of Miss Martineau. Mind you, I also have to thank Miss Martineau for Jane's philanthropic work in Soho, so maybe she is intent on ruining all my family.'

George had only recently begun to discuss his family and other problems with Hilary. Having by now established a satisfactory physical basis to their union, he found her so sympathetic, understanding and, above all, so full of such good practical common sense that he had started confiding in her as well. She always had something useful and sensible to say, and these things they usually discussed at dinner or in bed before he left.

'I cannot see it would hurt to see this lady,' Hilary said sleepily. Whenever she thought of Lady Vestrey it was as an invalid, somehow very old and infirm, rather than the mother of a young child who was not yet talking. It was a vague notion of a little crimped old lady tucked up in bed and lovingly protected by her eldest daughter. The fact that Agnes was actually younger than George seemed difficult to believe and almost impossible to visualize.

'All the doctors who have seen Agnes have pronounced her condition hysterical in origin. The longer she stays in bed the more difficult it becomes to cure her. Of course I am worried about Agnes, but it is the effect on Caroline that troubles me most. I can see Caroline becoming like Aunt Ruth, and I would not have that even though Ruth has had, by many standards, an enjoyable life without the burden of children and other worries. Caroline's nature is too rich; she has much more to offer than to spend her life looking after her mother. Anyway my dear, I will take note of what you say and speak sharply to Miss Jane Vestrey. Thank you for your good advice, as always.'

George bent over Hilary, so warm and sweet-smelling, and put his mouth to hers. He could see she was sleepy and he made her lie down while he tucked her up as though she were a small child. Her eyes were already closed before he tiptoed down the stairs and let himself into Elm Grove.

It was almost daylight and only the solitary, curious black-bird singing in the magnolia tree observed him.

CHAPTER FIFTEEN

If Mr and Mrs Ticehurst were in any way put out by the visit of Miss Jane Vestrey's relations they were too over-awed to say so. Soberly and discreetly dressed, the Vestrey family and their relations had trooped round Soho, carrying cans of soup, loaves of bread and warm clothing. James thought it was colossal fun and did twice as much as every-one else, but Polly was depressed and by lunch time very nearly in tears. Dalton grew more thoughtful and shocked by what he saw, the poverty, the dirt, the helplessness and filth.

But the room belonging to the Ticehurst family was quite different. It was neat and clean, even though Mr and Mrs Ticehurst and three of their children slept in it. Maggie Ticehurst lived at the hotel where she worked, and there was an older brother in the army and a younger one who was an apprentice printer and slept at the home of his employer. Mr Ticehurst was in bed, his nightshirt clean, he himself washed and shaved, the bedclothes fresh but frayed. Mrs Ticehurst sat by the small fire sewing and the four-year-old played on the floor.

Jane Vestrey went in first to prepare them for meeting her family and Mrs Ticehurst got up in a flurry to see if she had enough tea to give to the visitors.

'Oh pray do not!' Jane exclaimed. 'They have just had lunch at the Mission. They are helping us today.' She thought it was important to emphasize that they were helpers, not benevolent do-gooders seeing how the other half lived. The room overlooked a yard and was surrounded by buildings so that it was very dark inside and the candles by the side of Mr Ticehurst's bed and on the mantel gave a poor light. Dalton came in first, bending his head and peering round in the gloom while Mrs Ticehurst dropped a curtsey and Mr Ticehurst pulled his shawl round his shoulders as he sat propped up in bed trying to read a book.

When they were all in the room was overfull and Jane thought they should all go out again. Then Dalton, who had gone over to peer out of the window by the bed, glanced at the man in it and stopped. For some moments he and Mr Ticehurst gazed at each other and then the sick man put out a trembling hand which Dalton took and shook, the expression on his face one of undisguised dismay.

'It *is* Mr Dalton, sir. I thought so, being as how you are on the tall side and could hardly pass through the door. As soon as I saw you stoop, with your long thin frame if I may say so sir, I said to myself, "Mr Dalton Tangent". And sorry I am that you see me so reduced, Mr Dalton.' Mr Ticehurst hung his head and a tear stole down his face before, owing to the emotion of the encounter, he succumbed to a paroxysmal attack of coughing.

The whole family were stunned at Mr Ticehurst's revelation and Dalton sat on his bed still holding onto his hand.

'This is Edward Ticehurst,' he said, looking up. 'He was Sir Smithers' clerk for many years. We knew he was ill and he left the Chambers about eighteen months ago, but we had no idea he was so reduced.'

'Did you try and find out?' Jane said, a hard edge to her voice.

Dalton shrugged and looked embarrassed.

'I . . . of course *I* was not Mr Ticehurst's employer. I assumed Sir Smithers . . .'

'*Assumed* Sir Smithers . . .' Jane said witheringly. 'When did he ever think of anyone but himself, or the fat fees he commands?'

'Oh Jane I *beg* you,' Dalton said. 'Sir Smithers is a very important man, the head of the Chambers. It was hardly up to him . . .'

'Then who was it up to?' Jane asked. 'His faithful clerk for many years, you said. Didn't he want to *know* what had happened to him?'

Mrs Ticehurst came forward and put a pleading hand on Jane's arm.

'Please do not distress yourself, Miss Vestrey, on our behalf,' she said. 'Sir Smithers was always very good to Edward who first joined him when he was fifteen. He sent a hamper at Christmas and was very thoughtful to all his staff. But Mr Tangent is right. He was a very important man, powerful you know, Miss. It would hardly concern him what happened to my husband.'

'But do you not think it *ought* to have concerned him? I do.'

'Jane, how many servants has your father?' Polly said gently.

Jane, appearing startled, looked at her cousin, but said nothing.

'You don't know, do you?' Polly continued. 'Do you think he knows what happens to them *all* if they get sick? He hears they are ill, their wages are paid, maybe a cottage is reclaimed. Did you ever think of that?'

Jane turned away and stared out of the window. Her blood was boiling with anger, but her heart was troubled. It was true she had never thought, nor supposed her father or mother had, though everyone considered her father a good man. It was the bailiff's job to see to the servants, and heaven knew what became of them if they left because of illness. But unless it was a particularly close servant, a personal maid or one who had been in service for years, you couldn't possibly keep track of them. Sometimes one heard one had died and was very sorry; but there was very little thought to the widow and children apart from a small donation and some food sent over from time to time. She felt ashamed of herself.

'I'm sorry, Mrs Ticehurst,' she said. 'I think I have caused more trouble than I intended.'

'Not at all, not at all.' Dalton got up and came over to Mrs Ticehurst, standing with a worried frown on her face in front of the fire. 'I am very *glad* to have found out what happened to Mr Ticehurst, even though distressed to find you in such circumstances. I will speak immediately to Sir Smithers about this and see if he cannot . . .'

'Oh pray do not trouble Sir Smithers,' Mrs Ticehurst said urgently. 'We have a little money coming in from our elder children and Miss Goodey's Mission is so kind. I don't know what we would do without it and the daily visits from Miss Vestrey.'

In the gloom and confusion no-one had noticed that another person had entered the room until a slight form walked across the room to where Mr Ticehurst lay in bed and, putting a basket on the floor, stooped and kissed him. Then she turned and very shyly, self effacingly, went over to her mother handing her the basket.

'The chef sent these Mother, nourishing victuals for father.'

Mrs Ticehurst looked embarrassed and took the basket over to the corner of the room that had a basin, a jug and some pots and pans, serving as a sort of kitchen.

'This is my daughter, Maggie,' she murmured. 'She is a kitchen maid in Bentley's hotel and the chef occasionally sends something for father, like a junket or custard.'

Even in her kitchen maid's rags Maggie Ticehurst was a beautiful girl. She was tall with very curly black hair and that, hanging loosely, and her dark fiery eyes made her look like a gypsy. Her shawl, though closely wrapped round her did not conceal her slender figure and firm bosom, her slim hips and narrow waist. She appeared on the verge of going as Jane stepped forward.

'I am so pleased to see you, Maggie. I know you are the mainstay of the family.'

Maggie bobbed but avoided Jane's eyes.

'Thank you Miss, I'm sure. I know you are very good to Ma and Pa. I wish I could do more to help. I must get back now. Mr Parker the chef had just made some custard for the lunches and sent this to Pa while it was hot.'

Without another word she left the room as swiftly as she had come. Seeing that Mrs Ticehurst was anxious to serve the hot custard to her invalid husband Jane suggested that they should go and awkwardly, perhaps sorry that they had come to witness such intimate destitution proudly borne, they trooped towards the door, all except Dalton who looked at Mr Ticehurst.

'If Mr Ticehurst has no objection, I should like to stay and chat a while with him. He taught me most of my law. I owe him a great debt.'

Edward Ticehurst managed to chuckle and the colour rushed to his face.

251

'That is *very* good of you, Mr Dalton. I would like nothing better if it does not inconvenience you, sir. Don't forget I learned my chancery law from Sir Smithers *and* Lord Makepeace before him, who became Mr Justice Makepeace. But I would be very glad of your company, sir; though here, with poor heat and bad light . . .'

'Pray Mr Ticehurst, do not distress yourself,' Dalton said cheerfully. 'I am delighted to keep you company and it is quite warm enough for me in here.'

Outside the light was failing and Jane decided it was time to return to the Mission and home. James, who had other ideas, bade them good-bye outside the Ticehursts' humble dwelling. He thought it had all been a jolly lark and went gaily off to pass a couple of hours in Windmill Street seeing it was so close by. He had never paid any attention at all to Polly.

Queen Victoria's new baby had been a boy, Leopold, the first of her children to be delivered with the help of chloroform administered to her by Dr Snow whom Jane Vestrey knew from his work in Soho where he lived. A gentle, self-effacing utterly dedicated man, Dr Snow was shy and withdrawn and had never married. He had been trying for years to find the cause of cholera, the disease which so decimated parts of England, and especially the inner city areas with depressing regularity. He had advanced the theory that it was not breathed through the lungs but swallowed in drinking water. Some medical authorities took it seriously, but others treated it with a good deal of scepticism. There were so many theories abounding, that no-one quite knew which one to believe.

However cholera was not on anyone's mind when the family gathered at Chetwell Place for Easter. Emily was not in waiting but, as someone who had actually seen the new Royal Prince, was eagerly sought after and listened to by the many friends who called with Easter greetings or who sent gifts of fruit or flowers for the poor invalid.

Agnes delighted the whole family by consenting to take Easter day lunch in the dining-room. She had seldom sat in the dining-room since the birth of Rebecca. There was a great deal of commotion and preparation as she was wheeled in her chair to the table with its many places set for a large family gathering. Carefully her chair was placed facing Papa who himself made sure that she was comfortable, fussing over her in a most concerned and gratifying manner before he resumed his own seat.

Caroline recalled the previous Easter when Rebecca had been christened. Debbie had been alive and she and Emily had yet to quarrel about Rawdon Foxton. His name was never mentioned between them even now, though he continued to call and see her when he was at Saltmarsh and she knew that he escorted Emily to dances in London when she was not in waiting. She had once invited him to an evening party at Buckingham Palace.

Caroline tried to think of him once more simply as a friend of the family – as she used to in the days before they had become adults; but it was hard. It would be very suitable to be married to him. It would give her the status that, as an unmarried woman, she did not have; status in itself was of no importance except that, more than anything else, it would give her independence. It would free her from what was becoming a lifetime of servitude to Mama.

In the many moments that Caroline had to reflect upon her life, her one regret was that it was so uneventful; she seemed to have missed out on everything, to have achieved nothing. Whatever her fantasies about Rawdon, she did not really regret not being a wife, or having a home and servants of her own. The last eighteen months had shown an enormous void in her life that up to then she had not been aware of, and certainly didn't know how to fill. Neither marriage nor looking after Mama was what she really wanted, nor being the eldest daughter of the house; the one on whom everyone relied from Papa downwards.

Yet what did she want? What could an unmarried daughter of a nobleman, well educated, well brought-up, possibly want except for a husband and her own home or, alternatively, what she had now, an important task in fulfilling her duty to her family? Everyone relied on her, and baby Rebecca was such a treasure. It was like having her own child.

Caroline looked around the table – at her beloved family united once again, alas with the exception of Debbie. James looked happy and satisfied with life, as he usually did; one seldom saw him perturbed about anything. He fitted well into this niche, his place in society. He loved the army, he had many friends, he was discreet about women, he was kind and thoughtful towards his family. Who would James marry? No-one, Caroline thought, for a long time, if he could possibly avoid it.

Next to him was Jane. The sight of Jane displaced the happiness she always had in her heart when contemplating James. James was good to look at – a well-rounded, contented member of the human race. But Jane. Jane, in some subtle, indefinable way, had grown harsher, more positive; even, one would say, a little sour. She now criticized absolutely everything: the family, the style in which they lived, society, the government. It was tiresome and rather shocking, because the Vestreys had always supported the establishment and the status quo. Vestreys had always served and commanded, never criticized. One became rather apprehensive when Jane was about, knowing that the least thing said amiss would be leapt upon, and one would be lectured, bullied and otherwise abused until one either retracted what one had said or fell silent.

Oliver sat next to Jane, arguing with her as he always did. Oliver was seventeen and as tall as James. He was preparing to go to Oxford, a year earlier than was customary because he was so clever. His tutors said he would have a brilliant career. Caroline knew that Papa hoped Oliver would be the really outstanding member of his family – that he would go early into Parliament and rise rapidly in the ranks of government as William Pitt the Younger once had, Prime Minister at the age of twenty-four. Of course that couldn't happen now; but Oliver could have a seat in the Cabinet in his thirties if he fulfilled this early promise.

Oliver always kept his voice very level and measured in argument while Jane tended to shout.

'What the government is doing for the masses is *not* enough, Oliver,' she said, her voice rising. 'If you were not such a conceited young puppy you would come and see for yourself. What do the hallowed corridors of Eton teach you about the working classes? Don't you realize you are quite cut off from a whole section of society?'

'I have time to remedy it, Jane,' Oliver said, his tone low and agreeable. 'I will come with you this very vacation and see Soho for myself.'

George looked across at Caroline and winked.

'The response of a statesman, my dear boy. But really, Oliver, Jane is right. You *must* see for yourself; only I hope it will not make you as radical as it has her. I want a new Pitt or Melbourne in my family, not a Bentham or a Mill.'

'You need not fear that, father,' Oliver said smiling at his sister. 'I believe in the steady progress of society, not in violent radical change. It is solely due to the basic soundness of the English constitutional system, the rightness of our laws, that we did not succumb to the turmoil that swept through Europe in 1848 destroying so many of its institutions, toppling monarchs from their thrones.'

'How right you are,' George said approvingly. 'Although I can tell you that many of us were exceedingly worried about the conflagration spreading here. There *is* dissatisfaction among the masses, alas, no doubt of that, as the Chartist riots showed us. But they lack leaders, thank God, agitators to organize them and spread the seeds of revolt.'

'The people are too tired, ill and badly clothed and housed to rise up, father,' Jane said hotly. 'They could not riot even if they wished. They are underfed and can barely go from one day to the next . . .'

'Oh come, Jane it is not as bad as that,' Oliver protested.

'It *is* as bad as that!' Jane thumped her fork on the table. 'Every bit as bad as that.'

'Pray, dearest, have regard to your manners,' Agnes said in a small weak voice, passing her hand over her forehead in a characteristic gesture. 'And do lower your voice. I fear one of my "heads" might be beginning.'

'I'm sorry, Mama,' Jane murmured, but Caroline could see she was trembling. 'I do feel so passionately about this.'

'I'm sure you do, dear, and it does you credit,' her father said. 'But there is no need to throw the household in a furore because of it. Would you have us sell our lands and turn our house into an orphanage?'

'It would not be such a bad idea, Papa,' Jane looked at him boldly. 'After all, what has a large house like this with so few people . . .'

'Oh for heaven's *sake*, Jane!' Emily exclaimed, flicking her wrist in a little gesture of irritation. 'Be good enough to spare us your views at the lunch table. Those who wish to be enlightened may perhaps gather with you afterwards in the drawing-room to hear you expound them. I find it too tedious for words.'

Jane gaped at her sister, her mouth sagging open. Caroline had seldom seen her so taken aback, and tried to suppress a smile. Emily had become much more self-assured and sophisticated since she had been at Court. She had developed a kind of detachment, a remoteness from her family that seemed to emphasize her closeness to the Queen. Like James, Emily disliked having her composure or equanimity disturbed, and the thought of it threatening the stability of her universe was intolerable.

'You have no heart at all, Emily,' Jane said, making an effort to control herself. 'And you never had. You know people actually *starve* in great numbers in this country?'

Emily carefully put her knife and fork together and looked serenely at her sister. 'I refuse to be drawn into argument, Jane. I am sorry. Apart from my complete lack of sympathy with your anarchistic views, this commotion will bring on one of Mama's bad heads.'

The aunts, Ruth and Dorothy, who had been carefully listening to what threatened to become a family brawl, almost audibly breathed sighs of relief and resumed their conversation, while Agnes thankfully fanned herself with her handkerchief and asked Polly to pour her a fresh glass of water. George and John Tangent also looked thankful the storm had passed and resumed a discussion about new drainage proposals that threatened to bisect the Vestrey lands near the town.

Caroline was a meticulous housekeeper and saw to it that everywhere inside shone; the floors were waxed and polished, there were new covers on the chairs and some new drapes at the window and one or two rooms had been repapered, but in plain old-fashioned colours. But there was no new furniture. Papa drew the line at that; anyway what they had was mostly very old, well built, and very solid. Except out of vanity it did not by any stretch of the imagination need replacing. Aunt Ruth's transformation of the Park Street house was regarded by the conventional Vestreys of Chetwell as a bit of a joke.

Large bowls of daffodils stood in every room and there were little posies of spring flowers in the recesses and, now, on the gleaming dining-room table at luncheon.

Caroline's eye darted from the table to the servants, from the sideboard to the door that led to the kitchens, from the door back to the table again, making sure that all was as it should be, the right helpings by the right people, plenty of wine for Papa and Uncle John and also Aunt Ruth who liked one or two glasses, if not more. Aunt Dorothy was very chatty this lunchtime and her high voice was invariably to be heard whenever there was a lull. Aunt Ruth and Aunt Dorothy got on very well and were usually put next to each other, if there were not enough men and on this occasion there weren't. They liked to exchange gossip of all the things that had happened since they had last met, all the people they had seen or whose unusual and, hopefully, scandalous doings they knew about.

The subject now which came to Caroline, in waves from their end of the table, was the youngest daughter of Mr Nightingale of Embley House, Hampshire, who was an acquaintance of Aunt Ruth and also of Papa, through Mrs Nightingale's father William Smith. He had been a Member of the House of Commons and a near neighbour of the Vestreys for years in Park Street.

Mr Smith had a large family and Aunt Ruth had grown up along with them in the early years of the century. She was but two years younger than Fanny Smith who had married William Nightingale after her father had refused her permission to marry the Honourable James Sinclair, to whom she had given her heart, on the grounds that he had no money.

Aunt Ruth well remembered Fanny's bitterness, particularly since she was nearly thirty when the affair with Sinclair was brought to an end. But William Nightingale, although six years younger than Fanny, not only had money, but he had a lot of it. Besides, the Smiths had known him since he was a boy; he had been at school with Octavius, Fanny's younger brother. William was good looking and very clever, and Fanny was used to good company through her father's friends who had included men like Charles James Fox, Wilberforce and Sir Joshua Reynolds.

Even though the family still did not approve of her new choice – you could never please some people – Fanny and William had married and gone abroad. In fact they seemed to have become addicted to the continent and spent a good deal of time there. Both their daughters were born abroad.

Aunt Ruth rather lost touch with Fanny in these early years of her marriage. Now she saw her from time to time when she came to London, and had kept in touch with her sister Julia who had never married, a fact attributed by Aunt Ruth to her advanced views which often made her think of Jane. In her opinion men really could not abide clever women with strong political ideas, no matter how pretty they were, and Julia Smith, like all the Smiths, had been very good looking. Jane was a beauty, no mistake about that, but with her absurd socialist views, her hot-headed intolerance, what chance had she of finding a good stable man – someone, say, like Rawdon Foxton?

Caroline kept hearing snibbets of the conversation as the two women, heads together, nattered on and on, so absorbed that their food grew cold on their plates. Caroline found herself straining to hear and finally, in another lull – that is when everyone else *except* Aunts Dorothy and Ruth had stopped talking – said: '*What* is this about Florence Nightingale, Aunt Ruth?'

'Oh, you haven't heard? I thought Emily would have told you,' Aunt Ruth said eagerly, putting down her knife and fork yet again. 'Emily told me that Florence Nightingale, who has always been considered *most* peculiar, is going to take a job as the superintendent of a hospital!'

'It is quite true,' Emily said with that studied detachment she had cultivated since she became intimate with the highest in the land, 'and I do not think I am gossiping Papa, as everyone knows it.'

Her father smiled and inclined his head good humouredly. Really, he was so indulgent about everything these days, even the imprudence of his second daughter. Hilary had done him such a lot of good. He thought back fondly to their leavetaking the Wednesday before when he was just on the point of travelling to Chetwell for the vacation. An intimate little luncheon had been followed by two hours of delightful love making. It had been hard to wrench himself away. He had felt dejected when leaving her and told her how he wished she could have come to Chetwell, pointing out that in the old days, as Aunt Ruth's friend she could have, but now it would not be proper. He thought her silence enigmatic, her smile wistful. But she said nothing.

'Lady Canning is on the committee of the Institution for the Care of Sick Women in Distressed Circumstances. It is she who told me during our last waiting, that she had interviewed Miss Nightingale for the post. Mrs Herbert recommended her, as she and her husband are intimate friends of Miss Nightingale.'

'And is she going to accept?' George asked in some dismay. 'I have never heard anything like it, though even I have heard of Florence Nightingale's eccentricities. They are the talk of London.'

To Caroline, Florence Nightingale was only a name. She had never met any of the family or if she had she couldn't remember. However the very idea of a lady of quality becoming a nurse was extraordinary.

'How is Miss Nightingale eccentric, Papa?'

'Well,' George looked uncomfortable, aware that now he was gossiping. 'It is known that she is, what shall we say?, not like other young women. She is very intellectual, very forthright, very beautiful too. I know that she has been admired by a number of men and I believe that Mr Monkton Milnes was very taken by her, as were many other extremely eligible young men. But she refused them all. It is said she does not wish to marry which you may think unusual

259

enough. She has been pestering her family for years to let her nurse. I think she even did some training in Germany. *Most* singular when you consider the reputation of nurses for immorality. I have only met her briefly on occasions when the family stay in London, usually in Old Burlington Street. Mrs Nightingale likes to entertain and your aunt and I are sometimes invited. Jane, too, I think on the last occasion?'

'Yes, I met Miss Nightingale,' Jane said with indifference. 'I thought her very stuck up and bossy. If you say she does not like men I don't think she likes women either, or maybe she did not think I was intellectual enough for her.'

Miss Nightingale began to intrigue Caroline. Suddenly someone she had never heard of became important. A young woman of fortune and good birth who wanted to *nurse*, an intellectual who had turned down any number of eligible men, who was going to superintend a hospital? It seemed incredible.

'What age is Miss Nightingale, Jane?'

'Oh, she is quite old,' Jane said vaguely. 'Even older than you!'

Jane meant the effect to be good humoured but as it was said it sounded rude. Caroline blushed and averted her eyes from her sister. Jane was implying that she was an old maid who did nothing, not even good works. There was a little silence while everyone registered their disapproval of Jane, then Aunt Ruth said coolly:

'Florence is about thirty-two or three. She has an older sister, Parthenope, who is even more of a burden to her family than she is. She will not let Florence out of her sight and becomes hysterical if there is talk of her marrying or going away. She was even treated for a time by Sir James Clark. I must say those girls have been a trial to poor Fanny, but I sometimes think Fanny has brought it on herself. She is a very possessive mother; she would never let Florence leave the nest or do a thing for herself.'

There was another little silence which this time seemed directed at Caroline. Agnes, who had been half listening to Dalton sitting next to her, dropped her fork with a clatter and George leaned forward anxiously and asked if she were all right. Agnes passed a hand across her brow.

'Just a little tired, dear. This is my first day having luncheon with you all for a long time. It is a big treat, but an ordeal for me.'

George got up and came over to his wife, putting a hand on her shoulder and kissing her cheek. 'Do let me know if you wish to retire, my dear. I will take you up myself.'

Agnes clasped his hand and kissed it, an expression of marital harmony that few remembered seeing for years. Aunt Ruth smiled approvingly. Everything was being sorted out very nicely as far as George and Agnes were concerned.

'Parthenope sounds as though she could do with Mrs Chetwynd,' Jane said, sitting back in her chair and staring at her mother.

'*Who* is Mrs Chetwynd, dear?' Agnes said, vaguely aware that Jane's remark had been meant for her. She smiled pleadingly at George. He really was very loving and considerate these days. He had bought her a beautiful emerald brooch from Aspreys for Easter. He was like an especially dear and tender brother. Thank goodness he had resigned himself, or seemed to, to a life of chastity. It was far more satisfactory, more dignified too for parents of grown-up children. She thought guiltily of little Rebecca whom she didn't like very much at all. However Caroline adored her, so that made up for it. Jane was saying? She looked enquiringly at Jane after George had given her an answering smile.

'She is a friend of Miss Martineau, a healer, Mama. Miss Martineau was cured of a very debilitating illness by mesmerism and Mrs Chetwynd is a mesmerist.'

Agnes coloured and put a hand to her hot cheeks. Jane of course was getting at her again. She knew it.

'But what is that to do with the elder Miss Nightingale? I fail, I confess, to see . . .' She looked again for help to her husband, the poor little woman with her tremulous smile. George frowned. He thought Jane's remark was premature; he had intended to spend the whole of Easter leading up to it.

'Mesmerism is particularly suited to sorts of illnesses occasioned by . . .' Jane faltered, aware of her father's expression. 'Well, any illnesses of *any* description. I wondered if you would like to see her, Mama? She has a wonderful reputation.'

Agnes swayed in her chair and Dalton caught her elbow. She straightened herself, appeared to make a big effort, her breath coming quickly.

'If you are thinking of *me*, Jane dear.' she managed to say, 'you must know that I have seen the most eminent men that your father can find. Specialists have come from London and pronounced my case baffling. It is out of the question to see someone *unqualified*. Is it not, George?'

Appealed to for help George did not know what to say, and it was left to Caroline again to come to the rescue. Mama's help. 'Miss Martineau is a very well-known case, Mama. Much has been written about it including a pamphlet, I believe, by her brother-in-law who was himself a medical practitioner.'

'The Prince is very interested in mesmerism,' Emily observed. She seemed only to intervene in a conversation when she could mention the Royal Family. 'I believe he asked for a demonstration.'

'*Really?*' Agnes began to resume her normal colour and looked interested, even impressed. She was as much infatuated with the Royal Family as her daughter. There was not one single thing she could think of that they did wrong except, perhaps, that the poor Queen had too many children and that meant the Prince, despite his look of almost puritanical rectitude, must be just like George. Agnes did not like to think of the Queen and the Prince indulging in those sorts of antics at all – she shut her eyes at the very thought. What a lot she and the dear Queen would have to say if they could ever get together for an intimate gossip. Of course it was out of the question. One simply never discussed that kind of thing. Agnes regretted it though. She would also like to have told Her Majesty how she coped with George; what a wonderful relationship they had now developed. Maybe the Queen could do the same with Albert.

'Oh, it is quite medically acceptable, my love,' George said, clearing his throat. 'But, you know, I would wish on you nothing that you do not desire. It is only my hope that one day you will be well again as you used to be, and up and about.'

George looked lovingly at his wife who promptly mis-interpreted his gaze. George, of course, was thinking of *that* again. Up and about meant, to her, down and preg-nant. Well, he needn't. Agnes had not the slightest inten-tion of being up and about again as long as George had that look in his eye. She settled back comfortably in her chair.

'I don't think I care to discuss this further. Could we close the conversation? My head is beginning to throb.' Agnes put a hand on her brow, and shut her eyes.

Everyone resumed their meal, but Caroline had lost her appetite. Mama had not the slightest intention of ever being well again.

CHAPTER SIXTEEN

There was no doubt that Jane was a problem. She irritated her sisters and worried her parents and her Great Aunt Ruth, who felt some responsibility for her as it was primarily owing to her readiness to have Jane practically living at the Park Street house that had brought about the trouble in the first place. Also that Miss Martineau continued to correspond regularly with Jane, although their relationship had cooled a little after Miss Martineau wrote a somewhat critical review of Miss Brontë's new novel *Villette* in the *Daily News* in February. The thing Miss Martineau had objected to was the fact that the heroine, Lucy Snowe, had allowed herself to fall in love with not only one man but *two*. After praising the author's originality Miss Martineau opined that, in real life, women did not fall in love with two men, better not even with one, for 'There are substantial, heartfelt interests for women of all ages, and under ordinary circumstances, quite apart from love . . .'

For the Vestrey girls Miss Brontë's novels and heroines remained profoundly sympathetic and *Shirley* and *Villette* had, if anything, enhanced the deep impression made on them in their adolescence by *Jane Eyre*. Caroline, especially, identified with Charlotte Brontë's heroines, lonely unfulfilled women, a prey to their passions and vague yearnings. Jane was more interested in Miss Brontë's actual life, the circumstances of which Miss Martineau had graphically relayed to her in all its grim detail; the lonely parsonage on the moor and Miss Brontë living in isolation with her eccentric old father. Miss Brontë to Jane was a heroic figure; she had carved a life for herself that made her stand out above the rest of womankind. Although Miss Martineau assured Jane that Charlotte Brontë was a tiny, rather insignificant looking woman, she nevertheless had for her a solitary magnificence that Jane idealized and would have emulated if she could; a defiance against the tragedies and injustices of life.

Emily admired Miss Brontë's novels because they were considered scandalous, even titillating; they dwelt upon thwarted hopeless love, self sacrifice and, above all, passion. Besides, all the Queen's ladies read them secretly, and, some suspected, the Queen herself.

Shortly after Easter Jane made the bold decision to go to Soho by herself, just as Isabella Goodey did. George came down one morning and found Jane in hectic argument with Great Aunt Ruth who was hardly ever to be seen downstairs so early. Matthew was on the doorstep looking unhappy and confused and Aunt Ruth was barring the way, arms akimbo between Jane and the door. George could not recall ever seeing Ruth look so angry. In fact the disturbance in the hall had caused him to hurry with his dressing and had sent him running downstairs.

'And *if* this goes on, young lady,' Aunt Ruth was saying, wagging her finger at Jane, 'I shall not allow you to stay here. I shall insist that your father sends you home. I cannot continue to take the responsibility...'

'But Aunt, I am twenty years old!' Jane replied hotly trying to edge her way forwards. 'Isabella Goodey has been taking the walk by herself for years. I...'

'I care not *what* Miss Goodey does or may not do,' Aunt Ruth said, 'fond as I am of her, she is no responsibility of mine. Isabella is thirty-five years of age and perfectly able to make her own decisions, even though she remains, nominally I suppose, in the care of her father. When your father is not here I am responsible for you, Jane Vestrey, and I will not have you walking unaccompanied through the streets of London as long as I have breath in my body. Now either you go with Matthew or you stay at home and —' Aunt Ruth, hearing footsteps on the stairs, turned to face her nephew. 'George, I shall ask you to send Jane back to Chetwell immediately.'

'Yes of course, Aunt. I side with you completely.'

' 'Twas Matthew alerted me to the fact that Jane had dismissed the coach this morning. My maid got me out of bed.'

Matthew stood neither inside nor out and shamefacedly ran the brim of his hat through his hands, round and round, shuffling his feet.

'Pardon my lord, but I felt I could not . . .'

'You did perfectly right, Matthew,' George said, going up to him and putting a hand on his shoulder. 'Think no more of it. Now Jane, do you go as before or do you stay?'

Jane flung her head in the air and, almost pushing past the discomforted coachman, made her way to the coach which stood outside in the road and climbed into it by herself.

George Vestrey dearly loved his wilful daughter. He put off a morning engagement to discuss her with Aunt Ruth; he would liked to have done the same with Hilary, but he had a meeting with Lord Aberdeen and Lord Clarendon that afternoon. The situation regarding Russia and Turkey was worsening and there was the possibility he would have to go to Vienna. If so he was going to try and take Hilary with him, travelling separately of course.

The very idea was exhilarating, but first came his duties as a father. Sitting talking to Aunt Ruth in the morning-room he recalled the occasion just a year ago when his fate with Hilary had been decided. They even sat in the same chairs and at the same small table.

'Jane should be married,' Aunt Ruth said. 'She is dissatisfied. She has a passionate nature and this comes out in her work. She should be applying it to husband and children. Jane, more than any of your eldest girls, should be married. She needs to be disciplined, to be protected by a strong man. I am full of foreboding for her.'

'That is what Hilary says.' George peered at Aunt Ruth over the rim of his cup, saw her stiffening. From the day of the conversation in this room a year ago until now Hilary had never intruded except as a name. After she had quietly left Park Street Emily had asked what had happened to her, and had been told that she had been left some money and had bought herself a small house. Both girls were surprised and sorry she had not said good-bye but Aunt Ruth, in the circumstances, thought it hypocritical and wrong to confront the girls with their father's putative mistress quite so flagrantly.

Aunt Ruth returned George's gaze and said: 'What I don't know I don't know.'

'But you *do* know, you suggested it.'

'I told you to be discreet and not give me the details.'

'I have been very discreet; we have never discussed it since I told you she was agreeable. All the same she is part of my life, an important part.'

'I told you not to get involved, George.' Aunt Ruth allowed her stern expression to relax a little. 'Still, I am glad you are happy. I knew you were. It shows.'

'She is perfect,' George whispered. 'Discreet, tactful, charming. We are very happy.'

'I said you would be a fool to fall in love.'

'Then I am a fool. How can I help loving her? She gives me everything and asks nothing. She is my confidante, friend and . . . mistress.'

Aunt Ruth sighed and, rising, walked to the window. It was as though she remembered the time a year ago too and threw open the french windows to let in the sun.

'I should have known. I felt you were suited. She is, of course, too gently bred a woman for me to expect you would treat her like a whore. I was foolish, George.'

George got up and put an arm round her shoulders, squeezing her in a very un-Vestrey-like display of affection.

'You were not. You were right. You know I will never leave Agnes or neglect her or the children. It is unthinkable. Hilary enhances my life, gives me peace and happiness. Is it wrong that I should love her in return? Nothing will change except in me. In fact I think I love Agnes better than before. She doesn't irritate me so much . . .'

'I noticed it at Easter. You were very tender. Everyone commented on it.'

'Well, there you are. She is happy and I am happy. Hilary will never ask any more of me. She is perfect. I am very lucky.'

'Perhaps you are. Then I *am* glad,' Aunt Ruth said at last and turning, gave him one of her rare lovely smiles which showed what a beauty she must have been when young. 'I missed much in my life by knowing nothing of love, personally I mean. You know why I didn't marry, but at times I have regretted it. Yet you and your family have given me such happiness that I have never missed children of my own, but passion – yes, sometimes I have missed that, not to *know* what it is like. That is why I am anxious about Jane. I see too much of myself in Jane. I was a beauty too, you know . . .'

'I know,' George said, 'and you *still* are.'

'Oh come, flatterer.' Aunt Ruth mockingly pretended to tap his cheek. 'No, I was much sought after, even after Archie died. I was perhaps foolish to cling to his memory. But Jane clings to something else. She frightens me. I hope she does not give us the trouble Miss Nightingale is causing her poor parents. She has accepted the position at the Institution, and I hear her mother and sister are prostrate. Her father sided with her and settled upon her an allowance of her own to give her independence. I cannot imagine what has got into the man. If we are not careful we shall have another Florence Nightingale on our hands. No thank you.'

'But Jane is much younger.'

'It is the same sort of thing. A wilfulness. George you must make a point of speaking to her firmly and insist that she does the season. There must be any number of eligible young men about. Even that Pagan fellow would be better than . . .'

'Pagan! ' George cried, 'do you mean the artist?'

'He is doing well. He has talent. He is a nice young man.'

'I will *not* have my daughter marrying a penniless artist,' George said firmly. 'Even if he were a rich one I would not consider it. We know nothing about his family and, besides, what I saw I didn't very much care for. Pagan is not my idea of a son-in-law. I will talk to Jane and, dear Aunt Ruth, would you, for me, visit Hilary? She is very lonely. She feels she cannot go about in society.'

Aunt Ruth pursed her lips and appeared to consider the question.

'I don't think I can visit her, George. I should be appearing to condone it and, if Agnes should ever find out, I would never forgive myself. As it is now, I know nothing. No. I think I am best kept well out of it. It is just between the two of you. It is not a family matter, and I *am* family.'

'Perhaps you're right,' George said, dismissing it from his mind.

Great Aunt Ruth was very wise.

That summer of 1853 saw a great deal of complex diplomatic activity to try and prevent hostilities breaking out between Russia and Turkey. Much of it, for those concerned and far from the possible theatre of war, was pleasant. The Austrians had been selected as mediators in preference to the French or the British who had treaty obligations with Turkey, and thus Vienna became the centre of intrigue and counter-intrigue to try and avert war.

In many ways it was almost too late. Russia was bent on expansion and Turkey, the Sublime Porte, increasingly unable to defend its possessions. No-one wanted to see a Russian base on the Mediterranean Sea. In July Russia did its best to provoke hostilities by occupying the Danubian principalities of Moldavia and Wallachia, ostensibly to guarantee the freedom of worship of the minority of Greek Orthodox Christians living there. Towards the end of July the Allied powers, acting in concert, sent a very stiff Note to Russia and Turkey. As this had been drafted in Paris in a pro-Russian spirit, and secretly submitted to the Czar Nicholas, who had amended it before it ostensibly came from the four Allied powers, it was not surprising that the Russians accepted the note; nor should it have surprised anyone that the Turks rejected it.

In August the Queen piously expressed the hope in her speech closing the Parliament session that war would be averted.

Lord Aberdeen wanted to avert war at all costs; but he was increasingly in a minority. The belligerent Palmerston was anti-Russian, but Aberdeen distrusted the Turks. The movement towards war was growing. The Cabinet was split, with Clarendon and Lord John Russell joining the pro-war faction.

George Vestrey's considerable diplomatic skills came into their own in the negotiations that preceded the outbreak of the war that was, in actual fact, to begin the following March. All the tact and skill that he had shown in reconciling warring factions on the Exhibition Committee was but a prelude to what went on in Austria in the summer of 1853. The momentous debates – which, at the time, threatened to divide families and break old friendships – about the position of the fixed elms, the colour schemes, whether to permit alcohol to be consumed on the premises or not, how much to charge, which places should go to whom, were but a warming up, albeit a useful one, to the pros and cons of the various parties concerned on the Eastern Question.

The young Austrian Emperor, Franz Josef, was anxious to placate the Russians who had helped him defeat Kossuth, soon after his accession in 1848. On the other hand the new Emperor of the French, the recently self-proclaimed Napoleon III, and a nephew of the Great Napoleon, was determined to pose as the champion of liberal Europe against Russian tyranny. He was anxious to defend his uncle's humiliation in 1812 by subduing the autocratic Nicholas I who even declined to treat him as an equal.

That summer Lord Vestrey travelled from London to Vienna, Paris and back again taking orders from Lord Clarendon and submitting them to the British Ambassadors in Paris and Vienna. He was even empowered to deal directly with the Austrian Foreign Secretary, Count Buol, and tried to simplify the devious relations between the French and the Austrians. Both of them were juggling for positions, while Aberdeen was vainly trying to keep England in the role of honest broker, despite having agreed to send the British fleet to the Aegean and, much against his will, giving the Grand Elchi, Lord Stratford de Redcliffe, authority to summon it to Constantinople if necessary. By potentially breaking the Straits Convention of 1841, which closed the Dardanelles to foreign warships, this could be interpreted as an act of war, if it occurred, which Aberdeen was anxious to avoid. He considered that if Britain breached the Dardanelles it would make her appear the aggressor and give Russia a just cause for war.

If George Vestrey found his new role exhilarating it was no more so than his role as a lover, which also necessitated a good deal of clandestine manoeuvring such as he was experiencing in the diplomatic field. The only one who had any idea of his lordship's complicated emotional life was his secretary, Hugh Benson, who was not only a model of discretion and tact but a consummate organizer as well. He was able to make arrangements for Mrs Ashburne's arrival in Vienna or Paris to coincide with that of Lord Vestrey, in such a way that no-one other than his lordship knew of it.

For the first time Hilary felt she was living with her lover, as a person in love wants to live. They slept together, breakfasted together and, when George was not needed for the many counsels that were constantly taking place, he took her about, sightseeing in one of the most beautiful cities in the world.

The *Innerestadt*, the old city of Vienna, was full of crooked and narrow streets, houses which huddled together and seemed to lean over until they almost touched. Unlike the slums of London, however, old Vienna kept its medieval charm with its Elizabethan buildings, curious little courtyards and uneven cobbled streets. George and Hilary would sometimes leave their cab to wander together in this enchanting world where everything was old and somehow venerable and the small shops gave off enticing odours of newly baked bread, pastries and roasting meat. But already the houses were coming down and plans were being made to lay out fine avenues and gardens, and build imposing new dwellings in keeping with the capital of the Austro-Hungarian Empire.

Beyond the *Innerestadt* were the suburbs, surrounded by a high wall pierced with thirteen gates, and here more architectural improvements were under way. There were ambitious plans to raise the bed of the river, as Vienna had a very high death rate owing, some thought, to an indifferent supply of water. The new source would furnish an ample and excellent supply from the neighbouring Alpine

271

streams. The streets in the suburb, all of them converging on the centre of the old city, were broad and straight with fine tall buildings, made of brick, housing families in a system of apartments, each family to a different floor.

Vienna was full of palaces, churches and magnificent public buildings. They saw the ancient church of St Stephen, one of whose four steeples, a masterpiece of Gothic architecture, was, except for Strasbourg, the loftiest in Europe. The quiet interior was enriched with many beautiful altars, statues and monuments. The church of St Peter, modelled on St Peter's in Rome, was adorned with fine frescoes and oil paintings, and the elegant church of the Augustines contained a masterpiece of the artist Canova, the famous mausoleum of the Archduchess Christina, built at a cost of 420,000 ducats.

They saw the Imperial palace, the Burg and, through George's diplomatic connections, visited the jewel office which contained one of the most valuable collections of curiosities in Europe. There were also priceless works of art, collections of medals and an extensive museum of natural history. Next to the Burg was the impressive Imperial library, with a gallery some two hundred and fifty feet long and nearly half a million volumes and rare manuscripts.

They saw the Imperial chancery, the famous Imperial riding school, the splendid palace of the Archduke Charles, the mint, the university, the Palace of the Archbishop, the Imperial arsenal, containing one of the largest and finest collections of arms and armour in Europe, the bank and the many palaces of the nobility each splendid and containing fabulous works of art. Most of these places they merely passed in their cab, the driver slowing down before whisking them on to the next. But they visited the Ambras museum with its pictures by Van Dyke, Veronese and Titian, and saw inside the university founded by Duke Rudolph IV in 1365 and remodelled by Maria Theresa, which had become one of the finest medical schools in Germany.

Then the cab took them across the beautiful Asspern Bridge over the Danube Canal, and the elegant Schwarzenberg which passed over the dirty little river Wien from which Vienna got its name. This journey took them to the Schönbrunn, the country residence of the Emperor, Franz Josef, and the immense park in the suburb of Leopoldstadt called the Prater which was traversed by six noble avenues of chestnut trees. The Prater resembled Hyde Park at the height of the season, for all the fashionable *monde* came there to see and be seen, gorgeously gowned, magnificently bonneted women in their light carriages and handsome uniformed men prancing about on their richly caparisoned horses. Nearby, the Würstel Prater catered more for the lower orders who thronged there, especially on Sundays and holidays, to be diverted by the Russian swings, roundabouts and jugglers and the liquor shops and pastryshops which abounded.

Vienna in its long history – it was part of Charlemagne's Empire – had been pillaged by the Goths and Huns, attacked by the Turks and occupied, in 1808 and 1809, by the French. In 1848 the revolutionary party had occupied it for a short time and it was heavily bombarded. But now with the new young Emperor firmly in command and Europe, at least, at peace, it was in its heyday, a city of enchantment and pleasure, a seat of learning and culture, the capital of the great ancient Austro-Hungarian Empire. Railways were radiating from Vienna in all directions, an ambitious new opera house was planned. It was a city bursting with life and prosperity, something never to be forgotten by George and Hilary in the many delicious, stolen hours they had to explore its delights.

Vienna was large enough to encompass the lovers, but they still had to be discreet, dining in small restaurants where the diplomatic corps was unlikely to foregather. They dared not wander through the broad streets and parks, but rode in cabs which seemed somehow to add to the excitement, to enhance their passion.

When George was busy Hilary, beautifully dressed and accompanied by her maid, visited the shops and boutiques which proliferated in prosperous Vienna offering all that that industrious city made in silk, velvet, gold and silver, leather, porcelain and fine delicate lace. Vienna was famous not only for its fashionable clothes, designs and accessories but also for its manufacture of precious jewels, musical instruments, meerschaum pipes, watches, cutlery, silver plate, carriages, straw hats, gloves, watches and, of course, chocolates, cakes and sweetmeats of every description.

Hilary would sit at one of the many pavement cafes sipping hot chocolate and eating the sumptuous strudels and tortes piled high with cream and fruit, made so expertly by the sweet-toothed Viennese. She delighted in buying little gifts for her lover and each evening would present him with some small token of her affection; a meerschaum pipe, some onyx cufflinks, or silk handkerchiefs worked with his initials.

Merely to see Hilary so relaxed and pretty was enough to revive George, and he would change eagerly into evening dress and go to her room to sip champagne while they discussed the programme for the evening. Maybe she had not quite finished her toilette and he would embrace and caress her as she dressed, fastening her stays and the back of her gown, kissing the nape of her long beautiful neck, the top of her full white bosom.

For Hilary the whole thing was enchantment, a totally new world and way of life that she had scarcely ever been able to imagine, let alone hope to experience. Not only was visiting Vienna intensely exciting, but being near to her lover, part of his life, his chief means of relaxation and enjoyment, was even more precious. It made her more indispensable to him than ever, cemented their bond, made them closer, deepened their understanding and broadened their love beyond the close confines of the house in St John's Wood.

It was wonderful, she thought, to wake up by the side of the man she loved and share all those morning activities with him which were usually undertaken by each party separately. There was no hurried exit from the bed at dawn or late at night, no furtive peering round the door when he came and went to be sure that he was unobserved. Even though they had to be careful it was far freer, far more open than living in London. Besides, it was so exciting to receive a message from Benson, or perhaps a hasty personal visit from him to say that Mrs Ashburne should take such and such a train from Victoria Station either to Paris or Vienna, once even to Milan. The tickets were obtained, the hotel, coinciding with the one to be occupied by Lord Vestrey, booked and all arrangements made. All she had to do was pack her bags and, accompanied by her maid, do as she was told.

Then when she wasn't travelling or waiting for delicious messages of secret assignations she was shopping and having new gowns and hats made. Gradually as her credit-worthiness became established she grew bold enough to ask the dressmaker or milliner to visit *her*, as all the grand ladies did. With the naïveté of those unused to money, and as a tribute to her middle-class origins, she always paid her bills promptly. This way those who served her knew she was not from the upper classes.

Even though she and George rarely attended functions together they often did separately, Mrs Ashburne being squired by the obsequious Benson, so that a dance or two with Lord Vestrey would not appear, to any casual observer, to be untoward. In this their confidence was not altogether well founded, the English upper classes being incurably curious.

Hilary flourished in this new world of international glamour, so alien to anything she had ever known. Hitherto she had never left England. Now, in that summer and autumn of 1853, she was hardly ever there. It seemed to bring out a latent exhibitionism in her, a desire to be seen and admired. It was such a contrast to the dowdy, servile respectability of the poverty stricken life she had lived as a widow seeking employment. She took to her new courtesan-type role with zest; even her looks changed and became more startling, more flamboyant – infinitely more alluring. Her noble lover, the cause as well as the means of this transformation, was dazzled.

She was so attractive that George eventually wanted everyone to see them together. He wished to show her off, he was so proud of her. With what ease she carried herself, what dignity, rivalling even that of the inveterate schemer the celebrated Madame de Lieven, wife of the Russian Ambassador to Vienna, who intrigued with all the powers in turn. Though she had once been the mistress of Lord Palmerston during her days in London, she was on intimate terms with Lord Aberdeen and sent him copies of all her husband's correspondence.

In fact Madame de Lieven, observing them at a ball given by the Emperor, demanded to be introduced to the lovely young woman with whom George Vestrey danced with such regularity. Observing the cautious look in his eye as he advanced with Hilary, she promised that she would be *very* discreet.

It was only natural that not only the Princesse de Lieven noticed the beautiful young woman so frequently in the arms of Lord Vestrey. The men noticed her particularly and the women observed how well George Vestrey looked, years younger in fact. Then they winked and hid a smile behind their fans; but many envied Hilary and ached to know who she was. Few believed she was really with Mr Benson, that amiable nonentity, but when they sought to find out more, or perhaps to invite her to dinner or a soirée, she was not to be found. Like Cinderella she had disappeared from the ball.

CHAPTER SEVENTEEN

It was hot in Soho, such a contrast to the cold winter but the effects were just as bad, even worse. There was as much disease, even more, typhoid taking the place of influenza. The Mission was badly ventilated and stuffy and the door to the street stood open all day to try and introduce a little welcome air.

Jane stayed later at the Mission because the nights were longer. She looked at her watch and saw it was five. She turned to her cousin Polly who, since her visit, frequently came up to London to help, though Jane suspected the initial reason was to try and see more of James.

In this she was disappointed. Apart from dining once a week at Park Street, James appeared totally indifferent to his cousin and never attempted to take her out alone, or even in the company of others. Jane knew that James kept company with a fast set, and her heart ached for Polly whom she thought would do so well for James; she would quieten him down. Jane knew quite well that he went to brothels. She had once taxed him after seeing him coming out of one in Windmill Street. James didn't attempt to deny it. Jane was disgusted. She felt that prostitution demeaned both sexes, those who needed it and those who provided it. For weeks afterwards she didn't speak to her brother; but no-one took any notice. They were quite used to Jane's moods and she couldn't tell anyone the reason for this one.

Rawdon Foxton was also a frequent visitor to Park Street. He always seemed to be there when Emily had a night off from waiting. Even Jane was beginning to notice how often he came. She began seriously to think of him as a prospective brother-in-law, a prospect that didn't dismay her as much as it might have done. Rawdon had changed; he didn't seem quite so rigid and formal. The uncertainty about his father's health appeared to have made him realize how fragile life was. From her experiences in Soho she knew how misfortune changed people, not always for the better. But Rawdon had lost that rather aggressive superiority that, although it obviously attracted her sisters, always put Jane on edge. He seemed less certain about life and this new vulnerability made him more likeable in her eyes.

One day she had remarked on his frequent appearances to Emily who immediately bristled.

'So? Is that so very terrible? We have known him all our lives, you know.'

'Oh, is that all it is?' Jane pretended unconcern, and got on with the paper she was writing on the extent of malnutrition among immigrants in Soho.

Emily was writing letters to her many correspondents in all parts of the world. After nearly two years in waiting, Emily considered herself a person of some significance, and would recite the names of some of the people with whom she corresponded, not so much to elicit admiration as to impart matters of fact. There were German princesses, relations of the Queen, Spanish duchesses, French countesses and members of the Austrian, Italian and Russian nobility. They had all been to stay at some time or other at Windsor, Osborne or Balmoral, recently enlarged and rebuilt in a turreted, battlement-style to a design of the Prince.

The two sisters paused to stare at each other across the writing desks on their laps.

'I don't see what you're hinting at, Jane.' Emily carefully blotted her crested notepaper. She always made a habit of using stationery with one of the Royal addresses on it.

'I thought you liked him. After the row with Caroline I thought you were in *love* with him.'

'Oh, I shall have Rawdon Foxton one day,' Emily said complacently. 'When I am ready. And I am nearly ready. But the Queen would be unhappy if I left before completing two full years of service. It might reflect on future members of our family if I should displease her. We Vestreys have always had a tradition of loyalty to the Crown. Rawdon is just panting to marry; but he will have to wait.'

'Has he spoken at last?' Jane enquired in astonishment, wondering that Emily could keep such a momentous happening to herself.

'In a way. He keeps on paying me extraordinary compliments and, as you know, dances with me all the time. I think he does not speak for fear of a rebuff. He is waiting for a sign from me, that is all. I am certain of it. He knows how I feel about service to Her Majesty. He is content to wait.'

'I thought Rawdon liked Caroline,' Jane said quietly. 'He goes to Chetwell too, you know. Quite often.'

'Oh, I know. He feels it is his duty. He takes Jenny and Harriet with him usually. He tells me all about it.'

But Jane doubted if this were true. She noticed the little flush on Emily's face and wondered if it was irritation or embarrassment. Somehow Emily didn't behave like a woman really in love. Jane turned back to her work and consulted a paper of government statistics her father had obtained for her; but she kept one eye on her sister who, she noticed, seemed to have lost her interest in writing and spent a lot of time gazing out of the window.

Being in waiting had made a difference to Emily. She was now twenty-one and seemed at her peak – she was amusing, witty and very beautiful. She knew everyone and was so well informed. She dined with this head of state or that, sat next to eminent men in all walks of life. She was now completely *au courant* on the Eastern Question and shared the Queen's dread of war, though also her dislike of the Russians.

Compared to Emily, with her verve, charm and accomplishment Caroline appeared, even in the eyes of one who loved her like Jane, more and more like a simple country cousin. And since she maintained her distance towards Rawdon, Jane could not help wondering if he did feel affection for her. He was certainly very attentive to Emily. But then, she could never tell with either of her sisters.

Considering their disparate lives Jane and Emily got on quite well. Emily's new-found detachment, her knowledge of many different kinds of lives, helped considerably. She appeared to think that her younger sister had the right to lead what sort of life she wished, within reason, however peculiar some might consider it. She had even mentioned it to the Queen who was full of approval for Jane's philanthropy, and continually asked Emily to invite her to stay at Osborne or Windsor. She would so like to question her about the distress of the poor, and the immorality among women of the lower classes, matters which concerned the Queen and the Prince deeply.

Jane continued to think about her sisters after she had abandoned her academic exercise and gone to the Mission for the rest of the day. At four she consulted the pearl fob watch at her waist, a present from Aunt Ruth. She just had time to go and see the Ticehursts before going home. She had hardly seen them at all lately. Edward Ticehurst was much better, thanks to Dalton who had interested Sir Smithers in his plight. Doctors had been consulted and a new diagnosis made. All Edward Ticehurst needed, they said, was plenty of nourishing food and rest, preferably a change of air. Twice he had gone to Kent to stay with the Tangents at Chetwell Rectory. With the prospect of a recovery Dalton was trying to get him legal work in Folkestone or Hythe where he and his family would benefit from the proximity to the sea.

'I'll just pop in and see the Ticehursts,' Jane said, 'then I shall come back and collect you. Is that all right?'

'Perfectly,' Polly said rubbing her eyes. It was so hot and she was tired. She longed to get home and take a bath, change her clothes, make herself as pretty as possible for James. She never gave up trying.

'You know that the Ticehursts are going to move?' Polly was doing some accounts and didn't even look up to see the effect on Jane.

'No. Where to?'

'Dalton is getting Mr Ticehurst legal work in Hythe. He is trying to get your father to let them have an old cottage on the estate.'

'I think someone might have told me,' Jane said frostily. 'I, after all, introduced the Ticehursts in the first place.'

'Don't be angry on Dalton's account,' Polly pleaded. 'You know how it is with him, but should you mind?' Polly continued her addition.

'Mind? Mind *what*?'

'Dalton is interested in Maggie Ticehurst. Should you mind?'

Jane sat down abruptly.

'You mean he is *romantically* interested in Maggie?'

Polly looked up and smiled, her expression mild. 'Yes. He wants to marry her.'

Despite the heat and the fact that moments before she had been perspiring, Jane had gone white. 'But surely it is out of the question. Maggie is . . .'

Polly drew a line under the accounts, and put down her pen. She had such a good brain and a neat hand that Isabella Goodey liked to leave the week's accounts to her.

'Yes?' Polly looked up as though to see if Jane had something interesting to say.

Jane faltered under Polly's cool gaze. 'Well, she is . . . hardly for Dalton I would have thought.'

'You mean because she is a kitchen maid?'

'Yes, if you like. I mean I wouldn't have thought she would make him the kind of wife he would . . . well frankly, Polly, Dalton has no fortune. Your mother and father are anxious for him to make a good match.'

'*Mother* is anxious, not father. He wants Dalton to be happy.'

'Does anyone else know about this?'

'Outside the family? Only you. I only knew last week because Maggie came to stay with us, and her mother and father. Dalton told us then.'

'Oh my goodness. What did Aunt Dorothy say?'

'It wasn't very pleasant.' Polly frowned at the recollection. 'Luckily Maggie and her family had just gone. There was a terrible storm with Mama and she retired to bed, rather like Aunt Agnes, with a bad head. But Papa took it very well. He says he *likes* Maggie and thinks she will suit Dalton.'

'But . . .'

'She was only a kitchen maid, after all, because she could not get work and had to have somewhere to live. Before that she was a milliner. I mean she speaks nicely and Dalton says that she is quite well educated, likes to read. I should have thought you would have been pleased, Jane. After all, it *is* in line, is it not, with what you profess about people being equal?'

Jane stared at her cousin knowing that Polly was challenging her. Somehow the thought of her close family entering into such an intimate alliance with someone like the Ticehursts was deeply repulsive. They were very nice people, but . . . She was ashamed of her instincts, but instincts they were. They were very deep. It was in her mind quite wrong for Dalton Tangent, her father's nephew, to marry a girl who was a scullery-maid. It would damage the family, maybe Papa who was doing so well in his career. What Emily would say to the Queen, goodness knew. Jane put a hand to her cheeks, shaking her head.

'People *are* equal, certainly; but there is such a gulf here that I think it will embarrass everyone – Mama and Papa, *your* mother and father and the Ticehursts. How could they ever be comfortable about it? It is the sort of mistake that people live to regret, however well meaning. It will damage Dalton's career, that is for sure. And yet . . .' Jane slowly picked up her shawl. 'Papa says that this is an age of great change. People will go up and down in the world more than before. Maybe that is what is happening now. Perhaps I shouldn't go and see the Ticehursts after all. They might feel awkward. I promised last week to see the Carpenters in Wardour Street and now is a good time to keep my promise.'

'Should I not come with you?' Polly said. 'Isabella does like us to keep to the "pair" rule.'

'Oh, I hardly ever take any notice of that now,' Jane retorted. 'Especially in the summer. It is so light. What could happen? I'll see you soon.'

Jane waved to her cousin and ran lightly down the steps onto the hot pavement, deep in thought. Why, after all, was she so upset about Dalton? If it didn't worry Polly why should it upset her? Because she was a Vestrey, that was why, she thought bitterly, turning into Broad Street. Vestreys or their near kin didn't marry beneath them, or as far beneath as Dalton was contemplating. One Vestrey in the seventeenth century had married a gypsy; but she had turned out to be the natural daughter of an earl.

Jane had never been in Jove and, apart from her curiosity

about passion, had never wanted to marry anyone. She had briefly found Jeremy Pagan attractive; but the fact that he was an artist, that no-one knew his family, had been a factor in her failure even to try and enter into any deeper relationship with him. He had written to her constantly when he had been abroad; she hardly ever replied. Papa would never countenance an alliance with someone like Mr Pagan however gifted he was, however interesting the people he knew. It was simply a waste of time getting closer to anyone like Jeremy Pagan, and no well brought-up young lady contemplated getting close to a gentleman unless she had marriage in mind.

But none of her brother's friends or the young men she met at balls ever attracted Jane. She had never met anyone who, in intellect and looks, came anywhere near the ideal that Papa presented, the perfect man: aristocratic, humanitarian, intellectual.

Jane smiled to herself as she crossed into New Street. She would probably never be in love, and end up an old maid like Miss Brontë. That was what everyone prophesied for Caroline: Mama would keep her at home until she lost all chance to marry. Well, she and Caroline would keep house together, in that case. She knew that she would never find a man because she aimed too high. There were too few men around like Papa.

Jane sensed in her heart that, of all his children, she was closest to Papa, and she thought he loved her best although he tried not to show it. He was so tender with her, even when she upset him, as she had when she tried to do without the carriage. He would sit down and take her hand in his, look at her with his large brown eyes and gently upbraid her. She hated to upset Papa and she promptly agreed to do as she was told, to please him. Seeing the pain go from his eyes and the gentle smiling image she had of him return, was reward enough. Yes, there was a special closeness between her and her father. She loved him too much, she thought, much more than Mama who never did anything to please him, but made him sad and angry all the time.

Jane paused at a narrow entrance which led off New Street; here a maze of tiny lanes would take her more quickly into Berwick Street. It was a short cut to her destination. Cock Court was a narrow, mean little lane with houses so close together there was hardly any ventilation. Jane scarcely knew the meaning of personal fear; besides, it was broad daylight and she knew the area well. She went into Cock Court, hurrying her footsteps a little because the leaning narrow buildings had suddenly cut out the sun. Jane was aware there was no-one else in the street and thought she would be thankful when she came to the end; her footsteps seemed to echo over the cobbles, despite the fact that there were so many sounds and noises coming from the streets through which she had just come.

Suddenly a figure detached itself from the shadow and, before she had time to gasp, barred her way. Then she knew fear, looking into the eyes of the large, unkempt man who stood before her, his face twisted into a vicious leer.

'In a hurry are you, dearie? Will you not dally a moment with me in this doorway?'

He grasped at her fine shawl and Jane clasped it more securely round her bosom, saying scornfully to try and hide her fear: 'Get away from me, do you hear? Out of my way, man!'

'Oh we have a *lady* here have we, by the sound of your voice. Get away, my man, eh?' He mimicked her tone and did a little dance in grotesque imitation of her air of refinement. Jane was trying to slip by him when a huge fist suddenly came out and caught her arm, pulling her brutally into the shadow from which he had emerged. She tried to scream but no sound came. She only heard the sickening throbbing of her heart in her throat, the pulse hammering in her head.

The man ripped off her shawl and then tore at the lace fichu round her neck. The thought of his odious grasping paws on her body made her feel ill. The smell from him was indescribable, an amalgam of sweat and dirt from the body, drink from the mouth. She felt his large belly pressing her into the wall, and heard his heavy breathing, the thick incoherence of what he was trying to tell her in stinking mouthfuls as he clawed at her skirts. Jane took a deep breath and, summoning all the strength of which she was capable, kneed him right in the crotch before he had time to pinion her to the wall. He gave a scream of pain and his jaw fell open, slavering and wet with the spittle which poured from his mouth. His teeth, exposed with rage, were jagged, black and uneven. She tried to slip to one side but he lunged at her, succeeding at last in pulling her skirts over her thighs and thrust himself against her. Then his hands came up to her neck and, grasping it firmly, his fingers tightened on her windpipe. Through a blur she saw the frenzied look in his eyes and knew that he would rape her and strangle her. She tried to struggle but found she could not move. He started to bang her head against the wall, something large and obscene pressing against the underpart of her belly, and all she was aware of was filth, dampness and an enveloping, swirling mist that was gradually drowning all sound.

The man passing Cock Court heard the scream that finally came. A split second before or after and he would have missed it, drowned in the sounds of Soho, because it was such a narrow entrance. He paused and was about to go on when he saw a couple engaged in what looked to him like the act of copulation roughly performed. It was not uncommon to see couples entwined in the doorways of Soho's dark alleys, but there seemed an unusual commotion going on here. The woman was clearly struggling. Daniel Lévy thought he would just approach and be sure that the female party was willing. She was probably drunk too. He strode swiftly into the gloom just as the man grasped the woman's throat and started banging her head against the wall. This was no amorous dalliance; this was rape.

The man was a giant, and the woman had no earthly chance. Daniel couldn't even see her from where he stood, she was completely obscured by the thick bulk of her attacker. Daniel was a slight man but quite fearless. He grasped his stick firmly and, lifting it up, brought it down forcefully across the man's thick neck. The giant staggered and loosening his grip, turned with a roar to see his assailant. Daniel saw the woman slide down the wall to the ground, her face white, her eyes closed, her skirts lifted over her thighs. To his horror blood trickled from her mouth.

Even in the gloom and despite her dishevelled appearance he could see she was not only a beauty but, by her clothes and general mien even in the horrendous circumstances, a lady.

He drew back his stick again and with both hands brought it on top of the bewildered giant's head. The man was so much bigger than he was that he knew to lay a hand on him was useless. He would be killed. But his second assault had taken effect. The man roared and lurched drunkenly down the passage away from the girl. By this time the alley was filling with idle spectators. Windows overhead had opened, and those who dared not intervene before now found the spectacle entertaining and gave one or two encouraging cheers.

Daniel knelt by the girl and took her pulse. He felt no movement. As he looked up the giant started to stumble back again towards him and the girl but another person interposed, a man who had come running down the court and knelt by Daniel's side. When the giant saw two men he put his hands to his face and ambled away. Daniel wanted to run after him and have him apprehended for his murderous attack but he was too worried about the girl.

The door opposite opened and after looking carefully to right and left a woman came over.

'Is she dead?' she asked timidly.

'I do not know. She is badly hurt. May we take her into your house?'

The woman shrugged and looked fearfully after the retreating giant who kept half-turning as though he would come back.

'That's Black Jack. He's killed several people already, but they never get evidence to hang him. No-one ever sees nothin'. He attacks women and leaves them dead, or half dead.'

The woman looked at Jane and shook her head. 'She'll probably die, but bring her in, poor girl.'

Daniel and the man lifted Jane, whose head hung sideways in an alarming manner, her blood-stained tongue lolling against her chin. They took her inside the dark hovel and put her on a dirty unmade bed in the corner. Several small children immediately appeared from the corners like so many little beetles, all thin and pinched-looking, their clothes ragged, their dirty little fingers in their mouths. A bundle of rags moved from a tumble-down chair and proved to be an old woman who shuffled over and stared without curiosity but with an awful knowingness at Jane's recumbent form. The room continued to fill with silent gawping figures, blocking the doorway, filling every corner. Everyone had hopefully come to see a good death.

The woman who lived in the house made her way through the throng with a cloth which she had dipped in a bucket of foetid water. She knelt by Jane and dabbed at her face, the bruise by her eye, the blood at her lips. The blood didn't flow and Daniel felt a surge of relief. Maybe she had merely cut her lip. No-one said anything as the woman continued her ministrations, kindly and gently as if Jane had been a small child.

'Do you know who she is?' Daniel said.

'No, 'cept that she's a leddy by her clothes. What she was doing in these parts God knows. She's not dead. I don't think she'll die; see, the colour is returning to her face.'

Daniel took the pulse again and felt it gathering strength. He held her wrists and rubbed them.

'Thank heaven,' he said. 'Someone should go after that brute and fetch the police.'

'Oh, they'll never get Black Jack. They know, but they never get him.'

'But you all *saw* him. I saw him.'

The woman shook her head. 'No-one saw nothin'. Best forget you saw anything. We keep ourselves to ourselves here.' The woman eyed him. 'Better like that.'

Another woman from the edge of the crowd elbowed her way through the goggling mass and leaned over Jane, pointing a bony finger. 'That's the lady from the Mission. One of them. I saw her only this morning, in that dress too.'

'What Mission?' Daniel enquired.

'In Poland Street.'

'She comes from Poland Street?'

'Yes, the ladies work there looking after folks like us. That's why she'd have been here.'

'Then we must take her to the Mission,' Daniel said. 'They will know what to do.'

'I'd leave her until she comes round,' the first woman said. 'I'll send my boy to the Mission to get one of the ladies. Here Harry! Hurry up to the Mission and say what's happened.'

Harry ran off like an agile little fox after a rabbit. Gradually, as there was apparently to be no death, the room cleared. The children shuffled off to play, the bundle of rags returned to her chair and Daniel and the woman whose house it was were left alone with Jane, whose breathing was now apparent although shallow and irregular.

'What sort of people are they that leave one of their number to travel alone in a place like this?'

The woman shrugged. 'We have a lot of charity workers around here; but the Poland Street Mission is one of the best. They let you have what you need and leave you to yourself. Don't try and reform you or nothin'. The others try to get you into the workhouse. Oh, not *us*,' the woman drew herself up, 'we don't take from the Mission. My man is a drayman and most of our family are working.'

'What is your name?' Daniel asked.

'Mrs Parker.'

'You are very good, Mrs Parker. I can't understand why no one came to help her before.'

Mrs Parker shook her head and wiped her nose on her arm. 'Oh, we leave things alone here. Like I said. We don't interfere. Black Jack is terrible strong. We'd get killed ourselves.'

Mrs Parker had an Irish accent. Daniel decided she was one of the many Irish who had been driven to these parts by the famines that had inflicted their poor country several times already this century.

Mrs Parker went over to where a tin basin stood on the floor and rinsed out the cloth she had used on Jane's face. Daniel thought there was nothing more he could do until help arrived. He wished it would be soon.

It was. Harry proved a good messenger and within a very

288

short time Polly Tangent hurried through the door, her face
ashen with distress, and flung herself at Jane's side.

CHAPTER EIGHTEEN

George Vestrey travelled non-stop to be with his daughter, going from Vienna to Paris, and Paris to Boulogne and thence to London pausing only to change trains. In Paris he found out that Jane was not expected to die, but her condition was still critical. There he parted from Hilary and made his way on by himself. He felt very lonely without Hilary and wished he could have her support.

Caroline travelled up from Chetwell and Emily, not being in waiting, went to take her place with Mama. It was the first time Caroline had been away in nearly two years. Even going to nurse a sick sister was like having a holiday.

The young man who had saved Jane's life called at the house twice a day to ask about her. They couldn't thank him enough, a young foreigner who happened to be passing, and did not lack the courage to tackle Black Jack. People sent messages and flowers, the Queen enquired constantly, so did the Prime Minister and members of the House of Lords. The attack was reported in the main newspapers, many of which seized the opportunity to insist that vice pits like Soho should be pulled down. What should be done with the poor wretches who lived there they did not say. Nor had they when the railways had made so many homeless, large numbers of whom spilled into Soho. The Poland Street Mission came in for a good deal of publicity and people turned up at the door just to stare.

For a man so large, Black Jack just disappeared. The police knew he was lying low but not where. There would always be some woman willing to protect Black Jack – an attack on the gentry would be considered fair game.

Doctor Snow came to see Jane and so did Dr Jenner, the Queen's doctor. Sir James Clark sent to enquire if he was needed. He was getting old now.

Jane lay in a state between consciousness and unconsciousness for almost a week, long after Papa had arrived and gone straight to her room. As he stood looking at her the tears ran down his face and when Caroline came over to him he buried his head in his hands.

'She will be all right, Papa,' Caroline said. 'It will take time.'

Time was on Jane's side because of her youth. Otherwise, the doctors said, such a terrible assault would have killed her. Her windpipe was nearly crushed and some little delicate bones in her neck had been broken. Her pelvis had been broken and three ribs cracked. She was bruised from head to foot. But, thank God, she had not been raped and she was not dead. Thank God.

Isabella Goodey was so upset she wanted to close the Mission, but Caroline and Aunt Ruth begged her not to. Jane had disobeyed the rule about going round in pairs. The helpers should now be made to see how necessary it was to have these rules. Besides, Polly wanted to take Jane's place. In everyone's mind there was no question of Jane ever returning to Poland Street.

Agnes had been too prostrate to attempt to come and see her daughter. She returned to bed completely and didn't get up for weeks. This, added to the news about Dalton which Aunt Dorothy had finally plucked up courage to relay, was too much. Agnes was sure her own end could not be long delayed.

Jane knew Papa had come back; she saw him through half-closed eyes. Above all she felt his presence. As soon as he was there the atmosphere was different. She sensed it. She didn't need to speak or smile or do anything. As long as he was there, the only man she loved, she would be all right. Papa's strength would make her get better.

George was alone in the room when Jane opened her eyes properly and looked around, like a newborn baby blinking even in the half light. He was reading some reports sent on from Vienna. The Turks had refused to sign the Vienna note, unless it was modified. The Russians would not sign it if it was. Lord Aberdeen was increasingly agitated. Some thought the situation was making him ill, because he wavered and was so irresolute about everything, trying to please everyone. Prince Albert had told Papa that he thought Palmerston would have been more suitable in the circumstances, even though he and the Queen couldn't stand him. Palmerston was very firm and direct. He would have shown the Russians we meant business. But George wasn't so sure. Palmerston was too aggressive, too much of a bully. He went round saying quite openly that he wanted to make an example of these 'red-haired barbarians', meaning the Russians.

But George did wish Lord Aberdeen would stop accusing himself of all kinds of errors. It was quite pathetic at times to listen to him. After all, he *was* the Prime Minister; sometimes one forgot it.

When he put down his papers and saw Jane's eyes wide open and staring at him he went swiftly to the bed and took her hand. The tears stole down his face again, and he tried to brush them away.

'Why are you crying, Papa? Am I going to die?' Jane's voice was very faint and at the end she faltered.

George threw himself on his knees, kissing her thin pale hand. 'Oh no, my darling, no! You are going to be *well*. I am crying with happiness to see you open your eyes. You have been very ill my sweet girl, my little Jane.'

Jane said nothing, did not return the pressure with her hand. She felt so weak she was hardly capable of making the gesture. She looked at Papa's bowed head then round the room at all the flowers. She closed her eyes again and smelt that awful odour of the man who had attacked her; his great body crushed her against the wall. She wanted to cry and her heart started beating quickly. She would never forget either him or the smell as long as she lived.

Then Caroline came in and saw Papa's bent head, Jane's limp form, her eyes closed. She thought her sister had died. With an exclamation she went quickly over to the bed and took her other hand feeling the pulse. As she did Jane's eyes opened again and she made a feeble attempt at a smile. Caroline bent over and kissed her, very gently, on the forehead.

'I'm so glad, my darling, that you are better.'

'But look at all these flowers, Papa's tears. I am going to die. It is like a funeral.'

Caroline sat on the clean white counterpane and rubbed the pale hand.

'You are *not* going to die. You were near death but thank God the crisis is now past. You are bruised and shaken, but you are not going to die.'

'I'm glad,' Jane said and closed her eyes again. She dropped immediately into a deep, regular sleep. Caroline went over to George and shook his shoulder.

'I will sit with her, Papa. You must take some rest.'

George raised his tearstained face and looked at Caroline.

'I don't want ever to leave her, she is so precious to me.'

'I know, Papa; but you will make yourself ill if you worry so much and do not take enough rest. Jane will pull through. She can only get better now and not worse. As Doctor Jenner said, her youth has saved her.'

The door opened and Aunt Ruth tiptoed in, her eyes on Jane. She could see at once by the regular heaving of her chest that she was better; she had more colour too. She smiled at George.

'She is better, I can see. So, why do you cry?'

'Papa is upset,' Caroline said going to the table beside the bed and straightening the various bottles and boxes containing Jane's medicines. Papa did love Jane best; these days had taught her that. Would he have wept over her, sat for hours on end by her side, even though he was so busy helping to try and avert the war? Would anyone, even Mama? No, Mama certainly wouldn't; she depended on Caroline. Caroline would have no business being ill in bed. But did Mama love her, or did she regard her as some sort of pleasing nurse-gaoler – someone whose strength she needed as she had when Rebecca had been born? What other daughter would have stayed by her mother's side during such an event? Everyone who had heard about it – and a lot had, thanks to Aunt Dorothy – was very shocked. It was not the sort of thing that was done at all, an unmarried daughter by her own mother's bed in childbirth. Emily was loved and Jane was loved; but was she, Caroline, loved? Or was she too cold to inspire love, too capable?

'The young man who saved Jane is here, George,' Aunt Ruth said. 'I told him you wanted to see him.'

George raised his head and got up immediately.

'Of course I want to see him! He is downstairs?'

'Yes, in the morning room. Let me take your place.'

Aunt Ruth had brought her crochet work and put on her pincenez as she took George's chair. She gazed at him over the half rims. 'He is not what you would expect, not a gentleman exactly, but very nice.'

'I don't care what he is,' George cried, 'he saved my daughter's life, and I am *forever* beholden to him.'

He went swiftly from the room and hurried down the great stone staircase to the parlour.

Daniel Lévy stood at the open French windows, savouring the fine scents that came in from the garden. Although there was the slightest touch of autumn in the air the breeze was warm and the birds sang. It was a very different place from Soho where he had found Jane; it was worlds away yet, in distance, scarcely more than two miles. He turned as the door opened and a tall handsome man came into the room; a confident man, one used to respect, giving orders and being obeyed. He saw the likeness at once as the man came towards him, his hand outstretched. As Daniel reached for the hand he saw the tears still on the man's face.

'She is not worse, sir?' he said in alarm.

'No, no thank God. She has regained full consciousness. After a week.'

George clasped the young man's arm. He would like to have kissed him on the cheeks as they did on the continent; but it was not at all the sort of thing the English did. Instead he led him to a chair and saw him comfortably seated. Then he offered him a cigar. Daniel Lévy took it and let it roll between his fingers, feeling the silky smoothness. Then he smelt the tip and cut the end with the cigar cutter George handed to him. He wasn't quite sure whether you left the band on or off and wanted to do the right thing. Despite the fact that he instinctively hated and despised the aristocracy he wanted to do the right thing for Lord Vestrey.

George did not sit but stood in front of the young man.

'I can't ever thank you enough, my dear sir. I am George Vestrey Jane's father. I was in Vienna when this mishap – this terrible mishap occurred.'

294

'I know sir. They told me. As for thanking me, Lord Vestrey, I only did what any man would do. I could not stand by and see your daughter killed.' George closed his eyes and his large frame shook with an involuntary spasm of grief. Killed. The very word was unthinkable. 'As it was, I thought I was too late to save her. She bled from the mouth and I thought her injuries internal and very severe. It came, I was later told, from the fact she had bitten her tongue. It is so fortunate her lungs were not damaged.'

'You must tell me exactly what happened,' George said, his face very pale. 'But first I am going to send for a large brandy for each of us. I must have it to sustain me, and the memory will doubtless be painful for you. I mean to see this villain apprehended and hanged.'

Daniel Lévy watched as Lord Vestrey got up and pressed the ornate brass button by the fireplace. It was the very latest thing in household communication that Aunt Ruth had just had installed, replacing the great plush bell push that had formerly hung there. By pushing the bell a panel in the servants' quarters indicated which room required service, merely by a signal activating the panel. It was quite remarkable.

Cornwall came in and bowed, requesting his lordship's requirements.

'Pray bring a decanter of the best brandy for my young friend and myself, Cornwall.'

'My lord,' Cornwall murmured, retreating as silently as he had come in. Daniel Lévy had never seen such splendour in his life, such a fine house, such rich furnishing, so many servants to carry out instantly one's merest whim. It was a system he hated, but you could not help being impressed, especially if you were an exile with not a penny to your name or no clothes other than the ones in which you stood up.

Cornwall came back with the brandy and poured some into two large balloon glasses which he put before George and his guest. Then he bowed again and withdrew.

'Thank you, Cornwall.' George raised his glass. 'To you Mr Lévy, I think it is?'

'Yes sir, Daniel Lévy.' Daniel raised his glass. 'And to the recovery of Miss Vestrey.'

George also selected a cigar and putting aside the tails of his morning coat sat down in one of Aunt Ruth's large comfortable chairs.

'Please, Mr Lévy . . .'

Daniel cleared his throat and took a sip of the excellent French brandy which fired his gullet so that he nearly choked. He recovered himself and outlined the events which had happened in Cock Court only a week before. As he spoke and the narration got more harrowing he saw large tears fill Lord Vestrey's eyes. He did not attempt to stop them but allowed them to fall on his immaculately starched white shirt front. When Daniel had finished George's face was quite wet with tears and the front of his shirt likewise. Then, finally, he wiped his eyes and blew his nose.

'It was such a miracle that you were passing. God is very good.'

Daniel, who did not believe that God existed, bowed his head. The narration had moved him too. He still saw her white form lying on the dirty cobbles, her clothes disarrayed, blood trickling from her mouth. He shuddered.

'It was a horrible thing, sir. It was very fortunate that I was there.'

'And how came you to be passing, Mr Lévy? Though I know it is none of my business, and I shall not be offended if you do not reply. But I would like to know all about you; you will always be a close, respected friend of this family.'

Daniel lowered his eyes and stared at the floor. The distance between himself and Lord Vestrey was so vast he did not know where to begin. Telling of how he had saved Jane had been the easiest part. The rest would be more difficult.

'I am an exile, sir, from France. I am at present living in Dean Street, near to some friends of mine, Dr and Mrs Marx.'

'An *exile*, Mr Lévy?' George appeared not to understand and looked nonplussed. Then, as the truth dawned, he felt a shock that contrasted sharply with his happiness at his daughter's survival. Daniel saw the look and it made him braver. He would have to tell the truth, he wanted to, and then the noble lord would see if he *still* wished to have him for a friend. His eyes narrowed slightly with contempt and he flicked the ash from his cigar into a tray.

'Yes, I am a revolutionary, Lord Vestrey. You have probably not met with the likes of me before. I want to overthrow society by violent means and establish a just system of law and order. I took part in the troubles in 1848 in Germany and Hungary and then I joined the Monagnards in my own country under the leadership of Monsieur Ledru Rollin. When our demonstration failed in June 1848 I fled abroad and took part in further outbreaks organized by revolutionaries in central Europe. When I returned to my own country I was arrested by Louis Bonaparte's reactionary police. I spent two years in prison and last year, upon my release, I came here, for the authorities were looking for an excuse to imprison me again. I am a professional revolutionary, Lord Vestrey. I cannot hide it from you. I think you will not now wish to have me for a friend.'

George had let his cigar go out and now made a great fuss of relighting it again, looking at Daniel through the smoke it engendered. He saw a pleasant-looking serious young man of little more than twenty-six or seven, maybe thirty at the outside. He was not handsome, and not very tall – of a medium sized, slight build with short dark hair, a neat beard and a moustache and very black piercing eyes divided by a long semitic nose. His clothes, though neat and clean, were undoubtedly threadbare. His hands, George noted, were well kept. He was not a man who supported himself by manual labour.

He liked him, but he thought it was a pity he had been the one to save Jane Vestrey from death. He could foresee complications both in what Lévy might feel towards them and what they might feel about him. He was not anti-semitic – a close friend of Benjamin Disraeli could not be; but a foreign Jewish revolutionary was hardly the sort of person one would choose for an acquaintance, let alone a friend. George blew out the spill and puffed at his cigar. He looked directly at Daniel.

'You know my position, I think, Mr Lévy. I am a member of Her Majesty's Government. I am at this moment one of those striving to avert war between Turkey and Russia. I am a member of the House of Lords. I cannot, therefore, support revolution and anarchy. Thank God it has not yet undermined the fabric of our state and I pray it never will. It failed in Europe, did it not? And it failed here in the form of the Chartist movement. But as for you, sir, that is a completely different matter. I see you as a human being, a man who rescued my beloved daughter from dishonour and a foul death. I look up to you, sir, for it, because you put yourself in danger. You showed courage in going to her aid. You are a brave man, Mr Lévy, and for that I admire and respect you. Your politics are of no concern or interest to me unless they were to undermine my own society. And I am sure they will not.' George got up and went again to shake Daniel's hand. Lévy too rose and smiled at George.

'Thank you, Lord Vestrey. The English you know, are, they say, a race apart. I believe it. Whatever its imperfections in many ways this is a good country and you have been good to me and my friends, exiles like me. We have freedom here from government harassment, although not from spies sent by our own governments. They report back everything that we do in case they can catch us again on the continent and imprison us. In England we can breathe as free men. It is a good country, a noble country. As a member of the ruling class, and I must say I never met one before, thank you for it sir.'

'Capital!' George clasped Daniel's shoulder and led him to the door. 'I know we shall see you again for you kindly come to enquire after my daughter.'

'You still wish me to?'

Lévy glanced at George and for a moment stood still.

'Of *course*! You are our friend. Besides, when she is well Jane will want to thank you herself. You must come whenever you like, Mr Lévy and, very shortly, I want you to have dinner with us.'

Outside the door Cornwall was waiting with Mr Lévy's hat which he had given a good brush. Without much avail; nothing could be done to improve that hat. The velour was greasy in places and worn with years of handling. Cornwall looked at it doubtfully as he handed it to Lévy with the slightest of bows. He knew quite well the foreigner had no class. It was a great pity, in his opinion, that he had been the one to rescue Miss Jane. He was not the sort of person the Vestreys were accustomed to receive. However, his lordship had his arm about Mr Lévy's shoulder in a very friendly and familiar gesture. It was not his business to criticize the actions of his employer. Lord Vestrey stood in the porch waving to Mr Lévy, then he turned round, looked sharply at Cornwall, noting the expression on his taciturn face and made his way swiftly upstairs to the room of his beloved Jane.

Towards the end of September and early October, the Sublime Porte decided on a policy for declaring war on Russia. Russia, on the other hand, seemed to have changed its mind and wanted to hold back, offering to leave the principalities it had occupied. The Czar offered to recall his troops as soon as the Vienna note was signed.

Lord Aberdeen was delighted, a view not supported by most of his colleagues, and by the country where war fever was mounting. Their pessimism seemed justified when on 3 October Turkey declared war and Lord Aberdeen urged the Queen to return to London from Balmoral in anticipation of the possible downfall of his government. On 8 October the Cabinet ordered the British fleet into the Black Sea, again despite Aberdeen. The pro-war party was a strong one – Lansdowne, Palmerston, Clarendon and Lord John Russell. On Aberdeen's side were the Duke of Argyll and Sidney Herbert; Gladstone was also for peace but had been ill. Brunnow the Russian Ambassador was sure that opening up the Dardanelles meant war. Palmerston thought that war would be no calamity and said so. Clarendon deprecated the fact that England should embark on a war caused by 'two sets of barbarians' quarrelling over a form of words. At Windsor the Queen and Prince Albert were very worried indeed and Emily found herself close to royal counsels as her father, no time for romantic dalliance now, hurried between London and Vienna.

Jane's improvement was very slow; too slow for those about her who worried that, despite the fact that she was mended in body, her mind took so long to recover. At times she relapsed into such long silences, refusing to speak or answer questions, that Caroline, who chiefly looked after her, wondered if she would ever be completely well.

The only people who seemed able to bring Jane to life were her father, and he was so often away, and Daniel Lévy, who regularly visited her and sat with her sometimes for hours. His quiet presence, his softly accented mellifluous voice had both a calming and, paradoxically, a reviving effect on Jane, and when he was with her, Caroline knew that she could get on with other tasks in the house. Daniel read to her from Dickens, Thackeray or the classics, and then he often talked to her quietly telling her about his life, about the great revolutionary year of 1848 and about his political ideas and those of his friends.

Caroline felt she lived in a world peopled by shadows of the sick, Mama and Jane, Jane and Mama. She flew down to Chetwell to see that Mama was all right. If Emily was not in waiting she stayed there with her, or arranged for Aunt Dorothy to stay. Aunt Dorothy already missed her own daughter, worried in case what had happened to Jane might happen to her; she was also frantic about Dalton who had now announced he was betrothed to Maggie Ticehurst. Despite what her husband said, she didn't know how she would survive the shame. It was a great comfort to unburden herself to Agnes, and they could weep together for hours on end. Both agreed that, so far, children were a terrible disappointment, and they didn't know what the world was coming to. Women seemed no longer to know their place in society; nor, clearly, did Dalton know his.

One day after she had shown Daniel upstairs and sat a while with him and Jane, Caroline found Rawdon Foxton waiting for her in the hall. As she descended the stairs she was aware of his tall figure, dressed in military uniform, and the sight of him was so unexpected that, for a moment, she thought something might have happened to James, and she ran down the last few stairs and across the tiled floor.

'Rawdon! Is everything all right?'

Rawdon smiled and bowed.

'Perfectly, Caroline. I happened to be exercising my men in the park and took the opportunity of leaving it to a lieutenant to take them home while I slipped away here. I wondered how Jane was? James told me that last time he saw her he thought her progress very slow.'

Caroline led the way into the front parlour, asking Cornwall on the way to bring in tea.

'Pray sit down, Rawdon,' she pointed to a chair and took a seat opposite him. She had not seen him in uniform for a long time and thought how well the red jacket with its high collar, the marks of rank on his sleeve, became him. She realized then that she had not been alone with Rawdon for a long time either. Occasionally they would be alone at Chetwell but never in London – always Aunt Ruth or Emily or some visiting relative or friend was about. 'Jane makes a little progress. Her physical injuries are better, but it is her mental state that causes us concern. However thanks to the daily visits of Mr Lévy I am happy to report improvement there.'

'Mr Lévy calls daily?' Rawdon crossed an elegant leg giving Caroline the opportunity to note the high polish of his black riding boots.

'Oh yes. He is very good. He chats to her and reads to her and says that she helps him with his English.'

'But are you not worried about . . .' Rawdon trailed off gazing too at the excellent veneer on his boot. 'I know not quite how to say it.' He looked at Caroline and she was aware of the concern in his grey eyes, the warmth in his smile.

'I do not understand you, Rawdon. Worried about . . ?'

Rawdon twiddled his foot several times then put it down squarely on the floor.

'Well, that some, how shall I say, understanding may occur.'

'Oh no! That is quite out of the question.' Caroline looked up as a footman entered with the tea tray followed by a maid with plates of cakes and Cornwall to see that all was as it should be. 'Thank you,' Caroline said smiling at the butler. 'I'll pour, Cornwall; that will be all.'

'Thank you, Miss Vestrey.'

Cornwall shepherded his underlings out before him and closed the door.

'With milk, Rawdon?'

'Please.'

'No, anything of that nature is *quite* out of the question. He is not the sort of person who would be considered suitable for a Vestrey to marry. He is very nice of course, in his own way, but oh dear no. The idea would never occur to Jane, or Mr Lévy I am sure.'

'But Jane *is* a rather impulsive young woman. Are you not afraid?'

'Not a bit, not a bit!' Caroline vigorously stirred her tea and shook her head. 'However radical she might be Jane knows quite well that there could be no question of an alliance between Mr Lévy and herself. Oh dear no. It would never be considered.'

'I hope you are right. Excellent tea.' Rawdon looked at Caroline over the rim of his cup. 'And how are you, Caroline?'

Caroline coloured and it enabled him to see then how very pale she had been. Her cheeks were slightly hollow, and there were black smudges round her eyes as though someone with very dirty fingers had pressed them right into her sockets.

'Oh, I am tolerably well, Rawdon.' Caroline touched her hair and felt suddenly nervous, aware of something unusual in the way he was looking at her.

'I think you don't look well at all. You have got thinner. Too much is expected of you and you give, give all the time. Your family is draining you, Caroline, depriving you of your youth. As someone who has been a friend of yours for so many years it worries me.'

'Oh Rawdon,' Caroline faltered. 'I am *much* moved by your concern, but there is nothing else I can do. It is expected of me, as the eldest daughter, and indeed it *is* my duty. You too have been very aware of your duty, Rawdon; you were willing to sacrifice your career for your father if called . . .'

Rawdon stood up and came over to her. She suddenly felt very tired and rather sick as though she were getting a fever. She felt his hand under her chin and he tilted her face back and looked at her.

'Caroline, you know I am very fond of you. I have watched you and admired you so much during these years when you have devoted yourself to your family. You must know that I have feelings for you that are more than mere affection.'

Caroline bowed her head and folded her hands in her lap trying to stop the trembling.

'No Rawdon, I did not know.'

'Well, perhaps I do not wear my heart on my sleeve. Like you Vestreys, we Foxtons are also used to controlling our emotions. Besides I did not think you were in a position to consider any offer from me. Also I myself was undecided about the future.' Rawdon drew a chair closer to her and, sitting down, leaned over towards her. 'But this *is* clearer to me now Caroline, and I hope it is a picture that commends itself to you.' Caroline looked at him; he reached over taking her hand and bringing it to his lips. After he had kissed it he continued to hold it. 'There is going to be a war, Caroline. We have been training for it for months . . .'

'Oh no!' She looked at him, the blood rushing to her face.

'Oh yes. But it will be a little war, merely. A skirmish in the Balkans to put down the Russian menace. When I come back I shall buy myself out of the army and apply for the Diplomatic. I want you to marry me then, Caroline, if you will, if you wish it. I have reason to believe that you are not indifferent to me . . .' She looked up at him and smiled, her eyes luminous with tears. 'In six months or so or when the war is over, you will have been able to free yourself from your duties, I think. Is it not so? Are you willing?'

Caroline clasped his hand, blinking back the tears. She shook her head.

'I am sorry to be so . . . feeble, Rawdon. I had no idea.'

'You had *no* idea? But I thought I made my intentions clear; my visits, their frequency, my concern for you.'

'I thought it was my sister you were interested in.'

Caroline saw an expression of dismay replace the tenderness and love on his face.

'Jane? But you know . . .'

'*Emily*, Rawdon,' Caroline said quietly. 'I thought you were in love with Emily.'

Rawdon kissed her hand again and gently let it fall. Then he got up and walked towards the window, his back, ramrod straight in its scarlet coat, to her.

'I will admit that in the past I have not been indifferent to Emily's charms. They are considerable. She is beautiful and accomplished and witty but – ' he turned towards her, half of his face still in the shadow made by the light streaming through the window. 'Emily is not a homemaker. I confess that thoughts of asking either of you to be my wife have passed through my mind during the past years. You both have the famous Vestrey charm and would be equally acceptable as my wife.'

Caroline felt herself relaxing and a smile passed across her face.

'You could be happy with either, as *The Beggar's Opera* has it, Rawdon?'

He strode over and seized her hand.

'Oh no, my dearest Caroline! Since you asked me, I am being honest and saying that Emily has many qualities to commend her. But I do not think that, in the long run, we would be as happy as, say, I hope you and I shall be. Will you accept me? There, I believe this is how 'tis done. Is that better?'

Rawdon sank on one knee and smiled at her. Caroline stared at him with a feeling of unreality. It was like some illusion brought on by excessive fatigue, some derangement of her mind, maybe some measure of wishful thinking. He bowed his head under her gaze and she saw the firm outline of his jaw, the deep-set eyes that were hidden from her. She wanted to reach out and stroke his face; but she didn't know how to behave on an occasion like this. Nothing had ever prepared her for it; there was no guidance offered to young women as to how to accept, or reject, a proposal. She would make sure her daughters were prepared. Her daughters. The children of herself and Rawdon? Suddenly her heart was filled with an overwhelming sense of joy; a strong and terrible passion was unleashed, the violence of which almost shocked her. Yes, she wanted this man; she always had, and now she was going to have him. She put a hand timidly on his head, the first time she had ever touched a man other than Papa or her brothers, and she knew that there was something sisterly and filial in this hesitant gesture. His hair was greased as Papa's was; it was strong and wiry, thick under her fingers. She wanted to continue the gesture by stroking his cheek, the thick whiskers on his chin; but she thought she had gone far enough.

'If it is what you want, Rawdon, I will gladly accept you. It is what I want too.'

'Caroline.' Rawdon looked up and, seizing both her hands, brought them to his lips. 'Oh Caroline; you *will* be my wife.' He leaned forward and kissed her on the side of her cheek. Then he got unsteadily to his feet and brought her up with him until they stood very close together. She knew the particular smell of Rawdon, but had never been so near him, her bosom against his chest, his long legs just inches away from her skirts. He clasped her hands and drew her even closer and as his face got nearer she closed her eyes in anticipation of the impress of his lips on hers. The hair on his cheeks brushed her, and the smooth stubble of his upper lip. It was a powerful, masculine sensation and she felt frightened. But his lips did not linger and when she opened her eyes again he was smiling so gently and lovingly that her fear evaporated and she wanted to laugh with relief. To know that life would be complete after all, know she would be married, and to someone she had always loved, and be a mother, and . . . all the things she had secretly seen herself being deprived of would now after all be realized.

'Oh, but the war!' She pressed his hands tightly and he took advantage of her emotion to draw near to her again. She could even feel his calf against her skirts.

'My darling, the war will be a matter of a few shots, a bit of swordplay maybe and we shall send the Russians galloping off the field. It cannot last more than a few days.'

'I cannot believe it Rawdon; that you love me, that you want me. I feel very honoured.'

'Oh, typical Caroline.' Rawdon squeezed her hand again, longing to take her in his arms but not daring to yet. He did not want to lose control and shock or upset this beautiful fragrant creature who had promised one day to be his. He would wait for that day; he must. 'It is *I* who should feel honoured. Now may I ask your father?'

Suddenly Caroline thought of Emily. She could see the sad look in her violet eyes, sense the degree of her distress. Only she knew how Emily would feel. Rawdon obviously had no idea. She must have time to prepare Emily.

'Rawdon could we . . . wait until the war is over? I do not want my family to think I am deserting them. My Mama will panic and it may set back Jane's recovery. Could it be a secret between ourselves until then?'

'But what if there is no war?'

'Then say in six months' time. Is that all right Rawdon? Within six months I will have secured my freedom. I will have prepared my family. Is it too much to ask?'

'Oh my darling,' Rawdon murmured, drawing her to him again. He was so aware of her overpowering femininity, her desirability, that he wanted to marry her straight away. Why had he thought Emily so sensual and Caroline not? To feel the warmth of her body near him, inhale the perfume she used, touch her thick chestnut hair and stroke her pale cheek was to conjure up a sense of eternal, overpowering, mystifying womanhood. 'Oh my darling, you can ask anything. Six months or after the war, whichever is the sooner.'

He held her away and gazed at her. 'But Caroline, can I trust you to free yourself? This sense of duty of yours. What will you do about your Mama, what will happen to Jane?'

'Now that I know you are waiting for me and that you want me I will do it, Rawdon. Don't you see that you have given purpose to my life? At last it has a meaning. Before I did not know where I was going. Now I do.'

CHAPTER NINETEEN

In November Harriet Martineau appeared again in London for the publication of her translation of Comte's *Positive Philosophy*. Miss Martineau had been very active in writing about the coming war; she was all for it. Or rather, she was for the will of the Russian people to determine the sort of government they wanted and not be ruled over by despots like the Czar of Russia, a country she had never liked. Nor was she in favour of the alliance with Austria and, although she distrusted Louis Napoleon, who had now declared himself Emperor Napoleon III, she regarded the French *people* as important, not the man who governed them.

Miss Martineau swept in one day only just preceded by Cornwall who had scarcely a moment to announce her before she was there. Caroline was in the parlour with Rawdon Foxton and she was reluctant to see Miss Martineau. She and Rawdon so seldom had any time together. The secret of their engagement was more trying than she had anticipated and she began to wonder whether it had been a logical, sensible thing to do. She had to go on pretending that he was just a friend when all the time she nursed this frightening, overwhelming passion in her heart.

'I am Caroline Vestrey,' she said, advancing to greet her distinguished guest. 'Jane's sister.'

Miss Martineau stuck her ear trumpet firmly into her ear and beamed. She had grown rather corpulent and leaned heavily on a stick.

'I can see you are, dear, there is a family likeness. And how is my poor Jane? Have they apprehended the villain?'

'He has gone to ground, Miss Martineau,' Caroline said. 'But for the first time there is a witness who would testify against him if he is found. The young man whose timely intervention saved my sister.'

'Is *this* the young man?' Miss Martineau turned and smiled at Rawdon with approval. Though by no means a

307

comely woman, she had great charm when she chose to use it.

'This is Mr Rawdon Foxton, Miss Martineau, a very great friend of our family.'

'Are you related to Lord Foxton, young man?'

'His son, ma'am.' Rawdon bowed deeply and took her hand.

'Good, Foxton is for the war. I read his speeches in the House of Lords. I am sorry he has been ill. But he is much recovered I hear?'

'Indeed, ma'am. Well enough to attend the House of Lords and contribute to the debates. My father is of the opinion that we must stop the Russian menace, and the only way to do that is to fight.'

Whenever Caroline thought about the war she grew cold. And the reason, she knew, was because of what might happen to Rawdon and James. The Guards were on manoeuvres all the time, preparing to embark at a moment's notice.

'Rawdon is in the Grenadier Guards with my brother, Miss Martineau. They would be the first to go if there were a war.'

'Excellent,' Miss Martineau nodded approvingly and banged her stick on the ground in a war-like manner. 'If I could go I would.'

The thought of this rather large, deaf, elderly lady going to the front was so comical that they both smiled and Miss Martineau, not above seeing a joke against herself, laughed out loud, flourishing her trumpet in the air as if it had been a bugle.

'See! I would smite them with my horn as the trumpets sounded for the fall of Jerusalem. Now where is your sister, young woman? Not in Kent I trust.'

'No Miss Martineau, we have an invalid there too, as you know.'

'Then should they not be nursed together? You are referring to your mother, I take it?'

'Yes. She and Jane . . .' Caroline paused for the right word, 'find each other a little irksome. It is best that they are not together. No, she is upstairs and her rescuer, a

308

young man called Daniel Lévy, is with her reading to her.'

'May I go up?'

'Of course.'

Rawdon gave Miss Martineau his arm and, leaning heavily on it, she slowly mounted the stairs pausing every so often to get her breath. Caroline hurried ahead to prepare Jane, who was sitting in her chair by the window, her head thrown back, listening to Daniel reading *Pendennis* by Mr Thackeray.

It was such a charming, intimate scene that Caroline momentarily paused and, at the same time, a little tremor fluttered in her heart. For though Jane leaned against the cushions, her eyes were on Daniel's head bowed intently over the book, his earnest thoughtful expression making him look, in that instance, almost beautiful. And when he stopped reading and his soft expressive eyes were raised to her she knew why. Jane had found a lover. The sister who had sworn she would never give her heart was losing it to a penniless exiled Frenchman and he, if his eyes were anything to go by, reciprocated.

And Jane was so much better. Even in a week the improvement had been marked. She moved around more freely and was able to dress herself. And then, as she gazed at Daniel's bent head, as she saw Jane's eyes fixed on him and how he looked up at her as she interrupted his reading, Caroline knew the reason for her sister's sudden improvement. She wanted to be well for Daniel.

'Miss Martineau is here,' she announced. 'She is on her way up.'

Jane jumped out of her chair with none of the feebleness of an invalid.

'Miss Martineau here! Oh Daniel, I do so want you to meet her. She is the greatest friend. She has been so kind to me while I have been ill, writing and sending gifts. She has a very clear idea as to diet.'

'Martineau?' Daniel said, carefully marking the page in the book. 'She is French?'

'No, she is from an old Huguenot family. They settled here a hundred years ago. She was brought up as a Unitarian, but now believes in nothing. Oh, you will like her Daniel, and she . . .' Jane looked at him, her eyes shining, 'she will *love* you.'

Daniel smiled at her and said nothing, only moving closer to her as though wishing to present a united front with her. His feet were slightly apart, his hands behind his back, his head back, chin slightly thrust out. Although his clothes were decidedly worn his shirt was always clean and his shoes shiny, as though he were a man who took care about his personal hygiene.

As Caroline looked at them, hearing Miss Martineau on the landing outside, she saw them as a couple, grave, dedicated, concerned with causes rather than people. Alas, they were a perfect match.

Miss Martineau didn't stop talking all the way up the stairs and such was the way she infused one with her own certainty that Rawdon began to feel almost enthusiastic about the war. Rawdon was worried about the war for the same reason as Caroline – he didn't want to lose her.

Nothing had made him love her so much as the eventual declaration of that love that somehow he had not been sure he was going to make even minutes before he made it. For so long he had been in such a torment as, indeed, he had weighed the pros and cons between one sister and the other. He knew how attractive Emily was to him, but he had not been sure about Caroline. She had an enigmatic quality which those slanting hazel eyes and high cheekbones enhanced. Perhaps it was this very remoteness of Caroline, her inaccessibility that won him. Emily was a little too transparent; Caroline infinitely mysterious. In many ways she was his ideal woman – beautiful, remote, dutiful, chaste. And his mother and sisters were so much in favour of her. They were quite sure that she was much more suited to be the chatelaine of Saltmarsh Castle than her younger sister who would hardly ever be there, they said, so busy would she be dragging him round all the ballrooms of London.

Rawdon knew that he was to some extent dominated by the women in his family. What they said mattered a lot to him, Jenny most of all. Despite her distorted views and twisted mind Jennifer Foxton had an almost paralysing effect on Rawdon, and she had said that not at any price would Emily be suitable for a wife. In the first place she would despatch his mother and sisters to live elsewhere, whereas Caroline was so kind, so used to caring for others, so thoughtful.

In many ways he wished he had not agreed to delay the announcement. Maybe he should have been bolder and insisted on a wedding before the war? What if he were killed in the war, never having known the delight of having Caroline for a wife? He saw how anxious she was, how quiet she became when Miss Martineau started enthusing about the war. Was it for the same reason? Seeing her beside her sister and this strange tubercular-looking young man he suddenly felt very close to her, wanted her very badly.

Jane and Miss Martineau embraced and then she was introduced to Daniel who once again was congratulated upon his bravery, to which he smiled modestly as he always did. Daniel felt he had done nothing that no other man would not have done; the only misfortune was that, as a result, he had grown to care too much for the victim, a relationship which he knew would be full of pitfalls, certain of an unhappy ending.

Miss Martineau was immediately interested in Daniel and, as Rawdon drew up a chair for her to sit on, she patted the place next to her. But first she turned to the invalid seated in her comfortable chair looking over the Park Street garden and questioned her as to her health.

'You look very pale, my dear, and so thin. Is she getting plenty of claret, oysters, game, turtle and brandy, Caroline? My hampers from Fortnum and Mason have been especially selected for their nutritional value. To an ample consumption of these substances I owe my continuing survival. That and, of course, the wonders of mesmerism. See my dear,' she took a small book from her capacious reticule and put it into Jane's hands, 'I have brought you a small volume that I wrote based on my own dreadful experiences when I was an invalid in Tynemouth ten years or so ago. Of course I was a delicate child and have not enjoyed good health throughout my life, suffering both from physical afflictions and those of a nervous nature. You might find it useful or, if not you, then your poor Mama.'

Jane looked at the volume.

'*Life in the sickroom,*' she read out. 'Oh *thank* you, Miss Martineau. But I am much recovered. Thanks to Caroline's wonderful nursing and Daniel, here. He reads to me every day, to perfect his English.'

Miss Martineau gave Jane a shrewd look and turned to Daniel. 'Do tell me about yourself,' she said. 'You are a hero, I hear. And not from this country either?'

Daniel looked so foreign that Caroline suppressed a giggle, aware that Miss Martineau, while inviting confidences, was also trying to be polite. The thick black serge of his suit, the loosely tied cravat, the bristling black hair, beard and moustache, the steady gaze of the penetrating eye, all spoke of someone who had not been born and reared on these shores.

'I am from France, Madame.' Daniel bowed. 'I was born in Rouen, but lived most of my life in Paris.'

'Daniel is a revolutionary,' Jane said with a mischievous smile. 'He would overthrow society as it exists.'

Miss Martineau screwed her trumpet firmly into her ear and leaned forward.

'Revolutionary! Good! I applaud idealism in the young. But to overthrow society by violent means? No, never. Society will evolve and create its own critical mass from within which it will throw off the yoke of misgovernment and tyranny. In feudal times, while you had the baronial wars, the middle and lower classes had time to rise and grow in strength, thus shifting the forces of society. We saw in 1848, when I began my *History of the Thirty Years' Peace*, the colossal ferment of society which I approved of and still do. The communist and socialist movements are *not* aggressions, but symptoms pointing to a desire for change in society. We had the same thing with the Chartist movement here. They are all experiences of malaise, of discontent. You cannot contain the critical mass for ever. And these changes will come, young man, but by slow process of transformation, not by violence such as you propose, though I sympathize with you. The more experiments we have the better, as long as they are carried on by people who know what they are about, as I am *sure* you do.' Miss Martineau smiled at him warmly. 'I will give you a copy of my *History*; it was very well received and I am being asked to update it; but I am waiting to see what the outcome of the present crisis in Turkey will be. In fact I am at the moment preparing a long article for the *Westminster Review* on foreign policy. I think, I know, it will be for war. The Russians must be thrown back for once and for all, or rather that tyrant the Czar must, not the Russian people who, in the process of time, will achieve the independence they rightly seek.

'I have a great belief in the sensibility of the people as those who have read my works will know, so long as they are not led by dictators or demagogues. As I am in London for some weeks you must come to dinner and tell me everything you did in 1848! I am dying with curiosity for first-hand news. I am *delighted* to know you, young man!'

Miss Martineau's eyes blazed with sincerity and Caroline could see how completely overwhelmed Daniel was by her charm. For although she was a large, plain woman who used an ear trumpet and spoke too loudly and too much, her presence was such as to endear her to her listeners though many people, including a fellow liberal John Stuart Mill, could not abide her.

'Do you know Karl Marx, Miss Martineau?'

'Marx?' Miss Martineau looked thoughtfully into the air, then shook her head. 'I don't believe I know anyone called Marx.'

'But Dr Marx is also against the Russians, and shares your views though I think he goes much further. He writes for the *New York Tribune*.'

'Indeed? Then I should have heard of him, although I no longer write so much or so regularly for the American papers as I did. I am vigorously in support of abolition, as doubtless you know, and have contributed much to that cause, I like to think. But Marx? No. I have not heard of him.' Miss Martineau took it for granted that any person of intelligence had not only heard of her, but read her books as well.

'He is a very *great* man,' Daniel said with passion. 'His ideas will change the world. He was very active in 1848 and before, an exile from Germany. He is most learned, a doctor of philosophy.'

'And where does this singular gentleman live, pray?'

'*Here* madame, in this very city! In Dean Street in Soho where he writes and works.'

'How interesting. I would like to meet Dr Marx.'

'*And* his friend Friedrich Engels who thinks like him, lives and works in Manchester. He wrote a study of the working classes there in 1844. He was quite appalled by what he saw. It has not yet been published in this country.'

'I have not heard of him either; but I am *most* interested in all you have to say, especially if Dr Marx is to change the world – I feel I should meet him!'

Miss Martineau smiled enigmatically and looked at the fob watch in her belt.

'Now my dear Jane, I know I have neglected you. But you are obviously much better. I thought I might bring Mrs Chetwynd to see you; but it appears she is no longer necessary. I think Mr Lévy here is helping to heal you with his socialist theories, though what your Papa says about it I cannot think!' Miss Martineau laughed and was about to get up when Caroline bent over towards her and looked at her earnestly.

'Miss Martineau, do you think Mrs Chetwynd could be persuaded to see Mama? I think from what you say that she might do her good.'

'I have been *longing* for Mrs Chetwynd to see your mother, my dear child. The problem is, how? I understand she does not really wish to be cured.'

The sisters looked at each other. Miss Martineau had now boldly said openly what they only dared think.

'We know it is true, Caroline,' Jane said quietly. 'Mama does *not* wish to get better. She wants to tie you to her, yet you have been so much happier here with me away from Chetwell; you are a different person. Mama must be *made* to get better.'

'But your mother can do without you,' Miss Martineau said. 'You have been here some time, have you not?'

314

'But my sister is with her when she is not in waiting, and Aunt Dorothy is there too; but still Mama does not get better. She really can hardly move her legs. It is paralysis.'

'She is too used to ill health,' Miss Martineau said firmly. 'I confess that even someone as strong minded as myself, and I can say this with modesty though you might not think so, became accustomed to the life of an invalid. As you will see from my little book it is all too easy to be reduced by the life. Mind you, even when ill and confined to my couch I never stopped work. I wrote many pamphlets on all sorts of subjects and articles and did much to help reform the drainage system in Tynemouth, where I lodged. Not enough attention has been paid to these matters in my experience, though things have improved a great deal since I left Tynemouth and went to live in Ambleside. Mr Chadwick, whom I admire enormously, has clung to this matter most tenaciously. His great Health of Towns Report so excited me when he sent me a copy that it made me too ill, at the time, to write and tell him how much I admired it. But your Mama, it seems to me, is quite a different case from mine. I *wished* to get better in order to become more active. She, it appears, does not. She has not enough to do, the trouble with many women who, having servants to do everything, succumb to every kind of malady merely to relieve boredom.'

Rawdon, who had remained in the background listening, rather overawed by the flow of words that poured from Miss Martineau, stepped forward and stood by Caroline. 'I wish you would, Miss Martineau. Caroline has been chained to her home for too long. Her mother is a monster of selfishness, though I know Caroline and Jane will not thank me for saying it. But 'tis true. Caroline wishes to do what other women do, be free to go into society, to marry perhaps...'

Rawdon was suddenly embarrassed by his intemperate plea and stopped abruptly, looking at Caroline. Miss Martineau, though a comparative stranger to romance in her own life, was quite able to perceive it in others. She raised an eyebrow but did not comment. Jane too was rather surprised by Rawdon's outburst and began to wonder if something was going on between him and her sister that she knew nothing about. Was she too absorbed, yet again, in her own affairs?

'Caroline has a strong sense of duty,' Jane said quickly. 'It would stand in her way.'

'Well.' Miss Martineau seized her stick and rose clumsily with its aid to her feet. 'I will see what I can do. It seems to me your father is the one who should insist that your mother sees Mrs Chetwynd. I assure you once she is there there will be no trouble. Mrs Chetwynd has great charm. Your mother will love her. I have no doubt of that at all.'

For once Hilary was not at the door to greet him or in the front parlour. George looked inquiringly at the passive face of Hilary's maid Ada.

'Where is your mistress, Ada?' He gave her his hat and adjusted his cravat in the mirror. 'Is she out?'

'She is upstairs, my lord. Mrs Ashburne is unwell and begs that your lordship will excuse her.'

'Unwell?' George turned from approving his reflection in the ornate glass on the parlour wall.

'She would have sent a note my lord, but the attack overcame her suddenly, too late to let you know.'

George began to feel alarmed. He recalled Hilary's pallor of late, her seeming lack of energy. Suddenly the vision of his dying daughter came upon him and he strode to the door, suddenly frantic with apprehension.

'Attack? Pray God what kind of attack, Ada? You must take me immediately to your mistress. Has the doctor been called?'

Without waiting for an answer or even giving the maid the chance to lead the way George ran up the staircase to the first floor and, without pausing outside the bedroom of his beloved, threw open the door and went in. Hilary was lying on the bed. She seemed to be fully dressed, but covered by a knitted blanket. She was very pale and her eyes were closed, but as he sat down by the side of her on the bed he saw that her lids flickered and knew she was awake. He took her hand which was icy cold and found that she was trembling.

316

'Oh my love, speak to me.' George bent down and kissed her cheek. 'You have a fever. It is the influenza. The doctor must be sent for at once. And you should be in bed with a fire in the grate, not shivering with cold as you are, my dearest girl.'

George got up and began to draw back the blanket, but Hilary put out a hand to stop him. Her blue eyes were full of suffering, and something else that was not connected with illness – remorse, anxiety? The look alarmed George more than her pallor and he sat once again on the bed taking both her hands and rubbing them between his.

'Hilary what *is* it my darling?'

'I have not been well for some time George,' she whispered.

The panic struck at his heart again. He was going to lose her as he seemed to lose everything he loved – his wife, his daughter, his son who would go to the war.

'Hilary, you are so precious to me!' He leaned over and kissed her again; but her trembling grew worse. Yet her face was so cold. She had no fever. She was near death. 'Oh my God. I myself will go for the doctor.'

As he got off the bed, Hilary suddenly sat up, her hair falling over her face, her bosom heaving with agitation.

'No George, pray do not go. I have seen a doctor.'

The colour was returning to her face; a flush from her neck was creeping up to her cheeks. Her eyes were burning, as though from some inner torment. The panic ebbed from George. It was replaced by a feeling of bewilderment and something else, fear. She was afraid and her fear was contagious. Something terrible had happened or was going to happen.

'I am with child, George,' Hilary said in a thin tired voice, and as she uttered the words the burning in her eyes gave place to tears and she kneaded her fists in her eyes like a small child.

George was still standing by the door, and as she spoke the words he recalled, oh how he recalled, the many times he had heard this phrase 'I am with child, George'. In the beginning it was with happiness and pride, feminine affection, bubbling over with tears of joy. In time it became the

317

reproachful 'I am with child again, George'. And he had tried not to look ashamed of himself, to pretend it had nothing to do with him. The last time there had been a terrible storm. She had not told him but the doctor. Agnes yet *again* was pregnant, a woman in her forties, a prey to the baseness of a man's desires.

'Mrs Vestrey is with child, Mr Vestrey – *yet again*.' Tut tut, what was he going to do about it? Dr Woodlove had looked at him with distaste, as though some quite unmentionable happening had taken place.

But this time the voice was different, the look pleading. *She* had done wrong and was asking *him* to forgive her. It was her fault not his; she clearly felt that and despite the shock of what she had told him his heart went out to her in love – and forgiveness. Of course he would forgive her. He knelt by the side of the bed and took her hand.

'Oh my darling, thank God.'

Hilary looked at him with astonishment. The tears cleared from her blue eyes and her chin trembled as she tried to speak.

'You don't *mind*, George? You are pleased?'

George closed his eyes trying to arrange his emotions.

'My darling I am just so thankful you are not ill – not mortally ill. You are so cold, so ashen. I thought you were dying.'

George leaned his face on her belly and wept.

For a while Hilary looked at his dark head pressed into the soft blanket on her belly. Inside her was their child, placed there by him, yet surely not wanted by him? She had made herself ill thinking about it. And all he was now concerned about was her. She knew how preoccupied he was with work, how tired he was of his wife, his family worries, and here she was adding to them – and yet all he was anxious about was her. He had thought she was dying. She put a hand on his tousled curls and played with them, picking them up at random with her fingers, pulling the hair straight and then letting it spring back into a tight coil. He seized her hand, kissing it, and she could feel the wetness on his face.

'I do love you, Hilary. I cannot do without you.'

'Even with a baby, George?'

He got up and sat beside her again, pressing her hands between his.

'Of course with a baby. With or without a baby I love you.'

'I am so sorry, George. Believe me if there was a way . . .'

She looked at him and saw his fear replaced with indignation, even anger.

'How do you mean, *if* there was a way . . .'

'To have prevented it, George. Or to get rid of it.'

'Get rid of my child?' George cried, letting her hands fall. 'Prevention is one thing; that *is* desirable if it is possible; but, not being so, to get rid of it . . . Hilary you would not dream of such a thing?'

'No George; but I did think of it. To spare you. I was too afraid.'

'You were quite right to be afraid.' George started to pace along by the side of the bed. 'The danger is appalling. Do you know the statistics of the mortality caused by abortion? It is not to be thought of. Never think of it. My darling Hilary if you died I should wish to die too.'

Hilary gave a deep sigh. She had been in torment for so long. It seemed as though a great weight had been lifted from her. She was once again secure in the knowledge of his love.

'It was in Vienna, George. I am four months gone.'

'Four months? But my darling you have concealed it so well.' He looked admiringly at her belly still protected by its warm blanket. Somehow the thought that his seed had taken root in her stimulated him to erotic thoughts in a way it had never done with Agnes. His relationship with Hilary had been so carnal, so sensuous. He closed his eyes at the crude but delicious memories the thought conjured up. It would be too dangerous to lie with her again until after the birth.

As though reading his mind she smiled and pulled him gently down beside her.

'I know what you are thinking, George. It is still possible you know. If you are careful.'

George looked at her with delight and carefully drew the blanket away from her lovely voluptuous form.

He was very careful; very tender. He begged her not to exert herself, not to be overtired. He lay beside her afterwards, his hand on her naked belly. Yes it was quite plump; though he had seen her so often that he didn't notice its increasing rotundity.

'Four months,' he said thinking back to Vienna. 'It was a lovely time. Our baby will be full of the love we shared there. A happy child, please God.'

She put her hand over his hand. She could feel her warm pulsating flesh through his. Their skins were rather damp.

'It *is* wonderful to make love and not worry about being pregnant, George.'

'But how long can we go on?'

'My doctor says about another month. Then the baby really begins to grow.'

'Oh, I only have you for another month!' George turned and buried his face in her flesh. She was so warm, so vibrant. Her breasts were larger too and he touched them with his tongue, wanting her to feed him with the fluid that was forming for the baby. With her rounded belly and swollen breasts she was like a beautiful, fruitful, earth mother.

'George, you have made me so happy,' Hilary said, then laughing as she saw his expression, 'oh I do not mean by making love, though that always makes me happy. It is your attitude; by still loving me and continuing to care. I was so frightened for so long. I thought you would be furious; that you would reject me. You are the very best of men, George. And I am so grateful to you.'

George kissed the crease between her breasts and straightened the blankets over them. Then he put his head on his arm and gazed at the ceiling. It was so cold in the room that their breath spiralled above them like smoke. But the heat of their bodies made it warm and comfortable beneath the blankets. He felt for her hand by her side and squeezed it.

'There is just one thing, my darling. We are happy as new parents should be, that our love has been fruitful. I

320

confess I did not want more children; but now, the knowledge that I have given you a child fills me with exquisite happiness, something that I felt more than ever today when I loved you, knowing that inside you was a part of me – that we are forever united by this bond.' He turned to her and his finger ran down her cheek, so warm now and rosy with ardour, so different from that icy pallor that had made his blood run cold. She turned to him and took his finger in her mouth, biting it with her delicate little teeth. 'But my darling, one thing I must tell you, and say it now. I can never marry you – as long as Agnes is alive.'

'I know that, George. I would never expect it.'

'There is no reason for her to predecease me. She is younger than I am and very healthy although she would have us believe otherwise. But she is my wife; we have a bond cemented in the church. I will never divorce her.'

'Hush, hush, George. Do not worry about these things.'

'But you, Hilary, may feel differently afterwards. After the baby . . .'

'I won't, George; but seeing that you are being frank let me speak plainly too. You do want me to keep the baby?' George sat up on his elbow, an expression on his face that Hilary found so comical she burst out laughing. 'Oh do not explode, Lord Vestrey! I see that you *do* want me to keep the baby . . .'

'Give my baby away?' George said with mock fury. 'Give away a *Vestrey*? My darling, you keep my baby, and you keep it here with you. *I* will do all I can to make the circumstances easy for you. All that I am saying is, it will not always be easy, Hilary. There are difficulties ahead of which you are, alas, not yet aware. There are bound to be; and I am limited by who I am and what I do in the kind of assistance I can give you.'

He snuggled down beside her and again they clasped hands under the bedclothes.

'As long as you do not desert me, George, as long as I have your love, nothing will be too hard to bear. Nothing.'

CHAPTER TWENTY

Miss Martineau's prophecy was correct: Agnes Vestrey not only took to Sophie Chetwynd on sight; she was thrilled by her. The extraordinary thing was that Mrs Chetwynd did not, on first appearance, look like one to command such devotion. She was a small woman, rather plump, rather grey and with a plain square face. There was, however, an air of capability about her, of sympathetic understanding that proved almost irresistible to a person like Agnes who needed a little of all those qualities Mrs Chetwynd seemed to possess.

She had felt neglected by Caroline, and now that Jane was well could not understand why she had not come home to Chetwell for good, to her rightful place by her mother's side. Emily had returned to Windsor and Dorothy Tangent, with her endless moping about Dalton and the disgrace, was becoming a bore. Mrs Chetwynd, introduced by Lady Foxton, appeared at exactly the right time.

The diplomacy needed behind the scenes had been such as to tax the inventiveness of George Vestrey despite his great experience in the art. Anyone introduced by him was bound to be received with hostility by his wife. Anyone introduced by *any* member of the family was sure to be suspect. For days after Miss Martineau's visit the matter was pondered, debated and endlessly discussed. At one point it was mooted that Miss Martineau herself should go and see Mama but, taking that lady's forceful personality, her dislike of cant and humbug into account, it was decided that, apart from the inconvenience to Miss Martineau, she should not be asked to go lest Agnes should, wittingly or not, offend her.

It was Rawdon, acting out of desperation, who brought up the idea of his mother. She would be the ideal intermediary; she was someone whom Agnes liked, even admired and knew well. She was also a tiny little bit afraid of her because Sybil Foxton was beautiful, capable, composed, intelligent and many other things that Agnes was not. Lady Foxton had presence, everyone was agreed on that. She never said a wrong word, or took a wrong step; yet she was kind, thoughtful and very popular. Also she was very anxious for her eldest son to marry Caroline Vestrey. She could think of no better daughter-in-law, someone who would complement Rawdon in every way, rather as she felt she complemented her own husband who was, however, much more difficult and trying than Rawdon.

Rawdon himself, full of excitement, had come down to Saltmarsh to put the plan to his mother. She was the only one he had told about his secret engagement, and she was pledged to keep quiet about it. She was thrilled. She would do anything, she said, to free Caroline from the shackles of her home. Sybil hurried up to London to discuss it with George Vestrey and Aunt Ruth. Lady Foxton liked the intrigue, the excitement and the air of uncertainty. But first of all she had to meet Mrs Chetwynd who was summoned to Saltmarsh and given a good going over.

Mrs Chetwynd, alerted by her friend Miss Martineau, knew exactly what to do. She had formed a pretty accurate picture of Agnes just from hearsay; she was sympathetic, kind but firm. Lady Foxton sent a glowing account of Mrs Chetwynd to George, and so the whole thing was arranged and the meeting took place early in December.

Agnes was expecting only Lady Foxton when she arrived with Mrs Chetwynd. No-one had dared to tell her because, of course, she had heard the name mentioned months before, though she may have forgotten it. No-one wanted to take the risk of finding out. So Sybil Foxton arrived and Agnes made a special effort to pretty herself and go along to the first floor drawing-room. She didn't want to be at a disadvantage in front of Lady Foxton. Sybil had not only kept her looks but, whereas Agnes had grown more timid in life, Lady Foxton was stronger. She was successful, able and she could cope. Since Rebecca's birth Agnes felt she couldn't cope at all.

She was thus seated by the fire looking pale but pretty

in a gown of blue foulard over a domed cage-crinoline, which was increasingly becoming the fashion. She wore, as usual, a lot of fussy little bows and laces, her favourite form of adornment, and a day cap made of the same material as her dress and trimmed with lace on her blonde hair, which had been curled and dressed by her maid for hours that morning.

She didn't get up when Lady Foxton was announced but extended her arms, as a welcome to her guest. She was sure that, once again, the object of her visit was a possible match between Rawdon and one of her daughters. She intended to try and sow the idea that *Jane* would be a suitable bride, because she was the only elder daughter with nothing to do and, after her terrible accident, she would never return to that charitable work again. Caroline had her mother to look after, and Emily the Queen to serve. Jane would have Rawdon. A good marriage would keep Jane out of more mischief.

Lady Foxton sailed into the room hardly waiting to be announced, Mrs Chetwynd a few discreet steps behind her. This strategy had been decided upon so that Agnes should be obliged to see her whether she wanted to or not. Being a lady she could never throw a visitor out of the room, but she could refuse to see her.

'My dear,' Lady Foxton cried, bending and kissing Agnes on both cheeks. 'You look radiant! I hear you are so much better.' She backed some distance away from her and beamed, her hands raised in the air as though asking God to witness a miracle. 'I have brought Mrs Chetwynd to see you, but I don't think her ministrations will be necessary. You look so *well*! '

Agnes's smile rapidly vanished and she peered behind her guest. She was quite confused and rather annoyed. Lady Foxton had not indicated she was bringing anyone. Chetwynd. Agnes frowned thoughtfully. The name rang a bell. Chetwynd ...

Mrs Chetwynd came forward, dropping a slight curtsey in front of Agnes and then took her hand.

'Your ladyship, how do you do.'

Agnes liked the little curtsey and the deferential way

Mrs Chetwynd addressed her. She looked up and saw a short, rather dumpy, plain woman, no longer young and quietly, unfashionably dressed. Not the sort of person one would have looked at twice, and she was about to turn and talk to Sybil when Mrs Chetwynd's eyes seemed to draw her towards her again. They were very dark and deeply set in her puffy white face; they sparkled with a curious intensity that transformed their owner. Agnes found them rather alarming, but remarkable. They were the one unexpected feature in an otherwise drab exterior. She found the eyes held her and it was not until her guest turned towards Lady Foxton that Agnes reluctantly experienced a sense of release. It had been rather a frightening and yet thrilling experience, as though one was in the presence of some powerful and unknown force. She felt she wanted Mrs Chetwynd to turn those remarkable eyes on her again and she looked after her eagerly.

'Mrs Chetwynd, I have heard of her,' Agnes said. 'I think my husband spoke of her though I can't be sure exactly.'

'Mrs Chetwynd is a very great friend of Miss Martineau,' Lady Foxton said quickly. 'She has also been helping me with my rheumatism.' Sybil Foxton flexed her long thin fingers. This was untrue; she had rheumatism, but she was not being treated by Sophie Chetwynd for it. However a white lie had been agreed upon as part of the strategy. 'I begged her to come over with me, on the spur of the moment, to see if she could do anything for your legs, my dear Agnes.'

That was it, a faith healer or some such. Agnes suddenly remembered where she had heard the name. Last Easter Jane had mentioned her and at the same time George started looking at her in that meaningful way. Agnes felt an overwhelming weakness and fear and wished with all her strength that she could run from the room; but she was powerless to move. Her legs felt like wooden stumps. It was an awful feeling and as she gripped the arms of her chair sweat broke out on her forehead.

Mrs Chetwynd turned again and gave Agnes a smile of such warmth and understanding, such serene goodness, that the fear suddenly left her and, by wriggling them, she could feel her toes again. She returned Mrs Chetwynd's smile and suddenly felt uplifted and free. Those unusual eyes never wavered and Agnes found she could look at nothing else, not even at Sybil who was watching the butler set up the table for the light luncheon Agnes had asked to be served in the drawing-room. She hadn't been downstairs to the dining-room for months; but stayed on the same floor as her bedroom.

Everything in the background continued, regardless of Agnes or even of Mrs Chetwynd who sat next to her, slightly sideways so that she could look at her, the gentle smile playing on her lips, her soft plump hand fingering the large cameo fastening the lace at her throat, and the eyes, dark, appealing, commanding.

'I hear you have been very ill,' Mrs Chetwynd said in a low voice as though she didn't want anyone else to hear.

'Oh yes, *very*,' Agnes said wishing to pour out her troubles to this understanding person. 'I injured my spine during the birth of Rebecca and cannot walk. I have to be helped everywhere and mostly stay in bed to spare my daughters or the staff who look after me.'

'That is very tragic,' Mrs Chetwynd said. 'But I have helped all kinds of cases, some maybe even more difficult than yours.'

Agnes felt a withdrawal, a constriction in the throat that made her reluctant and unwilling to say more. This woman *did* want to cure her, to make her a prey to George and his animal demands. She would not, she . . .

Mrs Chetwynd saw the storm in Agnes's eyes and put a comforting plump beringed hand on her arm. 'Nothing will happen that you do not wish, my dear. I may not be able to help you physically at all; but in your mind I may be able to give you peace.'

The eyes were like whirlpools, shifting waters that were focused on a central gyration by some powerful force. They twirled round to a tiny pin-point of light and then disappeared, sucked down into the swirling white-flecked brown foam. Yes there was tremendous calm in those waters, a floating away from all difficulties, all emotional storms, from demanding husbands, difficult daughters, wilful sons, crying unwanted babies. Peace.

Agnes convulsively pressed Mrs Chetwynd's hand as Bryce the butler came over and extended his arm for her to lean on. 'The light luncheon you ordered is ready to be served, my lady.'

Bryce leaned over but Agnes looked at Mrs Chetwynd who stood up and took Agnes's elbow, helping her to her feet. She smiled at Bryce and tucked a hand through Agnes's arm leading her gently over to the table where a comfortable cushion-filled chair awaited her. Mrs Chetwynd looked at the shuffling feet, felt the stiffness, the reluctance to move in Agnes's body. She gripped her very firmly and Agnes felt enormously secure. As she was lowered in her chair she smiled up gratefully.

'Thank you. You see how bad I am.'

'When was your baby born, Lady Vestrey?'

Agnes shut her eyes, unable to bear the memory. She passed a hand over her brow, but no word came. Sybil Foxton watched her anxiously. Maybe Agnes really was ill, and not suffering from an imaginary illness as everyone seemed to think. She was so stiff and when she had tried to rise there was a sense of real pain. Maybe they had all misjudged poor Agnes, and her look of slight scepticism turned to one of pity.

'Rebecca was born in November 1851,' she said, 'the year of the Great Exhibition. She has just had her second birthday has she not, Agnes?'

Agnes nodded, her face twisted with pain. Suddenly she wanted Caroline with her, strong, understanding Caroline who had gripped her hand while she pushed and pushed. Her eyes remained shut in a tight spasm and her hands, tightly clenched, reached out to grasp the firm reassuring hand of Caroline who was always there by her side when she needed her, who *had* always been at her side when she needed her.

And her hand was taken in a firm grip and, as she unclenched her fingers, an answering strong, reassuring hand clasped her own, sending strength through her body, fire into her blood, warming, enlivening, reassuring, healing.

Caroline was always there when she needed her; her firm young hands . . .

Agnes opened her eyes and looked into those of Mrs Chetwynd. She gazed at their clenched hands, the white, rather plump hand of a woman much older than Caroline, yet so strong, so forceful – not like Caroline's long, lean brown hands but just as powerful, just as reliable. Dependable.

'There, Lady Vestrey, I am here,' Mrs Chetwynd murmured reassuringly and, as though she had been dealing with a child, unfolded her napkin and placed it on her lap, smoothing it with the short, stubby bejewelled fingers which seemed to exercise over Agnes the same strange fascination as her eyes.

Lady Foxton appeared unaware of all this drama and was continuing the narrative of Rebecca's birth and miraculous progress ever since, her docile disposition, her beautiful nature, her precocity. It was a gentle background murmur, and every now and then Mrs Chetwynd nodded and said something like 'Really, Lady Foxton?' or 'How interesting, Lady Foxton.'

Agnes hardly ate anything, a spoonful or two of soup and a little of the poached fish that had been ordered specially for her delicate digestion. She felt very tired and put down her knife and fork; a heavy band seemed to press against her temple. She was aware of Sybil's sympathetic look and the glances exchanged between her and Mrs Chetwynd.

'Would you?' Sybil Foxton was murmuring. 'I will ring for her maid.'

Mrs Chetwynd got up and tucked the same reassuring hand through Agnes's arm leading her slowly to the door, noticing again the shuffling feet, the awkward movement of the legs. It was, she thought, like having a stiff old tree in your arms, all the branches creaking and half dead while the sap scarcely rose at all. As she got to the door Bryce came in and took Agnes's other arm and, between them, they helped her along to her room on the same floor, where her maid stood at the door waiting to receive her and lead her to the one secure home she had, her bed.

Sybil Foxton sipped her coffee and gazed for a long time

across the lawns, across the gentle landscape of the Kentish hills. From this side there was a view not of the sea, but of a rich leisured landscape, mile upon mile of fertile arable land interspersed with hedgerows, copses and meandering streams.

She was very worried indeed about Agnes; she had not realized she was half so ill. Everyone seemed to take it as a bit of a joke, a malingering, including Rawdon, her daughters and her own husband George. Sybil Foxton screwed up her eyes at the thought of George. He was such a vigorous, powerful, handsome man. A greater contrast to delicate, petite Agnes could hardly be imagined. She thought of the stories she had recently heard of him in Vienna and Paris, how he danced constantly with a beautiful blonde young woman. Some said she was an Austrian baroness, some a Hungarian princess, a member of the great Esterhazy family. In Paris she was supposed to be a member of the old nobility; but all agreed she was fascinating, mercurial and absolutely elusive. Nobody had ever succeeded in pinning her down long enough to issue an invitation to dine.

So George had a mistress. Not surprising, and discreet of him not to flaunt her in London, because no-one could actually point the finger or say anything to her than that he was seen a good deal in the company of Madame X . . . or Princess, or Baroness. It was very fascinating; but then George was a very fascinating man.

Sybil looked at the clock on the mantel and realized that time had passed since Agnes and the curious Mrs Chetwynd had left the room arm in arm. Sybil could not help noticing how fascinating Agnes had found her; it was a case of instant attraction, almost like love. Very odd, but then the pretty little Agnes Tangent whom George Vestrey had loved and wooed twenty-five years ago was no longer a flighty young girl, but a very sick prematurely aged woman.

The door opened quietly and Lucy, Agnes's maid, put her head round the door.

'Ah you are here, Lady Foxton. Mrs Chetwynd wondered if you would come to Lady Vestrey.'

'Is her ladyship worse, girl?' Sybil Foxton got up quickly and went to the maid's side looking at her anxiously.

'Oh no. Madam is tranquil and resting; but Mrs Chetwynd wishes to do something to her and would like you to be there.'

Lucy, thin and pale, looked decidedly alarmed, as if all the goings on she had known in her years at Chetwell had never reached such a pass.

'There is no need to be alarmed, Lucy.'

Lucy still looked alarmed.

'Oh I am sure there is not, Lady Foxton; but what is she doing? She looks at her ladyship so oddly and her ladyship can't stop looking at her. Neither of them seemed to notice me all the time I was in the room. They didn't even appear to realize I was *there*. And then as Lady Vestrey lay looking at Mrs Chetwynd, who held her hand, she turned to me and said "Pray fetch Lady Foxton. I think your mistress is right for what I am about to do".'

Sybil Foxton suddenly felt very agitated and, beckoning to the maid, hurried from the room.

'Come, we must be quick. Oh, I *wish* my son or Lord Vestrey were here. I think this is more than I bargained for.'

The door of Agnes's room was ajar and, as they came to the threshold, she slackened her pace and gently pushed it open. Inside it was very quiet and there was an air of peacefulness and calm. From where she stood she could see that outside the sea and the sky were the same grey colour, divided by the dark line of the horizon.

Mrs Chetwynd sat in a chair close by the side of Agnes's bed, and in her hand was a lighted candle which she passed gently backwards and forwards across Agnes's face. She did not interrupt her action, but said in a quiet monotonous voice, 'Pray sit down, Lady Foxton, with Lucy, and do not talk or interrupt. Close the door and lock it; then take a chair, if you would, behind us.'

The usually imperturbable Sybil felt rather frightened. She clasped Lucy firmly by the hand and drew her round the side of the room to two chairs by the window. From there what light there was left of the winter's afternoon

330

shone on Agnes and cast Mrs Chetwynd in the shadows. The flickering lighted candle passed rhythmically backwards and forwards between her and Agnes, obscured for them by her body, but appearing at either side like a swung pendulum with monotonous regularity. Even Sybil felt herself becoming sleepy and had to shake her head to keep awake as Mrs Chetwynd's voice droned on and on, and the candle passed back and forth, back and forth.

Agnes couldn't remember how she got into bed, except that Lucy, her maid, had undressed her and helped her into her chemise while Mrs Chetwynd waited outside the door, returning as soon as she was ready. As Lucy went out of the door Mrs Chetwynd came in and her eyes immediately fastened on Agnes as she took her hands and led her to the bed.

Now Agnes lay there feeling deliciously warm and comfortable, slightly sleepy, but her eyes quite unable to close because of the tiny pinpoint of light that went backwards and forwards. At times it obscured Mrs Chetwynd completely, or rather part of her, for the eyes remained fixed over the light; and in them she saw another thousand lights and a great cave full of fanciful shadows gyrating like dark storm clouds in the sky. She saw herself as a child come out of the shadows in the long white dress she wore for the first birthday party she could remember, she must have been seven or eight. Her father was there and her mother and it was a beautiful day in June. All her family were around her and her Uncle Cully Allwood was there who had lost a leg in the Battle of Waterloo two or three years before. Cully was her favourite uncle, her mother's youngest brother, a soldier who had fought in India and all through the Peninsular war only to lose a leg at Waterloo. Uncle Cully had lost his gaiety with his leg; he had become mournful and depressive and took to drinking which made him very quarrelsome and he shouted and ranted a good deal.

But that day Uncle Cully was laughing too and he hopped about on his good leg putting out his false one before him and making faces. Oh they laughed; but then suddenly Cully's bad leg – the one he held out in front of him in that comical manner – fell off, and he slipped over onto his face before anyone could help him and lay twisted and in pain on the ground, the wooden leg at a distance from his short, stocking-covered stump.

It was a terrible moment seeing Uncle Cully helpless and unhappy and Agnes burst into tears and rushed away because she could not bear to look at it, could not bear to think of being unable to walk.

He couldn't walk, she couldn't walk . . . she tried to go back and comfort Uncle Cully, she was his favourite niece, but she couldn't walk to him, she couldn't help him. She stretched out her arms and cried and cried, but she couldn't move. It was as though someone was holding her back. She strained out a hand and it was grasped by someone calm and capable, strong and reassuring and a voice said:

'Now put your feet on the floor and walk over to the window, steadily now, one foot after the other. Steady. That's it.'

And she was walking, quite firmly, not limping, or tottering, not even feeling stiff, just as she used to before Uncle Cully lost his leg. After the accident he would never wear it again and a short time later he was dead, some said of drink, but some said of a broken heart. There was nothing in front of her but the window, no support, nothing to hold on to; but the voice, behind her, said 'go on' and she went on as she had been told, on and on firmly one foot in front of the other, until she reached the window and saw the sea very grey merging with the sky because it was nearly dusk, a late, wet December afternoon. Then she came to the sill and suddenly her legs gave way beneath her and she grasped it urgently to prevent herself from falling to the floor. But before that there were firm hands supporting her, lifting her up, preventing her from falling. Firm strong young hands, Caroline's hands.

She felt a soft cheek pressed against hers, a soft, downy cheek smelling of powder, that of a much older woman. She felt the strong hands squeeze under her armpits, press a little against her bosom, rather a thrilling sensual feeling it was, feeling the hands on the thin chemise that was all there was between her and her naked breasts. Then a soft, friendly, womanly body pressed against hers, supportive and protective, not that harsh, demanding, angular man's body always asking for hateful shameful things.

'There my dear, you did it.' Mrs Chetwynd's lips were very close against Agnes's ear. 'I told you I could make you well. All you have to do is trust me. You can trust me always, you know. Always.'

CHAPTER TWENTY-ONE

Benjamin Disraeli called it a 'just but unnecessary war'. Lord Aberdeen never forgave himself for allowing it to happen, but it did. Britain and France declared war on Russia at the end of March 1854. For months war fever had gripped the country and all those who dared speak against it were regarded to some extent as traitors. Wild rumours said that the Prince Consort was treasonably involved with Russia, and huge crowds gathered on Tower Hill to see him and Aberdeen committed to the Tower. When this failed to happen the angry crowd burnt their figures in effigy instead. A curious madness gripped the country that no-one could adequately explain unless it was that, as a nation, England had been too long at peace.

The Guards left for war a month before it was officially declared. They embarked in February 1854 and the Honourable Rawdon Foxton and the Honourable James Vestrey went with them. Sections of the British Army dispersed about the world were speedily being recalled, but the élite Brigade of Guards had been preparing for months for war.

What was so distressing was the fact that when it did come it was so sudden. There was hardly time for goodbyes, for saying all the things left unsaid until the last moment.

'Now that it has happened,' Rawdon whispered when he and Caroline were briefly alone at Chetwell the week before the Guards left, 'it will soon be over. By the summer we shall be wed.'

The fact that he was leaving emboldened him to kiss her full on the lips; not just a soft brush but a firm, lingering kiss. Caroline felt that they merged together; the hard masculinity of his body, the soft curves of hers. She felt desire as she had never known it before, a feeling in her loins that distressed her greatly when she thought about it afterwards. It was really quite wicked to be so abandoned with a man to whom one was not married. If he felt she was too willing he would lose all respect for her. Even someone as understanding as Rawdon.

She broke away and patted her ruffled hair, put cold hands on her burning cheeks.

'I'm sorry,' Rawdon said backing away. 'Forgive me Caroline, for losing control. Please do not think that I do not love and respect you more than my life. It is the thought of losing you . . .'

'But you will not lose me, Rawdon. I am here. I shall wait for you.'

'And write?'

'Of course. I shall write every day and tell you what is happening and how the seasons change; because, except for that, my life will be very dull.'

'But your Mama is so much better!'

'Yes, it is quite remarkable, although her joints had stiffened so much through inactivity that she hobbles about like an old woman.'

But there was no doubt about it. Agnes walked, and every day her steps got easier and quicker. She could walk down the stairs and into the dining-room; she had walked into the garden well wrapped up against the bitter January winds. She had even got into the carriage and driven over to see her brother, but she decided she was too unwell to attend Dalton's marriage to Maggie Ticehurst. Besides, the shock of this misalliance might undo all the good that had been done. This sad event, a very quiet affair indeed, took part at Chetwell Church with a surprising number of people unable to come apart from Agnes. In fact the refusals outnumbered the acceptances, Sir Smithers Rawlings being one of the many to send their regrets. The Ticehursts were now comfortably lodged in a cottage on the Vestrey estate and Dalton and his bride were living in a small house in Islington not too far from his chambers.

So Agnes had regained the use of her legs and mesmerism was generally judged to be miraculous. Miss Martineau wrote that she could hardly wait to see her, but she had had very little doubt as to the outcome. Once one succumbed to the benign influence, it was bound to succeed even in the most sceptical. She had now returned to Ambleside where she was pouring out leaders in the *Daily News* encouraging all good Englishmen to support the war.

Rawdon felt there was a dreadful inevitability about the way Agnes Vestrey had recovered, and Caroline had, theoretically, regained her independence just at the moment he was called abroad. For there was no doubt that Caroline had her independence; her mother's new constant companion was Sophie Chetwynd. She had been given a comfortable suite on the same floor as Agnes, a large room that had been made into a sitting-room and George's old dressing room as a bedroom so that she slept just next door to Agnes. They even left the interconnecting door open in order to call to each other from their respective beds. It was mutually comforting to be so near.

'And Jane is on the mend,' Rawdon continued, 'though I tell you I feel you will have trouble with that fellow. The times I have seen them together make me uncomfortable. His eyes are all over her. It is not at all seemly, Caroline.'

'No, it isn't. Now that you mention it, Rawdon, I *am* aware of it. I have noticed it too. I try not to leave them alone together. With a person of his sort you cannot be sure that he knows how to behave with ladies. Oh I know that sounds awful but . . .' Caroline put a hand to her mouth and stared at Rawdon. She felt suddenly ashamed of her views and knew how Jane would despise her if she could hear her.

Rawdon came over to her and gently took her hand – how he loved to touch her – looking into her eyes.

'No my darling, you are right. He is a man of no station at all, lowly born, who might well not know how to behave. Jane is so unconventional she might think it bold and unusual to fall in with his wishes. Now that she is so well I think it is time that Mr Lévy was sent packing.'

'Jane is to join me here,' Caroline said. 'I intend to tell her about our understanding when we are alone and ease her in to looking after Mama so that I can prepare for our wedding in the summer.' She smiled at him with that adoring yet unobsequious expression he loved so much. She loved him, but not slavishly. They would be equal partners with Caroline submissive, as a woman should be, but a companion too. Yes, she would be the perfect wife; the perfect partner.

'Do you think I should speak to your father, my dearest ... Just to prepare him?'

'No, no!' Caroline said, squeezing his hand, longing to be kissed by him again yet fearing the awful commotion such intimate contact aroused in her body. It was a really wonderful feeling; but it was decidedly carnal. It could not possibly be right. Rawdon would be shocked if he knew. She edged away from him so that she could not feel his thigh, encased in his smart tan uniform trousers, so near to that lower intimate part of her body although that too was well protected by her voluminous skirts and the long drawers that even, Emily told her, the Queen was said to wear. It had been whispered among the women of the court although of course no-one talked about it *openly*. They just rushed out and bought these interesting new garments brought quietly into vogue by the Queen.

'No, there is no point in telling Papa, Rawdon. He is so busy; so distressed. Besides, he would not keep it to himself. Let us wait until you come home and then you can ask him and we can plan the wedding at the same time.'

All day Caroline felt a pain in her breast, a dull ache of regret and longing. There was a risk in every war and the Guards were always to the forefront. Besides, Papa had said that regiments were being recalled from all over the world. It looked as though it was going to be a much bigger thing than anyone had thought; certainly more than a mere skirmish.

Rawdon and James left Chetwell together and went back to London by the coach they had driven down in, having first called at Saltmarsh to take leave of Rawdon's parents and sisters, his brothers especially summoned from school and university. They arrived in Park Street towards evening to find that George had prepared a farewell dinner for them and that Emily was expected too, having been given leave by the Queen.

They had sherry in the upstairs drawing-room before dinner, George sombre and careworn, Aunt Ruth apprehensive and worried. The next day the Guards were going to march through London before embarking. George raised his glass.

'To the Guards, especially to Captain Foxton and Captain Vestrey. God bless you and bring you safely back.'

George drained his glass and turned away, making a show of consulting his watch to hide his emotion. Aunt Ruth left the room to see to the dinner preparations.

'Emily is late. Jane is downstairs waiting for her young man.'

'Lévy is to be here, father?' James's brows knitted with anger. He had grown a moustache and although it made him look older it also made him, if anything, appear more dashing. 'Good God, what made you invite that fellow?'

George shrugged. 'Jane asked me to. She has a great deal of obligation you know . . .'

'Obligation, nonsense, father. Are you blind? She is in love with him.'

'Oh no!' George said shaking his head. 'That is not at all the case. It could not be. Jane is my daughter and knows her duty. Even she realizes how unsuitable such an alliance would be. I assure you you are mistaken, James. He would not presume, I know. She likes and admires him and, like us all, is grateful for what he did for her. That is all. Ah. I think I hear Emily.'

Through the half-open door he heard a commotion in the hall and light footsteps up the stairs.

'Oh Papa!' Emily burst in, radiant in a ball gown of white silk with a deep embroidered hem and pink bows going from the hem to the bodice. 'Oh Papa. Lady Fox-Hargreaves is giving an impromptu soirée and dance to say goodbye to the Guards. The Queen says I may go. Oh Papa *please* come, with Rawdon and James. Aunt Ruth says "yes".'

Aunt Ruth walked slowly into the drawing-room followed by Jane. She smiled ruefully at George. 'What could I do, George? I am sure you will agree.'

George laughed. 'What can I say? If Rawdon and James agree?'

'Of course father,' James said smiling at his excited sister. 'And Jane? Will you come too?'

'I don't think Daniel would like the dance, James. He does not incline to that sort of thing. We will spend a quiet evening here. Aunt Ruth will be here. It will be *quite* respectable, father.' Her eyes flashed and she looked at her father as though challenging him to refuse.

'Jane, just what is your intention with that fellow?'

James began stroking his silky new moustache aggressively. But George put out a warning hand.

'Please James, not on the eve of your departure. That is something that Jane knows quite well how to control. Lévy is a friend of this family. We owe him a great debt. Remember that. Now if you are to go to a dance we must eat at once. You men will not want to be bleary-eyed when you march through London tomorrow.'

It was difficult to take his eyes off her, she looked so beautiful. The white virginal gown and her white skin, her blonde hair chastely parted in the middle fastened with a broad pink bow. The whole effect was to seem to contrive innocence, but tantalizingly to miss doing so. She looked too desirable, too flirtatious. There was a tiny bunch of artificial flowers behind her right ear and she wore a necklace of rubies and diamonds, a twenty-first birthday present from her mother and father, which blended with the pink touches to her ensemble.

She had talked all during dinner, ignoring Rawdon in that splendid, calculated way she had and then capturing him as soon as they arrived at Lady Fox-Hargreaves', eagerly leading him on to the dance floor, tugging at his hands, teasing with her very blue eyes.

'You are so solemn, Rawdon! Surely it is not just because of the war?'

'Well, it is a solemn time Emily; though we are glad to be seeing service at last. Travel abroad is a fine thing, and to places we have never seen.'

'You are going to Malta first?'

'Yes; then to Turkey.'

'Look after my big brother.'

'Oh, I will.'

'And yourself. Especially yourself.'

Emily, in the privacy afforded by the mêlée of people on the dance floor, put her lips to his ear, whispering. Momentarily he felt a wetness and knew that her little pink tongue had darted out and licked the lobe of his ear. He blushed and tweaked it, looking round to see if anyone had observed such boldness.

'No one saw, you goose!'

'Please Emily, there *are* proprieties . . .'

But he was excited. The old flame that he thought his pure chaste love for Caroline had dampened flared up again, tormenting him anew. She was beautiful, she was lively, she was wicked and provocative. She was inflammable. Did he ever feel inflamed by Caroline? Yes, in a way . . . but not the same way; not the same tormented way he felt about Emily with erotic visions of sleepless nights and wild passionate days. It was quite ridiculous. He was engaged to her sister. *In love* with her sister; really in love, not just ensnared by some despicable, lustful emotion.

She saw the look in his eyes, the flush on his cheeks and felt triumph in her heart. She could hold him; she could trap him whenever she liked.

'You have not been very nice to me lately, Rawdon?' she simpered.

'No?' He pretended to be surprised, but his blush deepened. He tugged at his stiff upright collar and hoped she would think it was the heat, not the guilt he was feeling at betraying Caroline and deceiving Emily. 'You know I have been very busy Emily, preparing for this departure.'

He put his hand lightly about her waist as they stationed themselves for the waltz, and as the small orchestra broke into sound he placed his hand on her palm, aware of the steady pressure of her free hand on his shoulder.

'No there is something *more* than that, Rawdon Foxton. You have been avoiding me.'

'But *why* should I avoid you, Emily?'

The dance started, and easily, with the familiarity of many years of practice, they began dancing round Lady Fox-Hargreaves' large drawing-room while scarlet-coated guardsmen and their partners jostled all about them. Rawdon was still aware of that saucy gesture as her tongue had flicked his lobe. He thought he could still feel the moistness of her saliva. His heart thudded with the fierce, sensuous visions her gesture had stimulated.

'It must be your conscience,' Emily shouted above the din. 'Something you are ashamed of.'

'I am ashamed of nothing!' Rawdon shouted back and then their eyes met and they laughed as though from the memory of some shared naughtiness, as when they were children and their nursemaid had caught them together in some misdemeanour or the other.

Yes, he felt so close to the Vestrey girls; so near to them in spirit. They both enchanted him, still. They were part of him. It was very, very confusing, and, altogether, a good thing he was going away.

People at the dance observed, and reported it afterwards until it reached every small corner of London society where gossip was bred and from where it circulated to an ever increasing audience, that Rawdon Foxton and Emily Vestrey danced together all evening. The only dance Emily missed was when her brother claimed her and Rawdon was seen standing against a wall watching every step they made, as though he could hardly wait to reclaim her again.

And it was true. The fascination that Emily had exercised so powerfully over him before overwhelmed Rawdon yet again. He *had* been avoiding her. He *had* left early when she was due to arrive somewhere, or when she had already departed, because during these months, with the connivance of his family, he had convinced himself that it was Caroline he should choose. Caroline was right for him and Emily wrong.

Wrong? The dancing stopped early; there were tearful farewells in the corner of balconies, in alcoves, on the staircases, in small dimly lit parlours off the great hall and just outside the huge French windows of Lady Fox-Hargreaves' drawing-room which had been opened despite the cold, because it was so warm indoors.

For the first time in his life Rawdon Foxton had kissed Emily fully and passionately, in a way he had never kissed Caroline. He had pressed his body hard against hers as she stood by the stucco wall, damp from the evening rain, and felt her firm womanly bosom against his chest. He had kissed her mouth, her eyes and her neck, his lips lingering on her shoulders, his eyes on that full, enticing mound which erupted out of her tight white bodice.

And Emily responded to him with the practice of someone who either was used to the art of turning men's heads or who had given the matter much thought. She moaned and she writhed in his arms, she closed her eyes and sighed like the heroine of every romantic novel she had ever read. When he tried to draw away she pulled him to her again and put out her little tongue, demanding more.

Caught up in such a torrent of passion Rawdon needed some reminding of where he was and that it was time to go.

'The lights are going out inside,' he whispered hoarsely. 'The candles are dying in their sconces.' He looked at her in the dim light that came from the many windows of the house. There was no moon and the garden was very dark. If anyone found them here they would both lose their reputations. He would never forget how beautiful, how sensually abandoned, she looked, her head just twisted sideways a little regarding him, her full mouth slightly parted and her bosom heaving. He would remember her nose and her chin, her white skin, her golden hair and those enchanting violet eyes now very bright with tears.

'I will wait for you, Rawdon,' she whispered. 'I will wait until you come back. The Queen will release me when she knows how much in love I am. She will understand.'

'Oh Emily I cannot . . .' Rawdon felt a sudden panic. A need to rush in and explain everything; but he could not. Not only was he tongue-tied, but there was no time. She put a finger on his mouth, lovingly closed his lips.

'There is no need to say anything, silly goose. I know what you have had on your mind. I know how you feel. Besides, you knew how occupied I was with my duties; and I confess I have loved being in waiting at the greatest Court in the world. But I will free myself eagerly as soon as you wish it. No, do not speak my love.' She kept her finger firmly on his mouth and he could only look at her agonizingly, appealingly, lacking the courage and the will to do what he knew he should before it was too late. Much too late. 'Go to the war with your heart filled with the memory of this night. I will wait for you. And when you return, I will be here.'

Caroline felt a terrible void after Rawdon and James went back to London. Not only was she lonely; but she was afraid. England had been involved in no major war since Waterloo nearly forty years before, when Mama and Papa were small children, and there was something terrifying in a threat to the order and stability of her world that involved people she loved. Emily remained in waiting and Jane was reluctant to leave London and Daniel until Caroline wrote and begged her to come home for a few days.

Even home was no longer the friendly place it had been. Christmas, once the happiest family occasion of the year, had been the first anniversary of Debbie's death and a time for sorrow and mourning. Mama had not come down at all but stayed in her room waited on by the new member of the household, Sophie Chetwynd.

Mrs Chetwynd had been at first welcomed by the family; but now she was seen as an obtrusive, alien presence with unfamiliar ways and curious frightening powers. She moved about very stealthily and lurked in corners; she always appeared when least expected. Her obsequiousness and exaggerated respect for the family was cloying and irritating.

What could Caroline do in a house with such a presence? She was more lonely, more frightened now than after Christmas when the family had thankfully gone back to London at the earliest opportunity. She went to the station to meet Jane, holding on to her tightly all the way back in the carriage. Caroline's attitude worried Jane. The family were all so used to leaning on her that one never thought she could be in need.

Later that day when Jane had spent her dutiful amount of time with her mother – being nice to her and receiving insults and recriminations in return – the two sisters were able to be alone in the small parlour where Caroline did her accounts. They had read stories to Clare and Patrick, kissed them goodnight, kissed Mama goodnight, bade a

343

chilly goodnight to Mrs Chetwynd and now they were together with the evening before them.

The rain lashed against the house, blown in from the sea by a gale of immense force. Everything that moved in the house seemed to creak; doors were blown open and shut. Smoke kept on billowing down the chimney in great gusts that made them move back from the fireplace every so often, coughing and brushing themselves, spluttering with rueful laughter.

Even when the fire was roaring once again up the chimney and there was no need to move back from the smoke, Caroline paced restlessly up and down, drawing back the curtain to look out of the window into the blackness of the night, unable to see anything. She thought of the ships tossing on the sea and of Rawdon, who might be among them, borne away to a far distant land. Jane watched her, wishing she would settle and they could talk. She hugged her shawl about her and peered into the fire, seeing Daniel's thin, intent face in the shadows formed by the ashes of the wood that crackled and snarled before they subsided into the recesses of the great stone fireplace.

The attraction to Daniel had come gradually; she had never believed that she could be so interested in someone so unlike Papa. Papa was tall and robust, handsome and confident, with everything that went with good birth, wealth, health and possessions. Daniel was hardly taller than she was, with the thin, almost emaciated body of the tubercular. His face was also skeletal, the cheeks slightly concave, the head angular and delicate, covered with fine short hair. His beard, running from ear to ear, entirely covered his chin and upper lip and the small amount of skin that one could see was very white, while his brilliant black eyes surmounted by very fine delicate eyebrows appeared a curious incongruity. He did not look like a man who enjoyed good health, and he said that as a child he had been frail.

His teeth were white and even, seldom seen because he was always so grave and quiet, little given to laughter. At first he had seemed like a companion, a clever, learned, patient friend who came to read to her and talk to her partly to correct his own poor English and partly, too, out of loneliness.

She couldn't even remember when the feeling of physical intimacy had started, or the first glimmerings of desire for someone who she realized was a man as well as a friend. The neutrality of sex vanished and she became aware of his masculinity, the outline of his taut, wiry body, and knew that he saw her too as a woman.

They didn't try and resist what they knew was happening. People, naturally, had grown accustomed to leaving them alone. The day he kissed her had been very deliberate, assured and yet relaxed. It was full and passionate, a far cry from the timid kiss in the studio with Jeremy Pagan who, she realized, must have had as little experience as she. It seemed the most natural thing to do, to come together in this way, to want to come together more completely in a way that she didn't yet understand; but Daniel did.

Daniel told her that he had slept with women, had had a mistress in Paris for two years, who had died of typhoid shortly before he left for good. He told her that the body was beautiful, and carnal relations between men and women among the most precious and delightful. He kissed her so expertly and once or twice he felt inside her dress, his hands caressing the swell of her breasts. Then the desire in her loins, new and unexpected, had been almost overwhelming as she felt him touch and explore her nudity, imagined the act of removing all her clothes.

Their sessions together had become an attempt on his part to seduce her, and he made no bones about it. He wanted her and she knew she wanted him; but he never mentioned marriage, or anything except taking her to bed with him. At the time it all seemed so wicked and secretive in the house in Park Street with Aunt Ruth, or Emily or Caroline blissfully ignorant in the parlour downstairs. She was sure the passion and heat engendered by their kissing must be obvious to all; but no-one seemed to notice a thing. Everyone thought they were reading Thackeray, or Goethe in the original German.

Then he told her, in his earnest forthright way, how he felt about marriage. That it was bourgeois and wrong. That a mutual, free association between men and women was all he believed in. So, there was no question of their marriage, or having to ask Papa for her hand, as if he had any chance of getting it. She was simply to tell her family, if she wished, that they intended to live together. That this was the mid-nineteenth century, the age of enlightenment and freedom. It was time to cast off the bourgeois shackles of the past.

Then he left her for some time to think it over. He did not get in touch with her and she was desperate. When at last he did appear he wanted an answer; otherwise he said he no longer trusted himself to contain himself with her. There would be no point in their continuing to meet. He desired her too much. That time he exposed her breasts altogether and caressed under her skirt. That time she almost gave way.

And then the announcement that James was going to Turkey had momentarily put a stop to everything. It was out of the question to talk to Papa, to say anything to anyone. Thank heaven she had a respite, for she did not know what to say. No Vestrey, to her knowledge, certainly no women members of the family, had ever done anything like this ever before.

Something inside her now was bursting to tell, to say she was in love and loved, that she knew about physical love, that the fierce flame of passion had burned in her not once but many times. She was no longer as she had been, but a woman ready to give herself in love, without the blessing of family or church. But if only she could talk to Caroline; to enlist her help, her advice, her understanding . . .

Caroline finally stopped her pacing and came and crouched by the fire, poking the embers with a long iron poker. Jane wished she would begin the conversation, say something, say anything about what they both had on their minds. But it was in the Vestrey tradition to keep silent about what was uppermost in their hearts. Whatever they had to say to each other, they did not know how to begin. Then it was as though they both decided at the same moment to unburden themselves, and began talking at once.

'Do you think . . .' said Jane.

'Mama is . . .' Caroline began, speaking at the same time. Then they both paused, stared at each other and laughed.

'You were saying?' Jane inclined her head and Caroline continued poking the fire.

'Mama is certainly much better. Don't you think?'

'She has exchanged one sickness for another,' Jane replied. 'I can't bear the way she clings to Mrs Chetwynd as though she were her nurse.'

'She *is* her nurse. I must be thankful. She has superseded and released me.' Caroline sat back on her haunches and stared at the blaze she had created. 'For what?'

Jane, knowing the moment had come, the intimacy she wanted, decided to seize it and leaned forward.

'It has been very hard for you, Caroline, to be tied to Mama. Now that you are free, is it too late?'

'Too late for what?' Caroline looked up defensively.

'Because Rawdon has gone? Is that it?'

'You think I wanted to be free for Rawdon?'

'Didn't you?'

Caroline stared at Jane, surprised and rather moved by her perspicacity. What she had had to conceal from everyone else had been obvious to her sister. Was it because she, too, had been touched by love?

'Yes, I suppose I did. At one time I thought I wanted to do something for the world, you know, achieve something. But now I think the best one can do is to marry a good man, be his helpmeet in life and raise a family.'

Jane gazed at her sister, her chin resting on her knee. The colour of Jane's hair was closest, of all the Vestrey children, to George's, almost black and curly like his. She had difficulty in disciplining it to fit in with the current fashionable neat central parting, with a bunch of carefully curled ringlets at the back. She liked it best when she could let it hang loosely, as now, cascading onto her shoulders. This was how Daniel loved her. He lost no time, as soon as the door was closed and locked, in letting her hair loose and running his hands through it, burying his face in it.

Caroline was aware of Jane's steady regard, almost able to read her thoughts.

'I know you might despise me, Jane, and think me dull. But that is what I have decided. It is what I am best suited to, what my training has prepared me for.'

Jane reached out and took Caroline's hand.

'I *never* despise you, darling Caroline, I never shall.

347

Nothing you ever did would make me despise you. What you have done these last few years is really inspiring. You have taken over the family, replaced our mother. You have had the agony of watching our little sister die and succoured and comforted us all. I want you to be happy Caroline, with all my heart, even if it is in a way that would not make me happy. Yes, I do want to change the world. I do want to make some mark on life, though I know not how any more than you. I feel constricted by the chains that bind us women – the narrow tedium of our lives. I want to write and preach and form groups of militant women who will overthrow their oppressors, and . . .'

'Oh pray!' Caroline threw herself on the floor next to Jane and put a hand on her arm. 'Oh dearest Jane pray stop! This is a dream that has no future; it will only make you unhappy and unfulfilled. Gradually women may have a more important function in society; but that time is not yet, not for many years. In the meantime we must make what we can of our lives, in the roles to which we are accustomed. And yes, I do want to marry Rawdon.'

She turned shyly to her sister, her heart bursting to tell. Jane pressed her hand. 'He did ask you?'

'Yes, oh quite a long time ago, in the autumn when you were still very sick. But we agreed to wait because it seemed there might be a war, and also I wanted to prepare Mama and Emily . . .'

'Oh, Emily.' Jane was offhand. 'She has set her cap too obviously at Rawdon. I think he laughs at her.'

'Oh, he does not laugh at her!' Caroline protested. 'He likes her. But he loves me. I am so fortunate, so happy.'

Jane leaned over and kissed her sister's cheek, and Caroline briefly put an arm round her shoulder and squeezed it. In the light of the fire they looked very young and vulnerable as they squatted on the floor, their legs stretched out before them, Jane with her shoes off and her hair unbraided.

'But I do not want Emily to be sad.'

'Oh, Emily will always find a man. Anyway she is happy with her role at Court. I think she wanted Rawdon because you did. In a way she is envious of you. The big sister. Oh I cannot explain it, but do not concern yourself too much over our Emily, dear Caroline. Prepare for your own happiness. I am well and Mama . . . well Mama seems to have her own kind of health.' Jane clasped her knees and hugged herself, bursting with some secret. 'Oh Caroline, I am so happy for you . . . and for me. For I am in love too!'

Caroline felt a chill as though the door had opened and someone had come into the room bringing with them all the cold from outside. To look at her sister's happy, flushed face was to know what she had been dreading for so long, what Rawdon and James had warned her and Papa about.

'Daniel?' she whispered, rising slowly to her feet.

'Yes Daniel, Daniel . . .' Jane threw her arms in the air looking up at them as though she expected a lovely present to fall into her hands. She was completely transformed, not only from the sick person she had been a few months before, but from the girl she had been before that. Although she looked like an excited young woman, she also had another quality – there was a womanliness about her that gave Caroline a curious sense of misgiving. Much as she loved Rawdon she did not think that she looked like that.

Suddenly she recalled the tense and somehow heavy atmosphere when Jane and Daniel appeared together, especially after having been alone in her room. It was rather shocking to feel like this about one's sister; but Aunt Ruth had wondered openly if they should be left alone. 'After all, he *is* a man,' Aunt Ruth had said and Caroline and Emily had looked at her, too distressed to speak, but realizing that something innocent might have become dangerous.

'Has he spoken to you?' she said quietly.

'About what?'

'About . . . being together. Marriage, I suppose I mean.'

'Daniel does not believe in marriage. He thinks it is a bourgeois accretion of society.'

'Then what . . . ?' The enormity of the implication of what Jane was saying dawned on Caroline only gradually and after her sister, expressing her agitation, had also got up and started to pace the room.

'Daniel would like me to live with him as his wife, yet not be married. He says he cannot accept marriage and I believe him. Whether I can do as he wants I do not know.'

'But of course you *can't*!' Caroline spun round and faced her sister, both of them nearly colliding in the middle of the room. 'I have never *heard* of such a thing, for a girl like you with father in the position he has . . . It is absolutely impossible. Besides, you would not want it. Would you, Jane?'

Caroline remembered the storms through the years as Jane, difficult, moody, erratic, was growing up. She would try now and calm her down with sweet reason, with gentle understanding. She remembered she was the elder sister who, in many ways, had always taken the place of Mama who, even before the advent of Mrs Chetwynd, had ceased to be the focus of the household. The little ones had come rushing to her to be comforted. It was only when they grew up that the restraint began. Jane needed her and, unless she could respond with more sympathy, Jane would dry up and leave the room full of rage and resentment because once again she was not understood.

'Would you, Jane?' she said gently going over to her sister and placing her hand on her arm. She wanted to embrace her and comfort her as she sometimes had with Debbie; but Jane would recoil and wriggle out. Jane had always been angular, a wriggler, never cuddly.

'Yes, I would,' Jane said, meeting Caroline's eyes, putting her own hand on Caroline's, pressing it, understanding the comfort that Caroline wanted so much to give but found so hard to express. 'It *is* what I want. I admire him so much that his views are most precious to me. He is so honest and fearless; he never dissembles, he never lies or cheats. He wants to change the world and destroy all the bourgeois conventions which bind us, like marriage, the worship of money, war, family institutions. And I should join him in this; his partner, free and equal by his side. He is the most daring, the most unusual man I ever met. And yet, I know it is impossible . . . because I am a Vestrey, Papa's daughter. I would ruin his career. Everyone would talk about me. Emily would have to leave the Court. I could not do it. But I am in torment, Caroline. In hell.'

Jane unexpectedly put her cheek against her sister's bosom. Caroline stroked her head, realizing that Jane was quietly sobbing, her tears wetting the gingham of her dress.

She cradled her head as she had always wanted to, stroked her sleek black hair, pressed her close; tried, by her presence, to convey comfort.

The prospect was shattering, disturbing, out of the question. Of course Jane was a Vestrey, and Vestreys did what was expected of them, they obeyed the rules. Daniel was so unsuitable from every point of view. Jane might love him, find him the most fascinating man alive, but most of the family could hardly get two sensible words out of him. Besides he was not very prepossessing, small and rather ill-looking. They were at a loss to know what Jane could possibly find attractive about him. He was grave, polite, but utterly silent. He never argued or contradicted or volunteered any information. He merely replied to questions in his solemn taciturn way. He seemed in another world altogether – a strange, alien world with which the Vestreys were quite unfamiliar.

But that was when he was not alone with Jane. To see them together was to see them laughing, talkative, relaxed, at ease in each other's company. To see them walking in the garden, or alone in each other's company in a corner of the drawing-room, was to see two people totally self-contained and self-absorbed. Aunt Ruth had expressed her anxiety many times and so had Emily. But what could one do? Daniel could not be banned from Jane's company; he was doing her no harm. Had he not positively saved her life? Did the family not owe him the most enormous debt?

In love. In hell. For a Vestrey woman it had to be the same thing. Total abandonment was simply not possible in a family used to obeying the conventions, the norms of society. It was no use telling Jane that she would find a way because a way like the one Daniel suggested could simply not be found. It was impossible. Out of the question. Jane had to continue as she was with Daniel Lévy, in a state of platonic friendship, or do without him altogether. There was no other way. Jane knew it, and Caroline knew it, but here, today, with her sister weeping on her breast, she knew not how to say it.

CHAPTER TWENTY-TWO

Jane returned to London as soon as she could because, among other things, the sight of her mother and Mrs Chetwynd together sickened her. They were like love-birds cooing away in corners or giving each other mysterious little smiles and signs that only they could understand. Caroline didn't object to Mrs Chetwynd as much as Jane. As one who stood a good deal of Mama's caprices while ill anything was a release. She was content because, at least, Mama left her alone; she could plan the sort of life she now wanted. But what life? She was free; she could do what she liked, but what? What could she do until Rawdon came back? Having been for so long needed by so many people she felt restless and incomplete.

She accompanied Jane back to London because she wanted to be near her to help, if necessary, and continue the *rapport* they had established at Chetwell on the night of the storm. They had come closer then than at any time since they were very small and used to huddle together exchanging childish secrets. They had spent most of the night talking, confiding to each other in a way they seldom had before. As soon as they returned to London Daniel Lévy recommenced his visits and Caroline, knowing what she did, felt she carried a heavy burden because she could discuss it with no one, not Aunt Ruth or Papa or Emily. She did all she could to prevent Jane and Daniel being alone together. She insisted that, as Jane was better, they should meet in the parlour where she, not infrequently, contrived to join them.

Despite the war it was a gay season and the girls were out at parties every night, accompanied by Aunt Ruth or Papa just as though nothing had changed. Daniel was never asked to escort Jane; in fact he was seldom mentioned. His existence was like a large, forbidding yet unseen cloud hovering over the house.

After the declaration of war London was suddenly denuded of young, eligible men who had gone to rejoin their regiments; yet nothing else changed. It was as though, in many ways, nothing had happened at all. Everyone expected that there would be a skirmish or two and the war would be over. There had been no serious war involving England since Waterloo. In fact most of the commanders on their way to Turkey had never had experience of war, or fought in a battle or given commands on the field.

The commander-in-chief, Lord Raglan, who had served under Wellington, was sixty-six. He had let a surgeon amputate his right arm on the field of Waterloo with the utmost calm and detachment, his only apparent concern being to have back the ring that had been left on one of the fingers of the severed hand. 'Hey, bring my arm back. There's a ring my wife gave me on the finger.' The calm and detachment he carried with him to the Crimea, an attitude that, though in many ways commendable, was out of place in that particular theatre of war.

The youngest commander was the thirty-four-year-old Duke of Cambridge, the Queen's cousin, and he had never seen service before.

For some time after Hilary's announcement George Vestrey had continued to feel like a young bridegroom again, only more pleasantly so than on the first occasion. It was true that at twenty he had married a girl with whom he was very much in love, and nothing ever quite recaptured the peculiar joy of that state again. But there were many disadvantages of being a young bridegroom that one forgot about later on, owing to the ability of the human mind to banish unpleasant memories. There was the shock occasioned to a young girl at the duties expected of her in the intimacy of the married bed. That was very difficult for an innocent young man to adjust to, especially as what seemed so repugnant to her had been so pleasurable to him, an act eagerly awaited and looked forward to. It seemed very unfair that there was this duality of attitude towards something that was not only so very fundamental to the married state, but was going to last rather a long time.

Then there was the business of having one's own home.

One was no longer part of the parental establishment. A house had to be bought and servants engaged; one went about in society in a different kind of way now that one was always accompanied by a wife. Altogether more was expected of one. And then very soon babies arrived and one's life became even more responsible, more circumscribed, not because one had to look after them or actually do anything, but because, by being a father, one had ascended yet another grave step in social accountability.

No, George concluded, it was much more pleasant having the *spirit* of a young bridegroom again, but with the advantages of age and experience to help one. It was also delightful having as a bride not a young girl of virginal susceptibilities to shock and apparently abuse, but a mature woman; one not too experienced with men, but familiar enough with their habits and desires which she not only tolerated but appeared to enjoy. And she did enjoy them; when her belly began to swell and normal intercourse was judged inadvisable she permitted George to caress her and continue those little intimacies, those joys of lovemaking which were not confined to the essential act of procreation. She was also able to reciprocate for him, and perform many little pleasantries that were usually only on the periphery of the techniques of making love, but which were wholly delightful all the same.

Then Hilary had her home and knew how to run it; she did not tolerate impertinences from servants and exacted respect and consideration. She knew how to deal with trade and how to clothe herself, and where and what to buy. She was a delightful, stimulating, on occasions even erudite companion because she read *The Times* and belonged to a circulating library. He could talk to her, even sometimes discuss affairs of state as he would with a man at his club, or one of his clever daughters. How he wished Hilary could be part of the family too.

But the main thing was the joy they shared in their forthcoming child. The knowledge that it was part of them, a bond that would forever bind them together, was precious. For Hilary, especially important was the fact that, despite what George had said, he would acknowledge the baby, if not formally at first, at least in his heart, as his own.

However a child could not be kept a secret for ever. One of her maids had recently had to be dismissed for some lewd comment made to the cook about the expansion in her mistress's figure. It was agreed that, however brave the face one maintained, people would comment and laugh. One would lose status to all and sundry. It would be unpleasant for Hilary to go into the town, or even to the High Street, and one could not be expected to stay indoors for ever.

So, with the greatest reluctance, the happy but unmarried bride and groom agreed for a short time to part. Hilary would go into the country, as if on a visit, and George would occupy himself with trying to help end the war which had just started.

It was a sad emotional parting, but one they agreed was sensible. It would be as though Hilary were going on a holiday for a few months and would return with a lovely gift for George.

Thus, by March, George had not only settled down to being a father again but looked forward to it. It was very satisfactory, in a way, to have continuing proof of one's virility, especially with a much younger woman.

Aunt Ruth, always practical, arranged for Hilary to stay with another of her many genteel, but impoverished, acquaintances; a lady in her fifties, also a widow, who had some nursing experience and an almost constant pressing need of cash. Without asking any questions she agreed to look after the recently widowed Mrs Ashburne and see her through her confinement.

The reliable Benson had taken Hilary to the house in Hampshire, deposited her there and would return regularly to be sure that all was well. It had been agreed that, because of the importance of his position, it would be far too indiscreet for George to allow himself a visit, and he regretfully but sensibly put the matter out of his mind, knowing she was in good hands. He was now, though not in the Cabinet, one of Lord Aberdeen's chief supports and constantly consulted by him, being one of the very few who had stood out against the war even at the end. George was worried about Lord Aberdeen's health. The Prime Minister confess to him one day that he felt his hands were permanently bloodstained, and that every drop of blood that would be shed in the war would be upon his head. This seemed ridiculous to George who pointed to the men who had been eager for the war – Palmerston, Russell and Clarendon – but Aberdeen refused to be comforted. He said that the guilt would go with him to the grave, so convinced was he that something could have been done to prevent hostilities.

George felt no guilt; he had done all he could. He had been a good servant of the people, a skilled and painstaking advocate of peacetime policies, despite the country-wide lust for war. Now, as he looked around the room at one of Liz Herbert's soirées he felt a degree of contentment. His daughters looked well. Jane was completely recovered and Caroline free from her mother. She had done her duty, as a good daughter should. It was a pity her freedom coincided with young Foxton going to the war. About Agnes, he no longer thought very much at all. He considered Sophie Chetwynd odious and obsequious, but she was obviously just what Agnes needed. He would take care to keep out of both their ways.

These thoughts, and others, were running through Lord Vestrey's mind as he looked round the salon. He had escorted Jane and Caroline to the party. Emily, for once not in waiting, was confined to her room in Park Street with a chill. George thought how much happier Caroline looked away from Chetwell; she had filled out again and, although by no means fat, had regained her lovely figure, her vibrant healthy good looks. She went frequently to parties now, and he noticed how the young men sought her out, how in demand she was for dances or intimate, carefully chaperoned, candlelit suppers after concerts or visits to the opera. Social life in London continued as though there were no war at all.

At last Caroline was enjoying the season; and so was Jane. How lovely to have her about and so well too. Jane however did not go to balls and parties as much as Caroline. She spent a lot of time writing, or studying or attending meetings of some sort or another with Daniel Lévy (now considered by George a curse on the home, though once its

356

saviour). There were always ructions because Aunt Ruth insisted either that she go with Jane and Daniel or they took her maid When Daniel protested at this bourgeois convention George nearly lost his temper and threatened to throw him out of the house. Sometimes he wished he had. It seemed that gratitude had no bounds. It went on and on. George glowered at Jane, but he was thinking, darkly, of Daniel.

Liz Herbert came up and put a hand on his arm. 'A penny for them, my dear,' she whispered. 'You look very thoughtful.'

George smiled at the beautiful woman whom he both liked and admired. Sidney Herbert was Secretary at War, but had been one of the anti-war party. He was an old friend of George's, an enlightened, erudite gentleman, heir to the Earl of Pembroke, his half brother. He was, moreover, strikingly handsome and, despite his great gifts and high responsibilities, longed only for the peaceful life of a country gentleman at his beautiful country estate of Wilton.

Liz Herbert shared her husband's interests, his philanthropy, his intense Christian dedication, but she was a gay, eager woman with soft olive skin and flashing dark eyes.

'I am thinking that on the whole I am content, Liz,' George said. 'True, I deprecate the war. I did all I could to prevent it, but it has happened. Like Lord Aberdeen himself, I too have a son who immediately goes to join it, so we are not shirking the issue. My wife is better and so is my daughter Jane – see how well she looks tonight, Liz – and Caroline is free to pursue her own life now that Agnes is well though, alas, I feel she does not really know what she wants to do.'

'Surely Caroline will marry?' she said. 'There are any number of young men who would be grateful for the privilege.'

'I think there is one young man in particular,' George said, 'but I will not specify who. Alas he has just gone to the war. I may be wrong, but I feel there is some understanding between them; however he has yet to speak to me. I know Caroline felt duty bound to look after her mother;

357

so that until recently she has not felt free to leave the home. Tragedy that it undoubtedly was, it was no bad thing that she had to come to London to nurse Jane. It helped to loosen the ties. My elder daughters though are very individualistic, you know Liz. They all seem to want to do something besides marry, though I dare say they will be happy enough to settle for that when the time comes.'

'Oh dear, I hope you have not three Florence Nightingales in your family! Poor George. Florence as you must know has spurned the entreaties of her parents that she should marry, and now has finally found perfect satisfaction running a nursing home in Harley Street. Look how happy she is and, although she takes her duties so seriously, she does not neglect the soirées and parties of the season. And is she not lovely, George? She has not lacked for suitors I can assure you. Monkton Milnes was inconsolable when she refused him.'

'She is very good looking. I have met her before,' George nodded, 'but God forbid my daughters should wish to emulate her. I would hate any of them to have such intimate dealings with the sick, much as I pity them. It is no work for a gentlewoman. I wonder why Miss Nightingale cannot combine philanthropy with matrimony as you do, Liz, so well if I may say so, and I hear your children are a credit to you.'

'Oh, Florence is *very* special,' Mrs Herbert said, her fine eyes gleaming. 'I cannot express it to you, George. She is absolutely dedicated and says that there is no room for anything else in her life but her work. Sidney thinks she will quite change people's ideas not only about nursing, but also hospital reform. She has all the figures at her fingertips. Come, let me introduce Caroline to her, and you must say "How do you do?" again.'

Mrs Herbert advanced across the drawing-room, scooping up Caroline on the way, to where Florence Nightingale sat with her mother and sister talking to Lady Beresford and Lady Canning. Mrs Nightingale was fanning herself and looking about at the company, finding the talk of hospitals boring and longing for a glass of cordial. Parthenope, also bored but violently jealous of her sister, never let her eyes leave her for an instant, as though constantly seeking Florence's attention and approval.

'Dearest Flo,' Mrs Herbert said, 'you have met George Vestrey I believe.'

'I do know Lord Vestrey,' Florence Nightingale looked up at him smiling, her frank gaze contriving to appraise and flatter at the same time as though she both approved and liked what she saw. Yet there was nothing flirtatious in her manner.

'We met at Lady Canning's last year, Miss Nightingale. I think you also met my younger daughter Jane but not, I believe, my eldest daughter Caroline?'

'How do you do, Miss Vestrey.' Florence Nightingale held out a hand and Caroline took it, aware of an instant fascination such as she seldom found with women. Miss Nightingale clasped her hand firmly and then held on to it while her clear, grey eyes gazed at Caroline in a thoughtful, speculative way. At first she did not smile and her face was grave and pensive but then, as she dropped Caroline's hand, she gave her a most enchanting smile, full of merriment and charm and Caroline felt completely captivated. No wonder everyone talked about Florence Nightingale; she was indeed a very singular woman.

Miss Nightingale was thirty-four in 1854. She was tall and slight with short chestnut hair, a well moulded mouth, perfect teeth and a determined chin. Her father was wealthy and she had been gently reared; she was well educated, knowing Latin and Greek and having a strong interest in mathematics as a form of mental discipline.

Yet, despite the fact that fortune had appeared to favour her from birth, she had had a difficult life. Believing herself called by God to perform some gigantic task, she had deliberately chosen not to marry and had had years of frustration and ill health, and also trouble with her family, while she tried to discover what the will of God might be.

It was only in the last few years that she thought she had found it. Despite the opposition of her family, particularly her mother and sister, she had decided her vocation was to nurse, something unheard of for a well born girl in those days. After nearly a year as the superintendent of a hospital for distressed gentlewomen in Harley Street she had achieved happiness, repose, fulfilment and a form of peace such as she had never thought to have.

Her contentment showed in her demeanour, the glow in her face, the clear sparkling grey eyes. Gone were all the attacks of illness she had previously suffered from, and she had never felt better in her life.

People hung about Miss Nightingale as though hoping for a word or even a look. She was a magnet of attraction because of her charm, the intelligence and unusual nature of her conversation, and that indefinable quality that even those who knew her well could not describe. She had access to the highest echelons of society, she could have made a brilliant marriage – yet she chose the life of a hardworking hospital administrator and a practical, much loved working nurse. The patients in her hospital adored her, some waiting in cold corridors for hours just to see her and touch her. She took it all with detachment yet compassion; she had the right word at the right time, but the scorn of her tongue she saved for bungling officialdom and there was plenty of that about.

Lady Canning watched with interest the meeting between Caroline Vestrey and Florence Nightingale. It occurred to her that the two were very alike, not only in looks, with their chestnut hair, their similar stature, but also in temperament. They had a reciprocal gravity yet a capacity for enjoyment; they both had captivating smiles.

'I am so glad to hear of your mother's recovery, Caroline,' Lady Canning said. 'It must be a great relief and joy to your family.'

'Thank you, Lady Canning.' Caroline smiled gratefully at Charlotte Canning, an old friend of the family's and a great friend of Emily's, being one of the senior of the Queen's ladies in waiting.

Lady Canning, who had been married at eighteen, was one of the two beautiful daughters of Lord Stuart de Rothsay. Like her sister, Lady Waterford, she was childless; but she seemed to have transferred all her maternal devotion to the Royal family whom she had served since 1842 and she was as close to the Queen as a non-royal could ever get. Queen Victoria was convinced that a great, unbridgeable gulf was fixed between those who were of royal birth and those who were not, and that intimacy between the two was impossible. However devoted she was to her ladies, and they to her, there was always a formality which she maintained to the end of her life.

In fact such was Lady Canning's devotion to the Royal family that it was rumoured to have caused a rift between her and her husband, Viscount Canning, son of the great statesman, who was said to console himself elsewhere, despite the austerity of his nature. He had been in the government as postmaster general since 1853 and, although he and George Vestrey were not close, having natures that were too dissimilar, they liked and respected each other.

'The Queen is *so* fond of Emily,' Lady Canning said to Florence Nightingale. 'She has become very dear to her. Have you met Emily Vestrey, dearest Florence?'

'I think not, Charlotte,' Florence Nightingale replied. 'I know I met another Vestrey sister, the one I think who did such courageous work in Soho.'

'And was horribly attacked, which should be a warning to all girls who unwisely stray from home.' Lady Canning threw up her hands in horror. 'But she is much better too, is she not, Caroline?'

'Yes thank you, Lady Canning,' Caroline said, aware of Florence Nightingale's penetrating look whenever her eyes turned towards her. 'Thank God, as she was very badly hurt.'

'And you have nursed your mother *and* sister?' Florence Nightingale said in a firm yet silvery voice of great charm.

'Yes, Miss Nightingale,' Caroline replied trying, she knew not why, to avoid engagement with those knowing eyes.

'Alas, Caroline too had the sad duty of nursing her younger sister Deborah through the final stages of consumption, to her death,' Lady Canning continued. 'I know her family consider her an angel.'

'Yes, I had heard about the tragic death of Deborah Vestrey,' Florence Nightingale said, her voice warm with compassion. 'My mother wrote to Lord and Lady Vestrey at the time expressing the deep sympathy of our family.'

'I saw her kind letter, Miss Nightingale,' Caroline murmured. Even now she felt close to tears when Debbie's death was mentioned. It was still too vivid in her mind. She also felt that Debbie's death marked the end of her real affection for her mother, the end of filial love and respect. It was a time too full of sadness to recall without grief.

She saw that Florence Nightingale was not really interested in conversing with anyone but her and she pulled herself out of her reverie, sitting, as Florence indicated she should, in the chair next to her. The grey sympathetic eyes were clear and probing as though, with scientific detachment, she was viewing Caroline through an optical instrument of great power and clarity. Caroline felt rather discomforted, but not afraid. She met Miss Nightingale's gaze fearlessly, yet not without a slight sense of bewilderment at being subject to such close scrutiny.

'Is it something that you are attracted to, Miss Vestrey?' Florence enquired gently. 'The care of the sick?'

Caroline did not know. Was she attracted to nursing? She looked at the tall, dedicated woman before her. 'I cannot honestly say, Miss Nightingale. You see I am the eldest daughter of the house. It is my duty to look after my mother and sisters because I love them, and would do anything for them. Whether or not I could apply this care to people at large I cannot say. Certainly I never felt a vocation in this direction.'

'I can see you are dutiful,' Florence Nightingale nodded approvingly. 'Believe me, if you ever thought of doing anything worthwhile, you could do no better than undertake work for the sick. Give it some thought.'

'Oh Flo, *do* stop talking about your work,' Parthenope Nightingale said in a voice pent with frustration and anger. 'You would think there was *nothing* else in life.'

Florence turned her clear gaze to her sister, the sister who had caused her so much suffering over the years and yet whom she still loved.

'I don't think there is, dear Parthe. I would have thought

that you, of *all* people, would have known my mind on the subject by now.'

Parthenope dropped her eyes and flushed under her sister's curiously dispassionate gaze. Caroline suddenly felt chilled and looked with dismay at the blushing embarrassed sister who, in an instant, Florence had managed to quell. Yes, Miss Nightingale was chilling, awe-inspiring. Caroline was fascinated but slightly repelled. She would not like to make an enemy of Miss Nightingale. But then, it seemed extremely unlikely that they would ever be better acquainted than they were now. There was no reason in the world why their paths should ever cross, particularly as Miss Nightingale was something of a celebrity with her dedicated, worthwhile life, and Caroline was no-one at all, with nothing particular to do.

CHAPTER TWENTY-THREE

All the talk was about peace and going home. In June the siege of Silistria had been raised by a determined Turkish force and in July the Russians had finally abandoned Moldavia and Wallachia, the occupation of which a year before had done much to provoke the war in the first place. In fact the main object of the joint Anglo-French operation had now been fulfilled. The Turkish Empire was saved and the Russians were in full flight northwards across the River Pruth. Apart from the help of a small contingent of English troops the whole thing had been done by the Turks.

But a point had also been reached from which there was no return. The Russians *had* to be taught a lesson; the British public had to have its thirst for war quenched. The wholehearted effort was geared towards war, the placating of national aspirations and pride.

Aberdeen was the most unpopular man in the country. His tactless honesty was his undoing. Even the Queen gently reproached him for rushing to the defence of the Czar in the Lords. It was true, she said, that Aberdeen did *not* share the popular enthusiasm for the war, which even she and the Prince were inclining to, however reluctantly. After all a lot of glory could come from a war, and this the people seemed to need. But she urged him 'not to undertake the ungrateful and injurious task of vindicating the Emperor of Russia from any of the exaggerated charges brought against him and his policy, at a time when there is enough in it to make us fight with all our might against it.' The Queen was more of a realist than her chief minister, and, despite her remoteness, closer to the people.

The Cabinet had already authorized Lord Raglan to take the great Russian naval port of Sebastopol in the Crimea, and secret plans for the embarkation of troops stationed in and around the Bulgarian town of Varna on the Black Sea had already begun. But even there the rumour about peace persisted and the troops were bored, angry and losing patience. They blamed Aberdeen as much as anyone. They wanted a good fight.

The Guards, who had left before anyone else, were accordingly angrier than anyone else. They had been pottering about since February, first at Valetta in Malta where they trained in the use of the new Minié rifle which was replacing the famous 'Brown Bess'. It was quite a jolly time; many wives and sweethearts had come along too and there were balls, parties, and all kinds of festivities. Marshal Canrobert of France had actually stood in with a British Square on a battalion field day and admired the splendid physique of the men of the First Regiment of Footguards, the Grenadiers, with their red tunics, Oxford grey trousers and bearskins. Lord Raglan, the Commander in Chief, had also turned up. He had served in the Regiment as Fitzroy Somerset. Finally on 22 April the whole Brigade of Guards, thirty-five officers and nine hundred and forty-nine men, sailed for the Dardanelles.

They arrived at Scutari where they were put under canvas on a hill near the town. From here they had a view of some of the most magnificent scenery in the world including the snowy mountains of Asia Minor and Constantinople just across the Bosphorus. Below them were the huge, ugly, airless Turkish barracks of Scutari where Lord Raglan had his headquarters from which, among other discontents, he complained of 'an abominable smell and all sorts of filth'. Since the end of May the regiment had camped at Varna, an ugly, dirty little town, the houses ramshackle and made of wood, hardly any shops, and, until the French got going with their civilizing influence, a few cafés outside which squatted sullen looking Turks surrounded by clouds of smoke.

Yet the country around was beautiful, a vast plain into which the Lower Balkans descended, its blue hills covered with trees and vegetation. In the distance was the magnificent chain of the Balkan Mountains where the main centre of the war, what there was of it at that time, was being concentrated towards the Danube.

Parts of the land were cultivated by luxuriant crops of

barley but, for the most part, it consisted of turf covered with brushwood and prickly bushes which, when the troops arrived, were a mass of tiny yellow flowers. There were also burrage, roses, larkspur and heather, so that at times the countryside resembled England with sunny glades and thick leafy fields.

Animal life abounded, slow moving land tortoises, marmots and wild dogs which the troops liked to flush out of the bushes and hunt, to the disgust of the Turks who regarded such animals as sacred. Bird life too was abundant and included exotic orioles and hoopoes with large colourful topknots.

But the attractions of the countryside, the occasional excursion to Shumla or the front, the dog hunting and pony racing which the cavalry organized, the swimming in Devna Lake or the Black Sea, did little to make up for the frustration and boredom among the men, the irritation with the inadequate food and poor accommodation due to the faulty commissariat which even now was being blasted by William Howard Russell reporting in *The Times* to an astonished audience at home. 'Where,' he enquired, 'is the English Post Office? No-one knows. Where does the English General live? No-one knows. Where is the hospital to carry a sick soldier to? No-one knows. At present if a serious case of illness occurs in the camp the only conveyance for the sufferer is a bullock cart, and in that miserable springless vehicle he has to perform the tedious journey to Varna – enough to destroy all chance of recovery.'

Even before the war had begun Russell, who had been with the first of the expeditionary forces, warned of the deficiencies in organization, the shortages, the inefficiencies, the lack of good doctors, hospitals and experienced commanders. He had warned of horrors to come if the old creaking army structure which had atrophied during forty years of peace was not drastically reorganized.

From the beginning, noted Russell, nothing had gone right. At Malta he had recorded shortages of coal, candles and fuel, tents and forage. Administrative muddle abounded. There were too many people responsible, and yet insufficient to take any blame. At Scutari the troops had arrived to find the French comfortably installed in the best places with warm tents and nourishing food, whereas the British had to be content with a camp eight miles away in wretched conditions. Nobody seemed to be expecting them, or to know what to do when they were there.

At Varna things were little better. There was not enough to eat except of ship's biscuits and salt pork which was agony to the throats of men already parched by the heat which started to soar until at times it reached one hundred and fifteen degrees. Yet without warning the weather could change and the storms blew down tents and released floods of water which caused more chaos, confusion and disease. In the heat the troops had clothing that had been provided for the winter and sweated in their leather overalls. In the cold and rain they had insufficient protection. No-one was ready for anything. The disease had begun almost at once, but grew worse with the hot weather. There was dysentery, low fever and, finally, cholera.

The cholera which had started in the French camp in July quickly spread to the English. It speedily decimated not only the Guards but all the regiments stationed in the surrounding camps at Varna, Devna and Kotlubei. It was a frightening disease which struck without notice and killed a man in a few hours, reducing him to a blackened, unrecognizable skeleton. It swept through the camps mercilessly picking off officers and men alike, doctors, padres and camp servants.

No one realized then that the cholera was to do more to undermine the British army and reduce its effectiveness than all the casualties sustained in the entire eighteen months of the campaign.

Rawdon Foxton had buried his tenth cholera victim in three days. As one of the few officers who were not sick he was most often called upon to perform this duty. James sarcastically said that it was also because he had a beautiful voice that was admirably suited to the burial service.

Rawdon found that the act of burial became quite automatic, and one would go round the sick tents at night calculating who would be the victims in the next few hours or on the morrow. Often when he was not performing the burial service he supervised a flogging, for discipline in the army had to be maintained at all costs. The full penalty of fifty lashes reduced a man's back to the colour of an overripe plum, and every stroke drew blood.

He had just buried a man whose flogging he had supervised two days previously. He did not die from that, though the weakness he sustained would not have helped when cholera intervened. But Rawdon didn't think about that. This was a military life and it had nothing at all in common with anything he had known in England. None of the manoeuvres performed on Salisbury Plain or the mountains of Wales had prepared him for the harsh arid life at Varna, where there was little difference in the conditions between officers and men except that the former got beer and occasionally potatoes, whereas the latter seldom did. They all slept either under canvas or in the open; they all subsisted on the same diet of salt pork and ship's biscuits that, preserved in sacks of tar because of the rain, tasted more of tar than flour. Sometimes a cow walked into the camp and was immediately killed and put into the pot together with rice, scraggy chickens and anything else edible which came to hand.

Excursions made into Varna or Devna – an equally wretched town with houses built of mud and hurdles instead of wood – sometimes produced a few eggs which invariably turned out to be bad, and nothing else. Bread and milk were practically unheard of, though sometimes a sutler, a private trader, set up shop in the camp and things temporarily improved.

The cavalry regiments fared even worse because they had horses to feed and, as the days got hotter and drier, the horses' bones began to stick out from their emaciated bodies and they started to die like the human victims of the cholera.

Yet despite all this, Rawdon was happy. He found the change and challenge exciting. The tasks he had to do were rewarding though daunting. He found he feared for nothing, not even his health; the sparse diet suited him. He liked sleeping rough, and the informality of life in the heat where, despite the orders of their commanders, the officers pottered about with full beards and moustaches, and in clothes of every description, turbans folded thickly around wide-awake hats with a tail to protect the shoulders.

Pipes were smoked filled with fragrant Turkish tobacco and, although there was little to read as they had had to travel light, he found time to sketch the landscape, keep a journal and write numerous letters to his family and to Caroline.

Over the months 'My dear Caroline' had become 'My dearest Caroline', and he tried to write to her every day. The sparseness of his life, the rigour and deprivation made thoughts of Caroline especially dear and, to him, women became even more of an ideal – soft, protected creatures, fragrant, warm, loving, all-enveloping. If it was true about the peace and he went back now he would regret that he had seen no fighting, but it would mean that marriage to Caroline would not be long delayed. They had become closer in their letters than ever they had in the flesh.

Army life suited James Vestrey too, except that he missed women. His last encounters had been in Constantinople and terrified him for days afterwards lest he had contracted disease. Although Constantinople, when viewed from the Bosphorus, was of surpassing beauty, tall towers and minarets reaching into a sky of cloudless azure; seen from within it was a city of narrow streets, tumbledown dwellings and filth everywhere, beggars, mangy dogs and whores.

After his experiences even in the better Turkish brothels, that also provided massage and more sophisticated attractions such as officers were used to, James was quite happy for a while to put women out of his mind and discipline his body with the rigours of army life. But then, in time, the fantasies returned and the overwhelming desire for the carnal joys that he had known continually since he was a young man.

Rawdon puzzled James. There was no finer officer, no more decent a human being, yet the intricacies of Rawdon's character he found almost impossible to understand. He was straight, honest, had an attractive enthusiasm and gaiety when he wished, yet overall he was a man who revealed little of himself. Despite this James felt Rawdon was the best friend he had in the world and he was grateful for his solid presence here in the dreadful heat of the camp at Aludyn a few miles from Varna where the Guards were stationed. It was on the outskirts of a chain of marshy lakes and the medical officer attributed to this fact the amount of sickness they had had and was pressing for removal.

Rawdon found James in his tent sheltering from the sweltering heat, bare from the waist up. The door of his tent was open and just inside a Turkish servant squatted on his haunches waving a flapper made of horsehair to provide a breeze and keep the flies away. The man nodded somnolently and James was reading, a long Turkish pipe – the *chibouque* – in his mouth, a cool water-soaked cloth round his head.

'Sit, my dear fellow,' James said pointing to the ground beside him, 'and forgive the lack of comforts. Get Mahomed or whatever his name is to pour you some wine. This local stuff isn't bad, though the occasional gripe I get in the gut makes me think I am getting cholera.'

Rawdon took off his hat and shirt and poured himself some of the white wine which stood in a cool earthen pitcher of water. 'It is the best prevention we have of cholera. I think that is why comparatively few of the officers get it in comparison to the men.'

'Oh, you're thinking of Jane's theory!' James laughed.

'It is no theory,' Rawdon said seriously. 'Dr Snow is quite certain that cholera is borne by water; yet people mock at his ideas. Here the men drink water because beer is short and the officers wine when they can get it. I am going to stick to it, I can tell you.'

'What is that you have in your hand?' James enquired idly. 'Another letter from Caroline?'

'No, this is from my mother. My father is unwell again. She wants me to ask for home leave; but I cannot justify it to myself. People will think I am opting out like so many fellows who are trying to get home. Lord Dupplin has just gone home though they do say he is very sick. There is a rumour now that our destination is Odessa or Sebastopol.'

'Is that in your mother's letter?' James laughed. 'They say people at home know everything before we know it ourselves.'

'No, this does not come from Mr Russell but from Lord Erroll who told me so himself this very morning, and *he* had it, of course, from His Royal Highness.'

Lord Erroll was a member of the Staff of the Duke of Cambridge who commanded the Guards Brigade and the Highland Infantry.

'Then it did *not* come from Lady Erroll and her French maid,' James mocked, sipping more wine. 'A more ridiculous sight I have yet to see than her Ladyship parading everywhere in the Duke's retinue accompanied by a French maid carrying her parasol.'

'No, nor the maid neither,' Rawdon said patiently. 'But from the Duke himself. It has been decided to quell the discontent at home by taking Sebastopol.

'We shall still be home before winter,' James yawned, 'and thank God for it. This is a dull campaign – if campaign you can call it. Sebastopol will fall like a house of cards. I confess I am missing the comforts of London and this food will ruin my digestion forever.'

Rawdon sat down, his eyes glinting in the dim light of the tent. The swishing flapper gave a welcome breeze and he felt cooler. He had just buried four men in the sweltering heat, covered with flies which seemed to alight on anything and everything. He swatted a blue lizard which slid lazily across the floor and closed his eyes. 'I do not want to go home before we see action. Besides, the country is thirsting for war. I'd like to have a crack at those Russians.'

James laid down his pipe and looked at his friend.

'You are a most surprising man, Rawdon. So peace loving, so calm and yet with a wicked thirst for blood.'

'No, it is to justify myself as a soldier that I would like to see action. Since we joined, James, we have seen naught, not even India or Portugal or South Africa or Afghanistan, like some fellows, where a few skirmishes have taken place. Wellington Barracks has become a sort of second home, as protective as Chetwell or Saltmarsh. If I am to be a soldier I want to see some fighting and not endless guard duties and ceremonies of that sort. Besides I think Caroline would ... admire me more if ...'

'... you covered yourself with glory!' James hooted with laughter and tossed off his wine. 'No, that kind of thing has no appeal for my sister. Caroline, you know, is unimpressed by displays of warlike manliness. My other sisters might be, but not Caroline. Nothing like that would alter any feelings she might have for you. *Does* she have any feelings for you, Rawdon? I know you are getting a number of letters.'

Rawdon closed his eyes, aware only of the overpowering heat, the sound of flies, the burning merciless sun over their tent, over the graves of the men he had buried. Was it likely that he and James would get back from this terrible country with its torrid climate? Would James have asked him such an intimate, personal question anywhere else but here where men seemed to have no real defences, where the barriers created by society and birth disappeared, and emotions were unashamedly on display?

As though accepting an implied rebuff by Rawdon's silence James screwed up his nose and recommenced the book he was trying to read, though the pages where his fingers touched were damp.

'I have asked Caroline to marry me,' Rawdon said, still with his eyes closed, as though pondering the wisdom of the deed. 'I believe she *does* entertain feelings of affection for me.'

'My dear boy!' James wiped his sticky fingers and palms on a rag and got to his feet. 'My dear old fellow! Why have you said nothing about it before? That we are to be brothers-in-law?'

He leaned over and grasped Rawdon by the shoulder. Rawdon reached up and offered him a hand, opening his eyes and giving him a lazy smile.

'Do not exert yourself too much, James. We shall perish in this heat 'ere I can become a groom.' Solemnly they shook hands like gentlemen and James flopped back on the floor again. 'I proposed to Caroline last October. She asked me to wait until she had prepared her mother and made sure that Jane was well. We were to get married in six months' time if the war had not come. We decided, then, to wait until it ended before I should speak to her father.'

'My dear fellow, you will have a white beard before it

ends,' James muttered, also closing his eyes. 'You should have married Caroline and brought her with you.'

'God forbid,' Rawdon said. There was a long silence and the monotonous sound of the flapper seemed almost unbearably loud, like some persistent oriental instrument of torture. 'There is something else, James.'

James opened his eyes and looked at the top of the tent. Despite the vigilance of the servant many flies had penetrated the tent and had clustered on the canvas. The prying, ceaseless motion of their tiny bodies reminded James, except for the colour, of the tins of maggots he used to use for fishing in the Chet when he was a boy. They crawled and squirmed and probed in perpetual, futile activity. James looked at Rawdon and took up his pipe from the floor.

'Say on. I'm listening dear boy.'

'I think I have given Emily the impression that I am fond of her. In fact I know I have.' He felt in his pocket and drew out a crumpled letter showing, but not offering it, to James. 'She reproaches me for not writing.'

'I am not surprised Emily has that impression,' James said, laconically puffing smoke towards the flies. 'I had that impression too watching you look at her, watching you dancing together. I recall particularly the dance the night before we left London. You danced with her the whole time, and when you didn't dance you mooned.'

'I am fond of her,' Rawdon said in a flat unemotional voice.

'But you are engaged to Caroline?'

'Yes.'

'Then you are in a mess, *mon vieux*, as our French allies say. Really, Rawdon. Trifling with both my sisters!' James guffawed and nudged him in the ribs. 'Naughty.'

James knew that in the heat, and because of its delicate nature, this would be a protracted conversation, and he puffed quietly at his pipe thinking about women. James had never been in love or found anything to admire in women, apart from his family, besides physical satisfaction. In a way he despised them. For him there were two sorts of women – those like his mother, sisters and cousins who were comforters and providers for men, inviolable, pure and detached, and those who inhabited the brothels and who had simply one function in life.

To him marriage could never be to appease the longings of the flesh, but to procreate, to establish the family it was his duty to bear in order to preserve the Vestrey name. Women were either meant to be venerated and respected or despised; there was nothing in between and the two aspects could never go together. Respect and passion could never go together, he was sure. He wouldn't expect his wife to behave like the whores in the brothels did; wouldn't want her to. It was very unfortunate that there had to be anything of this nature with one's wife at all because, in his eyes, it was a function that demeaned women.

'I am not trifling with them,' Rawdon said after what seemed an interminable interlude even allowing for the heat and inertia of the day. 'I am very fond of them both.'

'But you want to marry Caroline?'

'Yes.'

'Are you sure?'

James poked his *chibouque,* realized it had gone out and started refilling it.

'I don't know how to say this,' Rawdon sat up crossing his legs as the natives did, 'but Caroline embodies for me all the womanly virtues. She is calm, she is beautiful, composed . . .'

'Oh, she is all those,' James said.

'She is ideal for a wife.'

'You are marrying a woman, Rawdon, not an idea,' James said quietly.

'Emily on the other hand, is very exciting.'

'Ah, now you're on different ground; but nearer the point maybe?'

Rawdon felt himself blushing even in the heat. 'I think, as a man, you understand what I mean, James?'

James looked enigmatically at his friend, stroking his blond moustache. 'As a man, certainly; but as a brother I must protect my sister's virtue.'

'Oh I would never *dream* . . .' A spasm of outrage contorted Rawdon's features and he regretted he had ever started the conversation. But for this accursed heat he was sure he never would have. It loosened men's tongues.

'And neither would Emily . . . of being your mistress. That is what you are thinking, Rawdon, isn't it?'

'No, I completely deny any such notion. I admire and respect Emily; but she does have a quality that, I admit, is very sensual.'

'But you see in Emily qualities that you would like in a mistress and in Caroline virtues that you require in a wife.'

'Exactly.' Rawdon breathed a sigh of relief and lay down again, closing his eyes. 'I confess I am ashamed to own it. Can you imagine us having a conversation of this nature in England?'

James ignored the last remark. 'But Caroline is very beautiful too.'

'In a different way, very.'

'Emily is a flirt, she dances well, she likes men, she wants above all to be admired by them. But, you know, the Queen finds her a remarkably accomplished maid-of-honour. She often specifically asks for her, so you see, Emily has those more cosy, home-making qualities as well.'

Rawdon didn't reply. He was thinking of Emily on the horse on the beach, her veil flying about her, her skirts billowing. Then he thought of his body crushing hers against the wall of Lady Fox-Hargreaves' residence in Berkeley Square as though she were some doxy ready to be fondled in a dark passage; but, oh the feel of her luscious body . . . He knew the veins had swelled in his neck and he swallowed hard opening his eyes in order to banish such a sensuous, carnal, erotic, altogether reprehensible vision the memory of the occasion conjured up.

'I must tell Emily about Caroline,' Rawdon said meditatively, his eyes half closed. 'This talk with you has made me reach a decision. I must write and tell her. She wants me to write and I can't. I must tell her the reason and apologize for my behaviour that night . . . at the dance.'

He looked guiltily at James who gave a tolerant smile. 'I think the behaviour of quite a few of us that evening at the dance, especially after it, might not be considered exactly what is expected of officers and gentlemen. I even think there may be one or two pregnant lasses about now, trips required to the country and that sort of thing. It is a very emotional time, when soldiers leave for war. Oh do not look so startled, Rawdon. I am sure *you* did not go so far with my sister because we both escorted her home and all I had with Sophia Hartley was a quick fumble, like you, in the garden. Only I was further down by the gazebo and you did not see me.'

'You saw me with Emily?'

'Oh yes. At first I did not know who it was, and then I knew it could be no-one else. I thought, "I shall have to knock the fellow out"; but then I thought, "Let us all enjoy ourselves for we might not return from the war", and I gave Sophia a smacking great kiss which took her breath away and forgot about you and my sister.'

'Caroline would never have behaved like that.'

'She might have. Did you ever try?'

'Really James, now you go too far. I can't even imagine Caroline indulging in behaviour of that kind, whatever the circumstances.'

James made himself more comfortable on the ground and motioned to the servant to pour him some more wine. 'You know, nor can I. To change the subject – I think we had better – and talking of letters, Jenny has made me one of her good causes. She sent me a parcel and a nice letter.'

'My sister?'

'Jennifer Foxton, no less. The idea of the war inspires her, she says, the thought of us men all sacrificing ourselves. She says any number of people are coming out and she would like to as well.'

'Well she will not. I'll put a stop to that,' Rawdon said bluntly. 'Besides Lady Erroll and the redoubtable Mrs Duberly there are too many women about here. None should have been permitted in my opinion, not even the few wives. I do not want my sister turning into a sort of camp follower.'

James chuckled at the thought of the rather plain, reserved Jennifer Foxton turning into a camp follower, and knocked out his *chibouque*. 'I agree we are best without women of that sort, although I would not mind one or two *real* camp followers to provide for a fellow's needs, such as they had in the Peninsular War. However until that happy day comes we must either hope for a speedy end to the war or a return to Constantinople.'

Rawdon, who knew of James's fears after his experiences there, glanced at him. His friend had a very short memory. He stretched his arms behind his head. The wine combined with the heat soon made one sleepy. A beetle climbed slowly up his bare chest and he watched its progress through his thick body hair. How big and strange he must seem to the poor creature. He flicked it off and thought of the dead he had buried this morning, of the sick in the camp who begged not to be sent to the hospital at Varna because of its reputation as a morgue. It was said that few ever left it alive, and men, even in the final stages of cruel illness, preferred to die where they were rather than go to the Varna General Hospital.

Yes, this was a terrible country, with few redeeming features. Yet, curious enough, it was where he wanted to be.

CHAPTER TWENTY-FOUR

At home Mr Russell's despatches to *The Times* began to cause acute embarrassment to the government. In the Commons Lord Aberdeen was accused of 'fluctuating and pusillanimous conduct that had rendered war inevitable'. And yet at the same time the public clamoured for war, despite the awful stories that were emerging about the sickness in Bulgaria, the state of the army, the lack of supplies, the confusion and maladministration. It certainly did not sound like an army prepared to do battle with an enemy whose numbers were growing all the time.

In August a huge fire at Varna burned for ten hours and destroyed valuable supplies and provisions intended for the already suffering troops. Some said the town had been fired in four places at once and that it was the work of the Russians. The temperature rose, interspersed by violent and devastating storms which caused chaos and spread disease already rampant.

In London, too, it was a hot sultry summer. The season had ended and yet Caroline and Jane were reluctant to return to Chetwell and kept on finding excuses not to go. So Emily returned to Chetwell alone because she was due to go to Osborne with the Queen and she wanted to see Mama.

Sophie Chetwynd troubled Emily least of all the girls, because she took the least notice of her. She regarded her as a sort of superior servant and treated her accordingly. When she wanted to be alone with her mother she ordered Mrs Chetwynd out of the room and, as if in obedience to one who was so close to the Sovereign, Mrs Chetwynd went.

'What is it you wished to say that was so particular, dear?' Agnes said when the door was shut and she and her daughter were alone in the drawing-room, the open French windows letting in a refreshing breeze from the sea.

'Have you heard from James, Mama?'

'Why yes, dear. I have a letter by my bed. Shall I ask Sophie to get it?'

'I'll look at it later Mama if I may. Does he say anything about Rawdon?'

'Rawdon?' Agnes blinked as though she had difficulty at first in placing the name. 'Rawdon Foxton?'

'Who else, Mama?'

'I don't think he does mention him.' Agnes took up her sewing and glanced sideways at her daughter. Emily was looking tired and, although usually pale, her cheeks looked pallid and unhealthy. Even Agnes, preoccupied with her own health, could see that. 'You must have a good rest before you go to Osborne, Emily dearest. The season has taken its toll. I would not like the Queen to think you were overdoing things. Did you meet anyone you particularly liked, dear?'

'How do you mean, Mama?' Knowing perfectly well what she meant, Emily gave her mother a long, hard look.

'Any young men?'

'I am not interested in young men. I find them tedious.'

Agnes put down her embroidery and gave a loud sigh of exasperation. She massaged her leg under her long skirt; it always gave her a twinge when she was upset, though sometimes she scarcely ever thought of it, or, if she did, Sophie would make a few mesmeric passes and all would be well.

'Oh I know not what to do with my daughters!' she exclaimed, beringed fingers waving in the air. 'Not *one* of you seems to think about marriage and settling down. I shall have you three old maids on my hands, and Papa will say I have failed in my duty as a mother. Your father will blame *me,* you know, not himself or your aunt. He will say that I have not entertained for you as I should, given balls and parties and the like . . .'

'That is nonsense Mama, if you will pardon me for saying so,' Emily said in her firm authoritative voice. 'We have plenty of opportunities to meet with those of the opposite sex. It is simply that we have not met anyone yet who interests us. Or rather *I* have not . . .'

Emily paused; her thoughts flew swiftly across the sea. She tried to imagine the camp at Varna once described so vividly by James. Why did Rawdon not write? Why? She had written to him twice. He must have got her letters because James had, and they were together. Well, she would not again. She would harden her heart and not throw herself at someone so callous, someone who had simply used her. Every time she thought of the episode in Lady Fox-Hargreaves' garden she felt bitterly ashamed. To have let herself go in such an abandoned fashion, like some servant girl who knew no better! She, a Vestrey, a member of the Court, and he, an officer in the Guards, a gentleman. How could two civilized people behave in such a way? And if he had encouraged her, well that was no excuse. She should have known how to control herself by removing herself from temptation.

Despite the lack of instruction in the matter, every girl knew that men had certain physical appetites which well brought-up young women did their best to ignore, whatever their own feelings. And these feelings were strong, Emily had ruefully to admit. Whatever the horror and repugnance they engendered afterwards, at the time her physical needs, her attraction to Rawdon, had seemed overwhelming.

The very memory made her hot and she put her hands to her cheeks, closing her eyes. That, of course, was why Rawdon had not written. She had disgusted him. Well, she would not do it again. She had learned her lesson.

'Do you think either Jane or Caroline is interested in anyone?' Agnes said, determined to pursue the matter as she resumed her embroidery. She refused to be affected by Emily's hectoring manner.

'Caroline I know not. I do not think so. Jane . . . well, there is Daniel.'

'*Daniel*?' Agnes said screwing up her eyes. 'I do not think I know . . . oh pray Emily, you do not mean that foreign gentleman?'

'If "gentleman" is the word,' Emily said grimly. 'She sees him constantly.'

'Oh, but I thought he had gone long ago. Surely back to France or somewhere?' Agnes put her finger to her brow, as if to recall the exact whereabouts which she had locked in her memory.

'No, Mama. He is not allowed in France. He is in London and paying court to Jane.'

'Oh!' Agnes put a hand on her heart and let her embroidery slip from her fingers. 'Oh pray, ring the bell for Sophie, quick before I lose my breath . . .'

Agnes started to pant and Emily, who had not seen one of these spasms for many months, went quickly to the door and opened it. Mrs Chetwynd, who had obviously been leaning against it, nearly fell into the drawing-room on her face.

'Mrs Chetwynd!' Emily said with an artificial brightness that was lost on that good, but simple woman. 'How convenient that you happened to be passing. Mama has an attack of breathlessness . . .'

She swept aside with an exaggerated gesture and Mrs Chetwynd, quickly recovering herself rushed over to her charge, who was leaning back in her chair, her bosom heaving, her hands limply by her side.

Gently Mrs Chetwynd cupped Agnes's cheeks between her hands.

'Agnes, do you hear me? Open your eyes Agnes, and look at me. I am here Agnes, with you, and there is no need to be afraid. Can you hear me, Agnes? Open your eyes.'

Emily watched with awful fascination as her mother opened her eyes and stared straight into those of Mrs Chetwynd. At first she looked bewildered and then fear was replaced by calm as she gazed steadily in front of her.

'I want you to continue looking at me, Agnes.' Mrs Chetwynd backed slowly away and began passing both her hands backwards and forwards in front of Agnes's face. 'There. You are calm; your breathing is regular. There is nothing to fear. I am here. Do you understand, Agnes?'

'Yes, Sophie.' Agnes nodded obediently.

'Now I want you to shut your eyes, and when you open them again you will have forgotten the episode and you will be quite well. Do you understand that, Agnes?'

'Yes, Sophie.'

Agnes obediently closed her eyes and when, after a few minutes, she opened them again she seemed surprised to see Mrs Chetwynd and smiled at her. 'Why Sophie dear, when did you come in? Emily and I were just saying – ' For a moment a look of perplexity crossed Agnes's face. '*What* were you saying, dear?'

Emily, who had watched the whole performance with an amazement which, in her case, verged on repulsion, gazed first at her mother then Mrs Chetwynd. She saw the warning light in Mrs Chetwynd's eyes and, although it was contrary to her inclinations, she thought she should heed it.

'I was just going, Mama, to my room. We were talking of James at Varna. You said there was a letter by your bed. May I take it to my room, then, and read it, Mama?'

'Of course, child!' Agnes gave her a smile of great sweetness and reached for her hand. 'It is so lovely to have my clever talented daughter with me, such a comfort. The Queen is so taken with her, Sophie. Did you know that?'

Emily stood with her hand still in her mother's, looking with ill-concealed dislike at Mrs Chetwynd.

'I know how very attached Her Majesty is to Miss Emily, my lady, because you have often told me so. Oh and I forgot – ' Mrs Chetwynd reached in the pockets of her capacious gown. She had grown quite fat since she had been living at Chetwell, Emily thought bitterly, living on the fat of the land and her gullible, simple-minded mother. She stared at the large white envelope Mrs Chetwynd held out to her. 'This has been forwarded from Windsor, Miss Emily. It came in the post and I was coming to find you to give it to you when you opened the door.'

Emily reached for the letter and saw that it was crumpled and rather grubby as though it had been travelling for some time. She stared at it.

'It is from Varna,' she said.

'Oh, from James!' Her mother looked at Sophie with delight. 'Is he not a good thoughtful boy. Would you like to read it to us, dear?'

Emily was gazing at the writing, familiar through the years, only a little changed since he was a beardless adolescent. Although Rawdon was now a grown man his writing was still rounded and rather boyish as though he concentrated a great deal in making the characters.

Little did Emily know how he had sweated over this one, how many painful, hot hours it had taken him, how many drafts he had made and discarded. She held it tightly with both hands showing it to her mother.

'May I take it and read it in my room, Mama? With the other?'

'Of course dear, and then read it to us over lunch. Sophie be good enough to close the windows. I am finding it draughty.'

'Oh but Lady Vestrey, it is such a warm day . . .'

Emily shut the door firmly behind her and then she stood for a moment, undecided whether to go to her room or the garden with the precious missive. She felt hot and ill at ease and she could hear them murmuring in the room she had left. Agnes! That creature had the impertinence to use her mother's Christian name when she had her under her influence. Agnes indeed. But 'Lady Vestrey' she noticed when Agnes recovered. She thought she should talk to Papa about Mrs Chetwynd. What she had just seen had made her very unhappy indeed.

The out of doors seemed to beckon her. Despite what her mother said, it was a very warm day. Emily walked slowly out of a side door and along a path that led to the sea. She studied the envelope, her name written in his handwriting. For a moment, before opening it, she pressed it to her heart. Then she sat on a bench under a tree, out of sight of the house but overlooking the sea, and opened it.

Camp Aludyn, Varna, Bulgaria. 18 July 1854

'My dear Emily,

Forgive me for not writing before; but our activities have made us short of time. This is an infernal country, very hot and uncomfortable.

Emily I ask your forgiveness for what happened between us at Lady Fox-Hargreaves'. I blame my self completely. The emotion brought on by the war made me lose control of myself in a way of which I am bitterly ashamed.

Nine months ago I asked your sister Caroline to marry me. She did me the honour to accept. I do not repent of that decision and I intend that the wedding shall take place upon my return.

I will always think of you, dear Emily, with the greatest

respect and affection of the fond brother-in-law I hope to have the good fortune one day to be.

I have the honour to be,
    Yours most sincerely,
        Rawdon Foxton.'

Emily, quickly perusing the letter for an idea of its contents, saw the words 'brother-in-law' before anything else. Then she read the letter very slowly, and again and again, before she let it fall and lie on her lap.

She didn't cry or move for a long time, but stared unseeingly, unblinkingly, out to sea.

Caroline was increasingly worried about Jane who was unwilling to leave Daniel. She saw him almost every day. She had become very friendly with some people called Marx, friends of Daniel who lived almost next door to them in Dean Street. Mrs Marx was a former German baroness and Dr Marx the cleverest man Jane had ever met, she said. She was fascinated not only by his intellect but his startling views on the development of society. He wrote constantly and was embarking on a great work that would change man's thinking.

Jane begged Caroline to ask the Marx family to dinner, and, left to herself, she would have. However she was afraid of the reaction of Aunt Ruth and Papa whose behaviour, since the war news had got so bad, was erratic.

But Caroline was worried enough about Jane to agree to go and see her new friends. She deplored the freedom with which Jane now chose to go where she pleased, see whom she liked. She tried to accompany her when she could, but supervision of a wilful twenty-one year old sister was not easy. She thought her father should have exercised more control than he did, but he clearly had other things on his mind.

She went one hot day towards the end of August and doubtfully followed Jane into the narrow building where the Marx family lived. She kept her disquiet to herself as she climbed the dirty, narrow stairs and wondered that her well-bred sister could possibly claim friendship with people who lived in a place like this.

On the landing two small girls waited to greet them and grasped Jane by the hand, squealing with joy and leading her into a front room that was obviously the parlour, though it was like nothing that Caroline had ever seen in her life. Not one piece of furniture appeared to be intact. One chair had three legs, and everything was dirty, torn and thick with dust. In the middle was a large table covered with an oil-cloth which could scarcely be seen under the books, manuscripts and newspapers that littered it, together with children's toys, cutlery, dirty crockery, pipes, tobacco and a half-empty bottle of wine.

Yet the man sitting at the table appeared quite indifferent to either the clamour or confusion that surrounded him. He was writing slowly and steadily on a sheet of paper and puffing at a large pipe stinking of cheap tobacco, his huge head surrounded by clouds of smoke.

'Papa, Papa, it is Jane!' the eldest of the two small girls called and, for the first time, the man became aware of his visitors and looked up, his dark powerful face lit with a smile of welcome.

'Ah, *mein liebe* Jane! It is always a pleasure to see you. And where is your sweetheart?'

Jane blushed and looked behind her to where Caroline stood nervously on the threshold, her features carefully composed in an effort to keep the horror and dismay at what she saw out of them.

'Dr Marx, I have brought my eldest sister Caroline to see you. Daniel is unwell and is at home in bed.'

'In your home?'

'No, his. He felt unwell yesterday.'

'Ah, I must go and see him.' Dr Marx got up and although he was of medium height he seemed to dominate the room, so powerful was his frame, so awesome his personality. He had a head of thick bushy hair turning grey, but his full beard was still quite black. However his eyes were his most astonishing feature – dark and fiery, almost demoniacal, as they stared at Caroline with frightening intensity. The sight of him made her feel quite weak. He spoke English quite well but had a guttural German accent. He took Caroline's hands and his clasp was strong and powerful so that she felt the blood draining from them.

'How do you do, Dr Marx?' she said, keeping her nervousness from her voice. 'Jane speaks a lot about you.'

'And she speaks a lot about *you* and your family. She is very proud of you, your father and your brother who is in the war. Do you have recent news of him?'

Caroline's face clouded and she let her hands fall from Dr Marx's.

'Yes. He is at Varna in Bulgaria. His camp is riddled with cholera and so many of the men have died or are very sick. We are very worried about him . . . and another close friend who is with him.'

Dr Marx spread his arms wide as though to encompass the whole world in this tiny room. 'But what are cholera and disease compared to fighting the Russian menace? Cholera will pass but, unless they are stopped, the Russians will expand until they have ports on the Mediterranean. There is no stopping the great Russian bear other than by war. You must read my articles on the subject.'

'I know, Dr Marx. But when you love someone . . .'

A woman entered the room, her hand holding that of a sick-looking child of about eight. The woman, besides being obviously pregnant, looked careworn and far from well. Marx turned to her gently and led her to the three-legged chair propping it up on a stout piece of wood.

'*Mein liebschen*, this is the eldest Miss Vestrey of whom Jane has told us so much. Miss Vestrey, my wife, Mrs Marx. But she is the daughter of a German Baron you know, an aristocrat like you!'

Marx smiled as though very proud of the fact and Mrs Marx looked at her feet, clearly embarrassed. She seemed older than her husband and Caroline thought how good looking she must have been when young; traces of a distinct beauty were still visible in her pallid features.

Jane had told her of the tragedies in the life of the family. They had spent so many years in exile and poverty, harried from one country to another, falling out with the authorities wherever they went. There was never enough to eat, no secure place to live. They had lost two children already and a third, the only boy, was very sickly. He now crouched beside his mother, his expression timid, his finger in his mouth, gazing up at her as though for protection. She tenderly put an arm about his shoulders and pressed him to her as though aware of his need.

'We are very fond of Jane, Miss Vestrey. She is very good to us. You may not appreciate how good. You know my husband is a refugee, and it is not always easy for us to make ends meet. Miss Vestrey brings food and clothes and sometimes money . . .'

'But it is not only that,' Marx boomed, taking the younger of his two daughters in his arms and giving her a huge kiss. 'She is so receptive to new ideas. She is not at all what I expected to find in a young English aristocrat! She has a large view of the world. Have you too, Miss Vestrey?'

'If you mean am I a Socialist sir, the answer is no,' Caroline said clearly, suddenly losing her fear of this awesome man. 'I am not interested in politics; but I am against the war like my father who resisted it very strongly. He is so worried and upset it has made him almost ill like poor Lord Aberdeen. That is how *I* feel, sir.'

Caroline gazed at him undeterred by the fierce unfriendly expression in his eyes. To her surprise he suddenly smiled and put his young daughter down, bending to kiss her dark head.

'There you are, my darling Laura. Go ask Lenchen to make us some tea and cake if there is any. This is my baby, Miss Vestrey, Laura. She is ten years old. A little Belgian by birth. And this –' Marx led the older child forward, 'is Jenny, a little Parisian. You see my family is very cosmopolitan because I have been harried by the police of all the European countries until I found refuge in your country. Run now darling, to Lenchen.'

Little Laura ran into the next room and Caroline wondered who Lenchen could be and how she could possibly fit into this already crowded apartment.

'And this –' Marx went over to the boy and lifted him, hugging him, 'is my little darling, my Mouche I call him though his real name is Edgar. He was also born in Brussels but he is not well at the moment. He will soon be better though Mouche, eh?'

Marx hugged him again and looked at him with such

love that Caroline was touched. Despite his formidable appearance, the unorthodoxy of his views, his threadbare clothes, the squalor in which he lived and was apparently content to live, she felt drawn to someone of such a warm and compassionate nature, someone who so obviously loved his family.

Suddenly she did not care about the dirt and sat unconcernedly in a chair that almost toppled over on its side, and undoubtedly harboured fleas, maybe worse, next to Mrs Marx. At that moment a stout motherly body came in from the next room carrying a tray on which was a battered teapot and a selection of chipped mugs. A huge loaf of bread dominated the centre of the tray.

'No cake,' the body said cheerfully, 'until you visit the pawnbroker again.'

'But Lenchen.' Dr Marx held up his feet which, Caroline noticed for the first time, were encased in worn-looking slippers. 'I am already not allowed to go out because I have no shoes!'

'Oh that is not so, dear,' Mrs Marx said, glancing nervously at Caroline. 'You must not mind my husband, Miss Vestrey. Though poor, we are not quite destitute.'

'But Papa's shoes *are* at the pawnbrokers,' Jenny said in a voice mature for one of ten or so years old. 'I took them myself.'

There was a silence broken only by the sound of Lenchen making tea on an ancient stove in the corner.

'Is it not possible for Dr Marx to find academic work?' Caroline said diffidently. 'I hear he is so brilliant. Maybe a university...'

Marx laughed throatily and cut himself a thick piece of bread which he proceeded to stuff unconcernedly into his mouth. 'You think anyone would employ me with my views? I am followed everywhere by the police. Spies come from all over to report on me. I have been expelled from Germany, France and Belgium, Miss Vestrey.' He stopped and looked at her for a moment as though proud of the fact. 'No one would give me work; they would prefer me to starve.'

'Besides, Dr Marx has his own work which is so impor-

388

tant,' Jane said. 'He is going to embark on a massive economic treatise . . .'

'A study of the capitalist system,' Marx said, glancing at her with approval. 'It will be monumental. It will destroy it completely and change the way men think. In the meantime, of course, I also write pamphlets and articles for which I am paid a pittance. I could not possibly do any other work. We have a very good friend, Friedrich Engels, who helps to support me, and from time to time other people give money, like your sister. We are not too proud to accept it, Miss Vestrey. There are some things that are much more important than money and the way we live. Do you understand?'

Caroline looked about her, at the beautiful children with their father's dark intelligent eyes, their mother's delicate features; at the frail woman who was soon to usher another life into the world; at the fat comfortable body who was obviously a retainer now placidly cutting up bread, and offering it without butter to the little ones. Yet, withal, there was an air of honesty, humour and warmth about this ramshackle hovel; a sense of creativity and energy, a powerhouse of intelligence at work. She had never seen anything like it in her life. Could someone like *this* transform the world? Looking at him she suddenly thought yes, he could.

'Yes I understand, Dr Marx. I think there *are* more important things, as you say; whether I would like to achieve them like this I do not know.'

Marx looked at her sadly; his eyes seemed to brim with tears and she perceived he was an emotional man. 'You mean by neglecting my family, Miss Vestrey? Letting them live in poverty? My wife, the daughter of a Prussian nobleman? Two of my children have already died, probably due to the conditions in which we live. My wife is constantly ill and oppressed; now she is pregnant again. What right have we, you may say, to introduce another child into all this?'

He gestured about with his hands at the untidy, hot little room, the sun scarcely able to penetrate the tiny window thick with dust. 'I should *work*, Miss Vestrey, you think, become respectable. I am a professor after all. But my work is in *here*.' Marx tapped his forehead. 'In here and – ' he placed a hand on his breast, 'in my heart. That is the most important place. What is the misery we share compared to that of the masses who work and suffer without a voice, without a hope of changing the terrible monotony and squalor of their lives? Compared to these unhappy creatures I live as a king. Have you ever been in a factory, Miss Vestrey, seen the conditions? The small children, scarcely old enough to leave their mothers, working eight and ten hours a day, often caught up in the terrible machinery which mangles them to pulp? Do you know these people can hardly crawl home at the end of a day, and when they do it is to hovels worse than this where they all sleep in one bed, if they have a bed at all. And when they get there there is nothing to eat, and too many mouths to feed and the next day it is just the same.

'Compared to these people, Miss Vestrey, these millions, this is a palace. We have friends who give us food and money, above all *hope*. We know we can change; they do not. They have no hope. Compared to these millions, Miss Vestrey, you do not know what life is. Yet, without them, Britain would not be as rich as she is, for she gets her prosperity only from the sweat and toil of the suffering underpaid masses. One day they will unite and overthrow this whole evil system. That is what I am fighting for, working for. Yes, letting my family suffer for.

'I want everything to change. I do not want to make things *better* like the philanthropists who flock about pretending to do good, Lord Shaftesbury and the like, even Jane's good friend Miss Martineau. They do not even scratch the surface. They make fine fancy speeches and at night they go home to a full table and fine linen on their beds . . .'

'But surely they do good . . .'

'They do *nothing*.' Marx thumped the table so that the pots on it jumped and shook about and kindly Lenchen looked at him reprovingly, for she almost upset the tea. 'I do not *want* to make things better. If anything, I want to make them *worse*, so that the masses will be driven to rise up against their oppressors. That is what I explained to Jane about her work in Soho. You will never really improve things with soup kitchens and charity. The masses are too inert, too hungry to care. Make things even worse so that they realize that by rising up they have nothing to lose, as Rousseau has said.

'I want to change the structure of society, and you can only do that by revolution!' Marx ended his peroration by holding both hands in the air resembling, Caroline thought, some mighty Old Testament prophet who would bring fire and brimstone, destruction in his wake.

Suddenly the warmth was gone and she felt afraid again. Marx would upset the whole order of the society into which she had been born. It would be like the French Revolution, with terror and the destruction of whole families like hers. Already she fancied she heard the sound of tumbrels.

'You frighten me, Dr Marx,' she said slowly. 'Somehow I hope you never achieve what you wish. I believe you can improve conditions by doing good, by peaceful means, and I know many who are trying just this. It will happen, but peacefully, not by war and revolution.'

'Mohr, you disturb our guest,' Mrs Marx said reproachfully, and passed a hand over her abdomen as though she had a cramp. Her tired faced tightened in a spasm of pain. Caroline wondered how such a gently born woman could stand such a life, knowing that it was not for the moment or a short time, but forever.

The expression on Marx's face had changed again and softened. She could see he was someone given to swift changes of mood. He went over to Caroline and took her hands, pressing them in his large firm ones.

'I do not mean to frighten you, my dear. But these are stirring times such as we never had before. They are dreadful times, because the masses have never been so oppressed. But we are not frightening people and we truly love your sister. Come and see us again, or better, come with us one day to Hampstead Heath! We love making excursions there and have a marvellous time.'

'Oh yes!' Jenny said. 'We take a picnic and there are always friends of Papa's like Daniel and Uncle Willy. We play hide and seek in the bushes. *Do* come with us.'

Caroline smiled, enchanted by the childish enthusiasm. Her good humour returned again and she imagined them all piling into a coach and driving to the Heath, tumbling about in their high spirits.

'I would love to,' she said. 'But now we must go. I think Jane wants to call on Daniel to see he is all right. Goodbye, Dr Marx. I will not forget this meeting. It has been very instructive. You must meet my father. I think he will change your mind. He is a very balanced man.'

Marx took her hand and shook his head sadly.

'I think Lord Vestrey and I would find little in common, *mein liebschen*. I *know* such men as your father. They cannot listen to people like me. You see, we are born before our time. But you I would like to see again. Yes, Hampstead Heath on a Sunday, why not? And you can bring a basket of good food and, mind, some strong shoes.'

'Shoes?' Caroline, startled, looked at him. 'You mean you *walk* from here?'

Marx threw back his head and laughed heartily. 'Of *course* we walk! All the way and back. It is nothing, it does us good. It only takes three hours or so, providing the little ones do not drag their feet too much. And there are such excellent sights to see on the way, and smells, all sorts of things to learn. Your Mr Dickens is a great walker too. It is the only way to find out how people live, you know that. You want to forget about your carriage, and walk!'

Marx looked at her kindly. She shook Mrs Marx's hand and smiled at Lenchen and the children. Then she carefully made her way down the creaking narrow stairs, knowing that Jane had stayed behind to have a few words with her friends, maybe find out how they liked her.

Friends. To think of such people being friends of Jane. And close friends. She saw a lot of them, knew them well. It was worse even than she thought, worse than the friendship with Daniel. Much as one could like Dr Marx and find him stimulating, his family appealing, his influence, she was sure, was ultimately pernicious and quite wrong for Jane. She felt she would have to talk to her father and say, however reluctantly, that Jane should be forced to live at Chetwell.

In the street it was hot and oppressive. There were few people about and only dogs and beggars lurked in the shadows trying to keep cool on the hot stones. The humidity seemed to rise from the uneven streets, and even the trees at the end of the street in Soho Square looked wilted. Caroline thought that in this narrow, dirty city-within-a-city smelling of garbage and putrid vegetables, thousands of people lived like the Marxes, some perhaps not quite so well off as Dr Marx seemed to think he was. She had seldom visited Jane at her Mission. Though aware of another kind of life, she had hardly ever thought about it, and remained completely untouched by it.

Suddenly tired, she leaned against the door frame listening to steps inside tumbling down the stairs, and then Jane burst out onto the street, an emanation of life and vigour compared to the sullen oppressive heat outside. How well Jane looked! Cool and beautiful in her yellow muslin dress – such a contrast to her dark, glowing skin – matching bonnet and a white silk shawl loosely held across her bosom by a large brooch, she was not a person for surroundings such as these, friends like the Marxes.

'Oh Caroline, aren't they marvellous! Don't you think Mohr is a treasure?'

'Mohr? Dr Marx? Is that what he's called?'

'Only by the family and special friends. They all have nicknames. Lenchen is really Helen. Jenny is sometimes called Qui-Qui, Laura Kakadu, and little Edgar always Mouche.'

'I would hardly call *him* a treasure,' Caroline said, beginning to walk along the street with Jane towards the Square. 'In many ways he is the most terrifying man I have ever met.'

'Terrifying? Mohr? He is a darling! Everyone loves him. Friedrich Engels has given his life entirely for him. He has gone back to work as an industrialist in Manchester, something he hates, just to support Marx and his work. He is so warm and kind and good. You see how he loves the children?'

'Yes, I saw that.' Caroline nodded. 'I must agree about that. They are a very devoted family. Where for heaven's sake do they all sleep?'

'Oh, in the little back bedroom. They only have two

rooms. But Mohr often works all night and sleeps during the day. Sometimes he doesn't sleep at all, but pours out his ideas aided by tobacco and a little wine.'

'A *little* wine, a lot of wine judging by the empty bottles I saw in the corner.'

Jane stopped and looked Caroline in the face, her eyes grave.

'Caroline, you must not judge Dr Marx by the standards of ordinary people. He is one of the cleverest men alive, also brave and dedicated. He cannot help what he does and, even though they are poor and, yes, some of their things are pawned, they have a special quality in their life that you should envy.'

'Well I don't envy it!' Caroline said firmly. 'I would like to think, if I were as clever as Dr Marx, that my family had somewhere decent to live, that my children didn't die of malnutrition or disease, and that my wife didn't look as ill and unhappy as poor Mrs Marx. *That*, to me, would be preferable to any number of ideals.'

'You just don't understand,' Jane said crossly, seizing her sister's arm and pulling her through another narrow doorway a few houses along from Number 28 where the Marxes lived. 'You simply don't understand. To change the world is what Christ did after all, and look how poor he was. Not that Mohr has *any* time for Christ of course,' she said quickly, beginning to climb stairs that if anything were more rickety than those at Number 28.

'Although he says the one good thing about Jesus was His love of children. All great men live peculiar lives, and those who love them accept to lead it with them willingly, that is why . . .' Jane paused and stood on a step higher than Caroline, looking down at her, her face flushed, a rare gleam of excitement in her eyes. 'That is why *I* think Daniel is great too, because he shares Mohr's compelling idealism.'

Caroline's heart sank. Nothing had changed Jane, nothing would. She still hankered after Daniel, and Caroline knew that the bonds which had hitherto bound her to her family were loosening. For one thing the frequent absence of Papa, and Mama's new life, meant that the family lacked its former cohesiveness. It was no longer united. Chetwell was not the focus as it had been. The girls rather came and went as they pleased and Oliver too who, since leaving Eton and going up to Cambridge, had seemed to do very much as he pleased, spending most vacations with numerous friends at home or abroad. The family had broken down. It must all be changed if Jane was to be saved.

She looked fearfully after Jane, who scampered up the stairs right to the top of the house with far more energy on this hot day than Caroline felt she had. They stopped at a door and Caroline caught her breath while Jane knocked. Her heart pounded with a kind of fear as well as the exertion. The events of the day were proving a strain; everything was so different, so alien to what one knew.

'Daniel,' Jane called. 'It is I, with Caroline.'

There was no reply and, after knocking again and calling, Jane's face changed from elation to concern. She listened against the door and then turned the handle. The door opened and Caroline heard her gasp and then run forward into the room, from which came a terrible stench.

Caroline felt her dread growing as she followed her sister into a tiny room which was really an attic, scarcely more than a boxroom, with one slanting window in the eaves and a bed in the corner. She put a hand to her mouth to stop herself from retching.

On the bed lay someone she hardly recognized. His face was almost black, and vomit ran down from his mouth onto the sheets. There was an indescribable smell from the bed, and the floor was stained with faeces which ran down from under the crumpled sheet covering the man. His head lolled to one side and his tongue protruded thickly at an unnatural angle.

'Oh *Daniel* . . .' Jane screamed and was about to throw herself on him; but, acting with an energy which surprised herself, Caroline shot out her hand and she clasped her sister's arm, drawing her back.

Cholera.

CHAPTER TWENTY-FIVE

Daniel Lévy was one of the many victims of the outbreak of cholera that reached Soho in the middle of August 1854, after travelling through many parts of the kingdom since September the previous year. However, either due to the weather or the close proximity in which its residents lived, it struck Soho with terrible ferocity and the daily victims were numbered in hundreds not tens.

Suddenly there was an exodus from Soho. People packed and left on such a scale that a week after the outbreak about three-quarters of their inhabitants had deserted the afflicted streets – thus saving the lives of many.

Dr Snow lived in Soho Square. Luckily he had been in when Jane flew to get him on the day she and Caroline found Daniel at death's door, and within hours had him admitted to the Middlesex Hospital a few streets away. To this timely intervention and the fact that Dr Snow was an expert on cholera, Daniel owed his life.

Awful as the outbreak was it led to the final eradication of cholera, though no-one knew it at the time. After studying the pattern of those afflicted by the epidemic, Dr Snow suspected that the pump in Broad Street, near the Poland Street Mission, was responsible. Accordingly he importuned the local Board of Guardians to have the handle removed. They resisted him, but eventually agreed. Soon after this was done the outbreak ended as quickly as it had begun.

In subsequent investigation Dr Snow was to show that the Broad Street pump was infected by a cesspool which served the nearest house to the pump, Number 40 Broad Street, where a baby had been attacked by cholera at the end of August.

The Broad Street pump had a reputation for the taste and purity of its water. A lady, a former resident in Soho, appreciated it so much that she even sent daily for it to be delivered to her home in Hampstead, and she died of cholera. So did a niece visiting her who also drank the water. However, none of the seventy employees of a brewery very near the pump caught cholera because they drank beer or water from the brewery's own well.

An army officer from St John's Wood dining in Wardour Street drank the water from the Broad Street pump and died, and Daniel Lévy, who had visited friends living in Berwick Street, into which Broad Street ran, also drank the water with such a high reputation. He was lucky. He only drank a little during the dinner he enjoyed with his friends and this, Dr Snow judged, had saved his life.

His friends were not so lucky. An entire family of French emigrés, mother, father and three children, were buried in St Anne's Churchyard together with hundreds of other victims. This virtually closed the churchyard because the following year a new London burial ground was bought at Woking.

Like other London hospitals, the Middlesex had a staff of professional nurses who were drawn from the lower ranks of society. They drank, slept with their male patients, and generally had a very cavalier attitude to their work. It was mostly a matter of luck whether the patient got better or not, rather than skilled nursing. Doctors tended to prescribe horse riding or sea air to treat disease in the absence of really efficient drugs. Those, such as mercury, that were used were often more lethal than the disease and the medical profession enjoyed, in some quarters, a reputation little higher than the nurses.

Dr Snow was an exception. He was a dedicated, scientific man who had studied not only cholera but chloroform. Since he had set up his plaque in Frith Street, Soho, he had done an enormous amount of good. He had been called to Jane Vestrey when she was attacked and, because of his admiration for the work of the Poland Street Mission, he had kept in touch with her. He also knew Emily through the service he had performed for the Queen in administering chloroform when Prince Leopold was born.

Through the influence of Dr Snow Jane practically moved into the Middlesex Hospital to nurse Daniel. It was severely understaffed anyway. Dr Snow said it was largely owing to her that his life was saved; her devotion, her care, and her complete fearlessness in the face of the dreadful disease. She washed his body herself, wiping away the vomit and the effects of the diarrhoea. She changed his nightshirt several times a day and bathed the sweat from his brow. She brought the chamber pot herself, stayed with him while he used it, then emptied it. Finally the dreaded blackness left his face and his normal pallor returned. Dr Snow said he would live. Jane Vestrey would make a fine nurse, he declared, should she ever have the inclination.

Caroline was much more disturbed by Daniel's illness than the mere fact that he might die. She knew how close one became to a sick person. Jane's already declared affinity was sure to deepen. Visiting the hospital to be with Jane she was appalled by what she saw. It was dirty, the patients were often unkempt and the nurses slovenly and disordered. A patient could be left for hours in a bed defecating or vomiting without help or assistance being given. She watched the faces turning black and death come soon after. The corpse was unceremoniously dumped on a trolley and taken off to the morgue by a whistling porter.

Aunt Ruth was beside herself as Matthew was summoned every day to take the girls to the hospital. But she could do nothing. George was in Scotland with Oliver staying at Lord Aberdeen's country home Haddo House, where he had gone for the grouse shooting. Caroline pointed out that she was nearly twenty-four and Jane twenty-one. She realized with a shock that a short time before she would never have spoken like this to her aunt; nor could she ever have imagined herself doing such a thing. But the chaos and suffering as the victims flooded into the Middlesex during that dreadful outbreak convinced her that something had to be done, and she had more experience than most in doing it.

She came across all sorts of opposition from the nurses and medical staff, but quietly she fetched chamber pots and buckets, changed soiled garments and bathed fevered brows. Too often she pulled the sheet up over the dead face. Dr Snow begged her only to drink water brought from home which she knew was uncontaminated and to wash her hands not once but many times a day, especially after being in contact with the faeces of fever patients.

One day Caroline was wearily making her way down the corridor carrying a bundle of soiled linen when a passing woman stopped and looked at her. The action was arresting enough for Caroline to pause. There was something familiar about the woman, but she could not place her and for a moment they stared at each other, their faces slowly breaking into smiles of recognition.

'Miss Vestrey, is it not?'

'Miss Nightingale.' Caroline remembered the meeting at Mrs Herbert's months before. 'How kind of you to remember me.'

'Oh I remember you, Miss Vestrey. I hoped we should meet again, but not in conditions such as these.' She looked Caroline up and down, the bundle in her arms. 'Are you by any chance a volunteer here?'

'Yes, I have come to help nurse the cholera patients.'

'There. I said you would find a reward in nursing,' Miss Nightingale said. 'I have been asked to supervise the nursing of the cholera patients. I am sure you can be of great assistance to me, Miss Vestrey.'

Caroline looked at the calm grey eyes and the attraction she had first felt towards this unusual woman flooded back again. Miss Nightingale wore a dark dress with a severe neckline and a little lace cap on her head. Her hairstyle was very simple, parted in the middle and drawn back behind her ears. Her height seemed to give her a strength that was not belied by her slimness. She looked the sort of person who could capably and calmly organize anything.

'I would be delighted to help you, Miss Nightingale. I am in the ward for women at the end of the corridor. May I put these sheets in the wash and come back to you?'

Miss Nightingale nodded and Caroline walked swiftly to a laundry basket that stood at the end of the corridor and hurried back.

'How long have you been here, Miss Vestrey?' Florence looked at her speculatively.

'A friend of my sister was taken ill two weeks ago. When

I saw how bad conditions were I decided to stay. Isabella Goodey of the Poland Street Mission is here too. There is a pressing need for helpers. The nursing is appalling; it is a wonder anyone recovers.'

'It is sheer *chance*, Miss Vestrey. The women are badly trained, lodged and ill paid. As you know they drink and their morality leaves much to be desired. I believe Lady Palmerston thinks the nurses quite good and their drinking justified to relieve the horror of their lives. Unfortunately, much as I like Lady Palmerston, I do not agree. For some time I have been engaged in studying conditions in hospitals. The Herberts are with me in this. I ...'

Miss Nightingale's further observations were drowned by the noise that came from the female ward into which they went. Beds were stacked everywhere and some patients lay on the floor on blankets. Some were half in and half out of bed and sometimes there were two or three to a bed. Chamberpots stood on the floor overflowing with excrement. Many of the women, half naked, appeared near death, one or two had certainly stopped breathing. There were many small children clutching their frantic mothers who rocked them in their arms regardless of the risk of contagion, trying to retain the flicker of life in their frail bodies. It was a scene of helpless horror, noise and confusion.

For some time Miss Nightingale stood on the threshold gazing at the scene. Then she shrugged and looked at Caroline.

'Well, there is much to do. Let us first try and get some order in the ward, see if we can requisition more beds and so on. If you would procure some paper and follow me, Miss Vestrey, we could begin by making a list.'

'But ought we not to be looking after the patients, Miss Nightingale?' Caroline enquired in surprise. 'Their needs are so great.'

'We shall help them better by restoring order, Miss Vestrey, giving each a bed, finding more chamber pots. This filth impedes their recovery. I know what I am talking about, I assure you. You should see my little hospital, which is regarded as a model of what good nursing ought to be.'

There was nothing self-satisfied about the way Miss Nightingale spoke. There was an authority and conviction in her voice that rang true. Caroline could see that by restoring order many patients would be helped; many would die anyway. She meekly got a pad from the head nurse's desk and followed Miss Nightingale down the ward, noting everything she said.

By mid-September the outbreak was over; the wards began to empty and were not immediately filled by fresh cases. Caroline had worked non-stop, often not even going home. The method of Miss Nightingale soon bore dividends though it was much resented by the staff, doctors as well as nurses, who said she was an interfering busybody and it gave them more work. She confined herself to the wards where she worked, and work she did with dedication. She dressed and bathed the patients every bit as devotedly as Caroline; she seemed to be particularly patient towards the prostitutes who were brought in reeking of drink, unkempt, and some infinitely pathetic in the final stages of disease.

She treated them just like everyone else, with compassion and also a degree of expertise that few of the professional nurses had ever seen before. She emptied chamber pots, wiped up vomit and excreta and made the last moments of many of the dying just a little less hard to bear. Occasionally she wept when a dead child gave its last gasp; it was particularly heartbreaking to see the young succumb, as many of them did very quickly, to this awful disease.

Caroline and Florence had very little chance to talk. When they were close to exhaustion they each went quietly home to snatch a few hours' rest, Miss Nightingale to Harley Street and Caroline to Park Street. There Aunt Ruth, though despairing of the way her nieces were developing – so unladylike – always got up to make sure she had a good meal and a chance to unburden herself about the day's events.

Daniel was at Chetwell being nursed back to health by Jane. Dr Snow was afraid that his serious illness would reactivate his tendency to consumption and sea air was recommended. George Vestrey had no hesitation in agreeing that the man who had saved his daughter's life should have the chance of recovery at his home. If he also was worried about Jane's relationship with Daniel he said nothing. He had too many preoccupations to concern himself with family affairs. The storm of criticism of the government was increasing, fuelled by *The Times* and reports of men who wrote home, and George saw his own chances of political preferment fading if his friend Lord Aberdeen fell from power. Besides, his grown-up daughters could surely take care of themselves; his paternal attention was now devoted to the son Hilary had borne him in May: Henry George Vestrey Ashburne.

Isabella Goodey had worked at the hospital from the inception of the cholera epidemic. So many of its victims were known to her because they were mostly centred round Broad Street which was bisected by Poland Street. Day by day she toured every wretched tenement in the area making sure that there were no victims too ill to make their plight heard. Those who could not be moved she helped to tend and then usually to bury; those who could be admitted to the hospital she visited and looked after, especially those without families. Cholera was a disease which struck swiftly. It could kill in hours or days and chose its victims without discrimination. It seemed, however, naturally to prefer those who were poor and forced to crowd together. This explains why the epidemic in August 1854 fell most heavily in the East End, Southwark, Lambeth and Soho, where the squalid dregs of humanity were packed like sardines.

A great happiness had recently entered the life of Miss Goodey, who was nearly thirty-seven years old. This helped to temper days which almost broke her with weariness and exhaustion. She had become engaged to one of the curates at St Marylebone Church, Mr Lancelot Spurgeon, a shy retiring bachelor as devoted to good causes as Miss Goodey and only two years her junior. They were fond of music and sang in the church choir where their fairly long acquaintance had deepened into affection.

Everyone rejoiced that two such good and worthy people, no longer in the first flush of youth, should find each other and have the chance of shared happiness. They were ideally suited; the pity of it was that they had not found this out before.

Lancelot Spurgeon came often to the hospital to help his fiancée and escort her home when her work was done. Sometimes this was in the small hours of the morning, and Miss Goodey was back in the Poland Street Mission supervising the cooking of nourishing food for the invalids just after dawn.

Caroline knew they all looked pale and worn, they were continually tired as their work gave them little respite. Many of the nursing staff had been attacked by cholera and many of the volunteers were more well-meaning than useful. But Isabella seemed to take more out of herself than anyone else. Her slim frame grew gaunt and her eyes became bright and feverish. She moved with a nervous intensity and could not seem to slow down. However the epidemic was nearly over, Caroline thought with relief one night in the second week of September. It had been a month since they had found Daniel on that hot day after visiting the Marx family, none of whom, luckily, had been touched by the outbreak.

The ward was quiet and orderly, thanks to Miss Nightingale. There were plenty of beds, chamber pots, buckets, jugs, bowls and other necessities for nursing the sick. The bed linen was clean and regularly changed, the floor well scrubbed and there were no overflowing chamber pots or kidney bowls. There were flowers on tables up and down the ward and a low light burned on the desk where Caroline was writing up her notes for the day.

She paused and looked over towards the sleeping patients. Thank heaven none were expected to die, although one or two were still very ill and now and then their groans penetrated the air. There were even some empty beds. Caroline sat back and gave a deep sigh. Yes, she had felt fulfilled working at the hospital, though it had been hard and strenuous requiring reserves of energy she didn't know she had. It had been rewarding. The time had passed so swiftly;

she had felt necessary and wanted. She knew she was capable and efficient, cool in a crisis, swift in an emergency. A sort of elation had possessed her even though the work was distressing, humbling and very hard.

But how she had come to admire Miss Nightingale, who had made them all seem like fumbling nincompoops, even Isabella Goodey who was almost Miss Nightingale's equal in administrative ability. Miss Nightingale's efficiency was frightening, yet not overwhelming. She was always quiet and collected; she could move swiftly but never appeared hurried; she cajoled rather than bullied. She was by the side of a patient scarcely before a cry had been uttered, soothing, speaking quietly, administering what was wanted. she did not shrink from the hard jobs, personal contact with disease and decay; she dressed and undressed patients and put on their turpentine stupes herself.

And, by her gentle persistence on cleaning up the wards first, she had been proved absolutely right. Lives had been saved by the use of carbolic, by ensuring that each patient had her own bed, by the ventilation that she had insisted on even though there were many who opined fresh air did one positive harm. Miss Nightingale had pointed out in her firm, tactful way that even the Queen herself was a known enthusiast of fresh air and it appeared to her to do the Royal Family little harm. On the contrary, Sir James Clark had assured her they thrived on it. So rusty catches were loosed and fresh air circulated through the wards for the first time for years. And, although this had little to do with death or survival, it at least made the lives, or what was left of them, of the afflicted more comfortable, their sufferings easier to bear. Many died in comfort and dignity instead of squalor and pain.

Caroline thought that this was one of the real mysteries of Florence Nightingale: she got what she wanted by a mixture of firmness and gentle persuasion. In no time at all things had improved. The hostility of the nursing staff towards her did not lessen, but some of the doctors had begun to appreciate her work. Caroline wondered if she should try and emulate Miss Nightingale and seriously consider nursing as a profession? Help her to improve its status

as she so earnestly wished? She too had a gift for administration, patients liked her and, although their sufferings
distressed her acutely, she found them bearable, and she
could do much to help them.

Caroline smiled in the dim light of the ward. She
imagined how Aunt Ruth would react if she told her – Jane
had caused enough distress, now it was Caroline's turn. No,
she would not bring this shock on her family until she had
thought about it a lot more. She knew that a task awaited
her at Chetwell where Daniel and Agnes certainly did not
get on and Mama was loudly calling for his removal, while
Papa deliberately stayed out of the way.

Papa. Caroline frowned as she thought of this beloved
parent, so careworn with his efforts during the year. She
felt that her father had grown away from them all; there
was a distance about him that was new. In a way she
blamed Mama. It was Mama who had caused that first little
rift in the family that now threatened to grow into a
chasm.

There was a movement behind her and Caroline turned.
Then she rose with alarm and went to the end of the ward
where Isabella Goodey was slumped in an attitude of utter
exhaustion, her head resting against the doorway.

'Isabella, are you all right?' Caroline cried with concern
and put her arm around her, leading her to a chair. Isabella
sat down and her head lolled onto her chest. Then her
expression became one of anguish and she put a hand to
her stomach.

'I have such a terrible cramp. Oh ...'

Isabella fell to the floor and a nurse, who had been
tending one of the patients, rushed over to her.

'What is it, miss?'

'Miss Goodey is unwell. I think she has been working too
hard. Would you go into the corridor, nurse, and see if her
fiancé has arrived to take her home? I think she must rest
for a few days.'

The nurse looked sharply at Caroline but decided to obey
her instructions. She got up and returned in a few moments
with not only Mr Spurgeon, but Miss Nightingale herself,
who had been about to leave the hospital by the main

entrance. Caroline had taken Isabella to an empty bed and was unfastening her tight bodice to allow some air to her lungs. To her horror she saw that her friend was almost unconscious, and Caroline knew that more was afflicting her than mere exhaustion.

Florence Nightingale, loosening her own cloak, came swiftly to her side and took her pulse; then she gently opened her mouth and looked at her tongue. Suddenly Isabella sat up almost vertically and, clutching her belly, was horribly sick. Miss Nightingale herself went for a bowl and, while Caroline and the nurse held the patient, Miss Nightingale mopped up the vomit and sponged the patient's mouth.

'We must get her into bed,' she said. 'She is very ill.'

Mr Spurgeon, a tall thin man with gold-rimmed spectacles, hovered anxiously on the fringe turning his hat round and round in his hands. His mild blue myopic eyes were anxious behind his thick pebbly lenses.

'Is she all right, Miss Nightingale? Is it exhaustion?'

Florence looked kindly at the anxious suitor, now only a few weeks away from the intended nuptials. She put a hand on his arm and pressed it firmly.

'She *is* very tired, Mr Spurgeon. But I am afraid she has also taken the cholera.'

Isabella Goodey lived for two days; even that was considered long because she fought so hard to stay alive. Her fiancé never left her side except for a few hours to take rest when Miss Nightingale insisted on it. Miss Nightingale nursed Miss Goodey herself; she too seemed so determined that she should live. Dr Snow was called and came several times; but nothing helped. She was too tired and too worn out to resist the virulent disease which had afflicted her. She died in the arms of the man whom she had so nearly married, but had met too late.

Caroline was inconsolable; she only kept what calm she could to help the bereaved fiancé. Miss Goodey's father himself came to take Mr Spurgeon to his home and said that he would always regard him as a son-in-law. Caroline felt it was too terrible, too unfair that the cholera had claimed such a good woman in the very last days of the epidemic.

'God does not choose between the good and the bad in disease, I know that,' Miss Nightingale said the day after Isabella's death. She was preparing to leave the hospital and take some rest at her family home at Lea Hurst in Derbyshire. 'He seems quite indiscriminating in this regard. Caroline – I may call you Caroline after what we have been through together, may I not? Would you like to take tea with me tomorrow in Harley Street? I am too tired to talk now, but I have something to ask you.'

Caroline, who had been about to leave for Chetwell first thing in the morning, looked curiously at Miss Nightingale. She wanted to ask if it could wait, but at that moment it seemed rude.

'Of course, Florence, I would be delighted,' she said. 'Now let me give you a lift back in our coach.'

The two women scarcely spoke during the short ride along Mortimer Street to Harley Street. Their weary heads nodded in rhythm to the clip-clop of the horses' hooves upon the cobbled street. Soon after she dropped Miss Nightingale at Number 1 Harley Street Caroline alighted at Park Street to be received for the last time by dear Aunt Ruth with a bowl of good hot broth.

Miss Nightingale had astonishing powers of recovery. At three the next afternoon it was hard to imagine she had spent weeks working in the cholera ward of a busy hospital and also not neglecting her duties at her own, which almost ran itself thanks to her genius for organization. But Miss Nightingale was becoming tired of her hospital. She had achieved what she had set out to do, and now she was looking to fresh pastures. She wanted to reform the entire structure of nursing, to produce a completely new kind of nurse. She was being pressed to become Superintendent of Nursing at King's College Hospital which was being reorganized and rebuilt.

But she was undecided. From the very beginning the news from Turkey had interested her – the emphasis on the lack of medical supplies, the absence of nursing and the high prevalence of illness. Part of her reason for volunteering to go to the Middlesex had been to gain more experience of the awful disease which was decimating the troops in Bulgaria in the same way that it had the population of Soho – cholera.

Miss Nightingale read the papers as the reports got worse, and she talked to the many highly placed friends she had in the government, particularly Sidney Herbert who, as Secretary at War, was responsible for the treatment of the sick and wounded. Despite her boredom with her job in Harley Street, where she had proved what she was capable of, and her undoubted interest in the work of King's College Hospital where she was offered a place by her friend Dr Bowman, she was reluctant to commit herself. Turkey seemed to beckon to her; once again, as she had in 1837 and 1853, she heard the voice of God speaking to her, calling her to some service, she knew not what. But her restlessness, her indecision and the overpowering interest in the war seemed to indicate to her what she should do.

Caroline sat facing Florence in her neat sitting-room in Harley Street drinking tea out of blue cups. Over the rim of hers Florence was regarding Caroline in that thoughtful, speculative way with which Caroline was by now familiar. It was as though Florence had singled her out from the beginning for some special attention, because she always seemed to look at her in that way.

'Are you rested now, Caroline?' Florence said, passing her a plate of madeira cakes.

'I do feel better thank you, Florence.' Caroline bit into one of the cakes noting that it was a trifle hard. 'I will do well to have a few days by the sea at our home in Chetwell.'

'And you are going there soon?'

'Tomorrow. I should have gone today but for your invitation.'

Florence put down her cup and folded her hands in the lap of her neat blue dress. She had the habit of folding her hands in this way and slightly leaning forward whenever she had something important to say.

'Caroline, chance or God, I know not which, has thrown

us together twice this year. Once to get acquainted and once to work together. I was attracted to you in the beginning because I saw in you someone not unlike myself – you had a seriousness and earnestness not possessed by every woman. Our dear friend Isabella, God rest her soul, was another. I urged that you should think about nursing but, doubtless, you dismissed it from your mind as a profession, if one may call it such, unbecoming to a gentlewoman.'

'My father has *very* decided views on the subject,' Caroline murmured. 'He would be quite aghast at the idea.'

'Oh.' Florence looked disappointed and poured herself a fresh cup of tea. 'I do not doubt that it would shock Lord Vestrey; but you see I too had this problem with my own family. You will never know the amount of opposition I had to endure. Both my mother and sister became ill and made me ill over it. My father only gave in at the very end and I was already over thirty! I know what families can do, my dear Caroline. They must be resisted at all costs!'

Florence pursed her lips and lightly reached for one of Caroline's hands, pressing it as she took it. Caroline was embarrassed by this gesture but, at the same time, she felt a curious trembling in her body, as though there was something electrifying about Florence's touch. She did not withdraw her hand but sat there, facing Florence, aware of a growing intimacy. It was almost like an attraction, like being in love. It rather disturbed and frightened her and her heart increased its pace.

As though sensing her effect on Caroline, Florence gently disengaged her hand and, standing up, went to the window which overlooked Harley Street.

'I think you are ready to detach yourself from your family, Caroline, to do something for the world. I am thinking of getting together a party to go to Turkey and I am asking you to join me.'

Florence turned and looked earnestly at Caroline who, once again, found herself captivated by that penetrating gaze.

'Turkey?' she murmured. 'Why Turkey?'

'Because of the war. You have heard what is happening

to our men in Varna; and now they have embarked for the Crimea and taken their disease with them. The Turkish barracks at Scutari have been turned into a hospital and I hear the conditions are appalling.'

'You want to go and *nurse* in Turkey?' Caroline said unbelievingly. 'But such a thing has surely never been heard of before?'

'A lot of things have never been heard of before,' Florence said briskly. 'A woman being the superintendent of a hospital, for one. You think I wanted merely to visit there? To go and gawp like so many other curious busybodies? Oh no: I want to be useful. *God*, I believe, wants to send me there. This is a new age, Caroline; a new era. Women have never nursed men at war, you say. Is there any reason *why* they should not?'

Under the compelling gaze of those wise grey eyes Caroline could only murmur that there was none that she could see.

'Well then. I believe you have a brother in Turkey? Would you not like to see him?'

James . . . Rawdon. Yes she would like to see both of them but especially Rawdon. She swallowed.

'You are asking me to come and nurse with you in Turkey, Florence? But I have so little experience.'

'Few women have,' Miss Nightingale said casually, 'and those who do are not the kind I want. I know you have nursed a sick mother and then your sisters. I saw the work you did in the Middlesex and admired your competence, your devotion, above all your common sense. Nursing is as much a matter of common sense as anything else, dearest Caroline.'

'There *is* something else,' Caroline said half-fearfully. 'I have decided to marry.'

The expression on Miss Nightingale's face became more disapproving than before and she rounded her mouth into another little 'Oh'. Then, after a pause: 'I am sorry to hear that, Caroline. Maybe you think it is a strange thing to say; but I think there is a much higher form of life than marriage, a life of dedication and service to humanity. We women are so conditioned to our lot, to marry, to be subservient, that we are expected to shut our minds to everything else. Do you not think that is so?'

Caroline looked away from her interlocutor and gazed for a moment out of the window. She could hear voices and the sound of carriages passing down Harley Street; opposite were the façades of elegant town houses like this one. Yet this had been transformed into a hospital, a place of service and dedication. Apart from this it was just like Park Street, a row of large houses where wealthy families lived and were comfortably looked after by servants. Where the women of the house sewed, read or played with their children, and the men went forth to their clubs or to ride in the park – very few to work unless they were like her father and engaged in a respectable profession or an honourable calling. But times were changing, and wealth was no longer confined to the nobility. Trade and commerce, such as Isabella Goodey's father participated in, were becoming respectable, and many fortunes were being made by people whose origins were very humble. Yet one mixed with them quite freely.

'I know what you mean, Florence. Oh I do know what you mean! My sisters and I, especially the younger, Jane, have had many qualms about the lot of women in this changing society. Jane wants to reform the world too, but through politics. I will own there was a time when I felt called to break the bonds of domesticity, when I was restless and disturbed, when I felt unfulfilled. But that was because I was so tied to my home, to my sick sister and a rather difficult parent. Then I realized what an important vocation *that* was – to be of succour to one's family; and my unhappiness gave place to satisfaction that I was doing my duty. And then . . .' Caroline lowered her gaze before the implacable expression that Miss Nightingale still maintained – the expression of one who has heard it all before and is not convinced by what she has heard – 'then I became attached to someone I have known for many years. I realized I loved him and was overjoyed to find that this affection was reciprocal. His name is Rawdon Foxton.'

'I know the Foxton family, of course.' Florence's countenance grew less severe. 'Mr Foxton is a delightful man,

411

attractive and good natured. His parents are amiable, most, but his sisters are another matter; a bane on anybody's life because, like the lilies of the field, they neither toil nor spin; but, unlike the lilies, they are not in the least comely. They have few redeeming features.'

Caroline's mind flew back to the picnic, to Jennifer's behaviour on that day. But the breach had been healed, the families were friendly again and, in any case, Jennifer would one day be part of *her* family – her sister-in-law.

'Oh, I think that is a little severe, Florence. Jennifer has many problems with which to contend. She would like to be a writer; that she is ill favoured is not her fault and she is resentful because of it. And Harriet . . .'

'I *know* you are a kind person, Caroline.' Florence interrupted her impatiently. 'You emanate charity and compassion. Mr Foxton is indeed a fortunate man; he has chosen well.' Miss Nightingale smiled at Caroline and then arched her brows, as though struck by a sudden thought. 'But is he not in Varna with the Guards suffering those terrible privations?'

'Oh yes,' the tone of Caroline's voice expressed her anxiety, 'and with my brother.'

'Then you would be near them both if you came with me.'

Miss Nightingale consulted the fob watch at her belt and rose abruptly, going to the bell push by the fireplace. 'You see, I do not give up easily. I know good material when I see it. I have sacrificed marriage, Caroline, and all that goes with it. By that I mean a certain status that marriage gives a woman, quite wrongly in my opinion, but it is so. Then, I am very fond of children. I have foregone the opportunity to have any of my own.' She looked, Caroline thought, momentarily sad as though seeing in front of her the shades of all her unborn offspring. Then her face brightened. 'But that is all in the past now.'

'Are you sure, Florence?' Caroline murmured, not wanting to give offence.

'Oh quite, quite sure. All that is behind me; but if it is what you really wish I would never try and dissuade you. *If* it is what you wish. Now I have my visits to do and a doctor to see. Will you think about what I have said to you? Call and see me again if you wish to talk about it. Or write to me at Lea Hurst. Lady Maria Forrester knows of my plans and is helping me. But, above all, you must tell no-one, not even your father – *especially* your father, so close to the Premier. If the government know about my plans, they will immediately try and interfere. And I am not ready for their interference – yet. I am even hopeful that they may *ask* me to go, and then my task will be much easier. But for you, my dear, this is an opportunity to find a life for yourself as an independent woman. It would be a wonderful chance. Your marriage would surely be enriched by your experience; you would not simply be encompassed by its stifling folds without knowing that there was something else in life.' Miss Nightingale appeared struck by a fresh thought and held up her hand. 'Maybe your sister Jane would be interested if . . .'

Caroline smiled. '*She* is in love too, Florence. But her man is *not* in Turkey.'

Florence smiled good humouredly. 'You Vestrey girls are too pretty; with all the men after you, who can blame you for succumbing? But, if the thought of seeing your fiancé again attracts you? Come to Turkey.'

The door opened and Mrs Clarke, Florence's devoted housekeeper, stood aside for Caroline to pass.

'There is one further thing, Florence.' Caroline paused at the door. 'My engagement is not yet known to my family. I beg you will be discreet about what I have told you.'

Florence said nothing, but seemed to understand and nodded, with that tantalizing, compelling smile on her face.

CHAPTER TWENTY-SIX

Mrs Hilary Ashburne brought home her infant 'nephew' when he was four months old. It was put about that her sister had sadly died in childbirth. He was a fine, chubby baby with a veritable thatch of dark hair and rather distinctive, aristocratic features. When asked if he resembled his mother or his father Mrs Ashburne replied rather vaguely, she thought his father; the colouring of her poor, lamented sister resembled her own.

People wondered that the father of such a fine boy should part with him so easily, but Mrs Ashburne let it be known that he was too bereaved to undertake such a responsibility. It was believed also that he would shortly leave for India where he had some sort of government post. The child was accordingly put in her custody.

Into this little world of lies and deceit Mrs Ashburne fell, alas, all too easily and naturally. It had really started eighteen months before when she became the mistress of Lord Vestrey, and a great deal of subterfuge was found necessary to protect his reputation. His, not hers, let it be understood.

Hilary thought that her own feelings had really been of very little account. At the time she was more grateful than complaining, counting her blessings, and delighted to be free from poverty and want. But the Hilary Ashburne who returned in September 1854 to the house in St John's Wood was not quite the same shy, diffident person as the one who had left it the previous March.

Six months was a long time to be away from home, and she had not enjoyed her forced sojourn in the country. She had not liked Mrs Parkington who, knowing part of her secret and guessing the rest, patronized her, mistaking her for some abandoned, destitute woman of easy virtue. She'd seen many in her life, some quite well born, who had come down in the world. In a way she was one of them herself.

Nothing that Hilary ever did or said seemed likely to disabuse Mrs Parkington of this conviction, especially when the father of the child never visited her. Mrs Parkington didn't believe for the moment the tale about recent widowhood. The circumstances were far too identifiable.

Hilary had had six months to brood about her relationship with George Vestrey. Their separation was of little comfort to her, nor were his lack of visits, the sparsity of his letters, their perfunctory nature when they arrived. Benson's monthly visits with news of his lordship were of little consolation for his absence during a long and difficult breach birth, the baby being delivered with the help of forceps.

It was of little consolation too, during the weeks of depression which followed – which extended the projected absence of four months into six – the patronizing, sometimes insulting air of Mrs Parkington, and the lack of hope about the future.

It was true that his lordship was very busy and worried about the war. He thought of her constantly, he assured her and Benson said the same. But what use were thoughts when he had spoken so tenderly of his love, persuaded her that without her he did not wish to live? Six months was ample time in which to forget the exigencies of passion. It also gave one the opportunity of reflecting on the nature of a love which could appear so remiss. It almost made one forget what the beloved looked like. In that time one had changed oneself, not only physically to bear a child, but mentally too. The prospect of being a mistress and a mother as well did not seem such a harmonious possibility as before.

But once back in St John's Wood things changed. New staff had been engaged and the place shone with polish. Everywhere there was a profusion of summer flowers ordered by his lordship who, unfortunately, was still in Scotland at Haddo House with Lord Aberdeen, but was expected back soon.

A nursemaid was engaged and Hilary thought it was time she had a butler. As the mother of the son of a peer surely her place had risen in the world? Moreover, as she awaited the advent of Lord Vestrey, she began to feel more

415

secure, more sure of him, just for this very fact. However he had behaved, Henry George Vestrey Ashburne was his son and even looked like him.

George detected the change in Hilary at once. She had matured, grown quite grand, waiting for the butler to announce him instead of flying to the door. She greeted him with some distance, holding out a hand and smiling in a rather brittle way. He thought she looked devastatingly attractive, more so than ever, more poised and sophisticated. Her figure was just a little rounder, her face a little fuller. Perfection. He had only been to the brothels a few times in six months and he felt a very urgent need of her. The mother of his fourth son. However much he had not wished it, they now had a bond that, to his surprise, he found he welcomed.

But Mrs Ashburne kept her distance to start with. She immediately took George up to the nursery and there he fell in love with his infant son as he had with every one of his children as soon as he saw them, a deep, paternal love for his own issue, blood of his blood. He kissed Hilary and thanked her for the gift of this son and then she allowed him to embrace her, to take her in his arms, but not yet to make love to her.

She was quite decided about not wanting to present his lordship with an offspring every year. Her country doctor had advised her on certain methods that one could adopt to prevent this; he was very forward for his time, and recommended an eminent London obstetrician whom she had yet to see.

She didn't try and explain to George why she refused him. One did not discuss things of that delicacy with anyone, even one's lover. George felt it was her way of rebuking him for his behaviour towards her, and he felt chastened.

'My darling, you realize it was impossible for me to come to the country? You do see that don't you?'

Hilary smiled and offered him a cup of tea. She said nothing, but the way she turned her back on him just at that juncture made him sense her reproach. He stirred his tea thoughtfully.

'He is a very beautiful baby, my darling. You know, I already love him as much as any of my children.'

416

'And how *are* your children?' Hilary said, changing the subject. She hadn't reproached him, or said a word about not writing or anything like that. She wanted him to feel that everything was as it had been – only subtly different. That she had become stronger, more independent. In fact, that she had a lever she hadn't had before: Henry George Vestrey Ashburne.

George frowned and gave a deep sigh, stretching out his long legs before him.

'My children are well but presenting something of a problem which, thank heaven, this little one does not yet. Jane is in love with a Communist revolutionary who is at present at our home making my wife ill again. Caroline is her usual imperturbable self, but is deeply disturbed about something. She does not say what. Emily, as usual, gives no trouble. If she loves anyone it is Prince Albert, and his affections are otherwise engaged. Oliver wants to leave Cambridge and join the army. Clare and Patrick are so far just normally naughty, Patrick a fraction more than Clare who, of course, is rapidly growing into a young woman. James is well but on his way to the Crimea and we are worried about the high incidence of fever out there. At the moment there seems to be little chance of injury from war as there is no fighting to speak of.'

'Will you allow Oliver to leave Cambridge?' Hilary said, her small dainty teeth biting into a light French pastry. She was careful about her figure, and ate sparingly. But these pastries from a new baker round the corner she found irresistible. 'I thought he was a good scholar.'

'I will try and stop him. He is not of age; but he has always admired James inordinately. He *is* a good scholar; he has a first rate brain; but he is also very active and patriotic. He has a fierce love for this country and a pride in her history. Military matters are his hobby; he collects model soldiers and books telling of famous exploits. I think I shall have to let him go, but with the war being so static I doubt he can come to much harm. We shall soon have him back and, having served his country, he can honourably settle down to his studies again.'

Hilary sat by George and placed her arm against the back

of the settee in an easy, rather proprietorial way, so that her hand lightly touched his back. She looked interested but detached and a remote smile played on her lips; George thought she looked tantalizing and he wanted to crush her in his arms.

'And Jane's revolutionary is the young man who saved her?'

'Yes, very unfortunately so. He is most unsuitable. He is also rather lazy and arrogant and angers the servants at Chetwell ordering them to do this, that and everything else, which is not what one would expect, or so I am led to believe, from a servant of the people such as he says he is.'

'But *why* is he there?'

'He was very ill with cholera. His lungs are affected and he needs the sea air, indefinitely I am afraid. Agnes has almost lost the use of her legs again and spends days in bed to keep out of his way. I have to go down and sort everything out soon.' George closed his eyes wearily and a hand encircled her waist. Oh if he could only have her now. He let a hand rest on her thigh, but she gently moved a little way down the sofa.

Well there was little he could do about it. She was no longer merely his kept mistress, but the mother of his son. It was not what he had wanted, but it was a fact. Their relationship had changed, and he now felt in some curious way beholden to her. He now had to please her, not simply expect to be pleased by her.

It really was a very worrying time altogether. The thought of Chetwell he dreaded; the government was in trouble . . .

'I wish you would be nice to me,' he whispered. 'I do need you so very much.'

She put an arm about his neck and pecked his cheek. Her perfume and the heady presence of her voluptuous, fragrant body were overpowering. Her soft womanly smells, the outline of her plump breasts, the graceful line of her throat . . . He leaned his head on her bosom and could hear her heart beating, not very quickly it was true. She was breathing quite deeply and regularly. She was not as unduly excited by his presence as he had hoped she would be.

'I will be very nice to you, George, of course,' she murmured into his ear, just letting her tongue flick over it ever so slightly and sending a delicious *frisson* running through him. 'But not just yet. There *is* a reason.'

'Ah – ' he looked at her. 'Your time . . .'

She put a finger on his mouth and pouted.

'George darling, there are certain things one simply does not talk about. But when you next come I will be very nice to you indeed.'

George felt relieved. For a moment he had feared that she might start making excuses like Agnes, but, of course, she was indisposed. How indiscreet of him to mention it. It was not that she did not want him. He realized how much he had dreaded that might be so. He put his arms round her and hugged her, aware of her thighs, enlarged through having his child, her belly where she had carried him. Her full breasts fed him and her arms held him. Every part of her was involved with him or his baby. She was more dear to him than ever. He loved her.

'My precious,' he murmured, 'my precious girl, I need you. I really do. I have missed you so very much.'

Caroline's thoughts were still full of Florence Nightingale, what she had said, the curious power she had to attract. She felt she wanted to see her again and be near her. She felt half in love with her and it was rather unnerving. People had told her that Miss Nightingale did have a powerful effect on women as well as men and Caroline remembered the devotion of her patients in the ward, far more than anyone gave to her or dear, good Isabella.

But Caroline couldn't decide what to do. She held back. She was a little frightened. Nursing was one thing, but going all that way to Turkey, ravaged by war and disease, was something quite else.

The atmosphere at home was awful. It had all the overtones of war and unrest that, she imagined, existed in Turkey. Mama showed her hatred of Daniel by confining herself, once again, to her room, and Daniel put everybody's backs up and showed no signs of ever going away. It was now early October and he had been here a whole month.

Caroline, to her surprise, found she didn't really dislike

Daniel. He was invariably polite to her, even friendly. He was informed, intelligent and his conversation was undoubtedly original even if she didn't agree with it. Even though he treated the servants as inferior beings in a way the Vestreys would not dream of, she thought it was because he didn't know any better. He seemed grateful for the care he was getting and the obvious improvement to his health.

In fact Daniel was the most relaxed of all apart from the young ones who seldom let anything interfere with their animal good spirits.

Jane was another matter. Caroline thought her sister looked ill and her spirits depressed. Gone was the gaiety, even of a month ago. She recalled how lovely Jane had looked that day in August, when they had visited the Marxes, in her yellow muslin, her pretty flower-decked bonnet. How bursting with life she had been, how full of vitality. Now she was drawn, pale and her eyes had a haunted unhappy look that Caroline had never seen before. If she was, indeed, in love, one could only say that it didn't seem to make her happy.

And yet her devotion to Daniel was all-absorbing. She supervised his meals, saw that he was well wrapped up against the breezes which blew in from the sea, presaging winter, made sure he had an afternoon rest and cosseted and fussed over him like a mother . . . or a wife. Caroline preferred not to think about that. With Daniel as an invalid surely they couldn't even contemplate . . .

But the real problem in the house was Mrs Chetwynd, who had rapidly made slaves not only of her mother, but the servants as well. Mrs Chetwynd, in some subtle way, had superseded Mama; she gave orders and the senior staff came to her for instructions as to what to do. Caroline was by-passed entirely, and Mama might as well not exist.

Caroline, emulating Emily, was quite impervious to Mrs Chetwynd's charm and knew that she knew it. She was perfunctorily polite but nothing more; but in her heart she had a real horror of what Mrs Chetwynd was doing. She was taking over Chetwell Place and the souls of everyone inside it. Caroline longed for her father to come and restore normality.

In the meantime she put the thoughts of going to Turkey out of her mind; but she wrote daily to Rawdon. He seemed the one sure bond in a changing and unsatisfactory world. 'My dearest Rawdon . . .' 'My very dear Rawdon . . .' But so often when she thought of Rawdon the face of Miss Nightingale interposed, quickly to be banished away. It was a very odd sensation indeed.

And now Papa *was* coming! He had taken Oliver back to Cambridge, firmly quashing his desire to join his brother in Turkey and for a time there was nothing he could really do about the war that was not yet a war. Everyone thought Sebastopol would fall in a few days, some of the more optimistic said hours, once the troops were there to take it. The war would certainly be over by Christmas. Few at home realized that the administrative chaos and confusion that had been noted in Valetta and Varna, had now followed the army to the Crimea. So had the disease and the inadequacy of medical arrangements.

The day Papa was due Caroline woke feeling for once, rested and at peace. She had a pleasant sense of anticipation. She had not seen her father to talk to for what seemed like months. Despite the presence of so many British and Allied troops in Turkey and the Crimea, the popularity of the war, attempts to find peace and prevent the conflagration spreading continued in Vienna and Paris. Her father was accordingly often bound across the Channel if he was not engaged in urgent meetings in London, in Windsor or Balmoral, where he was a frequent visitor.

The Queen's fondness for Emily was well known and this affection she extended to her father. She enjoyed Lord Vestrey's company. Besides, like her beloved Albert, he also danced and sang well and was thus good company after dinner. The Prince valued him ever since his work on the Exhibition committee and thought his views sound. He liked talking to him. There was talk of an important ambassadorial position for George if peace was declared, maybe Paris or Vienna.

Yes, Papa had become a man of affairs; he no longer belonged solely to the family.

George was weary as he travelled in the train down to

Chetwell. He had had any number of arguments with Oliver and even now feared he might abscond from Cambridge and find his way to the Crimea by underhand means. Neither was he altogether happy about Hilary. She had not actually done or said anything; but somehow, delicately, she had made him feel he had behaved badly towards her, and perhaps he had. Perhaps he *should* have gone to see her, or written more. He had possibly taken her too much for granted; seen her as a child-bearing, pleasure-giving chattel; something that belonged to him and that he paid for.

Put like that it didn't seem nice at all. In a way, Aunt Ruth *had* put it to him like that. Aunt Ruth, with her womanly insight, now saw only too clearly Hilary's point of view. She had even expressed her intention of visiting her new great nephew though George secretly wondered how Hilary would receive her. She really had changed; grown rather frightening. Hilary had suddenly developed presence, unseen but clearly felt. He was now slightly in awe of her in a way that he had certainly not been before.

With the thought of Papa coming, Caroline wasn't even annoyed by Mrs Chetwynd at breakfast, as she usually was when cook came to give her the day's recipes and seek her orders. Caroline breakfasted briefly in order to get things just right for Papa. She wanted to make sure that his room was ready, with fresh towels and flowers. She doubted whether Mrs Chetwynd would be quite so keen on the kinds of things that concerned Papa. She also wondered where Jane was. She had not come down to breakfast; Daniel never did.

Clare and Patrick had breakfasted earlier with their governess and were in the schoolroom with the Tangent children. Polly was due over today too with her mother. There was to be a dinner party to greet Papa. Caroline thought she might have been consulted on the menu for that. But no, nothing was going to put her out. She was not going to let it.

She looked in on the schoolroom on her way to Papa's room. All seemed to be going well there and she smiled at the governess and her pupils. As she was passing Daniel's room, she paused. She wondered if Daniel had had his breakfast. Jane usually saw to that. He was, after all, an invalid, or supposed to be. He had certainly gained weight during his stay here.

She was about to pass on and then decided not to. She never knew what decided her because, after all, Daniel was no concern of hers. He was devotedly enough looked after by Jane. And where was Jane? Had she breakfasted earlier perhaps? The dishes were left on the sideboard on hot plates for an hour. Caroline felt a vague sense of unease about the whole thing; she didn't know why.

She knocked at the door of Daniel's room. There was no reply. She knocked again, louder. Still no reply. She became alarmed. It was just after nine and the sun streamed into this part of the house, which faced the sea. She turned the knob and found that the door swung gently open.

In the bed on the far side of the room Daniel was asleep, his face turned away from the light. His eyes were closed and his chest rhythmically moved up and down. Next to him was her sister Jane. She was fast asleep too and the upper part of her body, completely unclothed, was slightly turned toward Daniel, one arm thrown across his bare chest.

Caroline couldn't move, either to go in or leave and shut the door. The horror of what she saw fixed her to the spot like Lot's wife. She couldn't take her eyes from Jane's breasts, her full, heavy nipples, the arm over Daniel. That proprietorial arm seemed more a proof of familiarity than, awful as it was, the nudity.

What she now observed left absolutely no room for misinterpretation.

Jane opened her eyes first and saw her. The eyes, fresh from sleep, opened very wide, staring at Caroline without fear, but with a look of complete surprise and astonishment on her face. She seemed, at first, to be unaware of where she was. Then, as Daniel grunted in his sleep and turned by her side, she drew her sheet up to cover her naked breasts and continued to stare, rather fixedly, at Caroline, as though willing her to disappear.

Daniel went on sleeping, which was rather a relief. After the initial shock Caroline felt the blood return to her legs, and was about to close the door when Jane suddenly leapt out of bed and, rushing to the washbasin standing on the tallboy, was violently sick. Caroline shut her eyes. Jane had no clothing on at all, and even Caroline had never seen her nude since they had bathed together as small children.

As Jane heaved over the basin the sight inevitably reminded Caroline of her experience at the hospital. Cholera. Now more apprehensive than shocked, she went rapidly over to Jane and put around her her robe which had lain on the bed, bending anxiously over her as she retched into the basin.

When she had finished she led her back to the bed and sat her down on the side, gently stroking her hair and wiping her lips. Daniel, by this time looking very startled, was sitting bolt upright against the pillows, the sheet drawn up to his chin. His very pale face with the dark beard and tousled hair made him look sinister, utterly alien, like the foreign, unwelcome masculine presence that Caroline felt he was.

Jane's head was slumped on her chest and her eyes shut. As she heaved, Caroline saw there were tears coming from her eyes, either from the effort as she vomited or for some other reason. Her alarm increased. She put her arm about Jane's shoulders and squeezed her reassuringly.

'Are you all right now?' she whispered.

Jane nodded but said nothing, her fingers frenetically kneading her white lawn robe. Caroline was conscious of her strong bare legs visible as the robe fell away on either side, of the little delta of dark pubic hair.

'Are you ill in any other way, Jane? Have you pains in the stomach?'

Jane shook her head, still saying nothing. Caroline didn't know what to do. She sat with her arms about her sister looking out of the window. She could just see the horizon, and a thin ribbon of the sea.

'Jane is pregnant, Caroline,' Daniel said in a level unemotional voice. 'She is sick every morning. It is one of the symptoms of pregnancy. That is why we slept so late; she is not well.'

Caroline was aware of the wooden frame of the window, of the curtains down either side, and beyond was the familiar sea. The tips of the trees in the park as they crested the hill were just visible from the level of the window sill. She concentrated very hard on this visual image as though time would somehow etch it permanently in her mind as a moment when another part of her safe, reliable world shattered. She felt it was important to fasten onto something visible and tangible to retain her own emotional grip on herself: the window and the thin line of the sea, the long green curtains and the tips of the brown, autumnal trees swaying in the park. This was home, familiar, something she could cling to.

'Thank God,' she heard herself saying. 'I thought it was the cholera.'

Beside her Jane trembled and, bursting into tears, threw herself against Caroline's bosom. Protectively, lovingly, Caroline put her arms about her sister and rested her cheek against her thick, black hair.

'There, there,' she murmured, remembering Jane, very small and dark, leaping in and out of the big bath tub in the nude when they were children. 'There. Why did you not tell me?'

Jane went on sobbing and shaking her head.

'She didn't know how,' Daniel said from behind. 'It is not an easy thing to tell.'

'But I am her sister.' Caroline didn't look at him.

'It is still not easy. It was not easy to tell me, in the circumstances.'

'How long have you known?'

Caroline thought this conversation, back to back, was a very curious one, comical even; but she did nothing to change it. She didn't particularly want to look at Daniel or observe the expression on his face, to see whether it was sorry or concerned, or smug as she rather suspected it would be. This man who had violated her sister.

'Jane is about four months pregnant,' Daniel went on in his unemotional voice. 'She saw Dr Snow in August, just before I was ill.'

'Dr Snow *knew*?'

'Yes.'

'And yet he let her nurse you?'

'I don't think he could do anything to stop it. Jane is a very determined young woman, as you know.'

'I'm surprised *you* let her, though.'

'I could not do anything either, Caroline,' Daniel said without emotion. 'She loves me.'

Yes, she loved him. Four months pregnant; yet she was so thin and pale. Caroline's arm tightened once more protectively about Jane's shoulder.

There was no question of her going to Turkey now. Jane would need her.

George Vestrey felt that there were times when God seemed to have turned His back on him and his family. He had felt this for quite a long time, and his enthusiasm for going to church had accordingly diminished. It seemed useless to pray when your prayers were so seldom answered, when disaster piled on disaster, and God did not seem to offer much comfort as the Church taught one to expect.

He had been hoping, despite the odds, for a little respite, a few pleasant days with his family, only to be told almost as soon as he stepped over the threshold that his favourite, most beloved daughter, still unmarried, was going to have a child. What was even worse, insupportable almost, was that Daniel said he had no intention of marrying her; that she had known this from the beginning and it was a risk she had gladly taken.

'*Gladly!*' George Vestrey thundered wanting to knock the fellow down. Suddenly at that moment Daniel Lévy, whom he had never really been able to like, had seemed utterly repugnant, offensive and detestable.

Jane, still not recovered from the shock of her family so abruptly discovering her secret, sat crouched in a chair in the corner of the drawing-room. Caroline, the only other one in the know, sat by her, very still and erect. She folded her hands in her lap as Miss Nightingale did when she had something important to say, her chin slightly raised, her eyes on her father.

Daniel, whether because he was nervous, or because he didn't care – it was so hard to tell from his placid features – lolled in a chair by the fireside opposite George. One leg was bent and the other straight, his right hand in his trouser pocket. In the other was a cigar which he puffed rather unconcernedly as he looked, good humouredly, at the man whose daughter he had dishonoured.

'*Gladly!*' George said, rising to his feet and standing threateningly over Daniel. 'You mean my daughter would *willingly* flout the conventions of society! She is a Vestrey, you know.'

'Oh I know that, Lord Vestrey. I am always being reminded of it, not by Jane but by everyone else, particularly her mother who dislikes me. I think even Jane has it constantly at the back of her mind. It seems to me to be a terrible burden to be a Vestrey; not a state to be envied at all.'

'My dear young man,' George's voice grew hoarse, 'whatever your relationship to my daughter I will have *no* hesitation in throwing you out of the house if you carry on in that impertinent way in front of me!'

Daniel's pale cheeks momentarily took on a little colour and he looked down at the chain strung across his waistcoat.

'I apologize, sir. I am, after all, a guest in your house.'

George put his hands under his coat tails and stood with his back to the fire. He looked at Caroline as though seeking help; but Caroline could think of nothing useful or helpful to say. Even though they had discussed what to do before her father summoned Daniel, nothing had come out right. George had never, in his wildest dreams, nor had Caroline, expected that this foreign little upstart, with no name or fortune of his own, would refuse to do the right thing by his daughter, as George had expected he would be glad to do. He had decided to allow them to marry; to give his daughter in matrimony to this, this French Casanova, as the lesser of two evils.

But the Casanova was not even grateful. He did not believe in marriage and said that Jane knew his views from the start. All the contempt and prejudice that, in his heart, George Vestrey felt for foreign revolutionaries came welling to the surface. No matter that this man had saved Jane's life, no matter that George was a liberal, enlightened diplomat and politician, a man speaking fluent French and German and used to consorting with people of all nationalities. In his heart he hated Daniel Lévy, he despised him and all he stood for, and he condemned him to hell.

'Well what is to be done then?' George said at last, trying desperately to keep the hatred from his voice, to sound decent and reasonable for Jane's sake. 'I want to do the best for my daughter, and my first grandchild. That is paramount in my mind.'

Jane suddenly got up and ran over to her father, throwing herself into his arms.

'Oh Papa, Papa. You are so good, too good. I did not expect this . . .'

George felt his eyes brim with tears and, catching her, drew her into his arms. Poor deluded bewildered girl, what had she anticipated? Was he such a fearful father?

'But, my darling, what did you expect? That I would throw you into the street? It is your . . . it is Mr Lévy whom I would like to throw into the street. But you, never, I am your father and I will always look after you and protect you, whatever you do.'

Jane went on sobbing and Caroline felt hot tears prick her own eyes. She loved her father more at that time than she ever had in her life. He was so good, so practical, so dependable, despite the terrible shock he had had. When she had first told him in the privacy of his study he had wept. She had seldom seen him cry before; but he had broken down and wept.

'Do you want to stay at Chetwell, 'my darling? Or . . .' George left the sentence unfinished. How could she stay here with Agnes who had yet to hear the news? He and Caroline had agreed that Agnes must be the last to know. They had hoped to have Jane safely married to the hated foreigner before she knew. Now not even that was possible. No, Jane could not stay here.

'I want to be with Daniel, Papa.' Jane lifted her head and looked into his eyes, her own suddenly dry. 'I love him and I do want to bear his child. I want to live with him as though we were wed.'

'And is this his wish too?'

Jane nodded and looked around at her lover, who appeared to be listening to the proceedings as though they had very little to do with him; as though he was quite easy as to the outcome, whatever it was.

'I think so, Papa.'

'You *think* so? You have not talked about it?'

'Jane has behaved as though it hadn't happened, sir,' Daniel said drily. 'As though by not talking about it, it would go away.'

'In her case I would have thought that a natural reaction,' George said frostily. 'In your position I would have thought it my duty to make plans immediately, even if you do not believe in doing the right thing by her and marrying her.'

'But what can *I* do, Lord Vestrey?' Daniel got up and threw the butt of his cigar into the fire. By the side of his lordship he appeared at a decided disadvantage, being much smaller and, by virtue of his recent illness, frailer looking than ever. But it didn't seem to perturb him and he put his hands behind his back just like George, and swung easily to and fro on his feet. 'I have no fortune, not even a home as I have been forced to give up the little room I had in Dean Street. I can offer Jane absolutely nothing.'

'But would you provide for her if you could?'

'Of course. But I cannot; so it is not a question over which I care to exercise my brain.'

'And I suppose for you, your brain is exercised over matters of world shattering importance, such as the enslavement of the masses over which you think you have some control?' George could not keep the menace out of his voice and Daniel, for the first time, looked at him rather uneasily and moved a few paces away.

'My views, by themselves, sir, can do little. But the brotherhood of man . . .'

'Like all of your kind that I have ever had to deal with,' George said, his voice constricted with emotion, 'I find you glaringly lacking in concern for the individual. In this case my daughter. You would put the welfare of the many before the good of the few, like Mr Mill to whose views doubtless you subscribe?'

'Oh, Mill does not go *nearly* far enough for me,' Daniel

said with asperity. 'He is no radical, sir, but one of these fireside philosophers, all talk and nothing much besides. Anyway, Lord Vestrey, apart from her condition, your daughter is in no way deprived as the masses are. I love her, you love her. She is protected in the bosom of her family ...'

'Oh you *do* love her then?' George could not keep the mockery out of his voice. 'I must say it is the first time I have heard you utter the word.'

'Of course I love her. Why should you doubt that I love her?' Daniel appeared genuinely surprised and put his forefingers in the pockets of his vest.

'I thought if you loved her you would do the right thing by her. It is not easy in the society in which we live for an unwed woman to have a child. You could give her respectability and you will not. A little sacrifice on your part would, to me, be a proof of your love. If you cannot take care of her materially, you could at least do that much. It is a moral matter.'

Jane stepped away from her father and went and stood by Daniel. She put her arm through his and drew him close to her.

'But *I* do not wish to marry Daniel, father,' she said, gazing at him. 'I *do* subscribe to his views; a free association based on love. It is the most glorious thing for two people, freely, to live with each other as we shall. It was not without hesitation that I did what I did, because it *was* against everything I had been brought up to believe. But having done it I do not regret it, and I do not regret the result. I am proud to have Daniel's child, and to be a pioneer in introducing the values of freedom of choice into this country, hidebound by tradition and old fashioned virtues.

'I was always kept back, father, by the fact that I was a Vestrey – that Emily was at Court, that you were in the government, a member of the House of Lords. Daniel has shown me how unimportant, how bourgeois these views are, how they keep us from a true appreciation of ourselves. Like him I feel that a new society is around the corner, and I want to be in the forefront; to share it with him.'

George Vestrey lowered his head and appeared to ponder

430

his daughter's words. Watching him, knowing his agony, Caroline ached for her father, but could do nothing.

One thing however was sure. If her sister and Daniel were to set up house together, undoubtedly paid for by their father, she would indeed be free. There was no place for her in this house with her mother, dominated by Mrs Chetwynd, and Jane would not need her, after all.

CHAPTER TWENTY-SEVEN

Sophie Chetwynd moved silently around the room, her plump little hands surprisingly deft as they opened the drawers of the dressing table, the large chest and the tall-boy, the fingers probing eagerly through the contents. Hardly a thing was disturbed, none of Emily's neat piles of handkerchiefs, stockings or underlinen. Everything about Emily was neat, her wardrobe, her shoes, the pile of books by the side of her trim narrow bed. Mrs Chetwynd even looked through the books, carefully riffling the pages to try and find what she sought.

The letter. The effect on Emily of the letter from Varna had been so remarkable that her mother could not get it out of her mind. It had agitated her ever since. Mrs Chetwynd had known it was not from James, familiar as she was with his writing from the letters he so diligently wrote to his Mama. Somebody else was writing to Emily; someone who had upset her. They were both curious, nay eager, to know who.

The day she received the letter she had stayed in her room, declining to come down to meals. She claimed that the heat had brought on a headache. But that night, standing outside Emily's room, in her secretive, insidious way, Mrs Chetwynd had heard the sound of tears smothered by a pillow, of deep heartrending sobs. Every night it was the same. During the day Emily continued to move about the house; but as someone sleep-walking. She neither smiled, laughed, frowned, nor wept. She seemed to be looking at something that only she could see, something far into the future or far far away. Agnes grew very alarmed indeed; but when she had tried to encourage Emily to confide in her she was rebuffed. Then Emily, still silent, went to Osborne, and shortly after that Caroline came back.

When Emily returned home in November she seemed her old self. Her month in waiting had restored her spirits.

Agnes soon forgot about the letter; but Mrs Chetwynd did not. It would please Agnes if she found it, and it would please her too because there was nothing about the Vestrey family that she did not wish to know. They obsessed her – their beauty, talent, richness, insouciance, arrogance. She knew quite well how they felt about her; how they despised her and resented her influence over Agnes. Any little score she could settle with any Vestrey would give her immense pleasure. Emily was sure to have brought that letter back with her. Sophie went on delving, very quickly, quietly, knowing that Caroline and Emily were visiting the Foxton family and would not be back until dark.

Then she found it. It was in the drawer of the little Adam table by Emily's bedside, unlocked. The last place someone as secretive as Sophie would have hidden it, or someone as devious as she would expect to find it – just tossed in an unlocked drawer. She saw the letter there as soon as she opened it; no attempt to conceal it at all. Of course with the supreme self confidence and arrogance of a Vestrey, so reasoned Mrs Chetwynd, Emily would not have expected anyone to look in her drawers. People like the Vestreys reckoned without the Chetwynds of this world.

As soon as they returned to the house Caroline and Emily realized that something untoward had occurred; there was an atmosphere of subdued panic about the ground floor with servants scurrying around, and the rooms on the first floor so lit up, that even as the carriage approached the house from a distance it gave them a feeling of unease. Caroline anxiously pulled off her gloves as she preceded Emily into the house and walked quickly into the hall. Bryce the butler, coming down the main staircase, moved with such speed that he nearly collided with Caroline.

'Bryce, whatever has happened?'

'Oh Miss Vestrey, pardon me Miss.' Bryce, pale and apologetic, stepped abjectly back. 'It is your mother, Miss. She was taken very bad this afternoon . . .'

'Oh . . .' Caroline clutched at her cloak which she was about to remove and started for the stairs.

'But she is all right again, Miss Vestrey. This time the

doctor did think it was a heart attack; but now he thinks it was not so.'

'He is still here?'

'No, he left a quarter of an hour ago, Miss Vestrey. He will return tomorrow. Mrs Chetwynd is with your mother.'

'Mama? What has happened to Mama?' Emily, coming in after Caroline, heard the end of Bryce's words. Quickly Caroline told her what had happened and the two girls prepared to mount the stairs. Bryce stepped forward and put his hand on the bannister.

'If I could, might I venture . . .' Bryce coughed. 'I do not think Miss Emily should approach your mother yet, Miss Vestrey.'

'But whyever not?' Startled, Caroline looked from him to Emily.

'I cannot say, Miss Vestrey. I do not know. But I understand your mother's distress has something to do with Miss Emily. It was that that occasioned the attack.'

'What nonsense! I have done nothing.' Briskly Emily began to run up the stairs calling over her shoulder. 'You will see, this is some mischief of Sophie Chetwynd. She is behind all the trouble in this house.'

Caroline looked at Bryce, but said nothing and ran up the stairs after her sister to their mother's room.

Agnes did indeed look unwell. Propped on her white pillows she appeared too ethereal to be alive; her eyes were closed and her mouth sagged slightly open. She was asleep and emitted tiny little grunts that sounded like pathetic cries of distress. Emily rushed to her mother's side and knelt by the bed.

'Oh Mama, Mama, what has happened?'

But Agnes didn't move. Sophie Chetwynd, looking unnaturally pale herself, and sitting by Agnes's bed, made no attempt to get up when the girls entered. She gazed rather dully at Emily as though even she was too shocked by what she had brought about to speak. However she braced herself and, leaning over, touched Emily's shoulder.

'Your Mama is drugged, Miss Emily. The doctor gave her a heavy dosage of laudanum. She should sleep until morning.'

'But is she all right? What happened?' Caroline stood behind Emily looking with concern at her mother. 'She looks simply terrible.'

'She had an attack, Miss Vestrey. It was so bad I thought she was dying . . .'

'What brought it about?'

Emily slowly got to her feet. Having satisfied herself that there was nothing she could do for her mother, she stood by Caroline's side staring at Mrs Chetwynd.

'Yes *what* brought this on, Mrs Chetwynd? The butler said it had something to do with *me*.'

Mrs Chetwynd hung her head while a heavy, dull flush gradually rose from her fleshy neckline to her overhanging cheeks. She shrugged her shoulders.

'Pray could we have a word with you downstairs?' Caroline said coolly. 'I would like to get to the bottom of this.'

'Oh, but I must stay with your mother.'

'I will send a servant up to keep an eye on her. We shall not be gone for long. Kindly step downstairs, Mrs Chetwynd.'

'Oh but . . .'

Mrs Chetwynd saw the expression on Caroline's face and decided to obey.

The three women stood facing one another in the drawing-room. The red velvet curtains were drawn for the night and a large fire, fuelled by logs from the estate, had been warming the room since morning. Although it was a cold day, and a cold evening, Caroline felt the atmosphere oppressive. It had taken her some minutes to digest the contents of the letter, which she now held limply in her hand.

'And you showed *this* to my mother?'

'Yes.'

'Having *stolen* it first!' Emily said, her pale, beautiful face now livid and mottled with rage. 'You are a common petty criminal, Sophie Chetwynd, and I will tell my father to throw you out of this house. To hand you over to the magistrate. To . . .'

Caroline put a hand out. 'Hush, Emily. How she got the

letter, though pertinent, is not really the point. Showing it to Mama is something quite else.'

'She stole it from my drawer!' Emily screamed. 'Stole it, stole it, stole it.'

Suddenly she ran over to Sophie Chetwynd and put her hands around her fat neck. Her lips were drawn back and her fine white teeth bared in a most un-Emily-like expression of uncontrolled savagery. Sophie Chetwynd's eyes rolled in her sockets and she looked like some heavy sack that was about to drop onto the floor. With an exclamation Caroline ran up to her sister and, with all the force she could muster, dragged her away, loosening her fingers from the folds of flabby flesh.

'Emily, if you kill her it will solve nothing.'

'She deserves it.' Emily's hands still reached for the throat on which two large weals were slowly appearing, and her face still had the rictus of dementia.

'Emily, Emily. Calm, please, or you will be ill too.'

Emily closed her eyes and momentarily leaned against her sister for support. Caroline put her arms round her and held her.

All this was her fault. She should have said something. She should have spoken months ago. She hugged Emily to her, bowed down by the weight of her own guilt and misery.

'Oh Emily, Emily.'

Mrs Chetwynd flopped into a chair and started rubbing her throat. 'I shall report this attack to the authorities, Miss Emily. At first light I shall . . .'

'You can certainly pack your bags and get out,' Caroline said. 'What you do after that is no concern of ours. We are not afraid of your threats, you miserable, mean minded, little sneak of a woman.'

The Vestreys wouldn't be, Sophie thought, choking. She rubbed her neck and glared vengefully at the two sisters. It had been a terrible day. She had been so triumphant when she found the letter and devoured its contents. She'd flown along the corridor to Agnes's room, waving it about like some triumphant banner.

'Your Mama had seemed so *well*,' she said plaintively. 'I never dreamed it would have this effect on her.'

'Well what *did* you think?' Caroline said, still clasping her sister around the waist. 'Did you think she would laugh and say "How droll"? What on earth did you think she would do? I thought you were some kind of medical practitioner?'

'I thought my power was strong enough to support her.'

'Well it certainly wasn't, you old fool.'

Mrs Chetwynd made a pathetic effort to straighten herself up. If only she didn't give in to all these lovely puddings and cakes the Vestrey cook made so well, she would have felt better able to confront those daunting Vestrey girls.

'I made an error of judgment, Miss Emily. To call me a "fool" is to fail to acknowledge the good I have done your Mama. I have cured her. Without me she will be ill again.'

Her statement of an obvious truth gave her confidence and she put a pudgy hand protectively on her large bosom smoothing the taffeta folds of her bodice.

'You don't mean that you feel you could stay on *here*,' Caroline said incredulously, 'after what has happened?'

'I do not know I would care to stay on here, Miss Vestrey. It would need considerable persuasion to make me after the attack made upon me today. But I know that, without me, you will be looking after your mother for the rest of your life. She will go down, down, down . . .' Mrs Chetwynd made a movement of her hands as though sliding them down a deep, slippery slope. 'So much for your chances of marriage to Mr Foxton then, Miss Vestrey.'

'Oh you . . .' Emily tried to hurl herself at the offensive woman again, but Caroline had felt Emily's muscles tense and anticipated her. Her grip round her waist tightened.

'I really think you should leave us,' Caroline said, not sure how long she could hold her sister. 'You have given us the facts. You know our point of view and we know yours. Maybe we should all sleep on this and talk again in the morning. Good night, Mrs Chetwynd.'

Caroline nodded curtly.

'May I go back to Lady Vestrey?' Mrs Chetwynd managed a docility that took Caroline by surprise. She looked almost pathetic as she stood up, so very small and plump beside the two tall elegant girls.

'I don't see why not.'

Caroline suddenly felt tired. She wanted to flop. As Mrs Chetwynd closed the door she let Emily go and slumped into a chair, passing her hand across her brow.

'Oh God, what a mess.'

Emily folded her arms and walked to the fireplace. For a long time she stood staring down at the crackling flames.

'Why didn't you tell me before?'

Caroline looked at her sister's bent head, loving her, pitying her, wanting to spare her suffering.

'I lacked courage. Forgive me. I knew that you felt for him . . .' Caroline faltered not quite knowing what to say. 'Well that you were fond of him too. Obviously, as he is of you.'

'For what happened between us . . .' The words, like writing on stone, had etched themselves into her brain ever since she first saw them. The shock about her mother, the anger with Mrs Chetwynd, were nothing compared to that awful admission *'for what happened between us'.*

'What *did* happen between you, Emily?' she said in a tight voice kept very closely under control. Emily, her head still bent towards the fire, closed her eyes. 'I want to know, Emily.'

Slowly Emily turned round and faced her sister. She had been so close to forgetting the pain. It had happened three months ago. She had thrown herself into her duties at the Court, talked herself dry, sung herself hoarse, danced until there were holes in her shoes. She had almost forgotten the pain of the letter, though never the memory of him. And now this.

'We kissed. That is all.'

As she stared at her Caroline got up.

'What did you say?'

'We kissed.' Emily raised her chin. 'We kissed against a wall in Lady Fox-Hargreaves' garden. We . . .'

She felt the sting of Caroline's hand on her cheek almost at the moment she saw her raise it to strike her. It was a swift, unpremeditated action, a reaction made scarcely without any thought at all.

Now Caroline looked like the vengeful vixen, her lips drawn back, her eyes flashing with hatred. Emily touched her cheek and moved towards the door. She had never seen Caroline strike anyone in her life; not even the children when they were especially naughty. The look in her eyes frightened her.

'A kiss isn't very important, Caroline,' she said timidly, wanting to placate this suddenly strange, fearsome being opposite her.

'It is very important to me, Emily. He is my fiancé.'

'I didn't know that. A woman doesn't take the initiative in these matters.'

'*You* do, Emily,' Caroline said bitterly. 'You have a flirtatious nature. You are a siren at heart, always leading the men on, ensnaring them. You have always had your eyes on Rawdon, always said that he wanted to marry you. Well he didn't. He wanted to marry me.' Caroline pointed at her breast. 'It was always me, never you; but you led him on, and flirted with him, danced your way into his heart. Rawdon loves *me*, not you, and if he kissed you that night then . . .' Caroline's face suddenly crumpled and she burst into tears, flinging herself onto the sofa, waving her feet in the air. Her great sobs echoed round the vast room and Emily became nervous lest the servants should hear. She wanted to comfort Caroline, but she dared not go near her. Caroline had hurt and frightened her. She could still feel the sting on her cheek. Besides she did love Rawdon; she did.

Emily gazed at her sobbing sister and crept over to the door. She opened it as quietly as she could and then slipped out, shutting it gently behind her.

It was agreed that Mrs Chetwynd should stay, for the time being. The intermediary was Dr Woodlove who found a state of *impasse* when he called at the house the next day. Lady Vestrey had certainly recovered; she had not sustained a heart attack and she was more composed. But she refused to have either of her elder daughters in her room. She was quite adamant about that and, fearing another attack, worse maybe than the last, no-one dared disobey her. Mrs Chetwynd thus reigned triumphant in Lady

439

Vestrey's bedroom; the girls remained closeted separately in theirs, refusing to meet or speak and Dr Woodlove, who had never in all his years of practice encountered a similar situation, consulted the Reverend and Mrs Tangent with all speed.

It was decided to send for Lord Vestrey as a matter of urgency.

George had never had such a pleasant reception from his wife for a long time. She even opened her arms as he walked into the room, having come down by train within hours of receiving the wire from his wife's brother who had met him at the station. He felt better knowing what had happened, though it was an extraordinary state of affairs. He too felt angry that he hadn't been told about Caroline and Rawdon. It helped to be angry with someone. He bent and kissed Agnes's cheek.

'You look very well, my dear. I am glad you have recovered.'

'This time yesterday was a very different matter,' Mrs Chetwynd said ominously, deferentially drawing a chair for his lordship up to her ladyship's bed. 'I thought your wife was dying.'

'Most unpleasant,' George said, eyeing his wife's companion uncomfortably. She was a difficult woman to take to. 'A severe shock; but how came she by the letter, Mrs Chetwynd?'

Sophie blushed and looked at the ground.

'I asked her to find it, George,' Agnes said with the equanimity provided by a further light dose of laudanum after lunch. 'We knew that Emily had received this letter from Varna but not from James, and that she was considerably disturbed by it. Sophie knew it was not James's handwriting, so who was it? We thought it must be an illicit follower.'

'When Lady Vestrey asked your daughter about it she refused to discuss it, my lord,' Mrs Chetwynd said indignantly. 'She was quite stubborn towards her mother.'

'But is Emily not old enough to receive letters, my dear?' George enquired reaching out to take Agnes's hand. She quickly withdrew it fearing that an overture of a carnal nature might be in the offing, and tucked it under her very white sheet, looking anxiously at Sophie.

'Not while she is in your care, George. You know that. You have a duty as a father to protect your daughters, however old they are, until they marry. I thought that if Emily was so upset something untoward was afoot, something possibly of a physical nature – knowing Emily's disposition.'

Agnes pursed her mouth grimly. Let Emily find out about being in love, what it really entailed, and then see if she was still keen to chase the men. Momentarily Agnes closed her eyes. She always felt quite sick at the thought of her daughters having to undergo the horror she had endured for so many years. But unfortunately it could not be avoided. It had to happen for the continuance of the race. She found it very difficult to understand how God could possibly have arranged such a state of affairs. Dorothy Tangent assured her it was the result of original sin – it was all Eve's fault apparently; otherwise procreation would have been a much simpler and more pleasant business, with nothing unseemly for the woman to do at all. It was God's way of punishing Eve for that business with the apple. She opened her eyes and looked at Sophie who nodded understandingly. Sophie always seemed able to read one's thoughts.

'As it was, you disturbed a hornets' nest,' George said thoughtfully.

'And they do not speak to each other . . . There was some great commotion after they had rudely dismissed Sophie who still happened to be outside the door . . .'

'Eavesdropping, Mrs Chetwynd . . .?' George enquired, wishing he had sensible Hilary by his side to help him.

'Oh *no*, my lord! But I was anxious about the girls. They were so overwrought. In matters of the heart,' Mrs Chetwynd dropped her eyes, 'your lordship knows how it is. Or rather, you must remember . . .'

Agnes looked at her warningly. The last thing she wanted was for George to be reminded of his courting days, when they were in love.

'I understand my daughters *hit* each other?'

'Well,' Mrs Chetwynd shrugged. 'That is what I *thought* I heard.'

George got up and straightened his waistcoat. It was not a pleasant duty, but one he had to do.

'I shall have to go and sort this out, my dear. Leave it all to me. At least, thank God, there is no concern on your part.'

'Oh George.' Agnes drew her hand from beneath the sheet and held it towards him. 'Oh George pray do not send Sophie away. She is the only friend I have. She will forgive the girls and stay here if you will permit it. She will overlook their awful behaviour, the things they said, for me. She acted on my instructions, not knowing the distress it would cause me. What *did* happen between Emily and Rawdon, George? To apologize for his *behaviour*? Oh George it can only have been something physical. Imagine someone like *Rawdon*. I always liked him so much. A man does not . . .'

Agnes put a hand to her heart and Sophie came speedily over with the *sal volatile*.

'There, deep breaths Agnes. I will make some soothing passes as soon as your husband has gone.'

George looked on with a curious sense of detachment as Sophie Chetwynd ministered to his wife, leaning over her bed, stroking her brow, calling her by her Christian name, tucking the sheets about her – performing all the little intimacies of a husband. Well; let her. Agnes was happy and he, despite all the anxieties provided by his family, had a deep and enduring source of happiness too. He thought of Hilary as he made his way along the corridor, up the stairs to the next floor and knocked on the door of his eldest daughter.

As she opened the door to her father George was shocked by the expression on Caroline's face, her pallor, the distraught expression in her eyes. His own concern was immediately apparent and as she closed the door she fell onto his chest, sobbing. George enfolded her in his arms and gazed over her head at her comfortable room with a view over the downs, away from the sea.

Caroline had one of the larger bedrooms because she was more in residence here than the others. When flowers were in season she had them arranged in vases or small posy bowls on her dressing table, her bedside table and the tall mahogany chest of drawers that matched her wardrobe and her bed. There were roomy armchairs and a small sofa dotted with cushions and draped with a fringed rug. Her books and sewing were left haphazardly, but not untidily, around the room.

Caroline made a room look lived in; she had the gift of homemaking. Emily's room always looked as though no-one lived there at all; all personal possessions were out of sight and one felt that, though scrupulously neat and clean, too scrupulously, it could belong to anybody. Jane's room was identified by its disorder. Despite the efforts of her maid, it had the appearance of accommodating five or six untidy people all living in a heap on top of one another. Clothes were on the floor, drawers and cupboards open and a variety of shoes scattered about.

George felt that the way they kept their bedrooms was very indicative of the sort of people his elder daughters were – each highly individualistic and different from the other. Caroline had never let herself go like this before, George thought, taking her over to the chair by the fire. On a table there was a tray with the food that had been brought up, apparently untouched. He sat her in the chair and drew one alongside. Caroline sat, her head bowed, her hand dabbing at her eyes with a fine lawn handkerchief. George saw that just by the initials there was what seemed like a spot of blood, a brown stain.

'Has your nose been bleeding, my darling?' He looked at her with concern and Caroline stared at him then, following the direction of his eyes, at the handkerchief. The sight made her start to cry afresh.

'Oh Papa. This is Debbie's handkerchief; the gift she worked for me and gave me for my birthday the day she died. I never meant to use it, Papa, but to keep it as a precious memory of her. Yet when I heard your knock I ran to a drawer and took out the first handkerchief I saw. Oh Papa, Papa...'

Caroline started to weep again and George put a hand on her shoulder.

'It is no matter, my dear. The blood . . . is her blood?'

'Yes, when she gave it to me she had a haemorrhage. The handkerchief fell. Oh Papa, I feel everything that has gone wrong in our house began with Debbie's death. Nothing has been right since.'

Caroline folded the handkerchief tenderly and put it on the table. Then she went to her drawer and, selecting another, gave her nose a good blow. It was pink and her eyes still very bright when she had finished; but she had stopped crying.

'I will iron the handkerchief myself. It is only stained with my tears. It is too precious ever to wash.'

'Do so, my darling,' George held out a hand and drew her back to the chair in which she had been sitting. He wanted to take her on his lap and comfort her as he might have done when she was a little girl; but Caroline was a woman. Next month she would be twenty-four. Agnes had already been married for seven years at that age, and had several children. What would happen now to Caroline? Why were his girls all so *different*?

'You look vexed, Papa.'

'Puzzled, my dear. Why are my daughters not like other girls?'

'I do not understand, Papa.'

'Oh no matter. I was merely thinking how different you all were; from each other but from others too. Most young women are married at nineteen or thereabouts.'

'Oh you are thinking of *marriage* again, Papa.' Caroline managed a slight smile.

George put his long elegant hands on his knees; he kept his nails beautifully pared and had a manicure every time he went to the barber. His hands looked like those of a surgeon, white and soft and capable. Caroline studied his hands; they were very much part of Papa. They went with his personality – wholesome and fresh, competent, incapable of anything mean; a man used to taking command, controlling his family. Now that Papa had come the warring element at Chetwell would soon be sorted out and sent into retreat.

'Why did you conceal your engagement from me, Caroline? It is this that seems to me the prime cause of the present trouble.'

'Papa, it was not an intention to conceal, but to delay. Rawdon asked me over a year ago. Jane was ill, Mama was still unwell. It was agreed that he should speak to you and we should marry if the war did not come. When it did our plans were delayed even further.'

'I still think Rawdon should have spoken to me.' George's tone was gentle and he pressed Caroline's hand to show he was more sorry than annoyed. 'Even if you did have an unofficial understanding it is one to which the father of the intending bride should be a party.'

'I know that now, Papa. I also knew that Emily felt very attracted to Rawdon, that she would be upset by our engagement . . .'

'She is a lot more upset now, my dear.'

'Yes Papa. One cannot always see the consequences of one's actions.'

Certainly one could not, George thought, settling back in his chair and stretching out his long legs in front of him. When he had lodged the attractive Mrs Ashburne at his expense in a house in St John's Wood it never occurred to him that within eighteen months they would have a son, that he would be madly in love with her and that this second home was becoming almost more important to him than his first, certainly much happier. He sighed.

'However, Papa,' Caroline sniffed into the new clean handkerchief. 'What sort of man is Rawdon if he can make a proposal to me and yet make love to my sister?'

'They made *love*?' George said, his eyes popping with incipient outrage.

'They kissed, Papa.'

'That is not quite the same thing, my dear.' George's naturally benign expression took control of his features again.

'It is to me,' Caroline raised her head and looked at her father. 'It is not honourable. It has diminished Rawdon

445

in my eyes. I do not even know if I still want to marry him.'

George leaned over and looked into Caroline's fine brown eyes, so like those of his mother whom he could only dimly remember. Yet it was agreed by all who had known her that her eldest granddaughter resembled her most. One never got over the loss of a mother in one's youth, George thought sadly. At least the children had Agnes, however inadequate. He had grown up with an aunt. Maybe this was why he was so dependent on the love of women; why he craved affection so badly. Did other men? He didn't know. Men were not given to confidences of this nature to one another.

'Caroline, my dear, it may be that you and Rawdon do not have the *chance* to marry. Oh I do not want to alarm you, merely to prepare you. We have had news of terrible battles in the Crimea, at Balaklava and, ten days ago, at Inkerman where the Guards distinguished themselves once again as they did on the River Alma. This is not after all going to be an easy war, a matter of a few skirmishes. It is going to be on the scale of the Peninsular war, and maybe last as many years. This is not to take into account the awful toll made by disease.' Caroline, horror-struck, stared at her father. The grim reality of war had touched her family, the man she loved, after all. 'That is the truth, my dear,' George went on. 'What worries you have may seem very trivial in comparison to what is going on out there where the weather, usually clement even in winter, is turning very cold. And despite everything, our men are ill equipped, badly prepared.'

'Oh Papa. I did not know.' Caroline put her face in her hands, her shoulders bowed. 'I am so ashamed of myself, Papa . . .'

'My dear, there is no need,' George said quickly. 'How could you know about the war? I only just learned myself; the news of Inkerman came through on the telegraph just before I left.'

'Not only that.' Caroline raised her face, the marks of her fingers still on her cheeks like the runnels made on a field of corn at harvest time. 'I am ashamed of my rage against Emily; for striking her. You know Papa, I have always been the eldest daughter of the house, used to being an example and keeping control. Yet last night I lost control. I hit my own sister, because of my passions. I have never done that in my life before. It shows that passion is an evil thing.'

George cupped her chin in his hand and looked into her eyes.

'No, my dear. Passion is not evil, but it can make us do strange things. I imagine your emotion for Rawdon, pent up over the months since his departure, is very strong and yet insecure. Then you learn that he has made advances to your sister. I do not wonder you snapped. Yet you must have regard for Rawdon's suffering too. Men do many things on the spur of the moment, and doubtless the thought of leaving for the war made him more emotional than is customary. That is obvious from his letter. He deeply repents of it. Men, you know, are prey to much stronger cravings than women. Very powerful forces are at work, that is well known. The thing is, what do we do now?'

George got up and stood with his back to the fire. 'Mrs Chetwynd must stay. There is no doubt of that. She has mesmerized Agnes to such an extent that if she left you, we, would have your mother on our hands again as a hopeless invalid. There is no question of her going. Oh, I do not like the woman, I dare say none of us does; but she is here, to stay as far as I can see. But neither you nor Emily can stay, for the time being, here in the same house with Mrs Chetwynd and your mother. Therefore I propose taking you back to London and asking Lady Tenby to have Emily for a while until she is next in waiting. You know how friendly Emily is with the Tenbys. How she enjoyed her holiday with them in the summer. I am sure they will be delighted.'

Caroline folded her hands on her lap and straightened her back. She raised her eyes to her father's, seeing how concerned he was, how loving. He would understand, if anyone would.

'Papa, Florence Nightingale asked me to go with her to

447

Turkey to nurse the sick and wounded. Now she might need me more than ever, if the war has begun in earnest. I hesitated to accept her proposal, but now I wonder if I should not, after all.'

'She has already gone, my dear.'

'Oh Papa, when?' Caroline's voice broke. Everything was failing her.

'She left at the end of October with a party of nurses. She will have arrived by now. Anyway it is out of the question for you to go. I would never agree to it.'

'But why not, Papa? What do you want me to do? There is nothing here. My mother can't abide me and I must say, Papa, with the greatest regret and respect, that the emotion is reciprocal. I have come to detest my mother – you can imagine how guilty I feel about *that*. I not only find her tiresome, I hate the sight of her and that sickening simpering creature she has by her side.'

'Caroline you must not talk like that about your mother.'

'But I *must*, Papa! If I cannot talk frankly to you, to whom can I? Jane is immersed in her own situation, and Emily and I cannot talk freely. I realized after Debbie's death how I really felt about Mama. Do you recall that day she refused to kiss her, for fear of contagion? It was such an unmaternal action that I felt my filial feelings towards Mama, which had slowly been eroding, disappear altogether. And Debbie forgave her and accepted it with the greatest docility because she loved her. But I thought, "How can a mother be so inhuman?"'

'Your mother did not realize that Debbie was dying, my dear. I know she reproached herself many times afterwards.'

'But that is not the point. She *should* have known it. She was here in the same house, yet none of us dared broach the matter for fear of upsetting *her*. And we regarded that as quite natural too – that Mama's peace of mind should be preserved at all costs.'

'It was a sensible thing to do,' George murmured, yet knowing his case was hopeless.

'But Papa, all the time we placated Mama she grew worse; she became more self-centred, more deeply dug into her own little hole. You moved out of her room, we all crept about doing this thing and that thing for her. Subtly she terrorized the whole family for fear that if we did not obey every whim instantly she would grow ill again.

'And you know, while Mama was like this, before the Chetwynd woman came, there were tasks she would let no-one do but me. Something a maid or Mary Oakshott could have performed perfectly well had to be done by me. That's why Mary left, she could not stand the sight of Mama so dominating and destroying me.'

'Oh my darling, I didn't realize it was so bad.' Of course he didn't, George thought remorsefully. He was busily engaged in an important love affair. Apart from his work he had very little thought for anything else except Hilary and their growing, exciting relationship.

'Well it was bad, Papa. And I am telling you now because Mama now is so far removed from me that the sight of her sickens me. Mama always has to have a slave and the latest, my successor, is Sophie Chetwynd. Fancy having that slug in a bed with you, Papa?' Caroline made a grimace of extreme distaste. 'Mama actually chooses to sleep with her. Do you not think it unnatural?'

What could he say? He had brought it about. At least Sophie Chetwynd wouldn't make Agnes pregnant. That was something to be thankful for.

'Sophie is like a nurse, nothing more. I think you must think of your mother as a sick person, my darling. Sick in mind if not body. Much of what she does she cannot help.'

Hilary had told him that. Without ever setting eyes on her she had made a very credible diagnosis of the mental condition of Agnes Vestrey. Oh, the insight of that remarkable woman!

'Well, I cannot help my feelings either, Papa. If I stay here I shall go mad like Jennifer Foxton, or maybe emulate Mama and take to *my* bed . . .'

'Oh pray . . .' George began to laugh, but the expression on Caroline's face silenced him.

'It is not funny, Papa. Ridiculous maybe; but it is absolutely true. I have an obsession about being with Mama. I can't bear it any more. And I have told you this at such length to explain why I must get away. Why, it would be so suitable for me, at this particular time in my life, to go to Turkey. It is like a call, as though God intended it for me in the same way as he called Florence Nightingale. I need to get far, far away, Papa. I must. Besides, I am an unmarried, useless girl. I am nearly twenty-four. I am not sure the man I love loves me – oh Papa, just because he is at the war and in danger does not make me any more sure. I am at loggerheads with my sister who also loves the same man. Is it not a farcical situation, father? Two sisters in love with one man?'

Caroline gave a bitter laugh that George could not recall hearing from her before. It made her seem older, more remote and the note of cynicism distressed him.

'I do not think it is like that, Caroline. I have tried to explain to you how it might have come about, this – er – incident at Lady Fox-Hargreaves'...'

'That may explain Rawdon but it does not explain Emily. Her feelings have never changed. They are strong. I know. I know her. We are each in love with Rawdon, Papa. And I think he is a bit in love with each of us.'

George didn't answer but looked into the fire, his brow puckered. How would Hilary have dealt with this? Oh, she would have had some sensible, eminently practical solution. She was so wise in the ways of the world. She would know what to do.

'You present me with a dilemma, my dear. Besides, Miss Nightingale has already left...'

'But may I not go, Papa? With Polly?'

'Polly Tangent?'

'Certainly, Papa. She is dying to go to Turkey. So is Jennifer Foxton but I think I would find her too unstable as a companion; besides she is engaged in writing yet another novel. The composition of unpublished novels seems to give her the repose she seeks, so no-one tries to interfere. But Polly is sensible. Polly is also frustrated at home.'

'I shall have to talk to John. But it offers a glimmer of hope. You should not be on your own. I shall talk to the Herberts when I return to London. We shall both go and see them, the day after tomorrow. How is that?'

Caroline was suddenly transported with a sense of joy, an emotion to which for such a long time she had been a stranger. Joy and hope, freedom. 'Oh thank you, Papa!' She threw her arms round his neck and hugged him. Laughingly he freed himself.

'But my darling, we are not through the wood. I may agree to let you go, if the Tangents release Polly. But you have to help me before you do. Jane is determined to live with this young man. How can I set my daughter up in a house in London, living unmarried with a man whose child she is expecting?'

'Jane is at Park Street now?'

George nodded. 'But every day her condition becomes more apparent. Oh Caroline, this gives me more agony than anything else that has happened, your mother, the war, or your own situation.'

Suddenly Caroline became the eldest daughter again. Things that were obscure to other people became quite clear to one when seen from a distance. It was one's own immediate problems that seemed insoluble.

'You must buy a little house away from the centre Papa, somewhere like Hampstead or St John's Wood.' She did not see George's guilty start and went confidently on. 'Jane would not go into society anyway in her condition. People would think she was here. It will become known Papa, in time; but there's nothing you can do about it. Things in this modern age are changing so quickly that I think you will be surprised by the ease with which people will accept, or at least become accustomed to the situation. It is a *fait accompli* already, is it not?'

George took her hand and lifted it to his lips. She was right, but his heart was heavy. With one daughter pregnant but unmarried, another about to go and nurse in the war, a third rebellious and in love, a younger son wanting to defy his wishes and join the army too, and a wife apparently in love with another woman, what chance was there of anything approaching a normal life for him?

What chance outside a little house tucked discreetly away in a small street in St John's Wood?

CHAPTER TWENTY-EIGHT

The baby, a pathetic underweight puny creature, lived only long enough to utter a despairing cry at the world which rejected it, and the mother died soon after.

Caroline put the baby in the emaciated arms of the mother, its thin wrists so brittle that they looked like old dead sticks, and covered them with a blanket. Before they were buried in the cemetery behind the hospital the blankets would be taken off and replaced by sacking. Blankets were too few, too valuable to be buried with the dead.

Caroline's brief midwifery experience, holding her mother's hand during the birth of Rebecca, had been augmented a hundredfold since her arrival in Turkey. She was now considered the chief midwife and delivered a baby almost every day. As soon as the women began their labour they called for Miss Vestrey because she was not only experienced, but the most tender and sympathetic – qualities at a premium among the poor women who lived below the Barrack Hospital at Scutari.

But whatever she did the mortality was about seventy per cent, and now she no longer cried, or even grieved, to see the tiny bodies briefly struggling for life in that dark foetid cellar before they quitted it for a better world. In many ways she thought it a merciful act of God to spare the innocents the universal suffering of hospital life.

She went into the corner of the cellar that served as an office and said to Lady Alicia Blackwood, busily writing in her store book: 'Dead. Baby Durrance and the mother. Now the whole family is dead. The father, Corporal Durrance, died upstairs last week from wounds received at the Alma.'

Caroline was about to turn, having made her routine report, but Lady Alicia called her back, her own eyes weary, but bright with sympathy.

'Miss Vestrey, should you not rest?'

Caroline looked at her, and her pale tired features were briefly lit by an ironic smile. 'Rest, Lady Alicia? And when did *you* last rest?'

'Last week we had two days in Therapia. I think you too should take a rest. I'll speak to Miss Nightingale.'

'Oh pray do not add me to Miss Nightingale's burden,' Caroline cried in alarm. 'I should not like that at all. She has far too much to do, without thinking of me. She never takes any rest herself. I can manage without rest, Lady Alicia. I am well and strong and, so far, thank God, free from disease. I just want to be allowed to carry on with my work. Anyway at least I get out of the hospital at night which is more than the poor wretches who live here do.'

She looked about the cellar which, unlike the silent wards of suffering men overhead, was a babble of sound, none of it pleasant. There were cries, shrieks, screams, groans and sometimes raucous laughter when some drunken old prostitute gave an account of her recent adventures to an appreciative audience. The smell of drink conflicted with the smell of vomit, faeces and urine and the wonder was that in time one ceased to notice it. Caroline always found it particularly pungent in the morning when the boat brought her and Polly the short distance across the Bosphorus from Constantinople.

The smell from the hospital wafted down to the water's edge, and the boatmen who brought them were glad to push off from the shore again. Some tied cloths across their faces, and the price of the trip had gone up alarmingly since she had been here. It was terrible to think that such a smell came *from* the hospital into which the sick, who flowed down from the Crimea, were crammed. The hospital was approached through an enormous gateway on which, Miss Nightingale is supposed to have said, should be written the words 'Abandon Hope All Ye Who Enter Here'.

By the end of December, when Caroline and Polly arrived, the hospital was apparently a paradise compared to what it had been when Miss Nightingale and her original band of thirty-eight nurses first arrived on 5 November. In six short weeks she had done wonders but even so the floors still ran with excreta, the walls with rain, or snow drifted in through the broken windows and settled on the beds of the men stretched out in draughty corridors.

The place was infested with bugs, lice and huge rats which leapt from the wooden benches – known as 'divans' – that lined walls which went back to the time when the hospital was the Barracks for the Turkish army.

The men's food was still cooked in large urns, meat being boiled in them just after they had been used to make tea. There were insufficient shirts, dressings, medicines, comforts of any description and, at one time, no operating table existed and limbs were hacked off on boards between two trestles in full sight of the ward containing wounded about to endure the same fate. A decree had gone out from Doctor Hall, the chief of medical staff in the Crimea, that chloroform should be sparingly used, as he considered 'the smart use of the knife is a powerful stimulant, and it is much better to hear a man bawl lustily than to see him sink silently into the grave'.

When she had arrived in Constantinople Caroline wasn't even able to see Miss Nightingale for days. She had unfortunately arrived almost at the same time as an unwelcome party of nurses and 'ladies' brought out by Miss Mary Stanley which Miss Nightingale refused to accept. Correspondence flew backwards and forwards between Constantinople, the Crimea, Scutari and London and, once again, Miss Nightingale found herself bogged down in the repetitive minutiae of administrative chaos and muddle which had plagued her since her arrival. She did not want the nurses; there was nowhere for them to sleep. She had not asked for them and she would not accept them. For days the party lingered at a house in Therapia belonging to the British Ambassador Lord Stratford, where the women started bickering with one another and most wished they had never come.

It was at this time that Caroline disembarked at Constantinople expecting to be welcomed by the woman who had begged her to come only a few months before. And when Florence Nightingale did at last see her, she failed to recognize her. It was a poor welcome and Caroline, who had fought so hard to come, began to regret it too. It had been a stormy journey from Marseilles and Polly had been confined to her bed with sickness.

Miss Nightingale sat at a bare deal table in the storeroom where she also slept, in a bed out of sight behind a screen. The room, which was terribly cold, had only one stove which would not draw so Miss Nightingale used it as a table and it was thick with papers. She did all her writing and requisitioning herself, and there were forms and papers everywhere as well as the stores which she had purchased from her own money and *The Times* fund which she administered.

Due to the terrible muddle that existed in the Purveyor's Department she did all her own purveying, making sure that every item was properly requisitioned by a doctor. She had complained to Sidney Herbert that she had become a general dealer rather than a nurse. The medical staff, who had begun by hating and ignoring her, now, with some exceptions, knew how much they depended upon her. She was the only one who had been able to create order out of the chaos as wave after wave of men descended on Scutari after the battles of the Alma, Balaklava and Inkerman which followed in rapid succession. The few men whose lives were saved probably owed them to her. Without her the hospital system would have collapsed completely.

She scarcely glanced at Caroline as she and Polly were brought forward by Lady Alicia Blackwood, who had arrived with her husband the previous month.

'Miss Vestrey, Miss Nightingale,' Lady Alicia said deferentially, having as much awe of its superintendent as anyone in the hospital. 'I believe you are acquainted. Miss Vestrey has been trying for some days to see you but Mrs Clarke has told me how busy you were.'

'And *am* . . .' Miss Nightingale said, her head bent towards her papers again, her pen flying furiously across the page.

Caroline gazed at her in some consternation. She wondered if this was the same delightful person who had given her tea from blue china cups in Harley Street only three months before. It hardly seemed possible.

She wore a black woollen dress with a white linen collar, linen cuffs and a white apron. On her head was a white cap under a black silk handkerchief. Her hair was short and scarcely visible, and her face had a pallor that Caroline had not seen even in August at the height of the cholera epidemic in London.

But as she put down her pen and looked up, rubbing her wrists from the cold, Caroline perceived the same haunting grey eyes that by now had attracted the devotion of hundreds of suffering soldiers on whom they had rested. For, as well as all the administrative work, Lady Alicia said, she still found time to spend hours on her knees dressing the wounds and sores of the men, whether suffering from the effects of battle or disease. When she could she attended all the amputations, standing by their side, her lips pursed, her hands clasped, managing to show that she was suffering with them, feeling the pain they felt, making it easier to bear.

If the authorities hated her, the men adored her and, in a very short time, her fame had spread through to the Crimea and to England simply by letters home from the common men whom the army, since before Wellington, had always despised. But with them she developed a special affinity, a transcendent love that in later years made her think of them as her children, whom she would never forget. And knowing that she loved them they called her an angel, the Lady-in-Chief, who stood by their side comforting and succouring them, who wrote letters home for them, attended them in their needs and stayed with them in death. It was her rule that, if she could help it, no man died alone.

It all showed now in the eyes that gazed calmly at Caroline, failing to recognize her, those eyes whose power had made her mother say sadly to Mrs Gaskell, 'We are ducks who have hatched a wild swan'.

'Miss Vestrey?' Miss Nightingale looked at her paper as though she would prefer to take up her pen and dash off another thousand words. She frowned. Then suddenly she got up and, coming over to Caroline, embraced her. For a moment Caroline felt that overwhelming sense of attraction that the touch of Florence Nightingale had induced in her before. There was something almost sensuous about the pressure of her body, still warm and sweet-smelling despite the cold and the terrible overpowering odour that assailed

456

the nostrils of all who visited the hospital until they could get used to it. The wife of the British Ambassador had been only once and vowed never to come again.

Then Florence stood back and looked at her, her arm still about her, her eyes shining.

'So you *came*! But you are too late! I am overwhelmed with nurses! I have no room. Nothing for you to do, much as I would like to keep you. You should have come with me when I asked.'

'I could not!' Caroline felt herself blushing under that reproachful gaze. 'I had problems at home that made it impossible.' Caroline glanced round to where Polly stood shyly behind her and drew her forwards. 'I have brought my cousin Polly, Miss Nightingale. She too . . .'

Miss Nightingale shook her head and the smile abruptly left her face. She sat down and picked up her pen and the almost perceptible mantle of greatness descended on her again – the administrator, the pioneer, the woman of vision, not just an ordinary person at all. The signs had been there in August at the Middlesex; now they were indisputable.

'No, my dear. I am sorry. You must go home. I am refusing a party of nurses brought out by a great friend, well – ' Miss Nightingale looked wryly at Lady Alicia, 'shall we say a *former* great friend, because I am afraid she hates me now. I must have my nurses tightly under my control. What work there is for them they are doing, but there are medical orderlies as well to look after the sick, though God knows most of them do little good.'

Miss Nightingale raised her eyes to heaven. 'I must co-operate with the authorities, Caroline. That is the only way I can do any good here at all. The situation is still indescribable, even though I have worked tirelessly for weeks. The men are ravaged by disease rather than the effects of war – dysentery, cholera, fever, typhus, gangrene, erysipelas, these are killing our men, far more than their wounds or the loss of limbs, unless they were fortunate enough to have them cut off on the field of battle. Here our losses from amputations are atrocious. The place is diseased, Caroline. Already a commission is looking into it and I am begging Sidney Herbert to send a proper Sanitary Commission which he has promised to do. See, I am at my desk all day writing, begging, reporting. And if that is not enough, I have religious and sectarian quarrels enough to derange the sanest of women, which at the moment I do not feel. The Protestants quarrel with the Catholics and both with the Dissenters. Many of my nurses try and proselytize and are more intent on capturing souls than saving lives. Now Miss Stanley has a large contingent of *nuns* with her who will only obey their superiors . . .' Miss Nightingale threw up her hands in a Gallic gesture of despair.

'Thank God I *am* surrounded by a few trusted friends and helpers – Mr and Mrs Bracebridge, Dr Blackwood and Lady Alicia, the Reverend Mother of the Bermondsey nuns who came with me, Mrs Roberts, Mrs Clarke and one or two others. If you had come with me maybe you would have been one, but now I do not need any more, for the moment. You must go back. I am sorry.'

She looked up to signify the interview was at an end and Caroline, downcast, took Polly's arm and turned towards Lady Alicia, who suddenly leaned over Miss Nightingale's table and said earnestly: 'Dearest Flo! I could do with help in my cellar. It is not important work like your nurses do for our brave soldiers; but it is important for the lives and the souls of the poor creatures you have entrusted to my care. I am almost by myself down there.'

Miss Nightingale looked from Lady Alicia to Caroline and, once again putting down her pen, folded her hands in an attitude of deep thought. It was almost as though she prayed silently for guidance as to what to do. Then she looked up. ,If that is what you want, and what *she* wants, you may have her. But is it what you want, Caroline?'

Caroline, still rather confused, looked searchingly from one to the other.

'I should explain, Caroline,' Miss Nightingale went on, 'that there is nothing heroic in looking after the poor creatures whom the army mistakenly allowed to come with the men. This is yet another of the many muddles we have had from the inception of the war last February. Many women accompanied the men to Malta, but some of the more hardy ones managed to come as far as Varna and now, forbidden to go to the Crimea, they are here. They are wives, sweethearts, but there are also children and babies of all ages and a number of unattached women, whose function I do not like to describe to a fellow gentlewoman in so many words, but which you might imagine for yourself. They drink, curse, swear and bring forth children with distressing regularity. Lady Alicia has done marvels in the short time she has been there by separating the more respectable women and getting them to wash clothes for the men. She has started a lying-in ward, and set up a proper system for the distribution of food. But it is sadly chaotic, and the disease and death rate are still appalling, for the infection spreads from the wards overhead. There is no natural light down there and little air, yet it is still freezingly cold for no fire will burn. I do not think you will want to stay there; but you are welcome to try.'

That was all she said. She took up her pen in her cramped fingers again and started writing without another word.

Caroline, Polly and Lady Alicia crept away as though leaving the presence of royalty, squeezing past the long patient queue of doctors, nurses, orderlies, soldiers and officials of various kinds who waited for a word with the most important person in the Barrack Hospital.

And so Caroline and Polly had stayed. The only bright thing was that Lord William Paulet, the new Military Commandant and a friend of the Vestreys, had procured for them a small house near the Embassy which they shared with other volunteers who had come out but for whom no work could be found. The house was very small and tumbledown, but at least it was clean and dry in the rain and snow that fell incessantly. It was not warm, because nothing was warm that winter in Turkey except, perhaps, the magnificent residence of the British Ambassador, the 'Great Elchi' himself. Here she was sometimes invited if only because Lady Stratford wished to hear at first hand about the horrors of the Barrack Hospital, even if she did not wish to see them for herself or do very much to alleviate them. It was nice to know what was happening opposite one's doorstep – not, thankfully, on it.

The view from the house was also something quite spectacular and every day in the light of dawn, as Caroline roused herself from an uneasy sleep, she would look out and see the great gleaming barracks deceptively golden and romantic in the morning sun. How much better it was to look at it than to be in it! The contrast between the beauty of Constantinople as one approached it through the Dardanelles and its reality seemed reflected everywhere in Turkey.

From the ship all one saw was a fairyland aspect of towers and minarets, flecked in blue, white and gold; in the streets all was dirt, noise, poverty and squalor. So it was with the barracks, magnificently perched on a hill overlooking the Bosphorus. Yet to get up to the barracks one had to clamber through a sea of mud which, owing to the weather, had turned into a quagmire so that one scrambled up the unmade path, fearing at any moment to slip back into the foaming waters beneath. Once or twice she couldn't even get to the hospital; because of the weather, no boat would cross the swirling waters; but mostly they managed.

Looking at the cellar that day in January 1855, having just assisted at yet another fatal delivery, Caroline thought how easily one became inured to death, dirt, danger and disease. The four 'Ds' she called them. The four 'Ds' became part of your life; yet you still contrived to live in a world of normality where you ate and slept, wore fresh clothes, wrote letters home and occasionally attended parties at the British Embassy which seemed to have suspended reality altogether, life there continuing as though the war had not really happened.

Thinking, two short months before, that there would be no need for *The Times* fund – as he had not taken the trouble to look into the Barrack Hospital – Lord Stratford had suggested that he might use the money to build a Protestant Church in Constantinople which badly needed one.

Yet in the wards, along the unheated corridors, in every nook and cranny, the terrible death rate continued. It was calculated, that January, that of the mighty British army assembled before Sebastopol only eleven thousand were in the field or in the cavalry, and twelve thousand were in the various hospitals, including those in the Crimea, of which most were the victims of cold, disease, bad provisioning and neglect rather than any action inflicted by the enemy.

Polly came out of the gloom over to Caroline; she was carrying a bowl, still half full of food.

'I can get Mrs Porter to take no nourishment, not even arrowroot laced with port wine.'

Caroline looked over to the corner to where a young woman lay on a straw bed, covered with a thin blanket. By her side crouched two underfed children with large round apathetic eyes who scarcely seemed to know where they were or what was going on, or, happily for them, to care. But if their mother died what would happen to the children? Their father was at the front. It was terrible that wives and children should ever have been allowed to accompany the troops. Yet it happened. This war, that Florence Nightingale now called a 'calamity unparalleled in the history of calamity', had been seen in those balmy days of the previous spring as just another campaign which would teach the Russians a lesson and be over very quickly. Women had always followed the men. They had gone with them to the Peninsular, to Africa, India, Afghanistan; to every farflung outpost of the expanding British Empire, every theatre of war where the army had a right or no right.

Why should anyone have thought that Turkey was different? In the spring very few had foreseen, could possibly have foreseen, that Turkey and the Crimea would have one of the worst winters for years, that the army administration would be so chaotic and its medical care so bad, and that disease would be so rampant, on such a gigantic, catastrophic scale.

Outside it was growing dark. If they missed their boat they would have to stay the night here, and that was the last thing Caroline wanted. She felt the only thing that kept her and Polly going was the knowledge that at night they could strip and wash from head to foot and sleep in a freshly made bed, though still invaded by a few bugs, and that they could have a decent meal away from the smells and horror of the Barrack Hospital. Without that to look forward to Caroline knew she would not be able to cope. She was no Florence Nightingale.

'Come on, Polly,' she said. 'We shall miss our boat.'

'But Mrs Porter . . .'

'I think she will not be here in the morning whatever you do,' Caroline whispered, looking at the distressing scene. 'And tomorrow is another day. Come, there may be news of James and Rawdon.'

The very thought of news from the front cheered Polly who, like everyone else, was pale and tired, but whose small frame otherwise bore up well to the rigours. All they knew to date was that Rawdon and James were alive. They had both survived the Battles of the Alma, Balaklava and Inkerman, though James had momentarily been missing in the mists at Inkerman for some hours and for a time was thought to be dead. He had narrowly evaded capture by the Russians.

They were thankful for that much because, although all the regiments had suffered, the Brigade of Guards, the very flower of English military prowess, had suffered, in the opinion of many, most of all.

Lord Rokeby, sent out to replace the Duke of Cambridge, wept when he first saw the condition of the Brigade of Guards camped before Sebastopol in February 1855. He was reading them flattering letters from the Queen but, in the face of such a pathetic remnant of a once fine fighting force, he broke down and could not go on. Only a month before he had been writing from England to their Colonel telling him to be sure the men were well drilled each day. Now that he saw the pitiable remains of the once mighty Brigade – three thousand men reduced to four hundred and fifty – it was too much for him to bear.

The Duke of Cambridge, the Queen's cousin, had returned home in December. Some said he had gone mad after Inkerman, quite potty in his yacht in Balaklava Bay, but this was proved to be a rumour. In December he had toured the Barrack Hospital at Scutari and made a number of complaints about what he saw there, particularly the quality of the food. After that, greatly to the Queen's relief, he went home. He was said to have a tendency to low fever; but some thought he had had as much as he could take.

But for the men, the common soldiers who were left, there was no going home. For some there would never be any going home. After the heat of Varna, and the fierce initial battles of the Crimean campaign, they settled down in the trenches before Sebastopol. There they gradually wasted away from hunger and disease brought on by the fact that what supplies there were, and there were plenty, remained at Balaklava, the roads between made impassable by eight miles of mud. Bales of clothing intended for men clothed only in rags were floating in Balaklava harbour and used as stepping stones in the mud on the wharf. Wood to be used for building much-needed huts, likewise was turned into planks for crossing through the mud in the Balaklava streets.

On the heights the men were suffering from frostbite, dysentery, cholera, fever and scurvy when, in Balaklava harbour, a ship-load of rotting cabbages was thrown into the sea because no one knew what to do with them. Plenty of barley and lime was sent to combat the effects of scurvy, but no-one had actually requisitioned it and so it stayed where it was. Eight miles away the effects of cold and malnutrition caused men's toes to drop off or be amputated and their wounds refused to heal; but when they became too ill there was no transport to take them down the heights to Balaklava because all the horses had died of starvation too.

The French, far better provisioned, less overworked and better organized, sent what transports they could to take the sick to the harbour. There they were unceremoniously dumped on board and left, their wounds untended for days, sometimes weeks, before they reached Scutari, three days' trip across the Black Sea.

By February, when Lord Rokeby burst into tears, the Guards were losing thirty men a day. Rawdon Foxton said that within six weeks they would no longer be in existence. The drafts who were being sent out to replace the sick and dead lasted, on an average, about three weeks. They were badly trained, poorly drilled, and less acclimatized than the veterans of the campaign. Their comrades scarcely cared what happened to them, so precious were the men who had been there from the beginning.

But if the Guards were in a bad way, many of the other regiments were more so. The Ninth and the Sixty-third had only a dozen men left in each regiment, and the cavalry had hardly a horse between them. Lord Lucan forbade any to be shot and those who were past help went round in a dazed, crazy condition until they dropped.

The Guards, owing to their legandary strength and fitness, had worked as hard as any digging the trenches that surrounded the besieged city of Sebastopol. For many they were digging their graves. They collapsed from cold or exhaustion and lay where they were, or a round shot from the Russian batteries got them and the mud simply covered them up. For many it was a blessing. That February the gales, coming after the snow of January, made the mud worse than ever; and slow progress was made on the railway line being constructed by specially imported navvies to run to the heights from Balaklava.

Rawdon Foxton and James Vestrey listened to Lord Rokeby quite dry-eyed. They were gratified by the gifts sent out personally by the Queen for her Brigade – the Guards were closer to the Sovereign than any other regiment, having been formed in the days of Charles I and II especially for the protection of the monarch. In all the muffetees and comforters, Lord Rokeby said, was a little bit worked by the Queen's own hands. Rawdon wondered what the Queen would have said to see how inadequate her comforts were to half-naked, dying men – some not yet twenty, but who looked about seventy as they crept round bowed down by rheumatism, scurvy, brown ague and fever. Those who attempted to desert were shot; some blew their brains out anyway.

The condition of the men was terrible, but the officers, though scarcely enjoying the kind of life they had been accustomed to, dared not complain. Although they slept continually in their clothes, and woke with them either hard with frost one morning or soaked with rain the next, and although they shared the same hazards as the men in the trenches, they had more comforts. Their tents were better equipped, servants looked after them, they had more money. Even in the Crimea, in that harsh bitter winter, money could buy most things. Their servants took their bât-horses over to Kamiesch or Balaklava to buy poultry, wine, vegetables, preserved meats; and their wealthy families sent boxes by the score full of warm clothing or hampers from Fortnum and Mason with *pâté de foie* and champagne.

For the commanders, life was even more remote from the men. Lord Raglan lived in a comfortable farmhouse and was seldom seen by his troops; many officers who had been with the army from the beginning of the campaign would not have recognized him if they saw him. Some said he travelled about incognito, unlike the Duke of Wellington who always had a large retinue; but others said he didn't care, and his remoteness and seeming indifference got him a bad reputation.

Many of the senior officers lived on their yachts in Balaklava harbour, well equipped and provisioned. After the Charge of the Light Brigade Lord Cardigan, who led it, went straight back to his yacht, bathed, drank a bottle of champagne and went to bed. For men like this the war was fought in the old style, with a certain elegance, far removed from the lives of the common soldier who perished in the bitter cold of the open plains and trenches before Sebastopol.

But Rawdon loved his men; he felt for them; he suffered with them. Men he had known for years, seen on sentry duty at St James's or Buckingham Palace, were suddenly there no more and sometimes no-one knew where they had gone – swept away by the mud or taken to Scutari to die of disease.

James had, throughout all the dreadful days, preserved much of his equanimity, his easy good nature. Even when he was ill with dysentery he managed to have a marvellous time in Balaklava Hospital. There Elizabeth Davis presided over the kitchens and made special pets of the young officers, whom she plied with all sorts of delicacies got specially from her friend the Purveyor-in-Chief.

Mrs Davis had come out with Miss Stanley and took an aversion to Miss Nightingale even before she saw her. ('I did not like the name of Nightingale.') Her experience at the Barrack Hospital confirmed her forebodings and she volunteered for the Crimea, against Miss Nightingale's wishes, where she quickly became friendly with many of her opponents. These included Dr Hall, the Medical Chief, and Mr Fitzgerald, the Purveyor-in-Chief, who provided those good things that helped to restore Captain the Honourable James Vestrey and others like him to good health.

Now he was back before Sebastopol again, congratulating Rawdon on the good news he had just received from Lord Rokeby and wishing it were he.

'Constantinople! My dear fellow, you will have a marvellous time! And you will see Caroline and Polly.'

During a brief lull in the weather Rawdon was exercising his horse. He and James had ridden over to Cathcart's Hill from where they had an excellent view of the green roofs, white houses and minarets of Sebastopol lying below. The sun had come out and shone on the simple crosses that marked the last resting places of so many dead, buried on the hillside named after Sir John Cathcart who had been killed at Inkerman. In front of them, behind the Russian lines fortified by the celebrated Russian engineering genius Colonel Todleben, stood two of the powerful redoubts, the Redan and the Mamelon, next to which was the Malakoff Tower. Below them men swarmed in the trenches on both sides, and every now and again the guns from the batteries spat out or a shell exploded, sending up great jets of mud which sprayed like a dirty firework display back on to the men underneath.

Rawdon did not want to leave this place where he had spent so many nights and days with his men. He knew the Guards were decimated, that the only hope for them was to retire to Balaklava to recoup. It was being said that this was what was going to happen, but until he knew for sure he wanted to stay. But because the Brigade was so depleted the commanding officers wanted to have back all the men they could. So each regiment was sending an officer to go to the hospitals at Scutari, Abydos and Smyrna to see who was nearly fit for duty.

Rawdon bent and patted his horse to calm him after a

burst of shell fire which seemed to have come rather close.

'It seems to funk it to go to Constantinople.'

'You are not funking it, you are being ordered to go! I wish I had your luck. I think everyone thought I had it too easy with Ma Davis, though there was not one nurse there that knew how to give a man a really good time.'

'I was not aware that was their function.' Rawdon raised an eyebrow sarcastically. 'Miss Nightingale's nurses are not allowed *near* the officers.'

'Ah, that is why I am glad I was not sent to Scutari. Come Rawdon, think of seeing Caroline again!'

Rawdon spurred his horse and turned for the camp. He wondered if, in his heart, that was why he didn't want to go. They had written so much that their relationship itself seemed to have undergone a change. They appeared to him more intimate, more affectionate, more in love. Ever since he had known she was so near he had longed to see her. But, now that it was going to happen he found the reality daunting. What *would* it be like actually to see Caroline again?

By February in the great Barrack Hospital at Scutari things had slightly improved, due to the work and determination of Miss Nightingale. The death rate was still much too high, and the men continued to pour in from Sebastopol in their hundreds so that the wards and corridors were as full as ever. However the organization had improved, there was more control, and the men were better looked after and had their limbs amputated on proper tables behind a screen. But the food was still bad, water was rationed, vermin proliferated and the smell was just as unpleasant as Caroline had found it in December. Only now she scarcely noticed it at all.

In January a number of Miss Nightingale's nurses had gone to Balaklava at the request of Lord Raglan with the rebellious Mrs Davis. Another rebel, Mother Bridgeman, and Mary Stanley, who felt that 'dearest Flo' expected far too much in the way of discipline – ('Few English women of education would submit to the kind of subjection she requires') – went with the remnant of the party she had brought with her to Koulali, where the Turkish Cavalry barracks had also been turned into a hospital. This was under the control of Lady Stratford, the Ambassador's wife, who determined to run it without all the difficulties which Miss Nightingale raised. Maids of all work were to do the uncongenial tasks and white fur coats and straw bonnets were ordered from home for the ladies.

However, as superintendent of all the hospitals in Turkey, Miss Nightingale could not quite wash her hands of the whole business, much as she would have liked to, for her strength was ebbing fast. Caroline, having proved herself by her strenuous, unselfish and largely thankless work in the cellar, was more and more called upon to assist the Lady-in-Chief in the wards upstairs. Such was her reputation for calm, compassion yet determination that she frequently assisted at amputations herself, or took Miss Nightingale's place at a deathbed. Florence gradually drew Caroline into the closed circle of those she relied on and trusted, while Polly was left to take her place in the cellar.

Polly had not worn so well. She had twice had fever and had once been sent to the Embassy villa at Therapia. Lady Stratford was concerned about her and wanted her to go home; but Polly wanted to stay. The very idea of coming to Turkey, in her mind, had been to see James, and when she heard he was ill in Balaklava she begged to be allowed to go. But Miss Nightingale would not hear of it. She did not want Polly to be spoiled and demoralized in the chaotic conditions she heard prevailed at Balaklava hospital. Were it not for the fact that she might thus lose Caroline, she rather wished Polly could be sent home too. It was not her intention to kill women with work for which they were unsuited.

And Polly was unsuited for the work. It didn't mould her character and spirit as it did that of Caroline. It began to destroy her. Suffering on such an intense scale was something her temperament, gently nurtured in the countryside of Kent, could not accommodate, and though she was brave and resilient and helped by her strong Christian faith, it wore her down. She became morbid and said sometimes that she felt she would never see her parents again.

Caroline begged her to go home. People, she said, were doing it all the time and there was no shame attached;

officers were openly proclaiming they could stand the war and conditions no longer. Even Lord George Paget, who had taken part in the Charge of the Light Brigade, had gone home but, being cut by his friends at his club, had been shamed into coming back.

'We are not called upon to be heroes and heroines,' Caroline gently pointed out. 'Just to do as much as we are able.'

But Polly refused. She wanted to see James. The mortality among officers was so great that she felt she would not see him again either, and she refused to go until she had.

But it was Rawdon who was to be sent down, not James. Polly cried the whole night long when she knew. Caroline stayed awake, but dry-eyed. She did not know what to think. So much had happened since November when there had been the fuss at Chetwell about the letter, and she had gone back to London with her father, that she had scarcely thought about her relationship with Rawdon at all. She had not even seen Emily to say goodbye which distressed her, but which Papa thought was for the best. They should both have time to think, he advised – and to try and forget and forgive. Time would show them things in perspective. As Emily made no effort to see her, despite knowing that she was going, Caroline concurred. But she sailed for Turkey with a bitter feeling in her heart. The family, as family, she felt, would never recover; everyone seemed to be at war with everyone else, just like the real war being fought in the Balkans.

And her work at the hospital, the horror of daily suffering and death had somehow, as Papa said it would, made herself and Rawdon seem that much smaller. What were the lives of two people, three if one included Emily, compared to the deprivation on such a scale of so many? Caroline found Florence Nightingale's example inspiring. Here was one who, completely and devotedly, was fulfilling her mission, doing what she said she had been created for. Could one perform such an act of self-sacrifice if one allowed human love to intervene?

Caroline pondered the question in the dark; but reached no solution before she finally fell asleep. She didn't know how it would be when she saw Rawdon again. In a way she dreaded it.

CHAPTER TWENTY-NINE

Florence Nightingale made the rounds of the hospital every night when she could, visiting those she had attended during the day, comforting new patients, seeing how others were progressing. She could not talk to them all, but she smiled or nodded, and those sick men who raised themselves on shattered limbs to see her were content and sank back on their beds.

She had an extraordinary effect on the men, on the atmosphere of the hospital and, had she not seen it with her own eyes and so often, Caroline would have found it hard to believe. She began her rounds when the hospital had grown quiet; the men had been fed, the orderlies, except for a few, had gone and those who could prepared themselves for sleep. Some were afraid to close their eyes in case they did not open them again; and some stayed awake simply to see Miss Nightingale or her shadow pass before they could rest.

Caroline had been in the wards all day and was more than weary. She and Polly had moved into a house on the Scutari side of the Bosphorus to be nearer the hospital. There had been too many rough seas during the winter, when the narrow strait between Scutari and Constantinople was closed and they had fretted at not being able to cross. It was this value that Caroline placed on her work which made her closer to Florence.

Polly had gone early, she knew, and she wished she could have gone with her. But many nurses were ill and the hospital was short staffed. Inspired by Florence, Caroline would never admit to being tired or depressed. 'Complain' was not a word that she allowed into her vocabulary. It was her duty; duty above all. She walked slightly behind Florence that night, her own lamp in her hand. One of the Sellonite sisters was with them and Doctor McGrigor, a staunch supporter of Miss Nightingale from the beginning. Occasionally they stopped to discuss a patient together, or Dr

McGrigor stepped back while Florence put down her lamp by the side of a suffering man to talk to him in her soft gentle voice because, perhaps, medicine was of no further help to him.

The Florence Nightingale Caroline saw in the wards on her rounds she never saw at any other time. It was truly as though she were possessed by something altogether unworldly, supernatural, eternal. Yet it was not religious at all; it was intensely practical and inspired by genuine compassion for the men, by love. Dimly Caroline could remember when she was a little girl, not feeling very well, and Mama would come creeping into her room, a candle in her hand. She would stoop over her bed and bend down smelling gorgeously of soap and perfume, her light flowing dress almost enveloping the bed as she kissed Caroline softly on the cheek or stroked her brow. That was a very long time ago, because over the years Mama had changed a lot, but it came back to her through the mists of the past . . . maternal. It was deep maternal love that flowed from Miss Nightingale to her men. Yes, her men. They belonged to her as they belonged to no-one else. Caroline was not to know that for the rest of her life Florence would always think of the men dead beneath the Crimean soil as her children, and write of them as such.

When Caroline, the doctor or the sister stopped, they appreciated it too. But they all wanted Miss Nightingale. There was, to them, no-one like her.

Thank God it was warmer, and a soft breeze stirred through the wards that was welcome after the harsh bleak winds of the previous month. Caroline suddenly glanced towards the entrance of the ward through which they were passing. The wards and corridors ran one into the other so that a continuous passage was possible. A tall, thin man stood with his arms clasped in front of him, looking at her. He had on a peaked cap and his cloak concealed his uniform. He wasn't looking at Florence or anyone else, but at her and, as she saw him, she felt such a spasm of emotion that she nearly dropped her lamp. But she continued with the procession as it passed through the ward, stopping to talk to a man here, to consult with Florence or Dr McGrigor there. All the time she tried to control the irrational clamour of her heart, the trembling of her limbs. But, occasionally, she glanced towards the doorway and he was still there; no mirage but a breathing, living human being. Rawdon.

Rawdon had not seen Caroline for a year. How much had happened since then. He had been seared by his experiences in this grim and bitter war; a war that was as much against the elements, against apathy and despair, as against the enemy. There had been no major battles since Inkerman; just skirmishes and the endless exchange of fire between the opposing forces in their respective trenches outside Sebastopol. Every day there were casualties, but not on a huge scale. The real victims were the men who perished from cold or disease, those who in their hundreds poured into the hospitals in Turkey and the Crimea with gangrene and frost-bitten limbs.

Even though it was late when he had arrived in Constantinople, he had begged to be allowed to go to Scutari. He had to see her again; he needed that vital link with his past, normal life; the security that was Caroline Vestrey. For a long time he gazed as her tall slim figure moved among the beds, very like Miss Nightingale who had been pointed out to him by the officer who had brought him.

As she got nearer, her lamp flickering in her hand, he saw how much older she looked, thinner and, even in the dim light, he was struck by the terrible pallor of her face. She had a little cap concealing her luxurious chestnut hair, like Miss Nightingale, and a black woollen dress with white collar and cuffs. There was a dedication about her that was suddenly frightening, until she looked at him and he knew that she recognized him. That she was pleased to see him. Then, he was frightened no longer.

Miss Nightingale came up to him first, pausing as she was about to go through the doorway into the corridor. She raised her lamp and searched his face.

'You are not one of our wounded, sir?'

'I am Captain Foxton of the Third Battalion the Grenadier Guards, Miss Nightingale. I am sent to Scutari to inspect the men of my battalion who are your patients here.'

Rawdon took off his cap and bowed.

Florence, her face lit by a faint enigmatic smile, turned and looked at Caroline. She stood back and made a gesture with her hand, ushering Caroline forward.

'Captain Foxton, Caroline,' she said. 'I did not recognize him. You will be pleased to see him.'

Caroline came slowly up to Rawdon and, gazing at him, gave him her hand. He clasped it to his breast before bending and kissing it.

'Caroline,' he murmured.

Florence had turned and was talking to Dr McGrigor, whether out of tact or not Caroline didn't know. She stared at Rawdon's bowed head, noting that his thick black hair was lustreless, that his cheeks were thin and sallow and that, when he looked up at her at last, his eyes had the stricken expression of one who had been emptied of emotion because of some overwhelming circumstance. She pressed his hand; but found she was too overcome even to utter polite words of greeting.

'Do not let us delay, Florence,' Caroline said at last with forced composure. 'Captain Foxton and I shall meet later.'

She smiled at Rawdon yet with a detachment that sent a chill through his heart. Yes, that look of dedication was frightening; momentarily he felt disorientated as though he had no right to be in this hospital, sacred because of all those who had perished between these walls, all those who still lingered, many in agony. He was out of place here. Yet Caroline was not; she belonged. She belonged to the shades of the dead, among the sick and to Florence Nightingale who, with a smile at Rawdon, said gently: 'You see, I have a helper of wonderful spirit in Caroline, Captain Foxton. She will let nothing interrupt her sense of duty.'

'I know that, ma'am,' Rawdon swallowed. 'Miss Vestrey has always been mindful of her duty. And please do not let me delay you. We all think the work you and your helpers do at Scutari is most admirable.'

'*All*, Captain Foxton?' Miss Nightingale permitted herself an ironic smile. 'Do you not know that I am opposed by three-quarters of the army and most of the medical establishment?'

'I hear only the praise of the men, ma'am, who come

back. The very few, Miss Nightingale, who come back.'
Rawdon's voice broke and he bowed his head. The emotion
of being in the hospital among such suffering, of seeing
Miss Nightingale and Caroline again, was almost too
much for him. The man who had never shed a tear all during the long and arduous campaign felt close to breaking
down.

'I see you are close to your men, Captain,' Florence said
gently. 'That is as it should be. Too many officers I know
think their men are of no importance. I see you are not one
of those.'

'Indeed I am not, ma'am. I fought with them, side by
side, at Inkerman particularly which was called the
"soldiers' battle" because, in the mist, there was no-one to be
seen to be in command. It was won by the common fighting
man who fought with such ferocity, regardless of personal
safety, and through a passionate love of his country and his
Queen. On that day the common soldier became a hero for
me, Miss Nightingale, and in the plains and trenches before
Sebastopol, where the conditions are still indescribable, he
remains one.'

Florence nodded her head with approval and, turning to
Dr McGrigor, she passed on while Rawdon fell in with the
little procession by Caroline's side, his face gazing at her
profile in the flickering light of her lamp.

Rawdon was appalled by the scale of the suffering he
witnessed as the procession passed through ward after ward.
Some men groaned and writhed in pain, others called out,
many were unnaturally still, others just lay and stared at the
high ceiling without moving. It was hard to tell whether
they were alive or dead. Those who could sat up and greeted
Miss Nightingale as she passed, and the many more unable
to move raised a hand in a gesture of silent blessing.

The Lady with the Lamp; she was already a legend. She
had become part of history. Florence Nightingale. And
Caroline Vestrey? Was she part of history too, he wondered, as he watched how absorbed she was in her work,
almost as though she had forgotten he was there. She
walked slightly behind Miss Nightingale and Dr McGrigor,
stopping as they stopped, consulting notes she carried in her

hand by the light of the lamp, quietly, efficiently answering the abrupt, exact questions that Florence or the doctor put, the facts at her fingertips, the knowledge hers to command.

It was nearly midnight when they reached the hall of the hospital and Miss Nightingale gently dismissed the doctor and the Sellonite sister with quiet words of thanks.

'Try and get some rest. I will see Miss Vestrey and Captain Foxton to the door.'

Rawdon doffed his cap and the doctor and the nurse nodded and hurried away.

'You will escort Caroline home, Captain Foxton?'

'Of course, Miss Nightingale.'

'You will have much to discuss. Caroline, if you would care to, please take tomorrow off.'

'Oh no, Florence! I would not dream of it. Nor would Rawdon wish it. Besides, he has his own work to do. Is it not so?'

'Yes.' The chill had not left his heart. She had hardly smiled at all, nor did she now as she looked at him. He could have been one of the patients she had spoken to as they lay on their palliasses on the by now well scrubbed floors of the hospital. Her gaze was friendly, compassionate but detached. Not the expression of a woman in love. *Did* she still love him?

'Yes, I have much to do here and in the other hospitals, Miss Nightingale. I have been most edified by what I saw tonight. Edified, and appalled.'

'It *is* appalling, Captain Foxton,' Florence said gently. 'And it was so much worse. Now take my helper away and see that she has a good night's sleep. Have you accommodation yourself for the night?'

'I believe I am billeted at a house a few doors along from Caroline and Polly. My servant took my things there before coming to the hospital.'

'Good.' Florence nodded and gazed at Rawdon, something in her expression seeming to ask him for help, as though imploring him. 'Do not take my right hand away from me will you, Captain Foxton? Not yet.'

The chill around his heart was like an icicle. He felt a

476

stab of pain. He wanted to reply but no words came. He bowed his head.

'Come, Rawdon.' Caroline touched his arm, a quick impersonal nurse's touch, and pressed Florence's hand. 'Now Florence, go straight away and rest. No more work tonight, I beg you. Do you promise me that?'

Florence smiled and returned Caroline's gesture, letting her long, slim hand linger on her arm. 'I promise, my dear. And thank you.'

She drew her shawl around her shoulders as Rawdon and Caroline walked away, observing the distance between them. They did not move close together, shoulders touching, like lovers; but walked well apart. Well, they had their business to sort out and she had hers. She watched them walk away, glad that it was a fine night. Gazing at the stars she sniffed the air. Surely spring was on the way at last . . . *and* the Sanitary Commission promised by Lord Penmure.

In the light from the doorway she saw Caroline and Rawdon turn and wave. Slowly she lifted her hand and waved back. Then she sighed and went indoors.

The constraint was almost intolerable at first. Rawdon broke the silence at last as they walked along the uneven road lit only by moonlight.

'You have not said a word to me yet.'

'I did not expect to see you.'

'You did not seem pleased to see me.' Rawdon stopped and she had to stop too. He faced her. 'Are you?'

Caroline lifted her hands to her face and then drew them down over her cheeks. She felt very tired. 'I don't know. It has been a very long time, Rawdon. So much has happened.'

'And to me too,' he said grimly.

'I know, I know.' Her voice broke with compassion; she wanted to touch him. To hold him to her as she did all those wounded men, many of whom had died as her arm gently cradled their heads. 'Oh Rawdon, you look so awful – pale and tired. You look so different.'

'Is that why you are not glad to see me?' He realized his voice was beginning to break with emotion.

'Of course not . . .'

She threw herself into his arms and, as they curved protectively around her, she wept. Now the tears flowed – the tears for Debbie, for her mother, for all the dead and the wounded, the women and children in the cellar as well as the men. She had not shed a tear all the time she had been at Scutari; she had not wept like this since the day she told Papa she wanted to leave home. Rawdon was like Papa – tall and sturdy and comforting, his clasp so warm and reassuring.

She felt his lips on her forehead, on her cheeks, seeking her mouth. She clung to him and the firm impress of his lips, the strong clasp of his arms, made her feel that she wanted to merge with him as she never had before. She wanted the security of his love and his body, to belong to him. A long time ago she had wanted him to take her away, and now she did again. No more fighting; no more being dutiful; no more trailing after Florence along those dark depressing wards. The intensity of her kiss, pleasing at first, startled him and he gently drew away, gazing down at her. Her eyes were still closed, her cheeks still wet, the lines round her mouth deeply etched in a way that had aged her.

'Oh Rawdon, do not leave me.' She opened her arms for him and he clasped her more strongly, pressing her to him, aware of her vulnerability. She was so soft, so feminine, so desirable. He started to tremble.

'Caroline,' he murmured, 'let us be wed. There is no more need for words. Let us be married by the Great Elchi himself while I am in Constantinople, and then you can come back with me to the front and ride around all day with Mrs Duberly gazing at the men dying in the trenches.'

Caroline laughed through her tears, a noise that emerged as a kind of croak. 'So Mrs Duberly *does* exist?'

'Oh yes. She accompanies her husband everywhere and he trots after her like a servant holding her horses while she inspects the corpses. We call her the Vulture, or rather some of the men do. I rather admire her myself, though I think she has more feeling for her horses than the poor fellows who are sick and wounded.'

'I do not *want* to be like Mrs Duberly.'

'But you do want to be my wife?'

'I don't know.' Caroline stepped back, drying her tears

on the corner of her shawl. 'So much has happened, Rawdon.'

'But you love me, my darling. What you have just done shows me you love me.'

Rawdon tried to take her in his arms again, but she stopped him with her hand.

'Does it? I have such a great need for human warmth and protection that I know not what to call it, Rawdon.'

'But it is love. It *is* love. You do love me.' He seized her shoulders and pressed her to him without trying to kiss her.

She let her head rest on his chest aware that his heart was hammering. She put her hand on it and felt it through his thick cloak. Thank God it beat so strongly! She thought of all the men by whom she had knelt feeling for a flicker of their hearts, but they were still in death. Now she wanted to lean against Rawdon and cry again for all the men who lived no more, whose hearts had ceased beating.

'What about Emily?' Caroline found herself saying, without passion, as though she was talking about an acquaintance.

'Emily?'

'Emily Vestrey.' Caroline leaned heavily on the surname. 'My sister.'

'But there was nothing with Emily ...'

She threw her head back and looked at him. She felt his grip on her tighten as though he was afraid to let her go. 'I know about Lady Fox-Hargreaves' ball, about the letter you wrote Emily. It caused a fair commotion in our household.'

Reluctantly he let her go. She felt cold and drew her shawl tightly around her. They fell into step and continued their walk. They had withdrawn from each other. Momentarily she regretted mentioning Emily, and then she knew it had to be. She had to know. But why now, when they were both so tired? No, she had to know now.

'You saw the letter?'

'Yes. Emily did not show it to me. One day I will tell you how all that came about. But I know that you kissed my sister passionately at Lady Fox-Hargreaves' ball the night before you left London. That your last memory of a woman's lips was hers, not mine.'

'And you have thought about that all these months?'

'I only found out in November last; but still four months seems a long time.'

'How could you doubt my love? My letters told you how much you meant to me.'

'I could only think about you kissing Emily instead of me. About your betrayal of our love.'

'But my darling, if . . .'

'Oh I know what you are going to say.' Caroline's tone grew mocking. 'You will say that if *I* had been at the ball you would have kissed me. Is that not so? Or is it that a kiss is not so important?'

He was hurt by the stridency of her tone, bewildered by the swift changes in mood.

'I know not what to say,' Rawdon said at last and felt the gulf between them suddenly widen.

'You have always loved Emily.'

'I have *not* always loved Emily! If I loved her I would not ask you to marry me. I love not Emily but you, though God knows you give me little enough cause at the present moment, playing with me this way and that, first kissing me and then pushing me away. I do not know where I am with you, Caroline.'

They had reached the house. Polly had put a lamp in the window to guide Caroline home. They both stared at the light as though seeking guidance – a symbol of hope in the dark.

'My mind is in a turmoil, Rawdon. Please understand that. I was very distressed about learning the truth about you and Emily. We have not spoken since on account of it.'

'You and Emily have not spoken?'

'No.' Caroline averted her eyes. 'It was also the reason I came out here, to burden my mind with something other than thoughts of self. Now I have lost myself completely in caring for others. I hardly thought of you until I knew you were coming, and then when I saw you again today. It is the truth Rawdon, and I am sorry. I put you from my mind. I no longer know how I feel about you. But I do know that as long as the war goes on I have a place here and work to do.'

Hearing voices Polly had opened the door and looked out. She felt nervous by herself in the house at night. Usually there were one or two other people there; but this night she was alone. Recognizing Rawdon's voice she ran towards them and threw herself into his arms. He caught her up and kissed her cheek, such was the happiness of the moment. Then she felt rather abashed by her impulsiveness and struggled to free herself.

It was very different from the way ladies conducted themselves in England.

'Oh Rawdon, how is *James*?'

'He is better, Polly. He is his old self and back with the regiment, chafing to get away but so are we all.'

'Get away? Do you not wish Sebastopol to fall?' Caroline asked in surprise, grateful for the interruption.

'Oh I mean get right away, finish the war. Of course we want it to fall; but will it? Our men are not fit to take it even if it fell. You have no idea of the feebleness of our army there, Caroline. I am sent to bring half dead men back to the lines.'

'I *do* know about the weakness of the army there,' Caroline said sharply, letting him go first through the door into the house. 'I talk to the men, you know. But what can be done?'

'We want a new army sent out from England; the present one rested and restored to health. God grant that I am there to see the fall of Sebastopol; but our men are quite unfit. Our army is just patched up and the new recruits die faster than the old ones . . .'

Caroline suddenly looked grave and shut the door behind her, leaning against it.

'Do not say that. I heard from father today that Oliver is to come out as an ensign. He is in the new draft.'

'But he has only just joined.'

'I know, three months ago. They are desperate for men and Oliver is so keen to come. He was hardly back at Cambridge before he was demanding to enlist. Father felt it was cowardly to go on refusing him.'

481

'Oh, he will be all right, as long as he takes care in the trenches. And the weather is improving. The railway from Balaklava is nearly complete so we shall have no trouble with supplies. And . . .' Rawdon faltered and looked at Caroline. 'If you were there you could keep an eye on him.'

'How could Caroline be there?' Polly asked in surprise. 'Do you not know she is Miss Nightingale's right hand woman?'

'Oh, I know,' Rawdon said bitterly. 'She is keeping her from me.'

Caroline took off her shawl and threw it onto a chair, into which she subsided, wearily closing her eyes. 'Please do not start that again, Rawdon. Florence is *not* keeping me from you. It is I who feel this is where my duty is. Here, in Scutari, for the time being. It is true that Florence does rely on me; but she is far too noble and humane a person to keep me from happiness, from doing something I desired. However she does need me, it is true, and I cannot let her down. But she cannot stay out here forever; she is too tired. Only those who know her well know how tired she is, and when she does lie down she does not sleep. I would never forgive myself if I deserted her. It is my duty to remain for a while longer.'

'But there are *thousands* of women longing to serve Miss Nightingale!' Rawdon roared, dashing his smart peaked cap to the ground. 'Balaklava is full of angry ladies she has rejected. My mother asks me all the time "Can you procure a place for so and so with Miss Nightingale?" I tell you . . .'

Polly intervened, smiling, and picking up Rawdon's discarded cap.

'You do not know Florence, Rawdon. Only a very few, special people are for her. Those she loves and trusts. Such a one is Caroline. I think it would break her heart if Caroline left, just now. She is very vulnerable!'

Rawdon snorted in disbelief. 'I hear she is as hard as a pair of army regulation boots, when you can get them!'

Polly shook her head. 'No, she is not. She only appears so on the surface. Many people have betrayed her and hurt her. You heard about Nurse Elizabeth Wheeler who caused all the trouble by her letter to *The Times*? She was most trusted by Miss Nightingale.'

'But Caroline isn't going to write to *The Times*. I want her to marry me here.' Rawdon looked appealingly at Polly.

'Oh, how romantic!' Polly clasped her hands and gazed at the ceiling in an attitude of ecstasy.

'But she will not.'

Polly was brought down to earth by the flatness of Rawdon's voice.

'Not *yet*,' Caroline said gently, remembering how, a short time ago, she had needed him, the passion of their embrace. Was that how he kissed Emily? Was as much feeling transmitted as had passed between them then? It was a rare experience for her, to feel desire so strongly. True he had briefly made her feel like that at Chetwell, but here the passion was different – as though they were warriors with warriors' needs. She knew more about passion than most gently reared young women, having learned of it at first hand from her sister. In the weeks she remained in England Jane had talked about it often, the floodgates of pent-up reserve opened at last, describing exactly how she had found herself unable to resist going to bed with Daniel Lévy, and why. Despite herself and though, of course, profoundly shocked, Caroline had found herself listening with a good deal of interest. Now she knew something of what Jane meant.

'It is certainly not a *good* time to wed,' Polly said judiciously. 'The war has upset everyone. Besides think how upset your families would be if they were not present – your Mama and Papa, Caroline, and yours Rawdon?'

'I feel if I do not marry Caroline now I never shall,' Rawdon said with desperation. 'I know not why but I do. Maybe I am to die or maybe . . .'

'Oh no, no, no!' Caroline flung herself out of her chair and into his arms. 'Oh do not say that . . .' She scrutinized his face, tracing the tired lines with her fingers, noting the sad, haunted expression in his eyes. '*Never* say that! But oh, my beloved, and you are beloved whatever I may say, do not press me now. Let us talk about it again when we are rested; when we have time to think.'

Suddenly Rawdon saw it was sensible. After all, they were still engaged. She had not rejected him. She merely wanted time to think. The war had changed her as it had them all. It was silly to say they would never marry because, of course, they would. One day the war would end and one day she would be his wife.

He took her hand and brought it to his lips, bowing his head in acquiescence.

CHAPTER THIRTY

Daniel Lévy came in from the small garden at the back of the house in Flask Walk, Hampstead, which Jane's father had purchased for them. The French windows led straight into his study, a room on which a lot of care, thought and, of course, money had been expended. As the place where the great man would give birth to his thoughts, committing them to paper for the benefit of posterity it had been given far greater importance than that other room devoted to the fruits of his fecundity, namely the nursery. That had been distempered and a cot made ready, but nothing more.

The study was painted white, lined with shelves which were now almost full of books. Two leather covered chairs flanked the grate in which a small fire was burning. By the window stood his desk which was very neat and tidy, like Daniel, and not covered over with a mass of papers and books and empty wine bottles like that of his friend Karl Marx. The parquet floor was kept immaculately polished by one of two maids, and was adorned with expensive oriental rugs that Aunt Ruth had put in the attic in Park Street when she started her mania for modernization.

Daniel went to the fireplace and selected his favourite pipe from a rack that stood on the mantelpiece, proceeding to fill it with choice tobacco, a gift from Jane's father. He lit a spill from the fire and, packing his tobacco tightly in the bowl, lit it slowly emitting great puffs of smoke. When he had completed this task Daniel sighed with satisfaction and tucked the thumb of one hand into the pocket of his waistcoat, surveying his little domain.

He then went over to sit at his desk, took a pen from a variety he kept neatly laid out in a tray, dipped it in a large bottle of ink and resumed his labours on his treatise: *The Emergence of the Proletariat as a Force in European Politics.*

After a while the door opened quietly, but Daniel continued to work, without turning his head. Jane was accustomed to this. One had to be, if one was to get used to cohabiting with genius. She was convinced he had a rare talent and that, in the order of things, it was her privilege to serve him. She had not realized what a transformation loving Daniel would make to her world. But at times it was hard existing side by side with genius and the world as it was.

She sank into a chair and tried vainly to get herself into a position that was in any way tolerable. If she lay too far forwards her shoulders ached and it was impossible to sit upright because she was so large. The pungent tobacco smoke swirled about Daniel's head assailing her nostrils. She closed her eyes and attempted to waft it away with her hand.

In early spring the little garden was just beginning to slough off the drab shreds of winter. George had sent one of the gardeners up from Chetwell, and in a week he had transformed what was a wilderness, though minute, into a neat orderly patch surrounded on three sides by a high wall. Along the wall he trailed honeysuckle and clematis, and he pruned the roses which clambered over the outside front and back of the little white house with its pink door and pink wooden shutters at the windows.

Shrubs had been brought from Chetwell and a tiny lawn created almost overnight. Jane got unsteadily from the chair and lumbered over to the French windows leaning against the jamb of the door, looking alternately at Daniel and at the pretty garden. A welcome breeze wafted into the room, and overhead the sky was blue.

'Will you take a walk this afternoon Daniel?'

Daniel went on writing. The smoke seemed to follow Jane about, and now she felt like some votary shrouded in incense. More irritably she wafted the smoke away again. 'If you don't like it you should keep out, my love,' Daniel said without looking up from his task. 'You know it makes you feel sick.'

Jane went over and twined her arms around his neck, pressing her cheek close to his. 'But I want to be with you. Is that so unnatural?'

Daniel shook his shoulders impatiently and Jane relaxed her hold. She gazed at the paper in front of him, at his very small neat handwriting well spaced and with ample margins at either side of the paper. Everything about Daniel was so orderly. She bent down and tried to read what he was writing. Daniel gave a deep sigh, placed his pen in its tray and lifted his head, looking at her with equanimity.

'My dear, you know I find it impossible to work while you look over my shoulder.'

'Or even while I am in the room,' Jane said.

Daniel shrugged. 'If you like, yes.'

'Mohr works surrounded by people.'

'Because he has to. He has no alternative. I have. My mind functions best when I am alone. Surely you realize that, my love? My work is so important.'

He put out a hand and took hers drawing her towards him. His beard and moustache were trimmed closely to his face, and his hair brushed sideways with a parting on the left. His suit was of the best black broadcloth, one of many made recently by George's tailor, and paid for by George too. His cravat was stylishly high and tied in an elaborate bow. His face, though still thin, had filled out and, below the line of his gold watch chain, there was the suspicion of a paunch due to the months of good living since he had become an honorary part of the Vestrey family. The cuffs of his freshly laundered shirt peeped out two or three inches from the sleeve of his coat, and as he crossed his legs his shiny black hand-made shoes enhanced elegant ankles covered in black silk socks.

Jane adored him. She felt more in love with him each day, and thought he grew even more handsome due to the prosperity they now enjoyed. How happy she was to have been the cause of it. It seemed to her now that her function in life was to smooth Daniel's path towards greatness. She bent down, her eyes ablaze with passion, and kissed him. Daniel laughed but moved his chair back, nearly causing Jane to lose her footing and fall.

'Oh my dear, I am sorry!' He held firmly on to her hand. 'But really you should not give vent to such passionate impulses in your condition.' He produced a very white handkerchief and delicately wiped his mouth with it before tucking it back into his breast pocket.

'But just because I am going to have a baby, Daniel, it does not mean I do not want to kiss you.'

'I thought women did not have such urges at this time. It seems most unnatural.' Daniel looked sideways at the papers on his desk and one foot began to tap impatiently against his leg.

'Well, I have!' Jane said petulantly. 'I love you and I want to show it.'

Daniel swung her hand and looked into her eyes. Some men found pregnant women attractive, but he had discovered he was not one of them. Although Jane's face had not changed, he found this distortion of her once beautiful body revolting and somehow wished, secretly, that she could be quietly put away until after the birth, and then be presented slim and attractive again for his delight.

Jane had seen the look on his face before, many times, as her body swelled and she found moving about so difficult. He appraised her with such an air of detachment that sometimes she felt she disgusted him. It added to the sense of isolation, of desperation that she had felt increasingly since Caroline had gone to Turkey and they had moved into the house in Flask Walk. Surely at a time like this a woman should feel loved, wanted and protected? But he never seemed to want to touch or be near her, and kept strictly to his own side of their large bed as though marking out his territory.

She let go of his hand and walked back to the chair by the fire. There was an ache low down, at the base of her spine. She put a hand on it and tried to straighten up.

'It will be any day now, Daniel.'

'Thank God for that.' Daniel got up and reached for a volume from one of the shelves. 'It pains me to see you in such discomfort.'

'Oh, does it?' Jane smiled for the first time since she had come into the room, her voice warm with gratitude. 'I thought it was that you did not like me to look like this.'

Daniel glanced at her from the pages of his book. 'My

dear, all women look like this when they are about to give birth. It is unfortunate, but it is true.'

'Oh, then you do *not* like it?'

Jane looked down at her swollen belly, her voice low and depressed. Daniel sighed and shifted his feet, turning quickly over the pages of his book with an expression verging on exasperation.

'I of course am used to it,' Jane continued when he did not reply, 'having seen Mama pregnant so often. Papa used to tell her she was very lovely when she was with child. Rubenesque he called it. He was always very attentive to Mama at this time.' She sat down again.

'And do you imply that I am *not*?' Daniel snapped the book shut and stood in front of her, his black eyes smouldering. Looking at him Jane felt just a tremor of fear. Those dark, Gallic good looks could also be a little frightening when he seemed as far away from her as he did now. Jane's chin started to tremble; she felt almost overwhelmed by this sense of loneliness and anxiety.

'If only Caroline were here,' she murmured.

'Caroline? What on earth could Caroline do?'

'Caroline would come up and look after me.'

Daniel threw himself into a chair opposite Jane with an exclamation of disgust.

'My dear *Miss* Vestrey, you are thoroughly spoilt. Here you have everything you want; me, *two* servants, a cook, a house, granted not of the size you are accustomed to, but adequate. Your father comes often, so does your aunt and if your sister – the hoity-toity one at Court – will have nothing to do with you that is no affair of mine. *I* didn't ask you to have a child.'

The pain in her lower lumbar region grew stronger. Jane shifted in her chair but nothing would ease it. 'I didn't ask to have a child either,' she whispered, tears involuntarily beginning to well in her eyes.

'But you knew the consequences of lying with me? You have just told me on how many occasions you observed your mother in a state similar to your own. You must have known all about how babies are conceived, Jane. It was a risk you took, and now you are paying for it.'

The tears tracked slowly down Jane's cheeks and she stared at Daniel. Although tenderness was a quality which had certainly been lacking from his attitude towards her in recent months, he had never spoken to her like this, not in this tone.

'*I* am paying for it Daniel? But you are paying for it too are you not? You have given up your dingy little room in Soho, your threadbare clothes and scuffed shoes, the diet you had that brought you close to malnutrition and out in spots, the . . .'

'And *freedom*!' Daniel jumped up and for a moment she thought he would strike her. 'The freedom to do as I choose, go where I wish, yes eat what I want, live how I please. That room was freedom to me, freedom to work and think and not have all the time a moaning, whining *ugly* woman around my neck threatening to tell her father about me or have my allowance cut . . .'

'I have never asked my father to cut your allowance!' Jane struggled unsuccessfully to get up.

'Well you said I was spending too much. That I should take care!'

'Because the money Papa has is *not* limitless,' Jane shouted, clinging desperately to the sides of the chair for support. 'The money has all been spent on clothes for you, books for you, furniture for you, hats for you, shoes for you. The rest of the house and the nursery are almost bare except for essentials. There is not a bottomless pit of Vestrey money like the widow's cruse just for you, Daniel Lévy!'

Daniel hit her twice, once across each cheek. It happened so quickly that Jane scarcely knew what had occurred; no time to feel either pain or shock because, suddenly, a much greater pain possessed her abdomen. She clung frantically to the sides of the chair to prevent herself screaming. But Daniel was not there to see it. The whole house reverberated as he slammed the front door and the sound of his quick footsteps could be heard retreating on the pavement outside.

George Vestrey arrived by cab just as Daniel disappeared in the direction of Hampstead High Street. He thought he saw his small elegant form but he could not be sure. He paid the cabbie and took the large bunch of flowers from the back seat as well as assorted parcels containing gifts for Jane and the baby. But nothing more for Daniel, George thought grimly, nothing.

The maid took a long time to answer the door. When she did her face was flushed and her voice confused. George anxiously stepped inside aware of some sort of atmosphere in the house.

'What is it, Aggie?'

'Oh sir, my lord, the mistress has started in labour. She is in agony on the floor of the master's study. Oh sir it is the new maid's day off, and the cook . . .'

George threw down his parcels and flew into the study, too shocked even to register what the maid had said. The cook was kneeling by Jane, who was stretched out on the floor writhing in pain, her garments disordered, her hands clutching at her swollen, heaving belly.

'But how has this happened?' George said, quickly squatting beside Jane and putting a hand on her brow. 'Where is the midwife, the doctor?'

'The baby was not quite due sir,' the cook muttered. ' 'Twas brought on by a row between . . .'

'Oh *please*,' Jane grasped the cook's hand and shook her head. 'Please do not distress my father. Get a doctor quickly.'

George stood up. 'I will get the doctor . . .'

'No Papa, I want you with me. Oh Papa, please.' She put out a hand and George knelt and took it, pressing it to his lips. He couldn't take his eyes off the extraordinary commotion in her belly, shifting first this way and then that. It seemed as though his daughter was about to disintegrate.

'Of course, my darling. Of course I will not leave you; but we must get you up to bed.'

Jane shook her head and gave his hand a convulsive squeeze. Together, it seemed, they suffered the next prolonged spasm of pain. George closed his eyes and gripped her hand, willing it to be over. Was this what happened to women in childbirth? His wife had borne him thirteen children, his mistress one and yet, apart from the pleasant act

491

of creation – pleasant, that is to say, as far as he had been concerned – he knew nothing at all about the actual production of the fruits of his labours.

When Agnes had the first twinges prior to giving birth he was spirited away to a far room where no unpleasant sounds or commotion could disturb him and given a glass of brandy. Usually he went across to his brother-in-law at the Rectory until the birth was over. It was a short, pleasant stroll. He was within reach if necessary, and well looked after. Twice he had actually been in London. No, all George Vestrey knew about childbirth was being ushered into his wife's bedroom an hour or two after the birth when she and baby were washed, scented and suitably clad to receive the progenitor himself, the father of creation.

Now his fourth child, his beloved Jane, was twisted and tormented, suffering agonies on account of that arrogant, stubborn, *ugly* little foreigner who, if George could get his hands on him ...

'Oh Papa. You must get a doctor, or I feel I will die. Send Aggie. Quickly.'

The frantic maid was bending over her mistress clutching her apron in her hands.

'Aggie,' George said, 'you must go at once to get Doctor, what is his name?'

'Harvey,' Jane muttered. 'Doctor Harvey, in Pond Street.'

'Pond Street. Do you hear that? Now run girl, run and say if he does not come this instance Lord Vestrey will have his hide.'

'Yes sir ...'

Aggie tore out of the room and through the front door leaving it swinging open behind her.

Jane's face was covered with sweat, and she tugged at the buttons on her loose dress. 'I am so uncomfortable, Papa, so hot ...'

George looked at the cook but she, a maiden lady of some sixty years, was more at a loss than George Vestrey, father, after all, of fourteen, when it came to the bringing forth of children. She looked as though she could do with a hefty sniff of *sal volatile* and, since her mistress's father had come, had done little but sway backwards and forwards on her knees wailing like a mourner at an oriental wake.

George leaned forward and began to unfasten the buttons of his daughter's dress. He was discomfited to see the naked, swollen breasts beneath, the mound of her distended stomach. It was such an alien, distressing sight and he quickly took out a handkerchief and wiped the sweat from her face, stroking back her thick curls away from her forehead. Her eyes were black with suffering and the hand which held so tightly on to his was hot and sticky.

'Little Jane . . .' he murmured tenderly. 'We will soon have help, my darling.'

'I feel the baby is very near, Papa. I have a terrible urge to push.'

'But my darling, babies are not born so easily or quickly,' George said looking at her distractedly. He wished that somehow she could arrange herself with more decorum; this thrashing on the floor with legs apart and clothes disordered, this primeval frenzy of bulging, tormented flesh was quite obscene. George didn't know what he had imagined childbirth to be like, but certainly nothing resembling this – and to his daughter too. It was not the style of his beautiful Jane at all. Had Agnes looked like this, and *Hilary*? 'Your mother was once in labour for twelve hours. There is plenty of time.'

'It was the shock,' the cook muttered grimly, looking on with disapproval as Jane, as if aware of her father's distress and embarrassment, compounded it by drawing up her legs and fumbling frantically at the folds of the dress which constricted them.

'Shock?' George said, noting with alarm this new aspect of his daughter's primitive behaviour. Surely this was the birth position, like the position for love – to receive and to bring forth? The association distressed him further.

'The master and mistress had a terrible row. He hit her . . .'

'He . . .'

'Oh Papa, Papa . . .'

Jane screamed and opened her legs wide. George saw the undulating belly give a gigantic heave and he expected that at any moment his grandchild would appear from under her skirts. He began to remove his coat, to make a blanket for it when, to his intense relief, the sound of running footsteps proclaimed not only the doctor, but also the midwife with whom he had been about to set out to attend another delivery.

'Oh thank God, doctor,' George said getting up. 'My daughter is about to give birth. Can we not move her? It is so unseemly on the floor.'

The doctor scrutinized his patient's face, felt her belly and put a probing hand beneath her skirts.

'Certainly not sir,' he said in a clipped Scottish accent. 'She is not quite ready, but there is no time to move her. She is very advanced for a first baby. Tell that woman to bring me some pails of hot water and clean towels. Your grandchild will be born on this floor, Lord Vestrey, and there is nothing you can do about it. Now sir, if you will remove yourself?'

George stood looking down at his daughter, her tormented, painracked face, the awkward ungainly position of her distended body. Her eyes were closed, her breathing was heavy and laboured. She seemed already to have passed into another sphere, another world. He felt a sharp catch in his throat.

'Will she be all right? Will she live?'

The doctor chortled, removing his coat and tying a large white apron about his middle. 'My dear Lord Vestrey, Mrs Lévy is a strong young woman – she will give you many, many more grandchildren, never fear. This is a little quick, a little premature, but your daughter is well and healthy. Now be off with you, and take that drivelling woman away, for God's sake.'

George helped the cook to her feet and together they staggered out of the room while Aggie struggled through the door, lopsided, with a large pail of water on either side.

For two hours more George paced up and down in the small front sitting-room, a practically untouched brandy in his hand, before he heard the sound he both dreaded and wanted. He had dreaded it because of the complications it

494

would bring to the life of his beloved daughter. Yet he wanted it because, as well as meaning that Jane was safely delivered, it would herald yet another Vestrey born into the world. His first grandchild.

When Daniel returned it was nightfall and Jane and her daughter were sleeping peacefully in the upstairs bedroom overlooking the back garden. Due to the speed of the birth Jane had been badly torn, and had to endure more pain while the doctor stitched her. But when it was over and she, exhausted but happy at last, had looked at her newborn infant, she tucked her hand confidently into that of her father and sank into a deep sleep.

George thought how calm she looked in sleep, her face presenting a lovely profile against the white pillowcase. He remembered how he had watched over her after the attack on her in Soho; how anxious and worried he had been then, how fearful for the outcome. But now the situation was completely different. He marvelled at how quickly women recovered from childbirth, now that he knew more intimately what happened to them during it. No greater contrast could be imagined between his daughter now, and the terrible turbulent spectacle she had presented a few hours before.

Her long black lashes curled upon her cheeks, which were a little flushed, the bloom of motherhood. His baby, his Jane, was a mother; the first of his daughters to bear a child. His heart swelled with pride, with joy and with gratitude that she was alive and well and peaceful. Would that the rest of her life could be as precious and tranquil at this moment. He held her hand very tightly, relishing this silent communion between his daughter and himself, when the door was pushed ajar and Daniel stood on the threshold, his eyes wide open with shock. George sighed deeply and prepared himself for an onslaught of mutual recrimination and reproach.

George put a finger to his lips and Daniel advanced very slowly and quietly into the room. Then he stood by the side of her bed and looked at the woman who had just given birth to his child. George felt no love or affection for the man who had brought such suffering on his daughter, and he looked at him sternly, continuing to hold Jane's hand.

'Well sir, where were you?'

Daniel did not reply, his small sculptured mouth pursed, his expression sanguine as he gazed at Jane. It was as though Lord Vestrey were not there. Then, at last, he looked at him as though seeing him for the first time.

'I understand it was very quick.'

'Three hours.'

Daniel nodded and put his hands behind his back. Then he walked over to the crib in the corner and peeped into it, drawing back the thick white shawl that covered the slumbering child.

'A girl,' he said. 'She is quite pretty.'

George had a fierce urge to rise up and strike his daughter's seducer, but then he recalled that he was also the father of his grandchild, and he curbed the impulse. Whether he liked it or not he and Daniel Lévy were related, without benefit of the bond of marriage, but related still, forever.

'She is beautiful,' George said. 'You are a fortunate man, Lévy, that so much was accomplished without you being incommoded in any way.'

Daniel stared down at his daughter, as if deep in thought. He let a hand rest on her small covered shoulder. It was an affectionate, tender gesture that was not lost on George. It mollified him, but he was still angry. He felt the ordeal he had undergone during the day was almost insupportable – alone with his daughter about to give birth, unaided except by an ignorant cook and a very stupid maid. He yearned to pour the whole tale into Hilary's sympathetic ears. Daniel patted his daughter again then, folding his arms, walked over to George. For a moment he stood and gazed at him, contempt in every finely wrought feature of his delicate, sensitive face.

'And you, Lord Vestrey, may I ask how many times *you* have been incommoded during the many occasions on which Lady Vestrey has presented you with a new offspring to adorn your distinguished house?'

George got up so as not to be disadvantaged by Daniel's

slight form. Even then Daniel did not seem overawed by the considerable height of his lordship but gazed up at him calmly, taking a few steps back so as to even out the distance a little.

'Thanks to you, sir, my daughter gave birth on the floor like a common washerwoman. There was not time to lift her onto a bed, scarcely to summon the doctor. Thanks to *you* sir I might have had to act as midwife, and then . . .'

'Certainly it was preferable you being here to myself, sir,' Daniel Lévy said jauntily, putting his hands in his pockets and leaning against the wall. 'Never having fathered children before, that I know of at any rate, I have no experience at all on which to call. It is fortunate you were here. You should be pleased your daughter was under your protection with you to look after her.'

'It is you who should have been here, Mr Lévy, the father of my daughter's child. My granddaughter.' George swallowed with emotion and his hand went to his collar which suddenly seemed to constrict him. 'I understand that you brought on this precipitate labour which could have threatened the life of Jane and her baby.'

'*I*, Lord Vestrey?' Daniel looked incredulous. 'It was her time. The baby was due any day. It was unfortunate I happened to be out of the house . . .'

'I understand you hit Jane.' George moved nearer and raised his hand in a threatening gesture. 'That you hit my daughter and then ran out of the house.'

Daniel righted himself from his lounging position against the wall as though to be ready to escape from George's curled fist should it be put into use. He straightened his waistcoat nervously. 'Lord Vestrey, if we are to understand each other, and I think this is your wish, let me say this to you sir. Let me say this.' Daniel moved into the centre of the room and folded his arms again thrusting out his chin. 'Jane Vestrey is a spoilt girl. She is used to servants, to having everything done for her, her merest wish satisfied. She snaps her fingers and people come running. But not me, sir. I am no member of the bourgeoisie or the servant class impressed by the nobility. I am a free man, my own master. I am her master too, the head of this house as you are the head of yours. While she is in this house she is under my control. She chooses to live with me as my wife; then she must behave like one and obey me, as I am sure Lady Vestrey obeys you. If she does not like it she can quit. But those are my conditions, and today I made them perfectly clear. I am tired of Jane's tantrums and her wilful ways. I am a scholar, a thinker. I am engaged in work of enormous importance to the whole of mankind, not just one particular, headstrong woman. I can do this work anywhere and am quite ready to resume life on my own in Soho or wherever, as this house belongs to you.

'Jane knows this. I told her so this morning. This is what brought on her labour: the realization that she is not her own mistress, but subject to me. I made that clear.'

Daniel Lévy turned and looked at Jane still asleep in the bed. George thought his harsh expression softened but he couldn't be sure. Such was his feeling of outrage that he no longer seemed to see Daniel in any reasonable light at all, his vision increasingly obscured by blind hatred.

'I regard Jane as my wife,' Daniel continued in a proprietorial manner. 'We now have a daughter. We are a family. Surely, with your bourgeois notions, you approve of *that*, Lord Vestrey?'

George closed his eyes. He did not know how to answer. He would have given anything to take Jane and the baby away from this monstrous self-centred man; but at that moment Jane opened her eyes. Her dark lashes fluttered on her cheeks and when she saw Daniel her eyes lit up with love and pride and she reached trustingly for his hand.

He took it and sat on the bed beside her, tucking her hand against his chest. He bent down and kissed her cheek.

'I am sorry I was not here, my love. Forgive my temper.'

'Oh Daniel, are you pleased?'

'Of course I am, my dearest. I am thrilled with our little daughter. But how I wish I could have been with you.'

He looked at her slim form outlined by the bedclothes. Thank heaven that hideous protuberance was gone. Soon she would be a beautiful slim woman again, the woman he desired. Inwardly he breathed a sigh of relief. She looked so beautiful with her hair loose on the pillow, her full breasts rising and falling as she breathed. Because he had abstained for so many weeks he felt a crude resurgence of desire and he pressed his face to hers. 'The thought of your suffering here without me makes me quite deranged.'

'It is no matter, my darling; there is nothing you could have done. I am glad you were not here. It would have distressed you. Even Papa was at a loss and he has had a lot of children. My pains came on so suddenly, with such force, that I could not be moved.'

'Oh I know, do not speak of it.' Daniel kissed her hand, his face puckered with distress. 'Next time we shall be sure to have the nurse in the house well before the baby is due, even the midwife shall move in. I shall *never* allow my darling to suffer so again.'

His lips brushed her forehead and he put an arm tenderly round her shoulders drawing her close to him. Jane's face grew ecstatic with happiness.

'*Next* time? Daniel, are you already talking of *next* time? For heaven's sake, how many children are we going to have?'

Daniel lowered his face so that his eyes were only inches from hers. He looked into them with a naughty, meaningful expression and murmured in her ear. Jane pretended to be shocked by what he had said and playfully smacked his hand, her face full of laughter. But then she nuzzled against him, and he lay half recumbent on the bed as if to show what rights he had over the woman by his side.

Neither of them so much as glanced at George. They had eyes only for each other. Lovers in a private, enclosed, irrational world.

George Vestrey sighed deeply, but already he had accepted the inevitable. Despite his treatment of her, his selfishness and his callousness, Jane was hopelessly in love with Daniel Lévy. Was, and probably would remain so because she was that kind of girl. Love would be for her a matter of principle as well as passion.

She plainly worshipped Daniel and thought that whatever he did was right, because in her eyes he was a great man, engaged in great work. They made him feel like an intruder.

George quietly opened the door and crept softly out of the room.

CHAPTER THIRTY-ONE

Emily had been a maid-of-honour to the Queen for nearly four years. She was also twenty-three years of age and, like her mother, could not help feeling she should be married.

When Caroline went to Turkey, Emily decided to give up all thoughts of Rawdon Foxton. Her passion for him had caused enough trouble. She deeply regretted the estrangement from Caroline and wanted so much to see her before she left; but Papa had forbidden it. He gave her news of Caroline and the terrible conditions in the hospital at Scutari in which she and Florence Nightingale worked. There was brief mention of Rawdon's visit to Scutari.

They seemed very much a couple. Emily determined to put Rawdon completely out of her mind and to find a mate before she became an old maid like the Foxton sisters.

Agnes talked about it to her whenever she got the chance, hoping that one of her elder daughters was remotely normal. It was a great privilege to be a maid-of-honour; but now it was time she made a suitable, hopefully a distinguished, marriage. She nagged George about it too, on the few occasions when she saw him alone. George and Aunt Ruth should be making sure that Emily met lots of rich, titled young men – they were, surely, not *all* at the war?

Emily knew she was pretty and attractive to men; but the Queen allowed no flirtations in her Court, so that side of her life was restricted. When she was not at Court she either stayed in London, visited friends or, reluctantly stayed at home at Chetwell where, like her sisters, she could not abide the presence of Mrs Chetwynd. Like them, she regretted the disruption Mama's illness made to the family life.

Emily went to all the parties and balls, and knew she was admired and liked. But she wasn't going to accept any offer just in order to have her own establishment. Besides, she was an intelligent woman and the excitement and glamour of the Court, particularly in these thrilling years of such momentous happenings abroad, made her feel that she was at the centre of things, in a vital position. She could talk intelligently with her father about the war and she grew increasingly close to him now that Caroline was in Scutari and Jane living a life of her own in Hampstead.

Since Jane had brought such disgrace on the family Emily refused to talk to her or see her. She would have nothing to do either with her or her 'paramour', as she slightingly referred to Daniel. It had been such a dreadful time with Jane declaring she was pregnant by a man to whom she was not married, moreover that she was going to live openly with him; and Caroline insisting that she was old enough to know her own mind and wanting to go to Turkey. And then, to crown it all, there was the fracas caused by Oliver finally throwing up his studies at Cambridge and enlisting in the Fifty-seventh Foot.

Oliver could easily have got into the Guards; but he refused to consider it even though, as a family, the Vestreys were linked with the Brigade. Oliver did not wish to be under the eye of his elder brother. He felt, much as he loved James, that he was now a man and wanted to be independent. Oliver had this fierce, stubborn streak in him. In many ways he was the family's male counterpart of Jane, unbending when he felt he was right, which was practically all the time.

George had accordingly purchased for him a commission as an ensign, and he was now at Sebastopol with the Fourth Division, under the command of Lord Bentinck. The Fifty-seventh Foot was a distinguished regiment with a particularly fine record in the Peninsular War.

Army life suited Oliver as it suited James. He thrived on it and wrote glowing letters home. By the time he arrived in March 1855 the weather had improved and eased the flow of supplies from Balaklava. The plain round Sebastopol was full of snowdrops, crocuses and small wild hyacinths. The mud had gone and the troops were comfortable and dry in tents and new huts, some of which even had fenced gardens around them with peas and beans growing, and chickens penned up to provide fresh eggs. The weather was hot and turbans were coming out again wound round wide-awake hats, and a lot of inter-regimental entertaining was done. There were regular pony races between the English and the French. The railway from Balaklava was complete, its engines puffing away much to the consternation of the Russians, and the electric telegraph was installed between Balaklava, Kadikoi headquarters and the right and left attack.

Those who survived the winter never tired of telling the new recruits what they had missed; but Oliver didn't care. He wanted to have a crack at the Russians and his eyes gleamed on his first visit to the trenches, his inspection of the Russian fortifications through the field glasses given to him by his father. He looked at the battered town lying in its once beautiful bay, at the six large redoubts which surrounded it, at the guns smoking in the batteries and he longed to cover himself with glory.

The patriotism of Oliver and Caroline made up a little for the betrayal of Jane. Acting on the advice of Lady Canning, Emily decided to make a clean breast of things to the Queen. If Her Majesty heard about Jane from elsewhere, and London society talked about little else, she would think less of her, Lady Canning advised. As usual, she was right. She even went with Emily to break the news to the Queen, who was sitting in her room at Windsor overlooking the great park.

It was not a very propitious time to seek the sympathy of one even as understanding as the Queen, as Emily knew her to be, and she trembled in the royal presence as she had never trembled before, even in her first days at Court.

The Queen was most anxious to hear news about Oliver and Caroline; such self-sacrifice, she said. She herself would embroider a comforter for Oliver and write a personal note to Caroline. She embraced Emily and congratulated her on such a heroic family. Even Lady Canning shed a tear.

'There is another thing, Your Majesty,' Emily said, standing first on one foot then another. 'It is about my sister Jane.'

The Queen dabbed at her eyes and extended her arms

towards Emily. 'Oh pray, do not tell me of *another* act of heroic self-sacrifice.'

'Well, no alas, Your Majesty. I scarcely know where to begin.' Emily looked at Charlotte Canning, who had known the Queen for so many years, for help. She was sure to know the *mots justes*.

Now aged thirty-five, Victoria had been on the English throne for seventeen years. She was never a beauty but, though small, she was a strong minded, determined woman who was both loved and slightly feared by those who served her. Over the years the diminutive Queen had grown plump, and her round face and light brown hair, together with a smile of almost child-like sweetness, made her seem much more innocent and protected from the world than she was.

The Queen had a hard core of practicality, of robust commonsense – probably inherited from her tough Hanoverian ancestors. Lady Canning, who had served the Queen for many years, knew she was not as narrowminded as everyone thought. She had so many relatives abroad who frequently misbehaved themselves, and to most of them she showed compassion, understanding and kindness, which she manifested in unexpected ways.

'It is not pleasant news about Jane, unfortunately, Your Majesty,' Lady Canning had said lowering her voice. 'Emily hesitates to distress Your Majesty, but she felt it her duty to tell you that . . .'

Lady Canning paused, groping for the right words to tell the dreadful tale, and the Queen began to look agitated and clasped her handkerchief more securely in her small hand, having it ready for active service once more on her eyes.

'Oh pray do go on, Lady Canning. What *is* it about Jane? I am so fond of her. I hope she is not ill again?'

'She has formed a liaison ma'am with a young man . . . She is living with him openly and has borne him a child, a daughter, Your Majesty.'

There was a regal silence which only the Queen knew how to make awkward by the way she pursed her tiny mouth and glared from her prominent blue eyes.

'Oh,' she said at long last. Mentally Emily prepared to pack her bags. No self-sacrifice on the part of Oliver or

Caroline could possibly atone for this. 'I am to gather she is not married to the – er – young man in question?'

'Yes ma'am. They do not wish to marry. The young man is a revolutionary, expelled from his country and taking refuge on these shores.'

The Queen looked indignant. 'How ungrateful!' she said wrathfully, 'and *then* to seduce one of our girls. I was always against being so merciful to these creatures and said so several times to my Uncle Leopold, as well as to my own ministers. Can nothing be done?'

'My father has tried everything, Your Majesty,' Emily's courage began to return. 'But because he is such a fond father and loves Jane he cannot cast her off. He has provided a small pension for them and a tiny house in a discreet part of Hampstead where their presence will not be too noticeable.'

The Queen relaxed and a tender, tearful look came into her eyes. 'How *kind* of Lord Vestrey. What a truly *good* man he is. Then if he will not condemn her, neither will I. But pray dear Emily, do not let this get to the ears of the Prince! I may have to tell him, but in my own time.' The Queen held up her arms and beckoned to Emily, who nervously came over and stooped to receive the embrace of her Royal mistress.

'You know I love you truly, my dear Emily, and your dear family. I even love Jane and like Our Lord, Our Master, we must show forgiveness as he taught us with the woman taken in adultery. I pray that Jane will be guided to do what is best, and also that she might find one more deserving of her good qualities which I know are considerable. Assure your dear father and mother of my tender interest and concern, and my gratitude to you, dearest Emily, for telling me this sad news. I would hate to have heard it from other sources. Now seeing that *I* shall not speak of it no one else will *dare*.'

The Queen took up the comforter she was working on for her poor soldiers and bade her ladies do the same to keep her company; but Emily's gratitude was too intense and she begged leave to be allowed to go and recover herself.

Outside the door she broke down and wept. The Queen's

graciousness was almost too much to bear. She fled to her room and wrote a long letter to her father about the goodness and humanity of their sovereign, and had much to say about the wretchedness of Jane and the immorality of her ways.

Jane was another blot on the perfect image of the Vestrey family that Emily so wished to have. Mama was one and now Jane was another. She began to hate both of them for spoiling a happy respectable family life. As much as she loved the Court she decided that she must seriously find a suitor and build up a happy family life of her own to take the place of the one that had gone. She knew she was beautiful, but it would not last. She was getting old.

Among Emily's many admirers was Sir Arthur Stamford, a Gentleman-in-Waiting to the Queen, a cousin of the Marquess of Ludstow and a distinguished soldier. He had fought in many of the minor skirmishes that had occurred overseas in the forty years since Waterloo and he regretted that he could not go out to the Crimea. Sir Arthur had lost his wife from fever in India and one of the reasons that he left the army was to look after his, then, young family, two boys and three girls. The youngest was now nineteen and Sir Arthur was only forty-nine. He knew Emily was much too young for him, that people would look askance at such a match; but he was a good looking vigorous man with normal impulses which he kept rigidly in check, and he was infatuated by her.

Sir Arthur was always very correct at Court, standing with the men on the far side of the room and never making his feelings obvious, until he heard that Oliver Vestrey had joined the Fifty-seventh which, by chance, happened to be another brother's old regiment. He himself had been a cavalry man. Emily regarded Sir Arthur rather as she thought of her father, with respect and affection. In fact he was even older than her father. He had a very military appearance with close-cropped brown hair and a large moustache which was slightly grey at the edges.

Sir Arthur first deliberately sought her out the day Emily told the Queen about Jane. He happened to be on the same waiting as her. At a household dinner the Queen made much of the fresh news concerning Oliver and Caroline, Emily blushing because, all the time, she was thinking of what the Queen, that lady of rectitude and propriety, knew about Jane.

After dinner when the household assembled for cards and chat Sir Arthur had left the men in the corner and approached Emily. He started to reminisce about India and the Fifty-seventh in which he had briefly served before leaving a foot regiment for the cavalry. Emily found him rather entertaining. It was the first time she had really noticed Colonel Sir Arthur Stamford as a person instead of a stately, rather remote, courtier.

She soon knew him very well; she also realized he was courting her. He had visited the house in Park Street twice, at first on the pretext of a slight acquaintance with her father and on the second occasion to ask her and her aunt to dine with him at his house in Ebury Street.

Emily didn't want to marry an old man with a grown-up family; but there was something very right about Sir Arthur. He was also good looking, if you stopped remembering that he was older than Papa, because he had kept his figure, danced well, had a beautiful singing voice, and all the grace and manners of the practised courtier. The Queen and the Prince were devoted to him.

Besides, if she married Sir Arthur she would not have to leave the Court. Or rather she would, but she would still be in the swim, as it were. She would know what went on; she would be asked often, although gentlemen did not have their wives with them in waiting, as ladies did not have their husbands. But Lord Canning was always about the place and other spouses of the various courtiers.

Other than Sir Arthur there was no one who appealed to Emily at all.

Emily was an intelligent girl, but she concealed it well. She prattled away and laughed a lot and was a great hit at balls and parties, but the young men who thronged about her really were as silly as she pretended to be. She knew that if she settled for any of them she would have to spend her life concealing her interests; her liking for politics and world affairs, her interest in serious art and literature. After even-

507

ing upon evening talking about nothing – not even the war –
to be with Sir Arthur was familiar and comforting. He
seemed to know what she wanted; he was a gourmet and
kept a good table. He took her and Aunt Ruth, and occasionally Papa, to a good restaurant where he ordered
grouse and oysters if they were in season and the finest
wines, of which he was a connoisseur.

Emily began to be attracted by Sir Arthur; to prefer his
company above anyone else's, to look out for him. When
she was not in waiting she was eager to hear from him,
anxious for his little notes delivered by one of his footmen
always accompanied by a bouquet of flowers. If it were not
for the difference in age she thought she could easily be in
love with him.

Rawdon Foxton arrived back in Constantinople after visiting all the hospitals through Asia Minor where his men were
being treated. He had gone as far afield as Corfu, Smyrna
and Abydos, and had visited the controversial hospital at
Kullali of which Miss Nightingale did not approve.

At Smyrna Rawdon found that a party of forty-two ladies
and nurses had arrived from England, without the consent
of Florence, that there were no arrangements to meet them
and nowhere for them to stay.

'They appealed to me to help,' Rawdon told Caroline on
his first night back, 'but what could I do? I believe they
were eventually found lodgings with a Greek merchant. On
the whole though, our men are well looked after. Smyrna is
such a beautiful town, on top of a hill, very clean, not like
most that I visited. Abydos is very favourably situated, for
the site and the air are most suitable for the treatment of
wounds; but there is a great scarcity of water. Alas, I found
very few of my men fit to return.'

'And did you visit wicked Kullali?' Caroline said with an
air of amusement.

'Oh yes, Lady Stratford reigns supreme. I must tell you,
however, that Miss Nightingale is much criticized everywhere for her dictatorial manner.'

'The only way you can win this war against disease,'
Caroline said, 'is by being a dictator. Florence is still opposed

by the medical authorities and interfering busybodies like Lady Stratford. Do you know that after visiting the Barrack Hospital her ladyship refused to come again for fear of disease, and subsequent meetings had to be conducted outside? If Florence were allowed her own way the numbers of men dying would fall by half.'

The weather had turned warm. Rawdon and Caroline were sitting by the open door of the rented house at Scutari. Polly was still at the hospital. Caroline had felt unwell for some days and had agreed at Florence's insistence to a day off to welcome Rawdon home. He looked at her worn face, her thin frame, and he suddenly felt angry and bitter.

'She is a slave driver,' he said, 'look what she has done to you.'

'A *slave* driver?' Caroline gazed at him with incredulity. 'I know not what you mean. Florence is the most admirable person I have ever known. If she drives us she drives herself too, ten times more. You have no idea the number of women she has sent home, or away to rest. But herself? Never. No, I admire her.' Caroline sat back in her chair and looked across the Bosphorus at the minarets of Constantinople glittering in the setting sun. The sky above the city was blood red, like a harbinger of terror, and the small black clouds that lingered in the sky did not seem to offer any hope of change. 'In fact I love her.'

Rawdon reached urgently for her hand. 'And me? Do you love me, Caroline?'

For a long time Caroline didn't reply, but swung his hand lightly between their chairs. His touch was strong and comforting; she brushed the silky hairs on the back of his hands with her thumb. His grip tightened as though the familiar gesture had stimulated him, and he repeated the question.

'I am not talking about my love for Florence as one does of that between a man and a woman, Rawdon,' she said looking at him gravely. 'That is quite different. I love Florence as a very special person – someone who is above mere mankind, much greater. If you knew her as I do you would love her too.'

'Somehow I cannot imagine loving Miss Nightingale,'

Rawdon said ruefully, 'except perhaps in the way you describe. I find her very forbidding.'

'That is because she *wants* to be forbidding – to you. But not to the sick or suffering, those who need her. She no longer cares to attract normal men; she has put all that sort of thing behind her as an antidote to her beauty. Thus her attitude is, I agree, offputting. It is intentional.'

'But she is not beautiful,' Rawdon protested.

'She was,' Caroline paused. 'She was once very beautiful; but the conditions here, her mental and physical deprivations have ravaged her. She is emaciated; but her soul is so beautiful and *that* is what matters, Rawdon Foxton.'

His smile faded as he looked at her. 'Caroline, you are beginning to alarm me. What is this talk about the soul, the abandonment of physical beauty?'

'Oh, I do not talk for myself.' Caroline let his hand fall and clasped hers together on her lap. 'But I do admire it. I wish I could be as selfless. Yet when I see you . . .' She looked at him again, and in her eyes he saw an expression he had not seen before. 'I know I want you to love me as a woman. To find me beautiful. I want you to love me, not my soul.'

'Oh my darling, I *do* love you.' Exulted by her words Rawdon came and knelt beside her, slipping an arm around her narrow waist. 'I love you as a woman, a beautiful, vital woman; but my darling, you are very pale and wan, you are too thin. I think you have had enough of this nursing, this dedication. Please marry me. Please marry me now, and come back with me to the Crimea. The war cannot last much longer. We will honeymoon, my darling, among the crocuses and hyacinths which they say are now blooming there, and . . .'

It was very tempting. Caroline closed her eyes and thought how it would be with Rawdon. They would have a little hut surrounded by crocuses and wild hyacinths. If she inhaled she could almost smell them. Then she would know those delights that she could only dimly imagine, the anticipation of which sometimes made her pulse race through her body, her blood overheat, her legs weaken. She felt an apprehension of it when she gripped his long, strong masculine hand;

this secure, certain man who loved her, who wanted to take her to his bed.

She opened her eyes and shook her head, put out a hand and touched his cheek. 'I cannot. I have promised Florence I will not leave her. You would not have us begin our life together on a broken promise, would you Rawdon? How can I be happy knowing that Florence is surrounded by enemies, by people who would undo all the good she has done? My dearest, you are a man of honour. You *must* know that.'

'I am tired of being a man of honour.' Rawdon rose abruptly from his knees and walked to the door. He could see the wooden doors of the giant Barrack Hospital only a few hundred yards away. It seemed to threaten their future, this monstrous place of suffering and death. Those great doors were a barrier to their happiness. 'I am very tired of living without you. I am a man, Caroline, and I want to marry. You know what I mean.'

Caroline lowered her eyes, disturbed by a rush of blood to her cheeks. She had just been thinking about bed, and now Rawdon was talking about it. This was what he meant. He wanted to lie with her and make love to her, behave as married people did.

'I know what you mean,' she said. 'You do not want to be like James.'

'Exactly.'

'And I do not wish to be like Jane.'

'I should hope you do not, my darling!' he said indignantly. 'That certainly is no way to happiness, especially for a woman. Mind you, it does not surprise me. Your sister . . .'

Caroline held up a hand. 'Please Rawdon, I beg you. Do not criticize Jane. I think she is very brave. She shows courage in her lack of concern about what society thinks of her; in her devotion to a penniless revolutionary. She has physical bravery too. Papa says she was marvellous when her baby was born so quickly and unexpectedly. He has the greatest admiration for her. And she *does* love Daniel. Papa realizes that, and says that, in his peculiar way, Daniel loves her.'

'Then he should show it by marrying her. You think I would dishonour *you* by lying with you without marriage?'

Caroline gave a world-weary smile. He certainly had bed on his mind. 'Why is it, I always ask myself, dishonourable without marriage but honourable in it? Yet it is the same thing, or so I understand.'

'Caroline how could you talk like that!' Rawdon turned from his contemplation of the hated Barrack Hospital to gaze at her with bewilderment. 'Sometimes I wonder if your experiences here have made you lose your sense of what is right and what is wrong. It is a *very* different thing being married and not. Otherwise women would not be so condemned for doing it.'

'But men are *not* so condemned?'

'Caroline, I do not understand what has got into you.' Rawdon threw himself down in the wicker chair, his chin slumped on his chest. 'You are being outrageous.'

'But it is true, Rawdon. My experiences here have certainly not demoralized me; but they *have* made me think. I see the poor victims of the lust of men – married and unmarried. They bring forth children just the same way as married folk do. Their sufferings are just as great, whether married or not. Being married does not make it easier to bear a child, Rawdon. You must remember that since I have been in this hospital I have seen many children born, some die and some live to face a hopeless life. I have assisted at as many births as the midwife. I know exactly what it is all about, and I have never yet seen a man suffer as much as a woman as a result of what he was responsible for in the first place.'

Rawdon shook his head. He was reminded of his discussion with James at Varna the previous summer. Conversations took place in this atmosphere that were impossible to imagine at home.

'You are confusing me. What has all this to do with what we are talking about?' He looked at her profile turned once again to the water. He was sure her jawline was somehow stronger, the dint in her chin deeper, giving her mouth a firmer definition. She had been changed by her experiences

512

and, although she still retained her own particular style of beauty, she was not quite as beautiful as she had been. Besides, what were these strange ideas? Everyone was quite right. Nursing *was* no business for respectable gently-reared women if it gave them notions like the ones Caroline had been voicing. 'You are too like your sister,' he said. 'Too like Jane. Your headstrong notions will undo you, Caroline. You Vestrey girls . . .'

Caroline got up quickly and dashed the cushion, on which she had been sitting, to the floor. Her eyes blazed as she turned on Rawdon.

'Oh pray, Rawdon Foxton, be good enough to spare me you thoughts on "we Vestrey girls". I fancy I have heard them before. You think my sister Jane is a harlot and I am not much better, while Emily, who makes so free with her kisses, is probably just as bad. When you talk about "we" Vestrey girls you are talking about passion, Rawdon Foxton – bed, and lovemaking and lust. It is all you have on your mind. I tell you I have seen too much of its effects to have romantic notions lingering in *my* mind about it.'

Rawdon stared at Caroline as if in an apoplectic trance. His mouth hung open and his handsome, good-humoured face looked about to explode. He sat on the edge of his chair and put his hands squarely on his knees. Then he got up and seized Caroline by the shoulders, turning her to face him.

'Now, my good woman, listen to this. I have *not* got passion on the brain. I do *not* think all the Vestrey girls are whores. I am a normal male, with normal desires and wishes. One of these is to marry; to have a wife by my side who will love me, supervise my household and, yes, give me children. If that is "passion" then it is what every other normal male of my acquaintance also wishes and most normal women too. We are all dominated by passion, if that is the case, your mother and father and mine, and . . .'

'Oh Rawdon, *stop*!' Caroline put her hands to her head and backed away from him. 'Stop, stop. I cannot endure any more. We are not suited, Rawdon. Let us break our engagement. I think Emily would suit you better than me. Her ideas would fit in more with yours. Despite her behaviour at balls she is very decorous by instinct and you would be well suited.'

'But I do not want Emily!' Rawdon banged his fists together and the rickety furniture in the room bounced about on the wooden floor. 'I want you, Caroline Mary Vestrey. I want you!'

Caroline was leaning against the whitewashed wall. Her breath came fast and her racing heart was almost painful. To see Rawdon thus roused was an awesome sight, an unfamiliar, almost frightening one. She thought she had recognized in Rawdon a man who was, like her, dutiful. One whom she could admire and look up to, like Papa. Would Papa behave like this – his face red and contorted, his eyes popping out of their sockets?

All the Vestrey girls, she knew, had, to a greater or lesser extent, the model of their father as the perfect man – and the men who most resembled him were the most likely recipients of their love. Caroline knew that Jane found qualities in Daniel which in her opinion resembled Papa, even if she herself couldn't see them. She could hardly think of anyone less like Papa than Daniel; but for Jane there was – she said it was his passion for principle, his disdain of convention and expediency; his determination to do what he thought was right.

Now Caroline thought that Rawdon *was* very like Papa. Indeed, he was not only like him in build and looks but in his dedication, his devotion to the war and his men. She knew he had been under pressure to go home and see his ailing father for some time; but he wanted to be among his troops. When so many men were suffering and the Brigade was reduced to a shadow of its former strength he had refused to seek compassionate leave and reduce his Battalion's strength even further.

But Rawdon, she knew now, was himself. He was not Papa. How silly to expect the man she wanted to marry to be a copy of the man who had created her. As she stared at him without replying, slightly shocked by his outburst, the colour ebbed from his face and he came over to her. He put his arms around her and leaned his head on her bosom.

'I am very tired,' he said. 'I am sorry.'

This she thought was the function of women. To comfort men. She was tired too; but she put her arms around him and her face close to his. She must forget her own exhaustion because of his needs. One saw what happened when women did not; they became selfish like Mama. Caroline knew how Papa had suffered on account of Mama. Because Mama *had* rejected him and withdrawn her love and her obedience, it had affected not only her father but all the family. Her grip on him tightened.

'I love you and I will marry you,' she said, freeing one of her hands and gently tilting back his head. 'I will marry you in the autumn at Chetwell. We shall ask for leave.'

'Oh Caroline . . .'

Her body against the wall was so female, so desirable. He forgot how haggard and wan she looked. He could feel her breasts against his shirt, his body moulded to the contours of hers. The look in her eyes was so womanly, so deep, so comforting. She was Caroline; he needed her.

Her hand travelled to the back of his tousled head and she drew it closer to her.

'Kiss me, like you kissed Emily,' she said.

CHAPTER THIRTY-TWO

Aunt Ruth approved of Sir Arthur Stamford, his impeccable family, his distinguished career. As far as she was concerned he was a young man, as she thought of George. He had demonstrated his virility and would give Emily children. He would start a new, young family, like George. She was very much in favour of encouraging the match. What with the disgrace Jane had brought on the family it was a wonder he still wanted her. Not everyone would wish to have that awful skeleton in the family cupboard, however distinguished the Vestrey family. Also, if anyone knew that Agnes now had Mrs Chetwynd sleeping in her own bedroom because she said she was afraid of the dark, they might have second thoughts too.

In Aunt Ruth's opinion she carried all the Vestrey family problems on her frail shoulders. She was sixty-five and at times she felt every year. The family was divided and fraught with troubles. Chetwell was no longer the centre of family life. She went to see Jane but she did not encourage her to come and see her; she hated the sight of Daniel Lévy. The only really good thing to have come out of the recent disturbances was the heroism of Caroline and Oliver, and that was a constant worry. At least James had not known what he was going to when the Guards left for Malta a year before. Oliver and Caroline had no doubt at all.

Aunt Ruth hoped that Caroline's peculiar behaviour – in Aunt Ruth's opinion no gentlewoman went out to *nurse* – might result in her becoming famous like Florence of whom the Nightingale family were now so proud. To hear Fanny and Parthe talk at the endless parties they went to, bragging away about Flo, no-one would have guessed they had done everything they could to prevent it.

There were two comforts to ease Aunt Ruth's old age, in her view. Never having had children of her own she loved babies and, unconventional as they were, she was besotted by Henry George Vestrey Ashburne, now eleven months old and Françoise Lévy Vestrey, the daughter of Jane and Daniel.

Henry's resemblance to George was very remarkable, and what a lovely child he was, jolly and bouncy and full of fun. He was a laughing child who gurgled a lot, and Hilary was an ideal mother, careful, tender and very proud. As well she might be. In Aunt Ruth's opinion she was extremely honoured to have had a son by George. Not every poverty stricken ex-governess, however genteel, became the mother of the son of a member of the House of Lords, the old and distinguished Vestrey family.

Hilary was exactly right with Aunt Ruth – deferential without being obsequious, pleasant without cringing. She quickly perceived Aunt Ruth as an ally and she cultivated her when she first made known her intention of visiting her the previous autumn. She decided that it was politic to forget about the fact that, for over a year, Aunt Ruth, though kind from a distance, had declined to see her. Now they met frequently and once Aunt Ruth had even taken tea with George, Hilary and Henry together. It was quite domestic, and George was so happy with the baby, with Hilary, with everything, despite his worries. It did a lot to make up for Jane.

Aunt Ruth wished to goodness that at least Jane had given her daughter a sensible name and not that silly foreign one. She, herself, would always call her Frances. But she was a lovely baby, petite and dark, unfortunately the image of Daniel with his blazing dark eyes and very white skin. Aunt Ruth hoped, in a way, that the baby would make him decide to marry Jane; but it seemed to make no difference at all. She only hoped Jane wouldn't have another. But how did one prevent these things? She would have to ask Hilary who obviously had discovered the secret, if her trim figure was anything to go by. If only ladies *could* discuss such matters. It would have to be done delicately.

Aunt Ruth, ruminating about family affairs, was sitting in the ground floor parlour sewing. Hilary and Henry were coming to tea. It was the first time she had invited Hilary to Park Street since George had established her in St John's

Wood, and she had not done it without some trepidation. However the girls were all away. Jane now never came to the house. By some tacit agreement Hampstead was accepted as her place of exile, and Aunt Ruth always visited her, not the other way round. She was certainly not forbidden the house; it was taken for granted, in the understood Vestrey way, that she should never come for fear of embarrassing the servants.

Emily was fulfilling the final duties in a hectic waiting. The French Emperor and his wife had just concluded a very successful State visit and Emily was exhausted. There had been a review of the Household troops at Windsor, a ball, a visit to the opera, Fidelio, a spectacle at the new Crystal Palace at Sydenham and numerous luncheons and parties. More solemnly there had been at least two Councils of War and the Emperor had been invested with the Garter. The Queen was very much taken by the Empress, apparently, and thought her very beautiful. Everyone was concerned about the Emperor's threat to go out and conduct the war in the Crimea in person. Those who knew him considered his interference with the plans of his generals on the spot bad enough. The French had several times failed to back up English initiatives, and Lord Raglan was furious with Canrobert and Pélessier, the French generals.

Lord Raglan's detachment and *sang froid* were legendary; nothing ever ruffled him. But the French were proving very tiresome, and the last thing he wanted on the field was the nephew of the Great Napoleon telling everyone what to do.

Emily was due home the following day, or the day after depending on whether she had to go with the French Court to Dover or stay behind with the Queen. George had been begging Aunt Ruth to invite Hilary to the house for some time. It was the final mark of acceptance that was so important to Hilary, seeing that the rest of the family was forbidden her.

Aunt Ruth had grown very fond of Hilary. She was certainly not the mild little governess of two years ago; she had blossomed and developed into a real lady. If she had had her way, Aunt Ruth suspected that she could become very grand indeed. But she was good for George; she kept him in order and gave him an anchor in his life, now that Agnes was so hopeless in this peculiar attachment to Mrs Chetwynd which no one quite understood, and certainly never discussed, and all the grown-up children were away from home.

George often slept at the house in St John's Wood quite openly, as long as none of the children were at Park Street, and kept changes of clothing there, instead of having to skulk back in the small hours of the morning. He was delighted with his new family, the sweet baby, Hilary's care and devotion to him. The whole thing, though not admirable, was in the circumstances very suitable. The best thing for George, so long as no-one ever got to hear about it.

George had settled down quite happily with Lord Palmerston, who, as the Queen had feared, had succeeded the unpopular Lord Aberdeen in February. He had accompanied Lord John Russell to the Peace Conference in Vienna that had begun in March where his long experience of the war, his mastery of the intricacies of the Four Points put forward by the allies as being necessary for peace, were appreciated.

Aunt Ruth heard a commotion in the hall and, hearing the sound of a baby crying, went quickly to the door just as it was opened by Cornwall.

'Mrs Ashburne is here ma'am,' he said impassively. 'She has an infant with her and a maid.'

'That is her nephew, Cornwall,' Aunt Ruth said, equally impassively. 'Pray ask Mrs Ashburne to come in and take her maid to the servants' hall and see that she has tea.'

Cornwall bowed but, in order to make her feel at ease, Aunt Ruth went into the hall, her arms extended.

'Hilary my dear, I am so glad you could come. And how is dear little Henry?'

Aunt Ruth seized his chubby cheeks between her fingers and gave them an affectionate pinch. Immediately he stopped crying at the unfamiliar surroundings and gurgled with delight.

'He knows me! You see? He knows me.'

'Of course he does, Miss Vestrey,' Hilary said, gliding into the parlour and beckoning to the nursemaid to follow.

'I wondered if Barnes would like to take tea in the ser-

vants' hall,' Miss Vestrey murmured, 'and we can be together with Henry. George may be here soon,' she said *sotto
voce.*

Hilary nodded. 'What an excellent idea, Miss Vestrey.
Barnes, pray go to the servants' hall with the butler and give
Master Henry to me.'

The nurse tenderly put her charge into his mother's arms
and meekly followed Cornwall to the door.

'I will send tea up directly, madam,' he said, closing the
door.

'Now let me hold him,' Aunt Ruth said putting out her
hands. 'Oh, he is such a darling, a lovely, cuddly baby.' She
took him and cradled his head against hers.

The likeness was there too, Hilary thought complacently;
the large Vestrey nose, the dark curly hair of which Henry
now had an abundance, the lofty forehead. She looked about
her, thinking back to two years before when she had been a
sort of unpaid domestic to Miss Vestrey. How things had
changed for the better, despite everything. Oh, so *much* for
the better. She removed her gloves and shawl and, unbidden,
sat in the large comfortable chair by the window.

'What mild weather we are having, Miss Vestrey. I was
quite hot in the coach.' She waved her hand back and forwards across her face and pretended to be short of air. She
now had her own small brougham, bought for her by George
and stabled in the mews behind her house where George
kept a spare horse, and she kept one too for riding in the
park.

She did look very lovely, Aunt Ruth thought, cuddling the
baby who was now almost too heavy for her to carry comfortably. The crinoline was at the height of fashion and
Hilary's was so large that as she sat down it extended in
front of her like a vast cage. The material was of flowered
moiré silk and she wore a little *gilet,* or waistcoat, which
was considered extremely in vogue if rather fast, with her
jacket bodice open over it. The *gilet* was closely shaped to
her figure and accentuated her very trim waist, her firm full
bust. Her bonnet was of the same stuff as her dress, and was
worn slightly back on the head to show her careful coiffeur
which was secured on top by a velvet bandeau to prevent

the bonnet slipping off. The inside of the brim was trimmed with tulle, and a small bunch of artificial spring flowers peeped coyly from the underside, just by her right ear.

Aunt Ruth was glad to see that Hilary wore little make-up and there was just the trace of a smell of lavender water as she had come into the room. Hilary had to be careful about her appearance; too much make-up, strong perfume and a flamboyant style of dress were not the marks of a lady. In her position she had to be very careful not to look like the kept woman she was. It would not have suited George at all.

'You look exquisite, my dear,' Aunt Ruth said approvingly.

'Did you say Lord Vestrey would be here?' In his aunt's presence Hilary always referred to her nephew by his title and never by his Christian name.

'He *hopes* to be home soon. Something to do with the Emperor's visit. He was so anxious for you and Henry to call.'

'I know.'

Hilary gazed at Aunt Ruth with a very slight smile. George had wanted to welcome his son in his house, but she knew Aunt Ruth had opposed it just as, for so long, she had refused to see her – even when she was the one who had introduced her to George! But Hilary had learnt no longer to care very much about this kind of thing. She knew what sort of people the Vestreys were; they were aristocrats and they were snobs. But you did not get their support by fighting them; nor by lying down and letting them walk all over you. You had to find some middle way, and she felt she had achieved just that. As she tried very hard to get her dress and appearance just right, she did the same with her manner. In a way it was a question of strategy, and she knew she had won.

And Henry had been such a blessing; such a useful ally in the campaign, if you could call it that. His aunt adored him.

Two maids and a footman came in bearing the tea things, supervised by Cornwall. There was Indian and China tea, cucumber, egg and tomato sandwiches, little jellies, fairy cakes and a plate of cold ham which George rather enjoyed if he came home in time.

Hilary leaned back and admired the Vestrey china and silver, the delicate lace cloth on the tea table, the particular attention that had been paid to every tiny detail. She was emulating this style in her own home. She bought a lot of good china and silver; she was becoming an expert in porcelain. She was beginning to appreciate painting and had purchased a few water colours which George admired.

Henry sat on Aunt Ruth's lap beaming, two big teeth showing when he smiled. He wore the shawl which Aunt Ruth had given him for his christening which had taken place quietly in St John's Wood Church just before Christmas, Aunt Ruth and Benson standing as godparents. This part George had not enjoyed. He wanted everyone to know about his son. But it was just not possible; not yet. As it was he had wished his youngest, and most disadvantaged, son to bear his grandfather's name – Henry. Thus his first three names firmly linked him to the family from which he was divided by the bar sinister. One day, George hoped, he would be accepted into it; but as yet he did not know how or when.

'Hilary,' Aunt Ruth said after a lot of inconsequential chat about the weather, the war and Henry's progress, 'there is a delicate little matter I wish to speak to you about.'

Hilary looked at Aunt Ruth just as she was putting a dainty fairy cake covered with white icing to her lips. The expression of acute embarrassment on Aunt Ruth's face alarmed her.

'Yes, Miss Vestrey?' She put the cake down on the Minton plate aware that the palms of her hands were perspiring. She wiped them on a white napkin with a big 'V' stitched in the corner.

'It is not the sort of thing ladies discuss, I know; but it is important . . . for Jane. I have Jane in mind.'

'*Jane?*' Hilary couldn't think what on earth Aunt Ruth was leading up to. She hoped that she was not going to start comparing her position with that of poor Jane's. Because of the similarity of the situation Jane, in fact, was carefully never, or seldom, mentioned between them.

'Well . . . I do not know how to put this,' Aunt Ruth floundered on. 'But . . . well I do not think, in her situation,

Jane, whatever her intention, should have more children. I mean Daniel, though to all intents and purposes a good father, is *not* suitable. I mean we do not want her, them, that is *I* do not want them, to have more children. You see that, don't you?'

Aunt Ruth's powdered, creamy, puckered face was very red by now. 'But how can I help in that, Miss Vestrey?' Hilary's tone had risen a little to indicate that Aunt Ruth was on dangerous ground. Very dangerous.

'I wondered about birth control.' Aunt Ruth dropped her voice to a whisper. 'I hear it does exist. And you . . .'

Hilary lifted her chin and wondered whether to be insulted or not. It was certainly *not* the sort of subject she expected to hear mentioned by a maiden lady not in the first flush of youth. But Aunt Ruth had obviously distressed herself considerably by mentioning it. It would not do to cut her.

Hilary reached for her reticule and took from it a small gold pad to which was attached a tiny pencil. Opening the pad she wrote for a moment on a piece of paper which she tore out, folded and handed to Aunt Ruth with a conspiratorial smile.

'I know exactly what you are trying to say, Miss Vestrey, and I appreciate your delicacy and concern. I think if you mention the name of this doctor to Jane you will find he can be of help. He is a very esteemed gynaecologist with a house in Welbeck Street. Jane could do no better than consult him.'

'Oh *thank* you, my dear,' Aunt Ruth said tucking the piece of paper in her bosom. What a saint Hilary was to be so understanding. What a perfect treasure George had in her.

The Queen, having perceived how tired dear Emily was, urged her to go home the moment the Imperial guests left for Dover and before the Court returned to Windsor. A few days at Chetwell was just what she needed, she advised. Emily was inclined to agree. Talking French all the time was exhausting, and one had always to be on show. But it had been fascinating and, once again, Sir Arthur was in waiting with her and she had plenty of time to admire how handsome and distinguished he looked in his elegant uniform of a Colonel in the Eighth Hussars. She was almost able to forget that he had a son who was older than she was.

Once again Emily drove to Park Street, accompanied by her maid, in one of the Queen's landaus. It was a warm afternoon and she was very tired, longing for tea. But she was excited and nervous, eager for an intimate chat with Aunt Ruth, desperate for advice.

She got quickly out of the carriage and ran up the stairs. The door was immediately opened by Cornwall who looked surprised.

'Why, Miss Emily, you were not expected until tomorrow or the day after.'

'The Queen has dispensed with me, Cornwall!' Emily hurriedly began untying her bonnet. 'I had to do the lion's share of talking French. *Parlez vous français*, Cornwall?'

Emily threw back her head and laughed and then, listening, became very quiet.

'Are there guests, Cornwall?'

'Er, Mrs Ashburne, Miss Emily . . . and her nephew.'

'Nephew? She has a nephew? My goodness, we haven't seen her for years. How does she come to be here?'

'I am sure Miss Vestrey will inform you, Miss Emily,' Cornwall said discreetly, being particularly friendly with Matthew the coachman and groom. He marched solemnly ahead and threw open the door of the parlour announcing Emily in a loud, clear voice.

At first Emily was quite sure that Cornwall was in error. The Mrs Ashburne she remembered, the dowdy little governess in a grey frock with white collar and cuffs, was no-one like this fine lady dressed in the latest mode, in one of the enormous crinolines, who sat before her with such an air of ease and elegance, obviously accustomed to style. But the lady looked at her with every appearance of recognizing her, though she did not get up but held out her hand, accompanying the action with a smile of great charm.

'How nice to see you again, Miss Emily. I doubt that you remember me.'

Emily shook her hand and looked into her eyes. The eyes had always been very fine, she remembered, a dark sapphire blue, clear and bright. Yes, it was Mrs Ashburne. How extraordinary. Aunt had said she had come into some sort of legacy.

'I do remember you, Mrs Ashburne, of course. How do you do? I am pleased to see you looking so well.'

'And you, Miss Emily. I hear you are a great favourite with Her Majesty.'

Mrs Ashburne's voice was the same, low and warm and well modulated. She always used to say the right thing, Emily remembered; only her manner had changed. It was no longer deferential, almost obsequious, as one expected from a sort of honourable family retainer as she then was. It was assured and there was a resonance, a *timbre* that was not there before. She felt Mrs Ashburne must have come into a very considerable fortune indeed to have changed so much.

Aunt Ruth had her arm about the baby and was feeding it rusks dipped in a bowl of warm milk. Her arm was very tight round the baby as though she were clutching something very precious and, for a moment, in her confusion, Emily wondered who the baby could possibly be. She looked at the baby and was reminded very much of Clare when she was tiny. How peculiar.

'Is *this* your nephew, Mrs Ashburne?'

For a moment Aunt Ruth and Mrs Ashburne looked at each other, just a glance, but Emily caught it. She thought they looked rather uneasy, and she suddenly began to feel uncomfortable. 'I'm sorry, have I said something wrong?'

'No dear, of course not. You were simply unexpected. Pray sit down and I will ring for fresh tea.' Aunt Ruth rapidly retrieved the situation and, handing Henry to his mother, briskly went to the fireplace and rang the bell. She felt some movement was necessary to enable her to recover her emotions which had undergone a violent jolt.

Once with his mother little Henry began to howl and reached out for Aunt Ruth to come back, banging his little fists angrily against his side. Emily smiled.

'He is very taken with *you*, Aunt Ruth. What is his name, Mrs Ashburne?'

'Henry, Miss Emily. Henry George.'

'He *is* a darling.' Emily leaned over and took a tiny wrist that was still waving angrily about. Henry stopped crying and his large dark eyes gazed into Emily's. Emily was still amazed at the family likeness, or rather, the resemblance to Clare who was the only dark Vestrey baby she remembered at all well. 'How old is he?'

'He was born last May, Miss Emily. He is nearly a year old.'

'And have you borrowed him for the afternoon?'

'Oh no. I have adopted him. He lives with me. My sister died giving birth to him. He is now my sole relation.'

For a moment Mrs Ashburne looked a little tearful and Emily felt a pang.

'How sad. I am so sorry to hear that. I must confess I had the impression that you were completely alone in the world. I do not recall mention of a sister; but then I did not know you well. Please accept my condolences in your bereavement.'

'Thank you, Miss Emily.'

For a moment Mrs Ashburne's voice assumed the docile note Emily remembered and the expression, as she dropped her eyes, was momentarily of humble submissiveness too. Then she smiled and brightened as Aunt Ruth came back and offered Henry more rusks, but not taking him on her knee this time.

'Now tell us *all* about the Royal visit,' Aunt Ruth commanded and Emily, though tired, revived as she had her tea and complied. She began with the arrival of the Emperor's yacht in fog-bound Dover and ended that morning when she had taken leave of the Empress Eugenie, who had presented her with a pretty brooch studded with diamonds which surrounded her likeness.

Aunt Ruth and Mrs Ashburne were examining it with rapture when George's voice was heard booming in the hall and everyone looked up.

'Oh Papa! Good. I am *dying* to see him.'

Emily got up and ran to the door; but George had reached it before her and, as he came in, she saw how his eyes flew to Hilary and the look on his face was soft and welcoming. Only then did his eyes drop to her and his expression altered from pleasure, almost rapture, to stupefaction. He did not seem pleased to see her at all.

'Emily! Why are you here?'

Emily's smile vanished and she stared at her father.

'Are you not pleased to see me, Papa?'

George cleared his throat and bent to kiss his daughter. 'Of course, my love. But it is unexpected. 'Twas a surprise.'

'But is it not a surprise too, to see Mrs Ashburne? She has not been here for two years.'

Emily turned and gazed at Mrs Ashburne who sat holding her nephew, her cheeks a little flushed, her eyes brilliant with something that looked like tears, or could have been amusement or consternation. It was difficult to tell. They sparkled, anyway, as they looked at George and, almost involuntarily, her lips had parted in a smile.

In that instant Emily's eyes went from her father to Mrs Ashburne and lingered on little Henry George, the baby nephew. She saw the expression in the baby's face, the way his arms went out to George, the two big teeth which appeared in the gurgle of delighted recognition. Then she knew.

'Excuse me, Papa,' she said, her eyes filling with tears, and she hurried past him, along the hall and up the stairs to her room.

George gazed after his daughter, then closed the door. For a moment no-one spoke.

'How unfortunate,' Aunt Ruth murmured, wishing she had her smelling salts to hand. But who could have anticipated that *sal volatile* would be called for on such a delightful, long planned for, occasion?

George came over to Hilary and kissed the top of her head, a gesture Aunt Ruth found more expressive of affection than any lingering embrace. He took little Henry in his arms and kissed him on both cheeks; then he gave him tenderly back to his mother.

'Tea, George? I have your plate of cold ham ready.'

'I think I will have something a little stronger, thank you, Aunt Ruth. I had a gruelling day – Lord John threatens resignation again because of the Third Point which it is felt he bungled – and now I have a family crisis on my hands.'

'You think she knows?' Hilary said, soothing little Henry

who wanted to be with his father. He always made a great fuss whenever George appeared.

George shrugged and went over to summon Cornwall. 'Emily is a most intelligent girl. She would not miss much. It was so unexpected to see her. At first I only saw you.'

'I must go up to her,' Aunt Ruth said. 'I will go in a moment so that it does not appear too obvious. If she has not guessed I may be able to soothe her.'

'And if she has?' George took his accustomed place in front of the fire, his hands beneath his coat tails.

'Then I must decide what to do. Emily has her own crisis, you know. I think she wanted to talk to you about that.'

'Sir Arthur?'

'Yes.'

'You think she will marry the fellow?'

'I think she wants to ask you.'

George looked at the ceiling as Cornwall came in. He asked for the decanter of whisky and some water and waited until the butler had withdrawn.

'I *like* the fellow well enough. I saw a good deal of him during the State visit. He was very civil to me. But I cannot get over the fact he is *older* than I am – and he wants to marry *my* daughter. I don't like it. I don't know why, but I don't.'

Hilary had tried to soothe George on this point already. They had discussed it ever since Aunt Ruth had mentioned the subject weeks ago. Sir Arthur had not declared himself, but his intentions were rather transparent. Hilary knew that George was jealous, maybe envious; but she couldn't tell him that. He had a natural repugnance that a very much older man, one with a grown-up family, should wish to marry his daughter, take her to his bed. That was the truth of the matter. There were all sorts of things Hilary understood, but which she could not say to George.

'See what Emily has to say first,' she said sensibly. 'She may have decided against him. She wants Rawdon Foxton, you know, and as he . . .'

George leapt out of the chair he had taken and fumbled in his pocket for a letter.

'Oh, *that* is the very news I had to tell you! Caroline and

Rawdon have definitely decided to marry in the autumn. Even if the war is not finished they will ask for leave and come home. Rawdon, as you know, wanted to marry in Turkey, but Caroline wishes it to be in the bosom of her family.' George scanned the letter rapidly. 'They are very happy. Caroline is to go up to the Crimea with Florence, so they will see each other again. Caroline writes that for a time she doubted her intention to marry Rawdon; but now she knows that she loves him without any doubt.

'He stayed in and around Constantinople for some weeks. They had much time together; time to talk and be with each other.' George glanced at Aunt Ruth. 'Alas, I daresay unchaperoned; but with a daughter a nurse what can one say?'

Aunt Ruth shrugged her shoulders sympathetically. 'Dear George, in these hard times of war and chaos you must expect anything. I am sure however that where Rawdon and Caroline are concerned nothing *unseemly* would have occurred.'

'Oh good gracious no.' George looked horrified. 'No such thought ever entered my mind, but still it is *not* the thing for young unmarried people to be thrown on their own. It leads to talk. People might think little enough of my daughter for being a nurse, and we know what reputations for immorality nurses have.'

'Oh, but not one of *Miss Nightingale's* nurses,' Hilary said primly. 'I think one can be quite sure of that.'

George waved the letter around. 'Anyway, good news at last eh? A wedding in the autumn. Certainly *one* wedding at least, of which I approve.'

'I am pleased for you, George,' Hilary said. 'Very pleased.' She cradled little Henry who began to show signs of going to sleep. She looked at George and felt very secure, nursing his child in her arms.

Sometimes she felt almost like a Vestrey, one of the family. She was consulted about intimate family matters and, now, here she was, at Park Street, the family home. And Henry with his confident, sunny affability, seemed at home here too.

Emily had heard the rumour that her father had been seen

in Vienna and Paris with a beautiful blonde woman. She was supposed to be an Austrian Countess or a French Princess. No-one quite knew. She was a woman of mystery. Sir Arthur had told her, when he had heard it from some diplomatic source, to try and spare her feelings; but she didn't believe it and laughed it off, and Sir Arthur had never mentioned it again.

It was ridiculous to think that Papa had a mistress, as Sir Arthur said the rumour insinuated. She, of all people, knew what a devoted family man he was despite Mama's illness. She was prepared to believe that he was attractive to pretty women and that he danced with them. Of course; being a diplomat he could hardly help it. But that he had a mistress? Papa? No!

But that moment in the parlour, looking from Papa to Mrs Ashburne, the picture suddenly fitted. Never in a thousand years, when Hilary was the ex-governess charity case helped by Aunt Ruth, would she have called her beautiful. She was completely unmemorable, and Emily had quickly forgotten her. But now seeing her so elegantly dressed, so assured and distinguished-looking, she saw how people, who did not know her, could have assumed she was of the foreign nobility. The frame also fitted perfectly.

And then there was the baby who had looked so like Clare. Of course he looked like Papa too, and Jane and Caroline. All the dark Vestreys resembled one another and they all had that rather prominent nose with the flared nostrils. Thank goodness she had not inherited it; but those who resembled Mama had not. It was just the dark Vestreys with the big noses who all looked alike, and baby Henry was undoubtedly a Vestrey. And, besides, there were the names – Henry for Grandpapa and George for Papa. How perfidious it all seemed; how wrong from a man like Papa who had taught them such high standards.

Emily wet her pillow with tears before Aunt Ruth stole softly into her room. Aunt Ruth had decided to let her work it out and compose herself before she came. She was also anxious to have George and Hilary out of the house and told George to take Hilary home. But he should come back to break the news about Rawdon and Caroline to Emily.

Poor Emily. It was a very bad day for her. One couldn't help feeling sorry for people who were used to having things going right for them, as Emily was, when they suddenly went wrong. You didn't think they deserved it, because one of the reasons their lives were uncomplicated was that they had planned them that way. Even if it made them rigid, as it did Emily who was so unkind to Jane, Emily's world did not permit of chaos and disorder, and so they hardly ever entered it. Now things were hopelessly wrong and yet none of it was her fault.

As she climbed the stairs towards Emily's room she also wondered what the effect on the family would be if Emily had guessed, as she was sure to have done. It was a pity, in a way, that darling Henry, even at eleven months, was so obviously a Vestrey. She had been very foolish to ask them to the house.

But it was all too late now.

Aunt Ruth sat by the still figure that was Emily and for a while neither spoke.

'Are you asleep?' Aunt Ruth whispered at last.

'No.'

'Can you tell me what is the matter?' Aunt Ruth paused and then said, hopefully, 'Is it Sir Arthur?'

'No.'

Aunt Ruth's brief hope faded and she felt a little afraid of what she was going to say.

'Are things well with Sir Arthur?' she ventured.

Emily propped herself up on her elbow and Aunt Ruth saw the extent of her weeping, the ravaged cheeks, the burning tear-filled eyes.

'Aunt Ruth you know quite well what is the matter! It is Papa . . . and . . . *her*!' Emily threw herself back on the bed and the weeping started again.

Aunt Ruth moved her chair a little nearer and reached for one of Emily's hands. 'Did you only know today?'

'Of course! When I saw how he looked at her, and she at him . . . and the . . . b-b . . . baby.' Emily went on crying, rhythmically squeezing Aunt Ruth's hand until it was wet too, and felt rather mangled. Aunt Ruth did not know what to say. 'I mind more about the baby than anything!'

'Of course.' Aunt Ruth murmured.

'It is a betrayal of Mama . . . and us! It is terrible!'

'I don't see how it *betrays* anyone,' Aunt Ruth said at last. 'He is a dear little baby and quite blameless and innocent in the sight of God. If anything is in question it is why humans behave in this way, and I do not quite know the answer to that. It causes much suffering. Hilary has suffered quite a lot over it and I suppose in time Henry will suffer too.'

'Serve her right!'

'Oh Emily, don't say that.' Aunt Ruth withdrew her hand. 'It was your father who was most persistent, and he is a very attractive man. She had nothing, no-one.'

'Don't I know it! Adventuress!'

In the face of Emily's obduracy, which she had quite expected, there seemed so little that one could say.

'You could, if you like, blame your mother,' she said gently, 'for refusing your father. A man must have a normal . . .' Aunt Ruth floundered. 'I don't quite know how to put it. But these things are not unknown, alas. I am told they are quite common.'

'What things?'

'Affairs between grown-up people. You have to accept them, Emily. They are part of life.'

'I don't accept them,' Emily said. 'I don't have to and I am not going to. Nothing like this ever goes on at Court, I can tell you. But our family seems to be addicted to them. It is disgraceful. But what I mind most about Papa is choosing *her.* She is no-one. Ha! The rumour was that he had an Austrian baroness as a mistress. He was seen dancing constantly with her in Vienna, and all the time it was *her,* the little governess. I think I would mind less about a mysterious foreign aristocrat. It would suit Papa's style.'

'Oh, there *was* a rumour?'

'Sir Arthur heard it and wanted to spare me in case I did. Of course I didn't believe it; but *her* . . .'

'She is very nice,' Aunt Ruth said mildly. 'She is discreet and has done your father a lot of good. He has not had a happy time either with your Mama and Jane, and . . .' But Aunt Ruth did not dare mention Caroline. She had suspected all along that what made Emily hesitate about Sir

Arthur, apart from his age, was the hope that when Rawdon came home it might be to her. Goodness knew what Emily would say when she heard the news.

She was very glad she was not to be the one to tell her about that.

CHAPTER THIRTY-THREE

An almost carnival-like atmosphere pervaded the scene of the Crimean campaign with the approach of summer. The weather grew warmer, the mud cleared – despite bouts of torrential rain which was characteristic of that unpredictable climate – vegetation and delightful species of flora flourished, and the army grew in health and strength.

Civilians flocked from England to visit their relatives camped on the plain before Sebastopol, and Lord Ward's steam yacht plied backwards and forwards across the Black Sea, flags waving merrily, carrying distinguished passengers who came to gawp at the war.

For, despite everything, the war did continue. It grew even more bitter as each side faced stalemate, thanks to their mutual endurance and the genius of Todleben in repairing the ravages that the allied guns made in his trenches and on his redoubts. Nightly, officers and men on both sides were killed in the trenches and sometimes there was intense hand to hand fighting in skirmishes.

But on the whole, the visitors regarded the war as an extension of the English love of good sport. If a battle were expected the following day news got round. Accordingly the spectators went to bed after a good dinner, rose early and galloped to the front to take up prominent, but safe, positions behind the line of fire, peering earnestly through their field glasses.

On 9 April the second bombardment of Sebastopol began and went on for ten days with heavy casualties, mostly on the Russian side. But bickering among the senior allied officers continued and Canrobert was continually harassed by Imperial edicts from Paris which grew more frequent when the telegraph from Varna to the Crimean headquarters was completed, thus giving France a direct link with the front.

Rawdon Foxton arrived back in the Crimea to find his

camp had moved to Balaklava and consisted of comfortable huts set in a lovely spot overlooking the sea. With him came Polly and Mr and Mrs Drinkwater and their two daughters, who had come to visit their son Captain Robert Drinkwater of the Fifth Dragoon Guards camped at Kidoki near Balaklava. But Caroline stayed behind; she was to come up with Florence at the beginning of May.

As soon as Polly knew that Rawdon had completed his hospital tour she begged to be allowed to go to the Crimea with him. She had been ill again and Lady Alicia was very anxious for her to have a change of scene. Caroline reluctantly consented. She felt that Polly was in her care and that she was responsible for her. But with Rawdon and Lady Alicia pleading for her to be allowed to go, and the Drinkwaters offering to chaperone her Caroline felt she had to give in. Besides, things were so much better.

The Sanitary Commission had started its work and found that the Barrack Hospital was built on sewers and cesspools and that the water supply for most of the hospital had been flowing through the carcass of a dead horse; the porous walls were soaked with filth and blew poisonous gases through the pipes of open privies to the wards and corridors which housed the sick and dying. They set to work at once putting cleansing operations into effect and the mortality rate immediately began to fall.

Also in March Alexis Soyer, chef of the Reform Club, had arrived at his own expense at Scutari and promptly set about reforming the kitchens and the diet of the men. He demonstrated how nutritious cooking was possible on a large scale using makeshift equipment, and even invited the British Ambassador and his wife to a gourmet meal cooked from army rations.

All these improvements, these changes for the better seemed to Caroline coincidental with the arrival of Rawdon. To him she attributed her own new uplift in spirits, her feeling of wellbeing, despite chronic tiredness and a poor diet. It was sufficient to know that she was loved and that she loved in return.

Caroline's happiness informed her whole being. It cheered the men in the hospital where she went dutifully every day, working long hours. No-one talked about it and it was never mentioned to Miss Nightingale – Caroline was not ready to break the news to her yet – but it was there, like an aura, for everyone to see.

Only Polly gave cause for concern and then, when it was time for Rawdon to go back, it was agreed she would go with him and take advantage of the sea journey and the benefit of the freshness and beauty of the Crimean spring. Soon, it was said, they would all meet again and then they would be together with James and Oliver. Caroline could hardly wait for the family reunion to take place. People said the war could not possibly last throughout the summer now that the troops were being re-equipped and reinforced. By the autumn, please God, they would all be home, safe and sound and preparing for a wedding at Chetwell Parish Church. Maybe two weddings: Caroline saw her cousin off knowing how much she wanted James but knowing, too, how fickle James was, how loving towards all women rather than one.

James thoroughly approved of the Brigade's move to Balaklava where he had a large hut with a beautiful view of the bay, plenty of room for the trophies he had collected, which included a large well padded armchair, and good stabling for his horses nearby. He would put his armchair out in the sun and doze, a bottle of wine by his side, his hat pulled over his eyes so that he could just see the beautiful bay beneath and the old castle ahead of him.

The bay at Balaklava was being cleansed by the Sanitary Commission of all the putrid flotsam and jetsam which floated upon it – the bloated carcasses of horses, the human remains of those who had died and been buried at sea, the excreta and effluence of drains which poured into it, to say nothing of the normal tons of rubbish tipped into it by all and sundry. The stench was so awful that frequently those working to clean it fainted. But here, well away from the smell, it looked very beautiful with the plethora of tall masted ships and yachts which crowded together, like a small colourful armada about to set sail, and the little sailing boats at anchor by the side.

Now Balaklava was once more a bustling, busy, prosperous little port, its streets clean, its inhabitants thriving and well fed, its shops bursting with provisions which the troops could now afford to buy. A Macadamed road was being built to provide yet another link between Balaklava and the front, and every day the railway was busy transporting guns and ammunition with which, finally, to defeat the enemy.

The trouble was that Sebastopol had never really been besieged, in the sense that it was surrounded and completely cut off. Russian supplies and troops continued to pour in through the northern and eastern approaches which were ineffectively controlled by the allies, and there was also access by sea. Those who had thought from the beginning that to besiege Sebastopol was impossible were being proved right; but there were also those who were still determined it should be taken, despite the tremendous loss of life and the seemingly interminable nature of the campaign. It was felt that the French and British Empires were at stake by some, mostly at home and away from the horrors, and by others that they had been there too long to give up. If they left now all the sacrifice would be in vain.

But James, like everyone else, speculated when that day might be. He sank further into his chair, the sound of bees buzzing about the crocuses and hyacinths in his little patch of garden lovingly tended by his servant, and half fell asleep. The sound of horses thudding up to his hut jolted him wide awake and he sprang up with the innate fear of a man who knows that the possibility of attack was always there. Cossacks often made foolhardy forages into the camps for the purposes of plunder and killing, no matter what the cost of them.

But this was no Cossack army. Three people came to a halt by his hut. Two men and a woman.

A woman. No, a lady. James stared at her and thought at that moment, on the hills above Balaklava with the sun scorching down, that she must be the answer to prayer. For that instant she seemed to him to embody everything that he most treasured in his heart about English womanhood — she was fair, petite, elegant with a good seat on a horse. Her riding habit was of a dark blue cloth with a close corsage buttoning up the front and a long plain skirt which permitted just the lower part of her boots with their smart military heels to be seen. Her sleeves had broad cuffs and her gloved hands held a short riding crop. On her very fair curly hair was a smart black beaver hat with a veil which half covered her face. As she reined and halted she thrust up her chin and looked at him with a challenging, yet almost fearful smile.

A vision. He put his hands to his eyes to keep out the glare and perceived, under the mesh of the veil, the large violet eyes, the pale skin and, below, the pretty bow shaped mouth.

'Polly,' he murmured unbelievingly. 'Polly Tangent.' He took his pipe out of his mouth and went over and stood by her horse gazing up at her. 'Who would have thought it?'

'Thought what, James?' She held out a hand and the smile grew more confident as she saw the approval in his eyes.

'I thought you were a vision.'

'Then you are disappointed?'

'Not at all.'

He reached up and helped her down while Rawdon and his brother Oliver dismounted and handed their horses over to James's servant who had come running.

'You look a sight I must say, James,' was Rawdon's first laconic greeting.

And indeed James looked like some caricature of the mad Englishman abroad with a turban wound about his broad-rimmed hat and flapping at the back, a pair of French Zouave trousers very loose at the bottom, a Cossack jacket which was one of his trophies of war, bound round by a large sash which he had been given by a French brother officer after a roisterous night out. On his feet, which were otherwise bare, were comfortable Turkish slippers with pointed toes. He wore several days' growth of beard and his hair had grown very blond in the sun.

But to Polly he looked marvellous. The most beautiful, most handsome man alive, tall, well over six feet and broad. The war had made him more muscular, as well as putting lines on his face and, for the first time, she observed the thick hair on his chest under his half-open Cossack jacket.

'Is this what an officer in the Guards wears on parade?' she said laughingly, but still embarrassed because of those appraising eyes of his which never left her face. She lowered her head and was thankful for the heat to hide her blushes.

'It *is* Polly,' James said again almost to himself.

'Of course it is Polly!' Oliver said impatiently, 'and give us something to drink for God's sake as we are all parched with thirst.'

'Hooper!' James roared. 'When you have finished with the horses will you fetch some more wine for my guests from our secret store.'

James winked. 'Hooper has constructed a cellar for me which is the envy of the Brigade. We have to mount an extra guard at night to defend it, and my life is thought to be in danger.'

James chuckled and Polly's susceptible heart turned over. How often across the years had she heard that deep, throaty chuckle which had started, even when he was a boy in the schoolroom, to fascinate her. Blond, arrogant cousin James, always ragging her like his sisters and at parties going after the girls but never her. She was too familiar to him; she was family.

For Polly Tangent, the eldest daughter of the Rectory, life had never been very easy in the shadow of the beautiful Vestreys – the clever, attractive Vestreys with their abundance of talk and striking good looks. If the Tangents had, as a family, a disadvantage apart from being poor it was that they were on the whole rather on the small side; neither their mother nor father were tall. Dalton was the exception being tall and thin; but Polly was tiny. She felt her height prevented her from being attractive to men and that was why she dressed carefully and when she could, like today, she wore high heels to make her taller.

What was more, whereas the Vestreys seemed to pulsate with life and energy and world-shaking things were always happening to them, nothing ever seemed to interfere with the day-to-day routine of the Rectory which had been the same now for many years. People were not always coming and going and doing interesting things as they were at the Big House – three of whose members had gone to the war, one to the Court and one to live in sin in a love nest in Hampstead. If all that was not eventful Polly wanted to know what was.

All that ever happened at home was that she had, after a great deal of persuasion, been allowed to go up to London for a few days to work at the Mission and Dalton had married into a family which, although very nice and amiable, did nothing to add lustre to the Tangent name. Not that this troubled Polly at all. She had her father's truly egalitarian principles and liked her sister-in-law and appreciated her good qualities, among which was an all-consuming love for Dalton. She was also pretty and lively and intent on making up for her lack of education; but somehow it was inevitable that a Tangent should marry a Ticehurst and not a Foxton or . . . a Vestrey. It was almost impossible to hope for that.

Until now. She had accepted James would greet her with his good-natured banter and then ignore her; but no. He was leading her to his special armchair and completely ignoring his brother and his close friend whom he hadn't seen for weeks.

But she must be careful. Caroline had tried to warn her about James, though it was difficult to put what she had wanted to say in so many words. But she hinted that Polly knew how James was, about women . . . it was no secret, and that he hadn't seen any respectable ones for a long time and . . . well, they both knew what Caroline meant. But Polly didn't dare hope that he would think of her in that way; or rather she hoped, but she was always disappointed because James didn't change.

James left them all to admire the view while he disappeared inside his hut and when he re-emerged fifteen minutes later it was to show a smooth chin, combed hair and a neat shirt tucked into well cut civilian trousers.

'There, even General Brown would approve of me now, I think.'

'He would not have before,' Rawdon said laughing. 'I think the presence of a lady is good for morale.'

'Indeed it is.' James lowered his voice and smiled at Polly.

'General Brown?' Polly said, once more to cover the confusion caused by that penetrating look.

'Sir George Brown!' James said, sitting down on a stool beside her. 'Commander of the Light Division and a stickler for smartness as well as an imbecile old bully. He was the only man to shave before the Battle of the Alma, his servant holding a mirror for him as the men began to ford the river. He wanted us all to keep smart whatever the circumstances.'

'No, I like Brown. He is brave,' Rawdon said, loosening his jacket. 'Goodness, it is hot. Well James, how have things been without me? Bring me up to date.'

James did so while Hooper brought two bottles of white wine in an ingenious cooler made out of a biscuit tin filled with cold water. The crystal glasses had been brought out by Oliver at James's request and had the Vestrey 'V' engraved on them, being part of the family collection. After so many months of deprivation and living hand to mouth, James was among the first to want to have the niceties of life restored. To him decent glass and plate were among these things as well as good food, wine and pleasant female company.

James glanced again at Polly. He had been very short of what anyone could call 'pleasant' female company for far too long. The brothels at Constantinople had answered a call of nature rather than appealing to any aesthetic part of a man's nature, and the nurses at the hospital were crude and always drunk.

The sight of Polly looking so fresh, elegant and very English induced in him a nostalgia for the ballrooms of London, the graciousness of society and good living. There was also, to his surprise, an erotic quality about her. He not only admired her for her civilizing qualities; he found her sensually attractive. He knew that he desired her, this companion of his schoolroom whom he had always put on a par with his sisters, whom, until she appeared over the brow of the hill on her horse, he had never really thought of as a woman.

He shifted uneasily on his stool, ashamed of his unabashedly carnal thoughts. It was very wrong of him to think like this about his cousin. He had been too long without women.

'When is Caroline coming up?' Oliver asked. For him Caroline was the beloved elder sister, the one who had always mothered him and looked after him while Mama was ill or tired or overburdened with one didn't quite know what. His childhood memories of his mother were very vague; but those of Caroline, five years his senior, were vivid. It was Caroline who came running and scooped you up and bathed a grazed knee or a cut arm; Caroline who rested your head in her lap when you were tired or fed up or did not want to go back to school.

And now Caroline was to be married. He had been rather shy of Rawdon that day when they had met by chance, just when he and Polly had alighted from the ship at Balaklava. Oliver had gone into the port to collect a box sent out from home. Rawdon was a very fine fellow and he was glad . . . but he was also a little jealous. Rawdon was going to take Caroline away from the family and, even though he was grown-up and a soldier, she was a warm, nostalgic part of his life which went back to the deep recesses of his infantile memories.

Oliver was enjoying the war. He loved the trenches and the sound of rifle shot and shell fire; he had already had several narrow escapes and had been warned by his commander about being foolhardy. His commander had even spoken to James about it and James had given him a dressing down. Oliver did not take enough care when under fire; and once or twice he had rushed out over the trenches towards the Russian lines in pursuit of a fleeing Cossack who had come too near.

'Caroline comes up with Miss Nightingale hopefully sometime in May,' Rawdon said, looking anxiously at James, having noted the dead set he had made at Polly. He half wished James had been able to go to Constantinople and satisfy his overpowering physical urges which Rawdon, thankfully, due to his lifetime habit of self-discipline, did not possess. Or rather he did, like any normal man, but he was happy to wait until marriage to Caroline gave him a right and proper release for them. Much as he loved James and admired him, he thought he was self-indulgent and that he had let his appetites get the better of him.

Marriage to Caroline. It was still difficult to think it was happening. They had written to her father and as soon as he approved it would be announced...and as soon as Miss Nightingale approved too, Rawdon thought ruefully. He was rather afraid of the effect of that awesome and determined lady on his beloved. If Caroline were not afraid of her, she certainly strongly *wished* for her approval and, in Rawdon's opinion, Miss Nightingale only approved of like-minded, dedicated, celibate people like herself. He recalled Eleanor Stanley, another of the Queen's maids-of-honour, telling his sister that Lady Canning had said that, despite Florence's 'quiet, rather stern manner she had an immense air of fun about her'. It was a quality that, in the very few times he had seen her, appeared conspicuously lacking. She looked tired, preoccupied and withdrawn – everyone said a shadow of her former self. Much as he admired her, he also feared her. He saw her undoubted influence on Caroline as a possible threat to their happiness.

'Lord Stratford is coming soon with his daughters the Misses Canning,' Rawdon continued. 'We shall have a merry party here.'

That night they dined with the Drinkwaters on the *Star of the South* in which they had arrived. Lord Rokeby was also there and some expected Lord Raglan, but he did not appear. He was known to be very annoyed with the French and to have called another meeting with General Canrobert. The men wore dress uniform and Polly a pink organdie crinoline with multiple flounces made of lace, and a tight-fitting bodice that came to a deep point at the waist back and front. Her *décolletage* was off the shoulder which revealed her smooth white breasts, so pushed up by her bodice as to appear very full at the top. It was trimmed with a silk bertha which dipped 'en coeur' and she wore no cap, but a small bunch of fresh Crimean flowers by her ear, and her curly hair was draped behind the ears and plaited at the back of her head to curb its unruliness.

James in the full uniform of the Grenadier Guards Officer thought she looked enchanting. He could scarcely take his eyes off her and those observing him, and who knew his reputation, were worried on Polly's account and those who didn't thought he must be hopelessly in love.

The following day the Drinkwaters went off to see their son and Rawdon went up to inspect the trenches with Oliver. James offered to escort Polly on a tour of the area, and they set off mid morning riding into the plain as far as the Woronzov Road where the lush pastureland and green fertile valleys reminded Polly of England. There was white may and mignonette, dog roses and larkspur and, as they cantered towards the Woronzov Heights Polly could hear the distant fire of guns and looked anxiously at James.

'Rawdon and Oliver are at the front.'

'Oh don't worry, they will take care of themselves.' James smiled at her, spurring his horse towards the Inkerman Ridge, and he showed her where the Russian battery had first opened fire in the grey light of dawn as their infantry stole towards them in the mist.

From the top of the hill they had a good view of the valleys and the ancient ruins of Inkerman. James re-enacted as much of the battle for her as he could, for it had been a terrible day with mist and rain and parts of his Brigade had become separated from the rest, each man fighting for his life.

As the sun rose high it became too warm and they turned their horses along the banks of the Chernaya River where they stopped to let them drink. Polly was hot in her habit and wished she could unbutton her corsage. James looked cool in a shirt and trousers, his wide-brimmed hat tipped over his face. It was suddenly very still in the valley, no sound of guns, just the call of birds and the noise of their horses greedily drinking.

'The war seems miles away now,' Polly said gazing at the river. She was aware of how near James was to her and as he put a hand on her shoulder she did not turn away but looked at him and faced him. Her heart was beating very fast. He was so tall that he loomed right over her and she went on nervously. 'It is terrible to think of the carnage of that day. The mist . . . It was before the terrible winter too. They say Lord Raglan only came late to the battle and . . .

'Do not let us talk about Raglan, Polly,' James said. 'He is a very dreary fellow.'

'Oh, I thought . . .'

But the expression of what she thought was lost, for his mouth touched hers and he grasped her under the arms and pulled her up to him. She felt suddenly faint and her head swam but, as she closed her eyes, she was overcome by a totally new and delicious feeling brought on by the proximity of his body, the insistent pressure of his lips against hers. She put her arms as far around him as she could and clung to him, letting him carry her where he would, sweep away her senses.

Slowly they sank on to the ground and, as he stretched alongside her, he gently unfastened her corsage and inserted a hand into her bosom.

'Oh James! ' She came rapidly to her senses and clasped his wrist. 'Please, no! '

'Sorry.' James gave her a guilty look and withdrew his hand, and then she was sorry for what she had done and she left her buttons unfastened.

'I know your reputation, James,' she went on, trying to be severe. 'I have been warned about you.'

James laughed and lay back, holding his hands behind his head. 'I promise you I will not do that again, Polly; so please don't be angry, and come out with me again.' He propped his head on his arm looking at her and noting that she had not fastened her buttons, and a rounded pink nipple was almost visible through the lace of her bodice. It was very tantalizing. He did not touch her again, but lay back to consider his strategy. He knew he must have her and he knew she wanted him; but he was her cousin and he was responsible for her. Women like Polly quite properly never lay with men until a wedding ring was firmly on their fingers . . . unless they were like his sister Jane.

'Did you see Jane before you came out? ' he said, putting

a blade of grass between his teeth. 'You know she had a baby daughter?'

'Yes. No, I didn't see her after she left Chetwell, and then of course I didn't know about . . .' She was silent. Much as Papa said he had compassion for her, he had also indicated that her name was not to be mentioned at the Rectory.

'And you disapprove, of course?'

'About Jane?' Polly looked at him. 'Well, I am sorry for her. Everyone says he is not a very nice man.'

'Though I knew him for a rogue, I rather liked him.'

'Oh? Did you? Why?'

'I thought him straight and uncomplicated. I do not disapprove of her and I am not sorry for her. They are doing what is natural to men and women . . .'

Polly suddenly felt nervous and got up, dusting her habit and rapidly doing up her buttons. 'James, I would like to go back. It is very hot here.'

'Of course.'

James got up and pulled back the horses from the river, helping Polly to mount hers, side-saddle. He caught a glimpse of a leg as she tucked it beneath her and the desire he had for her, for anyone, was almost unendurable. He tightened her stirrup and then strode slowly towards his horse.

On the way back they began to talk again, quite naturally as cousins and old friends, and he took her straight to her ship in the harbour before arranging to see her that night.

Every day from then on they cantered into the hills, once as far as the River Alma where the first battle of the war had been fought and where the Guards had distinguished themselves by maintaining perfect order, regardless of personal safety. Despite the fact that they had already been under heavy fire, they marched straight across the river and onwards in such a relentless manner, their line unbroken, that their enemy were completely nonplussed. However the Russian guns finally tore a great hole in the middle of their formation and Colonel Percy of the Grenadiers was told to retire.

'Retire?' he had said indignantly. 'What the devil can

they mean?' And instead the Guards reformed and began to fire with great accuracy into the Russian ranks, finally breaking them before the Great Redoubt.

As Polly listened to the account of the battle and heard how many officers and men had been killed her eyes filled with tears. Imagine, if James had been one of them and lay under the soil, or on Cathcart's Hill instead of standing alive and well here with her. He saw her weeping and stopped in consternation.

'What is it, my dear?'

'You might be dead,' she sobbed.

'Aye, and might be tomorrow too, or next week. We must live for today Polly.'

Polly suddenly stopped crying and looked at him. His expression was so resigned, so tender, so appealing. 'We must live for today.' What did that mean?

'But the war is nearly over!'

James shook his head. 'Oh no. It is not nearly over. Some think it has hardly begun. Come, my little one, or Mrs Drinkwater will think I have seduced you.'

He went over to her and began to lift her on to the horse. Since that first day he had never touched her other than to assist her off the horse or on, or at table or to dance with her in the evening very correctly. She had utterly rebuffed him, and he might have so little time to live. She looked at him as he took her arm, prepared to lift her clean onto the horse. As he was so big and she so small, he could lift her like a child. Instead, as he bent down she put her arms around him and caught him, bringing his mouth down to hers like that very first day.

'You can if you like,' she said.

Afterwards she wondered if he would despise her as men were said to do when a woman gave herself so freely. They lay on his bed in the hot little hut and the perspiration ran from their bodies soaking the blanket beneath them. She lay on her front because she still felt a sense of shame and he had half covered her with a sheet before falling asleep, one arm around her, the other flung down by the side of the bed. She had seen plenty of naked men in the wards of

547

Scutari, so a nude male was no shock to her. But one who had made love to her, whose body had penetrated hers, and who was clean and healthy and not covered with wounds and disease . . . she had never seen that before and she still looked at it half with shame and half with wonder, half wanting to look and half not.

She had unbraided her hair and lay on it on the pillow. It fell tangled and sticky on either side of her face. She felt very wanton, like a harlot. Surely only loose women, such as James was used to, behaved like this. It was nearly evening and the sky was growing dark.

'Little Polly,' he said suddenly and his hand ran over her back. 'Where are you?' He opened his eyes and saw her gazing at him, her face propped on her hand. She looked a little tearful. He stroked her cheek and smiled.

'Why do you look afraid?'

'Because . . .'

'Because what?'

'I think you will despise me.'

James sat up and pulled the sheet across the lower half of his body.

'But why should I despise you?'

'Because I know that men do. If a woman is . . . easy.'

James put an arm around her and pressed her tenderly to his damp, naked torso.

'I see; but I told you I did not despise Jane. Was what we did not beautiful? Did you not feel it? It is wonderful to make love, not shameful, and Jane has found that out.'

'I still think she should get married.'

There was a silence while a fly buzzed lazily against the small glass windowpane.

'But we can get married.'

Polly stared at him; but even in the gloom she could clearly see his face. It looked open and honest and truthful.

'Is it what you wish, James?'

'Of course. I *love* you, Polly. I loved you the very day you rode over the hill, and I love you more now. I want to marry you just as soon as we can. We shall have a double wedding in Chetwell Church, or sooner if you want.'

'Oh, James.'

She couldn't believe it; but he wasn't joking. She knew that he wouldn't be so cruel.

'Then what we have done isn't such a sin.'

'Did you think of it as one?'

'Yes. It is a sin; but if we are wed in spirit then it isn't.'

'But do you want to marry me?'

'Of course. I always have.'

'Well then. That's settled.'

James put a hand around her and caressed her breasts. But she didn't want to do it again. It had been painful and not really pleasant and very, very frightening.

But now that she knew he loved her and wanted to marry her, maybe it would get better.

Every day, or nearly every day, they made love in the hut and it did get a little better. Polly became less tense and, because she loved him, she wanted so much to please him. To know she was doing that was sufficient for her, even if she still did not like it very much and felt it was sinful.

That's what she could not get over: the sense of sin. She wondered how Jane did because she never could; but then Jane had always been considered unusual and had not been brought up in the Rectory as the Rector's eldest daughter. This was not the sort of thing the unmarried daughter of the Rector did at all. The very idea was horrifying and would horrify anyone she knew, except perhaps Jane.

James continually assured her that he loved her, that they were married in God's sight and that it was, therefore, not unclean and not sinful. But Polly thought it was. The only way that she could possibly excuse herself and make her hope that God would forgive her was James's expression by the Alma River and the thought of the phalanx of the Guards moving in a solid mass towards the enemy. One day it might happen again. Many officers and men had been picked out and fallen. James was not among them then; but he might still be. She was giving herself to him because he wanted her in this way and she loved him. It was a sign of her wifely docility towards him, that she was ready to obey him even before the wedding. So she tried to rationalize it; but she wasn't happy and she knew she wouldn't enjoy it, if ever, until they were married.

And then the next week Caroline arrived in Miss Nightingale's party and there was no more creeping off to the hut to make love. The idyll was at an end.

CHAPTER THIRTY-FOUR

The Times thoroughly approved of the occasion. It compared her to her illustrious predecessor Queen Elizabeth, and to the Empress Marie Theresa of Austria to 'show how successfully female sovereigns have aroused the military ardour of their subjects.' The presentation by Queen Victoria of the Crimean Medal to veterans of the war on 18 May 1855 was

> the most brilliant and interesting military spectacle ever witnessed in this country . . . when a monarch who has known how to unite the heroic courage of her race with the tenderness and sympathy of her sex puts herself at the head of her army and, with her own hands, distributes the decorations so gallantly won by her heroes of the Alma, Balaklava and Inkerman.

Emily had been in a state of excitement ever since she had peeped out of her window at Buckingham Palace just as dawn was breaking. She had observed the numbers who had spent all night in Green Park rousing themselves and hastening down the Mall to join those who, converging from all parts of London, wished for a good view of the procession, if not a view of the ceremony itself. They hurried along Constitution Hill from Kensington, Chelsea and Richmond, down Birdcage Walk from Pimlico, Camberwell and Streatham and through Green Park from Marylebone and as far north as Highgate and Hampstead, even beyond.

The crowd had started streaming into London from the suburbs before first light; they came by train, carriage, horse, anything on wheels or with four legs. Many of them used the two legs God had endowed them with and walked from Sidcup, Gillingham, Sevenoaks, Kingston-upon-Thames and Esher – most having started the previous day.

By nine o'clock when four flank companies of the Grenadiers, the Coldstream Guards and the Fusiliers marched bravely onto the Parade with their bands, the tightly packed crowd strained the barriers, stretched along the Mall into Green Park on one hand and spilling into Whitehall on the other.

For those with invitations huge galleries covered in crimson cloth had been erected at every point overlooking the Parade in front of Horse Guards. Those on the park side accommodated Members of Parliament and the House of Lords. Opposite them, attached to the Horse Guards on each side of the archway, were two other galleries also draped in crimson. The north one was devoted to the families of those participating in the ceremony, the south for members of the government, their families and friends.

A large balcony for the Royal Family, handsomely draped with scarlet cloth, projected from the lower central windows of Horse Guards. Further tiers of seats rose up on the south side of the parade near the residence of the First Lord of the Admiralty, and at the north end along Admiralty Gardens. People crammed the roofs and stone balconies of Horse Guards, the Admiralty, the Treasury and every house and building offering a view of the spectacle.

Between nine and ten o'clock the reserved seats were filled with ladies and gentlemen belonging to the privileged classes who had gone to no end of trouble and expense to deck themselves in apparel worthy of the occasion.

Ladies were in gorgeous dresses made of soft light materials in the gayest of spring colours. Some wore mantles and some did not, but all wore fashionable bonnets variously adorned and trimmed with lace ribbons and flowers. The menfolk, equally elegant but more restrained, wore tight trousers, waisted frock coats or overcoats with velvet collars and shining top hats.

But even this brilliant concourse was utterly eclipsed by the gorgeous uniforms of those assembled on parade. Hundreds of officers and men of every rank in the service wore the full uniform of their regiments, with the decorations to which they were entitled emblazoned on their chests, at their throats and on their sleeves. There were the Hussars with their loose pelisses slung jauntily under their shoulders, the Lancers with their picturesque caps, the light blue and silver of the East India Regular Cavalry, the gay semi-oriental uniform of the Nizam's Irregular Cavalry interspersed among the scarlet and gold of the Line, or the silver and gold of the Militia regiments.

Drawn up in smart formation in front of the Parade were two squadrons of the Life Guards with their shining cuirasses, a squadron of the Royal Horse Guards Blue, a squadron of the Sixth Dragoon Guards and, in the rear, the Foot Guards in front of those who were to receive medals.

At half past nine the band of the Royal Marines marched through Horse Guards Parade from Whitehall followed by officers and seamen of the Royal Navy, and at ten the thunderous cheering of those lining Whitehall announced the arrival of the Queen's cousin the Duke of Cambridge, who, in his uniform of a lieutenant general with the Riband Star of the Garter, took command of the parade. Shortly afterwards the royal carriages containing the Princess Royal and Princess Alice, the Duchess of Kent, mother of the Queen, the Duchess of Cambridge and other senior members of the British and foreign Royal families arrived and took their places on the central balcony.

But just as the clock on Horse Guards Parade struck the hour of eleven the cannons in the park thundered their salute and the throats of the crowd roared their loyal, vociferous tribute as the monarch herself entered the Parade accompanied by Prince Albert, the Prince of Wales and close members of her family. Emily, in a carriage just behind, had never heard anything like the noise. It sounded as though a million Londoners had burst spontaneously into cheers which echoed and re-echoed to those who could see nothing, or perhaps were not even near the spot where the ceremony was to take place. The birds, frightened by the noise, rose in a flurry of indignation, scattering across the trees to the buildings surrounding the park, to the safety of the gardens of the Palace which glittered across the water of the lake.

The sun shone brilliantly onto the Parade and the Queen, in a lilac and white dress, a green velvet mantle and a white bonnet, smiled and waved, looking as though her heart too was bursting with the same joy and pride, the same sense of occasion, as that of her subjects.

The massed bands struck up the rousing strains of 'God Save the Queen' as her carriage drove to the central dais, also splendidly lined in crimson cloth and containing a gilded state chair for Her Majesty and a smaller one for the Prince.

The Queen and her suite remained standing as the Duke of Cambridge ordered both lines of those who were to be decorated to form four deep and then the rear line, passing through the front line, marched until it arrived within a hundred feet of the dais when the word to halt was given. The crowd started to applaud as the gallant men who had defended the honour of their country amid such hardship formed up to receive their medals from the Queen and then, to the strains of the Coronation March from *Prophète*, passed before her in single file, their name, rank and whether wounded and, if so, in what battle, being read out by Major General Wetherall. The Minister for War Lord Penmure handed the medals, on their blue and yellow ribbons, to Her Majesty and she leaned forward to present them from the highest, the Duke of Cambridge, to the lowest, the many private soldiers who had taken part in the war.

The emotions of the crowd were heightened by the sight of these brave men, many of them bearing scars or signs of mutilation, moving slowly before their sovereign. A few hobbled pitifully upon crutches or were assisted by their fellows; some were clearly blinded and had to be led, and some wore black bands upon their arms to mourn a relative whose body lay for ever beneath the soil of the Crimea.

Some were overcome by emotion as they approached the Queen, moved beyond words by her presence, by the graciousness of her manner, by the words she said to the wounded whether soldiers or officers. Three officers unable to walk were wheeled before Her Majesty in bath-chairs, among them Sir Thomas Troubridge of the Seventh Fusiliers who had lost both feet at Inkerman. Emily observed how the Duchess of Kent raised her handkerchief to her eyes at the tender way the Queen leaned over Sir Thomas's chair to hand him his medal and, speaking quietly, informed him that she had made him one of her aides-de-camp.

The Royal Navy followed the Army to receive their medals while the band played 'Rule Britannia'. According to regulation the soldiers touched their hat to the sovereign, but the sailors removed theirs before they approached the dais.

There was hardly a dry eye on the Royal dais by the time the procession ended. The faces of so many of the men who marched past were still marked by suffering or intense despair; but although Emily's heart went out to them as she thought of what they had endured, she nevertheless remained dry-eyed. As the sister of two men still fighting at Sebastopol she felt it unseemly to weep.

But supposing one of those scarlet coated heroes, with missing limbs, or bandages around their eyes, had been James or Oliver . . . or Rawdon Foxton? Emily's impassive face gave no clue to her wayward thoughts. Still she didn't weep. Caroline must see men like this all the time, but not dressed up for the Queen to be paraded before her on a balmy morning in May; men whose clothes had been torn from their bodies, who were unwashed, running with lice or covered with congealed blood. Caroline wouldn't weep, so nor would she, her sister, Emily Vestrey.

By her side as equerry to the Queen stood Sir Arthur Stamford, dressed in his splendid uniform of a Colonel in the Hussars, the loose pelisse slung across his back giving him a decidedly rakish, even youthful air. He never moved a muscle all during the ceremony unless he was called on to help, and then everything he did was exactly right, military, precise. His whiskers and moustache were slightly grey, his close-cropped hair going white at the sides. But when he turned and looked at her his blue eyes were clear, not the eyes of an old man at all – not the eyes of a man with grey whiskers and white hair. His cheeks were pink, his figure excellent. He walked with the grace of a young man. He was forty-nine, a year older than Papa. His eldest son had three children.

The Royal Marines were the last to receive their medals and when all of them had passed to the line of sentries drawn up on the Admiralty side, it was the turn of the Guards to march resplendent in new scarlet tunic regimentals. But even the splendid sight of the Guards, many of them soon to go out and join her brother, did not move

555

Emily to tears. She felt in her bosom a fierce patriotic surge of pride that so many of her family, her friends and those near to her were willing to shed their blood in a hostile foreign land for the country they loved, the Queen she and they served.

Emily gazed at the vast concourse of people wondering at the excellence of the arrangements, at how it was possible to accommodate so many. She looked at the stands next to the Royal dais where the relatives of those participating were seated, members of the government and their friends. Suddenly she froze and the joy and pleasure of the day evaporated. Papa was sitting between Aunt Ruth and a lady dressed in a gown of apple green tulle with a basquin bodice, gabrielle sleeves and decorative ribbon bows, known as *jockeys*, at her shoulder and wrists. Her bonnet made of Dunstable straw had the fashionable Marie Stuart dip in the middle of the brim which was trimmed with lace and artificial apple blossom. Her hands were clasped over a tall parasol. Mrs Ashburne.

On the other side of her was Hugh Benson and around them were many people of Emily's acquaintance. Papa had obviously made up a party to include his mistress. She felt her cheeks burn with shame and if any time that day she came close to tears it was then. She thought Papa glanced at her but she could not be sure. She fastened her eyes on the parade before her and did not look at the stand again until it was time to go. Then she stood up and turned to look at Papa. Seeing her, he leaned forward and doffed his hat. She stared back at him impassively, her face unsmiling. She wanted to convey to Papa what she thought of this *gaffe* – and to have Aunt Ruth connive at it too. It was quite monstrous.

The Queen's eyes were full of tears and her bosom heaved with emotion as she left the dais and the Duchess of Sutherland murmured words of comfort to Her Majesty, discreetly offering her a white cambric handkerchief. A fresh roar rose from the crowd as the Queen's carriage left the Parade and the band burst into the National Anthem. A detachment of Life Guards took up escort duty and, as the procession broke into a trot, the sun, which had been obscured by cloud during the ceremony, suddenly shone forth illuminating in a blaze of colour the swords, the steel casques and cuirasses, the splendid reds, blues and greens of the uniforms on parade.

The cortège rode back along the Mall, through the crowds, all frantically waving and cheering, some scampering through St James's Park, some waving flags from the trees, and others diving in front of the horses and running alongside the procession until it swept through the gates of the Palace coming to a halt at the doors in the courtyard.

After a quick collation the Royal party went out again to the Queen's riding school in Pimlico where a repast had been prepared for the soldiers and non-commissioned officers who had received medals. Leaning on the Prince's arm the Queen walked among her men crowded respectfully around her and once again, her face full of emotion, she spoke to them about their experiences in the field of battle and how they received their wounds.

The sight of the men at close quarters affected Emily more than on the parade ground. Here one could see the extent of the wounds, see the grim light in so many eyes. The thought of Papa parading his mistress in public had upset her and at last tears welled at the back of her eyes. Sir Arthur observed her distress and hovered near her as they walked among the men. She singled out the representatives of the Guards' regiments to talk to, and all of them knew her brother and Rawdon and expressed themselves proud to serve under such officers.

'Captain Vestrey is quite fearless, miss! He always puts himself in the thick of the fight.'

'Thank you!' Emily smiled. 'Should you return to the Crimea say that you spoke to his sister Emily.'

The guardsman touched his forehead. His hand was bandaged and one of his eyes, deeply scarred, was closed. The expression in the remaining eye was bright but resentful and he burst out after Emily had spoken.

'I won't return if I can help it, miss. It is like hell out there. The authorities have let us down.'

Emily thought of Caroline and felt suddenly cold. With a

557

smile she quickly passed on to the next. She did not mention Rawdon or James again.

That night the Queen gave a concert for the Royal family, foreign ministers and members of the nobility and gentry who had attended the day's ceremonial. During the interval after Madame Novello and others had given a thrilling rendition of *Mentre Dormi* by Asilio, there was supper in the Green Drawing Room and once again Emily found Sir Arthur Stamford, immaculate in Court dress, by her side. She accepted the glass of champagne he held out; how thoughtful he was. She smiled at him gratefully.

'You look very tired, Miss Emily.'

'It has been such an exhausting day, Sir Arthur, and with Her Majesty's birthday celebrations yet to come! I fear I shall be quite worn out by the time we go to Osborne next week. How Her Majesty endures it without flagging I do not know.'

'Her Majesty is fortunate in possessing the stamina her ancestors were famous for,' Sir Arthur said. 'The Hanoverians have always been very robust. I think His Royal Highness suffers from exhaustion much more than she does. I thought he looked quite pale on the parade today. But you, Miss Vestrey,' Sir Arthur positioned himself in front of her and looked into her eyes, 'you were so courageous today. The sight must have reminded you of your own brave family, your brothers and your sister. Yet yours was the only dry eye I observed on the dais. Only later did you seem to break down.'

'I wanted to be brave like them, Sir Arthur. They would not care to see me in tears. We saw the fighting men recovered; think what my sister Caroline must see when they are brought in from the field.'

'It is too dreadful to consider, Miss Emily, and *so* unsuitable for a well bred woman. It must distress you to think of it.' Sir Arthur gave a shudder and drained his glass, the finger of his white gloved hand elegantly extended as though he were taking afternoon tea. Emily looked at him gravely. He really was so correct, even handsome if one could overlook his age. He had looked particularly fine in the uniform of the Hussars, and Court dress became him too. In fact he looked distinguished in whatever he wore and he could always be depended upon to say just the right word, to do what was expected, unlike many younger men one knew. A foot was never out of place, a word extraneous. The Queen and the Prince thought very highly of him indeed.

Maybe she should encourage him after all? The idea *seemed* ludicrous, but she had known many marriages where there was a big gap in the ages of the spouses. An uncle of hers had married a woman thirty-five years his junior. They had been apparently very happy and had ten children. Not that she liked to think about the intimate side of a relationship with Sir Arthur. It was the public aspect he presented which was attractive – his role as squire, provider and certainly wise counsellor. He would be steadfast, independent, grateful for her youth and beauty and correspondingly tender and considerate.

He seemed to be reading her thoughts because, with the air of one visited by a brilliant and unexpected idea, though doubtless one that had been carefully planned beforehand, he said suddenly: 'I wondered Miss Vestrey, if you and your aunt would care to visit my cousin the Marquess of Ludstow at Ludstow Castle some weekend when you are free? He would be delighted to make your acquaintance. The Marchioness is distantly related to Lord Raglan.'

Emily dropped her eyes. The Marchioness of Ludstow was also an intimate of the new Duchess of Wellington, formerly as Lady Douro lady in waiting to the Queen. It was all so very suitable.

'I am sure my aunt will be enchanted, Sir Arthur.'

'Then may I ask my cousin to write to her at Park Street?'

'Please do.' When she was a married woman, people would write to her, not her aunt. Yes, it was time she had her own household. Her eye was caught by a movement in the far corner. 'Oh, I think Her Majesty is signalling to me. Before dinner she mentioned my accompanying Princess Alice on the pianoforte. Excuse me, Sir Arthur . . .' She gave him a brilliant smile, a little wave and sped off to join the Royal family, Sir Arthur's gaze following her right across the room.

When it was bought in 1843 Queen Victoria called it 'our

559

dear little home'. It was just what she wanted for complete seclusion in a domestic setting with her beloved Albert, as well as for her growing family, and Sir James Clark, her physician, came down to make sure the air was suitable for the Royal lungs.

But by 1855 Osborne House in the Isle of Wight had been turned into a substantial mansion in the Palladian style, thanks to the architectural efforts of Prince Albert and Sir Thomas Cubitt. The new house had a loggia, a campanile and terraced gardens. Despite its Italianate grandeur the Queen was still able to refer to it as a 'little Paradise' even though she subsequently regretted the fact that 'the character of the little house is gone'.

After the hectic activities of the previous week, the presentation of the Crimean medals and the celebrations to mark the occasion of Her Majesty's thirty-sixth birthday, Emily was glad to escape to Osborne with the Royal party, travelling by train to Southampton by the South-Western Railway and crossing by steamer to Cowes. On the Saturday, the day before her birthday, Her Majesty had a drawing-room attended by sixteen hundred guests among whom had been her father and Aunt Ruth, who chatted for fully a quarter of an hour to the Duchess of Kent. Emily found her father reserved and preoccupied, whether by the progress of the war or on account of Mrs Ashburne she was unable to tell. He attributed her own coolness to being exceptionally busy with her duties.

Emily arrived at Osborne the following Tuesday feeling not only exhausted but depressed. She had heard that Caroline and Polly were now in the Crimea, and instead of the suffering one had been led to expect after the parade of troops the previous week, seemed from reports to be having a remarkably good, even festive time. Although Emily couldn't help envying Caroline her happiness, she had decided to put Rawdon Foxton most firmly out of her mind. Instead her thoughts turned increasingly to Sir Arthur Stamford who would be such an anchor in this world of shifting family relationships and treacheries, such as Jane unmarried and living in sin with a man and Papa deceiving Mama with his mistress.

Already by the weekend she felt rested. Days at Osborne were so well regulated, so tranquil. There were visits to the model farm, the kennels and the Swiss cottage that Prince Albert had imported from the continent, and had erected by their little plots of garden for the children. Oh, delightful times were had here being waited on by the Royal children in their pretence at housekeeping. Then there was riding, sketching, walking and those delightful after-dinner impromptu dances and concerts.

Often at Osborne the Queen and Prince preferred to dine alone, and then the household occasions were even more informal and relaxed, the laughter more unrestrained, the dances occasionally quite boisterous. In the summer the Queen would bathe in the sea from her bathing machine. This was pushed right into the water so that Her Majesty could drop straight from its curtained verandah into the sea, thus ensuring that the Royal body was not exposed to the eyes of the curious. But in May it was too cold and the bathing machine remained covered up.

On the Saturday following the arrival of the Royal party at Osborne, members of the household not required by the Queen or Prince were permitted to do as they liked after lunch until tea-time. Emily wished to sketch the house from the sandy beach where the Prince had designed a semi-circular beach hut.

She announced her intention at lunch and the Duchess of Kent, on a visit to her daughter, thought it an excellent idea and clapped her hands.

'And what will you do with the sketch, Emily?' she enquired, her voice not having lost its German accent despite a residence of nearly forty years in the country of which her daughter was now Queen.

'Give it to your Royal Highness, if I may be permitted,' Emily said, experience having taught her exactly how to answer Royalty's leading questions.

'Oh, I would love a sketch by you! You have such talent my dear.' The Duchess clapped her hands with enthusiasm.

'But not as much as Lady Canning,' Emily said with charming modesty, looking across the table at Sir Arthur, who was gazing at her with the admiration he seldom now took the trouble to conceal.

'On the contrary, Miss Emily, I think your talent very fresh. I am sure her Royal Highness agrees with me. May I be permitted to escort you to the beach? I promise I will take a book and not disturb you.'

'I do wish you would, Sir Arthur,' the Queen said with a glance at her mother. 'I do not like my ladies to be alone, even in sight of the house.'

Emily looked at Sir Arthur through lowered lashes. It was really barely worthwhile taking a sketch pad, never mind a book.

They left the house by a side entrance and strolled down the broad Royal Avenue, lined with cedars and ilexes which gave the house the air of a royal residence despite the attempts of the Queen and Prince to pretend otherwise. The Queen and Prince had delighted in landscaping the park, and the way in which the fauna and flora grew in this balmy climate amply rewarded their efforts.

Emily wore a simple dress of flowered muslin over a taffeta skirt and she had a blue silk bandeau restraining the curly blonde wisps of her baby-fine hair. Sir Arthur, as usual, was impeccably dressed, preferring formal attire when even the Royal family were inclined to be more comfortable for the seaside. He had on a pearl grey suit, narrow trousers and a morning coat with broad tails. His matching waistcoat had black stitched borders bound with tape; he wore his slim gold watch in his right hand pocket and a heavy gold chain with a guard passed through his button hole. Around his neck he wore a large neckcloth secured in the middle with a grey pearl pin and the edges of his stiff collar touched his chin. As usual he carried a grey top hat which he put firmly on his head once they were out of doors.

On occasions he wore a monocle, whether because he needed to or for affectation Emily didn't know. However it suited him, lending him an air of even greater distinction.

The day was a perfect one. A deep blue sky was interspersed here and there with little pink-lined fleecy clouds and the warmth of the gentle breeze seemed a harbinger of summer. As they came to the beach Sir Arthur unfolded the stool he had carried for her and, thanking him, she sat on it and propped her large sketch pad on her knee. Sir

Arthur stood by her side for a while and then he strolled around the beach hut and stood admiring the large ships that came into the Solent from Portsmouth and Spithead opposite them.

Emily sketched the large square Campanile, the leafy ilexes between the house and the sea. But her mind was not on her work. She was aware of Sir Arthur hovering, of his presence, stooping to make a picture with his stick in the sand, or standing behind her to gaze at her work, or her, she was not sure.

At last she looked up at him and threw her pencil on her pad.

'It's no good. I am not in the mood today. Her Royal Highness will have to accept a sketch from me another day.'

She knew she had extra colour in her cheeks and hoped that he would attribute this to the fresh air. He fastened his hands over the gold top of his stick, his eyes fixed on hers. Emily felt a lump come into her throat. Solemnly Sir Arthur removed his hat.

'I have the Queen's permission to ask you to marry me, Miss Vestrey.'

His courtier's imperturbability deserted him and Emily could see his Adam's apple working nervously up and down. His blue eyes seemed assailed by sudden doubt and he looked at her anxiously. 'I hope I have made my intentions clear and this is not a shock, Miss Vestrey. I know I am much older than you, but I would consider myself the luckiest man in the world if you would do me the honour; but . . . dare I hope? Have I misread the signs?'

His neckcloth with its pearl pin was level with her eyes if she looked straight at him. She could see the whiskers on his neck, a patch of grey stubble where the razor had not shaved him properly. Little folds of skin hung from his lean jowl and when he smiled his teeth, though good, were capped in places with gold. Next birthday he would be fifty. She knew because she had looked him up in Debrett. Next birthday she would be twenty-four. By that time she might be his wife.

His look of anxiety was becoming distressing. His cousin was a Marquess and his family were pre-Conquest. He was very wealthy and did not depend on the Court for his livelihood. He would probably agree, if she wished, to leave the Court and travel about the world. He was very accomplished, read Greek and Latin and spoke at least three modern languages.

'I will marry you, Sir Arthur,' she said with composure. 'Your proposal is not altogether unexpected, and it gives me great pleasure to accept it.'

To her consternation he flung his stick and hat impulsively to the ground and came and knelt in the soft sand beside her. She was disturbed at the thought of his well pressed trousers becoming soiled. He seized her hand and, bringing it to his lips, kissed it, closing his eyes as though with ecstasy at the touch. After a long time he opened them and gazed at her, the look in his eyes more worshipful than before.

'Oh my *very* dear Emily. Thank you. You do me such an honour. You make me the happiest of men, the most fortunate of creatures.'

'Thank you, Sir Arthur.' She pressed his hand, feeling uncomfortable.

'You must call me Arthur my dear, if we are to be married.'

'It would seem sensible – Arthur.'

It was not easy to say at first.

He got to his feet, brushing the sand off his knees; she gave him her hand and he helped her up taking her sketch pad from her. He drew her close to him and for a horrified moment she thought he was going to kiss her. Vividly the memory of Rawdon pressing her against the wall at Lady Fox-Hargreaves' dance came back to her and she felt herself tremble with apprehension. It was a moment she often recalled in her mind, sometimes unbidden, because, although it filled her with shame and remorse, it was undoubtedly exciting; but it was also the reason, surely, that Rawdon had rejected her? She had disgusted him. A woman who could so comport herself was hardly worthy to be called a lady. She never wanted anything like that to happen to her again. She would make quite sure it did not. Not that Arthur's kisses were likely to be like Rawdon's on that night; they would be proffered gently to the cheek with lips tightly closed.

But, being the true gentleman he was, he didn't attempt to kiss her, not even on the cheek, and after a while he let fall her hand and folded her stool tucking it under his arm.

'I cannot believe my good fortune,' he said, standing up straight. 'But my dearest, have you considered sufficiently well the difference in our ages?'

'Yes. I have, Sir Arthur.'

'And it does not distress you?'

'No. I regard you as a very suitable companion. I prefer older men. Men like Papa, or the Prince.'

'But I am *much* older than the Prince!'

'He seems very old, especially lately. Do you not think so, Sir . . . I mean Arthur?'

'His Royal Highness works too hard. But oh Emily, I know the one doubt Her Majesty had was that you might consider me too old.'

'That is because the Prince and she are the same age. I *like* older men. So have no fears on that score . . . Arthur. And shall you stay on at Court?'

'My dear, that is one of the many things I wish to discuss with you. I want to devote my life to pleasing you. I have worshipped you, Emily, you do not know for how long.' He tucked her hand under his arm and escorted her from the beach. 'Now, shall we go and tell Her Majesty the good news? I believe she may have prepared a little celebration on our behalf.'

'How kind of the Queen,' Emily said; but other than an awareness of Her Majesty's goodness, she felt no emotion at all. She, Emily Vestrey, was marrying a man she did not love. Brought up on romance, an admirer of the Brontë novels, she never for a moment had thought that would be her fate.

CHAPTER THIRTY-FIVE

Françoise Lévy Vestrey was a little enchantress; tiny, dark and even at three months full of vitality and personality. She captured hearts instantly and everyone seemed instinctively to want to take her and play with her, to hold out their arms and embrace her.

Daniel had said it was too cold for a picnic, but when the day came it was so warm that they decided to eat out of doors after all. Cook prepared an elaborate basket, or rather baskets, enough to feed twice as many people as there were.

Dr and Mrs Marx had not been well; they had been prostrated by the death of their son, little Mouche, the previous month. They would have not come on the picnic at all if Jane had not insisted on sending a cab for them, sending and paying for it too. The cab called at Flask Walk spilling out all the Marx family who, after admiring the house and the baby and everything else, set out to walk slowly to the heath with Daniel, Jane and baby Françoise.

Marx looked terrible. His eyes had a feverish gleam and his thick luxuriant beard was speckled with grey. Jane watched him all during the meal, saw how little he ate, how much he drank. He had the air of one who had suffered a deep and possibly fatal wound.

'Mohr, you have not eaten at all.'

He looked at her tenderly.

'*Mein liebe* Jane, so kind. Do you know I have scarcely been out since Mouche died? Once or twice to the Museum, no more. And poor Jenny . . .'

He looked at his wife who had hardly spoken at all.

'It is my first time out too,' she whispered. 'We miss him so much. Not a moment goes by . . .'

'Mama, Mama I think the baby is trying to walk!'

Dark-haired, vivacious Laura dandled Françoise from her hands and pretended to walk her along the rug that was spread out on the side of the heath overlooking the Vale of

Health. It was just far enough to walk from Flask Walk and the view of London was spectacular. Marx had sat for a long time with hands folded looking at it.

'She could not possibly walk at that age!' Young Jenny Marx laughed and steadied the baby with her hand. 'Tussy is more advanced, but a baby cannot walk until about nine months.'

Baby Eleanor Marx, called 'Tussy' by the family, had been born the previous January.

'Tussy has stayed behind with Lenchen,' Marx explained. 'She has not been well either.'

'How is your work, Mohr?' Daniel had brought a book so as not to waste time. He sat slightly apart from the picnickers in order to concentrate on his task.

'Oh, I cannot work.' Marx stretched out on the rug and put his hands under his head. 'We have had many misfortunes in our life but I have never known such a time as this, the death of our only son. I should be able to overcome it, but I cannot. Bacon says that important people have so much to interest them that they easily get over any loss; but I am not so fortunate. I am not great or important. I grieve terribly.' A tear stole down his face.

'You are *very* great, Mohr. You must not give in to despair.' Jane moved over to him and took his hand. Daniel frowned.

'I would have thought throwing yourself into work would help, Mohr,' he said. 'You must try.'

'I am obliged to you, Daniel.' Marx glanced sideways at the younger man, his expression irritable. 'I am sure you would always keep yourself perfectly under control.'

'I would certainly try,' Daniel bent over his book. 'But then I have never really been afflicted so I cannot say how I would behave.'

'No, you have not suffered, Daniel. That is what is the matter with you.'

Mrs Marx started up anxiously and looked at Jane who quietly removed her hand from Marx's arm.

'I was not aware that anything was the matter with me?' Daniel gave a polite slightly challenging smile. Jane recognized the dangerous edge to his clipped, accented voice.

'You are too smug, too self satisfied, too bourgeois. You . . .'

'*I* bourgeois?' Daniel was so affronted that he got to his feet, his book falling on the ground. Jane reached out a hand and tried to pull him down but he ignored her.

'Yes, contented, well fed, well housed and looked after. You must suffer, Daniel, in order to live.'

'I am exiled from my country.' Daniel stiffened. 'Without Lord Vestrey I would have no home.'

'Yes, but you *have* Lord Vestrey and you *have* a home and a beautiful girl who bears you a child and yet to whom you do not give your name.'

'Ah, that is what is the matter.' Daniel sank down onto the ground as though it was a subject of no consequence and picked up his book.

'It is true. You know I do not approve of this sort of behaviour. It is an affront to the social conventions by which we all live.'

'Neither does Miss Martineau. She has written to Jane telling her in no uncertain terms what she thinks too. You call me bourgeois? I say it is *you* and Miss Martineau and all who think like you who are bourgeois.'

'A woman needs protection,' Marx said. 'She has to be looked after.'

'Jane is looked after, by her father. He is very generous – well, up to a point . . .'

Daniel frowned again. He riffled through the pages of the book. He had lost his place and exclaimed and sighed with annoyance until he had found it again.

'But it is your duty to look after the woman you live with.'

Daniel put a marker in his page, sighed again and looked patiently at Marx as if he were a small, recalcitrant child.

'Do you look after *your* wife and family, Mohr? You do not work; you say now you do not even write, except for a few articles for the papers. Where would you be without Friedrich Engels?'

'It is Friedrich's mission to support me,' Marx said with an air of massive calm. 'He says it is his role in life. He enjoys it. It is his contribution to the Revolution.'

'Then I am sure that is how Lord Vestrey feels about me.

Not a contribution to the Revolution, certainly, but one of his roles in life. He provides for me and his daughter and granddaughter so that I may get on with more important work. Now Mohr, if you cannot work I can. I do not wish to argue with you. I want to read this book of statistics in order to write a little more when I return.'

'I don't think you should talk to Mohr like that.' Jane's eyes flashed angrily. 'He is upset and distressed. We have come here for a happy day, not to argue.'

'*I* am not arguing,' Daniel said indignantly. 'Mohr brought this on by accusing me of being bourgeois.'

'I said you had not suffered. It was a different thing. I am sorry, old friend. I am not myself. I don't want to upset Jane.' Marx sat up, brushing the crumbs off his stained waistcoat and patted Daniel on the shoulder. 'I do not want to quarrel with good friends like you, especially my dear Jane who I believe looks even more beautiful since she became a mother.'

Jane's eyes sparkled and she ran a hand over her trim waistline. 'Thank you, dear Mohr.'

'Now let us change the subject. How are your sisters?'

'They are *both* going to be married! Caroline to Rawdon Foxton in the autumn and Emily, I heard only yesterday, to a Sir Arthur Stamford who, like her, is at the Court.'

'Do you like Sir Arthur Stamford?' Mrs Marx said hesitantly. Even in her jaded, unhappy state the thought of a wedding immediately cheered her up. She was pale and her hair straggled in little wisps from under her hat. She spent part of every day in bed, in pain. She leaned back against a tree. Her two daughters had taken Françoise towards the pond at the bottom of the hill and she kept her eyes on them.

'I do not know him,' Jane said. 'Emily and I do not communicate. Emily does not approve of me . . .'

'Like *you*, Mohr,' Daniel said with a malevolent smile.

'I do not approve of Jane?' Marx's face clouded. 'That is certainly not true. I do not approve of *you*.'

'But I do not want to marry either, if Daniel does not wish it. Truly, Mohr.'

'I do not believe it,' Mrs Marx said. 'All your friends must ignore you.'

'They were not worth having,' Daniel turned on his stomach to shield his eyes from the sun.

'That is what you say!' Jane got to her knees and began to gather the picnic things together. 'I *do* miss my friends, and my sister. I valued knowing someone like Miss Martineau. People do not approve, Daniel, and it is no use denying it. But I am not saying that I mind. As long as I have you, and Françoise and Papa . . .'

Jane looked down at the plates in her hand. It was not true. She was very lonely. She felt cut off and Daniel was no real substitute, no true companion. He shut himself in his study for hours and sometimes hardly communicated for days. If Jane could do without the friendship of Miss Martineau, she missed Emily terribly. There had been no final word, no painful scene, no chance to plead. Emily simply refused to see her or to be where she was. Visits to Chetwell had to be made when Emily was not there and they were rare and perfunctory because of the hostility that Mama showed towards Daniel, and the fact that her aversion to Jane had intensified because of the enormity of her behaviour. She never went to Park Street where Emily lived most of the time, and so she felt very cut off and estranged from the deep roots of her former family life.

Her father often came to Flask Walk and did his best to be friendly and keep the peace with Daniel; but now that Daniel had been assimilated into the ranks of the English aristocracy he no longer felt awestruck by them. He felt under no obligation to placate his benefactor and enjoyed goading George. In fact he went out of his way to open up an argument on the war or the state of the nation or the condition of the working classes, and the failure of the likes of the Vestreys to do anything about them.

'I would like to work, Mohr, to do something as I did in Soho. I didn't want to lead a *useless* life like this. Both my sisters are working. Is it not strange that I, a radical, should be the one to stay at home?'

'Useless? You call it useless looking after me, seeing to my wants, our baby? It is what women, after all, are for, surely. You don't call being at the Court working?' Daniel said, brushing a lock of his straight black hair away from his eyes, which smouldered angrily.

'Yes I do, in a way. It is hard work being at the beck and call of a monarch. Why must you always attack my sisters, Daniel?'

'Because I don't like them. I don't like the Vestreys at all, really. The more I know them the less they appeal to me.'

Mrs Marx made a Germanic exclamation and put her hands to her face. Marx lumbered to his feet, like a giant waking up. He looked scornfully at Daniel.

'That is not a nice way to talk, Daniel. I think you are in a black mood today. The Vestreys have been good to you, I think. Jane is a Vestrey and you like her.' He looked at Jane and put out a hand, pulling her to her feet. Her fresh young face, so happy when they had set out, looked strained. He wanted to stroke it but dared not. She was like a daughter to him, a child he loved.

'My dear, if you are bored and want something to do, why not assist me? Yes. You will make me work again. You can look up references for me at the British Museum. That is if you would like to.'

Jane clasped her hands together and ran into his outstretched arms. 'Oh *Mohr*, I would love it . . .'

'And I have secretarial duties you could perform for me. The London Assistance Committee which exists to help refugees like myself – and Daniel – needs reorganizing. We need fresh funds. You have no idea of some of the conditions in which our people work. To give an example. Men, stark naked, at a German felt factory in the East End, get into barrels to stamp raw pelts which are to adorn rich ladies with boas and muffs. Maybe some of those are friends of yours, who knows? They work with their hands and feet from morning unto night, stamping away and the perspiration from their bodies soaks into the skins to give them their suppleness.'

'Oh Mohr!' Jane put her hands to her ears. 'I cannot bear to hear any more. Say it is not true.'

'But it is,' Marx insisted.

'Jane would be quite useless for the work you suggest,' Daniel said, getting up. 'Where is Françoise? It is time we went back.' He looked at Marx, straightening his neat waistcoat, brushing the grass from his good broadcloth coat. 'She is too sensitive, also she is not methodical. If she were she could employ herself arranging my papers – but she is too untidy. You should see her drawers, our bedroom. She is used to gracious living . . . the Honourable Jane Vestrey.'

'That is not true, Daniel! Why must you be so loathsome today?' Jane stood close to Marx, turning on her lover. 'Did I not work uncomplainingly in the Mission, did I not observe horrible sights there daily? Were not my papers there, my accounts, in order? I *would* like to work for Mohr. It would give me something to do, something important that I believe in, and it would mean that you could get me out of the way. Surely you would like that?'

'I forbid it,' Daniel said. 'I refuse to discuss it further. I made it quite clear to Lord Vestrey that I was the master in my home. If Jane defies me she can go back to her father and I shall return to my room in Soho. That way she will have lost her reputation for nothing.'

He shook himself and began to stroll purposefully down the hill calling to Jenny and Laura to bring the baby. Dr and Mrs Marx and Jane stood looking helplessly after him. Only now that his back was turned did Marx put a protective arm round Jenny.

'He has changed for the worse, I am afraid. He was always inclined to be a little dictatorial.'

'He has your arrogance,' Mrs Marx murmured, 'but not your humility. He has not suffered enough.'

'He has not suffered at *all*,' Marx said bending down and picking up the rug. 'Here, Jane, let us fold this or Daniel will scold us for being late.'

But Jane stood looking after Daniel, her chin thrust out, her hair, caught by a gust of wind that blew in from the heath, streaming behind her.

'He is a great man, Mohr,' she said. 'He really is. He is so dedicated, so sure. If I disturb him he cannot work. He is not always like this. Not when we are alone. He can be very loving, really; so gentle and kind – and patient. He reads to me and helps me to learn. I think when he is like this – especially with my father – it is to show that he is independent of the Vestrey money. That he is a pure revolutionary. But nevertheless I must do as he says. I would love to help you but I cannot unless Daniel changes his mind.'

Marx turned and, glancing at his wife, gave the other half of the rug to her. They shook it silently and folded it into a neat square. Then, gathering up the picnic things, they walked down the hill in Daniel's wake.

The sun was setting over the dome of St Paul's Cathedral, a tiny white speck in the distance not yet obscured by the smoke that rose from thousands of chimneys, the fruits of the Industrial Revolution that had made Britain great. It gave the city a magical, mysterious quality and one could forget quite easily about all the factories employing sweated labour such as Marx had described; the thousands of souls who had not enough to eat, nowhere to sleep and only rags to clothe them.

In prosperous Hampstead, lights were beginning to appear at the windows of the houses, and a mist arose insidiously from the vale below, the place where Londoners were supposed to have sought refuge from the Great Plague.

The trees of the heath stirred, the mist swirling around them, so that the air between here and London looked clinging, vaporous, resembling the enchanted garden of fairy stories – the incandescent spell of near-twilight.

As the sun sank lower the mist and smoke obscured St Paul's altogether, and there was nothing but a shimmering black and red band upon the horizon – the colours of the Revolution. The people enchained by their poverty were bound to rise up and overthrow their masters. One day, maybe, along that line the sky would be red with flames, the streets black with blood.

Marx pulled his threadbare coat about him and put an arm round the frail shoulders of his wife. She clung to him almost desperately, as though only he could save her from losing her footing on the uneven ground. With so much on his mind Marx couldn't think why he worried so much about Daniel and Jane. But he did. Daniel was turning into one of those unrealistic, idealistic socialists of whom Marx knew so many – they betrayed the meaning of revolution by their behaviour. Daniel was embracing all the evils of the bourgeoisie and capitalism without even attempting to destroy the society in which they lived. On the contrary, he was being integrated into it.

And Jane, why did he worry about her, the daughter of a wealthy man, a lord? Her hands were quite unsullied by toil, her soul unscarred by suffering, as yet. As yet. Marx's grip on his wife tightened as they walked past the houses and onto the flat of the heath. Ahead of them Jane had caught up with Daniel and her hand was placatingly tucked into his. His wife Jenny had once been like Jane. She had been a beauty, 'the prettiest girl in Trier', and had resisted any number of offers to wait for him. Like Jane, her father had been a prominent, wealthy man. Yet she had thrown herself wholeheartedly in with his life, attending his meetings, copying out his articles, researching for him, listening to him. He must never be turned into a moneymaking machine she had said. She had believed in him passionately. Did she still? Had he quenched her light, her fires, her faith, with years of poverty, unending travel, worry, child-bearing, death?

He glanced at her pale, drawn, careworn face and drew no comfort from it.

There was no comfort anywhere.

CHAPTER THIRTY-SIX

May was a very eventful month in the progress of the war in the Crimea. It started badly with an unsuccessful expedition to Kertch on the Sea of Azoff which was called off on instructions from the Emperor after it had started. The allies were furious and, shortly after that, Canrobert resigned and was succeeded by General Pélessier. Kertch was finally successfully captured and the Sea of Azoff opened to allied warships on 22 May.

On 8 May the Sardinian army arrived to join the allied cause under its colourful leader General de la Marmora who immediately became inflamed by the beautiful Lady George Paget who had arrived with the Stratfords aboard the yacht *Caradoc* at the end of April. She reciprocated by thinking him and his troops with their bandit-looking hats and long waving plumes 'quite ravishing', and he ordered his band to play beneath the *Caradoc* in Balaklava harbour night and morning.

To this extent the social life at the Crimea grew more flippant but another enemy, beside the war, had returned. Cholera began to claim a number of victims again with the hot damp weather and among the very first when she arrived in the Crimea at the beginning of May was Florence Nightingale, though in her case it was called Crimean fever.

She was very ill. She scarcely had time to inspect Sebastopol from the heights above it and the General Hospital at Balaklava when she succumbed. Owing to the unpleasant odour in the harbour she was transported from her ship to the Castle Hospital and there, nursed by Mrs Roberts and Mrs Bracebridge, she battled against death. When at last she was out of danger Lord Raglan personally telegraphed the Queen.

She refused to go back to England or Switzerland to convalesce because she still had so much to do; but she did go back to Scutari, leaving Caroline behind to fill in at the

575

General Hospital. There Soyer was installing new kitchens and Miss Weare, who was in charge, was proving so incompetent that, before her collapse, Florence had decided she would have to be replaced.

But Caroline wanted to stay behind for more than that. She was very worried about the relationship between James and Polly who to her surprise had announced their engagement. They did not seem like a happy, loving couple newly engaged as she and Rawdon were. There was a constraint between them, a lack of spontaneity and gaiety and Polly looked unhappy. Caroline thought she knew why. With the plethora of young women who had come to the Crimea with their families to visit brothers and cousins in the army, James found a happy stamping-ground again. He flirted with all the girls he saw; hardly ever danced with Polly and seemed content to ignore her, as though she were already a wife. This contrasted with Rawdon whose love seemed to surround and protect her, cocooning her against the battles with Miss Weare and Dr Hall because she was regarded as Miss Nightingale's spy.

On 6 June the third bombardment of Sebastopol began and the hospitals were again filled with wounded and, inevitably, the victims of cholera. Caroline called Polly in to help even though she looked ill herself.

'Why do you not go home?' she asked at the end of a very hot day when the conditions seemed to her once again to resemble Scutari, with wards overflowing and the limbs of the injured men piling up in heaps as amputations were performed in rapid succession. But there was a difference. It was warm and, though this helped to spread disease, it seemed better than the biting cold of the winter, and the nurses, even the bad ones, were that much more experienced.

'You mean you want me to leave James?' Polly said angrily, turning from a cupboard where she was counting bandages and splints.

'No. I don't think you look well. A voyage home, some rest . . . and then James will be back and you can get married.'

Caroline felt no conviction as she spoke. Somehow the

words seemed to echo in the cramped room as though expressing the sense of emptiness she felt about her brother's relationship with their cousin. So happy at the beginning to hear about it, she was now full of foreboding as she observed James's characteristic flirtatious, irresponsible behaviour.

'You think James *will* marry me?' Polly said bitterly.

'Of course. Don't you?'

Caroline lowered her voice in case any of the sick men near them heard.

'No I do not. You can see how he behaves towards other women. He doesn't love me at all.'

Caroline put down the tray she was about to carry into the ward and put an arm around Polly.

'Then why did you become engaged?'

'He told me he loved me, and you know I have always loved him. But I think he just wanted . . . wanted . . .'

Polly burst into tears and Caroline hurried her out of the ward and into a part of the corridor that had no sick and wounded in it.

'Wanted what?'

She was now filled with alarm. Polly looked so tired, so pale. Caroline suddenly remembered how Jane had looked when she was expecting her child at the beginning, wan and listless. She feared her worst forebodings about James and Polly had come true.

'You know, what men want. He told me he loved me to make it feel better. I was so ashamed, so guilty because of what I did. I said he would despise me and he does. He holds me in contempt because I gave in to him. He has almost told me as much.'

'And you are with child?' Caroline asked, trying to feel resigned. At least she knew that, unlike Daniel, James would do the right thing.

Polly started to cry afresh, kneading her apron into her eyes. 'No, no, no! Not that I know of. I wish I were. Then I would have him. Now I don't know.'

Caroline patted Polly's shoulder, her mouth pursed, her eyes grim.

'He will marry you, Polly. He will have to. He has dis-

577

honoured you and made you a promise. If it is the very last thing I do, I assure you that James will make you his wife. I am not saying you will be happy; but you will have as good a chance as most. You knew James and I warned you again him. To give in to him was the height of folly . . .'

'But he wanted it so much,' Polly sobbed onto her cousin's bosom.

'Of course he did. He always has. He was seduced by someone when he first went into the army and he has never been able to restrain his passions. I deprecate it, but it is a fact. I love James, he is my brother; but I deplore his morals and I always have. Alas, I knew how much you loved him, however unworthy . . .'

'I saw him in imagination on the battlefield. Dead. I felt that it was a premonition. At any time . . .'

'Of course.' Caroline could see the heroic James painting a very convincing picture of the soldier about to go to war. 'You did what you thought was right.'

'No, no,' Polly sobbed. 'I thought it was wrong. I still do. I feel unclean and evil.'

'You must not think that,' Caroline said gently. 'It is not unclean or evil, only foolhardy. You are not pregnant and James will marry you, as he has promised and as he must. No decent man would want for his wife a girl who was not a virgin. James would not, no matter what he does now.'

Polly started to sob again and Caroline began to flounder. She scarcely knew what she was talking about. She knew so little about physical passion. It was not something that she and Rawdon would ever feel tempted to do until the sacred bonds of matrimony united them.

What made James and Polly, and Jane so different? Jane and Polly, whom she loved so much, had behaved in a way so contrary to their upbringing. Why? This was the sort of thing reserved for women of easy virtue, prostitutes and courtesans, women quite outside the pale of society. No wonder James no longer respected Polly and humiliated her in public and now, reading between the lines of Jane's letters, she was beginning to see signs of unhappiness there. Jane no longer wrote of Daniel as she used to.

The wages of sin, if not death, was certainly unhappiness.

it was very clear for all to see and it made her very sad for the people she loved and was so close to.

On 8 June the French took the Mamelon Hill, the first allied victory of any magnitude. Those watching them through their field glasses from the Maison d'Eau, and they included Lord Raglan, commander-in-chief, accompanied by lovely Agnes Paget and other ladies, expected the French to press on and take the Malakoff and the Redan. But they were driven back because they had insufficient men in reserve, and the English too, who supported them, suffered many killed.

Oliver, who was in reserve, was eager to get behind the enemy lines. He was not the least deterred by the slaughter sustained by the Eighty-eighth and the Sixty-second Foot during the taking of the Mamelon.

But the allies felt that the initiative in the war was now theirs, despite the supplies that daily arrived in Sebastopol harbour and the steady stream of men and carts that were seen toiling up the slopes to re-equip the redoubts.

The atmosphere in the allied ranks was charged with expectation. Something was afoot. There was much activity in the trenches, guns being taken to new positions and regiments being moved from Balaklava to the front, including the Guards. Gradually it was known that at last a major attack was to be made on the Malakoff and the Redan to force Sebastopol into submission.

The day chosen was Monday 18 June, the anniversary of Waterloo.

For Caroline the day before was almost unendurable. The hospital was full of men suffering from wounds sustained in supporting the French in the Mamelon attack on the eighth. James and Rawdon came to see her before the Guards moved back to Sebastopol. She remembered why Polly had given in to James. Looking at her brother's strong confident features she wondered if he had had a foreknowledge of death? The mortality recently among the officers in all regiments had been enormous.

She kissed James, her eyes full of tears. 'Take care,' she whispered.

'I'll be all right, old girl, but, I say, if anything does happen, see Polly gets home safely.'

Caroline could not speak and turned to Rawdon. She looked into his eyes and knew he could see her fear. He smiled at her and grasped her shoulder. Around them were too many people for any more intimate form of communication.

'Whatever happens, Caroline,' he said, 'we have much to be thankful for. We knew what it was like to love each other.'

Caroline turned away, pretending to be busy with something and, when she looked back the men had slipped out of her ward. Vigorously she applied her attention to the sick and the wounded who lay groaning all around her, in order to take her mind off her own terrible feeling of apprehension and pain.

But in the event the Guards stayed in reserve, and the Fifty-seventh Foot were part of the storming party led by Colonels Windham and Yea. Alert in the trenches below the Redan, waiting for the order to rush out across the quarry in front and take the hill, Oliver remembered that it was the anniversary of Waterloo and, like his uncle, he was going to bring honour to the family name. He crouched down, his rifle in his hand, waiting for the signal; he wanted to be the first across the quarry after Colonel Windham.

But the plan had already misfired, though he did not know it. At one o'clock, an hour before, General Pélessier had told Lord Raglan that the planned bombardment of the Malakoff Round Tower and the Redan before the storming party attacked could not take place. He wanted to go at once. The idea had been to reduce the Russians in the Round Tower and the Redan by three hours of fierce bombardment, and then rush them at six in the morning. Pélessier said he could not wait; the concentration of his men was too thick, the Russians would see them, and the element of surprise would be lost. Reluctantly Raglan agreed and at three in the morning the order was given to go.

But the storming party by this time was in disorder. Instead of advancing in a solid phalanx it was all in twos and threes, some leaping over, some hesitating, expressing the confusion of its commanders. In some places scaling ladders were already in position, but some were lying on their sides, deserted by the scaling party which had brought them. Everyone wanted to know where were the allied guns that were meant to give support? The French had been expected to take the Malakoff first, which was next to the Redan, and to send out a rocket signal when they had succeeded. Some thought they heard the rockets and went and some didn't so they stayed behind.

Crouching in his pit Oliver saw Colonel Lacy Yea of the Seventh Fusiliers start over the quarry and then stop, vainly trying to stem the broken formation of the troops behind him when he saw how solid was the defence ahead.

'This will never do,' he shouted. 'Go back. Where is the bugler to call them back?'

But there was no bugler, and just then Colonel Yea fell, hit in the leg, and his men swarmed after him towards the Redan ditch. The colonel crawled along with his hat on his sword cheering on his men and then a Russian came behind him and shot him in the back.

That was enough for Oliver. He leapt out of the trench towards the Russian who had shot Colonel Yea and bayoneted him. Then, as the smoke of guns swirled about him, he crossed the quarry into the great ditch before the Redan which was full of Russians with fixed bayonets discharging their guns. One loomed up in front of him and he thrust his bayonet between the man's eyes, proceeding to crawl through the bodies of his comrades who had preceded him until he reached the tangle of trees and branches, known as the *abatis*, which protected the lower slope of the Redan.

He stood up and could see that the sky, though thick with smoke and dust, was blue; it was nearly daylight. He saw he was almost on his own, that the slope was full of red-coated bodies, some groaning and writhing, others lying still. He felt pain in his arm but did not heed it. Something told him he could get to the top and tear down the Russian flag. He felt overwhelmingly confident of his ability to succeed and take the Redan alone. He would show his brother James just what he could do.

Suddenly before him a Russian pointed a pistol at his

head, two feet away. Oliver lashed at him with his bayonet and got him with a fusillade of bullets. Then he tripped in the *abatis,* which was the purpose of the tangled foliage, and fell headlong on his face. A Russian loomed over him and Oliver thrust up his bayonet into the man's guts. He staggered up again and looked towards the Russian flag. Behind him a bugle was sounding the retreat. But Wellington had said to the Fifty-seventh Foot at Albuera : 'Fifty-seventh die hard!' And Oliver meant to do just that. He felt another pain in his leg and crashed to his knee; his head began to swim and he realized that he was bleeding everywhere. He suddenly saw beautiful Chetwell, tranquil in the Kent countryside with the smooth expanse of water before it, and knew that he would never see it again. Russians were tumbling from the battery at the top of the Redan, advancing angrily on this lone English redcoat, their bayonets ominously fixed.

Oliver lay on his stomach and began to shoot them as they approached; he saw one fall, another stagger, another. He felt a terrible weight on his body and a pain in his head; and the sea in front of his beloved home rose up and swept over him.

When Caroline reached Cathcart's Hill with the Drinkwaters and Polly the attack almost over despite the fact that it was only just dawn. Amidst the smoke and the din she saw the carnage below, wave upon wave of redcoats lying in grotesque positions on the ground. English visitors and spectators were impassively viewing the battle through their binoculars, although by now they were a little subdued, as when a favourite horse has lost a race. One or two were even drinking coffee, quite unperturbed, breaking their fast on the hill above the valley of death.

To her right she saw that the Brigade of Guards were forming into a column and marching back to camp. She put her head in her hands and wept with relief. The attack had failed, but the Guards hadn't even gone in. It was only a little later that someone told her about the number of losses sustained by the Fifty-seventh Foot in leading the assault.

James had watched the whole thing with horror, standing

with his Battalion in rigid formation on the lower slopes waiting to be called. To him it was the same thing that had happened to the cavalry at Balaklava, only this time it was the infantry. There had been a muddle of orders and a gross blunde. had again been committed – to go with all the others in this long and horrible war. A French flag had briefly waved from the Malakoff but soon it was replaced by a Russian. There may have been rocket fire or there may not; it was too noisy to tell. He could see the confusion among the storming party; some went and came back and some never got started. But a lot went after Colonels Yea and Windham, and dropped almost immediately. He saw Sir John Campbell rush out cheering his men and fall straight away; he had sent away his *aides-de-camp* as though reluctant to bring them into danger.

As the Guards and Highlanders, waiting in reserve, were given orders to retreat, James asked permission to stay. He had seen Oliver rush out and had then lost sight of him; but he knew he was hit. His commander, Colonel Wellesley, knew that he wanted to look for him and acceded to his request.

'You go and tell Caroline,' James hissed to Rawdon. 'You can do nothing here.'

Rawdon nodded, used to obeying reasonable commands. Through his glasses he had seen the Russians advance on Oliver half way up the hill. He thought he was dead. He had seldom seen such bravery as shown by that gallant red-coated figure making its solitary way up the side of the Redan like a lonely man climbing a mountain.

All day long the dead and wounded lay in the sweltering sun. Occasionally a shirt or a hat was waved in a frantic effort to signal to their comrades to come and get them. But the Russians were busy rebuilding their defences and would not grant a truce until four in the afternoon. They had stopped bayoneting the enemy wounded, as they had used to do, but some thought this was another form of barbarity to leave the men all day in the broiling Crimean heat.

As soon as the white armistice flag was hoisted from the Redan James leaped over the trench into the Russian quarries and began looking for Oliver. The ground was covered with grass and weeds and the graves of men buried in the last few days. The earth was scarred by huge gaping holes where shells and shot had fallen. The litter parties were performing their melancholy work with speed and care, lifting bodies and transporting them behind the allied lines. Every now and then James would stop one and ask for news of Ensign Vestrey; but no-one had seen him.

Some of the bodies were so badly decomposed by the heat that they were unrecognizable; worms and maggots had already buried themselves deeply in the putrid flesh and many faces were quite black and had swollen and burst. Sometimes the men carrying the stretchers stopped and vomited and, but for the pressing need to find his brother, James would have done the same – the appalling stench and the sight of the decaying corpses were so awful. James now, remembering Oliver's fresh youthful face, dreaded what he might find.

As he got nearer the *abatis* the red jackets grew fewer and, for a hopeful moment, James wondered if his brother might have been captured.

Then halfway up the hill he came across two or three Russian bodies huddled together and under them was a red arm. He threw back the bodies and saw his brother on his face, his arms stretched out. From the top half he looked as though he was relatively unharmed; but his legs were covered with blood. James knelt beside him and Oliver, as though knowing it was him, smiled although he could not see him.

'They got me, but I got three of them first, two more before that. Oh God, James, I thought I would be left here to die.'

And then, as though the mere presence of his brother was enough to save him, once again he fainted while James bitterly regarded his shattered body.

CHAPTER THIRTY-SEVEN

Caroline received permission to nurse her brother herself at the Castle Hospital, holding his hands while both his legs were amputated just above the knees. She thought she had seen enough horror in her life until this terrible duty of having to watch her young brother being maimed, as the surgeon sawed away at his bones which had been crushed by round shot. Chloroform was used, but it hardly had time to take effect because it was so urgent to remove Oliver's legs, half-eaten by gangrene owing to his long exposure in the sun. Caroline gripped his hands and, through his half closed eyes, he seemed to see her and take strength from her.

Caroline bathed and dressed his poor stumps and set them on rests which she had made herself only a few days before, never thinking on whom she would have to use them. He had received other injuries, cuts to his face and chest, a bullet graze on the arm. She sponged him tenderly, put a clean shirt on him and tended all the wounds. Then she sat by him for a long time holding his strong brown hands and trying not to look at the foreshortened body in the bed.

James and Rawdon came in the evening and sat with her while Oliver continued his silent fight for life, tossing in his bed, reliving the battle. Polly came but could not stay because the sight upset her so much. She began to weep, and no-one wanted Oliver to see tears should he regain consciousness.

Oliver's colonel came and praised his reckless bravery, saying that those who had seen him attack the Russians single handed had been inspired by the sight. Out of four hundred men of the Fifty-seventh more than a third had been killed or wounded, officers and men.

Oliver lived through the night and the next morning he recovered consciousness. When Caroline saw his blue eyes gazing at her she felt full of hope. He would be an invalid but he would live! There were things he could do on the estate; he could still have a useful and happy life. He looked at her, moving quietly round the hot little hut so calm and composed, and his heart filled with gratitude and love for his sister who was always there when she was needed. The tears ran down his cheeks and, seeing he was conscious, she came over to him and knelt by his bed.

'Oh Oliver, don't weep. I am here, darling, and I am going to get you better.'

Oliver shook his head. 'I am not weeping because I am wounded, but because by some miracle you are here. As I went up the slopes of the Redan I thought of home, of the house and the sea beyond and all the good times I had as a child.'

Oliver's voice trailed off and he fell asleep again. His sleep was disturbed by dreams and fears, because he tried to turn a lot in his narrow bed and Caroline had to keep him still by constantly sitting with him and holding him.

It was so hot and airless in the hut that she got a fly whisk and whoever sat with Oliver kept on wafting it backwards and forwards over his head, to keep away the flies and induce a small breeze.

Polly took turns in looking after him, and Rawdon and James came whenever they could. Dr Hall himself looked in and the prognosis was hopeful because of his youth and strength.

But for days Oliver lay in a semi-conscious state, sometimes having long lucid conversations with Caroline or whoever was with him, and sometimes talking nonsense in his delirium.

Caroline had seen many men suffer as badly as her brother, sometimes worse; but it was almost unendurable watching someone you loved so much suffering such agonies. He had never once asked about his legs, and whether it was because he didn't know or he didn't want to talk about it she couldn't tell. Rawdon would come alone sometimes, and sit with her or relieve her while she went to rest or eat; but in this situation she preferred having James with her because Oliver seemed to sense that it was just the family and he was at his best at these times, quite lucid. He had always been very attached to his home.

'I was always half scared of James,' he said one day. 'But I'm not now.'

'That is because you are a hero,' James said. 'I lost sight of you, but those who watched said they had never seen such singular bravery.'

'I remember thinking I could take the Redan myself,' Oliver said laughing. 'I was quite sure I would get to the top and tear down the Russian flag. It was not bravery. I could not help myself. I wanted to take that hill.'

'And we should have done,' James said bitterly, 'if Raglan hadn't given in to Pélessier, against his better judgement we now hear.'

'Then why *did* he?' Caroline was sitting by the open door wafting the fly whisk about so as to give them more air.

'Pélessier apparently thought the enemy were going to attack the Mamelon and he wanted to forestall them by going up the Malakoff and, indeed, half way they met the Russians coming down. Someone said for a time there was a French flag waving on the Malakoff, but I didn't see it.'

Polly came in quietly and stopped when she saw James.

'Oh James, I was going to relieve Caroline; but as you are here . . .'

'But do stay, Polly.' James got up and gave her his chair. 'I see so little of you.'

'We have so many sick and ill,' Polly sighed and sat down. 'Now Lord Raglan is sick; but they say there is no cause for concern.'

James looked at her small weary figure and he wished he could love her as he said he did. But he saw her now as he used to, one of the family, the cousin he had grown up with. Only he didn't even think of her like that, which would have been better than the way he did feel about her. He couldn't help himself. The thought of her giving herself so readily sickened him. She had *asked* him to seduce her! What kind of lady did that? It was something he could never forget, or forgive, the easy wanton way she had given herself, like some sort of tart, not the kind of woman a man wanted for a wife at all.

Yet he felt sorry for her. He knew how bitterly she regretted what had happened; but he had said he would marry her and he would. He smiled at her again.

'Would you like to dine with me tonight, Polly? I have some men coming over and one or two of the wives.'

Polly's face lit up and Caroline smiled at James approvingly. She could see how hard he was trying to be nice to her. Caroline pitied Polly; but there was nothing else she could do but marry James, and she wanted to. It was simply that she knew how he felt about her. Caroline hoped that in the ordered family life they would lead James would get over it and make her happy.

Oliver had been restless today. The heat was stifling and she bathed him down every few hours. She was unhappy about his stumps and the doctor had been to look at them. She thought she had detected discoloration, signs of the dreaded gangrene.

After James had left with Polly, Caroline sat in the chair between the open window and Oliver's bed wafting the fly whisk back and forth. She thought of Polly and James, herself and Rawdon, and Oliver lying maimed in the bed. She thought of Chetwell, as he had, the family home, and of Mama and Papa. If they had not become estranged would Oliver be here now? Would she? Would Jane be living with a man to whom she was not married and would Emily have become so thoroughly rigid and unfeeling?

Was it the fault of Mama and Papa, or would it have happened anyway? Hard to tell with these things.

'Caroline,' Oliver said, 'I have no legs, have I?'

He had not spoken much during the day but she had known he was awake.

'No. Are you in pain?'

'I felt them with my hands. They only went as far as the knee. I wish they had been left, Caro, just to see if I could recover.'

Caroline went over to him and sat on a chair by the narrow bed. She took one of his young hands, now grown pathetically thin.

'There was no chance of recovery if they were left, darling. They had to come off; they were too smashed. You had been too long in the hot sun and they would have become infected.'

Oliver squeezed her hand and smiled.

'You are so good to me, Caroline. I am so glad you are here. I always thought of you as mother, and not Mama ...'

'But Mama *loves* you, Oliver ...'

'Oh I know; but you showed it. If I was worried or hurt I always wanted you. I love you, Caroline, and now that I am going to lose you I love you more than ever.'

Caroline felt a lump in her throat; but she would not let the tears come. There must be no suspicion of them, no betrayal of Oliver's bravery.

'You are not going to lose me, darling. You will get well and go home, to Chetwell.'

'Not without my legs. What use is a man without legs?'

She sat beside him on the bed so that she could cradle his head in her arms and hugged him very tight.

'You must not talk like that, Oliver; you must not be defeated. You are a Vestrey, don't forget that, and we are a long, strong line. You have your mind and your brains and you can finish your degree. You can take over the estate and help Papa who, some say, may be made an ambassador.'

'What woman would look at a man without legs?'

'A good woman, a beautiful woman, one who loved you. She would not notice them; it will not affect your life or hers. You will ...'

Oliver took her hand and brought it to his lips. 'You are very good, Caroline, too good. You would spend your life looking after me as you did Mama. I would be a burden and you would not marry Rawdon, but stay with me. When I knew you were to marry I was jealous, but now I know he is a good man and will make you happy.'

'We would *both* look after you,' Rawdon said coming quietly into the room. He had been standing in the doorway, not knowing whether to come or go because of the intimate nature of the conversation he had accidentally overheard. 'But, like Caroline, I don't think it will be necessary. You will have wooden legs and a servant to help you walk and you will be quite independent, knowing you. You will be climbing hills in no time!'

Oliver looked at him and smiled. 'I want you to be happy with Caroline; make her happy. She is the best of women, the best of mothers.'

'I know,' Rawdon said.

'And I want the family to be happy again. Emily to forgive Jane, and Papa and Mama to live happily as they used to. I would like to think of that.'

'But Oliver, you will be *there* . . .'

Oliver shook his head and fell into another disturbed sleep, crying out this time and sometimes gasping for air. Rawdon stayed with Caroline and she felt the warmth of his love, his companionship. They sat at the door holding hands, looking at the lights of the boats in the bay, the lamps glittering in the hospital huts scattered over the hill.

'I love you very much, Caroline. You are a good woman.'

'I am not a good woman. I am very selfish. I want to turn back the clock and have Oliver whole again, and the family at Chetwell all happy and united. It *was* such a happy family. I look back on the days of our youth and realize how fortunate we were.'

'That is not being selfish. But you will have a new family, Caroline, our family, and you will be the best of mothers as you are the best of daughters, the best of sisters. To your family you have already been all three.'

He leaned over and kissed her cheek and she felt that need for him that she had when they first embraced, a longing to merge, to be of one flesh. What was evil about wanting to do that? What was wrong? Could Jane possibly be right, after all, and it was simply years of convention that made men and women so strange with each other? She loved Rawdon and wanted him, but if they made love he would despise her, as James despised Polly. Yet, within marriage, the same act was supposed to make a man love and respect a woman. It was very strange, very illogical.

She turned to him and kissed him, gently on the lips, and she felt him tremble and knew he felt as she did. Then they joined hands again, very aware of each other.

'Emily is engaged to be married,' Caroline said softly. She didn't look at Rawdon, but was aware of his hand in hers.

'I'm glad,' he said. 'To whom?'

'To someone called Sir Arthur Stamford. Do you know him?'

Rawdon let go of her hand and leaned forward as if in thought. 'I know Christopher Stamford, who was in the Eighth Hussars. But he is in his twenties. His father, Sir Arthur Stamford, must be quite old. Surely that can't be the same man to whom Emily is engaged?'

'Yes, it is. He has a grown-up family, Papa says. I don't think he is too happy about the marriage.'

'Well, is Emily happy? That is the important thing.'

Caroline got up to light the lamp. Every time they talked about Emily she felt ill at ease. And yet now Emily was engaged, no longer a threat to her happiness with Rawdon.

'Papa does not say. The word he uses all the time is "suitable". It is a very "suitable" match in every way. There is no word of love.'

In his mind's eye Rawdon saw Emily galloping away on the beach, enticing him. Whenever he thought of home that scene always came to mind – it was so English, so romantic and beautiful; a lovely woman on a horse with the sea in the background; the long stretch of white sands beneath her feet. He would always remember Emily like that. On that day they nearly fell in love.

Caroline was standing in front of him looking down at him.

'Of what are you thinking?'

'Oh, nothing.' Rawdon emerged from his reverie and reached for her hand.

'Of Emily?'

'Caroline, why must you always goad me about Emily?'

'I am not goading. I wondered how you would react to her engagement.'

'I am pleased for her sake.'

Caroline turned towards the bed. 'I always wonder about you and Emily, Rawdon, and I always shall:'

She leaned over Oliver who lay smiling at her, his eyes open and very blue. Even in the dusk she could see how bright and blue they were. She felt an exultation because it

591

seemed he was really getting better; she had begun to worry about him, his restlessness, the state of his stump wounds, but now . . .

She put a hand on his forehead, smiling down at him. Then her pleasure turned to terror. She called his name and put her ear to his heart. But he smiled at her still and nothing changed; nothing would ever change for Oliver again.

'God take you straight to paradise,' she whispered.

Rawdon came over and put his arms right around her, giving her strength. She clung to him for a moment and then she knelt by Oliver's side and recited some prayers she could remember. Rawdon knelt with her and said the Amens. Then she drew his lids over his very blue eyes and kissed them. For a long time she looked at that face she loved so well, that she had nursed as a baby and kissed as a little boy, worried over as a young man. She gently pulled a sheet over it and telling Rawdon to summon James and Polly, went over to the main hospital hut to report another death from wounds in the Crimean war.

They buried him on Cathcart's Hill the next day. It was early morning and the small procession stopped by the spot where so many of his comrades had been buried a few days before; General Campbell, Colonel Yea, Captains Agar, Shiffner and Shadforth and many others who, like Ensign Vestrey, had been killed on the fortieth anniversary of the Battle of Waterloo. The hill was full of fresh graves. Some had just been filled in, others were still open to receive the dead, like Oliver, covered in his country's flag.

From the hill Caroline could see the Redan, the Russian flag still flying and the place where he had been mortally wounded just above the large ditch. Rawdon held her very close as they lowered Oliver's body into the grave, and James threw the first handful of earth while the chaplain recited the burial prayers. Rawdon picked up some earth and gave it to Caroline and for the first time she nearly broke down as she saw its grains scattered on the flag of the country he had been so proud to serve.

But how had it served him and others like him, young, untrained men who had been thrown into a war that was still badly led? What tragic, wrong decision had cost Oliver his life? What unnecessary heroism had his been?

Everyone was saying that it had been madness to storm such a strongly fortified place as the Redan when no attempt had been made to silence its guns. Instead of being elated by the self-sacrifice of the men, their fellows were disgusted at the war that bumbled on and on, with such wholesale slaughter and no visible gain. The Russians, who had seldom seen such senseless bravery as the attack on the Redan, said that the allied forces were 'lions commanded by asses'. After the defeat at the Redan everyone was more depressed than ever because no end to the war could yet be seen.

But no-one grieved more for the failure than Lord Raglan himself, though few around him knew it because he was a man who had seldom shown his emotions. Within a week he was dead, officially of cholera, but most people said he died because his heart was broken by his latest and most costly failure in the war.

The Grenadiers formed a Guard of Honour as Lord Raglan's body was removed from his headquarters on 7 July and placed aboard Her Majesty's ship *Caradoc* which departed for England the same day.

Caroline prepared to return to Scutari with James and Polly who were taking a boat home from Constantinople. The war would go on; everyone said there would be a fresh campaign in the winter, and James obtained leave to be with his family to share their grief about Oliver and escort his fiancée back home.

Two days after the departure of Lord Raglan, Rawdon received a telegraphed message from Saltmarsh. He first saw his commanding officer and then went up to the hospital on the hill, now full of fresh wounded from the skirmishes following the fall of the Redan. Rawdon stayed watching Caroline for a while as she walked among the men, brisk but compassionate, detached yet at the same time involved with their sufferings. She saw him and paused. It reminded her of the night she had seen him in Scutari. He had the same grave look on his face. But something about him now alarmed her and she went quickly over to him.

593

'What is it, Rawdon?'

'I must speak to you. It is very urgent.'

She looked behind her at the ward and saw that it was quiet. 'I can step out for a few minutes.'

'You must get someone to relieve you. I want to talk.'

Caroline hurried inside and conversed with one of the nurses. Then she drew on her shawl and walked out of the door with Rawdon to the path along the cliff overlooking Balaklava Bay. It was nearly nightfall and the boats were already lit up, the sound of lilting music came from the ships at anchor and the little cafes in the harbour.

'It is like some festival,' she said. 'Oh, I feel the war will soon end.'

'Caroline, my father is dead.'

'Oh Rawdon . . .' Caroline caught her breath and turned to him. 'Oh my dear, I am so sorry.'

'I am to go home immediately. Sir James Simpson has given me permission.'

'Of course.'

She put a hand on his arm, knowing that this event would change their lives. He drew her into his arms until their faces almost touched.

'I want you to come with me.'

'But Rawdon, I cannot.' Caroline tried to back away but he held onto her.

'I need you, Caroline. I want you to be my wife. I need you by my side. Your duty is to *me* now. You have served our country well.'

He let go of her and turned to face the bay, to give her time to collect her thoughts. A yacht was coming into the harbour for the night. It was very warm and he wiped the sweat off his face.

'Rawdon, I cannot come now. You must see that. It is too sudden. I have to report back to Florence . . .'

'But you were leaving here anyway.' His voice began to rise with anger.

'Yes, but to go back to Constantinople; not to go to England. Florence's great friends the Bracebridges are restless and wish to go home. They have been here from the beginning, you know, and are elderly.'

'There are others . . .'

'Yes, but others cannot do the things that I can do.'

'Caroline, you will *never* leave here as long as Miss Nightingale remains. You promised me . . . in the autumn . . .'

Rawdon's voice broke. Caroline wanted to touch him but dared not, for fear she would break down too.

'My darling, it is not *yet* the autumn. I promise I will ask for leave if the war does not end. We all thought it would be over by now, didn't we Rawdon? Truthfully? We had that in our minds when we planned an autumn wedding.'

'We said we should get leave. You could come back to Turkey, to Florence, after the wedding.'

'But with all your father's affairs to sort out will you return? You are now Lord Foxton, Rawdon.'

'I know.'

Rawdon bowed his head. He thought not only of his father but of the responsibilities that would now multiply around him; his mother, his sisters, the estates.

'Oh Caroline. I do want you.'

'I will come in the autumn Rawdon, whether you return or not. There will be a lot for us both to do, my darling, and the time will soon pass. It will pass very soon, Rawdon.'

He took her in his arms and kissed the brow of her head. He could feel the tension, the resistance in her body, as though she were withholding herself from him. He felt an ominous chill in his heart to compound the grief he felt for his father. Would she always be like this, resisting him when he needed her? Was it not her duty to be by his side, now and forever?

Suddenly a feeling of bitterness overwhelmed him and he let her go. She looked surprised and her face paled as he thrust her from him.

'What is it Rawdon?

'I don't think you really want me, Caroline. You are stalling me. If you wanted me, if you loved me truly, you would come with me.'

Although it was hot, Caroline pulled her light silk shawl more closely about her, anxiety gnawing at her heart. 'I am sorry you feel like this. I thought we understood each other. I do want you, dearest; but I cannot renege on my duty, even for you. Were I just to follow you blindly, would you respect me . . .'

'Yes I would!' Rawdon interrupted rudely, knowing she had not finished. 'Of course I would respect you. You think of nothing but respect. "Respect" and "duty" – that is all you talk about. You have agreed to be my wife, we should have been married months ago. I confess Caroline, I have not too much time for women who embark on lives of their own. It is not really womanly; my experiences out here have not impressed me. I do not think women have a place in hospitals, and Miss Nightingale is still, as you know, most unpopular. People are talking about you too Caroline . . .'

'Oh, are they?' she murmured quietly.

'Yes. They are saying why is the Honourable Caroline Vestrey mixing with nurses who are mainly whores and doing demeaning work? Most of the nurses out here have terrible reputations. Now because I love you and know you are utterly pure, I admire you for it. I saw your devotion with Oliver, before that with your sister Debbie. I think you have great qualities; but they are misdirected. You have made your point; you have shown us what you can do. Now it is time you settled down with me as Lady Foxton, with all your great qualities, and applied your sense of duty to me, to my family and to Saltmarsh.'

When he finished Caroline looked at him with an expression of utter rebellion. Was this all he thought of her? As some appendage, some chattel? How could she love a man who could speak to her in this way, who could trample on her feelings, so heartily condemn her aspirations?

But yet, and she despised herself for it, his anger was attractive. The light in his eyes, the set of his strong mouth made her want him. He would be powerful and protective; she would never have to worry about being cared for. Life as Rawdon's wife would be secure, happy and, yes, important. Not that she valued importance for itself; but she would have a place in the world, in society and, because of her experiences in Turkey and the Crimea as Florence had said so long ago, she would be that much wiser.

'Perhaps it *is* time I settled down, Rawdon.' She bowed her head with unaccustomed docility. 'Although I do not agree with all your views, and some things you say are harsh and hurtful.'

'Oh my darling, I did not mean it!' Rawdon, immediately contrite, put a hand round her waist. He was overcome with relief. He had spoken from the heart without wondering how she would react. Would she reject him? But then he saw the change in her expression. No, she would not. At heart she was an obedient, well brought-up daughter of the house and a few strong words on his part would remind her of her obligations. Women never responded to weakness. His father had said so and his father was right. This war had unhinged everyone, made people do foolish things. He loved and respected women, but they had to know their place, otherwise one was not respected in return. A weak man was too easily dominated.

Caroline leaned against him feeling his protective, encircling arm. 'When I return to Constantinople I will talk with Florence. I will resign. You have my word.'

'My darling,' Rawdon murmured, stroking her hair. 'You are quite right to see it like that my own, darling Caroline.'

After a while he let her go and silently, hands together, they walked back to the hospital.

The following day, with only the chance for cursory farewells, he embarked on a naval ship that was going straight to England. Caroline, Polly and James stood on the quay waving as his ship sailed out of the harbour. A week later they left together for Constantinople.

James had been very affected by Oliver's death, because he thought it was so unfair. A young, untried ensign's life had been sacrificed for nothing when he and Rawdon had been out more than a year, fought hard in every engagement and had not sustained a scratch. 'I should have died instead of him,' he said to Caroline the night before he left. 'It will be a grief I shall always carry until I die.'

Caroline, helping to pack Polly's things, straightened up. 'You must never blame yourself, James. It was the will of God, surely an *act* of God. Oliver did what he wanted to, even though his glory was brief. He will forever live in our family's hearts and memories, and our children will tell of

597

his bravery and fearlessness and perhaps by his example he will help to inspire others in years to come.'

She went up to him and kissed his cheek.

'You must be good to Polly, James. Do that as your tribute to Oliver. Regard it as your task to make her happy.'

'I will,' James said, 'but I do not love her. She knows I do not love her.'

'Then you must hide it. It is your duty. You did a shameful, despicable thing in treating a member of your *own* family, your first cousin, like a whore. It is worse than if you had done it to anyone else.'

'I know. I am very ashamed.' James put a hand to his eyes. 'What a horrible time this has been.'

'Polly will make you a good wife, James.'

'How can a wife be good who gave herself so easily?'

Caroline looked at him coldly. 'You despise her and not yourself? I despise you. I admire her because what she did was for you. For her it was a noble, self-sacrificing act inspired by the highest motives of love for a man whom she thought at any moment might be killed. For you it was simply to ease your lust. It is disgraceful, James, and you must now devote your life to making Polly happy, to atone for what you have done to her. It is your duty as a Vestrey and a man. I expect it of you, and so would Papa if he knew which, God forbid, he never will.'

CHAPTER THIRTY-EIGHT

James remembered Caroline's words as he looked at the plaque set in the wall:

In memory of
Ensign the Honourable Oliver Vestrey
Fifty-seventh Foot
Born 2 February 1835
Died 24 June 1855 from wounds sustained before Sebastopol
Dulce et decorum est pro patria mori

It is sweet and fitting to die for one's country. Fitting. Died of wounds . . . without any legs. Remembering the awful carnage in the broiling heat of the terrible day they failed to capture the Redan, James thought how easily sickly sentiment glossed over what was ugly. He remembered the trenches full of corpses and the blackened, putrid bodies congealing in the sun. At least Oliver's death had been as comfortable as circumstances could make it, nursed by his beloved sister, and his burial had been dignified. Not everyone was so fortunate, if you could think of death as being in any way fortunate.

Next to Oliver's plaque was another to Colonel the Honourable Gerard Vestrey, who died at Waterloo. It was his father's intention to enshrine the memory of the two Vestrey heroes of this century in a stained-glass window. At his request Jane had already spoken to Mr Burne-Jones about the possibility of designing one. No doubt it would be very poignant and beautiful, with the rays of the sun shining down on faces uplifted to the heavens.

But James felt too bitter. He could not expunge the bitterness from his soul and did not think he ever would.

Oliver's death was a waste and unnecessary, as the whole war had been unnecessary. His father had said the Russians were demanding the restoration of Sebastopol, should it fall, as part of the peace treaty! Such an act would be a violation of the memory of gallant men, like Ensign Vestrey, who had truly and passionately loved their country and had, indeed, gladly died for it.

And making love to Polly had been so unnecessary too. Like Oliver's death one could only blame it on the circumstances created by war, when one did not reason or function as a completely rational man. Oliver charging alone up the Redan, however brave, was not the act of a sane man. James felt that his folly with regard to his cousin had somehow curtailed his life; ensured that his youth was well and truly over. But at least most people began marriage with some sort of hopeful expectations. He had none. He was marrying a woman he neither loved nor respected because she had so easily given herself to him. Caroline had said she had done it from the highest motives of love; but he knew that this was not quite true. She had wanted it; she had *asked* him to seduce her, like some low born doxy, and such behaviour in a woman who was about to be one's wife was not easily forgotten, however much he could forgive himself and blame it on the war. Far better to have taken some drunken nurse than Polly. Oh far, far better for both of them. But the banns were being called and the wedding would be within the month so that he could return to the Crimea.

Everyone said now there would be peace; that the Russians were getting ready to quit Sebastopol. But there had been talk of peace for so long that few believed it any more.

He looked across at Polly standing with her mother and brothers and sisters. Dalton was there with his pretty, pregnant wife Maggie. The Ticehurst family stood in the pew behind looking like respectful family retainers, Mr Ticehurst in a shiny new suit and Mrs Ticehurst, rather complacent and overblown, in a large purple crinoline. James shut his eyes. He would be related by marriage to the Ticehursts! That was almost worse than anything. Polly glanced at him and smiled nervously. He smiled back. She frequently had that nervous smile now. They never talked about themselves, or even about anything particularly interesting. That marvellously intimate, personal talk of the Crimea was gone. Instead there was guilt and inhibition. She wanted to forget

600

they had ever been lovers, and his memories too were blurred by disgust and self-recrimination. He had treated her like a whore and pretended to love her. It was despicable.

But supposing he *had* died? Ah, that would have been different. Would she have remembered it as something to glory in for the rest of her days, treasuring his memory, like Aunt Ruth who everyone thought had gone to bed with her Archie, so powerful and steadfast was her love.

But, instead of looking forward to his life, as he always had, James was filled with dread. He felt it was over, and that he was to be buried, not on Cathcart's Hill like Oliver, but in the stale confines of a loveless marriage to a woman he did not admire and into a family far inferior to his own. Caroline said it was his duty.

'He who would valiant be...'

He threw back his head and joined in the hymn.

After the memorial service they strolled back to Chetwell Place. The older members of the family and guests went by carriage. But Agnes walked up with George, holding onto his arm. They walked quite fast so as to receive the guests as they came in through the main door, and George marvelled at how agile Agnes had become.

'You fairly skip, my dear.'

'Oh that was a horrid thing, George, a thing of the past. I owe my recovery all to Sophie.'

She looked behind her. Mrs Chetwynd waved. She was never far away. She had promised Agnes that she would never leave her completely alone with George, she would always be there in sight, just in case George ever suggested they should have a proper marriage again.

Sophie had been such a comfort since the awful news came from the Crimea. Without her she could not have borne it; she would have gone mad. She slept in her bed at night and hugged her close, driving out the awful nightmares that followed Oliver's death. Never to see those beloved features again . . . Agnes had sobbed for days. She would always reproach George for letting him go. It was quite unnecessary.

Could he have stopped him? George had never ceased to

think about it since the news came; the terrible day that his clerk brought him the telegram from the War Office.

'Died of wounds sustained at Sebastopol. Ensign the Hon. Oliver Vestrey.'

James had said it was a glorious death, and Rawdon that it was an example he would remember all his life. But to George the death of a son aged twenty was not glorious. In a few short weeks his hair at the temples had gone quite white. It was as though he himself had suffered a wound from which he would never recover – an open suppurating wound, the pain of which kept him awake at night. Not even Hilary had been able to assuage the agony, and at times he felt guilty because of the pleasure she gave him. Had God punished him for this sin of adultery?

They came to the main door and the Vestreys formed themselves into a line to receive their guests. George and Agnes, Aunt Ruth, then James, Emily and Jane.

Sir Arthur Stamford had been asked to represent the Queen and he was received first, kissing Emily on the cheek as he passed her and then taking his place next to Jane so that he, too, became one of the family, as Emily's fiancé. When Polly shook hands she stood next to him. She was soon to be a member of the family too.

Daniel Lévy stood in the line next to Jane, just like a full member of the Vestrey family. Many of the people who had come to the ceremony were as intent on gawping at Jane and Daniel as mourning Oliver Vestrey. Some could not understand the way Lord Vestrey paraded his fallen daughter and her vile seducer about the place – vile, Jewish and foreign too.

Jane and Emily had not yet spoken. Jane and Daniel had come on the morning train from London and were late arriving at the church. As the line of guests came to an end the members of the family moved into the drawing-room to circulate among their guests. George took Emily by the arm and hissed into her ear:

'I wish you to speak to your sister.'

Emily gazed around as though wondering who on earth Papa could be referring to; but George was not deceived.

'Jane. *And* I want you to say hello again to Daniel.'

'I refuse, Papa.'

'You cannot. I insist.'

'I will summon Arthur.'

'Sir Arthur will know what is right.' Out of his eye George saw Emily's impeccably dressed fiancé coming towards them. He reached out an arm and drew him forward.

'Sir Arthur, I wish Emily to speak to her sister, to be civil to Jane's common law husband.'

Even Sir Arthur looked startled and stroked his grizzly moustache. The truth about Jane had slowly emerged during the course of their very correct courtship – it had been dragged out of Emily most reluctantly with the help of Charlotte Canning before she left for India where her husband was now Viceroy. Sir Arthur had, of course, taken it all in his stride. Many who remembered the Regency were inclined to be more indulgent towards morals among the upper classes than the new generation.

'Oh, I'm sure Emily will say how do you do, Lord Vestrey. He looks a remarkably civil fellow.'

'He is also the father of my grandchild.'

'Ah!' Sir Arthur put a firm hand on Emily's arm and drew her, protesting, towards Jane and Daniel who were standing slightly to one side of the society which was so interested in discussing their affairs, while so disapproving of them.

Jane watched Emily and Sir Arthur cross the room with apprehension. She clasped Daniel's arm. He was uneasy too, his revolutionary *sang froid* having deserted him in the midst of this full blown concourse of the English aristocracy. Emily and Jane came face to face with each other. Both were unsmiling, but Jane's eyes were flickering nervously from Emily to Sir Arthur, her lips practising a timid smile. Suddenly Emily bent towards her and pecked her cheek, then she brought forward her fiancé.

'Jane, may I present Sir Arthur Stamford. My sister Jane, Arthur.'

Sir Arthur bowed gallantly over Jane's hand and his genuine friendly smile melted some of her fear.

'My dear, I am charmed to make your acquaintance.'

'This is Daniel,' Jane said. 'Daniel Lévy.'

Daniel stepped forward fingering the gold watch, a present from George, which hung from a chain suspended across his waistcoat. His black beard and hair were immaculately combed, his face still white but less chalky than the previous year. Emily, speechless, gave him her hand and he bowed over it but did not kiss it. He gazed for a moment at her and then he shook hands with Sir Arthur.

Neither Jane nor Daniel seemed capable of saying a word until George, having anxiously observed the ceremonial, came over and put an arm round the shoulders of each of his daughters. He kissed each one on the cheek and squeezed them. At last Emily smiled. At the very least they had succeeded in pleasing Papa.

Like the rest of the assembly the sisters were dressed in black, a colour that became Emily more than Jane. A little cluster of blonde curls on her forehead made her black bonnet look attractive rather than severe and she had a bunch of fresh purple violets on her corsage. She looked beautiful, capable and a little formidable. She was no longer a young girl, her manner seemed to proclaim, but a woman about to be married with all the responsibilities, duties and privileges that state entailed.

'How is your daughter?' she said at last. 'Papa says she is beautiful.'

'She is lovely,' Jane said. Her eyes thanked Emily for speaking first. 'Would you like to see her?'

Emily looked at Sir Arthur who tucked her proffered hand under his arm.

'Your sister and I would be charmed to visit you, my dear. And when we are married you must come often to see us.'

'When will that be?' Daniel said, keen to impress one of the Queen's courtiers with his very correct English.

'Ah, the date is yet to be arranged. Her Majesty is reluctant to part with Emily.'

'Must you leave the court when you are married?' Jane looked at her sister with surprise.

'Alas for ladies, yes,' Sir Arthur said. 'For the time being. After Emily has settled and become accustomed to married life no doubt Her Majesty will offer her a position of lady-in-waiting if she so desires. But first Emily wants to travel and, well . . .' Sir Arthur looked delicately at his intended who lowered her head as a little flush rose up her long white neck. Sir Arthur was obviously referring to children, a subject Emily was very reluctant to discuss except in the most general terms.

'Of course,' Daniel said, understanding. 'Not for a long time.'

Everyone noticed the encounter between the sisters, the initiative taken by Sir Arthur, gentleman-in-waiting to the Queen. A little queue formed behind him to meet Mr Lévy and shake his hand and that of the fallen woman next to him. One, of course, would never think of inviting them to one's house; but it was rather a *risqué* thing to do, in this age of high morality, to meet a couple who were living in sin. The older ladies, especially, jostled for position and Sir Arthur took Emily by the arm and bowed and withdrew.

'That was not too bad my dear, was it?'

'He looks better than he did,' Emily murmured. 'Good living at my father's expense suits him.'

'I think he seems quite an interesting fellow. *All* these foreigners aren't bad you know.'

'*That* sort of foreigner is,' Emily said. 'You can't compare him to the Emperor of France.'

'Ah, that is very different.'

He and Emily had only just returned from accompanying the Queen and the Prince to a visit to the Court of Napoleon III. He was a man who, together with his beautiful wife, the Empress Eugenie, was greatly pleasing to the Queen, even though he was a descendant of the Great Napoleon and not the real Royal Family of France, the Bourbons. The Emperor went to great lengths to flatter the Queen and she was a woman who greatly responded to male admiration.

Emily had been aware of Rawdon from the moment he entered the church. Without turning her head, but by swivelling her eyes, she had just been able to see him standing between his mother and sisters. Lord Foxton. He looked older, but not as old as Sir Arthur. She kept to her old trick of pretending not to know he was there, even managing to look surprised to see him in the receiving line and merely shaking his hand.

Now, Sir Arthur in tow, she made for him quite deliberately and he knew it, because he had been aware of her too from the very beginning. The day as well as being a sad one for him was also mingled with a sense of pleasant anticipation, because he was going to see Emily.

She had, he knew, been manoeuvring to be near to him, the minx. Still the same Emily. Sir Arthur didn't look as old as he'd thought. Now she was beside him, scintillating, even more beautiful, the dark violet eyes just as alluring. She leaned towards him and he was almost taken by surprise.

'May I kiss you now that we are to be related, Rawdon?'

'Of course.'

Rawdon smiled and stooped, aware of her softness, the lovely fragrance as her lips delicately brushed his cheek. She seemed to linger just a moment longer than was necessary and then stepped back.

'Sir Arthur, may I present Lord Foxton? He was with my brother Oliver when he died. Rawdon, I don't think you know my fiancé, Sir Arthur Stamford.'

The men bowed and shook hands.

'How do you do, Sir Arthur,' Rawdon said. 'I do know your son Christopher. We played polo together before he left the Hussars to become a country gentleman. How is he?'

His son. Sir Arthur's son was Rawdon's contemporary. Emily gazed at him impassively, the laughter leaving her mouth. Had he deliberately asked after Arthur's twenty-seven year old son? No, he was merely being polite; Rawdon would never be so spiteful. But she knew that she would feel it all her life; this defensiveness about Arthur's age would never leave her.

'My son is very well thank you, Lord Foxton. Please accept my condolences on your own bereavement. Do you intend to return to the Crimea?'

'That I don't know.' Rawdon glanced at Emily. 'It depends on Caroline. I am hoping she will return home.'

'Caroline is to return home?'

Was it dismay in Emily's voice? Rawdon couldn't tell; but he knew her eyes never left his face.

'We are to be married before Christmas. Caroline has promised.'

'There are those who wonder you did not marry in the Crimea.'

Emily's voice was stilted and artificial; her eyes were very bright and her smile brittle.

'Caroline did not wish it. I did.' Rawdon looked at her and Sir Arthur, sensing undercurrents he did not understand, shuffled his elegant feet and murmured, 'Miss Vestrey surely wishes to be married in the bosom of her family, as you do, my dear. Quite so. Emily, your aunt seems to wish us to join her.' Sir Arthur pointed to where Aunt Ruth was chatting in a group. 'I think she is having a problem entertaining Lord Aberdeen. Occasions like this always bring on a morbid state in him, reminding him of the many bereavements in his own family. I hope we see you again soon, Lord Foxton.'

Rawdon smiled but said nothing. He saw the look in Emily's eyes as she turned away.

Jane remembered how Caroline had discovered them here a year ago in this same bed; what a fuss there had been then. Now the moonlight streamed across their bodies and the whole family knew where they were. Daniel was still awake. He had just put out the lamp and lay on his back gazing at the ceiling. She had pretended to be asleep for the past hour. His hand groped for her and she sighed and moved away as though in sleep.

'Are you awake?' She didn't reply. He turned towards her and slipped a hand beneath her nightgown. 'I know you are awake. Your breathing is not regular. Why don't you want to make love to me?'

She felt stiff and cold. At times she felt she hated him.

'Is it because of the memorial service or because you did not enjoy the day? Too many curious people who wanted to stare at us, but will not invite us to their homes? I thought it went off quite well. Even Lady John Russell spoke to me; she was quite interested in my views on France.'

He pulled her nightdress over her thighs and caressed her

hips and buttocks. She moved further across the bed, trying vainly to get out of reach.

'I like it here,' he said. 'I like this house by the sea. The air is very good. I enjoyed the day. Even your sister spoke to me though it cost her dearly, and as for that stuck-up courtier ...'

'I thought he was rather nice!'

'Ah, you *are* awake.'

He leaned over her and put a leg across one of hers in order to separate them. He always imprisoned a leg like this because he could manoeuvre himself into the right position for love if she did not respond to him. Sometimes she found it exciting and it roused her; but tonight she did not.

'I hated the day,' she whispered. 'I hated the people staring and talking behind their hands. I would like to go away and never see any of them again.'

'Even your family?'

'Well, I want to see Papa. But Mama and Emily ... no I do not care if I never see them again.'

'And I don't care if I don't see your father again.'

Daniel withdrew his leg and rolled over again on his back. One had only to mention Papa to produce in Daniel a sulkiness that could last for hours, sometimes cloud the entire day. It certainly impeded his ardour.

'Papa is very good to us, Daniel.'

'I hate that word "good". It means patronizing.'

'He does not patronize. He is a good man.'

'He doesn't like me.'

'You don't give him much cause. You are rude to him all the time, arguing with him at every opportunity. It is as though you want to put him in his place.'

'I do.'

Jane raised herself on the pillow and looked out of the window. The full moon shone in the sapphire sky, and before she had got into bed she had gazed for a long time at the sea. She thought of Françoise and the little house in Hampstead where Françoise would be asleep. She worried about her when she wasn't with her.

She was aware of her nightdress still over her hips. She had to live with Daniel or else she would admit the most

608

terrible defeat, to herself, to society, to all those people who were there today. She could never come back to Chetwell, and she could not live by herself. Daniel was a great man but a difficult one. Sometimes serving him was very hard; she felt demeaned by it. Perhaps if they had another child it would help.

She turned on her side towards him and groped for his face. He took her finger in his mouth and, giving a little sigh of pleasure, drew the nightgown right up to her neck and began fondling her breasts. So often he spoke best to her through the flesh and, although she sometimes thought it was the line of least resistance, she answered him best that way. Here they achieved a communion they seldom were able to in anything else.

He was a wonderful, exciting lover. That never changed. After they had made love they always felt better; but when you had spent the whole day quarrelling or in silence or being hurt, like today, you did not always want to begin.

'So you do want me?' he murmured, putting a hand on her belly.

'Of course I want you.'

He kissed her and then he looked at her, stroking her hair back from her face.

'You are a very silly girl, Jane. Why do you make things so difficult?'

'Do I? Sometimes I think you are the one who makes things difficult.'

He put a finger over her mouth. 'Now you are talking nonsense. I have to make a great effort sometimes to keep the peace with you. You are so moody, Jane – like today. You wanted to be accepted by these people, yet you know you have put yourself beyond them by your behaviour. You want them to admire you and treat you as they used to. But they won't. You knew that a year ago and you do not accept it.'

'I don't think it's fair.'

'Neither do I. But it will not change for many years. Instead you have me, my darling. I do love you so much, Jane.'

His voice, speaking gently in its soft, accented English,

the delicate, skilled touch of his fingers arousing her, exploring her most intimate parts – these things were familiar and so pleasurable. She was so used to him, so at one with him on occasions like this. Really, he was all she had in the world, him and Françoise. They were a family. Maybe if Caroline were here it would be different, but they replaced her own family who had grown alien to her, except for Papa. But Daniel hated Papa; he made it difficult for Papa to visit them with any sort of pleasure; there was always such tension and unease in the air.

But she had chosen Daniel instead of Papa, and when things with him were good, when he spoke softly, tenderly and they had an understanding like at this moment, they were thrilling.

She could feel the edge of his beard, the bristles of his moustache next to her cheek.

'I do not mean to hurt you, Daniel.'

'Of course you don't my darling. I know that.'

He kissed her and she drew him on to her, linking her hands tightly behind his back, so that his taut, lithe body with its down of soft black hairs was pressed very close.

CHAPTER THIRTY-NINE

On 8 September, the day after the Chetwell memorial service, the Russians, to everyone's surprise, suddenly moved out of Sebastopol and the eleven month siege was at an end.

At about the same time Caroline came up with Florence who had recovered from her illness and was anxious to restore order to the nursing establishment in the Crimea.

As usual she was met with hostility. Mother Bridgeman who had come over with Mary Stanley and had always questioned her authority had, without her permission and backed by Dr Hall, moved to the General Hospital at Balaklava. Miss Nightingale had had a very bad passage due to the weather, and been prostrated with sickness. Since the Bracebridges had returned to England she relied on Caroline more than ever and she, to her mortification, had lacked the courage to tell her of her intention to return home.

She had promised Rawdon she would do so, and because Florence showed no signs of going back herself, despite her exhaustion, she knew she had to. Although Sebastopol had fallen everyone saw another winter in the Crimea, even if the peace could not long be delayed.

It was probably a bad time to tell Florence but then no time was ever the right one. She was always harassed and bogged down by worries of one sort or another.

'But you cannot *leave* me,' Florence said looking up from the pad on which she was, as usual, incessantly writing, when Caroline at last broached the subject.

'I do not mean to, Florence. But, now that Sebastopol has fallen, Rawdon may send for me.'

'*Send* for you?' Florence said raising her eyebrows. 'And you will obey him, of course? I must say, I thought you had more spirit, Caroline. I cannot blame you, I suppose, for letting your emotions be swayed; but I am sorry for it. He is a very attractive man, and a nice one. I liked him. I could see you were attached. But I too was once attractive and attracted to men, Caroline. I did not, in my heart, lack passion. But I applied it to my duty to my fellow human beings; all the men who have died in my hospitals or on these fields are my children. Is that not a greater calling?'

Caroline looked at Florence, so much changed since her illness. Her hair which had been cut off when the fever was at its height, was still shorn and she was terribly thin and pale. She hardly resembled the woman Caroline had met in London the year before. Yet, although she was weaker and her looks had suffered, her morale and serenity had noticeably grown. She looked like one who had received and answered the call to greatness; she no longer resembled an ordinary human being at all. It was indefinable, but it was there. But Caroline was no longer afraid of her. Since the death of Oliver she found that nothing frightened her any more, neither Florence, nor the war nor death itself. She had grown stronger too.

'It *is* a great calling, dearest Flo. But I am not called to it. I thought I was, but I am not. I wish to be married to Rawdon Foxton. I have a duty to him, especially since his father's death and he now has greater responsibilities. That is why I think that, with the fall of Sebastopol, he may decide not to return to the army. Rawdon Foxton and I love each other. There are disagreements, difference , as we discovered when he was here, but he has convinced me that my duty is by his side. I gave him my promise that I would ask you to release me as soon as Sebastopol had fallen, and now it has.'

'So you want to go home?'

'Yes.'

Florence wearily got up and came over to Caroline. They were living in the ship that had brought them from Scutari and had been talking and working since early evening on Florence's papers. The boat was quite still on the calm waters and a cold breeze from outside wafted in through the porthole. Suddenly Caroline shivered. It seemed to presage another winter like the last and she thought of Florence, working alone, her strength fading more and more, even though she now had her beloved Aunt Mai with her sent out by the family for support. But Aunt Mai had no knowledge, as Caroline had, of the way Florence worked, of the problems and difficulties that beset her in superintending the hospitals under her control. Nor had she the first-hand knowledge of nursing that Caroline had. Florence's hair was growing in little curls and she looked very weak and vulnerable, almost child-like, as she came up to Caroline and put a hand on her arm.

'Please do not leave me, Caroline, until the war is over. Afterwards I wish you all the happiness in the world with Lord Foxton, and I am sure you deserve it. I do not ask you to follow me and do as I have done. I would not ask that of any woman who did not think she truly had a vocation for this life. It is hard to be alone, especially when one is scarcely ever appreciated. Just stay with me until the war ends, Caroline, and then I will come to your wedding.'

Caroline closed her eyes. Florence grasped her hands and she felt that strange compulsive power that Florence always seemed to exercise upon her. How long would the war go on? What would she say to Rawdon?

'I cannot, Flo. I have given my word. Please release me, do not distress me. You know I love you and would do anything for you.'

'But the call of Rawdon Foxton is stronger?'

Caroline thought she saw scepticism in Florence's fine eyes. 'Yes.'

'Because he is a man? He bids you do a thing and you do it? I am surprised at you Caroline. I thought you had more independence. You are just going to be like any other woman after all.'

'*Any* other woman, Flo? Is that fair?'

Florence let go of her hands and went back to the table on which she had been working. After all she had had many blows in the Crimea, and this was just another. She sat down and took up her pen.

'No, maybe it is not fair. You are an exceptional woman, Caroline. I am sorry you are still riven by a conflict I resolved many years ago, because you cannot have a vocation to serve others *and* be married. That is quite clear. Richard Monckton Milnes has gone on to great things you know. He and I were very close; he proposed several times, but I had to work by myself.'

'But what can I *do*, Florence?' Caroline went over to her and knelt by her side. 'I do not feel a vocation like you. I am not called to serve the sick and suffering.'

'Are you sure?' Florence put a finger under Caroline's chin, raising it and looking into her eyes. Caroline was very aware of Florence's hand on her face, her fingers on her neck. 'I would have thought you were. Are you *completely* happy with Lord Foxton? You say you had disagreements?'

'Well, all engaged people have disagreements.'

'Do they? I would have thought it a sunny, carefree time of life if two people were intending to spend their lives together. If they disagree then what will happen after they are wed?'

She took her hand away from Caroline and made a few quick strokes with her pen on her paper. Caroline remained sitting on the floor at her feet looking up at her.

'We had many disagreements. Many of a fundamental kind.'

'And yet you are returning to marry him?' Florence raised her eyebrows and tilted her head without looking up. 'I find that *very* strange. Or do I? I know you have been throwing yourself into your work, Caroline, as though you are trying to drive out something. Memories perhaps? But not happy ones? Am I right?'

Memories of the fierce altercations she had had with Rawdon, the sense of rebellion and frustration he often left her with. Now that he wasn't here to tantalize and attract her by his physical presence she could see his deficiencies more clearly.

'Rawdon Foxton is a very – conventional man, Flo. He is a good man, a brave man, kind and . . .'

'Rigid?' Florence suggested.

Caroline considered the word carefully, stretching out her legs before her and supporting herself on her hands. 'No, not rigid. Upright.'

'But an upright man can have flexible ideas. I gather that Lord Foxton is not flexible in his attitude to women?'

'How did you know that, Flo?'

'Oh I guessed. I can read people, you know, and much as I liked him, attractive as he is, I would not wish to marry a man like that. He will expect you to behave in a certain way, the way, I grant, in which most women are expected to behave and indeed wish to; but somehow I suspect you are not one of them. You will want to behave differently, to think and do things that are unacceptable to other people; Lord Foxton will not like that.'

Caroline drew her knees up and rested her chin on them, gazing at Florence.

'What is it you think I should do, Flo?'

'I think you should write and tell him that you will return when the war is over. You have work to do; that will give you the chance to think.'

'But I have thought so much. I must see him.'

'There. I have put doubts in your mind haven't I?'

'Yes, but they were there already. What *is* my vocation, Flo?'

'Maybe to nurse, to administer. You have a great gift for both; you are good with people. They love you and respond to you. You are compassionate, yet you do not succumb to violent emotion, as you showed when your brother died. The very next day, it was reported to me, you were at work in the wards, gentle and smiling, with the poor, sick and wounded men as though you had nothing on your mind but them, as though you had not just lost and buried a beloved brother. Would you waste these qualities on marriage, Caroline?'

'But I do not think you waste them in marriage. Surely they enhance your marriage? They work to the benefit of your husband, your children ...'

'They *can*. If you have the right husband and children. But I am not saying you should *never* marry; that is a natural, human emotion. What I say is, is Rawdon Foxton right for you? That is what I am asking. Will he let you grow or will he diminish you?'

'I must think about it,' Caroline said slowly getting up. 'I will think what to do, Flo.'

She looked gratefully at Florence, but the Superintendent

of the Female Nursing Establishment of the English Hospitals in Turkey was hard at work, her pen flying as usual rapidly across the page.

The Redan had held out until the very end; a final assault was made on it by the allies, but still it refused to yield, and when the Russians moved out of the town they abandoned it.

Caroline stood at the top looking down onto the slopes where Oliver had received his mortal wounds and where many British soldiers had been buried. Ahead of her was Cathcart's Hill where Oliver lay; behind the harbour of Sebastopol and the sea beyond.

She had told Florence she wanted to think and Florence, in her wisdom, had suggested she should visit Sebastopol with a party that was going, one of whose members was Colonel Windham, who had led the storming party on the Redan when Oliver had been wounded. He was now governor of the south side of the town appropriated to the English. Also there was Colonel Wellesley of the Guards, *aide-de-camp* to Lord Rokeby. Oliver's heroism on a day when there had been many brave acts was still spoken of. There was talk of a new medal for conspicuous gallantry, to be instituted especially by the Queen, and Lord Rokeby said that Oliver's name would be among those put forward to receive it.

But did it compensate for Oliver's death at twenty years of age, or make the war any more sensible? Did it justify the terrible conditions in which those who still remained in shattered Sebastopol had been found? In one of the hospitals a pile of rotting corpses contained men still living underneath, one of whom, an English officer taken prisoner, had gone stark mad.

It was easy to see how the Redan had withstood assault so many times. It was so well fortified, a mass of little batteries, each still containing two or three guns with traverses behind. And beneath the gabions and sandbags were huts where its defenders lived for days, maybe even for weeks. There were even traces of female occupation – a half burid shoe, a crushed hat lying amid the rubble.

Bodies still lay about, carcasses of horses and dogs, decayed and putrefied beyond recognition. Some lay in half-dried pools of blood, and there were remnants of blood-stained uniforms, caps and weapons. Leaning over the steep parapet of the Redan Caroline saw the freshly turned earth in the trench beneath where so many British men who had fallen were buried on the spot, neat little wooden crosses marking their last resting places. Over towards the Mamelon she could see a blue-coated French *picquet,* smoking and talking quietly in the shade of a tent made out of cloaks arranged on long stout branches. In front of them was the usual *pot-au-feu* – beloved by the French, who always managed to eat and drink well regardless of conditions – bubbling away on a fire made of twigs.

They rode down from the Redan into the town, towards the harbour. Everywhere there was the same desolation and an awful stench rose from the ruins, some of which were still smoking, even though it was days since the Russians had left the city. Shattered guns and broken transport carts, some with their dead horses still in the shafts, leaned on their sides, or up against broken walls, their wheels deep in dried mud. On the corner of a street a small heap of green, putrefied bodies was being shovelled into a cart by men with cloths tied round their faces. Even from a distance Caroline could still smell the stench and she raised her hand to her head, thinking she might faint. But purposefully her horse strode on with the rest of the party who said little, as though dazed and shocked by what they saw.

It was true that most of the civilians had long since left Sebastopol; but how could *anyone* have survived? Not a building stood intact and, particularly pathetic in Caroline's view, were the beautiful villas with large gardens long abandoned by their owners, many of them now without roofs and with gaping shell holes in their walls.

The harbour was still full of ships, some with broken masts, half-sunk in the water. Some had been destroyed by fire and their blackened burnt-out hulls had a ghostly appearance enhanced by the bright sunshine. A fragment of a bridge stopped abruptly over the water and, from a terrace that overlooked the harbour, they saw workshops, a foundry for the Russian dockyard and discarded implements and machinery lying everywhere.

The odour from the dry docks nearby was almost as

intolerable as that from the decaying bodies, and Caroline once more felt overcome by nausea. Captain Greave, from her dead brother's regiment, noticed her distress and passed her some water in a bottle made of hide.

Colonel Windham rode over to her and looked at her anxiously.

'I think you have had enough, Miss Vestrey. It is no sight for a woman.'

'Nor for anyone, Colonel,' Caroline replied gravely. 'I have seen many terrible sights this past year, but I never thought to see such awful deliberate destruction, such hopelessness. To think that, for eleven months, we have bombarded this place and reduced it to rubble. For what purpose, Colonel?'

'To finish the war, Miss Vestrey,' the Colonel replied with some asperity. 'The war one of your brothers gave his life for, and yet another fought to win for his country. The war that *you* yourself, a woman, have served in with such distinction. War is a thing in itself, Miss Vestrey. It has its own dynamic and, once embarked on it whether good or bad, we must contrive to win it.'

'My father is again in Vienna at the peace talks. God grant they will succeed.'

Caroline turned away, keeping the rest of her thoughts to herself. She would not expect a professional soldier to share them; Rawdon might, but not James. War was for glory and had little other meaning. It was, in a sense, this grandiose concept of war that had driven Oliver. She knew there were still those who wanted it to go on; for the actual campaigning and fighting to continue, until the Russians were driven out of the Crimea.

They rode past the custom house, past the Court of Justice and the ruined dwelling houses, and around the Little Redan where bodies of dead Russians still lay among the twisted metal and broken gabions of the shattered fortress. They rode past the Malakoff Tower which, Colonel Wellesley told her, was a miracle of engineering constructed by the ingenious Todleben so that a shell from without could do no harm unless it fell in exactly the right place. Todleben had been wounded just after the unsuccessful British attack on the Redan when Oliver had fallen, but he still continued to direct and repair the fortress until the end.

A little beyond the walls of the town they passed through a fertile ravine in which a church and a graveyard stood somewhat incongruously. The church had been reduced almost to rubble by the guns – the ravine standing between the French lines and the Russian batteries – but its lead green-painted minaret still stood, rising with a pathetic defiance to the sky. Among the broken tombstones and monuments in the graveyard were flowering laburnums and acacias, lilac in full bloom and tall trees with thick green leaves that gave a welcome shade in the heat.

Caroline paused a while under one of the trees, her eyes closed, listening to the sounds of humming bees. Not long ago this quiet valley had reverberated with the sound of gunfire night and day. Shell and round shot, fallen short, still littered the ground so that it seemed to be paved with it. She tried to imagine it twenty years hence when all traces of the war would have gone; the little church restored, the tombs mended, the living coming quietly to pray, and the dead resting peacefully in their graves.

But nothing disturbed the dead or their tranquillity, no matter what men did. One day the trenches would be filled in and the redoubts levelled down, fresh green grass would grow where the allied camps now stood, and no one in Sebastopol, except those old enough to remember, would ever be able to tell that a war had been fought over it for almost a year.

If war had any meaning, even a hopeless, futile war as this had been, it was that life was inextinguishable and flourished in the most unlikely places, like the beautiful flora in this derelict graveyard.

Those of the party who had not paused in the shade were making their way slowly up the precipitous slopes of the ravine and along the side of the hill where Oliver lay. Caroline moved out into the hot sun and climbed after them, her horse plodding slowly, as weary as she was. The proximity of Oliver's grave filled her with such strong emotion that she wanted to go and kneel by his side, fling herself onto the earth and shed all the tears she had kept dammed up inside her over the past year, during all the months in Scutari, during the terrible days when he fought for life, and long, long after he died. She had never allowed herself to break down or neglect her duty, she the eldest daughter of the house. Was there not a time to weep, as well as to laugh, and to keep oneself so strictly in control?

But his grave was so peaceful on the slope in the sun, a gentle breeze blowing in from the sea as it did at his home in Kent. Here, on this Crimean Hill far away from Chetwell, Oliver seemed in a curious way finally at home.

Home. Home was England, Chetwell, Rawdon. She thought of the castle at Saltmarsh from the top of whose twin turrets you could just see the English Channel. Was she meant to be its mistress? Was she meant to marry Rawdon? What would Oliver, that young man grown wise before his time, have told her if he could speak?

For a long while she looked towards his grave. And then she knew, as if Oliver had indeed spoken to her from the dead. He would tell her to go home, to speak again to Rawdon and the family, to consult with Papa; and then to see where her duty lay. And Florence would approve. Florence would think it was right, even if she wanted Caroline with her; because Florence, she was sure, would never sacrifice a human being to her own selfish motives. Florence was much too wise.

An unexpected, sudden upsurge of relief and hope filled Caroline's heart like an answer to a prayer. She had doubted, but now the doubts were gone. She knew what to do.

In the distance one of the party stopped and hailed her. Caroline waved and flicked her crop against the flank of her horse. She galloped towards the Woronzoff Road to join the rest, leaving Cathcart's Hill behind.

CHAPTER FORTY

The crowd gathered round the carriage to say goodbye seemed pitifully small – just family and a few close friends of James. It was not the society wedding that either Polly or her mother had imagined in their dreams; the wedding to the heir of Baron Vestrey.

Polly peeped out of the window once the carriage door was closed holding out her hand to her mother. There were, Emily was sure, tears in her eyes. Dorothy Tangent clasped her daughter's hand and pressed it; there were tears in her eyes too. Why should her daughter be so unhappy marrying the man she had loved for so long? She couldn't understand it. They had not been merely tears of joy.

Emily stood at the back of the crowd aware of Rawdon Foxton just behind her. He had been best man, Clare and Patrick bridesmaid and page. Like James, he wore uniform as though to emphasize that the reason for this hastily arranged, sparsely attended, joyless wedding was the war. The war to which James was returning the following week.

The crowd milled around on the terrace of Chetwell Place talking. It was a very mild October; the day had been warm, full of sunshine.

'I never saw a more dismal-looking couple.' Emily turned to Rawdon. 'Do you think they can possibly be in love?'

'I think they were nervous.'

'More than that. James was morose for days and Maggie Tangent says that Polly has kept on weeping. It looks like it too. *What* happened in the Crimea, Rawdon?'

Emily of course had been much more beautiful than the bride. Her gown, of pale blue silk, had a bodice deep pointed at the waist. The *décolletage* was trimmed with lace and the V-shaped front with wide lace revers. Epaulettes of lace concealed the very short sleeves. The blue silk overskirt, gathered to the waist and very full, reached just above the knees. The skirt underneath was made of lace and decorated with small flounces and the dark blue flowers that also adorned her *décolletage* and the sash on her dress. Her lace gloves came to her elbows and her hair was ornamented with the same flowers that decorated her dress.

Emily was a picture – Rawdon had scarcely been able to stop looking at her and, at the wedding breakfast, their eyes kept on meeting over the heads of the guests.

'They decided to get married,' Rawdon said unable to give an adequate answer to her question. 'They must have fallen in love.'

'But did they *seem* in love?'

Emily casually left the terrace and took a path that led around the side of the house, through the formal gardens to the rough grass that bordered the copse overlooking the sea. Rawdon followed, wandering behind her, gazing at her back, the lovely line of her shoulders, the angle of her head.

'For a time, yes. They seemed very much in love; but I was preoccupied. I was in love too.'

Emily glanced behind then paused so that he stopped very quickly and nearly bumped into her.

'*Was?*'

'Well,' he said as they resumed their slow walk. 'Am. Of course I am in love with Caroline.'

They reached the copse and through the trees they glimpsed the sea. Only a slight breeze stirred and a haze obscured far-off Dungeness. It was almost like midsummer. There was a bench on the brow of the hill – the same one that Emily had sat on a year ago, reading Rawdon's letter – and, carefully arranging her dress, Emily sat down, her hands clasped in her lap. She looked very grave and composed, open to confidences of an intimate, certainly secret nature.

'You don't seem very sure. James looked as though he was going to be executed, not married. Of course no-one could understand why he decided to marry Polly. I think he had second thoughts. I hope you do not.'

'Of course I shall not,' Rawdon hovered, looking uneasily at her. 'There is no question of that. But, all the same, Caroline has changed, Emily. Her experiences have not been altogether beneficial. She is not the girl she was.'

622

'Oh.' Emily stared at her hands. 'I am sorry to hear it. Papa finds her letters most uplifting.'

'Well I do not. She has developed a passion for argument; she has some most extraordinary views which I find quite out of place in our society. I hope she will lose them when she returns home, when we are married.'

'Because, of course, you still intend to marry Caroline?'

'Of course,' he looked at her. 'We are engaged. After asking her to return home it would be contemptible not to honour my promise.'

'What an odd thing to say; almost as though you were talking about marrying someone you no longer loved, Rawdon. I fancied James no longer loved Polly. What strange things the Crimea does to people.'

'It does, very strange. It is like being in another world. One does and says things one would not dream of doing and saying at home. Tongues are loosened and emotions become disoriented. That is why I am sure that Caroline will lose her odd views when she is restored to her family; when she is no longer under the spell of Florence Nightingale.'

'Miss Nightingale is a bad influence?' Emily raised her eyebrows. 'But she is a heroine.'

'She has heroic qualities, certainly; but it is the way she achieves her ends that people object to. She brooks no opposition, she is a despot.'

'Certainly one has heard disquieting rumours,' Emily admitted, 'but the Queen is full of admiration for her. She is planning to have a brooch, designed by the Prince, to be specially made in her honour.'

'How long will you remain at Court, Emily?'

'Until my marriage. That has not yet been decided. In a way I am reluctant to give up my liberty to undertake new and important responsibilities. One obviously has certain liberties as a married woman; but one is still circumscribed. Sir Arthur, of course, is very anxious for the marriage. It will probably be in the spring.'

She looked over the sea as she spoke, her beautiful eyes shadowed by her thoughts. She did not look like a happy bride. Rawdon wanted to sit down beside her and touch her; but he did not dare.

'Sir Arthur could not come to the wedding?'

'Sir Arthur was not invited,' Emily said softly. 'After all, it was a quiet affair and he is not yet a member of the family.'

For a moment she looked at Rawdon and then resumed her pensive, thoughtful gaze across the sea.

Agnes thought it quite bizarre that, as soon as the happy bridal couple had left, Rawdon and Emily should have been seen creeping off together round the side of the house. She asked George to go after them, but he refused. Slowly the guests had departed, but still Emily and Rawdon stayed away until even Jennifer seemed on edge, bobbing up and down every minute to peer out of the window.

Daniel was amused. He could see the apprehension on their faces.

'I don't think Emily will come to any harm,' he said when Jennifer had got up yet again and even Jane was looking restless.

'Of course Emily will not come to harm!' George said testily. 'They have gone for a walk to clear their heads. It was very hot in that church.'

'Stifling!' Agnes wafted her handkerchief across her face. 'Sophie, would you be good enough to fetch the *sal volatile*? I shall have to lie down if my head gets any worse.'

Sophie got up rather reluctantly; she felt out of sorts when the family were at home, as though she was constantly being put in her place. When she and Agnes were alone the servants did everything; when Lord Vestrey was here, and especially his detestable daughter Emily, she seemed to be invested with the invisible veil of servant status again and was always on the go.

Jane sat with Françoise on her lap. Her daughter was making one of her infrequent visits to her grandmother who never seemed especially grateful for the opportunity of seeing her. But George adored her. In a life that was increasingly full of tension and disagreeable things she and his infant son were his greatest sources of consolation – they and Hilary. She grew more delightful, even lovelier, more companionable. The only thing that irked her, and it irked him, was the secrecy with which they had to conduct their relationship. He could only ever be seen out with her in a crowd and, despite his care, he knew people still talked. Even Lord Palmerston, that well known rake, had told him to be careful.

His home reminded him of how unsatisfactory his family life had become. James was obviously not in love with Polly – it was such a dismal wedding, it was like a funeral; everyone had such heavy solemn faces. Jane and Daniel seemed to be increasingly alienated, at least in public, and now Emily had disappeared with Rawdon. Every time they were together he, if not anyone else, was aware of the undercurrents between them. They were almost tangible. It was most uncomfortable.

The horseman was coming up the hill as Rawdon and Emily strolled back through the garden, making a long detour among the formal lawns and parterres to prolong the period during which they could be alone. She was telling him about the State visit to France and he thought once again what a delightful companion she was, how effortless her conversation, sparkling but not overwhelming, how intelligent. She was no longer the vain young girl she had been. If there was a word he would apply to Emily now it was – sophistication. She was sophisticated without being remote, mature but not cold. Life with Emily would be so stimulating; with Caroline he was beginning to fear it would be an ordeal. They saw the horseman go round to the servants' entrance, and a few minutes later, just as they came to the front door, they heard him ride away again down the drive.

George held the telegram in his hands as they entered the drawing-room and everyone looked at them and then away, as though they had surprised a guilty secret. George waved the telegram, looking unsure as to whether or not he was giving them good news.

'It is from Caroline,' he said. 'She is coming home. She may have left already.'

At eighteen months Henry George Vestrey Ashburne was a precocious toddler. He crawled or walked into everything and his nurse dared not take her eyes off him for one moment. His father viewed his development with pride.

'He is certainly the most advanced of my children at that

age,' he said, crossing his legs and accepting a cigar from Hilary. 'Thank you, my darling.' He kissed her hand, holding it briefly to his lips. Then he relaxed in the chair exhaling smoke to the ceiling. 'Caroline is coming home. You would have thought I was announcing a death when I broke the news, except for Jane. Jane was pleased. Even Agnes looked horrified, and as for Rawdon . . .' George made an aperture with his fingers, 'his face fell about two inches. Like that.'

'How incredible.'

'He had just been away for over an hour with Emily. She did not look pleased either at the news; but then she and Caroline are still, officially, not on speaking terms. They do not even correspond.'

'You think Rawdon's affections for Caroline have cooled?' She tucked a little faldstool beneath his feet and in a familiar gesture – one born of long intimacy – unbuttoned his jacket as she knelt by the side of his chair.

'Rawdon has changed. Whether or not it is the death of his father or because of his experiences in the war I cannot say. But he scarcely ever smiles. He is a man cast in gloom except if Emily is there. Then he is different altogether.

'Sir Arthur was speaking to me the other day about the wedding. He wants to make arrangements now for St Margaret's Church at Westminster. A big society occasion he wants. He thinks even the Queen may attend, though I doubt it; but certainly the Princess Royal will and the Duke and Duchess of Cambridge, maybe the Duchess of Kent. It will be a very grand affair. I dread it I must say. Oh my darling, how I wish I had you constantly by my side.' He took her hand and pressed it. She nestled her face against his arm.

'I am by your side, George – always. Even when we are apart. I am there.'

'I know, my darling. I hear you whisper your good counsels to me.' George kissed her hair. 'But I wish it were real.'

The door opened and Master Henry came running in pursued by his red-faced nurse. He scampered up towards his father and climbed with agility onto his knee. The nurse put her hands on her hips.

'Master Henry. I told you . . .'

'Leave him, nurse.' George hugged his son, his arm still round the mother. 'I love to see my son. We have such little opportunity to be together as a family.'

At the end of November a meeting was held at Willis's rooms in St James's Street in honour of Florence Nightingale. The Duke of Cambridge was chairman and the audience a distinguished one, the speakers including Lord Stanley, the Duke of Argyle and Sidney Herbert; also Florence's former suitor Richard Monckton Milnes. The room was packed, the audience almost wild with adulation. It was proposed to set up a fund named after Miss Nightingale for the establishment of an institute to train nurses.

Afterwards the Nightingale family, who were too overwhelmed with emotion to attend the meeting, held a reception at the Burlington Hotel, to which Rawdon Foxton had escorted his mother and sisters, and Sir Arthur had taken Emily Vestrey. Rawdon watched her across the room as she moved gracefully about greeting people, having just the right word, the right expression, for everyone. What an adornment she would be to the diplomatic world.

Every now and then Rawdon's and Emily's eyes instinctively met. It was always the same when they were near each other – they wanted to speak, to touch, to hold hands. But they dared not. She was here with her fiancé and Caroline was expected any moment.

Sir Arthur was an old friend of William Nightingale and as he sat talking to him Emily quietly detached herself and circulated slowly around the room – yes, Caroline knew Florence intimately; yes, wasn't it wonderful she was coming home? She felt she was in the shadow of a heroine, her own sister. Jennifer and Harriet Foxton were talking excitedly to Parthe who now luxuriated in the glory reflected by her sister. Jennifer had just completed a new novel about the war and Parthe had read it. She had been so moved she had wept; she couldn't wait to send it to Flo.

They met in the centre of the room, surrounded by the crowd which enclosed them. They both smiled with relief that they were together because a chance, contrived meeting like this had been in their minds all evening. Rawdon looked

627

into her eyes and he knew that he must tell her; that the words must be spoken, the truth told. He stood very close to her, pressed together by the crowd. For all that, they could have been alone on the cliffs above Chetwell. Whenever he was with Emily it was a memory he treasured for long afterwards. Whenever he and Caroline had been together something unsatisfactory lingered in the mind.

'I *must* talk to you,' he whispered.

She seemed to understand and nodded her head, gazing quickly in the direction of Sir Arthur. His back towards her, he was still conversing with William Nightingale, the man whose continual support of his difficult daughter was only now vindicated. It had been an exhausting struggle with Fanny and Parthe. Even now he was not sure it was worth it.

'Come tomorrow afternoon to Park Street. At three if you can. I shall be there.'

Rawdon managed to squeeze her hand before they parted, their meeting so brief it had scarcely been observed in that crowded room.

'Lord Foxton, Miss Emily.'

Cornwall bowed and stood back as Rawdon came quickly through the door and Emily got up from the book she had been trying to read to greet him. They met in the middle of the small sunny parlour, used by the family for games and quiet chats, and Cornwall observed how, as they clasped hands, their bodies seemed naturally to come together, almost merge. Cornwall grimaced to himself as he closed the door. He had never seen the second daughter of the house greet Sir Arthur Stamford like that.

'You know what I have to say?' Rawdon held her hand and remained where he was, looking into her eyes. She was the smallest of the elder Vestrey girls, but still taller than the average young Englishwoman. The crown of her head came up to his chin, just a nice height. He would be able to clasp her hips so easily, but he did not dare. Her figure, the perfection of her body with its taut prominent bustline, drove him to distraction. She wore a plain gown of grey wool with the large cameo the Queen had given her at her neck, and her beautiful golden hair swept away at either side from the decorous parting in the middle. The clear azure blue eyes, the quality of unalloyed crystal, gazed up at him.

'I love *you*, Emily, not Caroline. I realize that now and I had to tell you. I thought I was merely attracted by your beauty and your sensuality, but I know I was deceived.

'Ever since I came home my only desire has been to see you, to be with you. Just to catch a glimpse of you enhances my day. I know not why I did not see the truth before; but I see it now.'

Emily remained gazing up at him, their hands still clasped. He saw by her expression, by the mobility of her features and the light in her eyes, that she knew what he had to say. When he had finished she lowered her head.

'It is too late, Rawdon. I am to be married, and so are you. Caroline is coming home because you asked her to; she is coming to marry you.'

'But how can I marry a woman I do not love?'

His eyes pleaded with her, but she released his hands and went to the window, her back to him.

'You *will* love Caroline. She is a wonderful person. She was always our mother, our main support. Everyone loves Caroline because of her remarkable qualities. You know what they are. You were right to love her, at first, better than me. I was jealous of her because I wanted you ...'

'You wanted me all the time?'

'Yes,' she nodded. 'For years and years. I thought at one time you might propose ...'

'The day on the beach?' He came and stood just behind her and his presence was so troubling that she started to tremble very slightly.

'Yes. I knew you loved me in a way, but that Caroline was more suitable. And she is! Rawdon she will make you a wonderful wife – good and dutiful, everything you could wish for.'

'But *you* are everything I could wish for. You have grown up since you have been at Court. I can think of nothing more perfect than to have you at my side. I intend to enter the Diplomatic Service, Emily. I saw Lord Clarendon today and he approves. Imagine Emily, our life in the courts of Vienna, Paris.'

Emily trembled more violently and shook her head.

'It is not to be. I too am engaged, Rawdon. Sir Arthur is a good man. He loves me very much. He has partly completed the purchase of a house in Eaton Square where we are to live. He has made such plans. How could I let Sir Arthur down?'

She turned to him appealingly; but he crushed his fist into the palm of his other hand.

'You do not love *him* either!'

'Ah.' She held up a hand. 'I have never loved him. It was always a marriage of convenience as far as I was concerned. A woman has to be married, Rawdon.' She raised her head and her eyes had a wise, sad expression. 'There comes a time when she can delay no longer. I did not wish to be like the Nightingale sisters, or your own if you do not mind me saying so. I am twenty-four. Mama never tires of reminding me how many children she had at my age . . .'

'But why *him*? His son is older than I am.'

'The idea does offend you, does it not? It repels my father too. I confess I am not attracted to Sir Arthur; but I do like him. Maybe I accepted him because he was the least like you of all the men who would have offered for me. If I could not have you I wanted no-one remotely like you. No, Rawdon, it is done. I cannot break my word now – and you cannot break yours. We each have our duty to think of. Yours to Caroline who comes home especially to be wed to you, and mine to Sir Arthur.'

Duty. It was that grim Victorian word. Duty. Country. Patriotism. But Emily was right. They would destroy the happiness of two people if they reneged on their word.

'I have been very unhappy this past year, Rawdon. My family has broken up. My mother is a complete nervous wreck; my sister forms a misalliance with an ill-mannered and intolerant revolutionary, and my younger brother is killed in the war. My elder brother is obviously not happily wed and I am estranged from my elder sister whom nevertheless I deeply love. We became estranged over *you*, Rawdon, and it grieved me desperately.'

'I know.' He bowed his head, aware of the dull heavy

beating of his heart. 'I know about the letter. I have behaved so badly, Emily, that I think it is God's way of punishing me. I loved both the Vestrey sisters and when it came to choosing I obeyed what I thought I should do rather than what I wanted to do.'

She gave a wan smile. 'You thought I was silly and vain ... Besides, your mother and sisters preferred Caroline.'

'You were neither silly nor vain but, yes, a different person and they *did* prefer Caroline. I do not think they would prefer her now if they could hear some of her views.'

'Views?' Emily looked amused. 'On what, pray?'

'Oh, she is for women having their own lives, regardless of their husbands' wishes. She thinks women ought to be able to work and have more independence. I am not too sure about her views on morality either.'

'Oh, that is *very* serious.' Emily pursed her lips to hide her laughter. Rawdon looked so very solemn. But how she loved him. Just to be in his presence was the occasion of so much joy. 'But Caroline is not immoral, *surely*?'

'No, but there are things she condones that I would not. She has some very peculiar views. I am sure they would distress my mother.'

'Then they would certainly distress mine!' Emily tried to laugh, but not very successfully. 'You see, Rawdon, in all this I needed a refuge. Sir Arthur opened his heart to me and gave me that protection. I owe it to him not to let him down. Besides we will be close, you and I. We shall be related. We can be very good friends.'

But that was not what Rawdon wanted. He stooped and kissed her neck and, at the feel of his lips on her bare skin, her trembling ceased. An arm stole round her waist and he pressed her fiercely against him. Then he kissed her.

CHAPTER FORTY-ONE

She had felt a sadness ever since she arrived, not joy, as one would have expected, at seeing her family again or being reunited with Rawdon. She was not like a young woman in love. Everyone thought the reason was because of her terrible experiences in the war. She was so sad because of all the death and misery that had surrounded her, so changed because she could not adjust to being at home.

Caroline flitted from Park Street to Chetwell and up to Hampstead to see Jane. She found it difficult to contain her restlessness, to stay in any one place for more than a day or two. Rawdon understood her least of all. She had come back to be with him yet they were hardly together, certainly never alone to discuss plans.

But Caroline wasn't sad or unsettled because of the memories she left behind. It was because she was at home, when she wanted to be back in Turkey where another hard winter was in progress. Florence was still locked in struggles with the incompetent bureaucracy surrounding her, she had been ill again and Caroline knew she was at a very low ebb.

'How can I be happy here when so much remains to be done in Turkey?'

George studied the tip of his cigar, his other hand curled round a balloon glass of good brandy.

'But my darling, I thought you returned to get married? Will you go back after that? What will Rawdon say? Will we have another quick, quiet wedding at Chetwell? Really I don't know what has happened to my children – they seem obsessed by Turkey and the Crimea. James writes that he is so delighted to be back even though his regiment has been sent from the Crimea to Scutari where the weather is terrible, the barracks knee deep in mud, almost as bad as the Crimea last winter. Yet he has left a young bride behind, and it seems you wish to leave a husband because Rawdon says he does not wish to return. What is Rawdon's mind on the matter?'

Caroline leaned back in her chair, her favourite chair in the small parlour which she had used as an office during her years as her mother's nurse and companion. It faced inland and so was spared the buffetings sustained by the other rooms which faced the sea. It was cosy and intimate, and she felt that something of her remained there after all those years of service – or was it servitude?

'I have not really spoken to Rawdon about it.'

'You appear hardly to have seen him!' George tapped his ash into the fire and took another puff at his cigar. He was upset by Caroline's appearance her thinness, her pallor, her lack of appetite. To him she was a deeply unhappy girl. 'I had so hoped this would be a happy time, the time of your return.'

'I will not be happy until the war has ended Papa, and I have done my duty.'

'Then *why* did you come?'

'Because I promised.'

'Well, you must sort it all out. Tomorrow we are due to take luncheon at Saltmarsh and we can consider it then.'

The following day Agnes announced that she was getting a very bad cold and so George and his daughter set out alone to drive the fifteen miles to Saltmarsh. Caroline sat impassively, her back to the horses, her gloved hand on the window ledge watching the countryside through which they passed, the countryside where she was born, of her childhood. Home. But was it still home? George, seated opposite, considered that she looked more rested. There was some colour now in her cheeks and her maid had washed and set her hair so that it gleamed with something of its former sheen. Maybe it was the thought of seeing Rawdon that had improved her appearance? A deep foreboding had possessed George, but it began to lift a little.

Rawdon came out on horseback to greet them and rode ahead of them leading the way to the castle. He had put his head in the carriage window and pressed Caroline's hand for several seconds before letting it go. Well, that seemed more like a man in love, in George's opinion, a little more.

The whole thing was very rum, and he was not sure he understood it.

Sybil Foxton, greeting Caroline for the first time since her return, embraced her warmly, and Jennifer and Harriet fussed about making her comfortable, pressing a hot drink into her hand and making sure she sat very near the fire.

'You look frozen, Caroline.'

'Well it was quite warm in the Crimea before I left; but we have terrible extremes of climate out there. Here it is just cold all the time.' She rubbed her hands in front of the fire and looked up at Rawdon to see him standing with his back to the flames staring at her; he glanced quickly away when he saw her expression. They never looked into each other's eyes these days.

The dining-room at Saltmarsh had fires at either end, but still Caroline was cold and had little appetite for the prodigious amounts of English roast beef with which she was plied. A sip or two of claret however brought more colour to her cheeks. She began to thaw.

'I have written a novel about the Crimea,' Jennifer said excitedly. 'Parthe Nightingale says it is tremendous. Florence has a very important part in it. I would like you to read it for me, Caroline, and check the details.'

'Gladly,' Caroline said smiling, noting an improvement in Jennifer since the previous year. 'But you should come out there yourself Jenny.'

'I would like to, but Papa would not permit it when he was alive and now Rawdon too forbids it.'

'Oh?' Caroline looked to the head of the table where Rawdon was very preoccupied with the contents of his plate. 'Do you not think she should have experience of the Crimea, Rawdon?'

'No, I do not.' He put his glass to his lips which he then wiped with a large napkin tucked into his waistcoat. How very much the family man he looked, Caroline thought, the head of the table, the head of the household, imperturbable because his word was law. His mother and sisters flocked about him like the inhabitants of a farmyard. Wherever Rawdon strutted about, there they were in his wake, like nervous ducklings, or anxious kittens. 'I do not think the

Crimea improves a woman. It is no place for someone gently reared to be. Caroline knows my feelings about this.'

'So you will not permit her to go back after you are married?' George glanced uneasily at his daughter and gave his plate to the footman hovering behind him. 'Yes thank you, I will take another slice of this excellent beef. From your own farm, Rawdon?'

'No, we are only sheep and dairy farming here. This is from one of my neighbours who is experimenting with a new breed of bull bred from the Charolais.'

'It is very good,' George said. 'Now, about Caroline and the Crimea.'

'Of course I would not permit her to go back.' Rawdon carefully carved a thick slice of the beef and put it on George's plate. He stood up to carve, his napkin falling over his front, his face concentrated in effort. He had put on weight since he had left the Crimea. He showed signs of becoming a prosperous country gentleman.

Caroline saw Rawdon a few years hence, presiding at his table in similar fashion, surrounded by doting, subservient children. But who would be facing him at the other end of the table? Herself?

'Would I have no say in the matter, Rawdon?' Caroline put her knife and fork neatly together and sat back. The plenitude of food slightly sickened her after the meagre rations she had been used to. Even the scraps from this table were more delectable than some of the dinners she had eaten.

'My dear Caroline, as my wife I would expect you to accede to my wishes. Would you not expect that as a normal thing, Lord Vestrey?'

Rawdon indicated to the footman to remove the dish of beef from in front of him and resumed his seat. Caroline noticed that he had piled his own plate high again. Obviously no qualms of conscience interfered with his appetite.

George shuffled uncomfortably in his chair, aware of an unpleasant undercurrent, of people hanging on his words, of everyone looking at him.

'I would expect Caroline's wishes to be in accordance with yours, Rawdon, yes. I would imagine that, as a happy newly-married couple, you would both instinctively desire the same thing.'

'Quite, Lord Vestrey, Caroline's wishes and mine being identical.' Rawdon nodded approvingly at his prospective father-in-law.

'And supposing they are not?'

'Really, Caroline,' George said uneasily. 'I wish you would not talk in that manner. You seem to wish to provoke difficulties.'

'But Papa, we must talk practically, must we not? Rawdon wishes one thing, I another. Our wishes in this matter decidedly do *not* coincide.'

'Then, as his wife, I am afraid you must defer to his opinion. That is what I would expect.' George bent his head to his plate, but Caroline stared in front of her, her eyes looking neither to right nor left.

'Anyway, that will be settled soon, I have no doubt,' Sybil Foxton intervened smoothly. 'The main thing is, *when* is the wedding to be, and where?'

There was a silence, made more awkward by the fact that no-one rushed to speak.

'Emily is going to have St Margaret's.' George spoke first. 'St Margaret's, in the spring.'

'I do not want anything so large or ostentatious,' Caroline said quietly. 'You know I love Chetwell.'

'Well then Chetwell, if Rawdon concurs.'

'Chetwell or anywhere.' Rawdon speared a piece of prime English beef and raised it to his mouth. 'I am quite happy to fall in with Caroline's wishes here. You see I am not obdurate at all. Chetwell will do very well, do you not think, Mama?'

'Well, I love Chetwell too of course; but St Margaret's *is* central. Don't forget you will want to invite a number of your London friends, Rawdon. And if you are to go into the Diplomatic...'

Caroline's face changed colour. It was as though the warmth had suddenly penetrated her cold body and her cheeks were suffused with a rush of blood.

'Rawdon is to go into the Diplomatic Service?'

'That is the idea, yes,' Rawdon said smoothly, surveying his empty plate with a replete expression. 'I have talked to the Foreign Secretary about it and he thinks it an excellent plan. I may be sent to America which would be very exciting, or Japan. Lord Clarendon has not quite made up his mind on this point.'

'Papa, did you know Rawdon was to join the Diplomatic Service?'

Caroline's voice was high. She ignored her fiancé and looked straight at her father.

'Emily *did* mention that he was thinking of it; but he has not yet discussed it with me.'

'My mind is not yet made up,' Rawdon said hastily. 'There are any number of factors dependent upon it. I assure you, Lord Vestrey, you will be properly informed when I have come to a decision.'

'And shall I?'

Rawdon saw the colour in her face and the indignation in her eyes. He got up and rounding the table took his fiancé by the shoulders.

'Of *course* you shall, my love. You shall be the very first. Now do not let us quarrel. We must not start off arguing before we are married. You know that I shall consult you at every opportunity and that goes for all our married life.' He kissed her cheek and went back to his place, ringing the bell for dessert to be served.

'St Margaret's then, I think,' he said at last. '*If* Caroline approves. Mama is right. A number of important people will have to be asked and Chetwell is very small.'

'Then if that is decided when is it to be?' Sybil Foxton looked brightly at her son. 'What is the date? It is now December.'

'The spring?' Rawdon suggested. 'Is that soon enough? It will give Caroline time to prepare, to have her trousseau made, to rest and get well after her ordeal.'

'*What* ordeal?' Caroline said, aware of the burning rage in her heart, the constriction in her throat, the harsh timbre of her voice.

'Why, your ordeal in Turkey, my love. It has sapped your zest and spirits. It has aged you. When I walk down the aisle with my bride I wish her to be the most beautiful woman in London.'

Caroline put a hand to her cheek. She could still feel the

burning. But she said nothing. She could see everyone was beginning to think she was churlish, even her father whose eyes looked sad and worried.

All afternoon it rained and by four o'clock George decided to return home. There had been no time for Caroline and Rawdon to talk privately, to take the walk in the grounds they had otherwise intended. He kissed her hand and her cheek in parting and whispered in her ear that he loved her. She wished she could have seen his face as he said it; but the hallway in the ancient baronial fortress was dark.

That night she stayed in her room, declining to come down to dinner. She pleaded a headache but George was not deceived. He was deeply concerned about his daughter.

'She is not like a woman in love,' he confided to Agnes at dinner.

'Caroline *is* very strange, I confess,' Agnes said. 'Do you not think so, Sophie?'

The three dined without Caroline. George was by now quite accustomed to having Mrs Chetwynd as part of the family. He could not like her, but neither could she be ignored.

'I think Miss Vestrey is disturbed by something; but I confess I have never found her an easy person to understand. She would certainly not confide in me.'

'Nor in me, her own mother,' Agnes said plaintively.

'Caroline wishes to return to Turkey.' George took a bunch of grapes from the middle of the dining-room table. The tension of the day as well as the good meal at Saltmarsh had left him with little appetite. He toyed with his food, and grapes, being small and light, suited his mood. He was glad he was returning to London the following day. He did not know how he would survive without Hilary to turn to at times like this. She would know just how to comfort him.

'*Turkey?*' Agnes seemed to have difficulty comprehending George. 'You don't mean that terrible place she has just come from?'

'I do.'

'Then she is clearly mad. She looks awful, quite ill and years older. It has impaired her health and her spirits. I wonder Rawdon still finds her attractive.'

George looked at Agnes, the thought obviously disturbing to him. Mrs Chetwynd, who had been listening with her usual absorption when anything to do with the Vestreys was discussed, leaned forwards, her eyes like little blackcurrants in her heavy suety face.

'But we *know* that he prefers Miss Emily now, do we not? In our hearts we all know that; yet no-one dares say it.'

George pushed back his chair and got irritably to his feet.

'That is palpable nonsense, Mrs Chetwynd. Rawdon and Caroline are very much in love. You can see it in their faces. Does not her coming back prove it? The wedding is fixed. It will be at St Margaret's Westminster in the spring and Caroline will not be going back to the Crimea. 'Twas all settled today. That is the end of the matter. There is nothing more to say.'

Sir Arthur Stamford bowed very low over Caroline's hand. It was the courtly bow he saved for foreign nobility who appreciated gestures of that kind.

'My dear Miss Vestrey, what a pleasure it is to make your acquaintance. You have no idea how often, and lovingly, your sister speaks of you.'

Sir Arthur stood back to allow Emily to come shyly forward. Now that the moment had come words had failed her. Her father had hastened forward to introduce Sir Arthur as soon as they came into the room as though in an attempt to break the ice. Sir Arthur was such an able diplomat.

As Emily approached her, Caroline saw the timid expression in her eyes. She seized her hands and impulsively clasped her to her bosom hugging her.

'Oh Emily, Emily.'

'Caroline.'

They hugged and they wept until finally George, almost overcome himself and relieved that the awkward meeting had passed off so well, gently went to part them.

'My darlings, happy as I am to see you united, I feel you should prepare for the ball.' He glanced at his watch. 'Rawdon will be here in an hour. As we are already dressed, Sir Arthur and I will smoke a cigar together.'

The girls parted, laughing when they saw each other's wet cheeks, almost ashamed of their emotion.

'Come, let us change together!' Emily grasped her sister's hand and they raced to the door pausing to bow to their father. Shutting the door after them George went over to the fireplace rubbing his hands.

'Well that was ably done, Sir Arthur.'

'Emily was *most* apprehensive.'

'Thank you for making it go so well. It was such a foolish misunderstanding they had a year ago.'

'What was its nature? Emily has never told me. Ah, thank you, Lord Vestrey.' Sir Arthur accepted the proffered glass of whisky and held it to his lips, silently toasting his host.

'It was a tiff between sisters. I really forget the details.'

George sat down opposite the man who was soon to become his son-in-law. He was still not completely happy about this but he couldn't help liking the fellow, and admiring him. He would do Emily a lot of good; he had done already. She was much more poised and womanly, more tactful and discreet, less a prey to her emotions. Not like the Emily of old.

'Well Sir Arthur, Caroline is to wed at St Margaret's too.'

'Really? You surprise me. I thought she was so anxious for it to be in the family church.'

'She is, but Rawdon is to join the Diplomatic Service as soon as he has arranged for the sale of his commission in the army. He feels his marriage should attract attention.'

'Oh, I agree with him. Make a splash. You only do it once, eh Lord Vestrey?'

'Quite.' His lordship lowered his eyes, whereupon Sir Arthur cleared his throat.

'Unless, that is to say, one has been bereaved as I had the misfortune to be.'

'Oh quite, that is a different matter altogether.'

'Emily will make me the happiest of men, Lord Vestrey.'

'I do hope so.' George tried to keep the doubt from his voice and got up from his chair to refill their glasses. It was quite clear to him that his daughter was making a loveless match.

Caroline felt the old excitement as she and Emily, giggling as though years had fallen away, got dressed together upstairs for the ball. One by one they held out dresses, discarded them and sent their maids scurrying about looking for new ones, as well as matching slippers and ribbons.

'This one. The pink,' Emily said holding an elaborate crinoline to her figure. 'And for you the blue.' She held the dress against her sister, approved her choice, put it on the bed and, in her long drawers and petticoat, came up to her and hugged her again.

'Oh Caroline I can't tell you how I have missed you, what joy it gives me to see you again. I was so nervous, I thought I should be sick.'

'There was no need to be.' Caroline put a hand on her arm and kissed her cheek. 'It was a silly thing, over and done with a long time ago. I never harboured any resentment and I longed to write to you.'

'Then *why* didn't you? I longed to write to you too.'

'Oh!' Caroline shrugged. 'I had no time for one thing, and then . . . I thought you might resent me still.'

'Oh darling, I will never resent you. I only want you to be happy. I quickly got over Rawdon. It was a foolish, girlish passion. I am *much* older now. Besides, he is so in love with you.'

'Is he?' Caroline's smile evaporated and she gently pushed Emily away. 'He has a very funny way of showing it.'

'Oh, how?' Emily sat on the bed, taking the silk stockings from her maid and drawing them on, one to each slender leg.

'He seems so very strict and abrupt, with me at any rate. I must do this, I cannot do that. I think being Lord Foxton has made him over-pompous.'

'Rawdon? Pompous? Oh he is never that. Not that I see him much . . .' Emily hastily drew her garters along her leg, avoiding her sister's eyes.

In fact they had not met since he had come here to Park Street and made his unfortunate, upsetting declaration of love. She had sent him away at once, her mouth still burning from his passionate embrace, her heart in a turmoil because of yet another transgression. How she had hated herself. He had written to her twice but she had not replied. But for the companionship of Sir Arthur she would never

641

have agreed to come to the Countess of Hartsmoor's Christmas Ball in Grosvenor Square.

Caroline looked reflectively at her sister, admiring her dainty precise movements, her precision as she adjusted her neat beribboned garter.

'I want to go back to Turkey.' She sat on the bed next to Emily, who patted her garter and then looked in astonishment at her sister.

'You mean *now*?'

'Yes. But Rawdon will not let me.'

'Well.' Emily got up, motioning to her maid to bring her hoop. 'I cannot say I blame him. After all he has been yearning for you all this time. Of course he does not wish to lose you again.'

'You think I should stay here?'

'Oh decidedly. Thank you, Doris. Now be careful how you put my dress over the hoop.' Emily looked critically at herself in the mirror and smiled at the maid behind her. 'You have done your duty, Caroline. Now it is your turn to be happy.'

'But I was happy there.' Caroline didn't stir from the bed to be dressed by her maid, but remained in her long frilly drawers and bodice. 'It is more than mere duty. I am *really* happy there. I did not realize it, but since I came home I have missed Turkey and the Crimea.'

Emily continued to look at her with amazement.

'You mean to say you miss all that? All that suffering and horror, all the . . .' She paused, utterly lost for words.

'Yes, all that. I felt needed and wanted and loved. I was useful.'

'But darling, you are wanted here.' Emily went and knelt down beside her on the floor, carefully arranging her dress. 'Rawdon wants you to be his wife. You will be loved and happy *and* useful.'

'It is not the same thing.' Caroline put a hand to her head and brushed back a lock that had fallen across her forehead. 'I can't explain it to you, Emily; but even when I was in England I was not altogether happy.'

'But that was because of Mama, and . . .'

'Yes; but I have always felt the need to do something with

my life. In Scutari I thought that maybe this was my vocation – to serve others. Florence thinks so too . . .'

'But you wanted Rawdon, you loved Rawdon Foxton.' Emily's voice began to take on a ring of indignation. 'We had such rows over him. Do you remember . . .'

'Oh I do not forget, I assure you. I *did* love him; you and I *were* jealous of each other. Now I am not so sure I am doing the right thing.'

Emily placed a hand on her hip and looking at their maids jerked her head in the direction of the door.

'Doris and Frances, please leave us. We will ring when we want you.'

The maids obediently tripped to the door shutting it carefully behind them. Their giggles and scampering feet could be heard from the corridor outside.

'Whyever did you do that?' Caroline looked at the door in surprise.

'Because I want to talk to you, Caroline, and it is not fit for the servants to hear us. You are saying that you are not sure you are doing the right thing in marrying Rawdon Foxton? I want to be certain I understand you correctly.'

Caroline noted her sister's quick even breathing, the warm flush on her cheeks. 'No, I am not sure. Rawdon opposes me in everything I wish to do. He says . . .'

'He said you had changed, that you had developed odd views. He said you no longer thought so highly of obedience, of women being the helpmeets of men.'

'It is true,' Caroline concurred, 'I do not. I have been independent too long. I have seen how inept men can be in their management of the war, how cruel to and abusive of someone as noble as Florence Nightingale and her few devoted helpers. Anyway, why should women be subservient to men? Can you tell me that?'

'Because it is the natural order,' Emily said promptly, starting to do her hair in the mirror. 'Even the Queen obeys Prince Albert in everything. She abhors women who seek to usurp the privileges of men. The Prince is the head of the Royal household. He sends directives and awards praise or blame, even to *her*! He determines who should reign in the Royal nursery. In only one matter is the Prince not supreme:

in matters pertaining to the government of the Realm. But in everything else he is above the Queen, and she wishes it that way. I have their example – and, believe me, it brings true happiness – constantly before me. And if the Queen of England thinks this is right, who are we not to agree? It is truly admirable to see her docility in his presence. Now I, as you know, am a spirited person with, I freely acknowledge, a liking for my own way; but I should always defer to my husband. I am convinced that God made men to be superior to us, in brain as well as physique, and we are their partners and helpers. We bear their children and preside over their household. It is a very special and privileged life we women have, and I am sure it is so ordained, under God. He means mutual respect between women and men, but one head. It is logical. I am quite happy with it.'

'Well, I am not.' Caroline got up and put on her own hoop. 'And neither is Florence Nightingale. There are others like us. Look at Jane . . .'

'Oh, Jane. Pray do not speak to me of her. Jane is completely under the domination of Monsieur Lévy. You have only to *see* them together. They were at Chetwell for the wedding. She jumps at his every wish.'

'Yes.' Caroline sighed. 'I have seen them together. I am surprised, I confess, how subordinate she is to him. I see little equality of partnership there.'

'Of course there is no equality. She does as she is told. And he is so inferior to her, by birth, breeding, everything; not like the Queen and the Prince, who are cousins! Now Jane *would* have a right to assert herself; but she does not. She is his creature. How I detest him!'

Emily tugged angrily at her hair and went to the door to summon the maids. 'Oh dear, I cannot handle my own locks. I am too spoiled, I am afraid.' She came over and stood in front of her sister, her great blue eyes so appealing and trusting. 'Caroline, do give up all these silly ideas. You will only make yourself unhappy. You are so lucky to have Rawdon. He is a fine man and I envy you.'

'You *still* envy me?'

'Yes. Oh, Sir Arthur is admirable in every way; but I do not love him. Ours will be a marriage of mutual respect;

nothing more, well, on my part anyway. I will, however, always be a most dutiful wife, needless to say.'

· Emily tossed back her hair and started to give it a hundred vigorous strokes of the brush before her maid curled her ringlets with the heated curling iron.

Rawdon was smiling at her, holding her waist quite tightly. She clasped his hand and tilted her head; but nothing sang in her heart. She wanted to be happy and in love but she was not. She wished to burst out of the cage that imprisoned her, but it was impossible.

'Are you happy, my dear? You look enchanting tonight, a feast for any man's eyes.'

'I am so glad I have improved, Rawdon.'

He frowned, the slight edge to her voice not lost on him. 'Pray do not say it like that, Caroline. It makes me sound too critical. I was thinking of you, my dear, how ill you looked on your return home. That was why I could not think of letting you go back to Turkey. You will soon be your old self again.'

But she didn't want to be her old self. She wanted to be the new Caroline, so changed, so different from the old one, not so complacent.

They danced until supper and then they all met in the dining-room where a long table ran the length of the wall and little tables were set out for supper. Papa was there with Aunt Ruth, Sir Arthur and Emily and Rawdon and herself. Surprisingly, Hugh Benson, Papa's secretary, was also there, and a woman she didn't know, a woman who looked at her as she sat down as though she knew her and seemed half inclined to rise and greet her. Papa held back her chair for her.

'My dear, may I present Mrs Ashburne? Hilary, my eldest daughter, Caroline.'

'How do you do?' The lady was charming, with a light musical voice and clear eyes of an unusual blue like aquamarine. Caroline had no idea who she was.

'I have heard so much about you, Miss Vestrey, about your nobility and heroism in the Crimea. I so admire you.'

'Oh pray do not talk of that, Mrs Ashburne. I assure you

645

one is not heroic who serves our wonderful fighting men. It is Rawdon and James and their brother officers, to say nothing of the ordinary soldiers, who are heroic.'

'But still, for a woman . . .' Mrs Ashburne looked at George, as though seeking his approval to continue. She really was extraordinarily pretty, Caroline thought. Quite a few people were looking at her, stopping for a moment at their table and smiling at George. One or two just stopped and stared without taking the trouble to smile. Their manner seemed quite rude, and Caroline felt a tremor of unease.

'Women can do things just as well as men can. I assure you, if you were . . .'

Rawdon put a hand on hers, his good-natured face looking strained, his eyes appealing.

'Caroline my dearest, pray do *not* bring all that up again. Let us have a happy evening for once without all the moralizing.'

'Oh I agree.' Emily smiled warmly at Rawdon. 'Not that Caroline moralizes exactly. It is just her point of view. Even Sir Arthur quite admires Miss Nightingale.'

Sir Arthur nervously stroked his moustaches, the brilliantine with which they were waxed shining in the light from the profusion of chandeliers hanging from the ceiling. The parting in his hair was so straight that his pink skin shone underneath, showing that his hair was getting a little sparse. He was very nearly balding, Caroline thought and then, with a shock, she remembered that this man was going to marry her sister.

At the end of the table Papa was engaged in animated, one could say even sparkling, conversation with the delectable Mrs Ashburne, and Benson was talking dutifully to Aunt Ruth. Next to her sat Rawdon and she could just see Emily's head bent towards him, her eyes on his face, her mouth with a ready smile of anticipation, as though she already knew she would approve of what ever he was going to say.

'Might I have the pleasure of the next dance, Miss Vestrey?'

Sir Arthur leaned forward, his pencil poised on his dance card. Caroline nodded and he quickly wrote down her name.

Papa got up and bowed to Mrs Ashburne, holding out his hand. She had hardly eaten anything, Caroline observed, but just sat sipping at her glass of champagne. She smiled at Caroline, who smiled back and gave a friendly little wave of her hand. Somehow she couldn't quite see where Mrs Ashburne fitted into the picture. Benson got up and escorted Aunt Ruth into the ballroom, and the scraping sounds of the band tuning up after supper could be heard.

Caroline rose too, putting her arm through that of Sir Arthur. On either side people bowed and smiled. She recognized a Captain in the Coldstream Guards who had lost an arm at Inkerman. He waved at her with the one he had left, his white gloved hand looking like a semaphore above the crowd. 'Go back,' it said. 'Go back to the Crimea. Fulfil your destiny.'

She smiled and bowed too but hardly saw those around her, the hundreds of laughing excited people preparing for Christmas. She saw instead the rows of mattresses on the floor, some soaked with urine and faeces or drenched with blood. On them men were writhing and turning, calling for help. From others blanketed corpses were being removed for burial in the overflowing graveyard behind the hospital.

All the faces around here were the faces of the long dead, the men who had sunk in the mud and vanished without trace. Many of them were never found. The mud round Sebastopol must have contained layers of bodies, layers and layers like a thick chocolate cake. She saw the heights above Balaklava and the bay beneath, the lights of the ships, the flotsam and jetsam that floated on the water. She heard the noise of the wounded and smelt the stench of gangrene, suppurating sores and vomit.

A woman held up her arms begging for water; blood poured from between her legs and her puny baby newly delivered lay dead by her side. In the corner another was screaming and two youngsters clad in rags were watching the proceedings with dispassionate, callous interest. They were used to nothing else there in the dark rat-infested cellar of the Barrack Hospital . . .

'Are you quite well, Miss Vestrey?'

The band struck up a waltz. Sir Arthur's amiable blue-eyed face peered into hers, the smile on his lips like the rictus of death. She put a hand on his shoulder and he led her onto the floor, expertly turning her in time to the music.

'I do like Strauss, do you not, Miss Vestrey?'

'Yes, I do – very much.'

The bands played from the ships in Balaklava harbour, and on the heights the men in the wards of the Castle Hospital used to clap their hands and cheer. Some ran up and down tapping with a fork on an old tin can or mug. The men always kept their spirits up, no matter how bad the pain, how near to the end they were. Florence admired the British serviceman more than anyone in her life. She had never seen such heroism, such stoicism and bravery without hope of reward. She called herself the mother of fifty thousand children. 'No-one,' she had told Caroline, 'can feel for the army as *I* do.'

Caroline knew then, without any doubt, that she did not belong in this place or among these people. Like Florence she was apart; she had joined the ranks of those who did not conform. She doubted if she had a place in normal society any more. But the solution was quite clear. It had been there all the time, before her eyes. She could see them now across the room quite oblivious of where they were, their eyes riveted spellbound upon each other, as they used to when they danced – oh so long ago it seemed, before the war.

They came nearer, Emily's pink crinoline sweeping the floor, the lace flounces bobbing up and down. Her blonde ringlets brushed on her bare shoulders, he head was flung back to gaze only at Rawdon – the man she alone had always been faithful to.

Of course they were so well suited in every way – in looks, in temperament, in their identical, conventional views of life. She loved them both but she, Caroline Vestrey, the eldest daughter of the house, was the one outside. She did not belong any more.

He was just the right height for her too, elegant and strong in his black evening clothes with his high white cravat and starched collar. What appeared arrogance to her was the sort of aristocratic disdain that Emily admired, by which Emily was surrounded in her life at Court. Rawdon was the epitome of the English gentleman, and Emily of the English gentlewoman. Correct, at ease anywhere; but apart from the mob. Special. Privileged.

Caroline felt a surge of joy, such as she had felt when she made that last important decision on Cathcart's Hill – to come home and face the truth. Now she had faced it.

She smiled with such happiness, such animal-like exhilaration, that she startled poor Sir Arthur, who only a minute ago had wondered if she were ill.

'Are you *sure* you are quite well, Miss Vestrey?'

'Quite wonderful, Sir Arthur,' she said, her eyes brimming. 'I have never ever felt better in my life. I am suddenly become someone quite new.'

Poor Sir Arthur. Caroline felt a pang of guilt. For if her plan succeeded the one who would suffer most would be him. She squeezed his arm impulsively, warm sympathy suddenly showing in her eyes; but he continued to look at her with concern.

Such moods, such volatility. He wondered if the poor girl, so unhinged by her terrifying experiences, were not, finally and completely, going off her head?

CHAPTER FORTY-TWO

Caroline heard the voices before she had even tried to close her eyes. She knew she would not sleep so she had taken her time going to bed, dismissing her maid, brushing her hair and getting undressed very slowly. She wanted the evening, which had been so unexpectedly happy, to end well. Without telling him of the unexpected transformation in her life, she had taken an affectionate leave of Rawdon, said how much she looked forward to seeing him over Christmas. They were all due to travel down to Kent in two days' time, her twenty-fifth birthday. Papa was giving a small dinner party at Chetwell in her honour that evening.

Caroline would tell them all then. By early January she would be back in Scutari. Slipping between the sheets she left the lamp alight. She was so wide awake she thought she might read; but instead she lay on her back looking at the shadows cast by the light on the ceiling.

Then she heard the voices. Voices raised in anger. She got swiftly out of bed and opened her door. A lamp glowed on the table in the corridor. Emily's door was open. The voices were coming from the first-floor drawing-room. Caroline went swiftly down the broad staircase, her footsteps muffled by the thick carpet; then she quickly crossed the landing to the drawing-room door, which was ajar. Emily was talking now, or rather shouting, her raised voice bordering on hysteria.

'You bring shame on us all, Papa! You flaunt your mistress at a public ball. Everyone could see! People are not all fools you know, not blind to life. It was quite obvious she was not Benson's companion. You danced with her so frequently and when you were not dancing you were ogling her . . .'

'I do not like the word "ogling", Emily.' George's voice was lower, still angry but more controlled. 'I do not . . .'

Caroline knocked on the door and pushed it open. One

solitary lamp burned on the small table in the middle of the room and George, still fully dressed in his evening clothes, stood on one side of it and Emily, in robe and slippers, on the other. The light cast by the lamp surrounded them with an ethereal glow, accentuating the whiteness of George's shirt front, and Emily's golden hair loose and brushed back from her forehead. It seemed like a halo on the head of an angel, and, judging by the look on her face, an avenging one at that.

But what interested Caroline more was the sight of the woman who sat in the corner, away from the pool of light. One arm rested on the arm of the chair and her chin was cupped in her palm. Her eyes were on George and Emily and her expression interested rather than affronted, tranquil rather than enraged; a mere spectator. Mrs Ashburne.

George, in the act of raising a warning hand to Emily, stopped as Caroline came through the door, pulling her robe tightly around her. Only embers glowed in the grate and it was very cold. She closed the door firmly behind her and went slowly into the room trying to appraise the situation.

'Papa, your voices travel to the top of the house. I thought the servants might come down.'

'Ah!' George looked disconcerted at the sight of Caroline and he joined his hands in front of him, his head bowed in an attitude of dejection. 'I'm sorry to have disturbed your slumbers, my dear.'

'I wasn't asleep. What has happened, Papa?' She glanced at Mrs Ashburne who now sat upright on her chair in the corner in an attitude of expectancy, her hands clasped in her lap, her eyes on Caroline.

'*This* is Mrs Ashburne, Caroline. Papa's mistress,' Emily said, her eyes burning wrathfully.

'I did meet Mrs Ashburne tonight.' Caroline nodded and smiled briefly at the woman in the corner as though to try and make up for Emily's rudeness.

'But did you *know* that she was his mistress? That he keeps her at a house in St John's Wood? That . . .'

'Emily, must you voice Papa's affairs so loudly in the middle of the night, or rather the small hours of the morning? I can't see what concern it is of yours.'

'But it *is* my concern.' Emily stamped her foot angrily. 'And yours – and Aunt Ruth's and that of all our family. People are talking about Papa and this woman. At one time he was content to keep her hidden. But they were together at the ceremony when the Queen presented the Crimean medals in the summer. They were together tonight. I do not doubt they are seen in public on many other occasions I do not know about. What will people think when Lord Vestrey parades his mistress in public? It reflects on us all, brings shame to our house.'

Emily collapsed into the chair behind her suddenly shaken by sobs. Caroline didn't know whether she felt most sorry for Emily, Papa or the silent woman in the corner. She remembered who Mrs Ashburne was now. She recalled her name. Although they had never met, she had once been Aunt Ruth's companion in Park Street, no doubt where she and Papa had first met.

'I am sorry, my dear, that you should learn like this.' Papa was ashen; he looked ten years older than he had at the ball. Obviously the presence of Mrs Ashburne rejuvenated Papa. 'I thought you were both in bed and brought Mrs Ashburne in before driving her home. Emily wished, doubtless, to challenge my right to bring a guest into my own house. I have tried to keep my affair with Mrs Ashburne discreet, but you see, Caroline, I love her very much. She is a real companion to me, a wife if you like. She has with tact, discretion and love fulfilled that role abdicated by your mother. She has been a great source of strength and consolation to me during these last difficult years – your Mama's illness, Debbie's death, Oliver . . .' Papa faltered and, drawing a large white handkerchief from his pocket, blew his nose vigorously. 'There, and Jane and Daniel, you going to the Crimea, all these things upset us a great deal my dear. My worries about the war. My work . . .'

Caroline went over to him and put her arms around his shoulders. Raising herself on tiptoe she kissed him. George gave a loud groan and, seizing her in his arms, hugged her as though he would squeeze the life out of her.

'Oh my darling, you do not condemn me? Oh thank you Caroline, my precious girl. There is, of course, not and

652

never has been any question of my marrying Mrs Ashburne. She understands that quite well. I would never distress your mother, or break up the family, or bring disgrace on my children by asking for a divorce.'

He gazed at her, his face illumined with gratitude and also humility, kissed her again, the presence of Emily and Mrs Ashburne forgotten. In his expression Caroline saw all the grief Papa had suffered these past difficult years, all the worries and anxieties that had weighed him down, Mama being one of the greatest. Could she blame Papa for seeking comfort in the arms of another woman? And a good woman too. Even during their brief acquaintance at the ball Caroline had been struck by the amiability of her countenance, the obvious sweetness of her disposition.

'Of course I do not condemn you, Papa. I, of all people, know what torments you have suffered; for you have always been the kindest of fathers, the most loyal of husbands until Mama's illness and subsequent malaise made it so difficult for you. We children were bound up in our own affairs, Papa, and could not see how much you needed someone to support you. I gave you no support, certainly, but expected it from you. How lonely you must have felt. I think your relationship with Mrs Ashburne is, in the circumstances, understandable, even to be welcomed. I am glad she supports you Papa, and loves you. I am relieved, however, to hear you do not contemplate divorce. That would certainly never do.'

She kissed him again and he leaned his cheek for a while against hers. Emily was wiping her eyes on the edge of her gown; but Mrs Ashburne remained quite composed, the slightest of smiles on her face.

'They have a son!' Emily said beginning to weep again. 'What do you think of *that*?'

Despite herself Caroline experienced a sharp sense of shock. However she quickly digested this completely unexpected piece of information and, gently disengaging herself from her father, went over to Emily and knelt by her side.

'A child is the outcome of love, darling. We are love children too. Is it so very evil?'

'I can't understand you, Caroline,' Emily whispered, wiping her eyes afresh. 'You condone adultery and now illegitimacy. What sort of standards have you forsaken? What have your experiences in Turkey taught you? Rawdon warned me you had changed.'

'Ah!' Caroline got to her feet and glanced again at Papa who had gone to stand by Hilary. They held hands, looking trustingly at Caroline as though in her they found an unexpected source of salvation. 'I expect he did. I am sure Rawdon would not countenance Mrs Ashburne. He is bound to share your sentiments.'

'He would indeed be horrified. So would Sir Arthur.'

'Sir Arthur less so, I think.' Caroline shook her head sadly. 'He is a man of surprising depth. But Rawdon would certainly not approve. Yes, my standards have changed, Emily dearest. I like to think they have not fallen, but that I have got a breadth of vision I had not before. I like to think I am better for it, but others might not agree.

'Anyway I am going back to Turkey. I was going to wait until my birthday, to tell you all together; but I can tell you now. I shall leave early in January and rejoin Florence at Scutari. I shall stay there, as I promised I would, until the war is over.'

'And then?' Emily's shocked whisper reverberated around the room.

'Then I shall come home,' Caroline said lightly. 'But not to marry Rawdon Foxton. I respect him and admire him, but I do not wish to be his wife.'

'My dear, do you know what you are saying?' George let Mrs Ashburne's hand fall and came quickly over to Caroline, his face anxiously searching hers.

'Oh yes, Papa. I know. Rawdon and I started to disagree in the Crimea. Because I loved him and thought him the man for me I would not allow myself to see the extent of our divergencies; or how Rawdon, as an honourable God-fearing member of the English aristocracy, would not be able to understand the changes circumstances had forced on me.'

'But *you* are a member of the English aristocracy too,' Emily spluttered. 'He has kept his standards, but you have abandoned those by which we were brought up. So has Jane.

So has . . . Papa.' Emily's voice assumed its tone of accusation and she looked dismissively at her father.

'I think it is a question of experience,' Caroline said gently. 'Things which seem quite straightforward in one set of circumstances do not in another. I am surprised, I confess, that Rawdon has not profited more from what he has seen and experienced of the horrors of war.'

'That is what is so noble about him.' Emily's voice rang with pride. 'He has not lost his standards. You and Florence Nightingale most certainly have.'

'Oh, do not speak so easily for Florence.' Caroline's voice broke with laughter. 'She has *very* set ideas about the harm done by passion. Anyway, enough of this. I am going back to Turkey with or without anyone's permission. I am twenty-five the day after tomorrow. From now on I am going to do as I like. I am my own woman, in charge of my own fate.'

From the corner came the sound of a soft handclap.

'Well done, Miss Vestrey. May God speed you in fulfilling your destiny.'

Mrs Ashburne got up and came over to Caroline, shyly proffering her hand. Impulsively Caroline leaned forward and embraced her.

'I am longing to see my little half-brother,' she said. 'How old is he?'

It was even colder than in England. The wind howled round the Barrack Hospital, tore through the corridors in which the men still lay on their mattresses for as far as the eye could see. Icicles had formed indoors by the side of the cracked windows. She had had to delay crossing the Bosphorus for a day owing to the gales that made the sea unpassable. All she had brought with her was a carpet bag containing a fresh change of clothing. The doorkeeper recognized her even in the dusk and joyfully threw the great wooden doors open to greet her.

She smiled at him with her gentle smile but did not stop, passing swiftly through the hall and up the stairs to Florence's room. There was no-one outside the door and she feared it would be empty. But inside a candle glowed at the ramshackle table still piled with papers and books, and

Florence sat on an old chair stuffed with threadbare cushions scribbling away, her back to the door. There was an acrid smell in the room which made her eyes smart.

'Aunt Mai, is that you?' She called in a thin breathless voice that filled Caroline's heart with pity. 'This brazier makes my head ache. I want it put out, and shall just have to use extra shawls.'

Caroline put down her bag and, removing her cloak, draped it around Florence's shoulders. Then she leaned down and pressed her cheek to hers. Florence turned round, an expression of astonishment on her pale drawn face. Her eyes once again looked racked with fever.

'Oh, it is not . . .'

'It is I, Florence. I have come home.'

Florence let the cloak fall and clasping Caroline's hands pulled her towards her.

'Home? Here in Scutari?'

'Yes, Florence. It is home to me. I felt such joy coming up the muddy path from the jetty; even the smells of the hospital seem to my nostrils like the perfumes of Araby.'

Florence coughed and bent her body in a painful spasm.

'Florence, you are very ill,' Caroline said, anxiously kneeling by her side.

Florence shook her head. 'No more than usual. I am quite acclimatized now having had Crimean fever, dysentery, rheumatism and now laryngitis and earache. I believe I can stand out the war with any man. But tell me about you. How did you decide what to do?' She hung onto Caroline's hands as though they were a link with life. Yet the wise, knowing expression in her eyes was just as familiar, just as compelling. How calm she looked, like one who had attained divine serenity.

'It was decided for me by fate, or God, or both, I know not which. Lord Foxton, although wanting us to marry, forbade me to return here if I should be his wife. The experience had completely corrupted me, he said, and made me unfit for normal society. In that case I thought I might as well return to the only place where I am understood.'

'Oh I understand, and I need you!' Florence's frame was suddenly racked by another harsh cough. 'Aunt Mai is my closest companion, but I need your strength. Dr Hall continues his persecution of me by undermining my authority. The saga of Miss Salisbury whom I put in charge of the "free gift" store from which she stole, has done unremitting harm. She has not told the truth and yet has the authorities at home on her side.'

'I never trusted Miss Salisbury from the start,' Caroline said, remembering the meek little woman who had succeeded Mrs Bracebridge in charge of the "free gift" store. 'I advised you not to use her.'

'How right you were in this as in so much else, dear Caroline. She was immediately in league with Miss Stanley when she returned to London, and accused me of neglecting my patients, and other horrors. Even at the Embassy Christmas Party Lady Stratford, who received me so graciously, was busy on the side telling everyone she believed Miss Salisbury! What an unmitigated hypocrite that woman is!

'Then, of course, Mr Bracebridge's lecture reported in *The Times* did me no good at all. I have had to write an official rebuttal. More work, more time taken up by trivia. Poor man, he only meant to draw attention to the terrible circumstances we endure here, but the Army Medical Department think his attack was instigated by me, and the opprobrium directed at me is worse than ever. But this is digressing . . .' Florence seized her pen. 'I believe the McNeil and Tulloch Report into the supply of the British Army in the Crimea, which is to be laid before Parliament, will exonerate me. I have powerful supporters.'

'You have, Florence, greatest among them the Queen. Oh Florence, Her Majesty sent for me hearing I was to return and was so kind. She fully understands why I wanted to go and gave me her firm support. She wanted to hear all about the conditions here and your work, and is so anxious to help you in any way she can.'

Florence fingered the large enamelled brooch which was the only adornment on her severe black dress. It had on it the Cross of St George in red enamel on which was inscribed the single word 'Crimea'. Encircling it was a phrase from the Bible: 'Blessed are the merciful'. She unfastened it to show Caroline who turned it, reading on the reverse side:

To Miss Florence Nightingale, as a mark of esteem and gratitude for her devotion towards the Queen's brave soldiers from Victoria R 1855

'Prince Albert designed this for me himself. I could have no further proof of my sovereign's regard.'

'No, Her Majesty has you constantly in her thoughts and prayers, and asked me to give you this.' Caroline drew a large white envelope from the pocket of her skirt and put it in Florence's hands. 'Besides expressions of regard written in her own hand, it is an invitation to visit Her Majesty as soon as you return home. She told me to tell you that whatever vicissitudes you might suffer she knows that God has spoken to you and that you are right. She gave us both her blessing.'

Florence fingered the letter and put it on her table, her voice thick with emotion. 'How good of Her Majesty. And you, Caroline? What did she say to you?'

'I also told her of my intention not to marry Lord Foxton. As Her Majesty has always been such a good friend to our family, so concerned for our welfare, I was bold enough to suggest that as my sister Emily had always been in love with him I thought they were very well suited. They have the same views and the same temperament. The Queen seemed to agree although she said she felt heartbroken on account of good Sir Arthur Stamford. However Her Majesty said that if it was the intention of Rawdon and Emily to marry they should speak to her and she herself would break the news to Sir Arthur, and advance him to a higher position in her Court by way of compensation. He is such a gentleman that Her Majesty was sure he would gracefully accede to Emily's wishes, indeed understand the reasons for them. Because Her Majesty married for love she is a sentimentalist at heart and the knowledge that Rawdon and Emily are truly in love she found most uplifting. For so great a Queen, she has *such* a human heart.'

'And how did that leave matters between you and Emily? I know what upheavals of the heart are caused by matters of love.'

Caroline glanced at her gratefully. It was so like Florence to think of others.

'It left us more united than ever. There was sharp sorrow on her part at first and disagreement between us. But when she realized Rawdon was to be free her feelings towards me underwent a complete transformation and I came away also with her blessing. We are now once again devoted sisters. I have asked her to show the same charity and compassion to our younger sister Jane, who does not have an easy passage through life at this moment. I have asked her to take my place, and share her confidences.'

Florence sat back, but already her eyes wandered to her work, her fingers itching to take up her pen and resume her latest impassioned report.

'Well, that all seems satisfactory. And you, my dear friend, you have made a great sacrifice, such as most women would not make. It does not though, necessarily mean you must eschew romantic passion for the rest of your life, as I have.'

Caroline took her hand and briefly pressed it. 'I have made no sacrifice, Flo. Lord Foxton and I did not suit. If I bestow my affections in this way again I hope it will be upon someone who shares, and understands, my ideals. But for the time being, I am content.'

'You are quite, quite sure?' Florence searched her face earnestly.

'Oh, quite sure. Now that I am no longer to wed him I find Lord Foxton once more an admirable man. How differently one sees a person according to whether one is in love or out of it. He received the news from me with great dignity, even regret. He came to see me off when I left Dover with infinite expressions of tenderness and regard. One understood that, in letting me go, he was making the supreme sacrifice. He was courtesy itself. I daresay, however, that when he has recovered from his grief which, for convention's sake he is bound to show, he and Emily will come to some understanding.'

Caroline got up, unfastened her carpet bag and took out a pair of white cuffs and a crisp white apron which had been carefully ironed for her by the maid who packed her bag the night before she left home.

The sight of the apron and the smooth, glacial stiffness of the starch, suddenly reminded her of all she had left behind. Silent footmen who automatically appeared in front of one to open doors and offer chairs; maids who called one in the morning, brushed one's hair, dressed one, washed and arranged one's nether garments between lavender bags in spacious drawers, pressed one's dresses. There was the continual, unquestioned comfort of large warm rooms, open fires, heated beds, elegance and leisure. Here she had no maid, one change of clothes which she would wash and re-wash herself and, like Florence, she would settle for a trestle bed in a corner of the hospital.

Yet it was freedom! She shook the apron in front of her gaily like a flag, and deftly began to fasten it around her. She felt like bursting into song, such was the joy in her heart.

'Well, this will not last for long; but it looks nice, does it not, Flo? It will be a reminder to us of what it is to live graciously.'

Florence began to laugh and her long thin hand clutched the brooch at her throat. A little colour came to her face and the pain in her eyes seemed for the time being to be replaced by happiness.

'Oh Caroline, it does me so much good to see you. I feel better already.'

Caroline finished tying her apron with a little jig and attached the starched white cuffs to the sleeves of her plain black dress.

'Now Florence, pray do not let me disturb you any longer. For have we not work to do?'

CHAPTER FORTY-THREE

Once again it was a day of great rejoicing for the people, a Royal occasion. After an absence of two and a half years the Guards were returning home and for several hours London stopped working and, metaphorically, threw its collective hat into the air in a giant gesture of welcome to greet the warriors. For although the Brigade of Guards had not exclusively won the Crimean War they had served with great honour and distinction, losing a third of their number. And, more than any other regiment, the Guards belonged to London because they were so personally associated with the monarch. That day, Wednesday 9 July 1856, monarch and people combined to pay homage to the veterans of the war.

Although it was but a short step, the Vestrey family had left home early in order to secure their seats in the park. Young Patrick had departed just after dawn with a footman, because he wanted to greet his brother at Nine Elms station and follow if possible his progress through the City.

George had obtained much coveted seats on one of the few stands that had been erected in Hyde Park. Theirs stood just in front of the saluting base and the enclosure which was to house government notabilities and the suite of the Queen. The stands towered over the heads of those who thronged every corner of the park from which a vantage point could be obtained, and also parts were absolutely nothing could be seen at all except the trees above and the backs of people squashed in front.

From where they sat, midway between Marble Arch and Apsley House, Park Lane, like the rest of the route through which the Guards were to march, presented a riot of colour with pink and crimson awnings above the houses and gorgeously dressed ladies and elegant gentlemen crowding the windows, balconies and in many cases the roofs. Little urchins swung from trees and lamp-posts; the top of Marble

Arch itself was alive with people, and through the crowd strolled pedlars, hawkers, prostitutes and pickpockets in search of business. The trade in Union Jacks and balloons was brisk and, for those who had been there since daybreak, the sight as well as the smell of warm muffins and hot roast chestnuts was so tempting as to be overwhelming.

The day before, the Queen's review of the general body of her troops at Aldershot had been almost ruined by rain; but on this day, to welcome the return of the Guards, nature was not only kind but profligate. The sun shone from a bright cloudless sky, and its warmth quickly dried the sodden grass and the streets washed by the deluge only twenty-four hours before.

George removed his top hat to salute an acquaintance. He knew many people in the stand, some of whom stopped to greet him and his by now extended family. There were many curious and friendly glances for the new Lady Foxton, and some equally curious but less friendly for Jane Vestrey and Daniel Lévy who had been prevailed upon to come, despite the former's dislike of ceremonial and the latter's disgust for the conditions of the Peace Treaty.

Aunt Ruth was there, dependent now on a stick but as alert and interested as ever. And Agnes, dressed in a pretty voile outfit of blue and yellow, the colours of the Crimean medal, had made the journey specially from Chetwell.

Many of those who stopped to chat commented on the robustness of Lady Vestrey's health, the excellence of her looks.

'My dear Agnes, you have lost *years.*'

'Thank you, dear Christine! I owe it all to mesmerism, you know.'

'Emily looks so enchanting.'

'She is very happy, thank you.'

Thank-you, thank-you . . . everyone chatted and nodded, smiled, bowed, and passed on to greet fresh friends and acquaintances. It was one of those days so beloved by the English gentry when, in pleasant surroundings, amidst a medley of colours and clad in a profusion of rich and varied dresses and accoutrements, well tailored suits and shining top hats, they greet one another, they see and are seen.

Such days belonged to the races or rowing regattas, to the Glorious Fourth at Eton and to any event such as this one graced by the presence of the Queen and members of her family. These occasions were tolerable even in bad weather; but when the sun shone and the heat beat down they were sublime.

'I didn't know we knew so many people, George,' Agnes said excitedly. 'And when you consider it, I don't think I have been to London since the opening of the Great Exhibition.'

George mopped his brow on a large spotless white linen handkerchief. Men in morning dress and high tight collars were going to swelter in this sun. 'I don't believe you have, my dear.'

The Great Exhibition. Five years ago plus two months. Was it really five years since he had taken all his family to the opening as a treat? Rebecca was not yet born, nor Henry Ashburne. Debbie was still alive, although she had not come up for the day, and Oliver had been so interested in the mechanical exhibits at the Exhibition. Clare, who then had been only eleven, was now sixteen and with them today. The only daughter of the house who had given him no trouble – as yet. He looked to where she was sitting excitedly on the edge of her seat next to him, her pointed face bright with the anticipation that only belongs to innocence, fingers pointing in all directions as she saw a friend, or some interesting or amusing event in the crowd below.

'Look, a pickpocket!' She grasped her father's hand. 'Oh Papa, I saw a man put his hand in the pocket of that gentleman there. Papa, the one in the blue coat. See that other man running away, scampering through the crowds. Oh Papa, what *can* we do?' She clutched his sleeve, and he patted her hand reassuringly.

'Not a thing I am afraid, my love. The police have their minds on other duties.'

People had always said she would be the most beautiful of the Vestrey girls when she grew up, and that prophecy was on the way to being fulfilled.

She had black curly hair, the despair of her maid as it refused to conform to a neat central parting and ringlets, the most electrifying blue eyes and very fair skin with permanent rosebuds on her cheeks. In temperament she was most like Emily. She was a flirt and liked admiration; but she also had something of Caroline's sagacity and Jane's intellectual ability. The best qualities of his daughters blended into one. He squeezed her arm and smiled at her. Please God she would spare him the heartaches all his other daughters had given him.

James Vestrey had never expected anything like this. Ever since they had arrived at Nine Elms station the Brigade had been fêted by a solid mass of waving, cheering people, varying in quality but not in enthusiasm, from the middle-class and even humbler reaches of Brixton and Vauxhall south of the river to the modish purlieus of the wealthy in Westminster, Whitehall and Park Lane.

The column of three thousand men – each regiment preceded by its own band – had marched along Wandsworth Road, over Vauxhall Bridge, along Millbank and Abingdon Street to Old Palace Yard. The great bells of Westminster Abbey had sounded in majestic yet tuneful accompaniment with those of the lesser churches which pealed with joyous enthusiasm as the Guards moved past the Houses of Parliament whose windows were crowded with peers, peeresses and members of the Commons. Along Whitehall the balconies of all the houses and offices were crammed to bursting point, with little apparent regard for danger; stands had been erected in the grounds of Montague House and Lady Dover had assembled a large party which thronged every window of her commodious mansion. Opposite Downing Street the Guards were met by a squadron of the Second Life Guards whose splendid uniforms, feathered plumes and shining casques and cuirasses provided a moving contrast to the faded uniforms of many of the Crimean veterans.

All along the route the picture was the same – overflowing windows, balconies and even roofs whether belonging to clubs, private residences or government offices. Streamers and flowers were thrown at the soldiers, even laurels from the distinguished and beautiful ladies who were with the Duke of Cambridge at one of the windows overlooking Horse Guards Parade.

Sometimes the men raised a spontaneous cheer if they recognized an officer they admired, like the Duke or Lord Cardigan who had ridden down the Mall on the famous charger that had carried him through the valley of death at Balaklava. It took the Brigade a full fifteen minutes to pass through Horse Guards Parade which they reached as the tower clock struck noon. Like everywhere else, the parade ground was packed with people from all walks of life clapping, huzzaing, cheering, blowing horns and whistles, weeping. While the various regimental bands thundered out 'The British Grenadiers', 'Home Sweet Home' and 'Here's a Health to All Good Lasses', the column passed into Cockspur Street and thence into Pall Mall.

The humour and merriment of the crowd was astonishing, its warmth more moving than many of the seasoned warriors liked to admit. Some of them, like James Vestrey, with heavy beards and four clasps to the Crimea Medal, had served in the campaign from the beginning. But their joy at their homecoming was tarnished and always would be by the memory of their experiences, the numbers they had left behind under the soil of the trenches around Sebastopol. In many an eye there was a bitterness that would not have been observed when the Guards had left in February 1854, marching along parts of this very route.

In Pall Mall the balcony of the War Office was hung with crimson cloth which, for James, cynically observing it as he marched past, typified not celebration but appeared to him as an allegory of all the blood that had been so needlessly shed. Was this why the people were turning out? To atone? No, it was because they were joyful, happy, informed by the mad, foolish patriotism that had driven Oliver up the Redan to his death. They thought the war had been won and a glorious victory achieved. For them there was nothing ignominious about the terms of the Peace Treaty which had seemed to mock the fighting man by restoring Sebastopol to the Russians, after that bloody eleven-month siege! As they sank deeper and deeper into the mud how many men, could they have spoken, would have thought their sacrifice worthwhile?

There was the Reform Club, the Army and Navy, the Carlton, the Travellers, the Oxford and Cambridge, places which as a young, unblooded officer he had often frequented. Now they were festooned with bunting, every window crammed with a preponderance of ladies eagerly leaning forward to acclaim the conquering heroes. In the background champagne corks would be popping like bullets, James thought. He grinned to himself. Well, tonight he would pop a few champagne corks too; he would allow himself to forget the dead and drink to the living. Hats and handkerchiefs appeared in windows like confetti and everywhere there were hands; hands waving, hands with flags, hands with hats, and empty hands, red and white palms, old and young, the rough and gnarled as well as those belonging to people who had never known a day's manual labour, or what it was to load a gun or plunge a bayonet into the breast of a Russian soldier.

'Hurrah! Hurrah!' cried the crowd. 'Welcome, welcome.' 'Hip hip hooray!' The bands thumped their resounding tunes and six thousand heavily-booted feet crunched the ground underfoot, while the horses of the Life Guards, gorgeously caparisoned in their snowy fleeces, clip-clopped elegantly along like flighty young debutantes out of place at a soldiers' ball.

Now they were reaching the end of Pall Mall and the disciplined column wheeled to the left past St James's Palace. It was a long ordeal for troops already tired, and the previous day they had paraded in the rain at Aldershot. In the evening he had seen Polly and the recollection of their meeting still caused James pain. He had very successfully put her out of his mind during the past eight months. Apart from her weekly letters, her parcels and his few and sparse replies, there was no real communication between them. He had greeted her last night politely as a stranger, and not as the wife of his flesh.

Flesh. James shuddered. During the long idle months in Constantinople he had not sought forgetfulness in the brothels as he had thought he would. He had fallen in love, seriously and for the first time. But this love was as doomed as any other, for the woman, Betty Furlong, was the wife of a fellow officer in the Coldstreams who was walking at this very moment not a hundred yards behind him. There was nothing but trouble ahead, as far as James could see. Trouble, all trouble.

The column passed Marlborough House and emerged into the freshness of St James's Park. In front of them the Palace rose up like some beautiful mirage in a sea of faces. James opened his eyes wide and gazed at the balcony.

For an hour before the drums heralded the approach of the Grenadiers, the Royal Family, its numerous guests, foreign relations and assorted dignitaries had been waiting in the ante-room from which the monarch was to review the procession from the Palace balcony. Sir Arthur Stamford hardly had time to think as he paved the way for kings, dukes and duchesses, princes of the blood and lesser royalty. Moving swiftly through the richly dressed throng in his own splendid uniform of the Hussars, he was able to ensure that everyone was in the right place as the windows were opened and the signal was given to go onto the balcony.

Prince Albert had already left. In his uniform of Colonel of the Grenadiers, his own regiment, accompanied by his aides, he had ridden up Constitution Hill towards Hyde Park in order to receive the Queen. Faint cheers had been heard for His Royal Highness, thankfully no boos. The contrast between her people's love for her and dislike of her husband pained Her Majesty dreadfully.

'Your Royal Highness . . .'

His arm extended, Sir Arthur bowed and pointed the way to the Duchess of Cambridge who swept past him with a smile and took up her place behind the Queen.

Sir Arthur stepped on to the balcony, craning his head. It was a spectacular sight. The column of Guards had just turned out of Marlborough Gate into the Mall, each regiment preceded by its band. The tall bearskins rose and fell in a regular, monotonous harmony which reminded Sir Arthur, a keen amateur naturalist, of the disciplined feet of a centipede.

The scarlet line marched purposefully through the crowds which for an instant, at the simultaneous appearance of their sovereign and the Guards, grew suddenly silent before giving vent to an enormous roar. The Queen who, even for her, had shown a most unusual degree of excitement, leaned enthusiastically forward over the balcony, waving her white handkerchief and bidding the Princess Royal and the Prince of Wales to do the same.

At the end of the Mall the Guards passed through the south gate of the Palace, right under the balcony parting the splendid assembly of people, many of the men in uniform, who thronged the enclosure. After the Grenadiers had entered the forecourt the enthusiastic crowd flung itself forward into the reserved space in a spontaneous gesture of emotion. There were several moments of confusion while the police and the Life Guards tried to make a passageway for the rest of the column, but the Fusiliers had to break rank and run through the crowd to reform the line in order to pass before the Queen. Very tiny, dressed in white with a blue bonnet and her ribands, she nevertheless looked every inch the sovereign of her people, the great Queen she was.

The Queen and the Royal Family waved their handkerchiefs furiously, the men responding with cheers before they left the enclosure by the North Gate to proceed via Constitution Hill to Hyde Park.

Yes, it was a stirring sight. Her Majesty's deep emotion affected them all. Sir Arthur had felt his eyes moisten as the men paraded beneath the balcony, their faces raised as they cheered the Queen. What tenderness and affection there was between monarch and fighting man. And how good the monarch was to him! Sir Arthur still swallowed compulsively when he recalled the night Her Majesty had called him into her sitting room at Windsor and told him about Emily, very gently and quietly after asking him to sit down. He remembered so vividly the motherly, concerned expression on her face as she entreated him to accept the inevitable and not to feel that he had personally been rejected.

'Emily is so sensible of your good qualities, Sir Arthur,' she had said. 'Her admiration for you is unbounded. Alas, it is not and, I think you know never has been, enhanced by love. Now she has a man who loves her and whose love she returns. Will you release her, Sir Arthur? Can you be so noble? As one who has been fortunate in marrying for love but who is *surrounded* on all sides by many instances of loveless marriages, I can only hope you will understand and forgive.'

Sir Arthur had kissed her hand in gratitude. Of course he would understand and forgive. The knowledge that she cared enough to break the news herself not only made him feel stronger but more indebted than ever to the British throne. Ever since then the Queen had gone out of her way to make him feel privileged in a manner he had not before. And he knew that his behaviour, correct as always, had increased her respect.

As she turned now she looked straight into his eyes. It was as though she knew that he was thinking of Captain Vestrey who was marching with his regiment. Of course, it could not be, but her smile was sympathetic, so warm and encouraging. He bowed and stood back as the Royal Family moved through the room to descend to the carriages waiting for them below.

The large oblong marked out as the saluting base and protected by barriers from the crowd, was now ready to receive Her Majesty. Shortly after eleven Prince Albert had ridden into the park at the head of those battalions of the Guards which had remained behind, and had seen no action in the war. These Guards formed in lines in front of the saluting base, facing Park Lane, with its rear resting in a clump of trees.

People still continued to pour into an already overcrowded park. Even in her blue muslin dress, with a broad brimmed bonnet of rice straw, Emily was hot. She kept on smiling and waving to people she knew, happy and proud and aware that she looked it. As a married woman she had achieved that necessary position in society. From time to time she clutched Rawdon's arm in a proprietorial manner, pointing out various things of interest to him.

'See, the Duchess of Wellington in her carriage. And there is Mrs Gladstone in the enclosure. I am sure she is looking at us. Do wave.'

Rawdon glanced at his bride of a month and smiled. 'My dear, Mrs Gladstone could not *possibly* see over this distance.'

He gazed at Emily, his own pride in her reflected in his eyes. Because of the slight whiff of scandal attached to their engagement, involving as it had the jettisoning of one of the Queen's favourite courtiers, they had settled for a quiet wedding at Chetwell after all. But nothing like this seemed important after the conflicts had been resolved and she was his. His wife, his partner, his mistress, his love. He adored her. She was really quite perfect in every way, amusing yet well informed, a good conversationalist and, of course, one of the most attractive women in London. He was envied by many men. Lady Foxton. *His* Lady Foxton. Moreover, she did not argue with him or contradict him. There was no need. As Lord Vestrey had once said, newly-married couples should be compatible. They were.

Rawdon wore a black frock coat, tight trousers and a dark waistcoat. Men's fashions were becoming rather severe. People said it was because of all the smoke pouring out of the chimneys now that coal was so common. Or maybe it was because of the seriousness of the age; the grim sense of purpose. Emily wasn't sure, but anyway black suited her husband, emphasizing his saturnine good looks.

Emily kept on glancing anxiously about her, fearful of seeing Mrs Ashburne. How awful it would be, how despicable if Papa had procured a seat for her, and she and Mama were to meet. Not a word had been said since the night she had surprised Papa and Mrs Ashburne embracing in the library when they thought she was in bed. She had gone downstairs to get a book from the library, being too excited to sleep, and had passed the open drawing-room door.

Not only might Mama meet Mrs Ashburne, but Rawdon too. There was so much to conceal, even as a married woman with a place in the world and society, so much of which still to be ashamed. How much less Rawdon would think of Papa if he knew; maybe also of her.

In the short space of a month Emily was fast learning how far you could go with Rawdon, how much you could tell him and how much you should keep to yourself, what you could expect of him and what you could not. But he was just the man she had known he would be, his public behaviour and private conduct hardly at variance. There were no surprises in Rawdon, no unexpected, unwelcome habits or quirks – or as far as she had discovered. She swivelled her eyes and looked at him adoringly, surreptitiously groping for his hand and giving it an ecstatic squeeze.

She glanced quickly along at Jane, thankfully separated from her by Papa, Aunt Ruth and Polly. Neither Jane nor Polly looked happy. Jane had good reason to sulk with that uncouth foreigner she lived with being so unpleasant to her and all the family; but Polly was newly married like her! Polly should be as excited as a young bride.

No-one ever understood why James hadn't allowed Polly to go to Constantinople. He said it was because of the risk of disease and the harshness of the winter. Maybe it was; but any number of officers' wives had gone and Polly had stayed in Chetwell Rectory in a state of semi-mourning, like a reclusive widow.

The crowd stirred. Many on the stands stood up. Again there was hushed expectancy in the air and then, to a beat of drums, the Guards entered the park by Apsley House and the masses went wild. Hats were thrown in the air, surely never to be recovered by their rightful owners, and a sea of small waving flags fluttered beneath them. All the Vestrey party got to their feet and Polly burst into tears as the column moved briskly to the open space prepared for it, while the bands blared out stirring music, and everyone craned, pushed and shoved for a sight of the Crimean heroes. As the comrades who had remained behind presented arms, the newcomers took their appointed places in the spaces left in the line of columns already formed.

Emily put a comforting arm round Polly.

'I think I can see James,' she pointed. 'Is it not James, Rawdon?'

Rawdon strained his eyes but, to his chagrin, found his vision obscured by tears. He shook his head. He felt like a broken man and knew that his place should have been with them. All the comradeship of those Crimean days came most palpably back to him. Now he was going to be a diplomat; he had a wife; a new exciting future in front of him. But an important part of Rawdon Foxton would always be there, with the Third Battalion of the Grenadier Guards in the Crimea.

'Oh look, how worn their uniforms are compared to the

men who stayed behind. And see the long beards some of them have, and their skins are so weather-beaten.'

Emily brushed a tear from her cheeks, and continued to hug Polly, gazing at the astonishing scene in front of them.

Agnes was feeling very happy, and so well. She had been reluctant to leave Sophie behind, but George insisted on it. He was very particular about the occasion of welcoming James back being strictly a family outing. Not even the Tangents or the Foxtons had been invited. Well, Agnes didn't mind giving in on little things, as long as she got her way where the big things were concerned.

The Prince was now leaving to receive the Queen. The men who had just arrived at the parade, after a march of nearly two hours, shuffled their feet until told to stand at ease by Lord Rokeby.

'Can you recognize James, George?' Agnes peered beneath her parasol which she had raised to keep off the heat.

'No my dear. There are too many beards, and Polly says James has one. I hope he soon shaves it off. But, look, there are Lord and Lady Palmerston struggling to get through into the enclosure. Really, it is too bad that the Prime Minister should have such difficulty of access.'

'It is due to the enthusiasm of the people, George,' Agnes said reprovingly. 'The heroes belong to *them*, too.'

George smiled faintly at his wife. She had started nagging again, a sure sign of improved health.

'Ah, Lady Palmerston has been given a seat in Lord Penmure's carriage.' George pointed over to the few carriages by the saluting area. 'How kind of his lordship.'

'Has he mentioned the Ambassadorship again, George?'

'I am not interested, I told you, Agnes. Your health would prevent you from enjoying such a harsh climate as that of St Petersburg.'

'Oh I don't know, George. Sophie thinks it would do us the world of good.'

'*Us?*' George looked at her with outrage.

'She and I. Of course Sophie would come too, as my companion. The Russian Court is so very interesting.'

'Well, I am not interested. No, I shall continue in foreign affairs, but in the House of Lords, not in St Petersburg. Besides, I have my family to think of.'

'But Clare would *love* Russia. She is so pretty. Think how popular she would be at diplomatic balls. And Patrick starts at his school anyway in September.'

George felt his anger rising. That Agnes, of all people, should want to leave home was the most unexpected part of the whole wretched affair which he now wished he had never mentioned to her. He had been quite sure that her refusal to consider it would give him the excuse he needed to decline.

'You would look so wonderful in an ambassador's uniform, George.' Agnes looked at him quite coquettishly. 'And I am sure you would be made an earl. Think of that.'

'I have no desire to be an earl.'

'Well, you should.' Agnes looked at him sharply. 'The Vestreys have been barons for too long. That would give you an advantage over your son-in-law.'

George looked at her in surprise.

'I wish no advantage over Rawdon, my dear. There is no rivalry between us.'

'It is a question of ambition, George. If you are both to be diplomats you should be by far the senior, and show it. Besides it would give James a title too and help him to settle down and forget the dreadful war.'

'Anyone would think you didn't like Rawdon, Agnes.'

Agnes pursed her lips in that familiar disapproving rosebud.

'I do like him, very much. But he is twenty years your junior. You should be an ambassador and you should be an earl. Then I might consider leaving Chetwell and taking my place by your side again.'

George felt a tremor of alarm. Agnes by his side? God forbid. George had been looking surreptitiously for Hilary ever since they had arrived. He had managed to get her tickets in the stand next to theirs, but separated by some stretch of ground so that a meeting would be unlikely.

She had taken a friend who was staying with her, an amiable unmarried lady, Miss Cooper, with whom she had been at school. Somehow the presence of Miss Cooper disquieted George. She had been there for nearly six weeks, and seemed disinclined to leave the comfortable house in St John's Wood. There was a disapproval about her so far

as he was concerned that reminded him of Mrs Chetwyn[d]
It also interfered miserably with his attempts to see hi[s]
mistress for those purposes for which he had bought her th[e]
house in the first place.

Suddenly, at exactly half past one, a fresh roar rose fro[m]
the crowd and the procession of Royal carriages entered th[e]
Park escorted by the Royal Horse Guards. The Princ[e]
received his wife at Hyde Park Corner and then, preceded b[y]
a detachment of Life Guards, they made their way to th[e]
saluting base. Immediately behind the Queen's carriag[e]
rode the new Duke of Wellington who was Master of th[e]
Horse.

'No, I am *delighted* with Rawdon as a son-in-law,' Agne[s]
said as though she had taken the occasion of the arrival o[f]
the Queen to ponder the matter. 'He is everything I woul[d]
wish, and is obviously making Emily very happy. Jane how[-]
ever I *am* very worried about. She is beginning to look i[ll]
George. Do you think she is expecting again?'

George glanced anxiously at Jane, who was sitting bac[k]
with an expression of extreme boredom; showing her cus[-]
tomary apathy towards public, and especially royal, occa[-]
sions. She had only agreed to come because George ha[d]
stressed the family nature of the day.

'Oh my dear, I pray not. If there is another child I sha[ll]
insist on a wedding.'

'How?'

'By cutting off his allowance. For all I care he can g[o]
back to France and we shall have Jane and her children wit[h]
us.'

Agnes felt her lower lip tremble. She closed her eyes a[t]
the prospect.

'In that case, let us sincerely hope she is not expectin[g]
But I know that look, George. It was how I felt so ofte[n]
myself.'

She managed to convey reproach by her voice, bu[t]
George's eyes were still on the next stand looking for Hilar[y]
He knew she resented these family occasions because she wa[s]
excluded, and he was anxious to placate her. There was n[o]
doubt, however, that she had been unusually cool with hi[m]
of late, even before the ceremony for the return of th[e]

Guards was announced. He wondered if that was partly the reason for Miss Cooper's long and unexpectedly protracted visit.

The noise of the crowd grew deafening as the Queen's cortège moved towards the saluting base. Everyone in the stands stood up again. Even Daniel who had pretended to be half asleep rose reluctantly to his feet. He knew the insolence he exhibited on these occasions annoyed the Vestreys and upset Jane. It was his way of asserting himself.

Jane gave him the kind of look that so frequently enraged him – the aristocracy looking down on the representative of the people. It seemed to imply that he was somehow beneath her. And yet he knew, because he often questioned her about it, that she was unaware of doing it. It was instinctive; it was all part of the Vestrey arrogance he hated so much.

Behind the Queen's carriage came seven carriages full of her own family, visiting royals and the ladies and gentlemen in waiting. Sir Arthur rode with the other equerries beside the procession which was escorted by a detachment of the Royal Horse Guards. If anyone in the Vestrey stand noticed him no-one pointed it out. Sir Arthur Stamford, Bart, was forgotten.

From the third carriage the newly-engaged Princess Royal, looking ridiculously young – she was only fifteen – received special cheers from the public and bowed and waved shyly, surprised by the acclaim. As the Queen arrived at the saluting point the troops, including those from the Crimea, presented arms and the massed regimental bands played the National Anthem. The Royal party then drove along the lines formed by the troops, now in total numbering over five thousand men, while the spectators roared their heads off waving not only Union Jacks but the flags of many nations and anything mobile that came to hand. Some even raised their dogs and small babies and waved them.

When the Royal party returned to the flagstaff the horses of the Queen's cortège were disengaged and the Prince and the Duke of Cambridge arranged themselves on either side of the Queen. A group of generals formed a line a short distance from her, the massed bands stationed in the midst of them. At a signal from the band major the band broke

675

into the strains of 'See the Conquering Hero Comes' and the whole of the Brigade swung into a brigade march past Her Majesty in open column and quick time.

This was the most exciting moment in an already exciting day. The enthusiasm of the crowd grew to frenzy pitch as the torn and tattered colours of each regiment were proudly borne past, colours which some men had given their lives to defend when battle was at its height. Many in the vast crowd wept openly at the sight of banners neatly inscribed with the names of Alma, Inkerman and Sebastopol to add to the faded ones of Corunna, Talavera and Waterloo at which the Guards had also distinguished themselves so many years before.

Everyone in the stands remained upright as the Guards marched past. George, waving his hat high above his head, was aware of the tears streaming down the faces of the women; even Emily had succumbed at last and Jane would not last the ceremony. Agnes had to sit down, she felt her palpitations coming on again, and Clare, having been briefed by Mrs Chetwynd, quickly passed her mother the *sal volatile*. Clare Vestrey, the youngest daughter of the house but one, was so proud of her family, of her brave soldier brothers, of her clever statesman father, of her sister Caroline, who had told them in a recent letter that she would soon be coming home.

Everything the Vestreys did made Clare proud to be one of them. She could think of no more fortunate family in the whole world. As the march past came to an end her tears were dry, the smile on her face rapturous, and she bent down to hug her mother.

At last the troops returned to their original positions and the Duke of Cambridge gave the order for the whole brigade to advance rapidly to the flagstaff for the Royal salute. For a moment there was silence, a moment of utter solemnity, and then as the Queen with a gracious gesture acknowledged her troops, they threw their bearskins in the air or waved them from their bayonets high aloft above their heads, their cheers for their sovereign drowned by the fresh roars of approval from the crowd.

The crowd continued its acclamation as the monarch and

her party reassembled in their carriages, equerries and troops ranging themselves beside her, and escorted her from the ground.

'She is to review them again from the Palace balcony,' George said, putting his top hat on his head. 'I hope that scamp Patrick is safe.'

'Oh, Burgess will take care of him,' Aunt Ruth assured him and got arthritically to her feet clasping her stick. 'George, I have so enjoyed myself. I remember the troops coming home from Waterloo, you know.' She sighed. 'Forty years ago. I was Caroline's age. How I wish she were here to see this sight.'

'Oh Papa, do look!' Again Clare excitedly seized his arm. 'The people have burst through the barriers and are racing towards the Guards.'

And indeed, like a vast relentless river coursing from every side, the humble people of London, those who did not have tickets for the stands or the enclosures and who had waited so patiently for many hours in the rain and now this brilliant sun, streamed across the enclosure. They threw their arms around relatives and friends among the troops whom they had not seen for so long, or around men they did not know at all, simply to praise and thank those who had helped to save the honour of the nation. The troops, who had remained in their squares, looked at first abashed at this spontaneous display of enthusiasm, until at a word from their commanding officer they turned and formed themselves into marching order, gently disengaging those enthusiasts who still clung to them.

'Come now. We must be home to welcome James.'

George motioned to his brood and slowly they climbed down the steps and assembled on the ground below, no longer distinguished from the crowd but now part of a vast, confusing concourse.

'We must take care not to separate,' George said, taking Agnes's arm firmly. 'Please be careful, ladies, not to lose your parasols and hold on to your bonnets, and gentlemen be careful of your wallets.' George got out his handkerchief and mopped his brow. 'I declare I have never seen anything like this crowd. What a wonderful occasion it has been. A day to be proud of. A day in which to rejoice. Mr Lévy, be so good as to take Jane's arm and Emily, will you hang on to Clare? Rawdon perhaps you would escort Aunt Ruth, and Agnes and I shall bring up the rear.'

Rawdon put on his top hat and smiled.

'A very successful ceremony, sir. What a tribute to the Guards. How well they marched. What a fine body of men.'

George looked at Lord Foxton with his customary approval. His sentiments were always just right; his words aptly chosen.

'It *has* been a wonderful occasion, Rawdon. And to have all my family about me, including you, is not the least of my reasons for rejoicing. Thank God James has come home safely to us. And may He bring Caroline speedily back too.'

'Amen to that,' Rawdon said softly, taking Aunt Ruth's arm.

Yes, five years since they had walked home through the park after the opening of Mr Paxton's great Crystal Palace which had been reassembled at Sydenham and opened by the Queen in June 1854. So much had happened since; too much. In many ways his family had been disrupted like the nation, and some had left it never to return.

The Vestrey family, George reflected, was a microcosm of England, and family life was very like the life of nations – good parts, even great, and bad parts, some very bad. In the last five years he had fathered a son and daughter and lost a son and daughter, both much beloved. Had the new ones taken their place? No. People never replaced others – they just made the memory of one's loss a little easier to bear. He had also acquired his first grandchild, a daughter-in-law, a son-in-law, a man who was the equivalent of a son-in-law but was not, and a mistress. His homes were intact, his wealth was increasing, due to wise investments, and his position in the government secure.

Much as it had been criticized, the Peace Treaty signed in Paris in March had been the best terms the allies could get, given the fact that there had been no devastating and final defeat of the Russians. He had helped to draft it and had been there when it was signed. He was an important man – a man whom people now looked up to, deferred to.

Today he would even be a happy man, if only Caroline

were here. Caroline, the eldest daughter of the house. Yet, instead of returning to a happy marriage like Emily, to a union which for all its faults seemed to satisfy Jane, what was she coming back to? She would be twenty-six in December. What possible future was there for her? Who would want to marry a woman who had so defied convention? Who had deliberately broken her engagement to nurse in a distant country at war?

'George, George.' Agnes tugged at his arm. 'We are losing the rest, dear. Why are you so thoughtful?'

'I was thinking about the day of the Great Exhibition we spoke about earlier.'

'What made you think of that again, George?'

George stood slightly behind her so that he could protect her from the throng which had got thicker as everyone streamed for the exits.

'Well, I was just thinking, you know, of how much has happened since then. What a lot of changes.'

'I don't think so *very* much has changed.' Agnes looked at him in surprise over her shoulder.

George bent towards her and smiled.

'Don't you think that depends a great deal, my dear, on how one sees things? From where I stand a great deal seems to have happened. You, quietly down at Chetwell most of these years, perhaps do not think so very much has changed.'

'Well, I have been *very* ill, George,' Agnes said peevishly. 'I think you sometimes rather selfishly forget that. The greatest change for me is that now I am well again. Surely that is the *most* important thing?'

Which observation, George thought, urging his wife across the road, proved his point. He stifled his bitterness that, in this one thoughtless remark, she had apparently forgotten all about the death of Debbie, Oliver's immolation, the tragedy of Jane and Caroline's sacrifice. She didn't really mean to exclude them because he knew that in her heart she, like him, had had her life permanently scarred by these events. After all, they had been married for twenty-eight years and had shared eleven living children. Even Agnes couldn't become a complete stranger, lost in her world of self absorption and self regard.

Agnes's horizon *was* very narrow, bounded by her limitations, and how you saw things in retrospect really did depend upon whether your eyes were blinkered, or open to the world – whether you were directing the war in London as you thought it ought to be or fighting it in the Crimea. Family life, with all its nuances, was just the same as directing wars or governing nations. It all depended on where you stood.

He ushered his family along Green Street and into Park Street. People pushed and shoved good humouredly, either trying to go home or to make for Green Park and Buckingham Palace.

Vestrey House remained tall and square, the huge Union Jack hanging in the still air from the flagpole over the portico. It was a solid, welcoming sight after the colourful chaos of the day. The front door was open, flanked by Cornwall and a footman to make sure that none of the vulgar obtruded themselves.

The servants bowed as the family entered and the master of the house paused on the threshold, comparing in his mind the vast, jostling, noisy crowds outside and the quiet spacious surroundings in which he had been brought up within. They seemed to represent the two halves of his life – peace on the one hand, busy commitment on the other.

'Has Master Patrick returned yet, Cornwall?'

'No, my lord. But your lordship need have no fear, he will be perfectly safe with Burgess.'

'Oh, I know that. Doubtless he will stay until the troops disperse. Did you get any chance to see the procession?'

'I did glance into the park, my lord, but saw very little. It was too crowded for my taste. Some of the servants had quite a good view.'

'I'm glad you all enjoyed yourselves. Now Cornwall, Mr James will soon be arriving. I hope everything is in readiness for him?'

'Oh everything, my lord. That is why I did not stay out long, in order to prepare for Mr James. I have laid out his evening clothes myself. As you know the large bed from the main guest room was moved into Mr James's old room, at Miss Vestrey's request. I believe Mrs James found the arrangement satisfactory when she slept there last night

Fresh warming pans have also been put into the bed today. It will be a long time since Mr James has slept in such homely comfort.'

'A long time. Nothing like one's own bed, Cornwall,' George nodded approvingly.

'Oh nothing, my lord. And cook has not stirred from the kitchen all day preparing a sumptuous dinner for this evening's celebrations.'

'How *very* thoughtful of her. I must thank her myself, Cornwall.'

'Cook would be most gratified, my lord. How very pleasant, if I may say so, to see Lady Vestrey in such good health, and Lord and Lady Foxton. What a *pleasure* to see Miss Emily looking so well.'

'Is it not?'

George smiled with satisfaction. Everything was in its place; just as it should be. Part of family life; part of England. His newly-married daughter was received with her husband in her father's house, his soldier son was returning from the war – a hero to a victor's spoils. Despite its tragedies this was a day for the family; for respect for family life and all it entailed. For joy. Impulsively he shook hands with Cornwall and clasped him on the shoulder.

'Thank you, Cornwall. It has been a great day for the nation, for my family. An emotional day for us all.'

'Yes indeed, my lord.'

Cornwall bowed and stood back, touched beyond words by his master's gesture.

Lord Vestrey stepped into the cool interior of his home, giving his hat to the butler, and the great doors of Vestrey House were gently closed behind him.

EPILOGUE

Florence Nightingale returned to England in August 1856 alone, and unwelcomed, as she wished.

The British forces suffered 18,058 fatalities in the Crimean War of whom 1761 were killed directly by enemy action; the rest died of wounds or disease.

The following books were of particular value to the author in checking the details of the actual historical events and people described in these pages:

Airlie, Mabel Countess of. *With the Guards We Shall Go: A Guardsman's letters in the Crimea 1854–1855.* London, 1922.

Askwith, Betty. *The Lyttletons.* London, 1975.

Askwith, Betty. *Two Victorian Families.* London, 1971.

ed. Benson, Arthur and Esher, Viscount. *Letters of Queen Victoria, 1837–1861* (3 vols). London, 1907.

Bloomfield (Baroness) Georgiana. *Reminiscences of Court and Diplomatic Life.* London, 1883.

ed. Bolitho, H. *Letters of Lady Augusta Stanley: A young lady at Court, 1849–1863.* London, 1927.

Bowle, John. *Politics and Opinion in the Nineteenth Century.* London, 1954.

Cassin-Scott, Jack. *Costume and Fashion in Colour 1760–1920.* Dorset, 1971.

Cunnington, C. W. and P. *Handbook of English Costume in the Nineteenth Century.* London, 1959.

ed. Delamont, S. and Duffin, L. *The Nineteenth Century Woman: her cultural and physical world.* London, 1978.

Duberly, Mrs Henry. *Journal Kept During the Russian War.* London, 1856.

ed. Erskine, Mrs Stuart. *Twenty years at Court: Correspondence of the Hon. Eleanor Stanley 1842–1862.* London, 1916.

ffrench Blake, R. L. F. *The Crimean War.* London, 1971.

ed. Fitzherbert, C. *Henry Clifford, VC: His letters and sketches from the Crimea*. London, 1956.

Gibbs-Smith, C. H. *The Great Exhibition of 1851*. London, 1950.

Hibbert, Christopher. *Illustrated London News Social History of Victorian Britain*. London, 1976.

Hobhouse, Christopher. *1851 and the Crystal Palace*. London, 1950.

Iremonger, Lucille. *Lord Aberdeen*. London, 1978.

Judd, Denis. *The Crimean War*. London, 1975.

Kapp, Yvonne. *Eleanor Marx: Vol 1; Family Life*. London, 1972.

ed. Kitson Clark, G. and Young, G. M. *Portrait of an Age: Victorian England*. London, 1977.

Longford, Elizabeth. *Victoria R.I.* London, 1964.

Longmate, Norman. *King Cholera*. London, 1966.

Lutyens, Mary. *Millais and the Ruskins*. London, 1967.

Martineau, Harriet. *Autobiography* (3 vols). London, 1877.

Marx, Karl and Engels, Friedrich. *On Britain*. London, 1954.

Nicolaievsky, Boris and Mänchen-Helfen, Otto. *Karl Marx: Man and Fighter*. London, 1963.

ed. Peel, Ethel. *Recollections of Lady Georgiana Peel*. London, 1920.

Pevsner, Niklaus. *Studies in Art, Architecture and Design Vol 2: Victorian and after*. London, 1968.

ed. Quennell, Peter. *Mayhew's London*. London.

ed. Richardson, R. G. *Nurse Sarah Anne: with Florence Nightingale at Scutari*. London, 1977.

Roebuck, Janet. *The Making of Modern English Society from 1850*. London, 1973.

Russell, W. H. *The War*. London, 1855.

Stedman Jones, Gareth. *Outcast London: a study of the relationship between classes in Victorian society*. London, 1971.

Surtees, Virginia. *Charlotte Canning*. London, 1975.

Taine, H. A. (Trans: Hyams). *Notes on England*. London, 1957.

Thomson, D. *England in the Nineteenth Century*. London, 1950.

Times, The. London, 1855–6.

Trevelyan, Raleigh. *A Pre-Raphaelite Circle.* London, 1978.

ed. Vincent, J. R. *Disraeli, Derby and the Conservative Party. Political Journals of Lord Stanley 1849–69.* London, 1978.

ed. Warner, Philip. *The Fields of War: A young cavalryman's Crimea campaign.* London, 1977.

Webb, R. K. *Harriet Martineau: A Radical Victorian.* London, 1960.

Wheatley, Vera. *The Life and Work of Harriet Martineau.* London, 1957.

Whitworth, R. H. *The Grenadier Guards.* London, 1974.

ed. Wohl, Anthony S. *The Victorian Family: structure and stresses.* London, 1978.

Woodham-Smith, Cecil. *Florence Nightingale.* London, 1950.

ed. Wyndham, Hon. Mrs Hugh. *Correspondence of Sarah Spencer, Lady Lyttleton, 1787–1870.* London, 1912.

Outstanding women's fiction in Panther Books

C L Skelton
Hardacre £2.50 ☐

Erich Segal
Oliver's Story £1.25 ☐
Man, Woman and Child £1.25 ☐

Nicola Thorne
A Woman Like Us £1.25 ☐
The Perfect Wife and Mother £1.50 ☐
The Daughters of the House £1.95 ☐
Where the Rivers Meet £2.50 ☐
Affairs of Love £2.50 ☐

Jacqueline Briskin
Paloverde £2.50 ☐
Rich Friends £2.50 ☐
Decade £2.50 ☐
The Onyx £2.50 ☐

Celeste de Blasis
The Tiger's Woman £2.50 ☐

Barbara Taylor Bradford
A Woman of Substance £2.95 ☐
Voice of the Heart £2.95 ☐

Alan Ebert & Janice Rotchstein
Traditions £2.50 ☐

Trevanian
The Summer of Katya £1.95 ☐

Raymond Giles
Sabrehill £1.95 ☐
Slaves of Sabrehill £2.50 ☐
Rebels of Sabrehill £2.50 ☐
Storm over Sabrehill £2.50 ☐
Hellcat of Sabrehill £2.50 ☐

Marcelle Bernstein
Sadie £2.50 ☐

To order direct from the publisher just tick the titles you want
and fill in the order form.

Outstanding women's fiction in Panther Books

Muriel Spark

Territorial Rights	£1.25	☐
Not To Disturb	£1.25	☐
Loitering with Intent	£1.25	☐
Bang-Bang You're Dead	£1.25	☐
The Hothouse by the East River	£1.25	☐
Going up to Sotheby's	£1.25	☐
The Takeover	£1.95	☐

Toni Morrison

Song of Solomon	£2.50	☐
The Bluest Eye	£1.95	☐
Sula	£1.95	☐
Tar Baby	£1.95	☐

Erica Jong

Fear of Flying	£2.50	☐
How to Save Your Own Life	£1.95	☐
Fanny	£2.50	☐
Selected Poems II	£1.25	☐
At the Edge of the Body	£1.25	☐

Ann Bridge

Peking Picnic	£1.95	☐

Anita Brookner

A Start in Life	£1.95	☐
Providence	£1.95	☐
Look at Me	£1.95	☐

To order direct from the publisher just tick the titles you want
and fill in the order form.

Outstanding women's fiction in Panther Books

Mary E Pearce

Apple Tree Lean Down	85p	☐
Jack Mercybright	85p	☐
The Land Endures	£1.50	☐
Apple Tree Saga	£2.50	☐
Polsinney Harbour	£1.95	☐

Kathleen Winsor

Wanderers Eastward, Wanderers West (omnibus)	£3.95	☐

Margaret Thomson Davis

The Breadmakers Saga	£2.95	☐
The Breadmakers	£1.50	☐
A Baby Might Be Crying	£1.50	☐
A Sort of Peace	£1.50	☐

Helena Leigh

The Vintage Years 1: The Grapes of Paradise	£1.95	☐
The Vintage Years 2: Wild Vines	£2.50	☐
The Vintage Years 3: Kingdoms of the Vine	£1.95	☐

Rebecca Brandewyne

Love, Cherish Me	£2.50	☐
Rose of Rapture	£2.50	☐

Pamela Jekel

Sea Star	£2.50	☐

Henry Denker

The Healers	£2.50	☐

Chloe Gartner

Still Falls the Rain	£2.50	☐

Nora Roberts

Promise Me Tomorrow	£1.95	☐

To order direct from the publisher just tick the titles you want
and fill in the order form.

All these books are available at your local bookshop or newsagent, or can be ordered direct from the publisher.,

To order direct from the publisher just tick the titles you want and fill in the form below.

Name _____

Address _____

_____

Send to:
Panther Cash Sales
PO Box 11, Falmouth, Cornwall TR10 9EN.

Please enclose remittance to the value of the cover price plus:

UK 45p for the first book, 20p for the second book plus 14p per copy for each additional book ordered to a maximum charge of £1.63.

BFPO and Eire 45p for the first book, 20p for the second book plus 14p per copy for the next 7 books, thereafter 8p per book.

Overseas 75p for the first book and 21p for each additional book.

Panther Books reserve the right to show new retail prices on covers, which may differ from those previously advertised in the text or elsewhere.